CODE

and

THE MAN FROM ST PETERSBURG

KEN FOLLETT

CODE TO ZERO

and

THE MAN FROM ST PETERSBURG

PAN BOOKS

Code to Zero first published 2000 by Macmillan. First published by Pan Books 2001.
The Man from St Petersburg first published 1982 by Hamish Hamilton. First published by
Pan Books 1998.

This omnibus edition published 2003 by Pan Books
an imprint of Pan Macmillan Ltd
Pan Macmillan, 20 New Wharf Road, London N1 9RR
Basingstoke and Oxford
Associated companies throughout the world
www.panmacmillan.com

ISBN 0 330 43670 8

Copyright © Ken Follett 1982, 2000

The right of Ken Follett to be identified as the
author of this work has been asserted by him in accordance
with the Copyright, Designs and Patents Act 1988.

1 3 5 7 9 8 6 4 2

A CIP catalogue record for this book is available from
the British Library.

Printed and bound in Great Britain by
Mackays of Chatham plc, Chatham, Kent

CODE TO ZERO

Historical note: The launch of the first American space satellite, Explorer I, was originally scheduled for Wednesday 29 January, 1958. Late that evening, it was postponed to the following day. The reason given was the weather. Observers at Cape Canaveral were puzzled: it was a perfect, sunny Florida day. But the army said that a high-altitude wind called the jet stream was unfavourable.

Next night, there was another postponement, and the same reason was given.

The launch was finally attempted on Friday 31 January.

'. . . from its beginning in 1947, the Central Intelligence Agency . . . has spent millions of dollars on a major program of research to find drugs and other esoteric methods to bring ordinary people, willing and unwilling alike, under complete control – to act, to talk, to reveal the most precious secrets, even to forget on command.'

Thomas Powers, from the Introduction to
*The Search for the 'Manchurian Candidate':
The CIA and Mind Control* by John Marks

PART 1

5 A.M.

The Jupiter C missile stands on the launch pad at Complex 26, Cape Canaveral. For secrecy, it is draped in vast canvas shrouds that hide everything but its tail, which is that of the Army's familiar Redstone rocket. But the rest of it, under the concealing cloak, is quite unique . . .

He woke up scared.

Worse than that: he was terrified. His heart was pounding, his breath came in gasps, and his body was taut. It was like a nightmare, except that waking brought no sense of relief. He felt that something dreadful had happened, but he did not know what it was.

He opened his eyes. A faint light from another room dimly illuminated his surroundings, and he made out vague shapes, familiar but sinister. Somewhere nearby, water ran in a cistern.

He tried to make himself calm. He swallowed, took regular breaths, and attempted to think straight. He was lying on a hard floor. He was cold, he hurt everywhere, and he had some kind of hangover, with a headache and a dry mouth and a feeling of nausea.

He sat upright, shaking with fear. There was an

3

unpleasant smell of damp floors washed with strong disinfectant. He recognized the outline of a row of washbasins.

He was in a public toilet.

He felt disgusted. He had been sleeping on the floor of a men's room. What the hell had happened to him? He concentrated. He was fully dressed, wearing some kind of topcoat and heavy boots, though he had a feeling that these were not his clothes. His panic was subsiding, but in its place came a deeper fear, less hysterical but more rational. What had happened to him was very bad.

He needed light.

He got to his feet. He looked around, peering into the gloom, and guessed where the door might be. Holding his arms out in front of him in case of invisible obstacles, he made his way to a wall. Then he walked crabwise, his hands exploring. He found a cold glassy surface he guessed was a mirror, then there was a towel roller, then a metal box that might be a slot machine. At last his fingertips touched a switch, and he turned it on.

Bright light flooded white-tiled walls, a concrete floor, and a line of toilets with open doors. In a corner was what looked like a bundle of old clothes. He asked himself how he got here. He concentrated hard. What had happened last night? He could not remember.

The hysterical fear began to return as he realized *he could not remember anything at all.*

He clenched his teeth to stop himself crying out.

Yesterday . . . the day before . . . nothing. What was his name? He did not know.

He turned toward the row of basins. Above them was a long mirror. In the glass he saw a filthy hobo, dressed in rags, with matted hair, a dirty face, and a crazy, pop-eyed stare. He looked at the hobo for a second, then he was hit by a terrible revelation. He started back, with a cry of shock, and the man in the mirror did the same. The hobo was himself.

He could no longer hold back the tide of panic. He opened his mouth and, in a voice that shook with terror, he shouted: 'Who am I?'

* * *

The bundle of old clothes moved. It rolled over, a face appeared, and a voice mumbled: 'You're a bum, Luke, pipe down.'

His name was Luke.

He was pathetically grateful for the knowledge. A name was not much, but it gave him a focus. He stared at his companion. The man wore a ripped tweed coat with a length of string around the waist for a belt. The grimy young face had a crafty look. The man rubbed his eyes and muttered: 'My head hurts.'

Luke said: 'Who are you?'

'I'm Pete, you retard, can't you see?'

'I can't—' Luke swallowed, holding down the panic. 'I've lost my memory!'

'I ain't surprised. You drank most of a bottle of liquor yesterday. It's a miracle you didn't lose your entire mind.' Pete licked his lips. 'I didn't get hardly any of that goddamn bourbon.'

Bourbon would explain the hangover, Luke thought. 'But why would I drink a whole bottle?'

Pete laughed mockingly. 'That's about the dumbest question I ever heard. To get drunk, of course!'

Luke was appalled. He was a drunken bum who slept in public toilets.

He had a raging thirst. He bent over a washbasin, ran the cold water, and drank from the tap. It made him feel better. He wiped his mouth, then forced himself to look in the mirror again.

The face was calmer now. The mad stare had gone, replaced by a look of bewilderment and dismay. The reflection showed a man in his late thirties, with dark hair and blue eyes. He had no beard or moustache, just a heavy growth of dark stubble.

He turned back to his companion. 'Luke what?' he said. 'What's my last name?'

'Luke ... something, how the hell am I supposed to know?'

'How did I get this way? How long has it been going on? Why did it happen?'

Pete got to his feet. 'I need some breakfast,' he said.

Luke realized he was hungry. He wondered if he had any money. He searched the pockets of his clothes: the raincoat, the jacket, the pants. All were empty. He had no money, no wallet, not even a handkerchief. No assets, no clues. 'I think I'm broke,' he said.

'No kidding,' Pete said sarcastically. 'Come on.' He stumbled through a doorway.

Luke followed.

When he emerged into the light, he suffered another shock. He was in a huge temple, empty and eerily silent. Mahogany benches stood in rows on the marble floor, like church pews waiting for a ghostly congregation. Around the vast room, on a high stone lintel atop rows of pillars, surreal stone warriors with helmets and shields stood guard over the holy place. Far above their heads was a vaulted ceiling richly decorated with gilded octagons. The insane thought crossed Luke's mind that he had been the sacrificial victim in a weird rite that had left him with no memory.

Awestruck, he said: 'What is this place?'

'Union Station, Washington, DC,' said Pete.

A relay closed in Luke's mind, and the whole thing made sense. With relief he saw the grime on the walls, the chewing gum trodden into the marble floor, and the candy wrappers and cigarette packs in the corners, and he felt foolish. He was in a grandiose train station, early in the morning before it filled up with passengers. He had scared himself, like a child imagining monsters in a darkened bedroom.

Pete headed for a triumphal arch marked 'Exit', and Luke hurried after him.

An aggressive voice called: 'Hey! Hey, you!'

Pete said: 'Oh-oh.' He quickened his step.

A stout man in a tight-fitting railroad uniform bore down on them, full of righteous indignation. 'Where did you bums spring from?'

Pete whined: 'We're leaving, we're leaving.'

Luke was humiliated to be chased out of a train station by a fat official.

The man was not content just to get rid of them. 'You been sleeping here, ain't you?' he protested, following hard on their heels. 'You know that ain't allowed.'

It angered Luke to be lectured like a schoolboy, even though he guessed he deserved it. He *had* slept in the damn toilet. He suppressed a retort and walked faster.

'This ain't a flophouse,' the man went on. 'Damn bums, now scram!' He shoved Luke's shoulder.

Luke turned suddenly and confronted the man. 'Don't touch me,' he said. He was surprised by the quiet menace in his own voice. The official stopped short. 'We're leaving, so you don't need to do or say anything more, is that clear?'

The man took a big step backward, looking scared.

Pete took Luke's arm. 'Let's go.'

Luke felt ashamed. The guy was an officious twerp, but Luke and Pete were vagrants, and a railroad employee had the right to throw them out. Luke had no business intimidating him.

They passed through the majestic archway. It was dark outside. A few cars were parked around the traffic circle in front of the station, but the streets were quiet. The air was bitterly cold, and Luke drew his ragged clothes closer about him. It was winter, a frosty morning in Washington, maybe January or February.

He wondered what year it was.

Pete turned left, apparently sure where he was

going. Luke followed. 'Where are we headed?' he asked.

'I know a gospel shop on H Street where we can get free breakfast, so long as you don't mind singing a hymn or two.'

'I'm starving, I'll sing a whole oratorio.'

Pete confidently followed a zigzag route through a low-rent neighbourhood. The city was not yet awake. The houses were dark and the stores shuttered, the greasy spoons and the news-stands not yet open. Glancing at a bedroom window hung with cheap curtains, Luke imagined a man inside, fast asleep under a pile of blankets, his wife warm beside him; and he felt a pang of envy. It seemed that he belonged out here, in the pre-dawn community of men and women who ventured into the cold streets while ordinary people slept on: the man in work clothes shuffling to an early-morning job; the young bicycle rider muffled in scarf and gloves; the solitary woman smoking in the brightly lit interior of a bus.

His mind seethed with anxious questions. How long had he been a drunk? Had he ever tried to dry out? Did he have any family who might help him? Where had he met Pete? Where did they get the booze? Where did they drink it? But Pete's manner was taciturn, and Luke controlled his impatience, hoping Pete might be more forthcoming when he had some food inside him.

They came to a small church standing defiantly between a cinema and a smoke shop. They entered by a side door and went down a flight of stairs to the basement. Luke found himself in a long room with a low ceiling – the crypt, he guessed. At one end he saw an upright piano and a small pulpit; at the other, a kitchen range. In between were three rows of trestle tables with benches. Three bums sat there, one at each table, staring patiently into space. At the kitchen end, a dumpy woman stirred a big pot. Beside her, a grey-bearded man wearing a clerical collar looked up from a coffee urn and smiled. 'Come in, come in!' he said cheerfully. 'Come into the warm.' Luke regarded him warily, wondering if he was for real.

It *was* warm, stiflingly so after the wintry air outside. Luke unbuttoned his grubby trench coat. Pete said: 'Morning, Pastor Lonegan.'

The pastor said: 'Have you been here before? I've forgotten your name.'

'I'm Pete, he's Luke.'

'Two disciples!' His bonhomie seemed genuine. 'You're a little early for breakfast, but there's fresh coffee.'

Luke wondered how Lonegan maintained his cheery disposition when he had to get up this early to serve breakfast to a roomful of catatonic deadbeats.

The pastor poured coffee into thick mugs. 'Milk and sugar?'

Luke did not know whether he liked milk and sugar in his coffee. 'Yes, thank you,' he said, guessing. He accepted the mug and sipped the coffee. It tasted sickeningly creamy and sweet. He guessed he normally took it black. But it assuaged his hunger, and he drank it all quickly.

'We'll have a word of prayer in a few minutes,' said the pastor. 'By the time we're done, Mrs Lonegan's famous oatmeal should be cooked to perfection.'

Luke decided his suspicion had been unworthy. Pastor Lonegan was what he seemed, a cheerful guy who liked to help people.

Luke and Pete sat at the rough plank table, and Luke studied his companion. Until now, he had noticed only the dirty face and ragged clothes. Now he saw that Pete had none of the marks of a long-term drunk: no broken veins, no dry skin flaking off the face, no cuts or bruises. Perhaps he was too young – only about twenty-five, Luke guessed. But Pete was slightly disfigured. He had a dark red birthmark that ran from his right ear to his jawline. His teeth were uneven and discoloured. The dark moustache had probably been grown to distract attention from his bad teeth, back in the days when he cared about his appearance. Luke sensed suppressed anger in him. He guessed that Pete resented the world, maybe for making him ugly, maybe for some other reason. He probably had a theory that the country was being ruined by some group he hated: Chinese immigrants, or uppity Negroes, or a shadowy club of ten rich men who secretly controlled the stock market.

'What are you staring at?' Pete said.

Luke shrugged and did not reply. On the table was a newspaper folded open at the crossword, and a stub of pencil. Luke glanced idly at the grid, picked up the pencil, and started to fill in the answers.

More bums drifted in. Mrs Lonegan put out a stack

of heavy bowls and a pile of spoons. Luke got all the crossword clues but one: 'Small place in Denmark,' six letters. Pastor Lonegan looked over his shoulder at the filled-out grid, raised his eyebrows in surprise, and said quietly to his wife: 'Oh, what a noble mind is here o'erthrown!'

Luke immediately got the last clue – Hamlet – and wrote it in. Then he thought: 'How did I know that?'

He unfolded the paper and looked at the front page for the date. It was Wednesday, 29 January 1958. His eye was caught by the headline U.S. MOON STAYS EARTHBOUND. He read on:

Cape Canaveral, Tuesday: The U.S. Navy today abandoned a second attempt to launch its space rocket, Vanguard, after multiple technical problems.

The decision comes two months after the first Vanguard launch ended in humiliating disaster when the rocket exploded two seconds after ignition.

American hopes of launching a space satellite to rival the Soviet Sputnik now rest with the Army's rival Jupiter missile.

The piano sounded a strident chord, and Luke looked up. Mrs Lonegan was playing the introductory notes of a familiar hymn. She and her husband began to sing 'What a Friend We Have in Jesus', and Luke joined in, pleased he could remember it.

Bourbon had a strange effect, he thought. He could do the crossword and sing a hymn from memory, but he did not know his mother's name. Perhaps he had been drinking for years, and had damaged his brain. He wondered how he could have let such a thing happen.

After the hymn, Pastor Lonegan read some Bible verses, then told them all that they could be saved. Here was a group that really needed saving, Luke thought. All the same, he was not tempted to put his faith in Jesus. First he needed to find out who he was.

The pastor extemporized a prayer, they sang grace, then the men lined up and Mrs Lonegan served them hot oatmeal with syrup. Luke ate three bowls. Afterwards, he felt much better. His hangover was receding fast.

Impatient to resume his questions, he approached the pastor. 'Sir, have you seen me here before? I've lost my memory.'

Lonegan looked hard at him. 'You know, I don't believe I have. But I meet hundreds of people every week, and I could be mistaken. How old are you?'

'I don't know,' Luke said, feeling foolish.

'Late thirties, I'd say. You haven't been living rough very long. It takes its toll on a man. But you walk with a spring in your step, your skin is clear under the dirt, and you're still alert enough to do a crossword puzzle. Quit drinking now, and you could lead a normal life again.'

Luke wondered how many times the pastor had said that. 'I'm going to try,' he promised.

'If you need help, just ask.' A young man who

appeared to be mentally handicapped was persistently patting Lonegan's arm, and he turned to him with a patient smile.

Luke spoke to Pete. 'How long have you known me?'

'I don't know, you been around a while.'

'Where did we spend the night before last?'

'Relax, will you? Your memory will come back sooner or later.'

'I have to find out where I'm from.'

Pete hesitated. 'What we need is a beer,' he said. 'Help us think straight.' He turned for the door.

Luke grabbed his arm. 'I don't want a beer,' he said decisively. Pete did not want him to dig into his past, it seemed. Perhaps he was afraid of losing a companion. Well, that was too bad. Luke had more important things to do than keep Pete company. 'In fact,' he said, 'I think I'd like to be alone for a while.'

'What are you, Greta Garbo?'

'I'm serious.'

'You need me to look out for you. You can't make it on your own. Hell, you can't even remember how old you are.'

Pete had a desperate look in his eyes, but Luke was unmoved. 'I appreciate your concern, but you're not helping me find out who I am.'

After a moment Pete shrugged. 'You got a right.' He turned to the door again. 'See you around, maybe.'

'Maybe.'

Pete went out. Luke shook Pastor Lonegan's hand. 'Thank you for everything,' he said.

'I hope you find what you're looking for,' said the pastor.

Luke went up the stairs and out into the street. Pete was on the next block, speaking to a man in a green gaberdine raincoat with a matching cap – begging the price of a beer, Luke guessed. He walked in the opposite direction and turned around the first corner.

It was still dark. Luke's feet were cold, and he realized he was not wearing socks under his boots. As he hurried on, a light flurry of snow fell. After a few minutes, he eased his pace. He had no reason to rush. It made no difference whether he walked fast or slow. He stopped, and took shelter in a doorway.

He had nowhere to go.

6 A.M.

The rocket is surrounded on three sides by a service gantry that holds it in a steel embrace. The gantry, actually a converted oilfield derrick, is mounted on two sets of wheels that run on wide-gauge rails. The entire service structure, bigger than a town house, will be rolled back three hundred feet before the launch.

Elspeth woke up worrying about Luke.

She lay in bed for a few moments, her heart heavy with concern for the man she loved. Then she switched on the bedside lamp and sat upright.

Her motel room was decorated with a space-programme theme. The floor lamp was shaped like a rocket, and the pictures on the walls showed planets, crescent moons and orbital paths in a wildly unrealistic night sky. The Starlite was one of a cluster of new motels that had sprouted among the sand dunes in the area of Cocoa Beach, Florida, eight miles south of Cape Canaveral, to accommodate the influx of visitors. The decorator had obviously thought the outer-space theme appropriate, but it made Elspeth feel as if she were borrowing the bedroom of a ten-year-old boy.

She picked up the bedside phone and dialled

Anthony Carroll's office in Washington, D.C. At the other end, the phone rang unanswered. She tried his home number with the same result. Had something gone wrong? She felt sick with fear. She told herself that Anthony must be on his way to the office. She would call again in half an hour. It could not take him longer than thirty minutes to drive to work.

As she showered, she thought about Luke and Anthony when she had first known them. They were at Harvard when she was at Radcliffe, before the war. The boys were in the Harvard Glee Club: Luke had a nice baritone voice and Anthony a wonderful tenor. Elspeth had been the conductor of the Radcliffe Choral Society and had organized a joint concert with the Glee Club.

Best friends, Luke and Anthony had made an odd couple. Both were tall and athletic, but there the resemblance ended. The Radcliffe girls had called them Beauty and the Beast. Luke was Beauty, with his wavy black hair and elegant clothes. Anthony was not handsome, with his big nose and long chin, and he always looked as if he were wearing someone else's suit, but girls were attracted to his energy and enthusiasm.

Elspeth showered quickly. In her bathrobe, she sat at the dressing table to do her make-up. She put her wristwatch beside the eyeliner so that she would know when thirty minutes was up.

She had been sitting at a dressing table wearing a bathrobe the first time she ever spoke to Luke. It was during a panty raid. A group of Harvard boys, some drunk, had climbed into the dormitory building through a ground-floor window late one evening. Now, almost twenty years later, it seemed incredible to her that she and the other girls had feared nothing worse than having their underwear stolen. Had the world been more innocent then?

By chance, Luke had come to her room. He was a math major, like her. Although he was wearing a mask, she recognized his clothes, a pale grey Irish tweed jacket with a red spotted cotton handkerchief in the breast pocket. Once alone with her, Luke had seemed embarrassed, as if it had just occurred to him that what he was doing was foolish. She had smiled, pointed to the closet, and said: 'Top drawer.' He had taken a pair of pretty white panties with a lace edging, and Elspeth felt a pang of regret – they had been expensive. But the next day he asked her for a date.

She tried to concentrate on her make-up. The job was more difficult than usual this morning, because she had slept badly. Foundation smoothed her cheeks and salmon-pink lipstick brightened her mouth. She had a math degree from Radcliffe, but still she was expected to look like a mannequin at work.

She brushed her hair. It was reddish brown, and cut in the fashionable style: chin-length and turned under at the back. She dressed quickly in a sleeveless shirtwaist dress of green-and-tan striped cotton with a wide dark brown patent-leather belt.

Twenty-nine minutes had elapsed since she had tried to call Anthony.

To pass the last minute, she thought about the number 29. It was a prime number – it could not be divided by any number except itself and 1 – but otherwise it was not very interesting. The only unusual thing about it was that 29 plus $2x^2$ was a prime number for every value of x up to 28. She calculated the series in her head: 29, 31, 37, 47, 61, 79, 101, 127 . . .

She picked up the phone and dialled Anthony's office again.

There was no reply.

1941

Elspeth Twomey fell in love with Luke the first time he kissed her.

Most Harvard boys had no idea how to kiss. They either bruised your lips with a brutal smackeroo, or opened their mouths so wide you felt like a dentist. When Luke kissed her, at five minutes to midnight in the shadows of the Radcliffe Dormitory Quad, he was passionate yet tender. His lips moved all the time, not just on her mouth but on her cheeks and her eyelids and her throat. The tip of his tongue probed gently between her lips, politely asking permission to come in, and she did not even pretend to hesitate. Afterwards, sitting in her room, she had looked into the mirror and whispered to her reflection: 'I think I love him.'

That had been six months ago, and the feeling had grown stronger since. Now she was seeing Luke almost every day. They were both in their senior year. Every day they either met for lunch or studied together for a couple of hours. Weekends they spent almost all their time together.

It was not uncommon for Radcliffe girls to get engaged in their final year, to a Harvard boy or a young professor. They would marry in the summer, go on a long honeymoon, then move into an apartment when they returned. They would start work, and a year or so later have their first baby.

But Luke had never spoken about marriage.

She looked at him now, sitting in a booth at the back of Flanagan's bar, arguing with Bern Rothsten, a tall graduate student with a bushy black moustache and a hardbitten look. Luke's dark hair kept falling forward over his eyes, and he pushed it back with his left hand, a familiar gesture. When he was older, and had a responsible job, he would put goop on his hair to make it stay in place, and then he would not be quite so sexy, she thought.

Bern was a communist, like many Harvard students and professors. 'Your father's a banker,' he said to Luke with disdain. 'You'll be a banker, too. Of course you think capitalism is great.'

Elspeth saw a flush rise at Luke's throat. His father had recently been featured in a *Time* magazine article as one of ten men who had become millionaires since the Depression. However, she guessed he was blushing not because he was a rich kid, but because he was fond of his family, and resented the implied criticism of his father. She felt angry for him, and said indignantly: 'We don't judge people by their parents, Bern!'

Luke said: 'Anyway, banking is an honourable job. Bankers help people to start businesses and provide employment.'

'Like they did in 1929.'

'They make mistakes. Sometimes they help the

wrong people. Soldiers make mistakes – they shoot the wrong people – but I don't accuse you of being a murderer.'

It was Bern's turn to look wounded. He had fought in the Spanish Civil War – he was older than the rest of them by three or four years – and Elspeth now guessed he was remembering some tragic error.

Luke added: 'Anyway, I don't aim to be a banker.'

Bern's dowdy girlfriend, Peg, leaned forward, interested. Like Bern, she was intense in her convictions, but she did not have his sarcastic tongue. 'What, then?'

'A scientist.'

'What kind?'

Luke pointed upward. 'I want to explore beyond our planet.'

Bern laughed scornfully. 'Space rockets! A schoolboy fantasy.'

Elspeth leaped to Luke's defence again. 'Knock it off, Bern, you don't know what you're talking about.' Bern's subject was French literature.

However, Luke did not appear to have been stung by the sneer. Perhaps he was accustomed to having his dream laughed at. 'I think it's going to happen,' he said. 'And I'll tell you something else. I believe science will do more than communism for ordinary people in our lifetime.'

Elspeth winced. She loved Luke, but she felt he was naive about politics. 'Too simple,' she said to him. 'The benefits of science are restricted to the privileged elite.'

'That's just not true,' Luke said. 'Steamships make life better for seamen as well as for transatlantic passengers.'

Bern said: 'Have you ever been in the engine room of an ocean liner?'

'Yes, and no one was dying of scurvy.'

A tall figure cast a shadow over the table. 'Are you kids old enough to drink alcoholic liquor in public?' It was Anthony Carroll, wearing a blue serge suit that looked as if he had slept in it. With him was someone so striking that Elspeth uttered an involuntary murmur of surprise. She was a small girl with a petite figure, fashionably dressed in a short red jacket and a loose black skirt, with curls of dark hair escaping from under a little red hat with a peak. 'Meet Billie Josephson,' said Anthony.

Bern Rothsten said to her: 'Are you Jewish?'

She was startled to be asked so directly. 'Yes.'

'So you can marry Anthony, but you can't join his country club.'

Anthony protested: 'I don't belong to a country club.'

'You will, Anthony, you will,' said Bern.

Luke stood up to shake hands, nudged the table with his thighs, and knocked over a glass. It was unusual for him to be clumsy, and Elspeth realized with a twinge of annoyance that he was instantly taken with Miss Josephson. 'I'm surprised,' he said, giving her his most charming smile. 'When Anthony said his date was called Billie, I imagined someone six feet tall and built like a wrestler.'

Billie laughed merrily and slid into the booth beside Luke. 'My name is Bilhah,' she said. 'It's biblical, she was the handmaiden of Rachel and the mother of Dan. But I was brought up in Dallas, where they called me Billie-Jo.'

Anthony sat next to Elspeth and said quietly: 'Isn't she pretty?'

Billie was not exactly pretty, Elspeth thought. She had a narrow face, with a sharp nose and large, intense, dark brown eyes. It was the whole package that was so stunning: the red lipstick, the angle of the hat, the Texas accent, and most of all her animation. While she talked to Luke, telling him some story about Texans now, she smiled, frowned, and pantomimed all kinds of emotion. 'She's cute,' Elspeth said to Anthony. 'I don't know why I never noticed her before.'

'She works all the time, doesn't go to many parties.'

'So how did you meet her?'

'I noticed her in the Fogg Museum. She was wearing a green coat with brass buttons and a beret. I thought she looked like a toy soldier fresh out of the box.'

Billie was not any kind of toy, Elspeth thought. She was more dangerous than that. Billie laughed at something Luke had said and swiped his arm in mock admonishment. The gesture was flirtatious, Elspeth thought. Irritated, she interrupted them and said to Billie: 'Are you planning to beat the curfew tonight?'

Radcliffe girls were supposed to be in their dormitories by ten o'clock. They could get permission to stay out later, but they had to put their name in a book, with details of where they planned to go and what time they would be back; and their return time was checked. However, they were clever women, and the complex rules only inspired them to ingenious deceptions. Billie said: 'I'm supposed to be spending the night with a visiting aunt who has taken a suite at the Ritz. What's your story?'

'No story, just a ground-floor window that will be open all night.'

Billie lowered her voice. 'In fact, I'm staying with friends of Anthony's in Fenway.'

Anthony looked sheepish. 'Some people my mother knows, who have a large apartment,' he said to Elspeth. 'Don't give me that old-fashioned look, they're terribly respectable.'

'I should hope so,' Elspeth said primly, and she had the satisfaction of seeing Billie blush. Turning to Luke, she said: 'Honey, what time is the movie?'

He looked at his wristwatch. 'We've got to go,' he said.

Luke had borrowed a car for the weekend. It was a two-seater Ford Model A roadster, ten years old, its sit-up-and-beg shape looking antiquated beside the streamlined cars of the early forties.

Luke handled the old car skilfully, obviously enjoying himself. They drove into Boston. Elspeth asked herself if she had been bitchy to Billie. Maybe, a little, she decided, but she was not going to shed any tears.

They went to see Alfred Hitchcock's latest film, *Suspicion*, at Loew's State Theatre. In the darkness,

Luke put his arm around Elspeth, and she laid her head on his shoulder. She felt it was a pity they had chosen a film about a disastrous marriage.

Around midnight they returned to Cambridge and pulled off Memorial Drive to park facing the Charles River, next to the boathouse. The car had no heater, and Elspeth turned up the fur collar of her coat and leaned against Luke for warmth.

They talked about the movie. Elspeth thought that in real life the Joan Fontaine character, a repressed girl brought up by stuffy parents, would never be attracted to the kind of ne'er-do-well Cary Grant had played. Luke said: 'But that's why she fell for him – because he was dangerous.'

'Are dangerous people attractive?'

'Absolutely.'

Elspeth turned away from him and looked at the reflection of the moon on the restless surface of the water. Billie Josephson was dangerous, she thought.

Luke sensed her annoyance and changed the subject. 'This afternoon, Professor Davies told me I could do my master's degree right here at Harvard if I want.'

'What made him say that?'

'I mentioned that I was hoping to go to Columbia. He said: "What for? Stay here!" I explained that my family's in New York, and he said: "Family. Huh!" Like that. Like I couldn't possibly be a serious mathematician if I cared about seeing my little sister.'

Luke was the eldest of four children. His mother

was French. His father had met her in Paris at the end of the First World War. Elspeth knew that Luke was fond of his two teenage brothers and doted on his eleven-year-old sister. 'Professor Davies is a bachelor,' she said. 'He lives for his work.'

'Have you thought about doing a master's?'

Elspeth's heart missed a beat. 'Should I?' Was he asking her to go to Columbia with him?

'You're a better mathematician than most of the Harvard men.'

'I've always wanted to work at the State Department.'

'That would mean living in Washington.'

Elspeth was sure Luke had not planned this conversation. He was just thinking aloud. It was typical of a man, to talk without a moment's forethought about matters that affected their whole lives. But he seemed dismayed that they might move to different cities. The solution to the dilemma must be as obvious to him as it was to her, she thought happily.

'Have you ever been in love?' he said suddenly. Realizing he had been abrupt, he added: 'It's a very personal question, I don't have any right to ask.'

'That's okay,' she said. Any time he wanted to talk about love, it was fine with her. 'As a matter of fact, I have been in love.' She watched his face in the moonlight, and was gratified to see the shadow of displeasure flicker across his expression. 'When I was seventeen, there was a steelworks dispute in Chicago. I was very political, in those days. I went to help, as a volunteer, carrying messages and making coffee. I worked for a young organizer called Jack Largo, and I fell in love with him.'

'And he with you?'

'Goodness, no. He was twenty-five, he thought of me as a kid. He was kind to me, and charming, but he was like that with everyone.' She hesitated. 'He kissed me once, though.' She wondered whether she should be telling Luke this, but she felt the need to unburden herself. 'We were alone in the back room, packing leaflets in boxes, and I said something that made him laugh, I don't even remember what it was. "You're a gem, Ellie," he said – he was one of those men who shorten everyone's name, he would have called you Lou for sure. Then he kissed me, right on the lips. I nearly died of joy. But he just went on packing leaflets as though nothing had changed.'

'I think he did fall in love with you.'

'Maybe.'

'Are you still in touch with him?'

She shook her head. 'He died.'

'So young!'

'He was killed.' She fought back sudden tears. The last thing she wanted was for Luke to think she was still in love with the memory of Jack. 'Two off-duty policemen, hired by the steelworks, got him in an alley and beat him to death with iron bars.'

'Jesus Christ!' Luke stared at her.

'Everyone in town knew who had done it, but nobody was arrested.'

He took her hand. 'I've read about that kind of stuff in the papers, but it never seemed real.'

'It's real. The mills must keep rolling. Anyone who gets in the way has to be rubbed out.'

'You make it sound as if industry were no better than organized crime.'

'I don't see a big difference. But I don't get involved any more. That was enough.' Luke had started talking about love, but she had stupidly moved the conversation on to politics. She switched back. 'What about you?' she said. 'Have you ever been in love?'

'I'm not sure,' he said hesitantly. 'I don't think I know what love is.' It was a typical boy's answer. Then he kissed her, and she relaxed.

She liked to touch him with her fingertips while they kissed, stroking his ears and the line of his jaw, his hair and the back of his neck. Every now and again he stopped to look at her, studying her with the hint of a smile, making her think of *Hamlet*'s Ophelia saying: 'He fell to such perusal of my face, as a would draw it.' Then he would kiss her again. What made her feel so good was the thought that he liked her this much.

After a while he drew away from her and sighed heavily. 'I wonder how married people ever get bored,' he said. 'They never have to stop.'

She liked this talk of marriage. 'Their children stop them, I guess,' she said with a laugh.

'Do you want to have children, some day?'

She felt her breath come faster. What was he asking her? 'Of course I do.'

'I'd like four.'

The same as his parents. 'Boys or girls?'

'A mixture.'

There was a pause. Elspeth was afraid to say anything. The silence stretched out. Eventually he turned to her with a serious look. 'How would you feel about that? Having four children?'

It was the cue she had been waiting for. She smiled happily. 'If they were yours, I'd love it,' she said.

He kissed her again.

Soon it became too cold to stay where they were, and reluctantly they drove back towards the Radcliffe dorms.

As they were passing through Harvard Square, a figure waved to them from the side of the road. 'Is that Anthony?' Luke said incredulously.

It was, Elspeth saw. Billie was with him.

Luke pulled over, and Anthony came to the window. 'I'm glad I spotted you,' he said. 'I need a favour.'

Billie stood behind Anthony, shivering in the cold night air, looking furious. 'What are you doing here?' Elspeth asked Anthony.

'There's been a muddle. My friends in Fenway have gone away for the weekend – they must have got the dates mixed up. Billie has nowhere to go.'

Billie had lied about where she was spending the night, Elspeth recalled. Now she could not return to her dorm without revealing her deception.

'I took her to the House.' He meant Cambridge House, where he and Luke lived. Harvard men's dormitories were called 'Houses'. 'I thought she could sleep in our room, and Luke and I could spend the night in the library.'

Elspeth said: 'You're crazy.'

Luke put in: 'It's been done before. So what went wrong?'

'We were seen.'

'Oh, no!' Elspeth said. For a girl to be found in a man's room was a serious offence, especially at night. Both the man and the woman could be expelled from the university.

Luke said: 'Who saw you?'

'Geoff Pidgeon and a whole bunch of men.'

'Well, Geoff's all right, but who was with him?'

'I'm not sure. It was half dark and they were all drunk. I'll talk to them in the morning.'

Luke nodded. 'What are you going to do now?'

'Billie has a cousin who lives in Newport, Rhode Island,' Anthony said. 'Would you drive her there?'

'What?' said Elspeth. 'But it's fifty miles away!'

'So it will take an hour or two,' Anthony said dismissively. 'What do you say, Luke?'

'Of course,' Luke said.

Elspeth had known he would comply. It was a matter of honour for him to help out a friend, regardless of inconvenience. But she was angry all the same.

'Hey, thanks,' Anthony said lightly.

'No problem,' Luke said. 'Well, there is a problem. This car is a two-seater.'

Elspeth opened the door and got out. 'Be my guest,' she said sulkily. She felt ashamed of herself for being so bad-tempered. Luke was right to rescue a friend in trouble. But she hated the thought of him spending two hours in this little car with sexy Billie Josephson.

Luke sensed her displeasure and said: 'Elspeth, get back in, I'll drive you home first.'

She tried to be gracious. 'No need,' she said. 'Anthony can walk me to the dorm. And Billie looks as if she might freeze to death.'

'Okay, if you're sure,' Luke said.

Elspeth wished he had not agreed quite so fast.

Billie kissed Elspeth's cheek. 'I don't know how to thank you,' she said. She got into the car and closed the door without saying goodbye to Anthony.

Luke waved and drove off.

Anthony and Elspeth stood and watched the car recede into the darkness.

'Hell,' said Elspeth.

6.30 A.M.

Stencilled on the side of the white rocket is the designation 'UE' in huge black letters. This is a simple code –

H	U	N	T	S	V	I	L	E	X
1	2	3	4	5	6	7	8	9	0

– so UE is missile number 29. The purpose of the code is to avoid giving clues as to how many missiles have been produced.

Daylight crept stealthily over the cold city. Men and women came out of the houses, narrowing their eyes and pursing their lips against the biting wind, and hurried through the grey streets, heading for the warmth and bright lights of the offices and stores, hotels and restaurants where they worked.

Luke had no destination: one street was as good as another when none of them meant anything. Maybe, he thought, he would turn the next corner and know, in a flash of revelation, that he was some place familiar – the street where he was brought up, or a building where he had worked. But every corner disappointed him.

As the light improved, he began to study the people he passed. One of these could be his father, his sister, even his son. He kept hoping that one of them would catch his eye, and stop, and embrace him, and say: 'Luke, what happened to you? Come home with me, let me help you!' But perhaps a relative would turn a cold face to him and pass by. He might have done something to offend his family. Or they might live in another town.

He began to feel he was not going to be lucky. No passer-by would embrace him with glad cries, and he was not suddenly going to recognize the street where he lived. Simply walking around fantasizing about a lucky break was no kind of strategy. He needed a plan. There must be some way to discover his identity.

Luke wondered if he might be a Missing Person. There was a list, he felt sure, of such people, with a description of each. Who kept the list? It had to be the police.

He seemed to remember passing a precinct house a few minutes earlier. He turned abruptly to go back. As he did so, he bumped into a young man in an olive-coloured gaberdine raincoat and matching cap. He had a feeling he might have seen the man before. Their eyes met, and, for a hopeful moment, Luke thought he might have been recognized; but the man looked away, embarrassed, and walked on.

Swallowing his disappointment, Luke tried to retrace his steps. It was difficult, because he had turned corners and crossed streets more or less at random.

34

However, he had to come across a police station sooner or later.

As he walked, he tried to deduce information about himself. He watched a tall man in a grey Homburg hat light a cigarette and take a long, satisfying drag, but he had no desire for tobacco. He guessed he did not smoke. Looking at cars, he knew that the racy, low-slung designs he found attractive were new. He decided he liked fast cars, and he was sure he could drive. He also knew the make and model names of most of the cars he saw. That was the kind of information he had retained, along with how to speak English.

When he glimpsed his reflection in a shop window, what he saw was a bum of indeterminate years. But when he looked at passers-by, he could tell if they were in their twenties, thirties, or forties, or older. He also found he automatically classified people as older or younger than himself. Thinking about it, he realized that people in their twenties seemed younger than he, and people in their forties older; so he had to be somewhere in between.

These trifling victories over his amnesia gave him an inordinate sense of triumph.

But he had completely lost his way. He was on a tawdry street of cheap shops, he saw with distaste: clothing stores with windows full of bargains, used-furniture stores, pawnbrokers, and grocery stores that took food stamps. He stopped suddenly and looked back, wondering what to do. Thirty yards behind him, he saw the man in a green gaberdine raincoat and cap, watching the TV in a store window.

Luke frowned, thinking: 'Is he shadowing me?'

A shadow was always alone, rarely carried a briefcase or shopping bag, and inevitably appeared to be loitering rather than walking with a set purpose. The man in the olive cap matched the specification.

It was easy enough to check.

Luke walked to the end of the block, crossed the street, and walked back along the side. When he reached the far end he stood at the kerb and looked both ways. The olive raincoat was thirty yards behind him. Luke crossed again. To allay suspicion, he studied doors, as if looking for a street number. He went all the way back to where he had started.

The raincoat followed.

Luke was mystified, but his heart leaped with hope. A man who was following him must know something about him – maybe even his identity.

To be sure he was being followed, he needed to travel in a vehicle, forcing his shadow to do the same.

Despite his excitement, a cool observer in the back of his mind was asking: 'How come you know exactly how to check whether you're being followed?' The method had popped into his head immediately. Had he done some kind of clandestine work before he became a bum?

He would think about that later. Now he needed bus fare. There was nothing in the pockets of his ragged clothes; he must have spent every last cent on booze. But that was no problem. There was cash everywhere: in people's pockets, in the stores, in taxicabs and houses.

He began to look at his surroundings with different eyes. He saw news-stands to be robbed, handbags that could be snatched, pockets ready to be picked. He glanced into a coffee shop where a man stood behind the counter and a waitress served the booths. The place would do as well as anything. He stepped inside.

His eyes raked the tables, looking for change left as tips, but it was not going to be that easy. He approached the counter. A radio was playing the news. 'Rocket experts claim America has one last chance of catching up with the Russians in the race to control outer space.' The counterman was making espresso coffee, steam billowing from a gleaming machine, and a delicious fragrance made Luke's nostrils flare.

What would a bum say? 'Any stale doughnuts?' he asked.

'Get out of here,' the man said roughly. 'And don't come back.'

Luke contemplated leaping the counter and opening the cash register, but it seemed extreme when all he wanted was bus fare. Then he saw what he needed. Beside the till, within easy reach, was a can with a slit in the top. Its label showed a picture of a child and the legend: 'Remember Those Who Cannot See.' Luke moved so that his body shielded the box from the customers and the waitress. Now he just had to distract the counterman.

'Gimme a dime?' he said.

The man said: 'Okay, that's it, you get the bum's

rush.' He put down a jug with a clatter and wiped his hands on his apron. He had to duck under the counter to get out, and for a second he could not see Luke.

In that moment, Luke took the collection box and slipped it inside his coat. It was disappointingly light, but it gave a rattle, so it was not empty.

The counterman grabbed Luke by the collar and propelled him rapidly across the café. Luke did not resist until, at the door, the man gave him a painful kick in the ass. Forgetting his act, Luke spun round, ready to fight. The man suddenly looked scared and backed inside.

Luke asked himself what he had to be angry about. He had gone into the place begging, and had not left when asked to. Okay, the kick was unnecessary, but he deserved it – he had stolen the blind children's money!

All the same, it took an effort for him to swallow his pride, turn around, and slink away like a dog with its tail between its legs.

He ducked into an alleyway, found a sharp stone, and attacked the can, venting his anger. He soon busted it open. The money inside, mostly pennies, amounted to two or three dollars, he guessed. He put it in his coat pocket and returned to the street. He thanked heaven for charity and made a silent promise to give three bucks to the blind if he ever got straight.

All right, he thought, thirty bucks.

The man in the olive raincoat was standing by a news-stand, reading a paper.

A bus pulled up a few yards away. Luke had no idea where it went, but that did not matter. He boarded.

The driver gave him a hard look, but did not throw him off. 'I want to go three stops,' Luke said.

'Don't matter where you want to go, the fare is seventeen cents, unless you got a token.'

Luke paid with some of the change he had stolen.

Maybe he was not being shadowed. As he walked towards the back of the bus, he looked anxiously out the window. The man in the raincoat was walking away with his newspaper tucked under his arm. Luke frowned. The man should have been trying to hail a taxicab. Maybe he was not a shadow, after all. Luke felt disappointed.

The bus pulled away, and Luke took a seat.

He wondered again how come he knew about all this stuff. He must have been trained in clandestine work. But what for? Was he a cop? Perhaps it was to do with the war. He knew there had been a war. America had fought against the Germans in Europe and the Japanese in the Pacific. But he could not remember whether he had been in it.

At the third stop, he got off the bus with a handful of other passengers. He looked up and down the street. There were no taxicabs in sight, and no sign of the man in the olive raincoat. As he hesitated, he noticed that one of the passengers who had got off the bus with him had paused in a shop doorway and was fumbling in his pockets. As Luke watched, he lit a cigarette and took a long, satisfying drag.

He was a tall man, wearing a grey Homburg hat.

Luke realized he had seen him before.

7 A.M.

The launch pad is a simple steel table with four legs and a hole in the middle through which the rocket jet passes. A conical deflector beneath spreads the jet horizontally.

Anthony Carroll drove along Constitution Avenue in a five-year-old Cadillac Eldorado that belonged to his mother. He had borrowed it a year ago, to drive to Washington from his parents' place in Virginia, and had never gotten around to returning it. His mother had probably bought another car by now.

He pulled into the parking lot of Q Building in Alphabet Row, a strip of barracks-like structures hastily erected, during the war, on parkland near the Lincoln Memorial. It was an eyesore, no question, but he liked the place, for he had spent much of the war here, working for the Office of Strategic Services, precursor of the CIA. Those were the good old days, when a clandestine agency could do more or less anything, and did not have to check with anyone but the President.

The CIA was the fastest-growing bureaucracy in Washington, and a vast multimillion dollar head-quarters was under construction across the Potomac

River in Langley, Virginia. When it was completed, Alphabet Row would be demolished.

Anthony had fought hard against the Langley development, and not merely because Q Building held fond memories. Right now the CIA had offices in thirty-one buildings in the government-dominated downtown neighbourhood known as Foggy Bottom. That was the way it should be, Anthony had argued vociferously. It was very difficult for foreign agents to figure out the size and power of the Agency when its premises were scattered and mixed up with other government offices. But when Langley opened, anyone would be able to estimate its resources, manpower, and even budget simply by driving past.

He had lost that argument. The people in charge were determined to manage the CIA more tightly. Anthony believed that secret work was for daredevils and buccaneers. That was how it had been in the war. But nowadays it was dominated by pen-pushers and accountants.

There was a parking slot reserved for him and marked: 'Head of Technical Services', but he ignored it and pulled up in front of the main door. Looking up at the ugly building, he wondered if its imminent demolition signified the end of an era. He was losing more of these bureaucratic battles nowadays. He was still a hugely powerful figure within the Agency. 'Technical Services' was the euphemistic name of the division responsible for burglary, phone tapping, drug testing and other illegal activities. Its nickname was Dirty Tricks. Anthony's position was founded on his record as a war hero and a series of Cold War coups. But some people wanted to turn the CIA into what the public imagined it to be, a simple information-gathering agency.

Over my dead body, he thought.

However, he had enemies: superiors he had offended with his brash manners, weak and incompetent agents whose promotion he had opposed, pen-pushers who disliked the whole notion of the government doing secret operations. They were ready to destroy him as soon as he made a slip.

And today his neck was stuck out farther than ever before.

As he strode into the building, he deliberately put aside his general worries and focused on the problem of the day: Dr Claude Lucas, known as Luke, the most dangerous man in America, the one who threatened everything Anthony had lived for.

He had been at the office most of the night, and had gone home only to shave and change his shirt. Now the guard in the lobby looked surprised and said: 'Good morning, Mr Carroll – you back already?'

'An angel appeared unto me in a dream and said: "Get back to work, you lazy son of a bitch." Good morning.'

The guard laughed. 'Mr Maxell's in your office, sir.'

Anthony frowned. Pete Maxell was supposed to be with Luke. Had something gone wrong?

He ran up the stairs.

Pete was sitting in the chair opposite Anthony's

desk, still dressed in ragged clothes, a smear of dirt partly covering the red birthmark on his face. As Anthony walked in he jumped up, looking scared.

'What happened?' Anthony said.

'Luke decided he wanted to be alone.'

Anthony had planned for this. 'Who took over?'

'Simons has him under surveillance, and Betts is there for back-up.'

Anthony nodded thoughtfully. Luke had got rid of one agent, he could get rid of another. 'What about Luke's memory?'

'Completely gone.'

Anthony took off his coat and sat behind his desk. Luke was causing problems, but Anthony had expected as much, and he was ready.

He looked at the man opposite. Pete was a good agent, competent and careful, but inexperienced. However, he was fanatically loyal to Anthony. All the young agents knew that Anthony had personally organized an assassination: the killing of the Vichy French leader Admiral Darlan, in Algiers on Christmas Eve in 1942. CIA agents did kill people, but not often, and they regarded Anthony with awe. But Pete owed him a special debt. On his job application form, Pete had lied, saying he had never been in trouble with the law, and Anthony had later found out that, as a student in San Francisco, he had been fined for soliciting a prostitute. Pete should have been fired for that, but Anthony had kept the secret and Pete was eternally grateful.

Now Pete was miserable and ashamed, feeling he had let Anthony down. 'Relax,' Anthony said, adopting a fatherly tone. 'Just tell me exactly what happened.'

Pete looked grateful, and sat down again. 'He woke up crazy,' he began. 'Yelling "Who am I?" and stuff like that. I got him calmed down . . . but I made a mistake. I called him Luke.'

Anthony had told Pete to observe Luke but not to give him any information. 'No matter – it's not his real name.'

'Then he asked who I was, and I said: "I'm Pete." It just came out, I was so concerned to stop him yelling.' Pete was mortified to confess these blunders, but in fact they were not grave and Anthony waved aside his apologies. 'What happened next?'

'I took him to the gospel shop, just the way we planned it. But he asked shrewd questions. He wanted to know if the pastor had seen him before.'

Anthony nodded. 'We shouldn't be surprised. In the war, he was the best agent we ever had. He's lost his memory, but not his instincts.' He rubbed his face with his right hand, tiredness catching up with him.

'I kept trying to steer him away from inquiring into his past. But I think he figured out what I was doing. Then he told me he wanted to be alone.'

'Did he get any clues? Did anything happen that might lead him to the truth?'

'No. He read an article in the paper about the space programme, but it didn't seem to mean anything special to him.'

'Did anyone notice anything strange about him?'

'The pastor was surprised Luke could do the crossword. Most of those bums can't even read.'

This was going to be difficult, but manageable, as Anthony had expected. 'Where is Luke now?'

'I don't know, sir. Steve will call in as soon as he gets a chance.'

'When he does, get back there and join up with him. Whatever happens, Luke mustn't get away from us.'

'Okay.'

The white phone on Anthony's desk rang, his direct line. He stared at it for a moment. Not many people had the number.

He picked it up.

'It's me,' said Elspeth's voice. 'What's happened?'

'Relax,' he said. 'Everything is under control.'

7.30 A.M.

The missile is 68 feet 7 inches high, and it weighs 64,000 pounds on the launch pad – but most of that is fuel. The satellite itself is only 2 feet 10 inches long, and weighs just 18 pounds.

The shadow followed Luke for a quarter of a mile as he walked south on 8th Street.

It was now full light and, although the street was busy, Luke easily kept track of the grey Homburg hat bobbing among the heads crowded together at street corners and bus stops. But after he crossed Pennsylvania Avenue, it disappeared from view. Once again, he wondered if he might be imagining things. He had woken up in a bewildering world where anything might be true. Perhaps the notion that he was being tailed was only a fantasy. But he did not really believe that, and a minute later he spotted the green raincoat coming out of a bakery.

'*Toi, encore,*' he said under his breath. 'You again.' He wondered briefly why he had spoken in French, then he put the thought out of his mind. He had more pressing concerns. There was no further room for doubt: two people were following him in a smoothly executed relay operation. They had to be professionals.

He tried to figure out what that meant. Homburg and Raincoat might be cops – he could have committed a crime, murdered someone while drunk. They could be spies, KGB or CIA, although it seemed unlikely that a deadbeat such as he could be involved in espionage. Most probably he had a wife he had left many years ago, who now wanted to divorce him and had hired private detectives to get proof of how he was living. (Maybe she was French.)

None of the options was attractive. Yet Luke felt exhilarated. They probably knew who he was. Whatever the reason for their tailing him, they must know something about him. At the very least, they knew more than he did.

He decided he would split the team, then confront the younger man.

He stepped into a smoke shop and bought a pack of Pall Malls, paying with some of the change he had stolen. When he went outside, Raincoat had disappeared and Homburg had taken over again. He walked to the end of the block and turned the corner.

A Coca-Cola truck was parked at the kerb, and the driver was unloading crates and carrying them into a diner. Luke stepped into the road and walked to the far side of the truck, positioning himself where he could watch the street without being seen by anyone coming around the corner.

After a minute, Homburg appeared, walking

quickly, checking in the doorways and windows, looking for Luke.

Luke dropped to the ground and rolled under the truck. Looking along the sidewalk at ground level, he picked out the blue suit pants and tan Oxfords of his shadow.

The man quickened his pace, presumably concerned that Luke had disappeared off the street. Then he turned and came back. He went into the diner and came out a minute later. He walked around the truck, then returned to the sidewalk and continued on. After a moment, he broke into a run.

Luke was pleased. He did not know how he had learned this game, but he seemed to be good at it. He crawled to the front of the truck and scrambled to his feet. He looked around the nearside fender. Homburg was still hurrying away.

Luke crossed the sidewalk and turned the corner. He stood in the doorway of an electrical store. Looking at a record player with an eighty bucks price tag, he opened the pack of cigarettes, took one out, and waited, keeping an eye on the street.

Raincoat appeared.

He was tall – about Luke's height – and his build was athletic, but he was about ten years younger, and his face wore an anxious look. Luke's instinct told him the man was not very experienced.

He spotted Luke, and gave a nervous start. Luke looked straight at him. The man looked away and continued walking, edging to the outside of the sidewalk to pass Luke, as anyone might to avoid contact with a bum.

Luke stepped into his path. He put the cigarette into his mouth and said: 'Got a light, buddy?'

Raincoat did not know what to do. He hesitated, looking worried. For a moment, Luke thought he would walk by without speaking; but then he made a quick decision, and stopped. 'Sure,' he said, trying to act casual. He reached into the pocket of his raincoat, took out a book of matches and struck one.

Luke took the cigarette out of his mouth and said: 'You know who I am, don't you?'

The young man looked scared. His training course had not prepared him for a surveillance subject who started to question the shadow. He stared at Luke, dumbstruck, until the match burned down. Then he dropped it and said: 'I don't know what you're talking about, pal.'

'You're following me,' Luke said. 'You must know who I am.'

Raincoat continued to act innocent. 'Are you selling something?'

'Am I dressed like a salesman? Come on, level with me.'

'I'm not following anyone.'

'You've been behind me for an hour, and I'm lost!'

The man made a decision. 'You're out of your mind,' he said. He tried to walk past Luke.

Luke moved sideways, blocking his path.

'Excuse me, please,' Raincoat said.

Luke was not willing to let the man go. He grabbed him by the lapels of the raincoat and slammed him against the shop window, rattling the glass. Frustration and rage boiled over. '*Putain de merde!*' he yelled.

Raincoat was younger and fitter than Luke, but he offered no resistance. 'Get your damn hands off me,' he said in a level voice. 'I'm not following you.'

'Who am I?' Luke screamed at him. 'Tell me, who am I?'

'How should I know?' He grasped Luke by the wrists, trying to shake his hold on the lapels of the raincoat.

Luke shifted his grip and took the man by the throat. 'I'm not taking your bullshit,' he rasped. 'You're going to tell me what's going on.'

Raincoat lost his cool, eyes widening in fear. He struggled to loosen Luke's grip on his throat. When that failed, he began to punch Luke's ribs. The first blow hurt, and Luke winced, but he retained his hold and moved in close, so that subsequent punches had little force. He pressed his thumbs into his opponent's throat, choking him. Terror showed in the man's eyes as his breath was cut off.

Behind Luke, the frightened voice of a passer-by said: 'Hey, what's going on here?'

Suddenly Luke was shocked at himself. He was killing the guy! He relaxed his grip. What was the matter with him? Was he a murderer?

Raincoat broke Luke's hold. Luke was dismayed at his own violence. He let his hands fall to his side.

The guy backed away. 'You crazy bastard,' he said. The fear had not left his eyes. 'You tried to kill me!'

'I just want the truth, and I know you can tell me it.'

Raincoat rubbed his throat. 'Asshole,' he said. 'You're out of your goddamn mind.'

Luke's anger rose once more. 'You're lying!' he yelled. He reached out to grab the man again.

Raincoat turned and ran away.

Luke could have chased him, but he hesitated. What was the point? What would he do if he caught the guy – torture him?

Then it was too late. Three passers-by had stopped to watch the fracas and were now standing at a safe distance, staring at Luke. After a moment, he walked away, heading in the direction opposite to that taken by his two shadows.

He felt worse than ever, shaky after his violent outburst and sick with disappointment at the result. He had met two people who probably knew who he was, and he had got no information.

'Great job, Luke,' he said to himself. 'You achieved precisely nothing.'

And he was alone again.

8 A.M.

The Jupiter C missile has four stages. The largest part is a high-performance version of the Redstone ballistic missile. This is the booster, or first stage, an enormously powerful engine that has the gargantuan task of freeing the missile from the mighty pull of Earth's gravity.

Dr Billie Josephson was running late.

She had got her mother up, helped her into a quilted bathrobe, made her put on her hearing aid, and sat her in the kitchen with coffee. She had woken her seven-year-old, Larry, praised him for not wetting the bed, and told him he had to shower just the same. Then she returned to the kitchen.

Her mother, a small, plump woman of seventy known as Becky-Ma, had the radio on loud. Perry Como was singing 'Catch a Falling Star'. Billie put sliced bread in the toaster, then laid the table with butter and grape jelly for Becky-Ma. For Larry she poured cornflakes into a bowl, sliced a banana over the cereal, and filled a jug with milk.

She made a peanut-butter-and-jelly sandwich and put it in Larry's lunch box with an apple, a Hershey bar and a small bottle of orange juice. She put the

52

lunch box in his school bag and added his home-reading book and his baseball glove, a present from his father.

On the radio, a reporter was interviewing sightseers on the beach near Cape Canaveral who were hoping to see a rocket launch.

Larry came into the kitchen with his shoelaces untied and his shirt buttons done up awry. She straightened him out, got him started on his cornflakes, and began to scramble eggs.

It was eight-fifteen, and she was almost caught up. She loved her son and her mother, but a secret part of her resented the drudgery of taking care of them.

The radio reporter was now interviewing an army spokesman. 'Aren't these rubbernecks in danger? What if the rocket goes off course and crash-lands right here on the beach?'

'There's no danger of that, sir,' came the reply. 'Every rocket has a self-destruct mechanism. If it veers off course it will be blown up in mid-air.'

'But how can you blow it up after it's already taken off?'

'The explosive device is triggered by a radio signal sent by the range safety officer.'

'That sounds dangerous in itself. Some radio ham fooling around might accidentally set it off.'

'The mechanism responds only to a complex signal, like a code. These rockets are expensive, we don't take any risks.'

Larry said: 'I have to make a space rocket today. Can I take the yoghurt pot to school?'

'No, you can't, it's half full,' she told him.

'But I have to take some containers! Miss Page will be mad if I don't.' He was near to tears with the suddenness of a seven-year-old.

'What do you need containers for?'

'To make a space rocket! She told us last week.'

Billie sighed. 'Larry, if you had told *me* last week, I would have saved a whole bunch of stuff for you. How many times must I ask you not to leave things until the last minute?'

'Well, what am I gonna do?'

'I'll find you something. We'll put the yoghurt in a bowl, and . . . what kind of containers do you want?'

'Rocket shape.'

Billie wondered if schoolteachers ever thought about the amount of work they created for busy mothers when they blithely instructed children to bring things from home. She put buttered toast on three plates and served the scrambled eggs, but she did not eat her own. She went around the house and got a tube-shaped cardboard detergent container, a plastic liquid-soap bottle, an ice-cream carton, and a heart-shaped chocolate box.

Most of the packaging showed the products being used by families – generally a pretty housewife and two happy kids, with a pipe-smoking father in the background. She wondered if other women resented the stereotype as much as she did. She had never lived in a family like that. Her father, a poor tailor in Dallas, had died when she was a baby, and her mother had brought up five children in grinding poverty. Billie herself had been divorced since Larry was two. There were plenty of families without a man, where the mother was a widow, a divorcee, or what used to be called a fallen woman. But they did not show such families on the cornflakes boxes.

She put all the containers in a shopping bag for Larry to carry to school.

'Oh, boy, I bet I have more than anyone!' he said. 'Thanks, Mom.'

Her breakfast was cold, but Larry was happy.

A car horn tooted outside, and Billie quickly checked her appearance in the glass of a cupboard door. Her curly black hair had been hastily combed, she had no make-up on except the eyeliner she had failed to remove last night, and she was wearing an oversize pink sweater ... but the effect was kind of sexy.

The back door opened and Roy Brodsky came in. Roy was Larry's best friend, and the boys greeted one another joyously, as if they had been apart for a month instead of just a few hours. Billie had noticed that all Larry's friends were boys now. In kindergarten it had been different, boys and girls playing together indiscriminately. She wondered what psychological change took place, around the age of five, that made children prefer their own gender.

Roy was followed by his father, Harold, a good-looking man with soft brown eyes. Harold Brodsky was a widower: Roy's mother had died in a car wreck. Harold taught chemistry at the George Washington University. Billie and Harold were dating. He looked at her adoringly and said: 'My God, you look gorgeous.' She grinned and kissed his cheek.

Like Larry, Roy had a shopping bag full of cartons. Billie said to Harold: 'Did you have to empty half the containers in your kitchen?'

'Yes. I have little cereal bowls of soap flakes, chocolates, and processed cheese. And six toilet rolls without the cardboard cylinder in the middle.'

'Darn, I never thought of toilet rolls!'

He laughed. 'I wonder, would you like to have dinner at my place tonight?'

She was surprised. 'You're going to cook?'

'Not exactly. I thought I'd ask Mrs Riley to make a casserole that I could warm up.'

'Sure,' she said. She had not had dinner at his house before. They normally went to the movies, to concerts of classical music, or to cocktail parties at the homes of other university professors. She wondered what had prompted him to invite her.

'Roy's going to a cousin's birthday party tonight, and he'll sleep over. We'll have a chance to talk without interruption.'

'Okay,' Billie said thoughtfully. They could talk without interruption at a restaurant, of course. Harold had another reason for inviting her to his house when his child would be away for the night. She glanced at him. His expression was open and candid – he knew what she was thinking. 'That'll be great,' she said.

'I'll pick you up around eight. Come on, boys!' He shepherded the children out through the back door. Larry left without saying goodbye, which Billie had learned to take as a sign that all was well. When he was anxious about something, or coming down with an infection, he would hang back and cling to her.

'Harold is a good man,' her mother said. 'You should marry him soon, before he changes his mind.'

'He won't change his mind.'

'Just don't deal him in before he puts his stake on the table.'

Billie smiled at her mother. 'You don't miss much, do you, Ma?'

'I'm old, but I'm not stupid.'

Billie cleared the table and threw her own breakfast in the trash. Rushing now, she stripped her bed, Larry's, and her mother's, and bundled the sheets into a laundry bag. She showed Becky-Ma the bag and said: 'Remember, all you have to do is hand this to the laundry man when he calls, okay, Ma?'

Her mother said: 'I don't have any of my heart pills left.'

'Jesus Christ!' She rarely swore in front of her mother, but she was at the end of her rope. 'Ma, I have a busy day at work today, and I don't have time to go to the goddamn pharmacist!'

'I can't help it, I ran out.'

The most infuriating thing about Becky-Ma was the way she could switch from being a perceptive parent to a helpless child. 'You could have told me *yesterday* that you were running out – I shopped yesterday! I can't shop every day, I have a job.'

Becky-Ma burst into tears.

Billie relented immediately. 'I'm sorry, Ma,' she

said. Becky-Ma cried easily, like Larry. Five years ago, when the three of them had set up house together, Ma had helped take care of Larry. But nowadays she was barely able to look after him for a couple of hours when he came home from school. Everything would be easier if Billie and Harold were married.

The phone rang. She patted Ma on the shoulder and picked it up. It was Bern Rothsten, her ex-husband. Billie got on well with him, despite the divorce. He came by two or three times a week to see Larry; and he cheerfully paid his share of the cost of bringing up the boy. Billie had been angry with him, once, but it was a long time ago. Now she said: 'Hey, Bern – you're up early.'

'Yeah. Have you heard from Luke?'

She was taken aback. 'Luke Lucas? Lately? No – is something wrong?'

'I don't know, maybe.'

Bern and Luke shared the intimacy of rivals. When they were young they had argued endlessly. Their discussions often seemed acrimonious, yet they had remained close at college and all through the war. 'What's happened?' Billie said.

'He called me on Monday. I was kind of surprised. I don't hear from him often.'

'Nor do I.' Billie struggled to remember. 'Last time I saw him was a couple of years ago, I think.' Realizing how long it was, she wondered why she had let their friendship lapse. She was just busy all the time, she guessed. She regretted that.

'I got a note from him last summer,' Bern said. 'He'd been reading my books to his sister's kid.' Bern was the author of *The Terrible Twins*, a successful series of children's books. 'He said they made him laugh. It was a nice letter.'

'So why did he call you on Monday?'

'Said he was coming to Washington and wanted to see me. Something had happened.'

'Did he tell you what?'

'Not really. He just said: "It's like the stuff we used to do in the war".'

Billie frowned anxiously. Luke and Bern had been in OSS during the war, working behind enemy lines, helping the French resistance. But they had been out of that world since 1946 – hadn't they? 'What do you think he meant?'

'I don't know. He said he would call me when he reached Washington. He checked into the Carlton Hotel on Monday night. Now it's Wednesday, and he hasn't called. And his bed wasn't slept in last night.'

'How did you find that out?'

Bern made an impatient noise. 'Billie, you were in OSS too, what would you have done?'

'I guess I would have given a chambermaid a couple of bucks.'

'Right. So he was out all night and he hasn't come back.'

'Maybe he was cattin' around.'

'And maybe Billy Graham smokes reefer, but I don't think so, do you?'

Bern was right. Luke had a powerful sex drive, but he craved intensity, not variety, Billie knew. 'No, I don't think so,' she said.

'Call me if you hear from him, okay?'

'Sure, of course.'

'Be seeing you.'

'Bye.' Billie hung up.

Then she sat at the kitchen table, her chores forgotten, thinking about Luke.

1941

Route 138 meandered south through Massachusetts towards Rhode Island. There was no cloud, and the moon shone on the country roads. The old Ford had no heater. Billie was wrapped up in coat, scarf and gloves, but her feet were numb. However, she did not really mind. It was no great hardship to spend a couple of hours in a car alone with Luke Lucas, even if he was someone else's boyfriend. In her experience beautiful men were tediously vain, but this one seemed to be an exception.

It was taking for ever to drive to Newport, but Luke seemed to be enjoying the long journey. Some Harvard men were nervous with attractive women, and chain-smoked, or drank from hip flasks, smoothed their hair all the time and kept straightening their ties. Luke was relaxed, driving without apparent effort and chatting. There was little traffic, and he looked at her as much as at the road.

They talked about the war in Europe. That morning in Radcliffe Yard, rival student groups had set up stalls and handed out leaflets, the Interventionists passionately advocating that America should enter the war, the America Firsters arguing the opposite with equal fervour. A crowd had gathered, men and women, students and professors. The knowledge that Harvard boys would be among the first to die made the discussions highly emotional.

'I have cousins in Paris,' Luke said. 'I'd like us to go over there and rescue them. But that's kind of a personal reason.'

'I have a personal reason too, I'm Jewish,' Billie said. 'But rather than send Americans to die in Europe, I'd open our doors to refugees. Save lives instead of killing people.'

'That's what Anthony believes.'

Billie was still fuming about the night's fiasco. 'I can't tell you how mad I am at Anthony,' she said. 'He should have made sure we could stay at his friends' apartment.'

She was hoping for sympathy from Luke, but he disappointed her. 'I guess you both were a little too casual about the whole thing.' He said it with a friendly smile, but there was no mistaking the note of censure.

Billie was stung. However, she was indebted to him for this ride, so she swallowed the retort that sprang to her lips. 'You're defending your friend, which is fine,' she said gently. 'But I think he had a duty to protect my reputation.'

'Yes, but so did you.'

She was surprised he was so critical. Until now he had been all charm. 'You seem to think it was my fault!'

'It was bad luck, mainly,' he said. 'But Anthony put

you in a position where a little bad luck could do you a lot of damage.'

'That's the truth.'

'And you let him.'

She found herself dismayed by his disapproval. She wanted him to think well of her – though she did not know why she cared. 'Anyway, I'll never do that again, with any man,' she said vehemently.

'Anthony's a great guy, very smart, kind of eccentric.'

'He makes girls want to take care of him, brush his hair and press his suit and make him chicken soup.'

Luke laughed. 'Could I ask you a personal question?'

'You can try.'

He met her eyes for a moment. 'Are you in love with him?'

That was sudden – but she liked men who could surprise her, so she answered candidly. 'No. I'm fond of him, I enjoy his company, but I don't love him.' She thought about Luke's girlfriend. Elspeth was the most striking beauty on campus, a tall woman with long coppery hair and the pale, resolute face of a Nordic queen. 'What about you? Are you in love with Elspeth?'

He returned his gaze to the road. 'I don't think I know what love is.'

'Evasive answer.'

'You're right.' He threw a speculative look at her, then seemed to decide that she could be trusted. 'Well, to be honest, this is as close to love as I've ever come, but I still don't know if it's the real thing.'

She felt a pang of guilt. 'I wonder what Anthony and Elspeth would think of us having this conversation,' she said.

He coughed, embarrassed, and changed the subject. 'Damn shame you ran into those men at the House.'

'I hope Anthony won't be found out. He could be expelled.'

'He's not the only one. You might be in trouble, too.'

She had been trying not to think about that. 'I don't believe anyone knew who I was. I heard one of them say "tart".'

He shot a surprised glance at her.

She guessed that Elspeth would not have used the word 'tart', and she wished she had not repeated it. 'I suppose I deserved it,' she added. 'I was in a men's House at midnight.'

He said: 'I don't think there's ever any real excuse for bad manners.'

It was a reproach to her as much as to the man who had insulted her, she thought with annoyance. Luke had a sharp edge. He was angering her – but that made him interesting. She decided to take the gloves off. 'What about you?' she said. 'You're very preachy about Anthony and me, aren't you? But didn't you put Elspeth in a vulnerable situation tonight, keeping her out in your car until the early hours?'

To her surprise, he laughed appreciatively. 'You're right, and I'm a pompous idiot,' he said. 'We all took risks.'

'That's the truth.' She shuddered. 'I don't know what I'd do if I got thrown out.'

'Study somewhere else, I guess.'

She shook her head. 'I'm on a scholarship. My father's dead, my mother's a penniless widow. And if I were expelled for moral transgression, I'd have little chance of getting another scholarship. Why do you look surprised?'

'To be honest, I'd have to say you don't dress like a scholarship girl.'

She was pleased he had noticed her clothes. 'It's the Leavenworth Award,' she explained.

'Wow.' The Leavenworth was a famously generous grant, and thousands of outstanding students applied for it. 'You must be a genius.'

'I don't know about that,' she said, gratified by the respect in his voice. 'I'm not smart enough to make sure I have a place to stay the night.'

'On the other hand, being thrown out of college is not the worst thing in the world. Some of the cleverest people drop out – then go on to become millionaires.'

'It would be the end of the world for me. I don't want to be a millionaire, I want to help sick people get well.'

'You're going to be a doctor?'

'Psychologist. I want to understand how the mind works.'

'Why?'

'It's so mysterious and complicated. Things like logic, the way we think. Imagining something that isn't there in front of us – animals can't do that. The ability to remember – fish have no memory, did you know that?'

He nodded. 'And why is it that just about everyone can recognize a musical octave?' he said. 'Two notes, the frequency of one being double that of the other – how come your brain knows that?'

'You find it interesting, too!' She was pleased that he shared her curiosity.

'What did your father die of?'

Billie swallowed hard. Sudden grief overwhelmed her. She struggled against tears. It was always like this: a chance word, and from nowhere came a sorrow so acute she could barely speak.

'I'm really sorry,' Luke said. 'I didn't mean to upset you.'

'Not your fault,' she managed. She took a deep breath. 'He lost his mind. One Sunday morning he went bathing in the Trinity River. The thing is, he hated the water, and he couldn't swim. I think he wanted to die. The coroner thought so too, but the jury took pity on us and called it an accident, so that we'd get the life insurance. It was a hundred dollars. We lived on that for a year.' She took a deep breath. 'Let's talk about something else. Tell me about math.'

'Well.' He thought for a moment. 'Math is as weird as psychology,' he said. 'Take the number *pi*. Why should the ratio of circumference to diameter be three point one four two? Why not six, or two and a half? Who made that decision, and why?'

'You want to explore outer space.'

'I think it's the most exciting adventure mankind has ever had.'

'And I want to map the mind.' She smiled. The grief of bereavement was leaving her. 'You know, we have something in common – we both have big ideas.'

He laughed, then braked the car. 'Hey, we're coming to a crossroads.'

She switched on the flashlight and looked at the map on her knee. 'Turn right,' she said.

They were approaching Newport. The time had passed quickly. She felt sorry the trip was coming to an end. 'I have no idea what I'm going to tell my cousin,' she said.

'What's he like?'

'He's queer.'

'Queer? In what way?'

'In the homosexual way.'

He shot her a startled look. 'I see.'

She had no patience with men who expected women to tiptoe around the subject of sex. 'I've shocked you again, haven't I?'

He grinned at her. 'As you would say – that's the truth.'

She laughed. It was a Texan colloquialism. She was glad he noticed little things about her.

'There's a fork in the road,' he said.

She consulted the map again. 'You'll have to pull up, I can't find it.'

He stopped the car and leaned across to look at the

map in the light of the flash. He reached out to turn the map a little, and his touch was warm on her cold hand. 'Maybe we're here,' he said, pointing.

Instead of looking at the map, she found herself staring at his face. It was deeply shadowed, lit only by the moon and the indirect torchlight. His hair fell forward over his left eye. After a moment he felt her gaze, and glanced up at her. Without thinking, Billie lifted her hand and stroked his cheek with the outside edge of her little finger. He stared back at her, and she saw bewilderment and desire in his eyes.

'Which way do we go?' she murmured.

He moved away suddenly and put the car in gear. 'We take . . .' He cleared his throat. 'We take the left fork.'

Billie wondered what the hell she was doing. Luke had spent the evening smooching with the most beautiful girl on campus. Billie had been out with Luke's room-mate. What was she thinking about?

Her feelings for Anthony had not been strong, even before tonight's calamity. All the same, she *was* dating him, so she certainly should not be toying with his best friend.

'Why did you do that?' Luke said angrily.

'I don't know,' she said. 'I didn't intend to, it just happened. Slow down.'

He took a bend too fast. 'I don't want to feel like this about you!' he said.

She was suddenly breathless. 'Like what?'

'Never mind.'

The smell of the sea came into the car, and Billie realized they were close to her cousin's home. She recognized the road. 'Next left,' she said. 'If you don't slow down you'll miss it.'

Luke braked and turned on to a dirt road.

Half of Billie wanted to arrive at the destination and get out of the car and leave behind this unbearable tension. The other half wanted to drive with Luke for ever.

'We're here,' she said.

They stopped outside a neat one-storey frame house with gingerbread eaves and a lamp by the door. The Ford's headlights picked out a cat sitting motionless on a windowsill, looking at them with a calm gaze, disdainful of the turmoil of human emotion.

'Come in,' Billie said. 'Denny will make some coffee to keep you awake on the return trip.'

'No, thanks,' he said. 'I'll just wait here until you're safely inside.'

'You've been very kind to me. I don't think I deserve it.' She held out her hand to shake.

'Are we friends?' he said, taking her hand.

She lifted his hand to her face, kissed it, and pressed it against her cheek, closing her eyes. After a moment she heard him groan softly. She opened her eyes and found him staring at her. His hand moved behind her head, he pulled her to him, and they kissed. It was a gentle kiss, soft lips and warm breath and his fingertips light on the back of her neck. She held the lapel of his rough tweed coat and pulled him closer. If he grabbed her now, she would not resist, she knew. The thought made her burn with desire. Feeling wild, she took his lip between her teeth and bit.

She heard Denny's voice. 'Who's out there?'

She pulled away from Luke and looked out. There were lights on in the house, and Denny stood in the doorway, wearing a purple silk dressing gown.

She turned back to Luke. 'I could fall in love with you in about twenty minutes,' she said. 'But I don't think we can be friends.'

She stared at him a moment longer, seeing in his eyes the same churning conflict she felt in her heart. Then she looked away, took a deep breath, and got out of the car.

'Billie?' said Denny. 'For heaven's sake, what are you doing here?'

She crossed the yard, stepped on to the porch and fell into his arms. 'Oh, Denny,' she murmured. 'I love that man, and he belongs to some woman!'

Denny patted her back with a delicate touch. 'Honey, I know *just* how you feel.'

She heard the car move, and turned to wave. As it swung by, she saw Luke's face – and the glint of something shiny on his cheeks.

Then he disappeared into the darkness.

8.30 A.M.

Perched on top of the pointed nose of the Redstone rocket is what looks like a large birdhouse with a steeply pitched roof and a flagpole stuck through its centre. This section, about thirteen feet long, contains the second, third and fourth stages of the missile – and the satellite itself.

Secret agents in America had never been as powerful as they were in January 1958.

The Director of the CIA, Allen Dulles, was the brother of John Foster Dulles, Eisenhower's Secretary of State – so the Agency had a direct line into the administration. But that was only half the reason.

Under Dulles were four Deputy Directors, only one of whom was important – the Deputy Director for Plans. The Plans Directorate was also known as CS, for Clandestine Services, and this was the department that had carried out coups against left-leaning governments in Iran and Guatemala.

The Eisenhower White House had been amazed and delighted by how cheap and bloodless these coups were, especially by comparison with the cost of a real war such as that in Korea. Consequently, the guys in Plans enjoyed enormous prestige in government circles

– though not among the American public, who had been told by their newspapers that both coups were the work of local anti-communist forces.

Within the Plans Directorate was Technical Services, the division that Anthony Carroll headed. He had been hired when the CIA was set up in 1947. He had always planned to work in Washington – his major at Harvard had been government – and he had been a star of OSS in the war. Posted to Berlin earlier in the fifties, he had organized the digging of a tunnel from the American sector to a telephone conduit in the Soviet zone, and had tapped into KGB communications. The tunnel remained undiscovered for six months, during which the CIA amassed a mountain of priceless information. It had been the greatest intelligence coup of the Cold War, and Anthony's reward had been the top job.

Technical Services was theoretically a training division. There was a big old farmhouse down in Virginia where recruits learned how to break into houses and plant concealed microphones, to use codes and invisible ink, to blackmail diplomats and browbeat informers. But 'training' also served as an all-purpose cover for covert actions inside the USA. The fact that the CIA was prohibited, by law, from operating within the United States was no more than a minor inconvenience. Just about anything Anthony wanted to do, from bugging the phones of union bosses to testing truth drugs on prison inmates, could be labelled a training exercise.

The surveillance of Luke was no exception.

Six experienced agents were gathered in Anthony's office. It was a large, bare room with cheap wartime furniture: a small desk, a steel filing cabinet, a trestle table and a set of folding chairs. No doubt the new headquarters at Langley would be full of upholstered couches and mahogany panelling, but Anthony liked the Spartan look.

Pete Maxell passed around a mug shot of Luke and a typed description of his clothes while Anthony briefed the agents. 'Our target today is a middle-ranking State Department employee with a high security clearance,' he said. 'He's having some kind of nervous breakdown. He flew in from Paris on Monday, spent Monday night in the Carlton Hotel, and went on a drinking binge on Tuesday. He stayed out all last night, and went to a shelter for homeless people this morning. The security risk is obvious.'

One of the agents, 'Red' Rifenberg, put up a hand. 'Question.'

'Go ahead.'

'Why don't we just pull him in, ask him what the hell goes on?'

'We will, eventually.'

Anthony's office door opened, and Carl Hobart came in. A plump, bald man with spectacles, he was head of Specialized Services, which included Records and Decrypting as well as Technical Services. In theory, he was Anthony's immediate boss. Anthony groaned inwardly and prayed that Hobart would not interfere with what he was doing, today of all days.

Anthony continued with his briefing. 'But before we

tip our hand, we want to see what the subject does, where he goes – who he contacts, if anyone. A case like this, he may just be having trouble with his wife. But it could be that he's giving information to the other side, either for ideological reasons or because they're blackmailing him, and now the strain has gotten to be too much for him. If he's involved in some kind of treason, we need all the information we can get *before* we pick him up.'

Hobart interrupted. 'What's this?'

Anthony turned to him slowly. 'A little training exercise. We're conducting surveillance on a suspect diplomat.'

'Give it to the FBI,' Hobart said abruptly.

Hobart had spent the war in Naval Intelligence. For him, espionage was a plain matter of finding out where the enemy was and what he was doing there. He disliked OSS veterans and their dirty tricks. The split went right down the middle of the Agency. The OSS men were buccaneers. They had learned their trade in wartime, and had scant respect for budgets and protocol. The bureaucrats were infuriated by their nonchalance. And Anthony was the archetypal buccaneer: an arrogant daredevil who got away with murder because he was so good at it.

Anthony gave Hobart a cool look. 'Why?'

'It's the FBI's job, not ours, to catch communist spies in America – as you know perfectly well.'

'We need to follow the thread to its source. A case like this can unlock a horde of information if we handle it right. But the Feds are only interested in getting publicity for putting Reds in the electric chair.'

'It's the law!'

'But you and I know it's horseshit.'

'Makes no difference.'

One thing shared by the rival groups within the CIA was a hatred of the FBI and its megalomaniac director, J. Edgar Hoover. So Anthony said: 'Anyway, when was the last time the FBI gave us anything?'

'The last time was never,' Hobart said. 'But I've got another assignment for you today.'

Anthony began to feel angry. Where did this asshole get off? It was not his job to hand out assignments. 'What are you talking about?'

'The White House has called for a report on ways to deal with a rebel group in Cuba. There's a top-level meeting later this morning. I need you and all your experienced people to brief me.'

'You're asking me for a briefing on Fidel Castro?'

'Of course not. I know all about Castro. What I need from you are practical ideas for dealing with insurgency.'

Anthony despised this kind of mealy-mouthed talk. 'Why don't you say what you mean? You want to know how to take them out.'

'Maybe.'

Anthony laughed scornfully. 'Well, what else would we do – start a Sunday School for them?'

'That's for the White House to decide. Our job is to present options. You can give me some suggestions.'

Anthony maintained a show of indifference, but inside he was worried. He had no time for distractions today, and he needed all his best people to keep an eye on Luke. 'I'll see what I can do,' Anthony said, hoping Hobart might be satisfied with a vague assurance.

He was not. 'My conference room, with all your most experienced agents, at ten o'clock – and no excuses.' He turned away.

Anthony made a decision. 'No,' he said.

Hobart turned at the door. 'This is not a suggestion,' he said. 'Just be there.'

'Watch my lips,' said Anthony.

Reluctantly, Hobart stared at Anthony's face.

Enunciating carefully, Anthony said: 'Fuck off.'

One of the agents sniggered.

Hobart's bald head reddened. 'You'll hear more about this,' he said. 'A lot more.' He went out and slammed the door.

Everyone burst out laughing.

'Back to work,' Anthony said. 'Simons and Betts are with the subject at this moment, but they're due to be relieved in a few minutes. As soon as they call in, I want Red Rifenberg and Ackie Horwitz to take over the surveillance. We'll run four shifts of six hours each, with a back-up team always on call. That's all for now.'

The agents trooped out, but Pete Maxell stayed back. He had shaved and put on his regular business suit with a narrow Madison Avenue tie. Now his bad teeth and the red birthmark on his cheek were more noticeable, like broken windows in a new house. He was shy and unsociable, perhaps because of his appearance, and he was devoted to his few friends. Now he looked concerned as he said to Anthony: 'Aren't you taking a risk with Hobart?'

'He's an asshole.'

'He's your boss.'

'I can't let him close down an important surveillance operation.'

'But you lied to him. He could easily find out that Luke isn't a diplomat from Paris.'

Anthony shrugged. 'Then I'll tell him another story.'

Pete looked doubtful, but he nodded assent and moved to the door.

Anthony said: 'But you're right. I'm sticking my neck all the way out. If something goes wrong, Hobart won't miss a chance to chop my head off.'

'That's what I thought.'

'Then we'd better make sure nothing goes wrong.'

Pete went out. Anthony watched the phone, making himself calm and patient. Office politics infuriated him, but men such as Hobart were always around. After five minutes the phone rang and he picked it up. 'Carroll here.'

'You've been upsetting Carl Hobart again.' It was the wheezy voice of a man who has been smoking and drinking enthusiastically for most of a lifetime.

'Good morning, George,' said Anthony. George Cooperman was Deputy Chief of Operations and a wartime comrade of Anthony's. He was Hobart's immediate superior. 'Hobart should stay out of my way.'

'Get over here, you arrogant young prick,' George said amiably.

'Coming.' Anthony hung up. He opened his desk drawer and took out an envelope containing a thick sheaf of Xerox copies. Then he put on his topcoat and walked to Cooperman's office, which was in P Building, next door.

Cooperman was a tall, gaunt man of fifty with a prematurely lined face. He had his feet on his desk. There was a giant coffee mug at his elbow and a cigarette in his mouth. He was reading the Moscow newspaper *Pravda*: he had majored in Russian literature at Princeton.

He threw down the paper. 'Why can't you be nice to that fat fuck?' he growled. He spoke without removing the cigarette from the corner of his mouth. 'I know it's hard, but you could do it for my sake.'

Anthony sat down. 'It's his own fault. He should have realized by now that I only insult him if he speaks to me first.'

'What's your excuse this time?'

Anthony tossed the envelope on to the desk. Cooperman picked it up and looked at the Xerox copies. 'Blueprints,' he said. 'Of a rocket, I guess. So what?'

'They're top secret. I took them from the surveillance subject. He's a spy, George.'

'And you chose not to tell Hobart that.'

'I want to follow this guy around until he reveals his whole network – then use his operation for disinformation. Hobart would hand the case over to the FBI, who would pick the guy up and throw him in jail, and his network would fade to black.'

'Hell, you're right about that. Still, I need you at this meeting. I'm chairing it. But you can let your team carry on the surveillance. If anything happens they can get you out of the conference room.'

'Thanks, George.'

'And listen. This morning you fucked Hobart up the ass in front of a room full of agents, didn't you?'

'I guess so.'

'Next time, try and do it gently, okay?' Cooperman picked up *Pravda* again. Anthony got up to leave, taking the blueprints. Cooperman said: 'And make damn sure you run this surveillance right. If you screw up on top of insulting your boss, I may not be able to protect you.'

Anthony went out.

He did not return to his office right away. The row of condemned buildings that housed this part of the CIA filled a strip of land between Constitution Avenue and the mall with the reflecting pool. The motor entrances were on the street side, but Anthony went out through a back gate into the park.

He strolled along the avenue of English elms, breathing the cold fresh air, soothed by the ancient trees and the still water. There had been some bad moments this morning, but he had held it together, with a different set of lies for each party in the game.

He came to the end of the avenue and stood at the halfway point between the Lincoln Memorial and the Washington Monument. This is all your fault, he thought, addressing the two great presidents. You made men believe they could be free. I'm fighting for your ideals. I'm not even sure I believe in ideals any more – but I guess I'm too ornery to quit. Did you guys feel that way?

The presidents did not answer, and after a while Anthony returned to Q Building.

In his office he found Pete with the team that had been shadowing Luke: Simons, in a navy topcoat, and Betts, wearing a green raincoat. Also there were the team that should have relieved them, Rifenberg and Horwitz. 'What the hell is this?' Anthony said with sudden fear. 'Who's with Luke?'

Simons was carrying a grey Homburg hat, and it shook as his hand trembled. 'Nobody,' he said.

'What happened?' Anthony roared. 'What the fuck happened, you assholes?'

After a moment, Pete answered. 'We, uh . . .' He swallowed. 'We've lost him.'

PART 2

PART 2

9 A.M.

The Jupiter C has been built for the Army by the Chrysler Corporation. The large rocket engine that propels the first stage is manufactured by North American Aviation, Inc. The second, third and fourth stages have been designed and tested by the Jet Propulsion Laboratory in Pasadena.

Luke was angry with himself. He had handled things badly. He had found two people who probably knew who he was – and he had lost them again.

He was back in the low-rent neighbourhood near the gospel shop on H Street. The winter daylight was brightening, making the streets look more grimy, the buildings older, the people shabbier. He saw two bums in the doorway of a vacant store, passing a bottle of beer. He shuddered and walked quickly by.

Then he realized that was strange. An alcoholic wanted booze any time. But to Luke, the thought of beer this early in the day was nauseating. Therefore, he concluded with enormous relief, he could not be an alcoholic.

But, if he was not a drunk, what was he?

He summed up what he knew about himself. He was in his thirties. He did not smoke. Despite appearances, he was not an alcoholic. At some point in his life he had been involved in clandestine work. And he knew the words of 'What a Friend We Have in Jesus.' It was pathetically little.

He had been walking around looking for a police station, but he had not come across one. He decided to ask for directions. A minute later, as he passed a vacant lot fenced with broken corrugated-iron sheeting, he saw a uniformed cop step through a gap in the sheeting on to the sidewalk. Seizing the chance, Luke said to him: 'How do I get to the nearest precinct house?'

The cop was a beefy man with a sandy moustache. He gave Luke a look of contempt and said: 'In the trunk of my cruiser, if you don't get the fuck out of my sight.'

Luke was startled by the violence of his language. What was the man's problem? But he was tired of tramping the streets, and he needed directions, so he persisted. 'I just need to know where the station house is.'

'I won't tell you again, shitbrain.'

Luke was annoyed. Who did he think he was? 'I asked you a polite question, Mister,' he snapped.

The cop moved surprisingly fast for a heavy man. He grabbed Luke by the lapels of his ragged coat and shoved him through the gap in the sheeting. Luke staggered and fell on a patch of rough concrete, hurting his arm.

To his surprise he was not alone. Just inside the lot was a young woman. She had dyed blonde hair and heavy make-up, and she wore a long coat open over a loose dress. She had high-heeled evening shoes and torn stockings. She was pulling up her panties. Luke realized she was a prostitute who had just serviced the patrolman.

The cop came through the gap and kicked Luke in the stomach.

He heard the whore say: 'For Christ's sake, Sid, what did he do, spit on the sidewalk? Leave the poor bum alone!'

'Fucker has to learn some respect,' the cop said thickly.

Out of the corner of his eye, Luke saw him draw his nightstick and raise it. As the blow came down, Luke rolled to one side. He was not quite fast enough, and the end of the stick glanced off his left shoulder, numbing his arm momentarily. The cop raised the nightstick again.

A circuit closed in Luke's brain.

Instead of rolling away, he threw himself towards the cop. The man's forward momentum brought him crashing to the ground, and he dropped the nightstick. Luke sprang up nimbly. As the cop got up, Luke stepped close to him, waltzing inside his reach so that the man could not punch him. He grabbed the lapels of the uniform coat, pulled the man forward with a sharp jerk, and butted him in the face. There was a snapping sound as the cop's nose broke. The man roared with pain.

Luke released his grip on the lapels, pirouetted on one foot, and kicked the man in the side of the knee.

His battered shoes were not rigid enough to break bones, but the knee has little resistance to a blow from the side, and the cop fell.

A part of Luke's mind wondered where the hell he had learned to fight like this.

The cop was bleeding from the nose and mouth, but he raised himself on his left elbow and drew his gun with his right hand.

Before it was out of the holster, Luke was on him. Grabbing the man's right forearm, he banged the hand on the concrete once, very hard. The gun immediately fell from the cop's grasp. Then Luke pulled the cop upright and twisted his arm so that he rolled onto his front. Bending the arm up behind the man's back, Luke dropped, driving both knees into the small of the cop's back, knocking the breath out of his lungs. Finally, he took the cop's forefinger and bent it all the way back.

The cop screamed. Luke bent the finger farther. He heard it snap, and the cop fainted.

'You won't beat up any more bums for a while,' Luke said. 'Shitbrain.'

He stood up. He picked up the gun, ejected all the shells, and threw them across the lot.

The whore was staring at him. 'Who the fuck are you, Elliott Ness?' she said.

Luke looked back at her. She was thin, and under the make-up her complexion was bad. 'I don't know who I am,' he told her.

'Well, you ain't no bum, that's for sure,' she said. 'I

never saw an alky that could punch out a big fat prick like Sidney here.'

'That's what I've been thinking.'

'We better get out of here,' she said. 'He's going to be mad when he comes round.'

Luke nodded. He was not afraid of Sidney, mad or otherwise, but before long there would be more cops on the scene, and he needed to be elsewhere. He stepped through the gap in the fence on to the street and walked away quickly.

The woman followed him, stiletto heels clicking on the sidewalk. He slowed his pace to let her catch up, feeling a kind of camaraderie with her. They had both been abused by Sidney the patrolman.

'It was kind of nice to see Sidney come up against someone he couldn't push around,' she said. 'I guess I owe you.'

'Not at all.'

'Well, next time you're feeling horny, it's on the house.'

Luke tried not to show his revulsion. 'What's your name?'

'Dee-Dee.'

He raised an eyebrow at her.

'Well, Doris Dobbs, really,' she admitted. 'But what kind of name is that for a good-time girl?'

'I'm Luke. I don't know my surname. I've lost my memory.'

'Wow. That must make you feel, like . . . strange.'

'Disoriented.'

'Yeah,' she said. 'That's the word was on the tip of my tongue.'

He glanced at her. There was a wry grin on her face. He realized she was making fun of him, and he liked her for it. 'It's not just that I don't know my name and address,' he explained. 'I don't even know what kind of person I am.'

'What do you mean?'

'I wonder if I'm honest?' Maybe it was foolish, he thought, to pour out his heart to a whore on the street, but he had no one else. 'Am I a loyal husband and a loving father and a reliable workmate? Or am I some kind of gangster? I hate not knowing.'

'Honey, if that's what's bothering you, I know what kind of guy you are already. A gangster would be thinking am I rich, do I slay the broads, are people scared of me?'

That was a point. Luke nodded. But he was not satisfied. 'It's one thing to want to be a good person – but maybe I don't live up to what I believe in.'

'Welcome to the human race, sweetheart,' she said. 'We all feel that way.' She stopped at a doorway. 'It's been a long night. This is where I get off the train.'

'So long.'

She hesitated. 'Want some advice?'

'Sure.'

'If you want people to stop treating you like a piece of shit, you better smarten yourself up. Have a shave, comb your hair, find yourself a coat that doesn't look like you stole it off a carthorse.'

Luke realized she was right. No one would take any

notice of him, let alone help him discover his identity, while he looked like a crazy person. 'I guess you're right,' he said. 'Thanks.' He turned away.

She called after him: 'And get a hat!'

He touched his head, then looked around. He was the only person on the street, male or female, without a hat. But how could a bum get a new suit of clothes? The handful of change in his pocket would not buy much.

The solution came fully formed into his head. Either it was an easy question, or he had been in this situation before. He would go to a train station. A station was generally full of people carrying complete changes of clothing, together with shaving tackle and other toiletries, all neatly packed in suitcases.

He went to the next corner and checked his location. He was on A Street and Seventh. On leaving Union Station early this morning, he had noticed that it was near the corner of F and Second.

He headed that way.

10 A.M.

The first stage of the missile is attached to the second by explosive bolts wrapped around with coil springs. When the booster is burned out, the bolts will detonate and the springs push the redundant first stage away.

The Georgetown Mind Hospital was a red-brick Victorian mansion with a flat-roofed modern extension at the back. Billie Josephson parked her red Ford Thunderbird in the parking lot and hurried into the building.

She hated to arrive this late. It seemed disrespectful of her work and her colleagues. What they were doing was vitally important. Slowly, painstakingly, they were learning to understand the mechanisms of the human mind. It was like mapping a distant planet, the surface of which could be seen only through breaks in the cloud layer that were tantalizingly brief.

She was late because of her mother. After Larry left for school, Billie had gone to get the heart pills and returned home to find Becky-Ma lying on her bed, fully dressed, gasping for breath. The doctor had come right away, but he had nothing new to say. Becky-Ma had a weak heart. If she felt breathless, she should lie

90

down. She must remember to take her pills. Any stress was bad for her.

Billie wanted to say: 'What about me? Isn't stress bad for me, too?' But instead she resolved anew to walk on eggshells around her mother.

She stopped by the admissions office and glanced at the overnight register. A new patient had been brought in late yesterday, after she had left: Joseph Bellow, a schizophrenic. The name rang a bell, but she could not recall why. Surprisingly, the patient had been discharged during the night. That was odd.

She passed through the day room on the way to her office. The TV was on, and a reporter standing on a dusty beach was saying: 'Here at Cape Canaveral, the question on everyone's lips is: "When will the army attempt to launch its own rocket?" It must be within the next few days.'

The subjects of Billie's research sat around, some watching TV, some playing games or reading, a few gazing vacantly into space. She waved to Tom, a young man who did not know the meaning of words. 'How are you, Tommy?' she called. He grinned and waved back. He could read body language well, and often responded as if he knew what people were saying, so it had taken Billie months to figure out that he did not understand a single word.

In a corner Marlene, an alcoholic, was flirting with a young male nurse. She was fifty years old, but she could not remember anything that had happened since she was nineteen. She thought she was still a young girl, and refused to believe that the 'old man' who loved and cared for her was her husband.

Through the glass wall of an interview room she saw Ronald, a brilliant architect who had suffered head injuries in a car crash. He was doing tests on paper. His problem was that he had lost the ability to deal with numbers. He would count with excruciating slowness on his fingers in the attempt to add three and four.

Many patients had forms of schizophrenia, an inability to relate to the real world.

Some of the patients could be helped, by drugs or electric-shock treatment or both; but Billie's job was to trace the exact contours of their disabilities. By studying minor mental handicaps, she was outlining the functions of the normal mind. Ronald, the architect, could look at a group of objects on a tray and say whether there were three or four of them, but if there were twelve and he had to count them, he would take a long time and might make a mistake. This suggested to Billie that the ability to see at a glance how many items are in a small group is a separate skill from the ability to count.

In this way, she was slowly charting the depths of the mind, locating memory here, language there, mathematics somewhere else. And if the disability was related to minor brain damage, Billie could speculate that the normal ability was located in the part of the brain that had been destroyed. Eventually, her conceptual picture of the mind's functions would be mapped on to a physical diagram of the human brain.

At her present rate of progress, it would take about two hundred years. However, she was working alone. With a team of psychologists she could progress much faster. She might see the map completed in her lifetime. That was her ambition.

It was a long way from her father's suicidal depression. There were no quick cures in mental illness. But the mind was still largely a mystery to scientists. It would be much better understood if Billie could speed up her work. And then, perhaps, people like her father could be helped.

She went up the stairs to the next floor, thinking about the mystery patient. Joseph Bellow sounded like Joe Blow, the kind of name someone might make up. And why had he been discharged in the middle of the night?

She reached her office and looked out of the window on to a building site. A new wing was being added to the hospital – and a new post was to be created to go with it: Director of Research. Billie had applied for the job. But so had one of her colleagues, Dr Leonard Ross. Len was older than Billie, but she had wider experience and had published more: several articles and a textbook, *An Introduction to the Psychology of Memory*. She felt sure she could beat out Len, but she did not know who else might be in the running. And she wanted the job badly. As Director, she would have other scientists working under her.

On the building site she noticed, among the workmen, a small group of men in business clothes – wool topcoats and Homburgs instead of overalls and hard hats. They looked as if they might be getting a tour. Looking more closely, she saw that Len Ross was with them.

She spoke to her secretary. 'Who are those guys being shown around the site by Len Ross?'

'They're from the Sowerby Foundation.'

Billie frowned. The Foundation was financing the new post. They would have a big say in who got the job. And there was Len making nice to them. 'Did we know they were coming today?'

'Len said he had sent you a note. He came by this morning to pick you up, but you weren't here.'

There had never been a note, Billie felt sure. Len had deliberately failed to warn her. And she had been late.

'Damn,' Billie said with feeling. She rushed out to join the party on the building site.

She did not think about Joseph Bellow again for several hours.

11 A.M.

Because the missile was put together in a rush, the upper stages use a rocket motor that has been in production for some years, rather than a new design. The scientists have chosen a small version of the tried-and-tested Sergeant rocket. The upper stages of the missile are powered by clustered assemblies of these small rockets, known as Baby Sergeants.

As Luke negotiated the grid of streets leading to Union Station, he found himself checking, every minute or two, to see whether he was being followed.

He had lost his shadows more than an hour ago, but they might now be searching for him. The thought made him fearful and bewildered. Who were they and what were they doing? His instincts told him they were malevolent. Otherwise, why watch him secretly?

He shook his head to clear it. This baseless speculation was frustrating. There was no point in guessing. He had to find out.

First he had to clean himself up. His plan was to steal a suitcase from a train passenger. He felt sure he had done this before, at some time in his life. When he tried to remember, French words came into his head: 'La valise d'un type qui descend du train.'

It would not be easy. His dirty, ragged clothing would stand out in a crowd of respectable travellers. He would have to move fast to get away. But he had no alternative. Dee-Dee the whore had been right. No one would listen to a bum.

If he were arrested, the police would never believe he was anything but a deadbeat. He would end up in jail. The thought made him shiver with fear. It was not prison itself that scared him so much as the prospect of weeks or months of ignorance and confusion, not knowing who he was and helpless to make any progress finding out.

Ahead of him on Massachusetts Avenue he saw the white granite arcade of Union Station, like a Romanesque cathedral transplanted from Normandy. Thinking ahead, he figured that after the theft he would have to disappear fast. He needed a car. The knowledge of how to steal one came into his mind immediately.

Close to the station, the street was lined with parked cars. Most would belong to people who had taken trains. He slowed his pace as a car pulled into a slot ahead of him. It was a two-tone Ford Fairlane, blue and white, new but not ostentatious. It would do fine. The starter would be operated with a key, not a handle, but it would be easy to pull out a couple of wires behind the dash and bypass the ignition.

He wondered how he knew that.

A man in a dark topcoat got out of the Ford, took a briefcase from the trunk, locked the car, and headed for the station.

How long would he be gone? It was possible he had some business at the station and would be back in a few minutes. Then he would report his car stolen. Driving around in it, Luke would be in danger of arrest at any minute. That was no good. He had to find out where the man was going.

He followed him into the station.

The grand interior, which this morning had seemed like a disused temple, was now bustling. He felt conspicuous. Everyone else seemed so clean and well dressed. Most people averted their eyes, but some looked at him with expressions of disgust or contempt. It occurred to him that he might run into the officious man who had thrown him out earlier. Then there would be a fuss. The guy was sure to remember.

The owner of the Ford joined a line at a ticket window. Luke got in line too. He looked at the ground, not meeting anyone's eye, hoping no one would notice him.

The line shuffled forward and his mark reached the window. 'Philadelphia, one-day return,' he said.

That was enough for Luke. Philadelphia was hours away. The man would be out of town all day. His car would not be reported stolen before he returned. Luke would be safe in it until tonight.

He left the line and hurried away.

It was a relief to be outside. Even bums had the right to walk the streets. He returned to Massachusetts Avenue and found the parked Ford. To save time later, he would unlock it now. He looked up and down the street. Cars and pedestrians were passing constantly.

The trouble was that he looked like a criminal. But if he waited until there was no one about, he could be here all day. He would just have to be quick.

He stepped into the road, walked around the car, and stood at the driver's door. Pressing his hands flat against the glass of the window, he pushed down. Nothing happened. His mouth felt dry. He looked quickly to either side: no one was paying him any attention yet. He stood on tiptoe, to add the weight of his body to the pressure on the window mechanism. At last the pane of glass slid slowly down.

When the window was fully open, he reached in and unlocked the door. He opened it, wound up the window, and closed the door again. Now he was ready for a fast getaway.

He considered starting the car now and leaving the engine running, but that might draw the attention of a passing patrolman or even just an inquisitive passer-by.

He returned to Union Station. He worried constantly that a railroad employee would notice him. It did not have to be the man he had clashed with earlier – any conscientious official might take it in to his head to throw him out, the way such a man might pick up a candy wrapper. He did everything he could to make himself inconspicuous. He walked neither slow nor fast, tried to keep close to walls when he could, took care not to cross anyone's path, and never looked anyone in the eye.

The best time to steal a suitcase would be immediately after the arrival of a large, crowded train, when the concourse was thronged with hurrying people. He studied the information board. An express from New York was due in twelve minutes. That would be perfect.

As he looked at the board, checking which track the train would come in on, the hairs on the back of his neck stood up.

He looked around. He must have seen something out of the corner of his eye, something that had triggered an instinctive warning. What? His heart beat faster. What was he afraid of?

Trying to be inconspicuous, he strolled away from the board and stood at the news-stand, examining a rack of daily papers. He took in the headlines:

ARMY ROCKET BLAST SOON
SLAYER OF 10 IS NABBED
DULLES ASSURES BAGHDAD GROUP
LAST CHANCE AT CAPE CANAVERAL

After a moment he looked back over his shoulder. A couple of dozen people criss-crossed the concourse, hurrying to or from suburban trains. A larger number sat on the mahogany benches or stood around patiently, relatives and chauffeurs waiting to meet passengers off the New York train. A maître d' stood outside the door of the restaurant, hoping for early lunch customers. There were five porters in a group, smoking . . .

And two agents.

He was quite certain what they were. Both were

young men, neatly dressed in topcoats and hats, their wingtip shoes well shined. But it was not their appearance so much as their attitude that gave them away. They were alert, raking the station concourse with their eyes, studying the faces of the people they passed, looking everywhere ... except at the information board. The one thing they were not interested in was travel.

He was tempted to speak to them. Thinking about it, he was overwhelmed by a need for simple human contact with people who knew him. He longed for someone to say: 'Hi, Luke, how are you? Good to see you again!'

These two would probably say: 'We are FBI agents and you are under arrest.' Luke felt that would almost be a relief. But his instincts warned him off. Every time he thought of trusting them, he asked himself why they would follow him around surreptitiously if they meant him no harm.

He turned his back to them and walked away, trying to keep the news-stand between him and them. In the shadow of a grand archway he risked a backwards look. The two men were crossing the open concourse, walking from east to west across his field of vision.

Who the hell were they?

He left the station, walked a few yards along the grand arcade of its front, and re-entered the main hall. He was in time to see the backs of the two agents as they headed for the west exit.

He checked the clock. Ten minutes had passed. The New York express was due in two minutes. He hurried to the gate and waited, trying to fade into the background.

As the first passengers emerged, a frigid calm descended on him. He watched the arrivals intently. It was a Wednesday, the middle of the week, so there were many businessmen and military types in uniform, but few tourists, and only a sprinkling of women and children. He looked for a man his own size and build.

As passengers poured through the gate, the people waiting surged forward and a traffic jam formed. The crowd around the gate thickened, then spread, with people pushing through irritably. Luke saw a young man of his size, but he was wearing a duffel coat and a wool watch cap: he might not have a spare suit in his haversack. Likewise, Luke dismissed an elderly traveller who was the right height but too thin. He saw a man who looked just right but carried only a briefcase.

By this time at least a hundred passengers had emerged, but there seemed to be many more to come. The concourse filled up with impatient people. Then he saw the right man. He was Luke's height, build and age. His grey topcoat was unbuttoned to show a tweed sport coat and flannel pants – which meant he probably had a business suit in the tan leather case he carried in his right hand. His face wore an anxious look, and he walked quickly, as if he were late for an appointment.

Luke slipped into the crowd and shoved his way through until he was directly behind the man.

The throng was dense and slow-moving, and Luke's target moved in fretful stops and starts. Then the crowd thinned a little, and the man stepped quickly into a gap.

That was when Luke tripped him. He hooked his foot firmly around the ankle in front of him. As the man moved forward, Luke kicked upward, bending the target's leg at the knee.

The man cried out and fell forward. He let go of both briefcase and suitcase, and threw his hands out in front of him. He crashed into the back of a woman in a fur coat and she, too, stumbled, giving a little scream, and fell. The man hit the marble floor with an audible thump, his hat rolling away. A split second later the woman went down on both knees, dropping a handbag and a chic white leather suitcase.

Other passengers quickly gathered around, trying to help, saying: 'Are you all right?'

Luke calmly picked up the tan leather suitcase and walked quickly away. He headed for the nearest exit arch. He did not look back, but he listened intently for shouted accusations or sounds of pursuit. If he heard anything, he was ready to run: he was not going to give up his clean clothes easily, and he felt he could probably outrun most people, even carrying a suitcase. But his back felt like a bull's-eye target as he walked briskly toward the doors.

At the exit, he glanced back over his shoulder. The crowd was milling around the same spot. He could not see the man he had tripped, nor the woman in the fur coat. But a tall man with an authoritative air was scanning the concourse keenly, as if looking for something. His head swivelled suddenly toward Luke.

Luke stepped quickly through the door.

Outside, he headed down Massachusetts Avenue. A minute later he reached the Ford Fairlane. He went automatically for the trunk, so that he could hide the stolen suitcase – but the trunk was locked. He recalled seeing the owner lock it. He looked back toward the station. The tall man was running across the traffic circle in front of the station, dodging cars, heading Luke's way. Who was he – off-duty cop? Detective? Nosy Parker?

Luke went quickly around to the driver's door, opened it, and slung the bag onto the back seat. Then he got in and slammed the door.

He reached under the dash and found the wires on either side of the ignition lock. He pulled them out and touched them together. Nothing happened. He felt sweat on his forehead, despite the cold. Why was this not working? The answer came into his head: Wrong wire. He felt under the dash again. There was another wire to the right of the ignition. He pulled it out and touched it to the wire on the left.

The engine started.

He pressed the gas pedal, and the engine raced.

He put the transmission into drive, released the parking brake, flicked the indicator, and pulled out. The car was pointing towards the station, so he did a U-turn. Then he drove off.

A smile crossed his face. Unless he was very unlucky, he had a complete set of fresh clothes in the bag. He felt he had begun to take charge of his life.

Now he needed somewhere to shower and change.

12 NOON

The second stage consists of eleven Baby Sergeant rockets in an annular ring around a central tube. The third stage has three Baby Sergeant motors held together by three transverse bulkheads. On top of the third stage is the fourth, a single rocket, with the satellite in its nose.

The countdown stood at X minus 630 minutes, and Cape Canaveral was buzzing.

Rocket men were all the same: they would design weapons, if the government wanted, but what they dreamed about was outer space. The Explorer team had built and launched many missiles, but this would be the first of them to break free of the Earth's pull and fly beyond the atmosphere. For most of the team, tonight's launch would be the fulfilment of a lifetime's hopes. Elspeth felt the same way.

They were based in Hangar D and Hangar R, which were side by side. The standard aircraft hangar design had been found to be well suited to missiles: there was a large central space where the rockets could be checked out, with two-storey wings either side for offices and smaller laboratories.

Elspeth was in Hangar R. She had a typewriter and

a desk in the office of her boss, Willy Fredrickson, the launch conductor, who spent almost all his time elsewhere. Her job was to prepare and distribute the launch timetable.

Trouble was, the timetable changed constantly. Nobody in America had sent a rocket into space before. New problems arose all the time, and the engineers were forever improvising ways to jury-rig a component or bypass a system. Here, duct tape was called missile tape.

So Elspeth produced regular updates of the timetable. She had to stay in touch with every group on the team, record changes of plan in her shorthand notebook, then transfer her notes to typed and Xeroxed sheets and distribute them. The job required her to go everywhere and know almost everything. When there was a hitch, she learned of it right away; and she was among the first to know about the solution, too. Her title was secretary, and she was paid a secretary's wages, but no one could have done the job without a science degree. However, she did not resent the low pay. She was grateful for a job that challenged her. Some of her Radcliffe classmates were still taking dictation from men in grey flannel suits.

Her noon update was ready, and she picked up the stack of papers and set out to distribute them. She was rushed off her feet, but that suited her today: it stopped her worrying constantly about Luke. If she followed her inclination, she would be on the phone to Anthony every few minutes, asking if there was any news. But that would be stupid. He would contact her if anything went wrong, she told herself. Meanwhile she should concentrate on her work.

Elspeth went first to the press department, where public relations officers were working the phones, telling trusted reporters that there would be a launch tonight. The army wanted journalists on the scene to witness their triumph. However, the information was not to be released until after the event. Scheduled launches were often delayed, or even cancelled, as unforeseen snags arose. The missile men had learned, from bitter experience, that a routine postponement to solve technical problems could be made to look like an abject failure when the newspapers reported it. So they had a deal with all the major news organizations. They gave advance notification of launches only on condition that nothing would be published until there was 'fire in the tail', which meant that the rocket engine had been ignited.

It was an all-male office, and several men stared at Elspeth as she walked across the room and handed a timetable to the chief press officer. She knew she was attractive, with her pale Viking looks and tall, statuesque figure; but there was something formidable about her – the determined set of her mouth, maybe, or the dangerous light in her green eyes – that made men who were inclined to whistle, or call her 'Honeybunch', think again.

In the Missile Firing Laboratory she found five shirt-sleeved scientists standing at a bench, staring worriedly at a flat piece of metal that looked as if it had been in a fire. The group leader, Dr Keller, said: 'Good afternoon, Elspeth.' He spoke in heavily accented English. Like most of the scientists, he was a German who had been captured at the end of the war and brought to America to work on the missile programme.

She handed him a copy of her update, and he took it without looking at it. Elspeth nodded at the object on the table and said: 'What's that?'

'A jet vane.'

Elspeth knew that the first stage was steered by vanes inside the tail. 'What happened to it?'

'The burning fuel erodes the metal,' he explained. His German accent became stronger as he warmed to his subject. 'This always happens, to some extent. However, with normal alcohol fuel, the vanes last long enough to do their job. Today, by contrast we are using a new fuel, Hydyne, that has a longer burning time and higher exhaust velocity – but it may erode the vanes so much that they become ineffective for steering.' He spread his hands in a gesture of exasperation. 'We have not had time to run sufficiently many tests.'

'I guess all I need to know is whether this is going to delay the launch.' She felt she could not stand a postponement. The suspense was already killing her.

'That's what we're trying to decide.' Keller looked around at his colleagues. 'And I think our answer is going to be: Let's take the chance.' The others nodded gloomily.

Elspeth felt relieved. 'I'll keep my fingers crossed,' she said, turning to leave.

'That's about as useful as anything we can do,' Keller said, and the others laughed ruefully.

She went outside into the scorching Florida sun. The hangars stood in a sandy clearing hacked out of the low scrub that covered the Cape – palmetto palms and scrub oaks and sharp sandspur grass that would cut your skin if you walked barefoot. She crossed a dusty apron and entered Hangar D, its welcome shade falling across her face like the touch of a cool breeze.

In the telemetry room Elspeth saw Hans Mueller, known as Hank. He pointed a finger at her and said: 'One hundred thirty-five.'

It was a game they played. She had to say what was unusual about the number. 'Too easy,' she said. 'Take the first digit, add the square of the second digit, plus the cube of the third, and you get the number you first thought of.' She gave him the equation:

$$1^1+3^2+5^3=135$$

'All right,' he said. 'So what is the next-highest number that follows the pattern?'

She thought hard, then said: 'One hundred and seventy-five.'

$$1^1+7^2+5^3=175$$

'Correct! You win the big prize.' He fished in his pocket and brought out a dime.

She took it. 'I'll give you a chance to win it back,' she said. 'One hundred thirty-six.'

'Ah.' He frowned. 'Wait. Sum the cubes of its digits.'

$$1^3+3^3+6^3=244$$

'Now repeat the process, and you get the number you first thought of!'

$$2^3+4^3+4^3=136$$

She gave him back his dime, and a copy of her update.

As she went out, her eye was caught by a telegram pinned to the wall: I'VE HAD MY LITTLE SATELLITE, NOW YOU HAVE YOURS. Mueller noticed her reading it and explained: 'It's from Stuhlinger's wife.' Stuhlinger was chief of research. 'She had a baby boy.' Elspeth smiled.

She found Willy Fredrickson in the communications room with two army technicians, testing the teletype link to the Pentagon. Her boss was a tall, thin man, bald with a fringe of curly hair, like a medieval monk. The teletype machine was not working, and Willy was frustrated, but as he took the update he gave her a grateful look and said: 'Elspeth, you are twenty-two-carat gold.'

A moment later, two people approached Willy: a young army officer carrying a chart, and Stimmens, one of the scientists. The officer said: 'We got a problem.' He handed Willy the chart, and went on: 'The jet stream has moved south, and it's blowing at 146 knots.'

Elspeth's heart sank. She knew what this meant. The jet stream was a high-altitude wind in the stratosphere between 30,000 and 40,000 feet. It did not normally extend over Cape Canaveral, but it could move. And if it was too fierce, it might throw the missile off course.

Willy said: 'How far south is it?'

'All over Florida,' the officer replied.

Willy turned to Stimmens. 'We've allowed for this, haven't we?'

'Not really,' Stimmens said. 'It's all guesswork, of course, but we figure the missile can withstand winds up to 120 knots, no higher.'

Willy turned back to the officer. 'What's the forecast for tonight?'

'Up to 177 knots, and no sign of the jet stream moving back north.'

'Hell.' Willy ran a hand over his smooth pate. Elspeth knew what he was thinking. The launch might have to be postponed until tomorrow. 'Send up a weather balloon, please,' he ordered. 'We'll review the forecast again at five o'clock.'

Elspeth made a note to add the weather-review meeting to her timetable, then she left, feeling despondent. They could solve engineering problems, but there was nothing they could do about the weather.

Outside, she got into a jeep and drove to Launch Complex 26. The road was a dusty, unpaved track through the brush, and the jeep bounced on the ruts. She startled a white-tailed deer that was drinking from a ditch, and it bounded off into the bushes. There was a lot of wildlife on the Cape, hiding in the low scrub. People said there were alligators and Florida panthers, but Elspeth had never seen either.

She pulled up outside the blockhouse and looked across to Launch Pad 26B, three hundred yards away. The gantry was a derrick from an oil rig, adapted for this purpose and coated with orange rust-resistant paint to protect it from corrosion by the humid, salty Florida air. At one side was an elevator for access to the platforms. The whole edifice was brutally practical, quite without grace, Elspeth thought; a functional structure bolted together with no regard for how it looked.

The long white pencil of the Jupiter C rocket seemed caught in the tangle of orange girders like a dragonfly in a spiderweb. The men called it 'she', despite its phallic shape, and Elspeth too thought of the rocket as female. A bridal veil of canvas covers had concealed the upper stages from prying eyes since it arrived here; but that had now been removed, and the missile stood fully revealed, sunshine gleaming off its spotless paintwork.

The scientists were not very political, but even they knew that the eyes of the world were on them. Four months ago, the Soviet Union had stunned the world by sending up the first space satellite, the Sputnik. In all the countries where the tug-of-war between capitalism and communism was still going on, from Italy to India, throughout Latin America and Africa and Indochina, the message was heard: Communist science is best. A month later the Soviets had sent up a second satellite, Sputnik 2, with a dog on board. Americans were devastated. A dog today, a man tomorrow.

President Eisenhower promised an American satellite before the end of the year. On the first Friday in December, at fifteen minutes to noon, the US Navy launched its Vanguard rocket in front of the world's press. It rose a few feet into the air, burst into flames, toppled sideways and smashed to pieces on the concrete. IT'S A FLOPNIK! said one headline.

The Jupiter C was America's last hope. There was no third option. If this failed today, the United States was out of the space race. The propaganda defeat was the least of the consequences. The American space programme would be in total disarray, and the USSR would control outer space for the foreseeable future.

All that, Elspeth thought, resting on this one rocket.

Vehicles were banned from the launch-pad area, except for essential ones such as fuel trucks, so she left her car and walked across the open space between blockhouse and gantry, following the line of a metal conduit that housed the cables linking the two locations. Attached to the back of the derrick at ground level was a long steel cabin, the same orange colour, containing offices and machinery. Elspeth entered by a metal door at the rear.

The gantry supervisor, Harry Lane, sat on a folding chair, wearing a hard hat and engineer boots, studying a blueprint. 'Hi, Harry,' she said brightly.

He grunted. He did not like to see women around the launch pad, and no sense of courtesy constrained him from letting her know it.

She dropped an update on a metal table and left. She returned to the blockhouse, a low white building with slit windows of thick green glass. The blast doors stood open, and she walked inside. There were three compartments: an instrumentation room, which ran the width of the building, and two firing rooms, A on the left and B on the right, angled towards the two launch pads served by this blockhouse. Elspeth stepped into Firing Room B.

The strong sunlight coming through the green glass cast a weird light over the whole place, so that it looked like the inside of an aquarium. In front of the windows, a row of scientists sat at a bank of control panels. They all wore short-sleeved shirts, she noticed, as if it were a uniform. They had headsets through which they could talk to the men on the launch pad. They could look over their panels and see the rocket through the windows, or check the colour television screens that showed the same picture. Along the back wall of the firing room, a row of pen recorders stood shoulder to shoulder, tracking temperatures, pressures in the fuel system, and electrical activity. In the far corner was a scale showing the weight of the missile on the launch pad. There was an air of quiet urgency as the men murmured into their headsets and worked their panels, turning a knob here, throwing a switch there, constantly checking the dials and counters. Over their heads, a countdown clock showed the minutes left to ignition. As Elspeth looked, the hand clicked down from 600 to 599.

She handed out her update and left the building. Driving back to the hangar, her mind turned to Luke and she realized she had a perfect excuse for calling

Anthony. She would tell him about the jet stream, then ask about Luke.

That perked her up, and she hurried into the hangar and up the stairs to her office. She dialled Anthony's direct line and got him right away. 'The launch is likely to be postponed until tomorrow,' she told him. 'There are strong winds in the stratosphere.'

'I didn't know there were winds up there.'

'There's one, it's called the jet stream. The postponement isn't definite, there's a weather-review meeting at five. How's Luke?'

'Let me know the upshot of that meeting, okay?'

'Of course. How's Luke?'

'Well, we have a problem there.'

Her heart missed a beat. 'What kind of a problem?'

'We've lost him.'

Elspeth felt cold. 'What?'

'He slipped away from my men.'

'Jesus help us,' she said. 'Now we're in trouble.'

1941

Luke arrived back in Boston at dawn. He parked the old Ford, slipped in through the back door of Cambridge House, and climbed the service stairs to his room. Anthony was fast asleep. Luke washed his face and fell into bed in his underwear.

Next thing he knew, Anthony was shaking him, saying: 'Luke! Get up!'

He opened his eyes. He knew that something bad had happened, but he could not recall what it was. 'What's the time?' he mumbled.

'It's one o'clock, and Elspeth is waiting for you downstairs.'

The mention of Elspeth's name jogged his memory, and he recalled what the calamity was. He did not love her any more. 'Oh, God,' he said.

'You'd better go down and see her.'

He had fallen in love with Billie Josephson. That was the disaster. It would make a train wreck of all their lives: his own, Elspeth's, Billie's and Anthony's.

'Hell,' he said, and he got up.

He stripped off his underwear and took a cold shower. When he closed his eyes he saw Billie, her dark eyes flashing, her red mouth laughing, her white

115

throat. He pulled on a pair of flannels, a sweater, and tennis shoes, then staggered downstairs.

Elspeth was waiting in the lobby, the only part of the building where girls were allowed, except on specially designated Ladies' Afternoons. It was a spacious hall with a fireplace and comfortable chairs. She was as eye-catching as ever, in a wool dress the colour of bluebells and a big hat. Yesterday, the sight of her would have gladdened his heart; today, the knowledge that she had dressed up for him just made him feel even more wretched.

She laughed when she saw him. 'You look like a small boy who can't wake up!'

He kissed her cheek and slumped into a chair. 'It took hours to get to Newport,' he said.

'You've obviously forgotten you're supposed to take me to lunch!' Elspeth said brightly.

He looked at her. She was beautiful, but he did not love her. He did not know whether he had loved her before, but he was sure he did not now. He was the worst kind of heel. She was so gay this morning, and he was going to ruin her happiness. He did not know how to tell her. He felt so ashamed it was like a pain in his heart.

He had to say something. 'Can we skip lunch? I haven't even shaved.'

A troubled shadow crossed her pale, proud face, and he realized that she knew perfectly well something was wrong; but her reply was carefree. 'Of course,' she said. 'Knights in shining armour need their beauty sleep.'

He told himself he would have a serious talk with her, and be completely honest, later in the day. 'I'm sorry you got dressed up for nothing,' he said miserably.

'It wasn't for nothing – I saw you. And your fellow housemen seemed to like my outfit.' She stood up. 'Anyway, Professor and Mrs Durkham are having a jolly-up.' That was Radcliffe slang for a party.

Luke stood and helped her into her coat. 'We could meet later.' He had to tell her today – it would be deceitful to let any more time pass without revealing the truth.

'That'll be fine,' she said gaily. 'Pick me up at six.' She blew him a kiss and walked out like a movie star. He knew she was faking, but it was a good act.

He returned woefully to his room. Anthony was reading the Sunday paper. 'I made coffee,' he said.

'Thanks.' Luke poured a cup.

'I owe you big time,' Anthony went on. 'You saved Billie's hide last night.'

'You'd do the same for me.' Luke sipped his coffee and began to feel better. 'Seems we got away with it. Has anyone said anything to you this morning?'

'Not a thing.'

'Billie's quite a gal,' Luke said. He knew it was dangerous to talk about her, but he could not help it.

'Isn't she great?' Anthony said. Luke observed with dismay the look of pride on his room-mate's face. Anthony went on: 'I kept asking myself: "Why shouldn't she go out with me?" But I didn't think she would. I don't know why, maybe because she's so neat and pretty. And when she said yes, I couldn't believe my ears. I wanted to ask for it in writing.'

Extravagant overstatement was Anthony's way of being amusing, and Luke forced a smile, but secretly he was appalled. To steal someone else's girlfriend was despicable in any circumstances, but the fact that Anthony was obviously crazy about Billie made everything even worse.

Luke groaned, and Anthony said: 'What's the matter?'

Luke decided to tell him half the truth. 'I'm not in love with Elspeth any more. I think I have to end it.'

Anthony looked shocked. 'That's too bad. You two are quite an item.'

'I feel like a jerk.'

'Don't crucify yourself. It happens. You're not married – not even engaged.'

'Not officially.'

Anthony raised his eyebrows. 'Have you proposed?'

'No.'

'Then you're not engaged, officially or unofficially.'

'We've talked about how many children we'll have.'

'You're still not engaged.'

'I guess you're right, but all the same I feel like a rotter.'

There was a tap at the door, and a man Luke had never seen before came in. 'Mr Lucas and Mr Carroll, I presume?' He wore a shabby suit, but had a haughty manner, and Luke guessed he was a college proctor.

Anthony leaped to his feet. 'We are,' he said. 'And

you must be Doctor Uterus, the famous gynaecologist. Thank God you've come!'

Luke did not laugh. The man was carrying two white envelopes, and Luke had a pessimistic feeling he knew what they were.

'I'm the clerk to the Dean of Students. He's asked me to hand you these notes in person.' The clerk gave them an envelope each and left.

'Hell,' Anthony said as the door closed. He ripped open his envelope. 'God damn it.'

Luke opened his and read the short note inside.

Dear Mr Lucas,

Please be good enough to come and see me in my study at three o'clock this afternoon.

Yours sincerely,

Peter Ryder

Dean of Students

Such letters always meant disciplinary trouble. Someone had reported to the Dean that there had been a girl in the House last night. Anthony would probably be expelled.

Luke had never seen his room-mate afraid – his insouciance always seemed unshakeable – but now he was pale with shock. 'I can't go home,' he whispered. He had never said much about his parents, but Luke had a vague picture of a bullying father and a long-suffering mother. Now he guessed the reality might be worse than he had imagined. For a moment, Anthony's expression was a window into a private hell.

Then there was a knock at the door, and in came Geoff Pidgeon, the amiable, chubby occupant of the room opposite. 'Did I just see the Dean's clerk?'

Luke waved his letter. 'Too damn right.'

'You know, I haven't said a word to anyone about seeing you with that girl.'

'But who did?' Anthony said. 'The only sneak in the House is Jenkins.' Paul Jenkins was a religious zealot whose mission in life was to reform the morals of Harvard men. 'But he's away for the weekend.'

'No, he's not,' Pidgeon said. 'He changed his plans.'

'Then it's him, damn his eyes,' Anthony said. 'I'm going to strangle the son of a bitch with my own hands.'

If Anthony were expelled, Luke realized suddenly, Billie would be free. He felt ashamed of such a selfish thought when his friend's life was about to be ruined. Then it struck him that Billie might be in trouble too. He said: 'I wonder if Elspeth and Billie have had letters.'

Anthony said: 'Why would they?'

'Jenkins probably knows the names of our girl-friends – he takes a prurient interest in such things.'

Pidgeon said: 'If he knows the names, we can be sure he reported them. That's what he's like.'

Luke said: 'Elspeth is safe. She wasn't here, and no one can prove she was. But Billie could be expelled. Then she'll lose her scholarship. She explained it to me last night. She won't be able to study anywhere else.'

'I can't worry about Billie now,' Anthony said. 'I have to figure out what I'm going to do.'

Luke was shocked. Anthony had got Billie into trouble, and by Luke's code he should be more worried about her than about himself. But Luke saw a pretext to talk to Billie, and he could not resist it. Suppressing a guilty feeling, he said: 'Why don't I go to the girls' dorm and see whether Billie's back from Newport yet?'

'Would you?' Anthony said. 'Thanks.'

Pidgeon went out. Anthony sat on the bed, smoking gloomily, while Luke quickly shaved and changed his clothes. Although he was in a hurry, he dressed with care, in a soft blue shirt, new flannel pants, and his favourite grey tweed jacket.

It was two o'clock when he reached the Radcliffe dormitory quadrangle. The red-brick buildings were arranged around a small park where students strolled in pairs. This was where he had kissed Elspeth, he recalled unhappily, at midnight on a Saturday at the end of their first date. He detested men who switched loyalties as readily as they changed their shirts, yet here he was doing the thing he disdained – and he could not stop.

A uniformed maid let him into the lobby of the dorm. He asked for Billie. The maid sat at a desk, picked up a speaking-tube of the kind used on ships, blew into the mouthpiece, and said: 'Visitor for Miss Josephson.'

Billie came down wearing a dove-grey cashmere

sweater and a plaid skirt. She looked lovely but distraught, and Luke longed to take her in his arms and comfort her. She, too, had been summoned to the office of Peter Ryder, and she told him that the man who had delivered her letter had also left one for Elspeth.

She showed him into the smoking room, where girls were allowed to receive male visitors. 'What am I going to do?' she said. Her face was drawn with distress. She looked like a grieving widow.

Luke found her even more ravishing than yesterday. He longed to tell her that he would make everything all right. But he could not think of a way out. 'Anthony could say it was someone else in the room, but he'd have to produce the girl.'

'I don't know what I'm going to tell my mother.'

'I wonder if Anthony would pay a woman, you know, a street woman, to say it was she.'

Billie shook her head. 'They wouldn't believe it.'

'And Jenkins would tell them it was the wrong girl. He's the sneak that reported you.'

'My career is over.' With a bitter smile, she said: 'I'll have to go back to Dallas and be a secretary to an oil man in cowboy boots.'

Twenty-four hours ago Luke had been a happy man. It was hard to believe.

Two girls in coats and hats burst into the lounge. Their faces were flushed. 'Have you heard the news?' said one.

Luke was not interested in news. He shook his head. Billie said desultorily: 'What's happened?'

'We're at war!'

Luke frowned. 'What?'

'It's true,' said the second girl. 'The Japanese have bombed Hawaii!'

Luke could hardly take it in. 'Hawaii? What the heck for? What's in Hawaii?'

Billie said: 'Is this true?'

'Everyone's talking about it on the street. People are stopping their cars.'

Billie looked at Luke. 'I'm frightened,' she said.

He took her hand. He wanted to say he would take care of her, no matter what.

Two more girls rushed in, talking excitedly. Someone brought a radio downstairs and plugged it in. There was an expectant silence while they waited for it to warm up. Then they heard an announcer's voice. 'The battleship *Arizona* is reported destroyed and the *Oklahoma* sunk in Pearl Harbor. First reports say that more than one hundred US aircraft were crippled on the ground at the Naval Air Station on Ford Island and at Wheeler Field and Hickam Field. American casualties are estimated to be at least two thousand dead and a thousand more injured.'

Luke felt a surge of rage. 'Two thousand people killed!' he said.

More girls came into the lounge, talking excitedly, and were rudely told to shut up. The announcer was saying: 'No warning was given for the Japanese attack, which began at seven fifty-five a.m. local time, just before one p.m. Eastern Standard Time.'

Billie said: 'It means war, doesn't it.'

'You bet it does,' Luke said angrily. He knew it was stupid and irrational to hate a whole nation, but he felt that way all the same. 'I'd like to bomb Japan flat.'

She squeezed his hand. 'I don't want you to be in a war,' she said. There were tears in her eyes. 'I don't want you hurt.'

His heart felt ready to burst. 'I'm so happy you feel that way.' He smiled ruefully. 'The world is falling apart, and I'm happy.' He looked at his watch. 'I suppose we all have to see the Dean, even though we're at war.' Then he was struck by a thought, and he fell silent.

'What?' Billie said. 'What is it?'

'Maybe there *is* a way for you and Anthony to stay at Harvard.'

'How?'

'Let me think.'

* * *

Elspeth was nervous, but she told herself that she did not need to be afraid. She had broken the curfew last night, but she had not been caught. She was almost certain this was nothing to do with her and Luke. Anthony and Billie were the ones who were in trouble. Elspeth hardly knew Billie, but she cared for Anthony, and she had a dreadful feeling he was going to be thrown out.

The four of them met outside the Dean's study. Luke said: 'I've got a plan,' but before he could explain, the Dean opened the door and summoned them inside. Luke had time only to say: 'Leave the talking to me.'

The Dean of Students, Peter Ryder, was a fussy, old-fashioned man in a neat suit of black coat and waistcoat with grey striped pants. His bow tie was a perfect butterfly, his boots gleamed with polish, and his oiled hair looked like black paint on a boiled egg. With him was a grey-haired spinster called Iris Rayford who was responsible for the moral welfare of Radcliffe girls.

They sat in a circle of chairs, as if for a tutorial. The Dean lit a cigarette. 'Now, you boys had better tell the truth, like gentlemen,' he said. 'What happened in your room last night?'

Anthony ignored Ryder's question and acted as if he were in charge of the proceedings. 'Where's Jenkins?' he said curtly. 'He's the sneak, isn't he?'

'No one else has been asked to join us,' the Dean said.

'But a man has a right to be confronted by his accuser.'

'This isn't a court, Mr Carroll,' the Dean said testily. 'Miss Rayford and I have been asked to establish the facts. Disciplinary proceedings, if such prove necessary, will follow in due course.'

'I'm not sure that's acceptable,' Anthony said haughtily. 'Jenkins should be here.'

Elspeth saw what Anthony was doing. He hoped Jenkins would be scared to repeat his accusation to Anthony's face. If that happened, the college might have to drop the matter. She did not think it would work, but perhaps it was worth a try.

However, Luke cut the discussion short. 'Enough of

this,' he said with an impatient gesture. He addressed the Dean. 'I brought a woman into the House last night, sir.'

Elspeth gasped. What was he talking about?

The Dean frowned. 'My information is that it was Mr Carroll who invited the woman in.'

'I'm afraid you've been misinformed.'

Elspeth burst out: 'That's not true!'

Luke gave her a look that chilled her. 'Miss Twomey was in her dorm by midnight, as the dormitory mistress's overnight book will show.'

Elspeth stared at him. The book *would* show that, because a girlfriend had forged her signature. She realized she had better shut up before she talked herself into trouble. But what was Luke up to?

Anthony was asking himself the same question. Staring at Luke, mystified, he said: 'Luke, I don't know what you're doing, but—'

'Let me tell the story,' Luke said. Anthony looked doubtful, and Luke added: 'Please.'

Anthony shrugged.

The Dean said sarcastically: 'Please carry on, Mr Lucas. I can't wait.'

'I met the girl at the Dew Drop Inn,' Luke began.

Miss Rayford spoke for the first time. 'The Dew Drop Inn?' she said incredulously. 'Is that a pun?'

'Yes.'

'Carry on.'

'She's a waitress there. Her name is Angela Carlotti.'

The Dean plainly did not believe a word. He said: 'I

was told that the person seen in Cambridge House was Miss Bilhah Josephson here.'

'No, sir,' Luke said in the same tone of immovable certitude. 'Miss Josephson is a friend of ours, but she was out of town. She spent last night at the home of a relative in Newport, Rhode Island.'

Miss Rayford spoke to Billie. 'Will the relative confirm that?'

Billie shot a bewildered look at Luke, then said: 'Yes, Miss Rayford.'

Elspeth stared at Luke. Did he really intend to sacrifice his career to save Anthony? It was crazy! Luke was a loyal friend, but this was taking friendship too far.

Ryder said to Luke: 'Can you produce this ... waitress?' He pronounced 'waitress' with distaste, as if he were saying 'prostitute'.

'Yes, sir, I can.'

The Dean was surprised. 'Very well.'

Elspeth was astonished. Had Luke bribed a town girl to pretend to be the culprit? If he had, it would never work. Jenkins would swear it was the wrong girl.

Then Luke said: 'But I don't intend to bring her into this.'

'Ah,' said the Dean. 'In that case, you make it difficult for me to accept your story.'

Now Elspeth was baffled. Luke had told an implausible tale and had no way to back it up. What was the point?

Luke said: 'I don't think Miss Carlotti's evidence will be necessary.'

'I beg to differ, Mr Lucas.'

Then Luke dropped his bombshell. 'I'm leaving the college tonight, sir.'

Anthony said: 'Luke!'

The Dean said: 'It will do you no good to leave before you can be sacked. There will still be an investigation.'

'Our country is at war.'

'I know that, young man.'

'I'm going to join the army tomorrow morning, sir.'

Elspeth cried: 'No!'

For the first time, the Dean did not have an answer. He stared at Luke with his mouth open.

Elspeth realized that Luke had been clever. The college could hardly pursue a disciplinary action against a boy who was risking his life for his country. And if there were no investigation, then Billie was safe.

A mist of grief obscured her vision. Luke had sacrificed everything – to save Billie.

Miss Rayford might still demand testimony from Billie's cousin, but he would probably lie for her. The key point was that Radcliffe could hardly expect Billie to produce the waitress Angela Carlotti.

But none of that mattered to Elspeth now. All she could think of was that she had lost Luke.

Ryder was muttering about making his report and leaving others to decide. Miss Rayford made a big fuss about writing down the address of Billie's cousin. But it was all camouflage. They had been outwitted, and they knew it.

At last the students were dismissed.

As soon as the door closed, Billie burst into tears. 'Don't go to war, Luke!' she said.

Anthony said: 'You saved my life.' He put his arms around Luke and embraced him. 'I'll never forget this,' Anthony said. 'Never.' He detached himself from Luke and took Billie's hand. 'Don't worry,' he said to her. 'Luke's too smart to get killed.'

Luke turned to Elspeth. When he met her eye he flinched, and she realized that her rage must be plainly visible. But she did not care. She stared at him for a long moment, then she raised her hand and slapped his face, once, very hard. He let out an involuntary gasp of pain and surprise.

'You fucking bastard,' she said.

Then she turned and walked away.

1 P.M.

Each Baby Sergeant motor is four feet long and six inches in diameter, and weighs fifty-nine pounds. Its motor burns for just six and a half seconds.

Luke was looking for a quiet residential street. Washington was totally unfamiliar to him, as if he had never been here before. Driving away from Union Station he had chosen a direction at random, and headed west. The road had taken him further into the centre of the city, a place of striking vistas and grandiose government buildings. Perhaps it was beautiful, but he found it intimidating. However, he knew that if he kept going in a straight line he must eventually come to a place where normal families lived in regular houses.

He crossed a river and found himself in a charming suburb of narrow streets lined with trees. He passed a building with a sign that read 'Georgetown Mind Hospital', and he guessed the neighbourhood was called Georgetown. He turned into a tree-lined street of modest houses. This was promising. People here would not have full-time household help, so there was a good chance of finding a place empty.

The street turned a corner and immediately dead-ended in a cemetery. Luke parked the stolen Ford facing the way he had come, in case he had to make a fast getaway.

He needed some simple tools, a chisel or screwdriver and a hammer. There was probably a small tool kit in the trunk – but the trunk was locked. He could pick the lock if he could find a piece of wire. Otherwise he would have to drive to a hardware store and buy or steal what he required.

He reached into the back and picked up the stolen bag. Rummaging through the clothes, he found a folder containing papers. He took out a paper clip and closed the case.

It took him about thirty seconds to open the trunk. As he had hoped, there were a few tools in a tin box next to the jack. He chose the largest screwdriver. There was no hammer, but there was a heavy adjustable wrench that would serve. He put them in the pocket of his ragged raincoat and slammed the lid of the trunk.

He took the stolen bag from inside the car, closed the door, and walked around the corner. He knew he was conspicuous, a ragged bum walking in a nice neighbourhood with an expensive suitcase. If the local busybody called the cops, and the cops had nothing much to do this morning, he could be in trouble in minutes. On the other hand, if all went well he might be washed and shaved and dressed like a respectable citizen in half an hour's time.

He drew level with the first house in the street. He crossed a small front yard and knocked at the door.

* * *

Rosemary Sims saw a nice blue-and-white car drive slowly past her house, and she wondered whose it was. The Brownings might have bought a new car, they had plenty of money. Or Mr Cyrus, who was a bachelor and did not have to stint himself. Otherwise, she reasoned, it must belong to a stranger.

She had good eyesight still, and she could watch most of the street from her comfy chair by the second-floor window, especially in winter when the trees were bare of leaves. So she saw the tall stranger when he came walking around the corner. And 'strange' was the word. He wore no hat, his raincoat was torn, and his shoes were tied up with string to stop them falling apart. Yet he carried a new-looking suitcase.

He went to Mrs Britsky's door and knocked. She was a widow, living alone, but she was no fool – she would make short work of the stranger, Mrs Sims knew. Sure enough, Mrs Britsky looked out the window and waved him away with a peremptory gesture.

He went next door and knocked at Mrs Loew's. She opened up. She was a tall, black-haired woman, who was too proud, in Mrs Sims's opinion. She spoke a few words with the caller, then slammed the door.

He went to the next house, apparently intending to work his way along the street. Young Jeannie Evans came to the door with baby Rita in her arms. She fished in the pocket of her apron and gave him something, probably a few coins. So he was a beggar.

Old Mr Clark came to the door in his bathrobe and carpet slippers. The stranger got nothing out of him.

The owner of the next house, Mr Bonetti, was at

work, and his wife Angelina, seven months pregnant, had left five minutes ago, carrying a string bag, obviously heading for the store. The stranger would get no answer there.

* * *

By now, Luke had had time to study the doors, which were all the same. They had Yale locks, the kind with a tongue on the door side and a metal socket in the jamb. The lock was operated by a key from outside and by a knob inside.

Each door had a small window of frosted glass at head height. The easiest way in would be to break the glass and reach inside to turn the knob. But a broken window would be visible from the street. So he decided to use the screwdriver.

He glanced up and down the street. He had been unlucky, having to knock on five doors to find an empty house. By now he might have attracted attention, but he could see no one. Anyway, he had no choice. He had to take the risk.

* * *

Mrs Sims turned away from the window and lifted the handset of the phone beside her seat. Slowly and carefully, she dialled the number of the local police station, which she knew by heart.

* * *

Luke had to do this fast.

He inserted the screwdriver's blade between the

door and the jamb at the level of the lock. Then he struck the handle of the screwdriver with the heavy end of the adjustable wrench, trying to force the blade into the socket of the lock.

The first blow failed to move the screwdriver, which was jammed up against the steel of the lock. He wiggled the screwdriver, trying to find a way in. He used the wrench again, harder this time. Still the screwdriver would not slip into the socket. He felt perspiration break out on his forehead, despite the cold weather.

He told himself to stay calm. He had done this before. When? He had no idea. It did not matter. The technique worked, he was sure of that.

He wiggled the screwdriver again. This time, it felt as if a corner of the blade had caught in a notch. He hammered again, as hard as he could. The screwdriver sank in an inch.

He pulled sideways on the handle, levering the tongue of the lock back out of the socket. To his profound relief, the door opened inward.

The damage to the frame was too slight to be seen from the street.

He stepped quickly inside and closed the door behind him.

* * *

When Rosemary Sims finished dialling the number, she looked out the window again, but the stranger had vanished.

That was quick.

The police answered. Feeling confused, she hung up the phone without speaking.

Why had he suddenly stopped knocking on doors? Where had he gone? Who was he?

She smiled. She had something to occupy her thoughts all day.

* * *

It was the home of a young couple. The place was furnished with a mixture of wedding presents and junk-shop purchases. They had a new couch and a big TV set in the living room, but they were still using orange crates for storage in the kitchen. An unopened letter on the hall radiator was addressed to Mr G. Bonetti.

There was no evidence of children. Most probably, Mr and Mrs Bonetti both had jobs and would be out all day. But he could not count on it.

He went quickly upstairs. There were three bedrooms, only one of which was furnished. He threw the suitcase on the neatly made bed. Inside it he found a carefully folded blue chalk-stripe suit, a white shirt and a conservative striped tie. There were dark socks, clean underwear, and a pair of polished black wingtips that looked only about half a size too big.

He stripped off his filthy clothes and kicked them into a corner. It gave him a spooky feeling, to be naked in the home of strangers. He thought of skipping the shower, but he smelled bad, even to himself.

He crossed the tiny landing to the bathroom. It felt great to stand under the hot water and soap himself

135

all over. When he got out, he stood still and listened carefully. The house was silent.

He dried himself with one of Mrs Bonetti's pink bath towels – another wedding present, he guessed – and put on undershorts, pants, socks and shoes from the stolen bag. Being at least half dressed would speed his getaway if something went wrong while he was shaving.

Mr Bonetti used an electric shaver, but Luke preferred a blade. In the suitcase he found a safety razor and a shaving brush. He lathered his face and shaved quickly.

Mr Bonetti did not have any cologne, but maybe there was some in the suitcase. After stinking like a pig all morning, Luke liked the idea of smelling sweet. He found a neat leather toiletry case and unzipped it. There was no cologne inside – but there was a hundred dollars in twenties, neatly folded: emergency money. He pocketed the cash, resolving to pay the man back one day.

After all, the guy was not a collaborator.

And what the heck did that mean?

Another mystery. He put on the shirt, tie and jacket. They fitted well: he had been careful to choose a victim his own size and build. The clothes were of good quality. The luggage tag gave an address on Central Park South, New York. Luke guessed the owner was a corporate big shot who had come to Washington for a couple of days of meetings.

There was a full-length mirror on the back of the bedroom door. He had not looked at his reflection since early this morning, in the men's room at Union Station, when he had been so shocked to see a filthy hobo staring back at him.

He stepped to the mirror, bracing himself.

He saw a tall, fit-looking man in his middle thirties, with black hair and blue eyes; a normal person, looking harassed. A weary sense of relief swept over him.

Take a guy like that, he thought. What would you say he does for a living?

His hands were soft, and now that they were clean they did not look like those of a manual worker. He had a smooth indoor face, one that had not spent much time out in bad weather. His hair was well cut. The guy in the mirror looked comfortable in the clothes of a corporate executive.

He was not a cop, definitely.

There was no hat or coat in the bag. Luke knew he would be conspicuous without either, on a cold January day. He wondered if he might find them in the house. It was worth taking a few extra seconds to look.

He opened the closet. There was not much inside. Mrs Bonetti had three dresses. Her husband had a sport coat for weekends and a black suit he probably wore to church. There was no topcoat – Mr Bonetti must be wearing one, and he could not afford two – but there was a light raincoat. Luke took it off the hanger. It would be better than nothing. He put it on. It was a size small, but wearable.

There was no hat in the closet, but there was a

tweed cap that Bonetti probably wore with the sport coat on Saturday. Luke tried it on. It was too small. He would have to buy a hat with some of the money from the sponge bag. But the cap would serve for an hour or so—

He heard a noise downstairs. He froze, listening.

A young woman's voice said: 'What happened to my front door?'

Another voice, similar, replied: 'Looks like someone tried to break in!'

Luke cursed under his breath. He had stayed too long.

'Jeepers – I think you're right!'

'Maybe you should call the cops.'

Mrs Bonetti had not gone to work, after all. Probably she had gone shopping. She had met a friend at the store and invited her home for coffee.

'I don't know ... looks like the thieves didn't get in.'

'How do you know? Better check if anything's been stolen.'

Luke realized he had to get out of there fast.

'What's to steal? The family jewels?'

'What about the TV?'

Luke opened the bedroom window and looked out on to the front yard. There was no convenient tree or drainpipe down which he could climb.

'Nothing's been moved,' he heard Mrs Bonetti say. 'I don't believe they got in.'

'What about upstairs?'

Moving silently, Luke crossed the landing to the

bathroom. At the back of the house there was nothing but a leg-breaking drop to a paved patio.

'I'm going to look.'

'Aren't you scared?'

There was a nervous giggle. 'Yes. But what else can we do? We'll look pretty silly if we call the cops and there's no one here.'

Luke heard footsteps on the stairs. He stood behind the bathroom door.

The footsteps mounted the staircase, crossed the landing and entered the bedroom. Mrs Bonetti gave a little scream.

Her friend's voice said: 'Whose bag is that?'

'I've never seen it before!'

Luke slipped silently out of the bathroom. He could see the open bedroom door, but not the women. He tiptoed down the stairs, grateful for the carpet.

'What kind of burglar brings luggage?'

'I'm calling the cops right now. This is spooky.'

Luke opened the front door and stepped outside.

He smiled. He had done it.

He closed the door quietly and walked quickly away.

* * *

Mrs Sims frowned, mystified. The man leaving the Bonetti house had on Mr Bonetti's black raincoat and the grey tweed cap he wore to watch the Redskins, but he was larger than Mr Bonetti, and the clothes did not quite fit.

She watched him walk down the street and turn the corner. He would have to come back: it was a dead end. A minute later the blue-and-white car she had noticed earlier came around the corner, going too fast. She realized then that the man who had left the house was the beggar she had been watching. He must have broken in and stolen Mr Bonetti's clothes!

As the car passed her window, she read the licence plate and memorized the number.

1.30 P.M.

The Sergeant motors have undergone 300 static tests, 50 flight tests and 290 ignition-system firings without a failure.

Anthony sat in the conference room, fuming with impatience and frustration.

Luke was still running around Washington. No one knew what he might be up to. But Anthony was stuck here, listening to a State Department time-server drone on about the need to combat rebels massing in the mountains of Cuba. Anthony knew all about Fidel Castro and Che Guevara. They had fewer than a thousand men under their command. Of course they could be wiped out – but there was no point. If Castro were killed, someone else would take his place.

What Anthony wanted to do was get out on the street and look for Luke.

He and his staff had put in calls to most of the police stations in the District of Columbia. They had asked the precincts to call in details of any incidents involving drunks or bums, any mention of a perpetrator who talked like a college professor, and anything at all out of the ordinary. The cops were happy to cooperate with the CIA: they liked the thought that they might be involved with international espionage.

The State Department man finished his talk, and a round-table discussion began. Anthony knew that the only way to prevent someone like Castro taking over was for the US to support a moderate reformist government. Fortunately for the communists, there was no danger of that.

The door opened and Pete Maxell slipped in. He gave a nod of apology to the chairman at the head of the table, George Cooperman, then sat next to Anthony and passed him a folder containing a batch of police reports.

There was something unusual at just about every station house. A beautiful woman arrested for picking pockets at the Jefferson Memorial turned out to be a man; some beatniks had tried to open a cage and free an eagle at the zoo; a Wesley Heights man had attempted to suffocate his wife with a pizza with extra cheese; a delivery truck belonging to a religious publisher had shed its load in Petworth, and traffic on Georgia Avenue was being held up by an avalanche of Bibles.

It was possible that Luke had left Washington, but Anthony thought it unlikely. Luke had no money for train or bus fares. He could steal it, of course, but why would he bother? He had nowhere to go. His mother lived in New York and he had a sister in Baltimore, but he did not know that. He had no reason to travel.

While Anthony speed-read the reports, he listened

with half an ear to his boss, Carl Hobart, talking about the US ambassador to Cuba, Earl Smith, who had worked tirelessly to undermine church leaders and others who wanted to reform Cuba by peaceful means. Anthony sometimes wondered if Smith were in fact a Kremlin agent, but more likely he was just stupid.

One of the police reports caught his eye, and he showed it to Pete. 'Is this right?' he whispered incredulously.

Pete nodded. 'A bum attacked and beat up a patrolman on A Street and Seventh.'

'A *bum* beat up a *cop?*'

'And it's not far from the neighbourhood where we lost Luke.'

'This might be him!' Anthony said excitedly. Carl Hobart, who was speaking, shot him a look of annoyance. Anthony lowered his voice to a whisper again. 'But why would he attack a patrolman? Did he steal anything – the cop's weapon, for example?'

'No, but he beat him up pretty good. The officer was treated in hospital for a broken forefinger on his right hand.'

A tremor ran through Anthony like an electric shock. 'That's him!' he said loudly.

Carl Hobart said: 'For Christ's sake!'

George Cooperman said good-humouredly 'Anthony – either shut the fuck up, or go outside and talk, why don't you?'

Anthony stood up. 'Sorry, George. Back in a flash.' He stepped out of the room, and Pete followed. 'That's him,' Anthony repeated as the door shut. 'It was his trademark, in the war. He used to do it to the Gestapo – break their trigger fingers.'

Pete looked puzzled. 'How do you know that?'

Anthony realized he had made a blunder. Pete believed that Luke was a diplomat having a nervous breakdown. Anthony had not told Pete that he knew Luke personally. Now he cursed himself for carelessness. 'I didn't tell you everything,' he said, forcing a casual tone. 'I worked with him in OSS.'

Pete frowned. 'And he became a diplomat after the war.' He gave Anthony a shrewd look. 'He's not just having trouble with his wife, is he.'

'No. I'm pretty sure it's more serious.'

Pete accepted that. 'Sounds like a cold-blooded bastard, to break a guy's finger, just like that.'

'Cold-blooded?' Anthony had never thought of Luke that way, though he did have a ruthless streak. 'I guess he was, when the chips were down.' He had covered up his mistake, he thought with relief. But he still had to find Luke. 'What time did this fight occur?'

'Nine-thirty.'

'Hell. More than four hours ago. He could be anywhere in the city by now.'

'What'll we do?'

'Send a couple of men down to A Street to show the photo of Luke around, see if you can get any clues where he might have been headed. Talk to the cop, too.'

'Okay.'

'And if you get anything, don't hesitate to bust in on this stupid fucking meeting.'

'Gotcha.'

Anthony went back inside. George Cooperman, Anthony's wartime buddy, was speaking impatiently. 'We should send in a bunch of Special Forces tough guys, clean up Castro's ragtag army in about a day and a half.'

The State Department man asked nervously: 'Could we keep the operation secret?'

'No,' George said. 'But we could disguise it as a local conflict, like we did in Iran and Guatemala.'

Carl Hobart butted in. 'Pardon me if this is a dumb question, but why is it a secret what we did in Iran and Guatemala?'

The State Department man said: 'We don't want to advertise our methods, obviously.'

'Excuse me, but that's stupid,' Hobart said. 'The Russians know it was us. The Iranians and the Guatemalans know it was us. Hell, in Europe the newspapers openly said it was us! No one was fooled except the American people. Now, why do we want to lie to *them*?'

George answered with mounting irritation. 'If it all came out, there would be a Congressional inquiry. Fucking politicians would be asking if we had the right, was it legal, and what about the poor Iranian shitkicking farmers and Spic banana-pickers.'

'Maybe those aren't such bad questions,' Hobart persisted stubbornly. 'Did we really do any good in

Guatemala? It's hard to tell the difference between the Armas regime and a bunch of gangsters.'

George lost his temper. 'The hell with this!' he shouted. 'We are not here to feed starving Iranians and give civil liberties to South American peasants, for Christ's sake. Our job is to promote American interests – and *fuck* democracy!'

There was a moment's pause, then Carl Hobart said: 'Thank you, George. I'm glad we got that straightened out.'

2 P.M.

Each Sergeant motor has an igniter that consists of two electrical matches, wired in parallel, and a jellyroll of metal oxidant encased in a plastic sheath. The igniters are so sensitive that they have to be disconnected if an electrical storm comes within twelve miles of Cape Canaveral, to avoid accidental firing.

In a Georgetown menswear store, Luke bought a soft grey felt hat and a navy wool topcoat. He wore them out of the store and felt, at last, that he could look the world in the eye.

Now he was ready to attack his problems. First he had to learn something about memory. He wanted to know what caused amnesia, whether there were different kinds, and how long it might last. Most importantly, he needed information on treatment and cures.

Where did one go for information? A library. How did one find a library? Look at a map. He got a street map of Washington at the news-stand next to the menswear store. Prominently displayed was the Central Public Library, at the intersection of New York and Massachusetts Avenues, back across town. Luke drove there.

It was a grand classical building raised above ground level like a Greek temple. On the pediment above the pillared entrance were carved the words:

SCIENCE–POETRY–HISTORY

Luke hesitated at the top of the steps, then remembered that he was now a normal citizen again, and walked in.

The effect of his new appearance was immediately apparent. A grey-haired librarian behind the counter stood up and said: 'Can I help you, sir?'

Luke was pathetically grateful to be treated so courteously. 'I want to look at books on memory,' he said.

'That'll be the psychology section,' she said. 'If you'd like to follow me, I'll show you where it is.' She led him up a grand staircase to the next floor and pointed to a corner.

Luke looked along the shelf. There were plenty of books on psychoanalysis, child development, and perception, none of which were any use. He picked out a fat tome called *The Human Brain* and browsed through it, but there was not much about memory, and what there was seemed highly technical. There were some equations, and a certain amount of statistical material, which he found easy enough to understand; but much of the rest assumed a knowledge of human biology he did not have.

His eye was caught by *An Introduction to the Psychology of Memory* by Bilhah Josephson. That sounded more promising. He pulled it out and found a chapter on disorders of the memory. He read:

The common condition in which the patient 'loses his memory' is known as 'global amnesia'.

Luke was elated. He was not the only person to whom this had happened.

Such a patient does not know his identity and will not recognize his own parents or children. However, he remembers a great deal else. He may be able to drive a car, speak foreign languages, strip down an engine, and name the Prime Minister of Canada. The condition would be more appropriately called 'autobiographical amnesia'.

This was exactly what had happened to him. He could still check whether he was being tailed and start a stolen car without the key.

Dr Josephson went on to outline her theory that the brain contained several different memory banks, like separate filing cabinets, for different kinds of information.

The autobiographical memory records events we have experienced personally. These are labelled with time and place: we generally know not only what happened, but when and where.

The long-term semantic memory holds general knowledge such as the capital of Romania and how to solve quadratic equations.

The short-term memory is where we keep a phone number for the few seconds in between looking it up in the phone book and dialling it.

She gave examples of patients who had lost one filing cabinet but retained others, as Luke had. He felt profound relief, and gratitude to the author of the book, as he realized that what had happened to him was a well-studied psychological phenomenon.

Then he was struck by an inspiration. He was in his thirties, so he must have followed some occupation for a decade. His professional knowledge should still be in his head, lodged in his long-term semantic memory. He ought to be able to use it to figure out what line of work he did. And that would be the beginning of discovering his identity!

Looking up from the book, he tried to think what special knowledge he had. He did not count the skills of a secret agent, for he had already decided, judging by his soft indoor skin, that he was not a cop of any kind. What other special knowledge did he have?

It was maddeningly difficult to tell. Accessing the memory was not like opening the refrigerator, where you could see the contents at a glance. It was more like using a library catalogue – you had to know what you were looking for. He felt frustrated, and told himself to be patient and think this through.

If he were a lawyer, would he be able to remember thousands of laws? If a doctor, should he be able to look at someone and say: 'She has appendicitis'?

This was not going to work. Thinking back over the last few minutes, the only clue he noticed was that he had easily understood the equations and statistics in *The Human Brain*, even though he had been puzzled by other aspects of psychology. Maybe he was in a profession that involved numbers: accountancy or insurance, perhaps. Or he might be a math teacher.

He found the math section and looked along the shelves. A book called *Number Theory* caught his attention. He browsed through it for a while. It was clearly presented, but some years out of date . . .

Suddenly he looked up. He had discovered something. He understood number theory.

That was a major clue. Most pages of the book in his hand contained more equations than plain text. This was not written for the curious layman. It was an academic work. And he understood it. He had to be some kind of scientist.

With mounting optimism, he located the chemistry shelf and picked out *Polymer Engineering*. He found it comprehensible, but not easy. Next he moved to physics and tried *A Symposium on the Behaviour of Cold and Very Cold Gases*. It was fascinating, like reading a good novel.

He was narrowing it down. His job involved math and physics. What branch of physics? Cold gases were interesting, but he did not feel that he knew as much as the author of the book. He scanned the shelves and stopped at geophysics, remembering the newspaper story headlined U.S. MOON STAYS EARTHBOUND. He picked out *Principles of Rocket Design*.

It was an elementary text, but nevertheless there was an error on the first page he looked at. Reading on, he found two more—

'Yes!' he said aloud, startling a nearby schoolboy who was studying a biology text. If he could recognize mistakes in a textbook, he had to be an expert. He was a rocket scientist.

He wondered how many rocket scientists there were in the United States. He guessed a few hundred. He hurried to the information desk and spoke to the grey-haired librarian. 'Is there any kind of list of scientists?'

'Sure,' she said. 'You need the *Dictionary of American Scientists*, right at the beginning of the science section.'

He found it easily. It was a heavy book, but nevertheless it could not include every single American scientist. It must just be the prominent ones, he thought. Still, it was worth looking at. He sat at a table and went through the index, searching for anyone named Luke. He had to control his impatience and force himself to scan carefully.

He found a biologist called Luke Parfitt, an archaeologist called Lucas Dimittry, and a pharmacologist called Luc Fontainebleu, but no physicist.

Double-checking, he went through geophysicists and astronomers, but found no one with any version of Luke as a first name. Of course, he thought despondently, he was not even certain that Luke was his name. It was only what he had been called by Pete. For all he knew, his real name might be Percival.

He felt disappointed, but he was not ready to give up.

He thought of another approach. Somewhere, there were people who knew him. The name Luke might not be his own, but his face was. The *Dictionary of American Scientists* carried photos of only the most prominent men, such as Dr Wernher von Braun. But

Luke figured he must have friends and colleagues who would recognize him, if only he could find them. And now he knew where to start looking – for some of his acquaintances must be rocket scientists.

Where did one find scientists? At a university.

He looked up Washington, DC in the encyclopedia. The entry included a list of universities in the city. He picked Georgetown University because he had been in Georgetown earlier and knew how to get back there. He looked for the university on his street map, and saw that it had a large campus covering at least fifty city blocks. It would probably have a big physics department with dozens of professors. Surely one of them would know him?

Full of hope, he left the library and got back into his car.

2.30 P.M.

The igniters were not originally designed to be fired in a vacuum. For the Jupiter rocket, they have been redesigned so that: (i) the entire motor is sealed in an airtight container; (ii) in case that container should be breached, the igniter itself is also in a sealed container; and (iii) the igniter should fire in a vacuum anyway. This multiple fail-safe is an application of a design principle known as 'redundancy'.

The Cuba meeting took a coffee break, and Anthony ran back to Q Building for an update, praying his team would have come up with something, any clue to Luke's whereabouts.

Pete met him on the stairs. 'Here's something weird,' he said.

Anthony's heart jumped with hope. 'Give!'

'A report from the police in Georgetown. A housewife comes back from the store to find that her home has been broken into and her shower has been used. The intruder has disappeared, leaving behind a suitcase and a pile of filthy old clothes.'

Anthony was electrified. 'At last – a break!' he said. 'Give me the address.'

'You think this is our guy?'

'I'm sure of it! He's fed up with looking like a bum, so he's broken into an empty house, showered, shaved, and put on some decent clothes. That's characteristic, he would hate to be badly dressed.'

Pete looked thoughtful. 'You know him pretty well, I guess.'

Anthony realized he had slipped again. 'No, I don't,' he snapped. 'I read his file.'

'Sorry,' Pete said. After a moment he went on: 'I wonder why he left stuff behind?'

'My guess is, the housewife came home before he was quite finished.'

'What about the Cuba meeting?'

Anthony stopped a passing secretary. 'Please call the conference room in P Building and tell Mr Hobart that I was taken ill with stomach pains and Mr Maxell had to drive me home.'

'Stomach pains,' she said, deadpan.

'Right,' he said, walking away. Over his shoulder he called: 'Unless you can think of something better.'

He left the building with Pete following, and they jumped into his old yellow Cadillac. 'This may need delicate handling,' he said to Pete as he headed for Georgetown. 'The good news is that Luke has left us some clues. Our problem is that we don't have a hundred men to chase up leads. So, my plan is to get the Washington Police Department working for us.'

'Good luck,' Pete said sceptically. 'What should I do?'

'Be nice to the cops, and leave the talking to me.'

'I believe I can handle that.'

Anthony drove fast and quickly found the address in the police report. It was a small one-family home on a quiet street. A police cruiser was parked outside.

Before going into the house, Anthony studied the opposite side of the street, scrutinizing the houses. After a moment he spotted what he was looking for: a face in an upstairs window, watching him. It was an elderly woman, with white hair. She did not step back from the window when she caught his eye, but returned his stare with unabashed curiosity. She was just what he needed, a neighbourhood busybody. He smiled and gave her a salute, and she inclined her head in acknowledgement.

He turned away and approached the house that had been broken into. He could see scratches and a little splintering on the door jamb where the lock had been forced; a neat, professional job with no unnecessary damage, he thought. That fitted Luke.

The door was opened by an attractive young woman who was expecting a baby – pretty soon, he guessed. She took Anthony and Pete into her living room where two men were sitting on the couch, drinking coffee and smoking. One was a uniformed patrolman. The other, a young man in a cheap sharkskin suit, was probably a detective. In front of them was a splayed-leg coffee table with a red Formica top. An open suitcase was on the table.

Anthony introduced himself. He showed his identification to the cops. He did not want Mrs Bonetti – and all her friends and neighbours – to know that the CIA was interested in the case, so he said: 'We're colleagues of these police officers.'

The detective was Lewis Hite. 'You know something about this?' he said guardedly.

'I think we may have some information that will help you. But first, I need to know what you've got.'

Hite spread his hands in a gesture of bafflement. 'We got a suitcase belongs to a guy named Rowley Anstruther, Junior, from New York. He breaks into Mrs Bonetti's house, takes a shower, and goes away, leaving his suitcase behind. Go figure!'

Anthony studied the case. It was a good-quality tan leather bag, less than half full. He looked through the contents. There were clean shirts and underwear, but no shoes, pants or jackets.

'Looks like Mr Anstruther arrived in Washington from New York today,' he said.

Hite nodded, but Mrs Bonetti said admiringly: 'How do you know that?'

Anthony smiled. 'Detective Hite will tell you.' He did not want to offend Hite by stealing his limelight.

'The bag contains clean underwear but no laundry,' Hite explained. 'The guy hasn't changed his clothes, so he probably hasn't yet spent a night away. That means he left home this morning.'

Anthony said: 'I believe some old clothes were also left behind.'

The patrolman, whose name was Lonnie, said: 'I got 'em.' He lifted a cardboard box from beside the couch. 'Raincoat,' he said, sorting through the contents. 'Shirt, pants, shoes.'

Anthony recognized them. They were the rags Luke had been wearing. 'I don't believe Mr Anstruther came to this house,' Anthony said. 'I think the bag was stolen from him this morning, probably at Union Station.' He looked at the patrolman. 'Lonnie, would you call the precinct nearest the railroad station and ask if such a theft has been reported? That's if Mrs Bonetti will permit us to use the phone.'

'Of course,' she said. 'It's in the hall.'

Anthony added: 'The theft report should list the contents of the bag. I believe you'll find they include a suit and a pair of shoes that are not here now.' They were all staring at him in astonishment. 'Please make a careful note of the description of the suit.'

'Okay.' The patrolman went into the hallway.

Anthony felt good. He had managed to take command of the investigation without offending the police. Detective Hite now looked at him as if waiting for instructions. 'Mr Anstruther must be a man of six foot one or two, about 180 pounds, athletic build,' he said. 'Lewis, if you check the size of those shirts, you'll probably find they're sixteen neck, thirty-five sleeve.'

'They are – I already checked,' Hite said.

'I should have known you'd be ahead of me.' Anthony flattered him with a wry smile. 'We have a picture of the man we believe stole the suitcase and broke into this house.' Anthony nodded to Pete, who handed Hite a sheaf of photographs. 'We don't have a name for him,' Anthony lied. 'He's six foot one, 180 pounds, athletic build, and he may pretend to have lost his memory.'

'So what's the story?' Hite was intrigued. 'This guy wanted Anstruther's clothes, and he came here to change?'

'Something like that.'

'But why?'

Anthony looked apologetic. 'I'm sorry, I can't tell you.'

Hite was pleased. 'Classified, huh? No problem.'

Lonnie came back. 'Dead right about the theft. Union Station, eleven-thirty this morning.'

Anthony nodded. He had impressed the hell out of the two cops. 'And the suit?'

'Navy blue, with a chalk stripe.'

He turned to the detective. 'So, you can put out a photo and description including the clothes he's wearing.'

'You think he's still in town.'

'Yes.' Anthony was not as sure as he pretended, but he could not think of any reason for Luke to leave Washington.

'I presume he's in a car.'

'Let's find out.' Anthony turned to Mrs Bonetti. 'What's the name of the white-haired lady who lives across the street, a couple of doors down?'

'Rosemary Sims.'

'She spends a lot of time looking out her window?'

'We call her Nosy Rosie.'

'Excellent.' He turned to the detective. 'Shall we have a word with her?'

'Yep.'

They crossed the street and knocked on Mrs Sims's

door. She opened it instantly – she had been waiting in the hall. 'I saw him!' she said immediately. 'He went in there looking like a bum, and came out dressed to the nines!'

Anthony made a gesture indicating that Hite should ask the questions. Hite said: 'Did he have a car, Mrs Sims?'

'Yes, a nice little blue-and-white model. I thought it didn't belong to anyone in this street.' She looked at them slyly. 'I know what you're going to ask me next.'

'Did you happen to notice the licence plate?' Hite asked.

'Yes,' she said triumphantly. 'I wrote it down.'

Anthony smiled.

3 P.M.

The upper stages of the missile are contained in an aluminium tub with a cast magnesium base. The upper-stage tub rests on bearings, allowing it to spin during flight. It will rotate at about 550 revolutions per minute to improve accuracy.

On 37th Street at the end of O Street, the iron gates of Georgetown University stood open. Around three sides of a muddy lawn were Gothic buildings of rusticated grey stone, and students and faculty hurried from one building to another in their cold-weather coats. As Luke drove slowly in, he imagined that someone might catch his eye, recognize him, and say: 'Hey, Luke! Over here!' And the nightmare would be over.

Many of the professors wore clerical collars, and Luke realized this must be a Catholic university. It also appeared to be all-male.

He wondered whether he was Catholic.

He parked in front of the main entrance, a triple-arched portico marked 'Healy Hall'. Inside he found a reception desk and the first woman he had seen here. She said that the physics department was directly below

161

where he stood, and told him to go outside and turn down a flight of steps that led beneath the portico. He felt he was coming nearer to the heart of the mystery, like a treasure hunter penetrating the chambers in an Egyptian pyramid.

Following her directions, he found a large laboratory with benches down the centre and doors on either side that led to smaller offices. At one of the benches, a group of men were working with the components of a microwave spectrograph. They all wore eyeglasses. Judging by their ages, Luke thought they were professors and graduate students. Some of them might easily be people he knew. He approached them with an expectant look.

One of the older men caught his eye, but there was no flash of recognition. 'Can I help you?'

'I hope so,' Luke said. 'Is there a department of geophysics here?'

'Goodness, no,' he said. 'At this university, even physics is considered a minor subject.' The others laughed.

Luke gave them all a chance to look at him, but none seemed to know him. He had chosen badly, he thought despondently; he probably should have gone to George Washington University. 'What about astronomy?'

'Why, yes, of course. The heavens, we study. Our observatory is famous.'

His spirits lifted. 'Where is it?'

The man pointed to a door at the back of the lab. 'Go to the other end of this building and you'll see it on the far side of the baseball diamond.' He returned his attention to the bench.

Luke followed a long, dark, dirty corridor that ran the length of the building. Seeing a stooped man in professorial tweeds coming the other way, Luke looked him in the eye, a smile ready to break out if the professor recognized him. But a nervous expression came over the man's face and he hurried by.

Undaunted, Luke walked on, giving the same look to everyone he passed who might possibly be a scientist; but no one showed any sign of recognition. Leaving the building, he saw tennis courts and a view of the Potomac river and, to the west across the sports field, a white dome.

He approached it with mounting anticipation. On the flat roof of a small two-storey house was a large revolving observatory, its dome having a sliding roof section. It was an expensive facility that indicated a serious astronomy department. Luke stepped inside the building.

The rooms were arranged around a massive central pillar that supported the enormous weight of the dome. Luke opened a door and saw an empty library. He tried another, and found an attractive woman about his own age sitting behind a typewriter. 'Good morning,' he said. 'Is the professor in?'

'You mean Father Heyden?'

'Uh, yes.'

'And you are?'

'Um . . .' Luke had stupidly not foreseen that he would have to give a name. Now his hesitation caused

163

the secretary to raise her eyebrows distrustfully. 'He won't know me,' Luke said. 'That is . . . he will know me, I hope, but not by name.'

Her suspicion grew. 'Still, you do have a name.'

'Luke. Professor Luke.'

'To which university are you attached, Professor Luke?'

'Um . . . New York.'

'Any particular one of New York's many institutions of higher learning?'

Luke's heart sank. In his enthusiasm he had failed to plan for this encounter, and now he saw that he was making a mess of it. When you were in a hole, it was best to stop digging, he thought. He turned off his friendly smile and spoke coldly. 'I didn't come here to be cross-examined,' he said. 'Just tell Father Heyden that Professor Luke, the rocketry physicist, has dropped by and would like a word with him, would you?'

'I'm afraid that won't be possible,' she said firmly.

Luke left the room, slamming the door. He was angry with himself more than with the secretary, who was only protecting her boss from being pestered by an apparent nutcase. He decided to look around, opening doors until either someone recognized him or he was thrown out. He went up the stairs to the second floor. The building seemed to be deserted. He climbed a wooden stair with no handrail and entered the observatory. It, too, was empty. He stood admiring the large revolving telescope with its complex system of cogs and gears, a real masterpiece of engineering, and wondered what the hell he was going to do next.

The secretary came up the stairs. He prepared himself for a row, but instead she spoke sympathetically. 'You're in some kind of trouble, aren't you,' she said.

Her kindness brought a lump to his throat. 'It's very embarrassing,' he said. 'I've lost my memory. I know I'm in the rocketry field, and I was hoping to run into someone who might recognize me.'

'There's nobody here right now,' she said. 'Professor Larkley is giving a lecture on rocket fuels at the Smithsonian Institution, as part of International Geophysical Year, and all the faculty are there.'

Luke felt a surge of hope. Instead of one geophysicist he could meet a whole roomful. 'Where's the Smithsonian Institute?'

'It's downtown, right in the Mall, around 10th Street.'

He had driven around Washington enough today to know that that was not far away. 'What time is the lecture?'

'It started at three.'

Luke checked his watch. It was three-thirty. If he hurried, he could get there by four. 'The Smithsonian,' he repeated.

'Actually, it's in the Aircraft Building, around the back.'

'How many people will be at the lecture, do you know?'

165

'About a hundred and twenty.'

Surely one of them would know him!

'Thank you!' he said, and he ran down the stairs and out of the building.

3.30 P.M.

Rotating the second-stage tub stabilizes the flight path by averaging the variations between the eleven individual small rocket motors in the cluster.

Billie was furious with Len Ross for trying to ingratiate himself with the people from the Sowerby Foundation. The post of Director of Research ought to go to the best scientist – not the most oleaginous. She was still annoyed that afternoon when the chief executive's secretary called and asked her to come to his office.

Charles Silverton was an accountant, but he understood the needs of scientists. The hospital was owned by a trust whose twin aims were to understand and alleviate mental illness. He saw his job as making sure that administrative and financial problems did not distract the medical people from their work. Billie liked him.

His office had been the dining room of the original Victorian mansion, and it still had the fireplace and the ceiling mouldings. He waved Billie to a chair and said: 'Did you speak to the people from the Sowerby Foundation this morning?'

'Yes. Len was showing them around, and I joined the party. Why?'

He did not answer her question. 'Do you think you could have said anything to offend them?'

She frowned, mystified. 'I don't think so. We just talked about the new wing.'

'You know, I really wanted you to get the job of Director of Research.'

She was alarmed. 'I don't like your use of the past tense!'

He went on: 'Len Ross is a competent scientist, but you're exceptional. You've achieved more than him and you're ten years younger.'

'The Foundation is backing Len for the job?'

He hesitated, looking awkward. 'I'm afraid they're insisting on it, as a condition of their grant.'

'The hell they are!' Billie was stunned.

'Do you know anyone connected with the Foundation?'

'Yes. One of my oldest friends is a trustee. His name is Anthony Carroll, he's godfather to my son.'

'Why is he on the board? What does he do for a living?'

'He works for the State Department, but his mother is very wealthy, and he's involved with several charities.'

'Does he have a grudge against you?'

For a moment, Billie slipped back in time. She had been angry with Anthony, after the catastrophe that led to Luke's leaving Harvard, and they never dated again. But she forgave him because of how he behaved toward Elspeth. Elspeth had gone into a decline, letting her academic work slide, and was in danger of failing to graduate. She walked around in a daze, a pale ghost with long red hair, getting thinner and missing classes. It was Anthony who rescued her. They became close, though the relationship was a friendship rather than a romance. They studied together, and she caught up enough to pass. Anthony won back Billie's respect, and they had been friends ever since.

Now she told Charles: 'I got kind of mad at him, back in 1941, but we made it up long ago.'

'Maybe someone on the board admires Len's work.'

Billie considered. 'Len's approach is different from mine. He's a Freudian, he looks for psychoanalytical explanations. If a patient suddenly loses the ability to read, he assumes they have some unconscious fear of literature, a fear that is being suppressed. I would always look for damage to the brain as the likeliest cause.'

'So there might be a keen Freudian on the board who is against you.'

'I guess.' Billie sighed. 'Can they do this? It seems so unfair.'

'It's certainly unusual,' Charles said. 'Foundations normally make a point of not interfering with decisions requiring professional expertise. But there's no law against it.'

'Well, I'm not going to take this lying down. What reason did they give?'

'I got an informal call from the chairman. He told me the board feels Len is better qualified.'

Billie shook her head. 'There has to be another explanation.'

'Why don't you ask your friend?'

'That's exactly what I'm going to do,' she said.

3.45 P.M.

*A stroboscope was used to determine exactly where weights
should be placed so that the spinning tub would be perfectly
balanced – otherwise the inner cage would vibrate within the
outer frame, causing the whole assembly to disintegrate.*

Luke had looked at his street map of Washington
before leaving the Georgetown University campus. The
Institute was in a park called the Mall. He checked his
watch as he drove along K Street. He would be at the
Smithsonian in about ten minutes. Assuming it took
him another five to find the lecture theatre, he should
arrive as the talk was ending. Then he would find out
who he was.

It was almost eleven hours since he had awakened
to this horror. Yet, because he could remember
nothing from before five o'clock this morning, it
seemed to have been going on all his life.

He turned right on 9th Street, heading south
towards the Mall with high hopes. A few moments
later, he heard a police siren blip once, and his heart
skipped a beat.

He looked in his rear-view mirror. A police cruiser
was on his tail, lights flashing. There were two cops on

the front seat. One pointed toward the right-hand kerb and mouthed: 'Pull over.'

Luke was devastated. He had almost made it.

Could it be that he had committed some minor traffic violation, and they wanted to ticket him? Even if that were all, they would still ask for his driving licence, and he had no kind of identification. Anyway, this was not about a minor traffic violation. He was driving a stolen car. He had calculated that the theft would go unreported until the owner got back from Philadelphia later tonight, but something had gone wrong. They intended to arrest him.

But they would have to catch him first.

He clicked into escape mode. Ahead of him on the one-way street was a long truck. Without further thought, he stamped on the gas pedal and pulled around the truck.

The cops switched on their siren and followed.

Luke pulled in front of the truck, going fast. Acting on instinct now, he yanked the parking brake and spun the wheel hard to the right.

The Ford went into a long skid, turning as it did so. The truck swerved left to avoid it, forcing the patrol car all the way over to the left side of the street.

Luke shifted into neutral to prevent the car stalling. It came to rest facing the wrong way. He put it into drive again and stepped on the gas, heading against the traffic on the one-way street.

Cars veered wildly left and right to avoid a head-on collision. Luke swung right to miss a city bus, then clipped a station wagon, but ploughed on amid a chorus of indignant horns. An old pre-war Lincoln swung onto the sidewalk and hit a lamp post. A motorcyclist lost control and fell off his machine. Luke hoped he was not badly hurt.

He made it to the next crossing and swung right onto a broad avenue. He raced two blocks, running red lights, then looked in his mirror. There was no sign of the police car.

He turned again, heading south now. He was lost, but he knew the Mall was to his south. Now that the patrol car was out of sight, he would have been safer to drive normally. However, it was four o'clock, and he was farther away from the Smithsonian than he had been five minutes ago. If he was late, the audience would have gone. He stepped on the gas again.

The southbound street he was on dead-ended, and he was forced to turn right. He tried to watch for street names as he sped along, swerving around slower vehicles. He was on D Street. After a minute he came to 7th and turned south.

His luck changed. All the lights were green. He hit seventy crossing Constitution Avenue, and he was in the park.

Across the lawn to his right, he saw a big dark-red building like a castle in a fairy tale. It was exactly where the map said the museum would be. He stopped the car and checked his watch. It was five past four. The audience would be leaving. He cursed and jumped out.

He ran across the grass. The secretary had told him the lecture was in the Aircraft Building around the back. Was this the front or the back? It looked like the front. To the side of the building was a path through a little garden. He followed it and came out on a wide two-way avenue. Still running, he found an elaborate iron gateway leading to the back entrance of the museum. To his right, beside a lawn, was what looked like an old aircraft hangar. He went inside.

He looked around. All kinds of aircraft were suspended from the ceiling: old biplanes, a wartime jet, and even the sphere of a hot-air balloon. At floor level were glass cases of aircraft insignia, flight clothing, aerial cameras, and photographs. Luke spoke to a uniformed guard. 'I'm here for the lecture on rocket fuels.'

'You're too late,' the man said, looking at his watch. 'It's ten past four, the lecture's over.'

'Where was it held? I might still catch the speaker.'

'I think he's gone.'

Luke stared hard at him and spoke slowly. 'Just answer the fucking question. Where?'

The man looked scared. 'Far end of the hall,' he said hastily.

Luke hurried the length of the building. At the end, a lecture theatre had been improvised, with a lectern, blackboard, and rows of chairs. Most of the audience had left, and attendants were already stacking the metal seats at the side of the room. But a small knot of eight or nine men remained in a corner, deep in discussion, surrounding a white-haired man who might have been the lecturer.

Luke's spirits fell. A few minutes ago, more than a

173

hundred scientists in his field had been here. Now there were just a handful, and it was quite possible that none of them knew him.

The white-haired man glanced up at him, then looked back at the others. It was impossible to know whether he had recognized Luke or not. He was speaking, and carried on without a pause. 'Nitromethane is almost impossible to handle. You can't ignore safety factors.'

'You can build safety into your procedures, if the fuel is good enough,' said a young man in a tweed suit.

The argument was a familiar one to Luke. A bewildering variety of rocket fuels had been tested, many of them more powerful than the standard combination of alcohol and liquid oxygen, but they all had drawbacks.

A man with a southern accent said: 'What about unsymmetrical dimethylhydrazine? I hear they're testing that at the Jet Propulsion Laboratory in Pasadena.'

Luke suddenly said: 'It works, but it's deadly poison.'

They all turned to him. The white-haired man frowned, looking slightly annoyed, resenting the interruption from a stranger.

Then the young man in the tweed suit looked shocked and said: 'My God, what are you doing in Washington, Luke?'

Luke felt so happy he could have wept.

PART 3

PART 3

4.15 P.M.

A tape programmer in the tub varies the speed of rotation of the upper stages between 450 r.p.m. and 750 r.p.m., to avoid resonance vibrations that could cause the missile to break up in space.

Luke found he could not speak. The emotion of relief was so strong it seemed to constrict his throat. All day he had forced himself to be calm and rational, but now he was close to breaking down.

The other scientists resumed their conversation, oblivious to his distress, except for the young man in the tweed suit, who looked concerned and said: 'Hey, are you okay?'

Luke nodded. After a moment, he managed to say: 'Could we talk?'

'Sure, sure. There's a little office behind the Wright Brothers display. Professor Larkley used it earlier.' They headed for a door to one side. 'I organized this lecture, by the way.' He led Luke into a small, spartan room with a couple of chairs, a desk and a phone. They sat down. 'What's going on?' said the man.

'I've lost my memory.'

'My God!'

177

'Autobiographical amnesia. I still remember my science, that's how I found my way to you guys, but I don't know anything about myself.'

Looking shocked, the young man said: 'Do you know who I am?'

Luke shook his head. 'Heck, I'm not even sure of my own name.'

'Whew.' The man looked bewildered. 'I never came across anything like this in real life.'

'I need you to tell me what you know about me.'

'I guess you do. Uh . . . where shall I start?'

'You called me Luke.'

'Everyone calls you Luke. You're Dr Claude Lucas, but I guess you never liked "Claude". I'm Will McDermot.'

Luke closed his eyes, overwhelmed by relief and gratitude. He knew his name. 'Thank you, Will.'

'I don't know anything about your family. I've only met you a couple of times, at scientific conferences.'

'Do you know where I live?'

'Huntsville, Alabama, I guess. You work for the Army Ballistic Missile Agency. They're based at Redstone Arsenal in Huntsville. You're a civilian, though, not an army officer. Your boss is Wernher von Braun.'

'I can't tell you how good it is to know this stuff!'

'I was surprised to see you because your team is about to launch a rocket that will put an American satellite in space for the first time. They're all down in Cape Canaveral, and word is it could be tonight.'

'I read about it in the paper this morning – my God, did I work on that?'

'Yeah. The Explorer. It's the most important launch in the history of the American space programme – especially since the success of the Russian Sputnik and the failure of the Navy's Vanguard.'

Luke was exhilarated. Only hours ago he had imagined himself a drunken bum. Now it turned out he was a scientist at the peak of his career. 'But I ought to be there for the launch!'

'Exactly . . . so do you have any idea why you're not?'

Luke shook his head. 'I woke up this morning in the men's room at Union Station. No idea how I got there.'

Will gave him a man-to-man grin. 'Sounds like you went to a great party last night!'

'Let me ask you seriously – is that the kind of thing I do? Get so drunk I pass out?'

'I don't know you well enough to answer that.' Will frowned. 'I'd be surprised, though. You know us scientists. Our idea of a party is to sit around drinking coffee and talking about our work.'

That sounded right to Luke. 'Getting drunk just doesn't seem interesting enough.' But he had no other explanation of how he had gotten into this scrape. Who was Pete? Why had people been following him? And who were the two men searching for him at Union Station?

He thought of talking to Will about all that, and

decided it sounded too strange. Will might begin to think he was nuts. Instead he said: 'I'm going to call Cape Canaveral.'

'Great idea.' Will picked up the phone on the desk and dialled zero. 'Will McDermot here. Can I make a long-distance call on this phone? Thank you.' He handed the phone to Luke.

Luke got the number from information and dialled. 'This is Dr Lucas.' He felt inordinately pleased to be able to give his name: he would not have thought it could be so satisfying. 'I'd like to speak to someone on the Explorer launch team.'

'They're in hangars D and R,' said the male operator. 'Please hold the line.'

A moment later a voice said: 'Army security, Colonel Hide speaking.'

'This is Dr Lucas—'

'Luke! At last! Where the hell are you?'

'I'm in Washington.'

'Well, what the bejesus are you doing? We've been going crazy! We got Army Security looking for you, the FBI, even the CIA!'

That explained the two agents searching in Union Station, Luke thought. 'Listen, a strange thing has happened. I lost my memory. I've been wandering around town trying to figure out who I am. Finally I found some physicists who know me.'

'But that's extraordinary. How did it happen, for Christ's sake?'

'I was hoping you could tell me that, Colonel.'

'You always call me Bill.'

'Bill.'

'Okay, well, I'll tell you what I know. Monday morning you took off, saying you had to go to Washington. You flew from Patrick.'

'Patrick?'

'Patrick Air Force Base, near Cape Canaveral. Marigold made the reservations—'

'Who's Marigold?'

'Your secretary in Huntsville. She also booked your usual suite at the Carlton Hotel in Washington.'

There was a note of envy in the colonel's voice, and Luke wondered briefly about that 'usual suite', but he had more important questions. 'Did I tell anyone the purpose of the trip?'

'Marigold made an appointment for you to see General Sherwood at the Pentagon at ten a.m. yesterday – but you didn't keep the appointment.'

'Did I give a reason for wanting to see the general?'

'Apparently not.'

'What's his area of responsibility?'

'Army security – but he's also a friend of your family's, so the meeting could have been about anything.'

It must have been something highly important, Luke reflected, to take him away from Cape Canaveral just before his rocket was to take off. 'Is the launch going ahead tonight?'

'No, we've got weather problems. It's been postponed until tomorrow at ten-thirty p.m.'

Luke wondered what the hell he had been doing. 'Do I have friends here in Washington?'

'Sure. One of them's been calling me every hour. Bern Rothsten.' Hide read out a phone number.

Luke scribbled it on a scratchpad. 'I'll call him right away.'

'First you should talk to your wife.'

Luke froze. His breath was taken away. Wife, he thought. I have a wife. He wondered what she was like.

'You still there?' Hide said.

Luke started to breathe again. 'Uh, Bill . . .'

'Yes?'

'What's her name?'

'Elspeth,' he said. 'Your wife's name is Elspeth. I'll transfer you to her phone. Hold the line.'

Luke had a nervous sensation in his stomach. This was dumb, he thought. She was his wife.

'Elspeth speaking. Luke, is that you?'

She had a warm, low voice, with precise diction and no particular accent. He imagined a tall, confident woman. He said: 'Yes, this is Luke. I've lost my memory.'

'I've been so worried. Are you okay?'

He felt pathetically grateful for someone who cared how he was. 'I guess I am now,' he said.

'What on earth happened?'

'I really don't know. I woke up this morning in the men's room at Union Station, and I spent the day trying to find out who I am.'

'Everyone's been looking for you. Where are you now?'

'At the Smithsonian, in the Aircraft Building.'

182

'Is someone taking care of you?'

Luke smiled at Will McDermot. 'A fellow scientist has been helping me. And I have a number for Bern Rothsten. But I really don't need taking care of. I'm fine, I just lost my memory.'

Will McDermot stood up, looking embarrassed, and whispered: 'I'm going to give you some privacy. I'll wait outside.'

Luke nodded gratefully.

Elspeth was saying: 'So you don't remember why you took off for Washington in such a hurry.'

'No. Obviously I didn't tell you.'

'You said it was better for me not to know. But I was frantic. I called an old friend of ours in Washington, Anthony Carroll. He's in the CIA.'

'Did he do anything?'

'He called you at the Carlton on Monday night, and you arranged to meet him for breakfast early on Tuesday morning – but you didn't show up. He's been looking for you all day. I'm going to call him now and tell him everything's all right.'

'Obviously something happened to me between Monday evening and Tuesday morning.'

'You ought to see a doctor, get yourself checked out.'

'I feel fine. But there's a lot I want to know. Do we have children?'

'No.'

Luke felt a sadness that seemed familiar, like the dull ache of an old injury.

Elspeth went on: 'We've been trying for a baby ever since we got married, which was four years ago, but we haven't succeeded.'

'Are my parents alive?'

'Your Mom is. She lives in New York. Your Pa died five years ago.'

Luke felt a sudden wave of grief that seemed to come from nowhere. He had lost his memories of his father, and would never see him again. It seemed unbearably sad.

Elspeth went on: 'You have two brothers and a sister, all younger. Your baby sister Emily is your favourite, she's ten years younger than you, she lives in Baltimore.'

'Do you have phone numbers for them?'

'Of course. Hold on while I look them up.'

'I'd like to talk to them, I don't know why.' He heard a muffled sob at the other end of the line. 'Are you crying?'

Elspeth sniffed. 'I'm okay.' He imagined her taking a handkerchief out of her handbag. 'Suddenly I felt so sorry for you,' she said tearfully. 'It must have been awful.'

'There were some bad moments.'

'Let me give you those numbers.' She read them out.

'Are we rich?' he said when he had written down the phone numbers.

'Your father was a very successful banker. He left you a lot of money. Why?'

'Bill Hide told me I'm staying in my "usual suite" at the Carlton.'

'Before the war, your Pa was an adviser to the Roosevelt administration, and he liked to take his family with him when he went to Washington. You always had a corner suite at the Carlton. I guess you're keeping up the tradition.'

'So you and I don't live on what the army pays me.'

'No, though in Huntsville we try not to live very much better than your colleagues.'

'I could go on asking you questions all day. But what I really want is to find out how this happened to me. Would you fly up here tonight?'

There was a moment of silence. 'My God, why?'

'To figure out this mystery with me. I could use some help – and companionship.'

'You should forget about it and come down here.'

That was unthinkable. 'I can't forget about this. I have to know what it's all about. It's too strange to ignore.'

'Luke, I can't leave Cape Canaveral now. We're about to launch the first American satellite, for heaven's sake! I can't let the team down at a moment like this.'

'I guess not.' He understood, but all the same he was hurt by her refusal. 'Who's Bern Rothsten?'

'He was at Harvard with you and Anthony Carroll. He's a writer now.'

'Apparently he's been trying to reach me. Maybe he knows what this is all about.'

'Call me later, won't you? I'll be at the Starlite Motel tonight.'

'Okay.'

'Take care of yourself, Luke, please,' she said earnestly.

'I will, I promise.' He hung up.

He sat in silence for a moment. He felt emotionally drained. Part of him wanted to go to his hotel and lie down. But he was too curious. He picked up the phone again and called the number Bern Rothsten had left. 'This is Luke Lucas,' he said when the phone was answered.

Bern had a gravelly voice and the trace of a New York accent. 'Luke, thank God! What the hell happened to you?'

'Everybody says that. The answer is that I don't really know anything except that I've lost my memory.'

'You lost your memory?'

'Right.'

'Oh, shit. Do you know how this happened to you?'

'No. I was hoping you might have a clue.'

'I might.'

'Why have you been trying to reach me?'

'I was worried. You called me on Monday. You said you were on your way here, you wanted to see me, and you would call me from the Carlton. But you never did.'

'Something happened to me on Monday night.'

'Yeah. Listen, there's someone you have to call. Dr Billie Josephson is a world expert on memory.'

The name rang a bell. 'I think I came across her book in the library.'

186

'She's also my ex-wife, and an old friend of yours.' Bern gave Luke the number.

'I'm going to call her right away. Bern . . .'

'Yeah.'

'I lose my memory, and it turns out that an old friend of mine is a world expert on memory. Isn't that a hell of a coincidence?'

'Ain't it just,' said Bern.

4.45 P.M.

The final stage, containing the satellite, is eighty inches long and only six inches across, and weighs just over thirty pounds. It is shaped like a stovepipe.

Billie had scheduled an hour-long interview with a patient, a football player who had been 'dinged' – concussed in a collision with an opponent. He was an interesting subject, because he could remember everything up to one hour before the game, and nothing after that until the moment when he found himself standing on the sideline with his back to the play, wondering how he got there.

She was distracted during the interview, thinking about the Sowerby Foundation and Anthony Carroll. By the time she got through with the football player and called Anthony, she was feeling frustrated and impatient. She was lucky, and reached him at his office on the first try. 'Anthony,' she said abruptly, 'what the hell is going on?'

'A lot,' he replied. 'Egypt and Syria have agreed to merge, skirts are getting shorter, and Roy Campanella broke his neck in a car wreck and may never catch for the Dodgers again.'

She controlled the impulse to yell at him. 'I was

passed over for the post of Director of Research here at the hospital,' she said with forced calm. 'Len Ross got the job. Did you know that?'

'Yeah, I guess I did.'

'I don't understand it. I thought I might lose to a highly qualified outsider – Sol Weinberg, from Princeton, or someone of that order. But everyone knows I'm better than Len.'

'Do they?'

'Anthony, come on! You know it yourself. Hell, you encouraged me in this line of research, years ago, at the end of the war, when we—'

'Okay, okay, I remember,' he interrupted. 'That stuff is still classified, you know.'

She did not believe that things they did in the war could still be important secrets. But it did not matter. 'So why didn't I get the job?'

'I'm supposed to know?'

This was humiliating, she felt, but her need to understand overrode her embarrassment. 'The Foundation is insisting on Len.'

'I guess they have the right.'

'Anthony, talk to me!'

'I'm talking.'

'You're part of the Foundation. It's very unusual for a trust to interfere in this kind of decision. They normally leave it to the experts. You must know why they took this exceptional step.'

'Well, I don't. And my guess is the step has not yet been taken. There certainly hasn't been a meeting about it – I'd know about that.'

'Charles was very definite.'

'I don't doubt it's true, unfortunately for you. But it's not the kind of thing that would be decided openly. More likely, the Director and one or two board members had a chat over a drink at the Cosmos Club. One of them has called Charles and given him the word. He can't afford to upset them, so he's gone along. That's how these things work. I'm just surprised Charles was so candid with you.'

'He was shocked, I think. He can't understand why they would do such a thing. I thought you might know.'

'It's probably something dumb. Is Ross a family man?'

'Married with four children.'

'The Director doesn't really approve of women earning high salaries when there are men trying to support a family.'

'For Christ's sake! I have a child and an elderly mother to take care of!'

'I didn't say it was logical. Listen, Billie, I have to go. I'm sorry. I'll call you later.'

'Okay,' she said.

When she had hung up, she stared at the phone, trying to sort out her feelings. The conversation rang false to her, and she asked herself why. It was perfectly plausible that Anthony might not know about machinations among the other board members of the Foundation. So why did she disbelieve him? Thinking back, she realized he had been evasive – which was not like him. In the end he had told her what little he knew, but reluctantly. It all added up to a very clear impression.

Anthony was lying.

5 P.M.

The fourth-stage rocket is made of lightweight titanium instead of stainless steel. The weight saving permits the missile to carry a crucial extra two pounds of scientific equipment.

When Anthony hung up the phone, it rang again immediately. He picked it up and heard Elspeth, sounding spooked. 'For God's sake, I've been on hold for a quarter of an hour!'

'I was talking to Billie, she—'

'Never mind. I just spoke with Luke.'

'Jesus, how come?'

'Shut up and listen! He was at the Smithsonian, in the Aircraft Building, with a bunch of physicists.'

'I'm on my way.' Anthony dropped the phone and ran out the door. Pete saw him and ran after him. They went down to the parking lot and jumped into Anthony's car.

The fact that Luke had spoken with Elspeth dismayed Anthony. It suggested that everything was coming unglued. But maybe if he got to Luke before anyone else, he could hold things together. It took them four minutes to drive to Independence Avenue and 10th Street. They left the car outside the back entrance to the museum and ran into the old hangar that was the Aircraft Building.

There was a payphone near the entrance, but no sign of Luke.

'Split up,' Anthony said. 'I'll go right, you go left.' He walked through the exhibits, scrutinizing the faces of the men as they gazed into the glass cases and stared up at the aircraft suspended from the ceiling. At the far end of the building he met up with Pete, who made an empty-hands gesture.

There were some restrooms and offices to one side. Pete checked the men's room and Anthony looked in the offices. Luke must have called from one of these phones, but he was not here now.

Pete came out of the men's room and said: 'Nothing.'

Anthony said: 'This is a catastrophe.'

Pete frowned. 'Is it?' he said. 'A catastrophe? Is this guy more important than you've told me?'

'Yes,' Anthony said. 'He could be the most dangerous man in America.'

'Christ.'

Against the end wall, Anthony saw stacked chairs and a movable lectern. A young man in a tweed suit was talking to two men in overalls. Anthony recalled that Elspeth had said Luke was with a bunch of physicists. Maybe he could still pick up the trail.

He approached the man in the tweed suit and said: 'Excuse me, was there a meeting of some kind here?'

'Sure, Professor Larkley gave a lecture on rocket

fuels,' the young man said. 'I'm Will McDermot, I organized it as part of International Geophysical Year.'

'Was Dr Claude Lucas here?'

'Yes. Are you a friend of his?'

'Yes.'

'Did you know he's lost his memory? He didn't even know his own name, until I told him.'

Anthony suppressed a curse. He had been afraid of this from the moment Elspeth had said she had spoken to Luke. He knew who he was.

'I need to locate Dr Lucas urgently,' Anthony said.

'What a shame, you just missed him.'

'Did he say where he was going?'

'No. I tried to encourage him to see a doctor, get himself checked out, but he said he was fine. I thought he seemed very shocked—'

'Yes, thank you, I appreciate your help.' Anthony turned and walked quickly away. He was furious.

Outside on Independence Avenue he saw a police cruiser. Two cops were checking out a car parked on the other side of the road. Anthony went closer and saw that the car was a blue-and-white Ford Fairlane. 'Look at that,' he said to Pete. He checked the licence plate. It was the car Nosy Rosy had seen from her Georgetown window.

He showed the patrolmen his CIA identification. 'Did you just spot this car illegally parked?' he said.

The older of the two men replied. 'No, we saw a man driving it on 9th Street,' he said. 'But he got away from us.'

'You let him escape?' Anthony said incredulously.

'He turned around and headed right into the traffic!' the younger cop said. 'Hell of a driver, whoever he is.'

'Few minutes later, we see the car parked here, but he's gone.'

Anthony wanted to knock their wooden heads together. Instead, he said: 'This fugitive may have stolen another car in this neighbourhood and made his getaway.' He took a business card out of his billfold. 'If you get a report of a car stolen nearby, would you please call me at this number?'

The older cop read the card and said: 'I'll make sure to do that, Mr Carroll.'

Anthony and Pete returned to the yellow Cadillac and drove away.

Pete said: 'What do you think he'll do now?'

'I don't know. He might go right to the airport and get a plane to Florida; he could go to the Pentagon; he may go to his hotel. Hell, he could take it into his head to go visit his mother in New York. We may have to spread ourselves kind of thin.' He was silent, thinking, while he parked and entered Q Building. Reaching his office, he said: 'I want two men at the airport, two at Union Station, two at the bus station. I want two men in the office calling all known members of Luke's family, friends and acquaintances, to ask if they're expecting to see him or if they've heard from him. I want you to go with two men to the Carlton Hotel. Take a room, then stake out the lobby. I'll join you there later.'

Pete went out and Anthony shut the door.

For the first time today, Anthony was scared. Now that Luke knew his own identity, there was no telling what else he might find out. This project should have been Anthony's greatest triumph, but it was turning into a foul-up that might end his career.

It might end his life.

If he could find Luke, he could still patch things up. But he would have to take drastic measures. It would no longer be enough simply to put Luke under surveillance. He had to solve the problem once and for all.

With a heavy heart, he went to the photograph of President Eisenhower that hung on the wall. He pulled on one side of the frame, and the picture swung out on hinges to reveal a safe. He dialled the combination, opened the door, and took out his gun.

It was a Walther P38 automatic. This was the handgun used by the German army in the Second World War. Anthony had been issued with it before he went to North Africa. He also had a silencer that had been specially designed by OSS to fit the gun.

The first time he had killed a man, it had been with this gun.

Albin Moulier was a traitor who had betrayed members of the French Resistance to the police. He deserved to die – the five men in the cell were agreed on that. They drew lots, standing in a derelict stable miles from anywhere, late at night, a single lamp throwing dancing shadows on the rough stone walls. Anthony might have been excused, as the only foreigner, but that way he would have lost respect, so he insisted on taking his chances with the rest. And he drew the short straw.

Albin was tied to the rusty wheel of a broken plough, not even blindfolded, listening to the discussion and watching the drawing of lots. He soiled himself when they pronounced the death sentence, and screamed when he saw Anthony take out the Walther. The screaming helped: it made Anthony want to kill him quickly, just to stop the noise. He shot Albin at close range, between the eyes, one bullet. Afterwards, the others told him he did it well, without hesitation or regrets, like a man.

Anthony still saw Albin in his dreams.

He took the silencer from the safe, fitted it over the barrel of the pistol, and screwed it tight. He put on his topcoat. It was a long camel-hair winter coat, single-breasted, with deep inside pockets. He placed the gun, butt down, in the right-hand pocket, with the silencer sticking up. Leaving the coat unbuttoned, he reached in with his left hand, pulled the gun out by the silencer, and transferred it to his right hand. Then he moved the thumb safety lever on the left of the slide up to the 'fire' position. The whole process took about a second. The silencer made the weapon cumbersome. It would be easier to carry the two parts separately. However, he might not have time to fit the silencer before shooting. This way was better.

He buttoned his coat and went out.

6 P.M.

The satellite is bullet-shaped, rather than spherical. In theory, a sphere should be more stable; but in practice, the satellite must have protruding antennae for radio communication, and the antennae spoil the round shape.

Luke took a taxicab to the Georgetown Mind Hospital and gave his name at the reception desk, saying he had an appointment with Dr Josephson.

She had been charming on the phone: concerned about him, pleased to hear his voice, intrigued to know that he had lost his memory, eager to see him as soon as she could. She spoke with a southern accent, and sounded as if laughter was forever bubbling up at the back of her throat.

Now she came running down the stairs, a short woman in a white lab coat, with big brown eyes and a flushed expression of excitement. Luke could not help smiling at the sight of her.

'It's so great to see you!' she said, and she threw her arms around him in a hug.

He felt an impulse to respond to her exuberance and squeeze her tightly. Afraid that he might do

197

something to cause offence, he froze, his hands in the air like the victim of a hold-up.

She laughed at him. 'You don't remember what I'm like,' she said. 'Relax, I'm almost harmless.'

He let his arms fall around her shoulders. Her small body was soft and round under the lab coat.

'Come on, I'll show you my office.' She led him up the stairs.

As they crossed a broad corridor, a white-haired woman in a bathrobe said: 'Doctor! I like your boyfriend!'

Billie grinned and said: 'You can have him next, Marlene.'

Billie had a small room with a plain desk and a steel filing cabinet, but she had made it pretty with flowers and a splashy abstract painting in bright colours. She gave Luke coffee and opened a package of cookies, then asked him about his amnesia.

She made notes as he answered her questions. Luke had had no food for twelve hours, and he ate all the cookies. She smiled and said: 'Want some more? There's another pack.' He shook his head.

'Well, I have a pretty clear picture,' she said eventually. 'You have global amnesia, but otherwise you seem mentally healthy. I can't assess your physical state, because I'm not that kind of doctor, and it's my duty to advise you to have a physical as soon as you can.' She smiled. 'But you look all right, just shook up.'

'Is there a cure for this type of amnesia?'

'No, there's not. The process is generally irreversible.'

That was a blow. Luke had hoped everything might come back to him in a flash. 'Christ,' he muttered.

'Don't be downhearted,' Billie said kindly. 'Sufferers have all their faculties, and are able to relearn what has been forgotten; so they can usually pick up the threads of their lives and live normally. You're going to be fine.'

Even while he was hearing horrible news, he found himself watching her with fascination, concentrating his attention first on her eyes, which seemed to glow with sympathy, then her expressive mouth, then the way the light from the desk lamp fell on her dark curls. He wanted her to carry on talking for ever. He said: 'What might have caused the amnesia?'

'Brain damage is the first possibility to consider. However, there's no sign of injury, and you told me you don't have a headache.'

'That's right. So what else?'

'There are several alternatives,' she explained patiently. 'It can be brought on by prolonged stress, a sudden shock, or drugs. It's also a side effect of some treatments for schizophrenia involving a combination of electric shock and drugs.'

'Any way to tell which affected me?'

'Not conclusively. You had a hangover this morning, you said. If that wasn't booze, it might be the after-effects of a drug. But you're not going to get a final answer by talking to doctors. You need to find out what happened to you between Monday night and this morning.'

'Well, at least I know what I'm looking for,' he said. 'Shock, drugs or schizophrenia treatment.'

'You're not schizophrenic,' she said. 'You have a real good hold on reality. What's your next step?'

Luke stood up. He was reluctant to leave the company of this bewitching woman, but she had told him all she could. 'I'm going to see Bern Rothsten. I think he may have some ideas.'

'Got a car?'

'I asked the taxi to wait.'

'I'll see you out.'

As they walked down the stairs, Billie took his arm affectionately.

Luke said: 'How long have you been divorced from Bern?'

'Five years. Long enough to become friends again.'

'This is a strange question, but I have to ask it. Did you and I ever date?'

'Oh, boy,' said Billie. 'Did we ever.'

1943

On the day Italy surrendered, Billie bumped into Luke in the lobby of Q Building.

At first she did not know him. She saw a thin man of about thirty in a suit that was too big, and her eyes passed over him without recognition. Then he spoke. 'Billie? Don't you remember me?'

She knew the voice, of course, and it made her heart beat faster. But when she looked again at the emaciated man from whom the words issued, she gave a small scream of horror. His head looked like a skull. His once-glossy black hair was dull. His shirt collar was too large, and his jacket looked as if it were draped over a wire hanger. His eyes were the eyes of an old man. 'Luke!' she said. 'You look terrible!'

'Gee, thanks,' he said, with a tired smile.

'I'm sorry,' she said hastily.

'Don't worry. I've lost some weight, I know. There's not a lot of food where I've been.'

She wanted to hug him, but she held back, not sure he would like it.

He said: 'What are you doing here?'

She took a deep breath. 'A training course – maps, radio, firearms, unarmed combat.'

He grinned. 'You're not dressed for ju-jitsu.'

Billie still loved to dress stylishly, despite the war. Today she was wearing a pale yellow suit with a short bolero jacket and a daring knee-length skirt, and a big hat like an upside-down dinner plate. She could not afford to buy the latest fashions on her army wages, of course: she had made this outfit herself, using a borrowed sewing machine. Her father had taught all his children to sew. 'I'll take that as a compliment,' she said with a smile, beginning to get over her shock. 'Where have you been?'

'Do you have a minute to talk?'

'Of course.' She was supposed to be at a cryptography class, but to heck with that.

'Let's go outside.'

It was a warm September afternoon. Luke took off his suit coat and slung it over his shoulder as they walked alongside the Reflecting Pool. 'How come you're in OSS?'

'Anthony Carroll fixed it,' she said. The Office of Strategic Services was considered a glamorous assignment, and jobs here were much coveted. 'Anthony used family influence to get here. He's Bill Donovan's personal assistant now.' General 'Wild Bill' Donovan was head of OSS. 'I'd been driving a general around Washington for a year, so I was real pleased to get posted here. Anthony's used his position to bring in all his old friends from Harvard. Elspeth is in London, Peg is in Cairo, and I gather you and Bern have been behind enemy lines somewhere.'

'France,' Luke said.

'What was that like?'

He lit a cigarette. It was a new habit – he had not smoked at Harvard – but now he drew tobacco smoke into his lungs as if it were the breath of life. 'The first man I killed was a Frenchman,' he said abruptly.

It was painfully obvious that he needed to talk about it. 'Tell me what happened,' she said.

'He was a cop, a gendarme. Claude, same name as me. Not really a bad guy – anti-Semitic, but no more so than the average Frenchman, or a lot of Americans for that matter. He blundered into a farmhouse where my group was meeting. There was no doubt what we were doing – we had maps on the table and rifles stacked in the corner, and Bern was showing the Frenchies how to wire a time bomb.' Luke gave an odd kind of laugh, with no humour in it. 'Damn fool tried to arrest us all. Not that it made any difference. He had to be killed whatever he did.'

'What did you do?' Billie whispered.

'Took him outside and shot him in the back of the head.'

'Oh, my God.'

'He didn't die right away. It took about a minute.'

She took his hand and squeezed it. He held on, and they walked around the long, narrow pool hand in hand. He told her another story, about a woman Resistance fighter who had been captured and tortured, and Billie cried, tears streaming down her face in the September sunshine. The afternoon cooled, and still the grim details spilled out of him: cars blown up, German officers assassinated, Resistance comrades killed in shoot-outs, and Jewish families led away to unknown destinations, holding the hands of their trusting children.

They had been walking for two hours when he stumbled, and she caught him and prevented his falling. 'Jesus Christ, I'm so tired,' he said. 'I've been sleeping badly.'

She hailed a taxi and took him to his hotel.

Luke was staying at the Carlton. The army did not generally run to such luxury, but she recalled that his family was wealthy. He had a corner suite. There was a grand piano in the living room and – something she had never seen before – a telephone extension in the bathroom.

She called room service and ordered chicken soup and scrambled eggs, hot rolls and a pint of cold milk. He sat on the couch and began to tell another story, a funny one, about sabotaging a factory that made saucepans for the German army. 'I ran into this big metalworking shop, and there were about fifty enormous, muscle-bound women, stoking the furnace and hammering the moulds. I yelled: 'Clear the building! We're going to blow it up!' But the women laughed at me! They wouldn't leave, they all carried on working. They didn't believe me.' Before he could finish the story, the food came.

Billie signed the check, tipped the waiter, and put the plates on the dining table. When she turned around, Luke was asleep.

She woke him just long enough to get him into the

bedroom and onto the bed. 'Don't leave,' he mumbled, then his eyes closed again.

She took off his boots and gently loosened his tie. A mild breeze was blowing in through the open window: he did not need blankets.

She sat on the edge of the bed watching him for a while, remembering that long drive from Cambridge to Newport almost two years ago. She stroked his cheek with the outside edge of her little finger, the way she had that night. He did not stir.

She took off her hat and her shoes, thought for a moment, and slipped off her jacket and skirt. Then, in her underwear and stockings, she lay down on the bed. She got her arms around his bony shoulders, put his head on her bosom, and held him. 'Everything's all right, now,' she said. 'You just sleep as long as you want. When you wake up, I'll still be here.'

* * *

Night fell. The temperature dropped. She closed the window and pulled a sheet around them. Soon after midnight, with her arms wrapped around his warm body, she fell asleep.

At dawn, when he had been asleep for twelve hours, he got up suddenly and went to the bathroom. He returned a couple of minutes later and got back into bed. He had taken off his suit and shirt, and wore only his underwear. He put his arms around her and hugged her. 'Something I forgot to tell you, something very important,' he said.

'What?'

'In France, I thought about you all the time. Every day.'

'Did you?' she whispered. 'Did you really?'

He did not answer. He had gone back to sleep.

She lay in his embrace, thinking about him in France, risking his life and remembering her; and she was so happy she felt her heart would burst.

At eight o'clock in the morning, she went into the living room of the suite, phoned Q Building, and said she was sick. It was the first day she had taken off for illness in more than a year in the military. She had a bath and washed her hair, then got dressed. She ordered coffee and cornflakes from room service. The waiter called her Mrs Lucas. She was glad it was not a waitress, for a woman would have noticed that she wore no wedding ring.

She thought the smell of coffee might wake Luke, but it did not. She read the *Washington Post* from cover to cover, even the sports pages. She was writing a letter to her mother in Dallas, on hotel stationery, when he came stumbling out of the bedroom in his underwear, his dark hair mussed, his jaw blue with stubble. She smiled at him, happy that he was awake.

He looked confused. 'How long did I sleep?'

She checked her wristwatch. It was almost noon. 'About eighteen hours.' She could not tell what he was thinking. Was he pleased to see her? Embarrassed? Was he wishing she would go away?

'God,' he said. 'I haven't slept like that for a year.'

He rubbed his eyes. 'Have you been here all the time? You look as fresh as a daisy.'

'I took a little nap.'

'You stayed all night?'

'You asked me to.'

He frowned. 'I seem to remember . . .' He shook his head. 'Boy, I had some dreams.' He went to the phone. 'Room service? Let me have a T-bone steak, rare, with three eggs, sunnyside up. Plus orange juice, toast and coffee.'

Billie frowned. She had never spent the night with a man, so she did not know what to expect in the morning, but this disappointed her. It was so unromantic that she felt almost insulted. She was reminded of her brothers waking up – they, too, emerged from sleep stubbly, grouchy and ravenous. But, she recalled, they generally improved when they had eaten.

'Hold on,' he said into the phone. He looked at Billie. 'Would you like something?'

'Yeah, some iced tea.'

He repeated her order and hung up.

He sat beside her on the couch. 'I talked a lot yesterday.'

'That's the truth.'

'How long?'

'About five hours straight.'

'I'm sorry.'

'Don't be sorry. Whatever you do, please don't be sorry.' Tears came to her eyes. 'I'll never forget it as long as I live.'

He took her hands. 'I'm so glad we met again.'

Her heart jumped. 'Me, too.' This was more like what she had hoped for.

'I'd like to kiss you, but I've been in the same clothes for twenty-four hours.'

She felt a sudden sensation inside, like a spring breaking, and she was conscious of wetness. She was shocked at herself: it had never happened this fast before.

But she held back. She had not decided where she wanted this to go. She had had all night to make a decision, but she had not even thought about it. Now she was afraid that once she touched him she would lose control. And then what?

The war had brought about a new moral laxity in Washington, but she was not part of it. She clasped her hands in her lap and said: 'I sure don't aim to kiss you until you're dressed.'

He gave her a sceptical look. 'Are you afraid of compromising yourself?'

She winced at the irony in his voice. 'Just what does that mean?'

He shrugged. 'We spent the night together.'

She felt hurt and indignant. 'I stayed here because you begged me too!' she protested.

'All right, don't get mad.'

But her desire for him had turned, in a flash, to equally powerful anger. 'You were falling down with exhaustion, and I put you to bed,' she said wrathfully. 'Then you asked me not to leave you, so I stayed.'

'I appreciate it.'

'Then don't talk as if I've acted like a . . . whore!'

'That's not what I meant.'

'It sure is! You implied I've already compromised myself so much that anything else I might do makes no difference.'

He gave a big sigh. 'Well, I didn't intend to imply that. Jesus, you're making a hell of a fuss about a casual remark.'

'Too darn casual.' The trouble was, she *had* compromised herself.

There was a knock at the door.

They looked at one another. Luke said: 'Room service, I guess.'

She did not want a waiter to see her with an undressed man. 'Get in the bedroom.'

'Okay.'

'First, give me your ring.'

He looked at his left hand. He wore a gold signet ring on the little finger. 'Why?'

'So the waiter will think I'm married.'

'But I never take it off.'

That angered her even more. 'Get out of sight,' she hissed.

He went into the bedroom. Billie opened the suite door and a waitress brought in the room-service cart. 'There you go, Miss,' she said.

Billie flushed. There was an insult in that 'Miss'. She signed the check but did not tip. 'There you go,' she said, and turned her back.

The waitress left. Billie heard the shower running. She felt exhausted. She had spent hours in the grip of a profound romantic passion, then in a few minutes it had turned sour. Luke was normally so gracious, yet he had metamorphosed into a bear. How could such things happen?

Whatever the reason, he had made her feel cheap. In a minute or two, he would come out of the bathroom, ready to sit down and have breakfast with her as if they were a married couple. But they were not, and she was feeling more and more uncomfortable.

Well, she thought, if I don't like it, why am I still here? It was a good question.

She put on her hat. It was better to get out with what dignity she had left.

She thought about writing him a note. The sound of the shower stopped. He was about to reappear, smelling of soap, wearing a dressing gown, his hair wet and his feet bare, looking good enough to eat. There was no time for a note.

She left the suite, closing the door quietly behind her.

* * *

She saw him almost every day for the next four weeks.

At first he was in Q Building for daily debriefing sessions. He would seek her out at lunchtime, and they would eat together in the cafeteria or take sandwiches to the park. His manner reverted to his characteristic relaxed courtesy, making her feel respected and cared for. The sting of his behaviour in the Carlton eased. Maybe, she thought, he too had never spent the night with a lover; and, like her, he was not sure of the etiquette. He had treated her casually, as he might treat his sister – and perhaps his sister was the only girl who had ever seen him in his underwear.

At the end of the week he asked her for a date, and they saw the movie of *Jane Eyre* on Saturday night. On Sunday they went canoeing on the Potomac. There was a spirit of recklessness in the Washington air. The city was full of young men on their way to the front or back home on leave, men for whom violent death was an everyday event. They wanted to gamble, drink, dance, and make love because they might never have another chance. The bars were jammed, and a single girl never needed to spend an evening alone. The Allies were winning the war, but the bubble of exuberance was burst daily by news of relatives, neighbours, and college friends killed and wounded on the front line.

Luke put on a little weight and started to sleep better. The haunted look went from his eyes. He bought some clothes that fitted him, short-sleeved shirts and white pants and a navy flannel suit that he wore for their evening dates. A little of his boyishness came back.

They talked endlessly. She explained how the study of human psychology would eventually eliminate mental illness, and he told her how men could fly to the moon. They relived the fateful Harvard weekend that had changed their lives. They discussed the war, and when it might end: Billie thought the Germans could not last much longer, now that Italy had fallen, but Luke believed it would take years to clear the Japanese out of the Pacific. Sometimes they went out with Anthony and Bern, and argued politics in bars, just as they had when they were all at college together, in a different world. One weekend Luke flew to New York to see his family, and Billie missed him so badly she felt ill. She never tired of him, never came near to being bored. He was thoughtful and witty and smart.

They had a major fight about twice a week. Each followed the pattern of their first row, in his hotel suite. He would say something high-handed, or make a decision about their evening's plans without consulting her, or assume he knew better about some subject, radio or automobiles or tennis. She would protest hotly, and he would accuse her of overreacting. She would get more and more angry as she tried to make him understand what was wrong with his attitude, and he would start to feel like a hostile witness under cross-examination. In the heat of the argument, she would exaggerate, or make some wild assertion, or say something she knew to be false. Then he would accuse her of insincerity, and say there was no point in talking to her, because she was willing to say anything to win an argument. He would walk out, more convinced than ever that he was right. Within minutes, she would be distraught. She would seek him out and beg him to forget it and be friends. At first he would be stony-faced; then she would say something that made him laugh, and he would melt.

But in all that time she did not go to his hotel, and

when she kissed him it was a chaste brush of the lips, always in a public place. Even so, she felt the liquid sensation inside every time she touched him, and she knew she could go no farther without going the whole way.

The sunny September turned into a chilly October, and Luke was posted.

He got the news on a Friday afternoon. He was waiting for Billie in the lobby of Q Building when she left for the day. She could see by his face that something bad had happened. 'What's wrong?' she said immediately.

'I'm going back to France.'

She was dismayed. 'When?'

'I leave Washington early on Monday morning. Bern, too.'

'For God's sake, haven't you done your share?'

'I don't mind the danger,' he said. 'I just don't want to leave you.'

Tears came to her eyes. She swallowed hard. 'Two days.'

'I've got to pack.'

'I'll help you.'

They went to his hotel.

As soon as they were inside the door she grabbed him by his sweater, pulled him to her, and tilted her face to be kissed. This time there was nothing chaste about it. She ran the tip of her tongue along his lips, top and bottom, then opened her mouth to his tongue.

She slipped off her coat. She was wearing a dress with blue-and-white vertical stripes and a white collar. She said: 'Touch my breasts.'

He looked startled.

'Please,' she begged.

His hands closed over her small breasts. She shut her eyes and concentrated on the sensation.

They broke apart, and she stared at him hungrily, memorizing his face. She wanted never to forget the particular blue of his eyes, the lock of dark hair that fell over his forehead, the curve of his jaw, the soft cushion of his mouth. 'I want a photo of you,' she said. 'Do you have one?'

'I don't carry photographs of myself around,' he said with a grin. In a New York accent he added: 'What am I, Frank Sinatra?'

'You must have a picture of yourself somewhere.'

'I might have a family photo. Let me look.' He went into the bedroom.

She followed him.

His battered brown leather bag lay on a suitcase stand where, Billie guessed, it had been for four weeks. He took out a silver picture frame that opened up like a small book. Inside were two photographs, one on each side. He slipped a picture out and handed it to her.

It had been taken three or four years ago, and showed a younger, heavier Luke in a polo shirt. With him were an older couple, presumably his parents, plus twin boys of around fifteen, and a little girl. They were all dressed in beach clothes.

'I can't take this, it's your picture of your family,' she said, although she longed for it with all her heart.

'I want you to have it. That's me, I'm part of my family.'

That was what she loved about it. 'Did you take it to France with you?'

'Yes.'

It was so important to him, she could hardly bear to deprive him of it – yet that made it even more precious to her. 'Show me the other one,' she said.

'What?'

'There are two photos in that frame.'

He seemed reluctant, but opened it. The second picture had been cut out of the Radcliffe year book. It was a photo of Billie.

'You had that in France, too?' she said. She could not breathe properly, her throat felt constricted.

'Yes.'

She burst into tears. It was unbearable. He had cut her picture out of the year book and carried it, alongside the photo of his family, all that time his life was in such danger. She had had no idea that she meant so much to him.

'Why are you crying?' he said.

'Because you love me,' she replied.

'It's true,' he said. 'I was frightened to tell you. I've loved you ever since Pearl Harbor weekend.'

Her passion turned to rage. 'How can you say that, you bastard? You left me!'

'If you and I had become lovers then, it would have destroyed Anthony.'

'To hell with Anthony!' She hammered his chest with her fist, but he did not seem to feel it. 'How could you put Anthony's happiness before mine, you son of a bitch?'

'It would have been dishonourable.'

'But don't you see, we could have had each other for two years!' The tears streamed down her cheeks. 'Now we've only got two days – two lousy goddamn days!'

'Then stop crying and kiss me again,' he said.

She put her arms around his neck and pulled his head down. Her tears ran between their lips and into their mouths. He began to unfasten her dress. Impatient, she said: 'Please, just rip it.' He pulled hard, and the buttons flew off down to her waist. Another tug opened it completely. She slipped it back off her shoulders and stood in her slip and stockings.

He looked solemn. 'Are you sure you want to?'

She was afraid he would become paralysed by moral misgivings. 'I have to, I have to, please don't stop!' she cried.

He pushed her gently back to the bed. She lay on her back and he lay on top of her, resting his weight on his elbows. He looked into her eyes. 'I've never done this before.'

'That's all right,' she said. 'I haven't either.'

* * *

The first time was over quite quickly, but an hour later they wanted it again, and this time it took longer. She told him she wanted to do everything, give him every pleasure he had ever dreamed of, perform every possible act of sexual intimacy. They made love all weekend, frantic with desire and sorrow, knowing they might never meet again.

After Luke left on Monday morning, Billie cried for two days.

Eight weeks later she discovered she was pregnant.

6.30 P.M.

Scientists can only guess at the extremes of heat and cold the satellite will suffer in space as it moves from the deep darkness of the earth's shadow into the glare of naked sunlight. To mitigate the effects of this, the cylinder is partially coated with shiny aluminium oxide in stripes one-eighth of an inch wide, to reflect the sun's scorching rays, and insulated with glass fibre, to keep out the ultimate cold of space.

'Yes, we dated,' Billie said as they went down the stairs.

Luke's mouth was dry. He imagined holding her hand, looking at her face over a candlelit table, kissing her, watching her slip out of her clothes. He felt guilty, knowing he had a wife, but he could not remember his wife, and Billie was right here beside him, talking animatedly and smiling and smelling faintly of scented soap.

They came to the door of the building and stopped. 'Were we in love?' Luke asked. He looked hard at her, studying her expression. Until now, her face had been easy to read, but suddenly the book had been closed, and all he could see was a blank cover.

'Oh, sure,' she said, and although her tone was

light, there was a catch in her voice. 'I thought you were the only man in the world.'

How could he have let a woman like this slip away from him? It seemed a tragedy worse than losing all his memories. 'But you learned better.'

'I'm old enough now to know there's no Prince Charming, just a bunch of more or less flawed men. Sometimes they wear shining armour, but it's always rusty in spots.'

He wanted to know everything, every detail, but there were too many questions. 'So you married Bern.'

'Yes.'

'What's he like?'

'Clever. All my men have to be smart. Otherwise I get bored. Strong, too – strong enough to challenge me.' She smiled the smile of someone with a big heart.

He said: 'What went wrong?'

'Conflicting values. It sounds abstract, but Bern risked his life for the cause of freedom in two wars, the Spanish Civil War and then the Second World War – and for him, politics came above all else.'

There was one question Luke wanted to ask more than any. He could not think of a delicate, roundabout way of putting it, so he blurted it out. 'Do you have anyone now?'

'Sure. His name's Harold Brodsky.'

Luke felt foolish. Of course she had someone. She was a beautiful divorcée in her thirties, men would be queueing up to take her out. He smiled ruefully. 'Is he Prince Charming?'

'No, but he's smart, he makes me laugh, and he adores me.'

Envy stabbed Luke's heart. Lucky Harold, he thought. 'And I guess he shares your values.'

'Yes. The most important thing in his life is his child – he's a widower – and after that comes his academic work.'

'Which is?'

'Iodine chemistry. I feel the same about my work.' Billie smiled. 'I may not be starry-eyed about men, but I guess I'm still idealistic about unravelling the mysteries of the human mind.'

That brought Luke back to his immediate crisis. The reminder was like an unexpected blow, shocking and painful. 'I wish you could unravel the mystery of my mind.'

She frowned, and despite the weight of his problems he noticed how pretty she was when her nose wrinkled in puzzlement. 'It's strange,' she said. 'Maybe you suffered a cranial injury that left no visible trace, but in that case it's surprising you don't still have a headache.'

'Nope.'

'You're not an alcoholic or a drug addict, I can tell by looking at you. If you'd suffered some terrible shock, or been under prolonged stress, I probably would have heard about it, either from you or from our mutual friends.'

'Which leaves . . .?'

She shook her head. 'You certainly aren't schizophrenic, so there's no way you could have been given the combination drug-and-electrotherapy treatment that could have caused—'

She stopped suddenly, looking alluringly startled, mouth open, eyes wide.

'What?' Luke said.

'I just remembered Joe Blow.'

'Who's he?'

'Joseph Bellow. The name struck me because I thought it sounded made up.'

'And?'

'He was admitted late yesterday, after I'd gone home. Then he was discharged in the night – which was real strange.'

'What was wrong with him?'

'He was a schizophrenic.' She paled. 'Oh, shit.'

Luke began to see what she was thinking. 'So this patient . . .'

'Let's check his file.'

She turned and ran back up the stairs. They hurried along the corridor and entered a room marked Records Office. There was no one inside. Billie turned on the light.

She opened a drawer marked 'A—D', flipped through the file, and pulled out a folder. She read aloud: 'White male, six feet one inch tall, one hundred and eighty pounds, thirty-seven years old.'

Luke's guess was confirmed. 'You think it was me,' he said.

She nodded. 'The patient was given the treatment that causes global amnesia.'

'My God.' Luke was dismayed and intrigued at the

same time. If she was right, this had been done to him deliberately. That explained why he had been followed around – presumably by someone keen to make sure the treatment had worked. 'Who did this?'

'My colleague, Dr Leonard Ross, admitted the patient. Len's a psychiatrist. I'd like to know his rationale for authorizing the treatment. A patient should normally be kept under observation for some time, usually days, before any treatment is given. And I can't imagine the medical justification for discharging the patient immediately afterwards, even with the consent of relatives. This is very irregular.'

'Sounds like Ross is in trouble.'

Billie sighed. 'Probably not. If I complain, people will accuse me of sour grapes. They'll say I'm bitter because Len got the job I wanted, Director of Research here.'

'When did that happen?'

'Today.'

Luke was startled. 'Ross got promoted *today*?'

'Yes. I guess it's not a coincidence.'

'Hell, no! He was bribed. He was promised the promotion in return for doing this irregular treatment.'

'I can't believe it. Yes, I can. He's real weak.'

'But he's someone else's tool. A superior in the hospital hierarchy must have got him to do it.'

'No.' Billie shook her head. 'The trust that's funding the post, the Sowerby Foundation, insisted on Ross for the job. My boss told me. We couldn't figure out why. Now I know.'

'It all fits – but this is almost as baffling as before. Someone in the Foundation wanted me to lose my memory?'

'I can guess who,' Billie said. 'Anthony Carroll. He's on the board.'

The name rang a bell. Luke recalled that Anthony was the CIA man mentioned by Elspeth. 'That still leaves the question why.'

'But now we have someone to ask,' Billie said, and she picked up the phone.

While she dialled, Luke tried to organize his thoughts. The last hour had been a series of shocks. He had been told he was not going to get his memory back. He had learned that he had loved Billie and lost her, and he could not understand how he could have been such a fool. Now he had discovered that his amnesia had been deliberately inflicted on him and that someone in the CIA was responsible. Yet he still had no clue as to why this had been done.

'Let me speak to Anthony Carroll,' Billie said into the phone. 'This is Dr Josephson.' Her tone was peremptory. 'Okay, then tell him I need to speak to him urgently.' She looked at her watch. 'Have him call me at home in exactly one hour from now.' Her face suddenly darkened. 'Don't jerk me around, buster, I know you can get a message to him any time of the day or night, wherever he is.' She slammed the phone down.

She caught Luke's eye and looked abashed. 'Sorry,' she said. 'The guy said: "I'll see what I can do," like he was doing me a darn favour.'

Luke remembered Elspeth saying that Anthony Carroll was an old buddy who had been at Harvard with Luke and Bern. 'This Anthony,' he said. 'I thought he was a friend.'

'Yeah.' Billie nodded, a worried frown on her expressive face. 'So did I.'

7.30 P.M.

The temperature problem is a key obstacle to manned space flight. To gauge the efficacy of its insulation, the Explorer carries four thermometers: three in the outer shell, to measure skin temperature, and one inside the instrument compartment, to give the interior temperature. The aim is to keep the level between forty and seventy degrees Fahrenheit — a comfortable range for human survival.

Bern lived on Massachusetts Avenue, overlooking the picturesque gorge of Rock Creek, in a neighbourhood of large homes and foreign embassies. His apartment had an Iberian theme, with ornate Spanish colonial furniture, twisted shapes in dark wood. The stark white walls were hung with paintings of sun-baked landscapes. Luke recalled Billie saying that Bern had fought in the Spanish Civil War.

It was easy to imagine Bern as a fighter. His dark hair was receding now, and his waist hung over the belt of his slacks a little, but there was a hard set to his face and a bleak look in his grey eyes. Luke wondered if such a down-to-earth man would credit the strange story he had to tell.

Bern shook Luke's hand warmly and gave him

strong coffee in a small cup. On top of the console gramophone was a silver-framed photograph of a middle-aged man in a torn shirt holding a rifle. Luke picked it up. 'Largo Benito,' Bern explained. 'Greatest man I ever knew. I fought with him in Spain. My son is named Largo, but Billie calls him Larry.'

Bern probably looked back on the war in Spain as the best time of his life. Luke wondered enviously what had been the best time of his own life. 'I guess I must have had great memories of something,' he said despondently.

Bern gave him a sharp look. 'What the hell is going on, old buddy?'

Luke sat down and related what he and Billie had discovered at the hospital. Then he said: 'Here's what I think happened to me. I don't know if you're going to buy it, but I'll tell you anyway, because I'm really hoping you can shed some light on the mystery.'

'I'll do what I can.'

'I came to Washington on Monday, right before the launch of the rocket, to see an army general for some mysterious purpose that I wouldn't tell anyone about. My wife was worried about me and called Anthony, to ask him to keep an eye on me. Anthony made a breakfast date with me for Tuesday morning.'

'It makes sense. Anthony's your oldest friend. You were room-mates already when I met you.'

'The next bit is more speculative. I met Anthony for breakfast, before going to the Pentagon. He put something in my coffee to make me fall asleep, then got me into his car and drove me to Georgetown Mind

Hospital. He must have gotten Billie out of the way somehow, or maybe waited until she left for the day. Anyway, he made sure she didn't see me, and checked me in under a false name. Then he got hold of Dr Len Ross, whom he knew might be bribed. Using his position as a board member of the Sowerby Foundation, he persuaded Len to give me a treatment that would destroy my memory.'

Luke paused, waiting for Bern to say the whole thing was ludicrous, impossible, a figment of an overactive imagination. But he did not. To Luke's surprise, he simply said: 'But for God's sake, why?'

Luke began to feel better. If Bern believed him, he might help. He said: 'For the moment, let's concentrate on how, rather than why.'

'Okay.'

'To cover his tracks, he checked me out of the hospital, dressed me in rags – presumably while I was still unconscious from the treatment – and dumped me in Union Station, along with a sidekick whose job was to persuade me that I lived like that, and at the same time to keep an eye on me and make sure the amnesia treatment had worked.'

Now Bern did look sceptical. 'But he must have known you'd find out the truth sooner or later.'

'Not necessarily – not all of it, anyway. Sure, he had to calculate that after a few days or weeks I would figure out who I was. But he thought I'd still believe I had gone on a bender. People do lose their memories after drinking heavily, at least according to legend. If I did find it hard to believe, and asked a few questions, the trail would have gone cold. Billie probably would have forgotten about the mystery patient – and in case she remembered, Ross would have destroyed his records.'

Bern nodded thoughtfully. 'A risky plan, but one with a good chance of success. In clandestine work, that's generally the best you can hope for.'

'I'm surprised you're not more sceptical.'

Bern shrugged.

Luke pressed him. 'Do you have a reason for accepting the story so readily?'

'We've all been in secret work. These things happen.'

Luke felt sure Bern was keeping something back. There was nothing he could do but plead. 'Bern, if there's something else you know, for God's sake, tell me. I need all the help I can get.'

Bern looked anguished. 'There is something – but it's secret, and I don't want to get anyone into trouble.'

Luke's heart leaped in hope. 'Tell me, please. I'm desperate.'

Bern looked hard at him. 'I guess you are.' He took a deep breath. 'Okay, then, here goes. Toward the end of the war, Billie and Anthony worked on a special project for the OSS, the Truth Drug Committee. You and I didn't know about it at the time, but I found out later, when I was married to Billie. They were looking for drugs that would affect prisoners under interrogation. They tried mescaline, barbiturates, scopolamine, and cannabis. Their test subjects were soldiers suspected of communist sympathies. Billie and Anthony went to military camps in Atlanta, Memphis and New Orleans. They would win the confidence of the suspect soldier, give him a reefer, and see whether he betrayed secrets.'

Luke laughed. 'So a lot of grunts got a free high!'

Bern nodded. 'At that level, the whole thing was faintly comical. After the war, Billie went back to college and did her doctoral thesis on the effects of various legal drugs such as nicotine on people's mental states. When she finally became a professor, she continued to work on the same area, concentrating on how drugs and other factors affect memory.'

'But not for the CIA.'

'That's what I thought. But I was wrong.'

'Christ.'

'In 1950, when Roscoe Hillenkoetter was Director, the Agency started a project codenamed Bluebird, and Hillenkoetter authorized the use of unvouchered funds, so there was no paper trail. Bluebird was about mind control. They financed a whole series of legitimate research projects in universities, channelling the money through trusts to conceal their true source. And they financed Billie's work.'

'How did she feel about that?'

'We fought about it. I said it was wrong, the CIA was planning to brainwash people. She said that all scientific knowledge could be used for good or evil, she was doing invaluable research and she didn't care who paid the bill.'

'Is that why you divorced?'

'Sort of. I was writing a radio show called *Detective Story*, but I wanted to get into movies. In 1952 I wrote a screenplay about a secret government agency that brainwashed unsuspecting citizens. Jack Warner bought it. But I didn't tell Billie.'

'Why not?'

'I knew the CIA would get the film cancelled.'

'They can do that?'

'You bet your goddamn life.'

'So what happened?'

'The movie came out in 1953. Frank Sinatra played the nightclub singer who witnesses a political murder, then has his memory wiped by a secret process. Joan Crawford played his manager. It was a huge hit. My career was made – I was deluged with big-money offers from the studios.'

'And Billie?'

'I took her to the première.'

'I guess she was angry.'

He smiled ruefully. 'She went ape. She said I'd used confidential information that I got from her. She was sure the CIA would withdraw her funding, ruin her research. It was the end of our marriage.'

'That's what Billie meant when she said you had a conflict of values.'

'She's right. She should have married you – I never really understood why she didn't.'

Luke's heart missed a beat. He was curious to know why Bern had said that. But he postponed the question. 'Anyway, to return to 1953, I assume the CIA didn't cut off her funding.'

'No.' Bern looked bitterly angry. 'They destroyed my career instead.'

'How?'

'I was subjected to a loyalty investigation. Of course, I had been a communist, right up until the end of the war, so I made an easy target. I was blacklisted in Hollywood, and I couldn't even get back my old job in radio.'

'What was Anthony's role in that?'

'He did his best to protect me, Billie said, but he was overruled.' Bern frowned. 'After what you've just told me, I wonder if that was true.'

'What did you do?'

'I had a couple of bad years, then I thought of *The Terrible Twins*.'

Luke raised an eyebrow.

'It's a series of children's books.' He pointed to a bookcase. The bright jackets made a splash of colour. 'You've read them, as it happens – to your sister's kid.'

Luke was pleased he had a nephew or niece – or maybe several. He liked the idea of reading aloud to them.

There was so much he had to learn about himself.

He waved a hand at the expensive apartment. 'The books must be successful.'

Bern nodded. 'I wrote the first story under a pseudonym, and used an agent who was sympathetic to the victims of the McCarthy witch-hunt. The book was a big bestseller, and I've written two a year ever since.'

Luke got up and took a book from the shelf. He read:

Which is stickier, honey or melted chocolate? The twins had to know. That was why they did the experiment that made Mom so mad.

He smiled. He could imagine children loving this stuff. Then he felt sad. 'Elspeth and I don't have any kids.'

'I don't know why,' Bern said. 'You always wanted a family so badly.'

'We tried, but it didn't happen.' Luke closed the book. 'Am I happily married?'

Bern sighed. 'Since you ask, no.'

'Why?'

'Something was wrong, but you didn't know what. You called me one time, to ask my advice, but I couldn't help you.'

'A few minutes ago, you said Billie should have married me.'

'You two used to be nuts about each other.'

'So what happened?'

'I don't really know. After the war, you had a big quarrel. I'm not too sure what it was about.'

'I'll have to ask Billie.'

'I guess.'

Luke put the book back on the shelf. 'Anyway, now I understand why you didn't react with total incredulity to my story.'

'Yes,' Bern said. 'I believe Anthony did this.'

'But can you imagine why?'

'I don't have the slightest idea.'

8 P.M.

If temperature variations are higher than expected, it is possible that the germanium transistors will overheat, the mercury batteries will freeze, and the satellite will fail to transmit data back to Earth.

Billie sat at her dressing-table, freshening her make-up. She thought her eyes were her best feature, and she always did them carefully, with black eyeliner, grey eye shadow, and a little mascara. She left the bedroom door open, and she could hear television gunfire downstairs: Larry and Becky-Ma were watching *Wagon Train*.

She did not feel like a date tonight. The events of the day had stirred up strong passions. She was angry about not getting the job she wanted, bewildered by what Anthony had done, and confused and threatened to find that the old chemistry between herself and Luke was as powerful and dangerous as ever. She found herself reviewing her relationships with Anthony, Luke, Bern and Harold, wondering whether she had made the right decisions in life. After all that had happened, the prospect of spending the evening watching the Kraft Theater on TV with Harold seemed insipid, fond of him though she was.

233

The phone rang.

She jumped up from her stool and crossed the room to the extension by the bed, but Larry had already picked up in the hallway. She heard Anthony's voice say: 'This is the CIA. Washington is about to be invaded by an army of bouncing cabbages.'

Larry giggled. 'Uncle Anthony, it's you!'

'If you are approached by a cabbage do not, repeat, do not attempt to reason with it.'

'A cabbage can't talk!'

'The only way to deal with them is to beat them to death with sliced bread.'

'You're making this up!' Larry laughed.

Billie said: 'Anthony, I'm on the extension.'

Anthony said: 'Get your jammies on, Larry, okay?'

'Okay,' said Larry. He hung up.

Anthony's voice changed. 'Billie?'

'Here.'

'You wanted me to call – urgently. I gather you chewed out the duty officer.'

'Yeah. Anthony, what the hell are you up to?'

'You'll have to ask me a more specific question—'

'Don't screw around, for Christ's sake. I could tell you were lying last time we spoke, but I didn't know what the truth was then. Now I do. I know what you did to Luke at my hospital last night.'

There was a silence.

Billie said: 'I want an explanation.'

'I can't really talk about this on the phone. If we could meet some time in the next few days—'

'The hell with that.' She was not going to let him procrastinate. 'I want your story right now.'

'You know I can't—'

'You can do anything you damn well please, so don't pretend otherwise.'

Anthony protested: 'You ought to trust me. We've been friends for two decades.'

'Yeah, and you got me into trouble on our first date.'

There was a smile in Anthony's voice as he said: 'Are you still mad about that?'

Billie softened. 'Hell, no. I want to trust you. You're my son's godfather.'

'I'll explain everything if you'll meet me tomorrow.'

She almost agreed, then she remembered what he had done. 'You didn't trust me, last night, did you? You went behind my back, right in my own hospital.'

'I told you, I can explain—'

'You should have explained *before* you deceived me. Tell me the truth or I'll go to the FBI the minute I hang up. You choose.'

It was dangerous to threaten men – it often made them obstinate. But she knew how the CIA hated and feared interference from the FBI, especially when the Agency was working on the borderline of legality, which was most of the time. The Feds, who jealously guarded their exclusive right to hunt spies within the USA, would relish the chance to investigate illegitimate acts by the CIA on American soil. If whatever Anthony was doing was strictly on the up-and-up, then Billie's threat was empty. But if he were overstepping the limits of the law, he would be scared.

He sighed. 'Well, I'm on a pay phone, and I guess it's unlikely your line is tapped.' He paused. 'You may find this hard to believe.'

'Try me.'

'Well, here goes. Luke is a spy, Billie.'

For a moment she was dumbstruck; then she said: 'Don't be absurd.'

'He's a communist, an agent for Moscow.'

'For Christ's sake! If you think I'm going to fall for that—'

'I'm past caring whether you believe it or not.' Anthony's tone was suddenly harsh. 'He's been passing rocket secrets to the Soviets for years. How do you think they managed to put their Sputnik into orbit while our satellite was still on the laboratory bench? They're not ahead of us scientifically, for God's sake! They have the benefit of all our research as well as their own. And Luke is responsible.'

'Anthony, we've both known Luke for twenty goddamn years. He's never been interested in politics!'

'That's the best cover of all.'

Billie hesitated. Could it be true? No doubt a serious spy would pretend to have no interest in politics, or even to be a Republican. 'But Luke wouldn't betray his country.'

'People do. Remember, when he was with the French Resistance he was working with the communists. Of course, they were on our side then, but obviously he continued after the war. Personally, I think the reason he didn't marry you was that it would conflict with his work for the Reds.'

'He married Elspeth.'

'Yeah, but they never had children.'

Billie sat down on the stairs, feeling stunned. 'Do you have evidence?'

'I have *proof* – top-secret blueprints he gave to a known KGB officer.'

She was bewildered now, not knowing what to believe. 'But even if all this is true – why did you wipe out his memory?'

'To save his life.'

Now she was totally baffled. 'I don't understand.'

'Billie, we were going to kill him.'

'Who was going to kill him?'

'Us, the CIA. You know the army is about to launch our first satellite. If this rocket fails, the Russians will dominate outer space for the foreseeable future, the way the British dominated America for two hundred years. You have to understand that Luke was the worst threat to American power and prestige since the war. The decision to terminate him was made within an hour of our finding out about him.'

'Why not just put him on trial as a spy?'

'And have the whole world know that our security is so lousy the Soviets have been getting all our rocket secrets for years? Think what that would do to American influence – especially in all these underdeveloped countries that are flirting with Moscow. That option wasn't even tabled.'

'So what happened?'

'I persuaded them to try this. I went right to the top. Nobody knows what I'm doing, except the Director of the CIA and the President. And it would have worked, if Luke hadn't been such a resourceful fucking bastard. I could have saved Luke *and* kept the whole thing secret. If only he had believed that he lost his memory after a night of heavy drinking, and lived the life of a bum for a while, I could have kept the lid on. Even he would never have known what secrets he gave away.'

Billie had a selfish moment. 'You didn't hesitate to blight my career.'

'To save Luke's life? I didn't think you'd want me to hesitate.'

'Don't be so goddamn blasé, it always was your worst fault.'

'Anyway, Luke fouled up my plan – with your help. Is he with you now?'

'No.' Billie felt the hairs prickle on the back of her neck.

'I need to talk to him before he does himself any more damage. Where is he?'

Acting on instinct, Billie lied. 'I don't know.'

'You wouldn't hide anything from me, would you?'

'Sure I would. You've already said your organization wanted to kill Luke. It would be dumb of me to tell you where he is, if I knew. But I don't.'

'Billie, listen to me. I'm his only hope. Tell him to call me, if you want to save his life.'

'I'll think about it,' Billie said; but Anthony had already hung up.

8.30 P.M.

*The instrument compartment has no doors or access hatches.
To work on equipment inside, engineers at Cape Canaveral
have to lift the entire cover. This is awkward but saves
precious weight, a critical factor in the struggle to break free
of Earth's gravity.*

Luke put down the phone with a shaky hand.

Bern said: 'For Christ's sake, what did she say? You
look like a ghost!'

'Anthony says I'm a Soviet agent,' Luke told him.

Bern narrowed his eyes. 'And . . .?'

'When the CIA found me out, they were going to
kill me, but Anthony persuaded them that it would be
just as effective to wipe my memory.'

'A vaguely plausible story,' Bern said coolly.

Luke was devastated. 'Jesus Christ, could it be
true?'

'Hell, no.'

'You can't be sure of that.'

'Yes, I can.'

Luke hardly dared to hope. 'How?'

'Because I *was* a Soviet agent.'

Luke stared at him. What now? 'We could both have

been agents, without knowing about each other,' he said.

Bern shook his head. 'You ended my career.'

'How?'

'You want some more coffee?'

'No, thanks, it's making me dizzy.'

'You look like hell. When did you last eat?'

'Billie gave me some cookies. Forget food, will you? Tell me what you know.'

Bern stood up. 'I'm going to make you a sandwich, before you faint.'

Luke realized he was painfully hungry. 'That sounds great.'

They went into the kitchen. Bern opened the refrigerator and took out a loaf of rye bread, a stick of butter, some corned beef, and a bermuda onion. Luke's mouth began to water.

'It was in the war,' Bern said as he buttered four slices of bread. 'The French Resistance was divided into Gaullists and communists, and they were manoeuvring for post-war position. Roosevelt and Churchill wanted to make sure the communists couldn't win an election. So the Gaullists were getting all the guns and ammunition.'

'How did I feel about that?'

Bern layered corned beef, mustard, and onion rings on the bread. 'You didn't have strong feelings about French politics, you just wanted to beat the Nazis and go home. But I had another agenda. I wanted to even things up.'

'How?'

'I tipped off the communists about a parachute drop we were expecting, so they could ambush us and steal our ordnance.' He shook his head ruefully. 'They screwed up royally. They were supposed to run into us on our way back to base, apparently by accident, and demand a friendly share-out. Instead, they attacked us at the drop point, as soon as the stuff hit the ground. So you knew we had been betrayed. And I was the obvious suspect.'

'What did I do?'

'You offered me a deal. I had to stop working for Moscow, right then, and you would keep quiet about what I had done, for ever.'

'And . . .?'

Bern shrugged. 'We both kept our promises. But I don't think you ever forgave me. Anyhow, our friendship was never the same afterwards.'

A grey Burmese cat appeared from nowhere and miaowed, and Bern tossed a sliver of meat to the floor. The cat ate it delicately and licked its paws.

Luke said: 'If I'd been a communist, I would have covered up for you.'

'Absolutely.'

Luke began to believe in his own innocence. 'But I might have become a communist after the war.'

'No way. It's something that happens to you when you're young, or not at all.'

That made sense. 'I might have spied for money, though.'

'You don't need money. Your family is wealthy.'

That was right. Elspeth had told him. 'So Anthony is mistaken.'

'Or lying.' Bern sliced the sandwiches and put them on two non-matching plates. 'Soda?'

'Sure.'

Bern took two bottles of Coke from the refrigerator and opened them. He handed Luke a plate and a bottle, picked up his own, and led the way back into the living room.

Luke felt like a starved wolf. He finished the sandwich in a few bites. Bern was watching with amusement. 'Here, have mine,' he said.

Luke shook his head. 'No, thanks.'

'Go ahead, take it. I ought to go on a diet anyway.'

Luke took Bern's sandwich and tore into it.

Bern said: 'If Anthony is lying, what was his *real* reason for making you lose your memory?'

Luke swallowed. 'It has to be connected with my sudden departure from Cape Canaveral on Monday.'

Bern nodded. 'Too much of a coincidence otherwise.'

'I must have learned something very important, so important that I had to rush to the Pentagon to talk to them about it.'

Bern frowned. 'Why didn't you tell the folks at Cape Canaveral what you had learned?'

Luke considered. 'It must be that I didn't trust anyone there.'

'Okay. Then, before you got to the Pentagon, Anthony intercepted you.'

'Right. And I guess I trusted him, and told him what I had found out.'

'And then?'

'He thought it was so important that he had to wipe my memory to make sure the secret never got out.'

'I wonder what the hell it was.'

'When I know that, I'll understand what happened to me.'

'Where will you start?'

'I guess my first step is to go to my hotel room and look through my stuff. Maybe I'll find a clue.'

'If Anthony wiped your memory, he must have gone through your possessions too.'

'He would have destroyed any obvious clues, but there may be something he didn't recognize as relevant. Anyway, I have to check.'

'And then?'

'The only other place to look would be Cape Canaveral. I'll fly back tonight . . .' He checked his watch. It was after nine o'clock. 'Or tomorrow morning.'

'Stay the night here,' Bern said.

'Why?'

'I don't know. I don't like the idea of you spending the night alone. Go to the Carlton, pick up your stuff, and come back here. I'll take you to the airport in the morning.'

Luke nodded. Feeling awkward, he said: 'You've been a heck of a good friend to me over this.'

Bern shrugged. 'We go back a long way.'

Luke was not satisfied with that. 'But you just told

me that after that incident in France, our friendship was never the same.'

'That's true.' Bern gave Luke a candid look. 'Your attitude was that a man who betrayed you once would betray you twice.'

'I can believe that,' Luke said thoughtfully. 'I was wrong, though, wasn't I?'

'Yes,' Bern said. 'You were.'

9.30 P.M.

The instrument compartment tends to overheat prior to take-off. The solution to this problem is typical of the crude but effective engineering of the rushed Explorer project. A container of dry ice is attached electromagnetically to the outside of the rocket. A thermostat switches on a fan whenever the compartment gets warm. Just before take-off, the magnet is disconnected and the cooling mechanism falls to the ground.

Anthony's yellow Cadillac Eldorado was parked on K Street between 15th and 16th, tucked in behind a line of taxis waiting to be summoned by the doorman of the Carlton Hotel. Sitting in the car, Anthony had a clear view of the hotel's curving driveway and brightly lit carriage porch. Pete was in the hotel, using the room he had rented, waiting for a phone call from one of the agents who were watching out for Luke all over town.

A part of Anthony hoped that none of them would call, that Luke would somehow make his escape. Then, at least, Anthony would be able to avoid making the most painful decision of his life. The other part of him was desperate to find out where Luke was and deal with him.

Luke was an old friend, a decent man, a loyal husband and a terrific scientist. It made no difference in the end. During the war, they had all killed good men who just happened to be on the wrong side. Luke was on the wrong side in the Cold War. It was knowing the guy that made it so hard.

Pete hurried out of the building. Anthony rolled down the window. Pete said: 'Ackie called in. Luke is at the apartment on Massachusetts Avenue, Bernard Rothsten's place.'

'At last,' Anthony said. He had posted agents outside Bern's building and Billie's house, anticipating that Luke might go to his old friends for help, and it gave him bleak satisfaction to have been right.

Pete added: 'When he leaves, Ackie will follow him on the motorcycle.'

'Good.'

'Do you think he'll come here?'

'He may. I'll wait.' There were two more agents in the hotel lobby who would alert Anthony if Luke should go in by another entrance. 'The other main possibility is the airport.'

'We have four men there.'

'Okay. I think we have all the exits covered.'

Pete nodded. 'I'll get back to the phone.'

Anthony brooded over the scene to come. Luke would be confused and uncertain, wary but keen to question Anthony. Anthony would try to get Luke alone somewhere. Once they were on their own, it would only be a few seconds before Anthony had the

246

chance to draw the silenced gun from the inside pocket of his topcoat.

Luke would make a last-second bid for life. It was not his nature to accept defeat. He would jump at Anthony, or dive at the window, or run for the door. Anthony would be cool, he had killed before, he would keep his nerve. He would hold the gun steady and pull the trigger, aiming for Luke's chest, firing several times, confident of stopping Luke. Luke would fall. Anthony would move close to him, check his pulse, and if necessary administer the *coup de grâce*. And his oldest friend would be dead.

There would be no trouble about it. Anthony had the dramatic evidence of Luke's betrayal, the blueprints with Luke's handwriting on them. He could not actually prove that they had been taken from a Soviet agent, but his word was good enough for the CIA.

He would dump the body somewhere. It would be found, of course, and there would be an investigation. Sooner or later the police would discover that the CIA had been interested in the victim, and would start asking questions; but the Agency was experienced in fending off inquiries. The police would be told that the Agency's link with the victim was a matter of national security and therefore top secret, but had nothing to do with the murder.

Anyone who questioned that – cop, journalist, politician – would be subjected to a loyalty investigation. Friends, neighbours and relatives would be interviewed by agents who referred darkly to suspected communist affiliations. The investigation would never reach any conclusion, but all the same it would destroy the credibility of the subject.

A secret agency could do anything, he thought with grim confidence.

A taxicab pulled into the hotel's driveway, and Luke got out. He was wearing a navy topcoat and a grey hat that he must have bought or stolen sometime today. Across the street, Ackie Horwitz pulled up on his motorcycle. Anthony got out of his car and strolled toward the hotel entrance.

Luke looked strained, but wore an expression of grim determination. Paying the taxi driver, he glanced at Anthony but did not recognize him. He told the driver to keep the change, then walked into the hotel. Anthony followed.

They were the same age, thirty-seven. They had met at Harvard when they were eighteen, half a lifetime ago.

That it should come to this, Anthony thought bitterly. That it should come to this.

* * *

Luke knew he had been followed from Bern's apartment by a man on a motorcycle. Now he was strung taut, all his senses on alert.

The lobby of the Carlton looked like a grand drawing room, full of reproduction French furniture. Opposite the entrance, the reception desk and concierge's desk were set into alcoves so that they did not spoil the regular rectangle of the space. Two women in fur coats chatted with a group of men in tuxedos near the entrance to the bar. Bellhops in livery and desk staff in black tailcoats went about their business with quiet efficiency. It was a luxurious place, designed to soothe the nerves of jangled travellers. It did nothing for Luke.

Scanning the room, he quickly identified two men who had the air of agents. One sat on an elegant sofa reading a newspaper, the other stood near the elevator, smoking a cigarette. Neither looked as if he belonged here. They were dressed for work, in raincoats and business suits, and there was a daytime look to their shirts and ties. They definitely were not out for an evening in expensive restaurants and bars.

He thought of walking right out again – but where would that leave him? He approached the reception desk, gave his name, and asked for the key to his room. As he turned away, a stranger spoke to him. 'Hey, Luke!'

It was the man who had walked into the hotel behind him. He did not look like an agent, but Luke had vaguely noticed his appearance: he was tall, about Luke's height, and might have been distinguished, except that he was carelessly dressed. His expensive camel-hair topcoat was old and worn, his shoes looked as if they had never been shined, and he needed a haircut. However, he spoke with authority.

Luke said: 'I'm afraid I don't know who you are. I've lost my memory.'

'Anthony Carroll. I'm so glad I've caught up with you at last!' He held out his hand to shake.

Luke tensed. He still did not know whether Anthony was enemy or friend. He shook hands and said: 'I have a lot of questions to ask you.'

'And I'm ready to answer them.'

Luke paused, staring at him, wondering where to begin. Anthony did not look like the kind of man who would betray an old friend. He had an open, intelligent face, not handsome but appealing. In the end Luke said: 'How the hell could you do this to me?'

'I had to do it – for your own good. I was trying to save your life.'

'I'm not a spy.'

'It's not that simple.'

Luke studied Anthony, trying to guess what was in his mind. He could not decide whether he was telling the truth. Anthony looked earnest. There was no expression of slyness on his face. All the same, Luke felt sure he was holding something back. 'No one believes your story about my working for Moscow.'

'Who is no one?'

'Neither Bern nor Billie.'

'They don't know everything.'

'They know me.'

'So do I.'

'What do you know that they don't?'

'I'll tell you. But we can't talk here. What I have to say is classified. Shall we go to my office? It's five minutes away.'

Luke was not going to Anthony's office, not before

a whole lot of questions had been answered to his satisfaction. But he could see that the lobby was not a good place for a top-secret conversation. 'Let's go to my suite,' he said. That would get him away from the other agents, but leave him in control: Anthony on his own would not be able to overpower him.

Anthony hesitated, then seemed to make up his mind and said: 'Sure.'

They crossed the lobby and entered the elevator. Luke checked the number on his room key: 530. 'Fifth floor,' he said to the operator. The man closed the lift gate and threw the lever.

They did not speak as they went up. Luke looked at Anthony's clothes: the old coat, the rumpled suit, the nondescript tie. Surprisingly, Anthony managed to wear his untidy garments with something of a careless swagger.

Suddenly, Luke saw that the soft material of the coat sagged slightly on the right side. There was a heavy object in the pocket.

He felt cold with fear. He had made a bad mistake.

He had not thought that Anthony would have a gun.

Trying to keep his face expressionless, Luke thought furiously. Could Anthony shoot him right here in the hotel? If he waited until they were in the suite, no one would see. What about the noise? The gun might have a silencer.

As the elevator stopped at the fifth floor, Anthony unbuttoned his coat.

For a fast draw, Luke thought.

They stepped out. Luke did not know which way to go, but Anthony confidently turned right. He must have been to Luke's room already.

Luke was sweating under his topcoat. He felt as if this sort of thing had happened to him before, more than once, but a long time ago. He wished he had kept the gun of the cop whose finger he had broken. But he had had no idea, at nine o'clock this morning, what he was involved in – he had thought he had simply lost his memory.

He tried to make himself calm. It was still one man against another. Anthony had the gun, but Luke had guessed Anthony's intentions. It was about even.

Walking along the corridor, his heart racing, Luke looked for something to hit Anthony with: a heavy vase, a glass ashtray, a picture in a solid frame. There was nothing.

He had to do something before they entered the room.

Could he try to take the gun away from Anthony? He might succeed, but it was risky. The gun could easily go off in the struggle, and no telling which way it might be pointing at the crucial moment.

They reached the door and Luke took out his key. A bead of perspiration ran down his face. If he went inside, he was dead.

He unlocked the door and pushed it open.

'Come in,' he said. He stood aside to let his guest enter first.

Anthony hesitated, then walked past Luke and through the doorway.

Luke hooked his foot around Anthony's right ankle, put both hands flat on Anthony's shoulder blades, and pushed hard. Anthony went flying. He crashed into a small Regency table, knocking over a large vase of daffodils. In desperation he grabbed at a brass floor lamp with a pink silk shade, but the lamp fell with him.

Luke pulled the door shut and ran for his life. He hurtled along the corridor. The elevator had gone. He burst through the Fire Exit door on to the staircase and ran down. On the next floor, he crashed into a maid carrying a stack of towels. 'I'm sorry!' he called as the maid screamed and towels flew everywhere.

A few seconds later, he reached the foot of the staircase. He found himself in a narrow corridor. To one side, up a short flight of steps, through a small archway, he could see the lobby.

* * *

Anthony knew, before he did it, that it was a mistake to enter the room first; but Luke left him no choice. Fortunately he was not seriously hurt. After a stunned moment, he picked himself up. He turned, strode to the door, and opened it. Looking out, he saw Luke haring along the corridor. As he gave chase, Luke turned aside and disappeared, presumably into the stairwell.

Anthony followed, running as fast as he could, but he was afraid he might not be able to catch Luke, who was at least as fit as he. Would Curtis and Malone in the lobby have the sense to apprehend Luke?

On the next floor down, Anthony was momentarily delayed by a maid who was kneeling on the floor, picking up scattered towels. Anthony guessed Luke had crashed into her. He cursed, and slowed his pace to manoeuvre around her. As he did so, he heard the elevator arrive. His heart leaped: maybe he was in luck.

A dressed-up couple emerged, obviously tipsy from a celebration in the restaurant. Anthony barged past them into the elevator and said: 'Ground floor, and quick about it.'

The man slammed the doors and threw the lever. Anthony stared impotently at the descending floor numbers as they lit up in slow succession. The elevator reached the ground floor. The door slid aside and he stepped out.

* * *

Luke emerged into the lobby next to the elevator doors. His heart sank. The two agents he had spotted earlier were now standing in front of the main entrance, blocking his way out. A moment later, the elevator door opened beside him and Anthony stepped out.

He had to make a split-second decision: fight or flee.

He did not want to fight three men. They would almost certainly overpower him. Hotel security would join in. Anthony would show his CIA identification, and everyone would defer to him. Luke would end up in custody.

He turned and ran back along the corridor, into

the depths of the hotel. Behind him, he heard the pounding footsteps of Anthony giving chase. There had to be a back entrance – supplies could not possibly be delivered through the main lobby.

He pushed through a curtain and found himself in a little courtyard decorated like a Mediterranean outdoor café. A few couples were swaying on a small dance floor. Barging between the tables, he made it to an exit door. A narrow corridor stretched away to his left. He ran along it. He must be near the back of the hotel now, he figured, but he could see no way out.

He emerged into a kind of butler's pantry, where the finishing touches were applied to dishes cooked elsewhere. Half a dozen uniformed waiters were heating food in chafing dishes and arranging plates on trays. In the middle of the room was a staircase leading down. Luke pushed through the waiters and took the stairs, ignoring a voice that called: 'Excuse me, sir! You can't go down there!' As Anthony charged after him, the same voice said indignantly: 'What is this, Union Station?'

In the basement was the main kitchen, a sweaty purgatory where dozens of chefs cooked for hundreds of people. Gas jets flared, steam billowed, saucepans bubbled. Waiters shouted at cooks, and cooks shouted at kitchen hands. They were too busy to pay attention to Luke as he dodged between the refrigerators and the ranges, the plate stacks and the barrels of vegetables.

At the back of the kitchen, he found a staircase going up. He guessed it led to the delivery entrance. If not, he would be cornered. He took the chance and raced up the stairs. At the top, he burst through a pair of doors into the cold night air.

He was in a dark yard. A dim lamp over the door showed him giant garbage bins and stacked wooden pallets that looked as if they had contained fruit. Fifty yards away to his right was a high wire fence with a closed gate and, beyond that, a street which his sense of direction told him must be 15th.

He ran for the gate. He heard the door behind him bang open, and guessed that Anthony had come out. And they were alone.

He reached the gate. It was closed and secured with a big steel padlock. If only a pedestrian would come strolling by, Anthony would be afraid to shoot. But there was no one.

Heart pounding, Luke scrambled up the fence. As he reached the top, he heard the discreet cough of a silenced pistol. But he felt nothing. It was a hard shot, a moving target fifty yards away in the dark, but not impossible. He flung himself over the top. The pistol coughed again. He staggered and fell to the ground. He heard a third muffled shot. He sprang to his feet and ran, heading east. The gun did not speak again.

At the corner, he looked back. Anthony was nowhere in sight.

He had escaped.

* * *

Anthony's legs felt weak. He put a hand against the cold wall to steady himself. The yard smelled of rotting vegetables. He felt as if he were breathing corruption.

It had been the hardest thing he had ever done. By comparison, killing Albin Moulier had been easy. Pointing his gun at the figure of Luke scrambling over a wire fence, he had almost been unable to pull the trigger.

This was the worst possible outcome. Luke was still alive – and, having been shot at, he was on full alert, determined to learn the truth.

The kitchen door burst open, and Malone and Curtis appeared. Anthony discreetly slid the gun back into his inside pocket. Then, panting, he said: 'Over the fence – go after him.' He knew they would not catch Luke.

When they were out of sight, he started to look for the slugs.

10.30 P.M.

The design of the rocket is based on the V2 bomb used against London during the war. The engine even looks the same. The accelerometers, relays and gyros are all out of the V2. The pump for the propellants uses hydrogen peroxide passed over a cadmium catalyst, releasing energy that drives a turbine – and this, too, comes from the V2.

Harold Brodsky made a good dry martini, and Mrs Riley's tuna bake was as tasty as promised. For dessert, Harold served cherry pie and ice cream. Billie felt guilty. He was trying so hard to please her, but her mind was on Luke and Anthony, their shared past and their puzzling new entanglement.

While Harold made coffee, she called home and checked that all was well with Larry and Becky-Ma. Then Harold suggested they move to the living room and watch television. He produced a bottle of expensive French brandy and poured generous measures into two oversize snifters. Was he trying to stiffen his own courage, Billie wondered, or lower her resistance? She inhaled the vapours of the cognac but did not drink any.

Harold, too, was thoughtful. He was normally an

entertaining talker, witty and clever, and she generally laughed a lot when she was with him, but tonight he was preoccupied.

They saw a thriller called *Run, Joe, Run!* Jan Sterling played a waitress involved with ex-gangster Alex Nichol. Billie could not get interested in the imaginary dangers on the screen. Her mind drifted to the mystery of what Anthony had done to Luke. In OSS they had broken all kinds of laws, and Anthony was still in clandestine work, but all the same Billie was shocked that he had gone this far. Surely different rules applied in peacetime?

And what was his motive? Bern had called and told her of his confession to Luke, and that had confirmed what all her instincts told her, that Luke could not be a spy. But did Anthony believe it? If not, then what was the real reason for what he had done?

Harold turned off the TV and poured himself another brandy. 'I've been thinking about our future,' he said.

Billie's heart sank. He was going to propose. If he had done it yesterday, she would have accepted him. But today she could hardly think about it.

He took her hand. 'I love you,' he said. 'We get on well, we have the same interests, and we both have a child – but that's not why. I believe I'd want to marry you if you were a waitress who chewed gum and liked Elvis Presley.'

Billie laughed.

He went on: 'I just adore you, for no reason other than you're you. I know it's real, because it's happened to me before, just once, with Lesley. I loved her with all my heart, until she was taken away from me. So I'm not in any doubt. I love you, and I want us to be together for ever.' He looked at her, then said: 'How do you feel?'

She sighed. 'I'm fond of you. I'd like to go to bed with you, I think it would be great.' He raised his eyebrows at this, but did not interrupt. 'And I can't help thinking how much easier life would be if I had someone to share the burdens.'

'This is good.'

'Yesterday, it would have been enough. I would have said yes, I love you, let's get married. But today I met someone from my past, and I remembered what it was like to be in love at the age of twenty-one.' She gave him a candid look. 'I don't feel that way about you, Harold.'

He was not totally discouraged. 'Who does, at our age?'

'Maybe you're right.' She wished she could be crazy and wild again. But it was a foolish desire for a divorcée with a seven-year-old. To give herself time, she lifted the brandy goblet to her lips.

The doorbell rang.

Billie's heart leaped.

'Who the heck is that?' Harold said angrily. 'I hope Sidney Bowman doesn't want to borrow my car jack at this time of night.' He got up and went out to the hall.

Billie knew who it was. She put down her brandy untouched, and stood up.

She heard Luke's voice at the door. 'I need to talk to Billie.'

Billie wondered why she was so inordinately pleased.

Harold said: 'I'm not sure she wants to be disturbed right now.'

'It's important.'

'How did you know she was here?'

'Her mother told me. I'm sorry, Harold, I don't have time to dick around.' Billie heard a thump, followed by a cry of protest from Harold, and she guessed Luke had forced his way into the house. She went to the door and looked into the hallway. 'Just hold your horses, Luke,' she said. 'This is Harold's house.' Luke had ripped his coat and lost his hat, and he looked very shaken. 'What's happened now?' she said.

'Anthony shot at me.'

Billie was shocked. 'Anthony?' she said. 'My God, what got into him? He shot at *you*?'

Harold looked scared. 'What's this about a shooting?'

Luke ignored him. 'It's time to tell someone in authority about all this,' he said to Billie. 'I'm going to the Pentagon. But I'm worried I may not be believed. Will you come and back me up?'

'Sure,' she said. She took her coat off the hall stand.

Harold said: 'Billie! For God's sake – we were in the middle of a very important conversation.'

Luke said: 'I really need you.'

Billie hesitated. It was very hard on Harold. He had

obviously been planning this moment for some time. But Luke's life was in danger. 'I'm sorry,' she said to Harold. 'I have to go.' She lifted her face to be kissed, but he turned away.

'Don't be like that,' Billie said. 'I'll see you tomorrow.'

'Get out of my house, both of you,' Harold said furiously.

Billie walked out, with Luke behind her, and Harold slammed the door.

11 P.M.

The Jupiter programme cost 40 million dollars in 1956 and 140 million in 1957. In 1958 the figure is expected to be more than 300 million.

Anthony found some hotel stationery in the desk drawer of the room Pete had rented. He took out an envelope. From his pocket he took three distorted slugs and three cartridge cases, the rounds he had fired at Luke. He put them into the envelope and sealed it, then stuffed it into his pocket. He would dispose of it at the first opportunity.

He was doing damage control. He had very little time, but he had to be meticulous. He needed to wipe out all trace of this incident. The work helped to distract his mind from the self-loathing that tasted so bitter in his mouth.

The assistant manager on duty came into the room, looking wrathful. He was a small, neat man with a bald head. 'Sit down, please, Mr Suchard,' Anthony said. He showed the man his CIA identification.

'CIA!' Suchard said, and his indignation began to deflate.

Anthony took a business card from his billfold. 'The

card says State Department, but you can always reach me at that number if you need me.'

Suchard handled the card as if it might blow up. 'What can I do for you, Mr Carroll?' He had a slight accent which Anthony thought might be Swiss.

'First, I want to apologize for the little fracas we had earlier.'

Suchard nodded primly. He was not going to say it was okay. 'Fortunately, few guests noticed anything. Only the kitchen staff and a few waiters saw you chasing the gentleman.'

'I'm glad we didn't disrupt your fine hotel too much, even over a matter of national security.'

Suchard raised his eyebrows in surprise. 'National security?'

'Of course, I can't give you the details . . .'

'Of course.'

'But I hope I can rely on your discretion.'

Hotel professionals prided themselves on their discretion, and Suchard nodded vigorously. 'Indeed, you can.'

'It may not be necessary even to report the incident to your manager.'

'Possibly . . .'

Anthony took out a roll of bills. 'The State Department has a small fund for compensation in these instances.' He peeled off a twenty. Suchard accepted it. 'And if any staff members seem discontented, perhaps . . .' He slowly counted another four twenties and handed them over.

It was a huge bribe for an assistant manager. 'Thank

you, sir,' said Suchard. 'I'm sure we can meet your requirements.'

'If anyone should question you, it might be best to say you saw nothing.'

'Of course.' Suchard stood up. 'If there's anything else . . .'

'I'll be in touch.' Anthony nodded dismissively, and Suchard left.

Pete came in. 'The head of security for the army at Cape Canaveral is Colonel Bill Hide,' he said. 'He's staying at the Starlite Motel.' He handed Anthony a slip of paper with a phone number, and went out again.

Anthony dialled the number and got through to Hide's room. 'This is Anthony Carroll, CIA, Technical Services Division,' he said.

Hide spoke with a slow, unmilitary drawl, and sounded as if he might have had a couple of drinks. 'Well, what can I do for you, Mr Carroll?'

'I'm calling about Dr Lucas.'

'Oh, yes?'

He seemed faintly hostile, and Anthony decided to butter him up. 'I would appreciate your advice, if you could spare me a moment at this late hour, Colonel.'

Hide warmed up. 'Of course, anything I can do.'

That was better. 'I think you know that Dr Lucas has been behaving strangely, which is worrying in a scientist in possession of classified information.'

'It sure is.'

Anthony wanted Hide to feel in charge. 'What would you say is his mental state?'

'He seemed normal last time I saw him, but I talked to him a few hours ago and he told me he'd lost his memory.'

'There's more to it than that. He stole a car, broke into a house, got in a fight with a cop, stuff like that.'

'My God, he's in worse shape than I thought.'

Hide was buying the story, Anthony thought with relief. He pressed on. 'We think he's not rational, but you know him better than we do. What would you say is going on?' Anthony held his breath, hoping for the right answer.

'Hell, I think he's suffering some kind of breakdown.' This was exactly what Anthony wanted Hide to believe – but now Hide thought it was his own idea, and he proceeded to try to convince Anthony. 'Look, Mr Carroll, the army wouldn't employ a nutcase on a top secret project. Normally, Luke is as sane as you or me. Obviously something has destabilized him.'

'He seems to think there's some kind of conspiracy against him – but you're saying we shouldn't necessarily credit that.'

'Not for a minute.'

'So we should soft-pedal this stuff. I mean, we shouldn't alert the Pentagon.'

'God, no,' Hide said worriedly. 'In fact, I'd better call them and warn them that Luke seems to have lost his marbles.'

'As you wish.'

Pete came in and Anthony raised one finger for him to wait. He softened his voice and said into the phone: 'By happenstance, I'm an old friend of Dr and Mrs

Lucas. I'm going to try to persuade Luke to seek psychiatric help.'

'That sounds like a good idea.'

'Well, thank you, Colonel. You've set my mind at rest, and we will proceed along the lines you have suggested.'

'You're welcome. If there's anything you want to ask me or discuss with me, call me any time.'

'I sure will.' Anthony hung up.

Pete said: 'Psychiatric help?'

'That was just for his benefit.' Anthony reviewed the situation. There was no evidence here at the hotel. He had prejudiced the Pentagon against any report Luke might make. That just left Billie's hospital.

He stood up. 'I'll be back in an hour,' he said. 'I want you to stay here. But not in the lobby. Take Malone and Curtis and bribe a room-service waiter to let you into Luke's suite. I have a feeling he'll come back.'

'And if he does?'

'Don't let him get away again – no matter what.'

12 MIDNIGHT

The Jupiter C missile uses Hydyne, a secret, high-energy fuel that is 12 per cent more powerful than the alcohol propellant used in the standard Redstone missile. A toxic, corrosive substance, it is a blend of UDMH – unsymmetrical dimethyl hydrazine – and diethylene triamine.

Billie drove the red Thunderbird into the parking lot of the Georgetown Mind Hospital and killed the engine. Colonel Lopez from the Pentagon pulled alongside her in a Ford Fairlane painted olive drab.

'He doesn't believe a word I say,' Luke said angrily.

'You can't blame him,' Billie reasoned. 'The assistant manager of the Carlton says no one was chased through the kitchens, and there are no cartridge cases on the ground at the loading dock.'

'Anthony cleaned up the evidence.'

'I know that, but Colonel Lopez doesn't.'

'Thank God I've got you to back me up.'

They got out of the car and walked into the building with the colonel, a patient Hispanic man with an intelligent face. Billie nodded to the receptionist and led the two men up the stairs and along the corridor to the records office.

'I'm going to show you the file of a man named Joseph Bellow, whose physical characteristics match Luke's,' she explained.

The colonel nodded.

Billie went on: 'You'll see that he was admitted on Tuesday, treated, then discharged at 4 a.m. on Wednesday. You have to understand that it's very unusual for a schizophrenic patient to be given treatment without observation first. And I hardly need to tell you that it's unheard of for a patient to be released from a mental hospital at four o'clock in the morning.'

'I understand,' Lopez said non-committally.

Billie opened the drawer, pulled out the Bellow file, put it on the desk, and opened it.

It was empty.

'Oh, my God,' she said.

Luke stared at the cardboard folder in disbelief. 'I saw the papers myself less than six hours ago!'

Lopez stood up with a weary air. 'Well, I guess that's it.'

Luke had the nightmare feeling that he was living in a surreal world in which people could do what they liked to him, shoot at him and mess with his mind, and he could never prove it had happened. 'Maybe I am schizophrenic,' he said sombrely.

'Well, I'm not,' Billie said. 'And I saw that file too.'

'But it's not here now,' said Lopez.

'Wait,' Billie said. 'The daily register will show his admission. It's kept at the reception desk.' She slammed the file drawer shut.

They went down to the lobby. Billie spoke to the receptionist. 'Let me see the register, please, Charlie.'

'Right away, Dr Josephson.' The young black man behind the counter searched around for a moment. 'Dang, where did that thing go?' he said.

Luke muttered: 'Jesus Christ.'

The receptionist's face darkened with embarrassment. 'I know it was here a couple of hours ago.'

Billie's face was like thunder. 'Tell me something, Charlie. Has Dr Ross been here tonight?'

'Yes, mam. He left a few minutes ago.'

She nodded. 'Next time you see him, ask him where the register went. He knows.'

'I sure will.'

Billie turned away from the desk.

Luke said angrily: 'Let me ask you something, Colonel. Before we saw you tonight, had someone else talked to you about me?'

Lopez hesitated. 'Yes.'

'Who?'

Reluctantly, he said: 'I guess you're entitled to know. We got a call from a Colonel Hide down in Cape Canaveral. He said the CIA had been watching you and they reported that you were behaving irrationally.'

Luke nodded grimly. 'Anthony again.'

Billie said to Lopez: 'Hell, I can't think of anything else we can do to convince you. And I don't really blame you for not believing us, when we have no evidence.'

'I didn't say I don't believe you,' Lopez said.

Luke was startled, and looked at the colonel with new hope.

Lopez went on: 'I could believe you imagined that a CIA man chased you around the Carlton Hotel and shot at you in the alley. I might even accept that you and Dr Josephson conspired to pretend there used to be a file and it disappeared. But I don't believe that Charlie here is in on the conspiracy. There must be a daily register, and it's gone. I don't think you took it – why would you? But then who did? Someone has something to hide.'

'So you believe me?' Luke said.

'What's to believe? You don't know what this is all about. I don't know either. But something sure as hell is going on. And I believe it must have to do with that rocket we're about to launch.'

'What'll you do?'

'I'm going to order a full security alert at Cape Canaveral. I've been there, I know they're lax. Tomorrow morning they won't know what's hit them.'

'But what about Anthony?'

'I have a friend at the CIA. I'm going to tell him your story, and say I don't know whether it's true or not, but I'm concerned.'

'That's not going to get us far!' Luke protested. 'We need to know what's going on, why they wiped my memory!'

'I agree,' Lopez said. 'But I can't do any more. The rest is up to you.'

'Christ,' Luke said. 'So I'm on my own.'

'No, you're not,' said Billie. 'You're not on your own.'

PART 4

1 A.M.

The new fuel is based on a nerve gas and is very dangerous. It is delivered to Cape Canaveral on a special train equipped with nitrogen to blanket it if any escapes. A drop on the skin will be absorbed into the bloodstream instantly and will be fatal. The technicians say: 'If you smell fish, run like hell.'

Billie drove fast, handling the Thunderbird's three-speed manual gear change with confidence. Luke watched in admiration. They sped through the quiet streets of Georgetown, crossed the creek to downtown Washington, and headed for the Carlton.

Luke felt energized. He knew who his enemy was, he had a friend at his side, and he understood what he had to do. He was mystified by what had happened to him, but he was determined to unravel the mystery, and impatient to get on with it.

Billie parked around the corner from the entrance. 'I'll go first,' she said. 'If there's anyone suspicious in the lobby, I'll come right out again. When you see me take my coat off, you'll know it's all clear.'

Luke was not comfortable with this plan. 'What if Anthony's there?'

'He won't shoot me.' She got out of the car.

Luke contemplated arguing with her and decided against it. She was probably right. He presumed that Anthony had thoroughly searched his hotel room, and had destroyed anything he thought might be a clue to the secret he so badly wanted to keep. But Anthony also needed to maintain a semblance of normality, to support the fiction that Luke had lost his memory after a drinking bout. So Luke expected to find most of his own stuff. That would help him reorient himself. And there might be a clue that Anthony had overlooked.

They approached the hotel separately, Luke remaining on the opposite side of the street. He watched Billie go in, enjoying her jaunty walk and the swing of her coat. He could see through the glass doors into the lobby. A porter approached her immediately, suspicious of a glamorous woman arriving alone so late at night. He saw her speak, and guessed she was saying: 'I'm Mrs Lucas, my husband will be along in a moment.' Then she took off her coat.

Luke crossed the road and entered the hotel.

For the porter's benefit he said: 'I want to make a call before we go upstairs, honey.' There was an internal phone on the reception desk, but he did not want the porter to hear his conversation. Next to the reception desk was a little lobby that had a payphone in an enclosed booth with a seat. Luke went inside. Billie followed him and closed the door. They were very close together. He put a dime in the slot and called the hotel. He angled the handset so that Billie could hear. Tense though he was, he found it deliciously exciting to be so near to Billie.

'Sheraton-Carlton, good morning.'

It *was* morning, he realized – Thursday morning. He had been awake for twenty hours. But he did not feel sleepy. He was too tense. 'Room five-thirty, please.'

The operator hesitated. 'Sir, it's past one o'clock – is this an emergency?'

'Dr Lucas asked me to call no matter how late.'

'Very good.'

There was a pause, then a ringing tone. Luke felt very conscious of Billie's warm body in a purple silk dress. He had to resist the urge to put his arm around her small, neat shoulders and hug her to him.

After four rings, he was ready to believe that the room was empty – then the phone was picked up. So Anthony, or one of his men, was lying in wait. That was a nuisance; but Luke felt better knowing where the enemy was deployed.

A voice said: 'Hello?' The tone was uncertain. It was not Anthony, but it might have been Pete.

Luke put on a tipsy voice. 'Hey, Ronnie, this is Tim. We're all waitin' for ya!'

The man grunted with irritation. 'Drunk,' he muttered, as if speaking to someone else. 'You got the wrong room, buddy.'

'Oh, gee, I'm sorry, I hope I didn't wake—' Luke broke off as the phone was hung up.

'Someone there,' Billie said.

'Maybe more than one.'

277

'I know how to get them out.' She grinned. 'I did it in Lisbon, during the war. Come on.'

They left the phone booth. Luke noticed Billie discreetly pick up a book of matches from an ashtray by the elevator. The porter took them up to the fifth floor.

They found Room 530 and went quietly past it. Billie opened an unmarked door to reveal a linen closet. 'Perfect,' she said in a low voice. 'Is there a fire alarm nearby?'

Luke looked around and saw an alarm of the type that could be set off by breaking a pane of glass with the little hammer hanging next to it. 'Right there,' he said.

'Good.' In the closet, sheets and blankets stood in neat stacks on slatted wooden shelves. Billie unfolded a blanket and dropped it on the floor. She did the same with several more until she had a pile of loose fabric. Luke guessed what she was going to do, and his conjecture was confirmed when she took a breakfast order from a doorknob and lit it with a match. As it flared up, she put the flame to a pile of blankets. 'This is why you should never smoke in bed,' she said.

As the flames blazed up, Billie piled on additional bedlinen. Her face was flushed with heat and excitement, and she looked more alluring than ever. Soon there was a roaring bonfire. Smoke poured out of the closet and began to fill the corridor.

'Time to sound the alarm,' she said. 'We don't want anyone to get hurt.'

'Right,' Luke said, and again the phrase came into

his mind: *They're not collaborators.* But now he understood it. In the Resistance, blowing up factories and warehouses, he must have worried constantly about innocent French people getting injured.

He grasped the little hammer that hung on a chain next to the fire alarm. He broke the glass with a light tap and pressed the large red button inside. A moment later, a loud ringing shattered the silence of the corridor.

Luke and Billie retreated along the corridor, moving away from the elevator, until they could only just see the door of Luke's suite through the smoke.

The door nearest them opened and a woman in a nightdress came out. She saw the smoke, screamed, and ran for the stairs. From another door, a man in shirtsleeves emerged with a pencil in his hand, obviously having been working late; then a young couple wrapped in sheets appeared, looking as if they had been interrupted making love; then a bleary-eyed man in rumpled pink pyjamas. A few moments later, the corridor was full of people coughing and fumbling through the smoke toward the stairwell.

The door to Room 530 opened slowly.

Luke saw a tall man step into the corridor. Peering through the murk, Luke thought he had a large wine-coloured birthmark on his cheek: Pete. He drew back to avoid being recognized. The figure hesitated, then seemed to make a decision and joined the rush for the stairs. Two more men came out and followed him.

'All clear,' Luke said.

Luke and Billie entered the suite, and Luke closed the door to keep the smoke out. He took off his coat.

'Oh, my God,' said Billie. 'It's the same room.'

* * *

She stared around, wide-eyed. 'I can't believe it,' she said. Her voice was hushed, and he could hardly hear her. 'This is the very suite.'

He stood still, watching. She was in the grip of a strong emotion. 'What happened here?' he asked her at last.

She shook her head wonderingly. 'It's hard to imagine that you don't remember.' She walked around. 'There was a grand piano in that corner,' she said. 'Imagine – a piano in a hotel room!' She looked into the bathroom. 'And a phone in here. I had never seen a phone in a bathroom.'

Luke waited. Her face showed sadness, and something else he could not quite make out. 'You stayed here in the war,' she said at last. Then, in a rush, she added: 'We made love here.'

He looked into the bedroom. 'On that bed, I guess.'

'Not just on the bed.' She giggled, then became solemn again. 'How young we were.'

The thought of making love to this enchanting woman was unbearably exciting. 'My God, I wish I could remember,' he said, and his voice sounded thick with desire.

To his surprise, she blushed.

He turned aside and picked up the phone. He dialled the operator. He wanted to make sure the fire did not have a chance to spread. After a long wait, the phone was answered. 'This is Mr Davies, I sounded the alarm,' Luke said rapidly. 'The fire is in a linen closet near room five-forty.' He hung up without waiting for a reply.

Billie was looking around, her emotional moment over. 'Your clothes are here,' she said.

He went into the bedroom. Lying on the bed were a pale grey tweed sport coat and a pair of charcoal flannel pants, looking as if they had come back from the dry cleaner. He guessed he had worn them on the plane and sent them for pressing. On the floor was a pair of dark tan wingtip shoes. A crocodile belt was neatly rolled up inside one of the shoes.

He opened the drawer of the bedside table and found a billfold, a cheque book and a fountain pen. More interesting was a slim appointments diary with a list of phone numbers in the back. He looked quickly through its pages and found the current week.

Sunday 26th
Call Alice (1928)

Monday 27th
Buy swim trunks
8.30 a.m. Apex mtg, Vanguard Mtl

Tuesday 28th
8 a.m. Bkfst w A.C., Hay Adams coffee shop

Billie stood beside him to see what he was reading. She put a hand on his shoulder. It was a casual gesture, but her touch gave him a thrill of pleasure. He said: 'Any idea who Alice might be?'

'Your kid sister.'

'How old?'

'Seven years younger than you, which makes her thirty.'

'So she was born in 1928. I guess I talked to her on her birthday. I could call her now, ask her if I said anything unusual.'

'Good idea.'

Luke felt good. He was reconstructing his life. 'I must have gone to Florida without my swimsuit.'

'Who thinks of swimming in January?'

'So I made a note to buy one on Monday. That morning I went to the Vanguard Motel at eight-thirty.'

'What's an Apex meeting?'

'I think it must have to do with the curve followed by the missile in flight. I don't remember working on it, of course, but I know there's an important and tricky calculation that has to be made. The second stage has to be fired precisely at the apex, in order to put the satellite into a permanent orbit.'

'You could find out who else was at the meeting and talk to them.'

'I will.'

'Then, on Tuesday, you had breakfast with Anthony in the coffee shop of the Hay Adams hotel.'

'After that, there are no appointments in the book.'

He turned to the back of the diary. There were phone numbers for Anthony, Billie and Bern, for

Mother and Alice, and twenty or thirty others that meant nothing to him. 'Anything strike you?' he said to Billie. She shook her head.

There were some leads worth following up, but no obvious clues. It was what he had expected, but all the same he felt deflated. He pocketed the diary and looked around the room. A well-worn black leather suitcase rested open on a stand. He rummaged through it, finding clean shirts and underwear, a notebook half full of mathematical calculations, and a paperback book called *The Old Man and the Sea* with a corner turned down at page 143.

Billie looked into the bathroom. Shaving gear, toiletry bag, toothbrush.

Luke opened all the cupboards and drawers in the bedroom, and Billie did the same in the living room. Luke found a black wool topcoat and a black Homburg hat in a closet, but nothing else. 'Zilch,' he called out. 'You?'

'Your phone messages are here on the desk. From Bern, from a Colonel Hide, and from someone called Marigold.'

Luke figured that Anthony had read the messages, judged them harmless, and decided there was no point in creating suspicion by destroying them.

Billie said: 'Who's Marigold, do you know?'

Luke thought for a moment. He had heard the name at some point during the day. It came back to him. 'She's my secretary in Huntsville,' he said. 'Colonel Hide said she had made my flight reservations.'

'I wonder if you told her the purpose of the trip.'

'I doubt it. I didn't tell anyone at Cape Canaveral.'

'She's not at Cape Canaveral. And you might trust your own secretary more than anyone else.'

Luke nodded. 'Anything's possible. I'll check. It's the most promising lead so far.' He took out the diary and looked again at the phone numbers in the back. 'Bingo,' he said. 'Marigold – home.' He sat at the desk and dialled the number. He wondered how much longer he had before Pete and the other agents came back.

Billie seemed to read his mind, and started packing his stuff into the black leather bag.

The phone was answered by a sleepy woman with a slow Alabama accent. Luke guessed from her voice that she was black. He said: 'I'm sorry to call so late. Is this Marigold?'

'Dr Lucas! Thank God you've called. How are you?'

'I'm fine, I think, thank you.'

'Well, what in heaven happened to you? No one knew where you were at – and now I hear tell you lost your memory. Is that so?'

'Yes.'

'Well, now, how did that come to pass?'

'I don't know, but I'm hoping you might help me figure it out.'

'If I can . . .'

'I'd like to know why I suddenly decided to go to Washington on Monday. Did I tell you?'

'You sure didn't, and I was curious.'

It was the answer Luke expected, but still he felt disappointed. 'Did I say anything that gave you a hint?'

'No.'

'What *did* I say?'

'You said you needed to fly to Washington via Huntsville, and you asked me to make reservations on MATS flights.'

MATS was the military airline, and Luke guessed he was entitled to use it when on army business. But there was something he did not understand. 'I flew via Huntsville?' No one else had mentioned that.

'You said you wanted to stop over here for a couple of hours.'

'I wonder why.'

'Then you said something kind of strange. You asked me not to tell anyone that you were coming to Huntsville.'

'Ah.' Luke felt sure this was an important clue. 'So it was a secret visit?'

'Yes. And I've kept it secret. I've been questioned by army security and the FBI, and I didn't tell either one of them, because you said not to. I didn't know if I was doing right or not, when they said you had disappeared, but I figured I better stick with what you told me. Did I do right?'

'Gosh, Marigold, I don't know. But I appreciate your loyalty.' The fire alarm stopped ringing. Luke realized he had run out of time. 'I have to go now,' he told Marigold. 'Thanks for your help.'

'Well, you bet. Now you just take care, hear?' She hung up.

'I've packed your stuff,' Billie said.

'Thanks,' he said. He took his own black coat and

hat from the closet and put them on. 'Now let's get out of here before the spooks come back.'

* * *

They drove to an all-night diner near the FBI building, around the corner from Chinatown, and ordered coffee. 'I wonder when the first flight to Huntsville leaves in the morning,' Luke said.

'We need the Official Airline Guide,' Billie said.

Luke looked around the diner. He saw a pair of cops eating doughnuts, four drunk students ordering hamburgers, and two underdressed women who might have been prostitutes. 'I don't think they'll keep it behind the counter here,' he said.

'I bet Bern has one. It's the kind of thing writers like. They're always looking stuff up.'

'He's probably asleep.'

Billie stood up. 'Then I'll wake him. Got a dime?'

'Sure.' Luke still had a pocket full of the change he had stolen yesterday.

Billie went to the payphone beside the restrooms. Luke sipped his coffee, watching her. As she talked into the phone she smiled and tilted her head, being charming to someone she had woken up. She looked bewitching, and he ached with desire for her.

She returned to the table and said: 'He's going to join us and bring the book.'

Luke checked his watch. It was two a.m. 'I'll probably go straight to the airport from here. I hope there's an early flight.'

Billie frowned. 'Is there a deadline?'

'There might be. I keep asking myself: What could have made me drop everything and rush to Washington? It has to be something to do with the rocket. And what could that be if not a threat to the launch?'

'Sabotage?'

'Yes. And if I'm right, I have to prove it before ten-thirty tonight.'

'Do you want me to fly to Huntsville with you?'

'You have to take care of Larry.'

'I can leave him with Bern.'

Luke shook his head. 'I don't think so . . . thanks.'

'You always were an independent son of a gun.'

'It's not that,' he said. He wanted her to understand. 'I'd love you to come with me. That's the trouble – I'd like it too much.'

She reached across the plastic tabletop and took his hand. 'It's okay,' she said.

'This is confusing, you know? I'm married to someone else, but I don't know how I feel about her. What's she like?'

Billie shook her head. 'I can't talk to you about Elspeth. You have to rediscover her yourself.'

'I guess so.'

Billie brought his hand to her lips and kissed it softly.

Luke swallowed. 'Did I always like you so much, or is this new?'

'This is not new.'

'It seems we get on really well.'

'No. We fight like hell. But we adore one another.'

'You said we were lovers, once – in that hotel suite.'

'Stop it.'

'Was it good?'

She looked at him with tears in her eyes. 'The best.'

'Then how come I'm not married to you?'

She began to cry, soft sobs that shook her small frame. 'Because . . .' She wiped her face and took a deep breath, then started crying again. At last she blurted out: 'You got so mad at me, you didn't speak to me for five years.'

1945

Anthony's parents had a horse farm near Charlottesville, Virginia, a couple of hours from Washington. It was a big white timber-framed house with rambling wings that contained a dozen bedrooms. There were stables and tennis courts, a lake and a stream, paddocks and woodland. Anthony's mother had inherited it from her father, along with five million dollars.

Luke arrived there on the Friday after Japan surrendered. Mrs Carroll welcomed him at the door. She was a nervous blonde woman who looked as if she had once been very beautiful. She showed him to a small, spotlessly clean bedroom with a polished board floor and a high old-fashioned bed.

He changed out of his uniform – he now held the rank of major – and put on a black cashmere sport coat and grey flannel pants. As he was tying his tie, Anthony looked in. 'Cocktails in the drawing room whenever you're ready,' he said.

'I'll be right there,' Luke said. 'Which room is Billie's?'

A worried frown flickered across Anthony's face. 'The girls are in the other wing, I'm afraid,' he said.

'The Admiral is old-fashioned about that sort of thing.'
His father had spent his life in the navy.

'No problem,' Luke said with a shrug. He had spent
the last three years moving around occupied Europe
at night: he would be able to find his lover's bedroom
in the dark.

When he went downstairs at six o'clock he found all
his old friends waiting. As well as Anthony and Billie,
there were Elspeth, Bern, and Bern's girlfriend Peg.
Luke had spent much of the war with Bern and
Anthony, and every leave with Billie, but he had not
seen Elspeth or Peg since 1941.

The Admiral handed him a martini and he took a
satisfying gulp. This was a time to celebrate if ever
there was one. The conversation was noisy and high-
spirited. Anthony's mother looked on with a vaguely
pleased expression, and his father drank cocktails
faster than anyone else.

Luke studied them all over dinner, comparing them
with the golden youths who had been so worried, four
years ago, about being expelled from Harvard. Elspeth
was painfully thin after three years on iron rations in
wartime London: even her magnificent breasts seemed
smaller. Peg, who had been a dowdy girl with a big
heart, was now smartly dressed, but her skilfully
made-up face looked hardened and cynical. Bern at
twenty-seven looked ten years older. This had been his
second war. He had been wounded three times, and
he had the gaunt face of a man who has known too
much suffering, his own and other people's.

Anthony had come through best. He had seen some

action, but had spent most of the war in Washington. His confidence, his optimism and his offbeat humour had survived intact.

Billie, too, seemed little changed. She had known hardship and bereavement in childhood, and perhaps that was why the war had not bruised her. She had spent two years undercover in Lisbon, and Luke knew – though the others did not – that she had killed a man there, cutting his throat with silent efficiency in the yard behind the café where he had been about to sell secrets to the enemy. But she was still a small bundle of radiant energy, gay at one moment and fierce at the next, her constantly changing face a study that Luke never tired of.

It was remarkably lucky that they were all still alive. Most such groups would have lost at least one friend. 'We should drink a toast,' he said, lifting his wine glass. 'To those who survived – and those who did not.'

They all drank, then Bern said: 'I have another. To the men who broke the back of the Nazi war machine – the Red Army.'

They all drank again, but the Admiral looked displeased and said: 'I think that's enough toasts.'

Bern's communism was still strong, but Luke felt sure he was no longer working for Moscow. They had made a deal, and Luke believed Bern had kept the bargain. Nevertheless, their relationship had never returned to its old warmth. Trusting someone was like holding a little water in your cupped hands – it was so easy to spill the water, and you could never get it back. Luke was sad every time he recalled the comradeship he and Bern had shared, but he felt helpless to regain it.

Coffee was served in the drawing room. Luke handed the cups around. As he offered cream and sugar to Billie, she said in a low voice: 'East wing, second floor, last door on the left.'

'Cream?'

She raised an eyebrow.

He smothered a laugh and passed on.

At ten-thirty the Admiral insisted the men move to the billiard room. Hard liquor and Cuban cigars were laid out on a sideboard. Luke refused more booze: he was looking forward to sliding between the sheets next to Billie's warm, eager body, and the last thing he wanted to do then was fall asleep.

The Admiral poured himself a big tumbler of bourbon and took Luke to the far end of the room to show him his guns, standing in a locked display rack on the wall. Luke's family were not hunters, and guns to him were for killing people, not animals, so he took no pleasure in them. He also felt strongly that guns and liquor made a bad combination. However, he feigned interest in order to be polite.

'I know and respect your family, Luke,' the Admiral said as they examined an Enfield rifle. 'Your father is a very great man.'

'Thank you,' Luke said. This sounded like the preamble to a rehearsed speech. His father had spent the war helping to run the Office of Price Administration, but the Admiral probably still thought of him as a banker.

'You'll have to think of your family when you choose a wife, my boy,' the Admiral went on.

'Yes, sir, I will.' Luke wondered what was on the old man's mind.

'Whoever becomes Mrs Lucas will have a place waiting for her in the upper reaches of American society. You must pick a girl who can carry that off.'

Luke began to see where this was going. Annoyed, he abruptly put the rifle back in the rack. 'I'll bear that in mind, Admiral,' he said, and he turned away.

The Admiral put a hand on his arm, stopping him. 'Whatever you do, don't throw yourself away.'

Luke glared at him. He was determined not to ask the Admiral what he was getting at. He thought he knew the answer, and it would be better if it were not said.

But the Admiral was determined. 'Don't get stuck with that little Jewess – she's not worthy of you.'

Luke gritted his teeth. 'If you'll excuse me, this is something I'd rather discuss with my own father.'

'But your father doesn't know about her, does he?'

Luke flushed. The Admiral had scored a point. Luke and Billie had not met one another's parents.

There had hardly been time. Their love affair had been conducted in snatched moments during a war. But that was not the only reason. Deep in Luke's heart a small, mean-spirited voice told him that a girl from a dirt-poor Jewish family was not his parents' idea of the right wife for their son. They would accept her, he felt sure – indeed, they would come to love her, for all the reasons he loved her. But at first they might be a little disappointed. Consequently, he was eager to introduce her to them in the right circumstances, on a relaxed occasion when they would have time to get to know her.

The fact that there was a grain of truth in the Admiral's insinuation made Luke even angrier. With barely controlled aggression, he said: 'Forgive me if I *warn* you that these remarks are personally offensive to me.'

The room went quiet, but Luke's veiled threat passed right over the head of the drunk Admiral. 'I understand that, son, but I've lived longer than you, and I know what I'm talking about.'

'Pardon me, you don't know the people involved.'

'Oh, but I think I may know more about the lady in question than you do.'

Something in the Admiral's tone sounded a warning, but Luke was angry enough to ignore it. 'The hell you do,' he said with deliberate rudeness.

Bern tried to intervene. 'Hey, guys, lighten up, will you? Let's shoot some pool.'

But nothing could stop the Admiral now. He put his arm around Luke's shoulders. 'Look, son, I'm a man, I understand,' he said with an assumption of intimacy that Luke resented. 'So long as you don't take matters too seriously, there's no harm in pronging a little tart, we've all—'

He never finished the sentence. Luke turned towards him, put both hands on his chest, and shoved him away. The Admiral staggered back, arms flailing, and his glass of bourbon went flying through the air.

He tried to regain his balance, failed, and sat down hard on the rug. Luke shouted at him: 'Now knock it off before I close your filthy mouth with my fist!'

Anthony, white-faced, grabbed Luke's arm, saying: 'Luke, for Christ's sake, what do you think you're doing?'

Bern stepped between them and the fallen Admiral. 'Calm down, both of you,' he said.

'The hell with *calm*,' Luke said. 'What kind of man invites you to his house then insults your girlfriend? It's about time someone taught the old fool a lesson in manners!'

'She is a tart,' the Admiral said from his sitting position. 'I should know, goddam it.' His voice rose to a roar. 'I paid for her abortion!'

Luke was stunned. 'Abortion?'

'Hell, yes.' He struggled to his feet. 'Anthony got her pregnant, and I paid a thousand dollars for her to get rid of the little bastard.' His mouth twisted in a spiteful grin of triumph. 'Now tell me I don't know what I'm talking about.'

'You're lying.'

'Ask Anthony.'

Luke looked at Anthony.

Anthony shook his head. 'It wasn't my baby. I told my father it was, so that he'd give me the thousand dollars. But it was your baby, Luke.'

Luke blushed to the roots of his hair. The drunk old Admiral had made a complete fool of him. He was the ignorant one. He thought he knew Billie, yet she had kept something as big as this a secret from him.

He had fathered a child, and his girlfriend had had an abortion, and they knew about it but he did not. He was utterly humiliated.

He stormed out of the room. He crossed the hall and burst into the drawing room. Only Anthony's mother was there: the girls must have gone to bed. Mrs Carroll saw his face and said: 'Luke, my dear, is something wrong?' He ignored her and went out, slamming the door.

He ran up the stairs and along the east wing. He found Billie's room and went in without knocking.

She was lying naked on the bed, reading, her head resting on her hand, her curly dark hair falling forward like a breaking wave. For a moment, the sight of her took his breath away. Light from a bedside lamp painted a line of gold at the edge of her body, from her neat small shoulder, along her hip, and down one slender leg to her red toenail. But her beauty only made him angrier.

She looked up at him with a happy smile, then her face darkened when she saw his expression.

He yelled: 'Have you ever deceived me?'

She sat upright, scared. 'No, never!'

'That fucking admiral says he paid for you to have an abortion.'

Her face paled. 'Oh, no,' she said.

'Is it true?' Luke shouted. 'Answer me!'

She nodded, began to cry, and buried her face in her hands.

'So you did deceive me.'

'I'm sorry,' she sobbed. 'I wanted to have your baby

– wanted it with all my heart. But I couldn't talk to you. You were in France, and I didn't know if you were ever coming back. I had to decide all on my own.' She raised her voice. 'It was the worst time of my life!'

Luke was dazed. 'I fathered a child,' he said.

Her mood changed in a flash. 'Don't get maudlin,' she said scornfully. 'You weren't sentimental about your sperm when you fucked me, so don't start now – it's too damn late.'

That stung him. 'You should have told me. Even if you couldn't reach me at the time, you should have told me at the first opportunity, the next time I came home on leave.'

She sighed. 'Yes, I know. But Anthony thought I shouldn't tell anyone, and it's not difficult to persuade a girl to keep something like that a secret. No one need ever have known, if not for Admiral goddamn Carroll.'

Luke was maddened by the calm way she talked about her treachery, as if the only thing she had done wrong was to get caught. 'I can't live with this,' he said.

Her voice went quiet. 'What do you mean?'

'After you've deceived me – and over something so important – how can I ever trust you again?'

She looked anguished. 'You're going to tell me it's over.' He said nothing. She went on: 'I can tell, I know you too well. I'm right, aren't I?'

'Yes.'

She began to cry afresh. 'You idiot!' she said through the tears. 'You don't know anything, do you, despite the war.'

'The war taught me that nothing counts as much as loyalty.'

'Bullshit. You still haven't learned that when humans are under pressure, we're all willing to lie.'

'Even to people we love?'

'We lie *more* to our loved ones, because we care about them so damn much. Why do you think we tell the truth to priests and shrinks and total strangers we meet on trains? It's because we don't love them, so we don't care what they think.'

She was infuriatingly plausible. But he despised such easy excuses. 'That's not my philosophy of life.'

'Lucky you,' she said bitterly. 'You come from a happy home, you've never known bereavement or rejection, you have troops of friends. You had a hard war, but you weren't crippled or tortured, and you don't have enough imagination to be a coward. Nothing bad has ever happened to you. Sure, you don't tell lies – for the same reason Mrs Carroll doesn't steal cans of soup.'

She was incredible – she had convinced herself that he was in the wrong! It was impossible to talk to someone who could fool herself so thoroughly. Disgusted, he turned to leave. 'If that's how you think of me, you must be glad our relationship is over.'

'No, I'm not glad.' Tears ran down her face. 'I love you, I've never loved another guy. I'm sorry I deceived you, but I'm not going to prostrate myself with guilt because I did a bad thing in a moment of crisis.'

He did not want her to prostrate herself with guilt. He did not want her to do anything at all. He just wanted to get away from her and their friends and Admiral Carroll and this hateful house.

Somewhere in the back of his mind, a small voice told him he was throwing away the most precious thing he had ever had, and warned that this conversation would cause him a regret so bitter that it would burn in his soul for years. But he was too angry, too humiliated, and too painfully wounded to listen.

He went to the door.

'Don't leave,' she pleaded.

'Go to hell,' he said, and he went out.

2.30 A.M.

The new fuel and a larger fuel tank have boosted the Jupiter's thrust to a force of 83,000 pounds, and extended the burning time from 121 seconds to 155 seconds.

'Anthony was a true friend to me then,' Billie said. 'I was desperate. A thousand dollars! There was nowhere I could find that kind of money. He got it from his father, and he took the blame. He was a mensch. That's why it's so hard to understand what he's doing now.'

'I can't believe I gave you up,' Luke said. 'Didn't I understand what you'd been through?'

'It wasn't all your fault,' Billie said wearily. 'I thought it was, at the time, but now I can see my own role in the whole mess.' She looked as if the telling of the story had exhausted her.

They sat in silence for a while, hushed by regret. Luke wondered how long it would take Bern to drive here from Georgetown; then his thoughts reverted to the story Billie had told. 'I don't much like what I'm learning about myself,' he said after a while. 'Did I really lose my two best friends, you and Bern, just by being unforgiving and pig-headed?'

Billie hesitated, then she laughed. 'Why mince words? Yes, that's exactly what you did.'

'And so you married Bern.'

She laughed again. 'You can be so egocentric!' she said amiably. 'I didn't marry Bern because you left me. I married him because he's one of the best men in the world. He's smart, he's kind, and he's good in bed. It took me years to get over you, but when I did, I fell in love with Bern.'

'And you and I became friends again?'

'Slowly. We always loved you, all of us, even if you could be a stiff-necked son of a gun. I wrote to you when Larry was born, and you came to see me. Then, the following year, Anthony had a huge party on his thirtieth birthday and you showed up. You were back at Harvard, getting your doctorate, and the rest of us were in Washington – Anthony and Elspeth and Peg working for the CIA, me doing research at George Washington University, and Bern writing scripts for radio – but you came to town a couple of times a year, and we would get together.'

'When did I marry Elspeth?'

'Nineteen fifty-four – the year I divorced Bern.'

'Do you know why I married her?'

She hesitated. The answer should have been easy, Luke thought. She should have said: 'Because you loved her – of course!' But she did not. 'I'm the wrong person to answer that question,' she said at last.

'I'll ask Elspeth.'

'I wish you would.'

He looked at her. There was an edge to that last

remark. Luke was figuring out how to tease out her meaning when a white Lincoln Continental pulled up outside, and Bern jumped out and came into the diner. Luke said: 'I'm sorry we woke you.'

'Forget it,' Bern said. 'Billie does not subscribe to the belief that when a man is asleep you should leave him be. If she's awake, everyone should be awake. You'd know that, if you hadn't lost your memory. Here.' He tossed a thick booklet on to the table. The cover said: OFFICIAL AIRLINE GUIDE – PUBLISHED MONTHLY. Luke picked it up.

Billie said: 'Look for Capital Airlines – they fly to the south.'

Luke found the right pages. 'There's a plane that leaves at six fifty-five – that's only four hours from now.' He looked more closely. 'But, shit, it stops at every small town in Dixie, and gets to Huntsville at two twenty-three this afternoon, local time.'

Bern put on a pair of spectacles and read over his shoulder. 'The next plane doesn't leave until nine o'clock, but it has fewer stops, and it's a Viscount, so it gets you to Huntsville earlier, a few minutes before noon.'

'I'd get the later plane, but I don't relish hanging around Washington any longer than I have to,' Luke said.

Bern said: 'You have two more problems. Number one, I think Anthony will have men at the airport.'

Luke frowned. 'Maybe I could leave here by car, and pick up a plane somewhere down the line.' He looked at the timetable. 'The early flight's first stop is a place called Newport News. Where the hell is that?'

'Near Norfolk, Virginia,' Billie said.

'It lands there at two minutes past eight. Can I get there in time?'

'It's two hundred miles,' Billie said. 'Say four hours. You can make it with an hour to spare.'

Bern said: 'More, if you take my car. It has a top speed of a hundred and fifteen.'

'You'd lend me your car?'

Bern smiled. 'We've both saved each other's lives. A car is nothing.'

Luke nodded. 'Thanks.'

'But you have a second problem,' Bern said.

'What's that?'

'I was followed here.'

3 A.M.

The fuel tanks contain baffles to prevent sloshing. Without the baffles, the movement of the liquid is so violent that it caused a test missile, Jupiter 1B, to disintegrate after 93 seconds of flight.

Anthony sat at the wheel of his yellow Cadillac a block from the diner. He had parked tight up against the rear of a truck, so that his distinctive automobile was mostly shielded from view, but he could clearly see the diner and the stretch of sidewalk brightened by the light spilling from its windows. It appeared to be a cop hang-out: there were two patrol cars parked outside, along with Billie's red Thunderbird and Bern's white Continental.

Ackie Horwitz had been stationed outside Bern Rothsten's apartment, with instructions to stay there unless Luke showed up; but, when Bern left in the middle of the night, Ackie had had the good sense to disobey orders and follow on his motorcycle. As soon as Bern arrived at the diner, Ackie had called Q Building and alerted Anthony.

Now Ackie came out of the diner in his motorcycle leathers, carrying a container of coffee in one hand

and a candy bar in the other. He came to Anthony's window. 'Lucas is in there,' he said.

'I knew it,' Anthony said with malevolent satisfaction.

'But he's changed his clothes. He has a black coat and a black hat now.'

'He lost his other hat at the Carlton.'

'Rothsten is with him, and the girl.'

'Who else is in there?'

'Four cops telling dirty jokes, an insomniac reading the early edition of tomorrow's *Washington Post*, and the cook.'

Anthony nodded. He could not do anything to Luke with the cops present. 'We wait here until Luke comes out, then we both follow him. This time, we're not going to lose him.'

'Gotcha.' Ackie went to his motorcycle, behind Anthony's car, and sat in the saddle to drink his coffee.

Anthony planned ahead. They would catch up with Luke in a quiet street, overpower him, and take him to a CIA safe house in Chinatown. At that point Anthony would get rid of Ackie. Then he would kill Luke.

He felt coldly determined. He had suffered a moment of emotional weakness at the Carlton earlier, but afterwards he had hardened his heart, resolving not to think about friendship and betrayal until this was all over. He knew he was doing the right thing. He would deal with regrets after he had done his duty.

The door of the diner opened.

Billie came out first. The bright lights were behind her, so Anthony could not see her face, but he recognized her small figure and the characteristic sway of her walk. Next came a man in a black coat and black hat: Luke. They went to the red Thunderbird. The figure in the trench coat bringing up the rear got into the white Lincoln.

Anthony started his engine.

The T-bird moved away, followed by the Lincoln. Anthony waited a few seconds, then pulled out. Ackie tucked in behind on his motorcycle.

Billie headed west, and the little convoy followed. Anthony stayed a block and a half behind, but the streets were deserted, so they were sure to notice they were being tailed. Anthony felt fatalistic about it. There was no further point in deception: this was the showdown.

They came to 14th Street and stopped for a red light, and Anthony came up behind Bern's Lincoln. When the light turned green, Billie's Thunderbird suddenly shot forward, while the Lincoln remained stationary.

Cursing, Anthony reversed a few yards, then threw the shift into drive and stamped on the gas pedal. The big car shot forward. He swung around the standing Lincoln and raced after the others.

Billie zigzagged through the neighbourhood at the back of the White House, shooting red lights, defying No Turn signs, and driving the wrong way on one-way streets. Anthony did the same, desperately trying to stay on her tail, but the Cadillac could not match the T-bird for manoeuvrability, and she drew away.

Ackie passed Anthony and stayed right on Billie's

tail. However, as she increased her lead over Anthony, he guessed that her game plan was first to shake the Cadillac by twisting and turning, then get on to a freeway and outrun the motorcycle, which could not match the T-bird's top speed of 125. 'Hell,' he said.

Then luck intervened. Screeching around a corner, Billie ran into a flood. Water was gushing out of a drain at the kerbside, and the entire width of the road was two or three inches under. She lost control of her car. The tail of the Thunderbird swung around in a wide arc, and the vehicle spun through a half-circle. Ackie veered around her, his bike slipped from under him, and he fell off and rolled in the water, but got up immediately. Anthony jammed on the brakes of the Cadillac and skidded to a halt at the intersection. The Thunderbird came to a halt slewed across the street, with its trunk an inch from a parked car. Anthony pulled across its front, blocking it in. Billie could not get away.

Ackie was already at the driver's door of the Thunderbird. Anthony ran to the passenger side. 'Get out of the car!' he yelled. He drew the gun from his inside pocket.

The door opened, and the figure in the black coat and hat got out.

Anthony saw immediately that it was not Luke, but Bern.

He turned and looked back the way they had come. There was no sign of the white Lincoln.

Rage boiled up inside him. They had switched coats, and Luke had escaped in Bern's car. 'You fucking idiot!' he screamed at Bern. He felt like shooting him on the spot. 'You don't know what you've done!'

Bern was infuriatingly calm. 'Then tell me, Anthony,' he said. 'What have I done?'

Anthony turned away and stuffed the gun back into his coat.

'Wait a minute,' Bern said. 'You've got some explaining to do. What you did to Luke is illegal.'

'I don't have to explain one goddamn thing to you,' Anthony spat.

'Luke's not a spy.'

'How would you know a thing like that?'

'I know.'

'I don't believe you.'

Bern gave him a hard look. 'Sure you do,' he said. 'You know perfectly well that Luke is not a Soviet agent. So why the hell are you pretending otherwise?'

'Go to hell,' Anthony said, and he walked away.

* * *

Billie lived in Arlington, a leafy suburb on the Virginia side of the Potomac river. Anthony drove along her street. As he passed her house, he saw on the other side of the road a dark-coloured Chevrolet sedan belonging to the CIA. He turned a corner and parked.

Billie would come home in the next couple of hours. She knew where Luke had gone. But she would not tell Anthony. He had lost her trust. She would stay loyal to Luke now – unless Anthony put her under extraordinary pressure.

So that was what he would do.

Was he crazy? A small voice in his head kept asking if the race was worth the prize. Was there any justification for what he was about to do? He pushed his doubts aside. He had chosen his destiny long ago, and he was not to be deflected from it, not even by Luke.

He opened the trunk of his car and took out a black leather case, the size of a hardcover book, and a pencil flashlight. Then he walked back to the Chevy. He slid into the passenger seat beside Pete and sat looking at the dark windows of Billie's little house. He thought: This will be the worst thing I have ever done.

He looked at Pete. 'Do you trust me?' he said.

Pete's disfigured face twisted in an embarrassed grin. 'What kind of question is that? Yes, I trust you.'

Most of the young agents hero-worshipped Anthony, but Pete had an extra reason for being loyal to him. Anthony had discovered something about Pete that could get him fired – the fact that he had once been arrested for soliciting a prostitute – but he had kept it secret. Now, to remind Pete of that, he said: 'If I did something that seemed wrong to you, would you still back me up?'

Pete hesitated, and when he spoke his voice was choked with emotion. 'Let me tell you something.' He looked ahead, through the windscreen, at the lamplit street. 'You've been like a father to me, that's all.'

'I'm going to do something you won't like. I need you to trust me that it's the right thing to do.'

'I'm telling you – you got it.'

'I'm going in,' Anthony said. 'Honk if anyone arrives.'

He walked softly up the driveway, circled around the garage and went to the back door. He shone his flashlight through the kitchen window. The familiar table and chairs stood in darkness.

He had lived a life of deception and betrayal, but this, he thought with a surge of self-loathing, was the lowest he had ever sunk.

The kitchen door had an old-fashioned two-way lock with a key on the inside. Anthony could have opened it with a pencil. He put the flask in his mouth, then unzipped the leather case and took out an instrument like a dental probe. He slid it into the keyhole, pushing the key out on the far side. It fell on to the mat with no sound. He twisted the probe and unlocked the door.

Silently, he stepped into the darkened house. He knew his way around. He checked the living room first, then Billie's bedroom. Both were empty. Next he looked in on Becky-Ma. She was fast asleep, her hearing aid on the bedside table. Last he went into Larry's room.

He shone his flash on the sleeping child, feeling sick with guilt. He sat on the edge of the bed and switched on the light. 'Hey, Larry, wake up,' he said. 'Come on.'

The boy's eyes opened. After a disoriented moment, he grinned. 'Uncle Anthony!' he said, and he smiled.

'Time to get up,' Anthony said.

'What time is it?'

'It's early.'

'What are we going to do?'

'It's a surprise,' Anthony said.

4.30 A.M.

Fuel shoots into the combustion chamber of the rocket engine at a speed of about 100 feet per second. Burning begins the instant the fluids meet. The heat of the flame soon evaporates the liquids. Pressure rises to several hundred pounds per square inch, and the temperature soars to 5,000 degrees Fahrenheit.

Bern said to Billie: 'You're in love with Luke, aren't you.'

They were sitting in her car outside his building. She did not want to go in: she was impatient to get home to Larry and Becky-Ma.

'In love?' she said evasively. 'Am I?' She was not sure how much she wanted to share with her ex-husband. They were friends, but not intimate.

'It's okay,' he said. 'I realized long ago that you should have married Luke. I don't think you ever stopped loving him. You loved me, too, but in a different way.'

That was true. Her love for Bern was a gentle, calm feeling. With him she had never felt the hurricane of passion that engulfed her when she was with Luke. And when she asked herself what she felt for Harold –

the easy affection or the whirlwind of excitement – the answer was depressingly obvious. Thinking about Harold gave her a pleasant but mild sense of pleasure. She had little experience of men – the only ones she had slept with were Luke and Bern – but instinct told her that with Harold she would never have the feeling Luke gave her of a sexual craving that left her weak and helpless with desire.

'Luke's married,' she said. 'To a beautiful woman.' She thought for a moment. 'Is Elspeth sexy?'

Bern frowned. 'Hard to say. She could be, with the right guy. To me she seemed cold, but she never had eyes for anyone but Luke.'

'Not that it matters. Luke is the faithful type. He'd stay with her if she was an iceberg, just out of a sense of duty.' She paused. 'There's something I have to say to you.'

'Okay.'

'Thank you. For not saying "I told you so." I sure appreciate your restraint.'

Bern laughed. 'You're thinking about our great quarrel.'

She nodded. 'You said my work would be used to brainwash people. Now your prediction has come true.'

'All the same, I was wrong. Your work had to be done. We need to understand the human brain. People may use knowledge to do evil, but we can't hold up scientific progress. But, listen, do you have a theory about what Anthony is up to?'

'Best I could come up with: I imagine Luke

313

discovered a spy down there at Cape Canaveral, and came to Washington to tell the Pentagon about it. But the spy is really a double agent, working for us, so Anthony is desperate to protect the guy.'

Bern shook his head. 'Not good enough. Anthony could have dealt with that simply by telling Luke that the spy was a double. He didn't have to wipe his memory.'

'I guess you're right. And Anthony *shot* at Luke a few hours ago. I know this secret agent work tends to go to men's heads, but I can't believe the CIA would actually kill an American citizen to protect a double agent.'

'Sure they would,' Bern said. 'But it wouldn't have been necessary. Anthony could just have trusted Luke.'

'Do you have a better theory?'

'No.'

Billie shrugged. 'I'm not sure it matters any more. Anthony has deceived and betrayed his friends – who cares why? Whatever strange purpose has driven him to this, we've lost him. And he was a good friend.'

'Life sucks,' Bern said. He kissed her cheek and got out of the car. 'If you hear from Luke tomorrow, call me.'

'Okay.'

Bern walked into the building, and Billie drove off.

She crossed the Memorial Bridge, skirted the National Cemetery, and zigzagged through the suburban streets to her home. She reversed into the driveway, a habit she had developed because she was usually in a hurry when leaving. She entered the house, hung her coat on the hall stand, and went straight upstairs, unbuttoning her dress and pulling it off over her head as she did so. She threw it over a chair, kicked off her shoes, and went to check on Larry.

When she saw the empty bed, she screamed.

She looked into the bathroom, then Becky-Ma's room. 'Larry!' she yelled at the top of her voice. 'Where are you?' She ran downstairs and went into every room. Still in her underwear, she left the house and looked in the garage and the yard. Going back inside, she went into every room again, opening closets and checking under beds, looking into every space large enough to hold a seven-year-old.

He had gone.

Becky-Ma came out of her bedroom, fear written on her lined face. 'What's happening?' she said shakily.

'Where's Larry?' Billie shouted.

'In his bed, I thought,' she said, her voice becoming a moan of misery as she realized what had happened.

Billie stood still for a moment, breathing hard, fighting down panic. Then she went into Larry's bedroom and studied it.

The room was tidy, with no signs of struggle. Checking his closet, she saw the blue teddy-bear pyjamas he had worn last night neatly folded on a shelf. The clothes she had set out for school today had gone. Whatever had happened, he had got dressed before leaving. It looked as if he had gone with someone he trusted.

Anthony.

At first she felt relief. Anthony would not harm

Larry. But then she thought again. Wouldn't he? She would have said Anthony would not harm Luke, but he had shot at him. There was no telling any more what Anthony would do. At the very least, Larry must have been frightened, to be woken up so early and made to get dressed and leave the house without seeing his mother.

She had to get him back fast.

She ran downstairs to call Anthony. Before she got to the phone, it rang. She snatched it up. 'Yes?'

'This is Anthony.'

'How could you do it?' she screamed. 'How could you be so cruel?'

'I have to know where Luke is,' he said coolly. 'It's unimaginably important.'

'He's gone—' She stopped herself. If she gave him the information, she would have no weapons left.

'Gone where?'

She took a breath. 'Where's Larry?'

'He's with me. He's fine, don't worry.'

That enraged her. 'How could I not worry, you dumb prick!'

'Just tell me what I need to know, and everything will be all right.'

She wanted to believe him, to blurt out the answer and trust him to bring Larry home, but she resisted the temptation fiercely.'Listen to me. When I see my son, I'll tell you where Luke is.'

'Don't you trust me?'

'Is that a joke?'

He sighed. 'Okay. Meet me at the Jefferson Memorial.'

She felt a small surge of triumph. 'When?'

'Seven o'clock.'

She checked her watch. It was after six. 'I'll be there.'

'Billie . . .'

'What?'

'Be alone.'

'Yeah.' She hung up.

Becky-Ma was standing by her side, looking frail and old. 'What is it?' she said. 'What's going on?'

Billie tried to give an impression of calm. 'Larry's with Anthony. He must have come in and got him while you were asleep. I'm going to pick him up now. We can stop worrying.'

She went upstairs and threw on some clothes. Then she picked up the dressing-table chair and placed it in front of the wardrobe. Standing on the chair, she took a small suitcase from on top of the wardrobe. She placed the case on the bed and opened it.

She unwrapped a cloth to reveal a .45 Colt Automatic.

They had all been issued with Colts in the war. She had kept hers as a souvenir, but some instinct made her clean and oil it regularly. Once you had been shot at, you were never comfortable unless you had a firearm someplace, she guessed.

She pressed the thumb release on the left side of the grip, behind the trigger, and drew the magazine

317

out of the grip. There was a box of bullets in the case. She loaded seven into the magazine, pushing them in one by one against the spring, then slid the magazine back into the butt until she felt it lock. She worked the slide to chamber a round.

She turned around to see Becky-Ma standing in the doorway, staring at the gun.

She looked back at her mother in silence for a moment.

Then she ran out of the house and jumped into her car.

6.30 A.M.

The first stage contains approximately 25,000 kilograms of fuel. This will be used up in two minutes and thirty-five seconds.

Bern's Lincoln Continental was a joy to drive, a sleek, long-legged car that cruised at a hundred, effortlessly flying over the deserted roads of sleeping Virginia. In getting out of Washington, Luke felt he was leaving the nightmare behind, and his early-hours journey had the exhilarating air of an escape.

It was still dark when he arrived at Newport News and pulled into the small parking lot next to the closed airport building. No lights showed except the solitary bulb of a phone booth next to the entrance. He turned off his engine and listened to the silence. The night was clear, and the airfield was starlit. The parked planes seemed peculiarly still, like horses asleep on their feet.

He had been up more than twenty-four hours, and he felt desperately weary, but his mind was racing. He was in love with Billie. Now that he was two hundred miles away from her, he could admit that to himself. But what did it mean? Had he always loved her? Or

319

was it a one-day infatuation, a repeat of the crush he had developed so quickly back in 1941? And what about Elspeth? Why had he married her? He had asked Billie that, and she had refused to answer. 'I'll ask Elspeth,' he had said.

He checked his watch. He had more than an hour until take-off. There was plenty of time. He got out of the car and went to the phone booth.

She picked up fast, as if she was already awake. The hotel operator advised her that the phone charge would be added to her bill, and she said: 'Sure, sure, put him on.'

Suddenly he felt awkward. 'Uh, good morning, Elspeth.'

'I'm so glad you called!' she said. 'I've been out of my mind with worry – what's happening?'

'I don't know where to begin.'

'Are you okay?'

'Yes, I'm fine, now. Basically, Anthony caused me to lose my memory, by giving me a combination of electric shock and drugs.'

'Good God. Why would he do a thing like that?'

'He says I'm a Soviet spy.'

'That's absurd.'

'It's what he told Billie.'

'So you've been with Billie?'

Luke heard the note of hostility in Elspeth's voice. 'She's been kind,' he said defensively. He recalled that he had asked Elspeth to come to Washington and help him, but she had refused.

Elspeth changed the subject. 'Where are you calling from?'

He hesitated. His enemies might easily have tapped Elspeth's phone. 'I don't really want to say, in case someone is listening.'

'All right, I understand. What are you going to do next?'

'I need to find out what it was that Anthony wanted me to forget.'

'How will you do that?'

'I'd rather not say over the phone.'

Her voice betrayed exasperation. 'Well, I'm sorry you can't tell me anything.'

'Matter of fact, I called to ask you some things.'

'Okay, fire away.'

'Why can't we have children?'

'We don't know. Last year, you went to a fertility specialist, but he couldn't find anything wrong. A few weeks ago, I saw a woman doctor in Atlanta. She ran some tests. We're waiting for the results.'

'Would you tell me how we came to get married?'

'I seduced you.'

'How?'

'I pretended to have soap in my eye, in order to make you kiss me. It's the oldest trick in the book, and I'm embarrassed that you fell for it.'

He could not tell whether she was being amusing, or cynical, or both. 'Tell me what the circumstances were, how I proposed.'

'Well, I didn't see you for years, then we met again

in 1954, in Washington,' she began. 'I was still with the CIA. You were working at the Jet Propulsion Laboratory in Pasadena, but you flew in for Peg's wedding. We were seated together at the breakfast.' She paused, remembering, and he waited patiently. When she resumed, her voice had softened. 'We talked and talked – it was as if thirteen years had never happened, and we were still a couple of college kids with all of life ahead of us. I had to leave early – I was conductor of the 16th Street Youth Orchestra, and we had a rehearsal. You came with me . . .'

1954

The children in the orchestra were all poor, and most of them were black. The rehearsal took place at a church hall in a slum neighbourhood. The instruments were begged, borrowed, and bought from pawnshops. They were rehearsing the overture from a Mozart opera, *The Marriage of Figaro*. Against the odds, they played well.

Elspeth was the reason. She was an exacting teacher, noticing every false note and rhythmic misstep, but she corrected her pupils with infinite patience. A tall figure in a yellow dress, she conducted the orchestra with enormous verve, her red hair flying, her long, elegant hands drawing the music from them with passionate gestures.

The rehearsal lasted two hours and Luke sat through the whole thing, mesmerized. He could see that all the boys were in love with Elspeth and all the girls wanted to be like her.

'These children have as much music in them as any rich kid with a Steinway in the drawing room,' she said in the car afterwards. 'But I get into lots of trouble.'

'Why, for God's sake?'

'I'm called a nigger-lover,' she said. 'And it's pretty much ended my career at the CIA.'

'I don't understand.'

'Anyone who treats Negroes like human beings is suspected of being a communist. So I'll never be more than a secretary. Not that it's a great loss. Women never get higher than case officer anyway.'

She took him to her place, a small, uncluttered apartment with a few pieces of angular modern furniture. Luke made martinis and Elspeth started to cook spaghetti in the tiny kitchen. Luke told her about his job.

'I'm so happy for you,' she said with generous enthusiasm. 'You always wanted to explore outer space. Even back at Harvard, when we were dating, you used to talk about it.'

He smiled. 'And in those days, most people thought it was a foolish dream of science-fiction writers.'

'I guess we still can't be sure it will happen.'

'I think we can,' he said seriously. 'The big problems were all solved by German scientists in the war. The Germans built rockets that could be fired in Holland and land on London.'

'I was there, I remember – we called them buzz-bombs.' She shuddered briefly. 'One nearly killed me. I was walking to my office in the middle of an air raid, because I had to brief an agent who was to be dropped into Belgium a few hours later. I heard a bomb go off behind me. It makes a horrible noise like *crump*, then there's the sound of breaking glass and masonry collapsing, and a kind of wind full of dust and little bits of stone. I knew that if I turned around to look, I'd panic and throw myself to the ground, and just curl up in a ball with my eyes shut. So I looked straight ahead and kept walking.'

Luke was moved by the picture of the young Elspeth walking through the dark streets as the bombs fell around her, and he felt grateful that she had survived. 'Brave woman,' he murmured.

She shrugged. 'I didn't feel brave, just scared.'

'What did you think about?'

'Can't you guess?'

He recalled that whenever she was idle she thought about math. 'Prime numbers?' he hazarded.

She laughed. 'Fibonacci's numbers.'

Luke nodded. The mathematician Fibonacci had imagined a pair of rabbits that produced two offspring every month, offspring that began to breed at the same rate one month after birth, and asked how many pairs of rabbits there would be after a year. The answer was 144, but the number of pairs of rabbits each month was the most famous sequence of numbers in mathematics: 1, 1, 2, 3, 5, 8, 13, 21, 34, 55, 89, 144 ... You could always work out the next number by adding up the previous two.

Elspeth said: 'By the time I got to my office, I had worked out the fortieth Fibonacci number.'

'Do you remember what it is?'

'Of course: one hundred and two million, three hundred and thirty-four thousand, one hundred and five. So, our missiles are based on the German buzz-bombs?'

'More on their V2 rocket, to be exact.' Luke was not supposed to talk about his work, but this was Elspeth, and anyway she probably had a higher security rating than he did. 'We're building a rocket that can take off in Arizona and explode in Moscow. And, if we can do that, we can fly to the moon.'

'So it's just the same thing on a larger scale?'

She showed more interest in rocketry than any other girl he had ever met. 'Yes. We need larger engines, more efficient fuel, better guidance systems, that kind of thing. None of these problems are insurmountable. Plus, those German scientists are working for us now.'

'I think I heard that.' She changed the subject. 'And what about life in general? Are you dating someone?'

'Not right now.' He had dated several girls since his break-up with Billie nine years ago, and had slept with some of them, but the truth – which he did not want to tell Elspeth – was that none had meant much.

There had been one woman he might have loved, a tall girl with brown eyes and wild hair. She had the kind of energy and *joie de vivre* that he loved about Billie. He had met her at Harvard while he was doing his doctorate. Late one evening, as they strolled together through Harvard Yard, she had taken his hands and said: 'I have a husband.' Then she had kissed him and walked away. That was the nearest he had come to giving his heart.

'How about you?' he asked Elspeth. 'Peg's married, Billie's already getting divorced – you've got some catching-up to do.'

'Oh, you know about us government girls.' The

phrase was a newspaper cliché. So many young women worked for the government in Washington that they outnumbered single men by five to one. Consequently they were stereotyped as sexually frustrated and desperate for dates. Luke did not believe Elspeth was like that, but if she wanted to evade his question, she was entitled.

She asked him to watch the stove while she freshened up. There was a big pan of spaghetti and a smaller one of bubbling tomato sauce. He took off his jacket and tie, then stirred the sauce with a wooden spoon. The martini had made him mellow, the food smelled good, and he was with a woman he really liked. He felt happy.

He heard Elspeth call out, with an uncharacteristic note of helplessness: 'Luke – could you come here?'

He stepped into the bathroom. Elspeth's dress hung on the back of the door, and she stood in a strapless peach-coloured brassiere and matching half-slip, stockings and shoes. Although she was wearing more clothes than if she had been on the beach, Luke found it unbearably sexy to see her in her underwear. Her hand was to her face. 'I got soap in my eye, damn it,' she said. 'Would you try to wash it out?'

Luke ran cold water into the washbasin. 'Bend down, get your face close to the bowl,' he said, encouraging her with his left hand between her shoulder blades. The pale skin of her back was soft and warm to his touch. He cupped water in his right hand and raised it to her eye.

'That helps,' she said.

327

He rinsed her eye again and again until she said the stinging had stopped. Then he stood her upright and patted her face dry with a clean towel. 'Your eye is a little bloodshot, but I guess it's okay,' he said.

'I must look a mess.'

'No.' He looked hard at her. Her eye was red and her hair on that side was wet in patches, but nevertheless she was as stunning as she had been on the day he first set eyes on her, more than a decade ago. 'You're absolutely beautiful.'

Her head was still tilted up, though he had stopped drying her face. Her lips were parted in a smile. It was the easiest thing in the world to kiss her. She kissed him back, hesitantly at first, then she put her hands behind his neck and pulled his face to hers and kissed him hard.

Her bra pressed against his chest. It should have been sexy, but the wiring was so stiff that it scratched his chest through the fine cotton of his shirt. After a moment he pulled away, feeling foolish. 'What?' she said.

He lightly touched the brassiere and said with a grin: 'It hurts.'

'You poor thing,' she said with mock pity.

She reached behind her back and unfastened the bra with a swift movement. It fell to the floor.

He had touched her breasts a few times, all those years ago, but he had never seen them. They were white and round, and the pale nipples were puckered with excitement. She put her arms around his neck and pressed her body to his. Her breasts were soft and warm. 'There,' she said. 'That's how it should feel.'

After a while he picked her up, stepped into the bedroom, and laid her on the bed. She kicked off her shoes. He touched the waistband of her half-slip and said: 'May I?'

She giggled. 'Oh, Luke, you're so polite!'

He grinned. It was kind of silly, but he did not know how else to be. She lifted her hips and he pulled off the slip. Her pink panties matched the rest of her underwear.

'Don't ask,' she said. 'Just take them off.'

When they made love it was slow and intense. She kept pulling his head to hers and kissing his face while he moved in and out of her. 'I've wanted this for so long,' she whispered into his ear; and then she cried out with pleasure, several times, and lay back, exhausted.

Soon Elspeth fell into a deep sleep, but Luke lay awake, thinking about his life.

He had always wanted a family. For him, happiness was a big, noisy house full of children and friends and pets. Yet here he was, thirty-three and single, and the years seemed to go by faster and faster. Since the war, his career had been his priority, he told himself. He had gone back to college, making up for the lost years. But that was not the real reason he was unmarried. The truth was that only two women had ever touched his heart – Billie and Elspeth. Billie had deceived him, but Elspeth was here beside him. He looked at her voluptuous body in the faint glow of the lights of Dupont Circle outside. Could there be anything better than spending every night like this, with a girl who was smart, brave as a lion, wonderful with children, and – on top of all that – stunningly beautiful?

At daybreak he got up and made coffee. He brought it into the bedroom on a tray, and found Elspeth sitting up in bed, looking sleepily delectable. She smiled happily at him.

'I have something to ask you,' he said. He sat on the edge of the bed and took her hand. 'Will you marry me?'

Her smile disappeared and she looked troubled. 'Oh, my God,' she said. 'Can I think about it?'

7 A.M.

*The exhaust gases pass through the nozzle of the rocket like a
cup of hot coffee being poured down the throat of a snowman.*

Anthony drove up to the Jefferson Memorial with Larry
sitting in the front seat between him and Pete. It was
still dark, and the area was deserted. He turned the
car around and parked so that its headlights would
shine at any other car that came along.

The monument was a double circle of pillars with a
domed roof. It stood on a high platform approached
by steps at the rear. 'The statue is nineteen feet high
and weighs ten thousand pounds,' he told Larry. 'It's
made of bronze.'

'Where is it?'

'You can't see it from here, but it's inside those
pillars.'

'We should have come in the daytime,' Larry
whined.

Anthony had taken Larry out before. They had gone
to the White House and the zoo and the Smithsonian.
They would get hot dogs for lunch and eat ice cream
in the afternoon, and Anthony would buy Larry a toy
before taking him home again. They always had a good

time. Anthony was fond of his godson. But today Larry knew something was wrong. It was too early and he wanted his mother and he probably sensed the tension in the car.

Anthony opened the door. 'Stay here a second, Larry, while I talk to Pete,' he said. The two men got out. Their breath misted in the cold air.

Anthony said to Pete: 'I'll wait here. You take the kid and show him the monument. Stay this side, so that she'll see him when she arrives.'

'Right.' Pete's voice was cold and abrupt.

'I hate this,' Anthony said. In truth, he was past caring. Larry was unhappy, and Billie was frantic with fear, but they would get over it, and he was not going to allow sentiment to get in his way. 'We're not going to harm the kid, or his mother,' he said, trying to reassure Pete. 'But she'll tell us where Luke has gone.'

'Then we give back the kid.'

'No.'

'We don't?' Pete's expression was concealed by the darkness, but his voice betrayed dismay. 'Why not?'

'In case we need more information from her later.'

Pete was troubled, but he would acquiesce, at least for now, Anthony thought. He opened the car door. 'Come on, Larry. Uncle Pete's going to show you the statue.'

Larry got out. With careful politeness he said: 'After we've seen it, I think I'd like to go home.'

Anthony's breath caught in his throat. Larry's bravery was almost too much. After a moment,

Anthony replied in a calm voice: 'We'll check with Mommy. Now go ahead.'

The child took Pete's hand and they walked around the monument toward the steps at the back. A minute later they appeared in front of the pillars, lit by the car's headlights.

Anthony checked his watch. Sixteen hours from now, the rocket would have taken off, and it would all be over, one way or another. Sixteen hours was a lot, plenty of time for Luke to do unlimited damage. Anthony had to catch him, fast.

Billie should be here by now. He suffered a pang of doubt. Surely she would come? She was too frightened and panicky to call the cops, or pull any kind of stunt, he felt certain.

He was right. A few moments later, another car arrived. Anthony could not see the colour, but it was a Ford Thunderbird. It parked twenty yards from Anthony's Cadillac and a small, slight figure jumped out, leaving the engine running.

'Hello, Billie,' said Anthony.

She looked from him to the monument and saw Pete and Larry up on the raised platform, looking into the circle. She stood frozen, staring.

Anthony walked toward her. 'Don't try anything dramatic – it would upset Larry.'

'Don't talk to me about upsetting him, you son of a bitch.' Her voice cracked with strain. She was near to tears.

'I had to do this.'

333

'Nobody *has* to do something like this.'

Her hostility was hardly surprising, but all the same her contempt stung him. He said: 'Do you know the quote from Thomas Jefferson that appears inside this monument, in letters two feet high? It says: "I have sworn upon the altar of God eternal hostility against every form of tyranny over the mind of man." That's why I'm doing it.'

'The hell with your motives. You've lost sight of whatever ideals you once had. Nothing good can survive this kind of treachery.'

It was a waste of time arguing with her. 'Where's Luke?' he said abruptly.

There was a long pause. At last she said: 'Luke caught a plane to Huntsville.'

Anthony breathed a deep sigh of satisfaction. He had what he needed.

He was also surprised at the answer. 'Why Huntsville?'

'It's where the army designs the rockets.'

'I know that. But why would he go there today? Florida is where it's all happening.'

'I don't know why.'

Anthony tried to read her face, but it was too dark. 'I think you're holding something back.'

'I don't care what you think. I'm going to take my son and leave.'

'No, you're not,' Anthony said. 'We're keeping him for a while.'

Billie's voice was a cry of anguish. 'Why? I've told you where Luke went!'

'There may be other ways you can help us.'

'It's not fair!'

'You'll live.' He turned away.

That was his mistake.

* * *

Billie had been half-expecting this.

As Anthony stepped towards his car, she rushed him. With her right shoulder, she hit him in the small of the back. She weighed only 120 pounds, and he had to be fifty pounds heavier, but she had surprise and rage on her side. He stumbled and fell forward, coming down on his hands and knees. He grunted with surprise and pain.

Billie took the Colt from her coat pocket.

As Anthony tried to get up, she charged him again, this time from the side. He crashed to the ground, rolling. As he came face up, she dropped to one knee beside his head and shoved the barrel of the gun forcefully into his mouth. She felt a tooth break.

He froze.

Deliberately, she moved the safety catch up to the firing position. She looked into his eyes and saw fear. He had not expected the gun. A trickle of blood appeared on his chin.

Billie looked up. Larry and the man with him were still gazing at the monument, unaware of the fracas. She returned her attention to Anthony. 'I'm going to take the gun out of your mouth,' she said, panting. 'If you move, I'll kill you. If you're still alive, you're going to call to your colleague and tell him what I say.' She took the gun out of Anthony's mouth and pointed it at his left eye. 'Now,' she said. 'Call him.'

Anthony hesitated.

She touched the barrel of the pistol to his eyelid.

'Pete!' he shouted.

Pete looked around. There was a pause. Pete said in a puzzled tone: 'Where are you?' Anthony and Billie were outside the range of the headlights.

Billie said: 'Tell him to stay where he is.'

Anthony said nothing. Billie pressed the gun into his eye. Anthony shouted: 'Stay where you are!'

Pete put his hand to his forehead, peering into the dark, looking for the source of the voice. 'What's happening?' he called. 'I can't see you.'

Billie shouted: 'Larry, this is Mom. Get in the T-bird!'

Pete grabbed Larry's arm.

'The man won't let me!' Larry screamed.

'Stay calm!' Billie yelled. 'Uncle Anthony's going to tell the man to let you go.' She pressed the gun barrel harder into Anthony's eye.

'All right!' Anthony cried. She eased the pressure. He shouted: 'Let the kid go!'

Pete said: 'Are you sure?'

'Do what I say, for Christ's sake – she's got a gun on me!'

'Okay!' Pete released Larry's arm.

Larry headed toward the back of the monument then reappeared, seconds later, at ground level. He ran towards Billie. 'Not this way,' she said, struggling to keep her voice calm. 'Get in the car, quickly.'

Larry ran to the Thunderbird and jumped in, slamming the door.

With a quick lashing movement, Billie hit Anthony on both sides of his face with the gun, as hard as she could. He cried out in pain, but before he could move she pushed the gun into his mouth again. He lay still, groaning. She said: 'Remember that if you're ever tempted to kidnap a child again.'

She stood up, withdrawing the gun from his mouth. 'Stay still,' she commanded. She backed towards her car, keeping the gun on him. She glanced up at the monument. Pete had not moved.

She got into her car.

Larry said: 'Have you got a gun?'

She stuffed the Colt inside her jacket. 'Are you okay?' she asked him.

He started to cry.

She shoved the gearshift into first and tore away.

8 A.M.

The smaller rockets that power the second, third and last stages use a solid fuel known as T17-E2, a polysulphide with ammonium perchlorate as oxidizer. Each rocket generates about 1,600 pounds of thrust in space.

Bern poured warm milk over Larry's cornflakes while Billie beat up an egg for french toast. They were giving their child comfort food, but Billie felt the adults needed comfort too. Larry was eating heartily and listening to the radio at the same time.

'I'm going to kill that son of a bitch Anthony,' Bern muttered, speaking quietly so that Larry would not hear. 'I swear to God, I'll fucking kill him.'

Billie's rage had evaporated. Pistol-whipping Anthony had gotten rid of it all. Now she was worried and frightened – partly for Larry, who had had a nasty fright, and partly for Luke. 'I'm afraid Anthony may try to kill Luke,' she said.

Bern dropped a knob of butter into a hot frying pan, then dipped a slice of white bread into the egg mixture Billie had made. 'Luke won't kill easy.'

'But he thinks he's escaped – he doesn't know I've told Anthony where he is.' While Bern fried the egg-

338

soaked bread, Billie walked up and down the kitchen, biting her lip. 'Anthony is probably on his way to Huntsville now. Luke's on a slow plane. Anthony could get a MATS flight and be there first. I have to find a way to warn Luke.'

'Leave a message at the airport?'

'It's not reliable enough. I think I have to go there myself. There was a Viscount that left at nine, wasn't there? Where's that airline guide?'

'Right on the table.'

Billie picked it up. Flight 271 left Washington at exactly nine. Unlike Luke's flight, this one stopped only twice, landing at Huntsville four minutes before noon. Luke's flight did not land until two twenty-three. She could be waiting for him at the airport. 'I can do it,' she said.

'Then you should.'

Billie hesitated, looking at Larry, torn by conflicting urges.

Bern read her mind. 'He'll be okay.'

'I know, but I don't want to leave him, today of all days.'

'I'll take care of him.'

'Would you keep him out of school?'

'Yes, I think that'd be a good idea, at least for today.'

Larry said: 'I've finished my cornflakes.'

Bern said: 'Then you must be just about ready for some french toast.' He slid a slice on to a plate. 'Want some maple syrup with that?'

'Yeah.'

'Yes, what?'

'Yes, please.'

Bern poured syrup from a bottle.

Billie sat opposite her son and said: 'I want you to skip school today.'

'But I'll miss swimming!' he protested.

'Maybe Daddy will take you swimming.'

'But I'm not sick!'

'I know, honey, but you had kind of a tiring morning, and you need to rest.' Larry's protests reassured Billie. He seemed to be recovering fast. All the same, she would not be comfortable letting him go to school, not until this whole business was over.

But she could leave him with his father. Bern was a trained agent and could protect his kid from just about anything. She made a decision. She would go to Huntsville. 'Have a fun day with Daddy and maybe you'll go to school tomorrow, okay?'

'Okay.'

'Mommie has to go now.' She did not want to make a drama of saying goodbye, for that would only scare the child. 'I'll see you later,' she said casually.

As she went out, she heard Bern say: 'I bet you couldn't eat another slice of that french toast.'

'I could too!' Larry replied.

Billie closed the door.

PART 5

PART 5

10.45 A.M.

The missile will take off vertically, then be tilted into a trajectory inclined forty degrees to the horizon. The first stage is guided, during powered flight, by aerodynamic tail surfaces and by movable carbon vanes in the engine exhaust jet.

Luke fell asleep as soon as he had fastened his seat belt, and he was unaware of the take-off from Newport News. He slept heavily while the plane was in the air, but woke up every time it bumped down at yet another airstrip on its stop-go flight west across Virginia and North Carolina. Each time his eyes opened he felt a rush of anxiety, and checked his watch to see how many hours and minutes were left until the launch. He would fidget in his seat while the little aircraft taxied across the apron. A few people would leave, one or two more would get on, and the plane would take off again. It was like riding the bus.

The plane refuelled at Winston-Salem, and the passengers got off for a few minutes. Luke called Redstone Arsenal from the terminal and got his secretary, Marigold Clark, on the phone.

'Dr Lucas!' she said. 'Are you okay?'

'I'm fine, but I only have a minute or two. Is the launch still scheduled for tonight?'

'Yes, ten-thirty.'

'I'm on my way to Huntsville – my plane lands at two twenty-three. I'm trying to figure out why I went there on Monday.'

'You still don't have your memory back?'

'No. Now, you don't know why I made that trip.'

'Like I said, you didn't tell me.'

'What did I do there?'

'Well, now, let me see. I met you at the airport in an army car and brought you here to the base. You went into the Computation Lab, then drove yourself down to the south end.'

'What's there, at the south end?'

'The static test pads. I imagine you went into the Engineering Building – you sometimes work there – but I don't know for sure, because I wasn't with you.'

'And then?'

'You asked me to drive you to your home.' Luke heard a prim note enter her voice. 'I waited in the car while you stepped inside for a minute or two. Then I took you to the airport.'

'That's it?'

'That's all I know.'

Luke grunted with frustration. He had felt sure Marigold would come up with some clue.

Desperately, he cast about for another line of questioning. 'How did I look?'

'Okay, but your mind was someplace else. Preoccupied, that's the word I'm searching for. I figured you were worried about something. Happens all the time with you scientists. I don't let it trouble me.'

'Wearing my usual clothes?'

'One of them nice tweed jackets.'

'Carrying anything?'

'Just your little suitcase. Oh, and a file.'

Luke stopped breathing for a moment. 'A file?' he said. He swallowed.

A stewardess interrupted him. 'Time to board the aircraft, please, Dr Lucas.'

He covered the mouthpiece with his hand and said: 'Just one minute.' Then he said to Marigold: 'Was it any special kind of file?'

'A standard army file folder, thin cardboard, buff-coloured, large enough to hold business letters.'

'Any idea what was in it?'

'Just papers, it looked like.'

Luke tried to breathe normally. 'How many sheets of paper? One, ten, a hundred?'

'Maybe fifteen or twenty, I guess.'

'Did you happen to see what was on the sheets?'

'No, sir, you didn't take them out.'

'And did I still have this file when you took me to the airport?'

There was a silence at the other end.

The stewardess returned. 'Dr Lucas, if you won't board the plane, we'll have to go without you.'

'I'm coming, I'm coming.' He began to repeat his question to Marigold. 'Did I still have the file—'

'I heard you,' she interrupted. 'I'm trying to remember.'

He bit his lip. 'Take your time.'

'Whether you had it at the house, I can't tell.'

'But at the airport?'

'You know, I don't believe you had it then. I'm picturing you walking away from me into the terminal, and I see you have your bag in one hand, and in the other . . . nothing.'

'Are you sure?'

'Yes, now I am. You must have left that file here somewhere, either at the base or at home.'

Luke's mind was racing. The file was the reason for his trip to Huntsville, he felt sure. It contained the secret he had found out, the one that Anthony was so desperate for him to forget. Maybe it was a Xerox copy of the original, and he had stashed it somewhere for safe keeping. That was why he had asked Marigold not to tell anyone of his visit. It seemed ultra-cautious, but not doubt he had learned such habits in the war.

Now, if he could find the file, he could discover the secret.

The stewardess had abandoned him, and he saw her running across the tarmac. The plane's propellers were already turning.

'I think that file could be very important,' he told Marigold. 'Could you look around and see if it's there?'

'My lord, Dr Lucas, this is the army! Don't you know there must be a million of them buff-coloured file folders here? How would I know which is the one you were carrying?'

'Just check around, see if there's one someplace

346

where it shouldn't be. As soon as I land at Huntsville, I'll go to the house and search there. Then, if I don't find it, I'll come to the base.' Luke hung up and ran for the plane.

11 A.M.

The flight plan is programmed in advance. During flight, signals telemetered to the computer activate the guidance system to keep it on course.

The MATS flight to Huntsville was full of generals. Redstone Arsenal did more than design space rockets. It was the headquarters of the Army Ordnance Missile Command. Anthony, who kept track of this kind of thing, knew that a whole range of weapons were being developed and tested at the base – from the baseball-bat-sized Redeye, for ground troops to use against enemy aircraft, up to the huge surface-to-surface Honest John. The base undoubtedly saw a lot of brass.

Anthony wore sunglasses to conceal the two black eyes Billie had given him. His lip had stopped bleeding, and the broken tooth showed only when he talked. Despite his injuries, he felt energized: Luke was within his grasp.

Should he simply take the first opportunity to kill him? It was temptingly simple. But he worried that he did not know exactly what Luke was up to. He had to make a decision. However, by the time he boarded the plane he had been awake for forty-eight hours straight, and he fell asleep. He dreamed he was twenty-one again, and there were new leaves on the tall trees in Harvard Yard, and a life full of glorious possibilities stretched before him like an open road. Next thing he knew, Pete was shaking him as a corporal opened the aircraft door, and he woke up inhaling a warm Alabama breeze.

Huntsville had a civilian airport, but this was not it. MATS flights came down on the airstrip within Redstone Arsenal. The terminal building was a small wooden hut, the tower an open steel gantry with a one-room flight-control post on top.

Anthony shook his head to clear it as he walked across the parched grass. He was carrying the small bag that held his gun, a false passport, and five thousand dollars in cash, the emergency kit without which he never caught a plane.

Adrenalin enlivened him. In the next few hours he would kill a man, for the first time since the war. His stomach tensed as he thought of it. Where would he do it? One option was to wait for Luke at Huntsville Airport, follow him as he left, and gun him down on the road somewhere. But that was high-risk. Luke might well spot the tail and escape. He would never be an easy target. He could yet slip away, if Anthony were not extremely careful.

It might be best to find out where Luke was planning to go, then get there ahead and ambush him. 'I'm going to make some inquiries at the base,' he said to Pete. 'I want you to go to the airport and keep watch. If Luke arrives, or anything else happens, try to reach me here.'

At the edge of the airstrip, a young man in the uniform of a lieutenant waited with a card that read: 'Mr Carroll, State Department.' Anthony shook his hand. 'Colonel Hickam's compliments, sir,' the lieutenant said formally. 'As requested by the State Department, we have provided you with a car.' He pointed to an olive-drab Ford.

'That'll be fine,' Anthony said. He had called the base before catching his plane, brazenly pretending he was under orders from CIA Director Alan Dulles, and demanded army cooperation for a vital mission the details of which were classified. It had worked: this lieutenant seemed eager to please.

'Colonel Hickam would be glad if you would drop by headquarters at your convenience.' The lieutenant handed Anthony a map. The base was enormous, Anthony realized. It stretched several miles south, all the way to the Tennessee River. 'The headquarters building is marked on the map,' the soldier went on. 'And we have a message, asking you to call Mr Carl Hobart in Washington.'

'Thank you, Lieutenant. Where's Dr Claude Lucas's office?'

'That'll be the Computation Laboratory.' He took out a pencil and made a mark on the map. 'But all those guys are down to Cape Canaveral this week.'

'Does Dr Lucas have a secretary?'

'Yes – Mrs Marigold Clark.'

She might know Luke's movements. 'Good.

Lieutenant, this is my colleague Pete Maxell. He needs to get to the civilian airport to meet a flight.'

'I'd be glad to drive him there, sir.'

'I appreciate that. If he needs to reach me here at the base, what's the best way?'

The lieutenant looked at Pete. 'Sir, you could always leave a message at Colonel Hickam's office, and I would try to get it to Mr Carroll.'

'Good enough,' Anthony said decisively. 'Let's get going.'

He got into the Ford, checked the map, and started out. It was a typical army base. Arrow-straight roads ran through rough woodland broken by neat rectangles of lawn close-cropped like a conscript's haircut. The buildings were all flat-roofed structures of tan brick. It was well signposted, and he easily found the Computation Lab, a T-shaped building two storeys high. Anthony wondered why they needed so much space to make calculations, then realized they must have a powerful computer in there.

He parked outside and thought for a few moments. He had a simple question to ask: where in Huntsville did Luke plan to go? Marigold probably knew, but she would be defensive of Luke and wary of a stranger, especially one with two black eyes. However, she had been left behind here when most of the people she worked with had gone to Cape Canaveral for the big event, so she was probably also feeling lonely and bored.

He went into the building. In an outer office were three small desks, each with a typewriter. Two were vacant. The third was occupied by a Negro woman of about fifty wearing spectacles with diamanté rims, and a flowered cotton dress printed with daisies. 'Good afternoon,' he said.

She looked up. He took off his sunglasses. Her eyes widened in surprise at his appearance. 'Hello! How can I help you?'

With mock sincerity, he said: 'Ma'am, I'm looking for a wife who won't beat me up.'

Marigold burst out laughing.

Anthony pulled up a chair and sat to one side of her desk. 'I'm from Colonel Hickam's office,' he said. 'I'm looking for Marigold Clark. Where is she?'

'That's me.'

'Oh, no. The Miz Clark I'm looking for is a grown woman. You're just a young girl.'

'Now, you stop your jive,' she said, but she smiled broadly.

'Dr Lucas is on his way here – I guess you knew that.'

'He called me this morning.'

'What time do you expect him?'

'His plane lands at two twenty-three.'

That was useful. 'So he'll be here around three.'

'Not necessarily.'

Ah. 'Why not?'

She gave him what he wanted. 'Dr Lucas said he's going home first, then he'll stop by here.'

That was perfect. Anthony could hardly believe his luck. Luke was going from the airport straight to his house. Anthony could go there and wait, then shoot Luke as soon as he walked in the door. There would be no witnesses. If he used the silencer, no one would even hear a shot. Anthony would leave the body where it fell and drive away. With Elspeth in Florida, the corpse might not be found for days.

'Thank you,' he said to Marigold. He stood up. 'It was a pleasure to meet you.' He left the room before she could ask his name.

He returned to the car and drove to the headquarters building, a long three-storey monolith that looked like a prison. He found Colonel Hickam's office. The colonel was out, but a sergeant showed him to an empty room with a phone.

He called Q Building, but did not speak to his boss, Carl Hobart. Instead he asked for Carl's superior, George Cooperman. 'What's up, George?' he said.

'Did you shoot at someone last night?' said Cooperman, his smoker's voice sounding even more gravelly than usual.

With an effort, Anthony put on the swashbuckling persona that appealed to Cooperman. 'Aw, hell, who told you that?'

'Some colonel from the Pentagon called Tom Ealy in the Director's office, and Ealy told Carl Hobart, who had an orgasm.'

'There's no proof. I picked up all the slugs.'

'This colonel found a hole in the fucking wall about nine millimetres wide and he guessed what caused it. Did you hit anybody?'

'Unfortunately not.'

'You're in Huntsville now, right?'

'Yeah.'

'You're supposed to come back immediately.'

'Then it's a good thing I didn't talk to you.'

'Listen, Anthony, I always cut you as much slack as I can, because you get results. But I can't do any more for you on this one. You're on your own from here, buddy.'

'That's how I like it.'

'Good luck.'

Anthony hung up and sat staring at the phone. He did not have much more time. His Billy the Kid act was wearing thin. He could disobey orders for only so long. He needed to wrap this up fast.

He called Cape Canaveral and got Elspeth on the phone. 'Have you talked to Luke?' he asked her.

'He called me at six-thirty this morning.' She sounded shaky.

'Where from?'

'He wouldn't say where he was, where he was going, or what he intended to do, because he was afraid my phone might be tapped. But he told me you were responsible for his amnesia.'

'He's on his way to Huntsville. I'm at Redstone Arsenal now. I'm going to your house to wait for him there. Will I be able to get in?'

She answered with another question. 'Are you still trying to protect him?'

'Of course.'

'Will he be okay?'

'All I can do is my best.'

There was a moment's pause, then she said: 'There's a key under the bougainvillea pot in the back yard.'

'Thanks.'

'Take care of Luke, won't you?'

'I said I would do my best!'

'Don't snap at me,' she said with some of her more usual spirit.

'I'll take care of him.' He hung up.

He stood up to go, and the phone rang.

He wondered whether to answer. It might be Hobart. But Hobart did not know he was in Colonel Hickam's office. Only Pete knew that . . . he thought.

He picked up.

It was Pete. 'Dr Josephson's here!' he said.

'Shit.' Anthony had felt sure she was out of the picture. 'She just got off a plane?'

'Yeah, it must have been a faster flight than the one Lucas is on. She's sitting in the terminal building, like she's waiting.'

'For him,' Anthony said decisively. 'Damn her. She's come to warn him that we're here. You have to get her out of there.'

'How?'

'I don't care – just get rid of her!'

12 NOON

The Explorer's orbit will be at thirty-four degrees to the equator. Relative to the Earth's surface, it will head south-east across the Atlantic Ocean to the southern tip of Africa, then north-east across the Indian Ocean and Indonesia to the Pacific.

Huntsville Airport was small but busy. The single terminal building had a Hertz desk, some vending machines and a row of phone booths. As soon as she arrived, Billie checked on Luke's flight and learned it was running almost an hour late, and would land in Huntsville at three fifteen. She had three hours to kill.

She got a candy bar and a Dr Pepper from a machine. She put down the attaché case that contained her Colt and stood leaning against a wall, thinking. How was she going to handle this? As soon as she saw Luke, she would warn him that Anthony was here. Luke would be on his guard, and could take precautions – but he could not go into hiding. He had to find out what he had done here on Monday, and for that he would need to move around. He had to take risks. Could she do anything to help protect him?

As she was racking her brains, a girl in Capital

356

Airlines uniform approached her. 'Are you Dr Josephson?'

'Yes.'

'I have a phone message for you.' She handed over an envelope.

Billie frowned. Who knew she was here? 'Thanks,' she muttered, tearing it open.

'You're very welcome. Please let us know if there's any way we can be of further service.'

Billie looked up and smiled. She had forgotten how polite people were in the South. 'I sure will,' she said. 'I appreciate that.'

The girl walked away, and Billie read her message: 'Please call Dr Lucas on Huntsville JE 6-4231.'

She was bewildered. Could Luke be here already? And how had he known she would be here?

There was only one way to find out. She dropped her pop bottle in a trash can and found a payphone.

The number she dialled answered immediately, and a man's voice said: 'Components test lab.'

It sounded as if Luke was already at Redstone Arsenal. How had he done that trick? She said: 'Dr Claude Lucas, please.'

'Just one moment.' After a pause the man came back. 'Dr Lucas stepped out for a minute. Who is this, please?'

'Dr Bilhah Josephson, I have a message to call him on this number.'

The man's tone changed immediately. 'Oh, Dr Josephson, I'm so glad we found you! Dr Lucas is very concerned to contact you.'

357

'What's he doing here? I thought he was still in the air.'

'Army security pulled him off the plane at Norfolk, Virginia, and laid on a special flight. He's been here more than an hour.'

She felt relieved he was safe, but at the same time she was puzzled. 'What's he doing there?'

'I think you know.'

'Okay, I guess I do. How is it going?'

'Fine – but I can't give you details, especially over the phone. Can you get yourself down to us?'

'Where are you?'

'The lab is about an hour out of town on the Chattanooga road. I could send an army driver to pick you up, but it would be quicker for you to get a cab, or rent a car.'

Billie took a notebook out of her bag. 'Give me directions.' Then, remembering her Southern manners, she added: 'If you would, please.'

1 P.M.

The first-stage engine must be switched off sharply, and separated immediately, otherwise gradual thrust decay could cause the first stage to catch up with the second and misalign it. As soon as pressure drops in the fuel lines, the valves are closed, and the first stage is separated five seconds later by detonation of spring-loaded explosive bolts. The springs increase the speed of the second stage by 2.6 feet per second, ensuring that it separates cleanly.

Anthony knew the way to Luke's house. He had spent a weekend there, a couple of years back, soon after Luke and Elspeth had moved from Pasadena. He reached the place in fifteen minutes. It was on Echols Hill, a street of large older homes a couple of blocks from downtown. Anthony parked around the corner, so that Luke would not be forewarned that he had a visitor.

He walked back to the house. He should have felt quietly confident. He held all the cards: surprise, time, and a gun. But instead he was nauseated with apprehension. Twice already he had felt he had Luke in his hands, and Luke had eluded him.

He still did not know why Luke had chosen to fly

to Huntsville rather than Cape Canaveral. This inexplicable decision suggested there was something Anthony did not know about, an unpleasant surprise that might leap out at him at any moment.

The house was a white turn-of-the-century Colonial with a pillared verandah. It was too grand for an army boffin, but Luke had never pretended to live on what he made as a scientist. Anthony opened a gate in a low wall and entered the yard. The place would have been easy to break into, but that would not be necessary. He circled around to the back. By the kitchen door was a terracotta planter with bougainvillea spilling out of it, and under the pot was a big iron key.

Anthony let himself in.

The outside was pleasantly old-fashioned, but the interior was right up to the minute. Elspeth had every kind of gadget in the kitchen. There was a big hall decorated in bright pastel colours, a living room with a console TV and a record player, and a dining room with modern splayed-leg chairs and sideboards. Anthony preferred traditional furniture, but he had to admit this was stylish.

As he stood in the living room, staring at a curved couch upholstered in pink vinyl, he recalled vividly the weekend he had spent here. He had known within an hour that the marriage was in trouble. Elspeth had been flirtatious, always a sign of tension with her, and Luke had adopted a forced air of cheery hospitality that was quite uncharacteristic.

They had given a cocktail party on the Saturday night and invited the young crowd from Redstone

Arsenal. This room had been full of badly dressed scientists talking about rockets, junior officers discussing their prospects for promotion, and pretty women gossiping about the intrigues of life on a military base. The gramophone had been stacked with long-playing jazz records, but that night the music had sounded plaintive, not joyous. Luke and Elspeth had got drunk – a rare thing for both of them – and Elspeth had grown more flirty while Luke became quieter and quieter. Anthony had found it painful to see two people he liked and admired so unhappy, and the whole weekend had depressed him.

And now the long drama of their interwoven lives was playing out its inevitable conclusion.

Anthony decided to search the house. He did not know what he was looking for. But he might turn up something that would give him a clue to why Luke was coming here, and warn him of unforeseen danger. He put on a pair of rubber gloves that he found in the kitchen. There would be a murder investigation eventually, and he did not want to leave fingerprints.

He started in the study, a small room lined with shelves full of scientific books. He sat at Luke's desk, which looked out on to the back yard, and opened the drawers.

Over the next two hours, he searched the house from top to bottom. He found nothing.

He looked in every pocket of every suit in Luke's well-filled closet. He opened every book in the study to check for papers concealed between the pages. He took the lids off every piece of Tupperware in the enormous double-door refrigerator. He went into the garage and searched the handsome black Chrysler 300C – the fastest stock sedan in the world, according to the newspapers – from its streamlined headlamps to its rocket-ship tail fins.

He learned a few intimate secrets along the way. Elspeth coloured her hair, used sleeping pills that were prescribed by a doctor, and suffered from constipation. Luke used a dandruff shampoo and subscribed to *Playboy* magazine.

There was a small pile of mail on a table in the hall – put there by the maid, presumably. Anthony shuffled the letters, but there was nothing of interest: a flyer from a supermarket, *Newsweek*, a postcard from Ron and Monica in Hawaii, envelopes with the cellophane address window that indicated a business letter.

The search had been fruitless. He still did not know what Luke might have up his sleeve.

He went into the living room. He chose a position from which he could see through the venetian blinds to the front yard, and also through the open door into the hallway. He sat down on the pink vinyl couch.

He took out his gun, checked that it was fully loaded, and fitted the silencer.

He tried to reassure himself by imagining the scene ahead. He would see Luke arrive, probably in a taxicab from the airport. He would watch him walk into the front yard, take out his key, and open his own front door. Luke would step into the hall, close the door, then head for the kitchen. As he passed the living room, he would glance through the open doorway and see Anthony on the couch. He would stop, raise his eyebrows in surprise, and open his mouth to speak. In his mind would be some phrase such as: 'Anthony? What the hell—?' But he would never say the words. His eyes would drop to the gun held perfectly level in Anthony's lap, and he would know his fate a split second before it happened.

Then Anthony would shoot him dead.

3 P.M.

A system of compressed-air nozzles, mounted in the tail of the instrument compartment, will control the tilt of the nose section when in space.

Billie was lost.

She had known it for half an hour. Leaving the airport in a rented Ford a few minutes before one o'clock, she had driven into the centre of Huntsville, then taken Highway 59 toward Chattanooga. She had wondered why the components testing laboratory should be an hour away from the base, and imagined it might be for safety reasons: perhaps there was a danger that components would explode under testing. But she had not thought very hard about it.

Her directions were to take a country road to the right exactly thirty-five miles from Huntsville. She had zeroed her trip meter on Main Street, but when the revolving figures reached 35 she could not see a right turn. Feeling only mildly anxious, she went on and took the next road on the right, a couple of miles farther.

The directions, which had seemed so precise as she wrote them down, never quite corresponded with the roads on which she found herself, and her anxiety grew, but she carried on, making the likeliest interpretation. Obviously, she thought, the man she had spoken to had not been as reliable as he had sounded. She wished she had been able to speak to Luke personally.

The landscape gradually became wilder, the farmhouses ramshackle, the roads potholed and the fences broken-down. The disparity between what she expected and the landmarks she saw around her grew until she threw up her hands in despair and admitted to herself that she could be anywhere. She was furious with herself and with the fool who had given her directions.

She turned around and tried to find her way back, but soon she was on unfamiliar roads again. She began to wonder if she were going around in a huge circle. She stopped beside a field where a Negro in dungarees and a straw hat was turning the hard earth with a walking plough. She stopped her car and spoke to him. 'I'm looking for the components testing lab of Redstone Arsenal,' she said.

He looked surprised. 'The army base? That's all the way back to Huntsville and across to the other side of town.'

'But they have some kind of facility out this way.'

'Not that I ever see.'

This was hopeless. She would have to call the lab and ask for fresh directions. 'Can I use your phone?'

'Ain't got no phone.'

She was about to ask him where the nearest pay

phone was when she saw a look of fear in his eyes. She realized that she was putting him in a situation that made him anxious: alone in a field with a white woman who was not making sense. She quickly thanked him and drove away.

After a couple of miles, she came upon a dilapidated feed store with a payphone outside. She pulled over. She still had Luke's message with the phone number. She put a dime in the slot and dialled.

The phone was answered immediately. A young man's voice said: 'Hello?'

'May I speak to Dr Claude Lucas?' she said.

'You got the wrong number, honey.'

Can't I do anything right? she thought desperately. 'Isn't this Huntsville JE 6–4231?'

There was a pause. 'Yep, that's what it says on the dial.'

She double-checked the number on the message. She had not made a mistake. 'I was trying to call the components testing lab.'

'Well, you reached a payphone in Huntsville airport.'

'A *pay*phone?'

'Yes, mam.'

Billie began to realize she had been hoodwinked.

The voice at the other end of the line went on: 'I'm about to call my Mom and tell her to come get me, and when I pick up the phone I hear you asking for some guy named Claude.'

'Shit!' Billie said. She slammed the phone down, furious with herself for being so gullible.

Luke had not been taken off his plane in Norfolk and put on an army flight, she realized, and he was not at the components testing lab, wherever that was. That whole story was a lie designed to get her out of the way – and it had succeeded. She looked at her watch. Luke must have landed by now. Anthony had been waiting for him – and she might as well have been in Washington, for all the use she had been.

With despair in her heart, she wondered if Luke were still alive.

If he was, maybe she could still warn him. It was too late to leave a message at the airport, but there must be someone she could call. She racked her brains. Luke had a secretary at the base, she remembered; a name like a flower . . .

Marigold.

She called Redstone Arsenal and asked to speak to Dr Lucas's secretary. A woman with a slow Alabama voice came on the line. 'Computation Laboratory, how may I help you?'

'Is that Marigold?'

'Yes.'

'I'm Dr Josephson, a friend of Dr Lucas.'

'Yes.' She sounded suspicious.

Billie wanted this woman to trust her. 'We've spoken before, I think. My first name is Billie.'

'Oh, sure, I remember. How are you?'

'Worried. I need to get a message to Luke urgently. Is he with you?'

'No, mam. He went to his house.'

'What's he doing there?'

367

'Looking for a file folder.'

'A file?' Billie saw the significance of that immediately. 'A file he left here on Monday, maybe?'

'I don't know nothing about that,' said Marigold.

Of course, Luke had told Marigold to keep his Monday visit secret. But none of that was important now. 'If you see Luke, or if he calls you, would you please give him a message from me?'

'Of course.'

'Tell him Anthony is in town.'

'That's all?'

'He'll understand. Marigold . . . I hesitate to say this, in case you think I'm some kind of nut, but I guess I should. I believe Luke is in danger.'

'From this Anthony?'

'Yes. Do you believe me?'

'Stranger things have happened. Is this all tied up with him losing his memory?'

'Yes. If you get that message to him, it could save his life. I mean it.'

'I'll do what I can, Doctor.'

'Thank you.' Billie hung up.

Was there anyone else Luke might talk to? She thought of Elspeth.

She called the operator and asked for Cape Canaveral.

3.45 P.M.

After discarding the burnt-out first stage, the missile will coast through a vacuum trajectory while the spatial-attitude-control system aligns it so that it is exactly horizontal with respect to the Earth's surface.

Everyone was bad-tempered at Cape Canaveral. The Pentagon had ordered a security alert. Arriving this morning, eager to get to work on the final checks for the all-important rocket launch, staff had been made to wait in line at the gate. Some had been there for three hours in the Florida sun. Gas tanks had run dry, radiators had boiled over, air-conditioners had failed, and engines had stalled, then refused to restart. Every car had been searched – hoods lifted, golf bags taken out of trunks, spare wheels removed from covers. Tempers frayed as all briefcases were opened, each lunch pail unpacked, and every woman's purse dumped out on to a trestle table so that Colonel Hide's military police could paw through her lipsticks, love letters, tampons and Rolaids.

But that was not the end of it. When workers reached their laboratories and offices and engineering shops, they were disrupted all over again by teams of men who went through their drawers and filing cabinets, looked inside their oscillators and vacuum cabinets, and took the inspection plates off their machine tools. 'We're trying to launch a goddamn rocket here,' people said again and again, but the security men just gritted their teeth and carried on. Despite the disruption, the launch was still scheduled for 10.30 p.m.

Elspeth was glad of the upset. It meant nobody noticed she was too distraught to do her job. She made mistakes in her timetable and produced her updates late, but Willy Fredrickson was too distracted to reprimand her. She did not know where Luke was and she no longer felt sure she could trust Anthony.

When the phone at her desk rang a few minutes before four o'clock, her heart seemed to stop.

She snatched up the handset. 'Yes?'

'This is Billie.'

'*Billie?*' Elspeth was taken by surprise. 'Where are you?'

'I'm in Huntsville, trying to contact Luke.'

'What's he doing there?'

'Looking for a file he left here on Monday.'

Elspeth's jaw dropped. 'He went to Huntsville on Monday? I didn't know that.'

'Nobody knew, except Marigold. Elspeth, do you understand what's going on?'

She laughed humourlessly. 'I thought I did . . . but not any more.'

'I believe Luke's life is in danger.'

'What makes you say so?'

'Anthony shot at him in Washington last night.'

Elspeth went cold. 'Oh, my God.'

'It's too complicated to explain right now. If Luke calls you, will you tell him that Anthony is in Huntsville?'

Elspeth was trying to recover from the shock. 'Uh . . . sure, of course I will.'

'It could save his life.'

'I understand. Billie . . . one more thing.'

'Yeah.'

'Look after Luke, won't you?'

There was a pause. 'What do you mean?' Billie asked. 'You sound like you're going to die.'

Elspeth did not answer. After a moment, she broke the connection.

A sob came to her throat. She fought fiercely to control herself. Tears would not help anyone, she told herself severely. She made herself calm.

Then she dialled her home in Huntsville.

4 P.M.

Explorer's elliptical orbit will take it as far as 1,800 miles into space and swing it back within 187 miles of the Earth's surface. Orbiting speed of the satellite is 18,000 miles per hour.

Anthony heard a car. He looked out of the front window of Luke's house and saw a Huntsville taxicab pull up at the curb. He thumbed the safety catch on his gun. His mouth went dry.

The phone rang.

It was on one of the triangular side tables at the ends of the curved couch. Anthony stared at it in horror. It rang a second time. He was paralysed by indecision. He looked out of the window and saw Luke getting out of the cab. The call could be trivial, nothing, a wrong number. Or it could be vital information.

Terror bubbled up inside him. He could not answer the phone and shoot someone at the same time.

The phone rang a third time. Panicking, he snatched it up. 'Yes?'

'This is Elspeth.'

'What? What?'

Her voice was low and strained. 'He's looking for a file he stashed in Huntsville on Monday.'

Anthony understood in a flash. Luke had made not one but two copies of the blueprints he had found on Sunday. One set he had brought to Washington, intending to take them to the Pentagon – but Anthony had intercepted him, and Anthony now had those copies. Unfortunately, he had not imagined there might be a second set, hidden somewhere as a precaution. He had forgotten that Luke was a Resistance veteran, security-conscious to the point of paranoia. 'Who else knows about this?'

'His secretary, Marigold. And Billie Josephson – she told me. There may be others.'

Luke was paying the driver. Anthony was running out of time. 'I have to have that file,' he said to Elspeth.

'That's what I thought.'

'It's not here – I just searched the house from top to bottom.'

'Then it must be at the base.'

'I'll have to follow him while he looks for it.'

Luke was approaching the front door.

'I'm out of time,' Anthony said, and he slammed down the phone.

He heard Luke's key scrape in the lock as he ran through the hall and into the kitchen. He went out the back door and closed it softly. The key was still in the outside of the lock. He turned it silently, bent down, and slipped it under the flowerpot.

He dropped to the ground and crawled along the verandah, keeping close to the house and below window level. In that position he turned the corner and reached the front of the house. From here to the street there was no cover. He just had to take a chance.

It seemed best to make a break for it while Luke was putting down his bag and hanging up his coat. He was less likely to look out of the window now.

Gritting his teeth, Anthony stepped forward.

He walked quickly to the gate, resisting the temptation to look behind him, expecting at every second to hear Luke shout: 'Hey! Stop! Stop, or I shoot!'

Nothing happened.

He reached the street and walked away.

4.30 P.M.

The satellite contains two tiny radio transmitters powered by mercury batteries no bigger than flashlight batteries. Each transmitter carries four simultaneous channels of telemetry.

On top of the console TV in the living room, next to a bamboo lamp, was a matching bamboo picture frame containing a colour photograph. It showed a strikingly beautiful redhead in an ivory silk wedding dress. Beside her, wearing a grey cutaway and a yellow vest, was Luke.

He studied Elspeth in the picture. She could have been a movie star. She was tall and elegant, with a voluptuous figure. Lucky man, he thought, to be marrying her.

He did not like the house so much. When he had first seen the outside, and the wisteria climbing the pillars of the shady verandah, it had gladdened his heart. But the inside was all hard edges and shiny surfaces and bright paint. Everything was too neat. He knew, suddenly, that he liked to live in a house where the books spilled off the shelves, and the dog was asleep right across the hallway, and there were coffee rings on the piano, and a tricycle stood upside down in the driveway and had to be moved before you could put your car in the garage.

No kids lived in this house. There were no pets, either. Nothing ever got messed up. It was like an advertisement in a women's magazine, or the set of a television comedy. It made him feel that the people who appeared in these rooms were actors.

He began to search. A buff-coloured army file folder should be easy enough to find – unless he had removed the contents and thrown away the folder. He sat at the desk in the study – *his* study – and looked through the drawers. He found nothing of significance.

He went upstairs.

He spent a few seconds looking at the big double bed with the yellow-and-blue covers. It was hard to believe that he shared that bed every night with the ravishing creature in the wedding photo.

He opened the closet and saw, with a shock of pleasure, the rack of navy blue and grey suits and tweed sport coats, the shirts in bengal stripes and tattersall checks, the stacked sweaters and the polished shoes on their rack. He had been wearing this stolen suit for more than twenty-four hours, and he was tempted to take five minutes to shower and change into some of his own clothes. But he resisted. There was no time to spare.

He searched the house thoroughly. Everywhere he looked, he learned something about himself and his wife. They liked Glen Miller and Frank Sinatra, they read Hemingway and Scott Fitzgerald, they drank

Dewar's scotch and ate All-Bran and brushed their teeth with Colgate. Elspeth spent a lot on expensive underwear, he discovered as he went through her closet. Luke himself must be fond of ice cream, because the freezer was full of it, and Elspeth's waist was so small she could not possibly eat much of anything at all.

At last he gave up.

In a kitchen drawer he found keys to the Chrysler in the garage. He would drive to the base and search there.

Before leaving, he picked up the mail in the hall and shuffled the envelopes. It all looked straight-forwardly official, bills and suchlike. Desperate for a clue, he ripped open the envelopes and glanced at each letter.

One was from a doctor in Atlanta.

It began:

Dear Mrs Lucas,

Following your routine check-up, the results of your blood tests have come back from the lab, and everything is normal.

However . . .

Luke stopped reading. Something told him it was not his habit to read other people's mail. On the other hand, this was his wife, and that word 'However' was ominous. Perhaps there was a medical problem he should know about right away.

He read the next paragraph.

377

*However, you are underweight, you suffer insomnia,
and when I saw you, you had obviously been crying,
although you said nothing was wrong. These are
symptoms of depression.*

Luke frowned. This was troubling. Why was she depressed? What kind of husband must he be?

*Depression may be caused by changes in body
chemistry, by unresolved mental problems such as marital
difficulties, or by childhood trauma such as the early
death of a parent. Treatment may include antidepressant
medication and/or psychiatric therapy.*

This was getting worse. Was Elspeth mentally ill?

*In your case, I have no doubt that the condition is
related to the tubal ligation you underwent in 1954.*

What was a tubal ligation? Luke stepped into his study, turned on the desk lamp, took from the bookshelf the *Family Health Encyclopedia*, and looked it up. The answer stunned him. It was the commonest method of sterilization for women who did not want to have children.

He sat down heavily and put the encyclopedia on the desk. Reading the details of the operation, he realized that this was what women meant when they spoke of having their tubes tied.

He recalled his conversation with Elspeth this

morning. He had asked her why they could not have children. She had said: 'We don't know. Last year, you went to a fertility specialist, but he couldn't find anything wrong. A few weeks ago, I saw a woman doctor in Atlanta. She ran some tests. We're waiting for the results.'

That was all lies. She knew perfectly well why they could not have children – she had been sterilized.

She *had* gone to a doctor in Atlanta, but not for fertility testing – she had simply had a routine check-up.

Luke was sick at heart. It was a terrible deception. Why had she lied? He looked at the next paragraph.

This procedure may cause depression at any age, but in your case, having it six weeks before your wedding—

Luke's mouth fell open. There was something terribly wrong here. Elspeth's deception had begun shortly before they got married.

How had she managed it? He could not remember, of course. But he could guess. She could have told him she was having a minor operation. She might even have said vaguely that it was a 'feminine thing'.

He read the whole paragraph.

This procedure may cause depression at any age, but in your case, having it six weeks before your wedding, it was almost inevitable, and you should have returned to your doctor for regular consultations.

Luke's anger subsided as he realized how Elspeth had suffered. He reread the line: 'You are underweight, you suffer insomnia, and when I saw you, you had obviously been crying, although you said nothing was wrong.' She had put herself through some kind of personal hell.

But although he pitied her, the fact remained that their marriage had been a lie. Thinking about the house he had just searched, he realized that it did not feel much like a home to him. He was comfortable here in the little study, and he had felt a start of recognition on opening his closet, but the rest of the place presented a picture of married life that was alien to him. He did not care for kitchen appliances and smart modern furniture. He would rather have old rugs and family heirlooms. Most of all, he wanted children – yet children were the very thing she had deliberately denied him. And she had lied about it for four years.

The shock paralysed him. He sat at his desk, staring through the window, while evening fell over the hickory trees in the back yard. How had he let his life go so wrong? He considered what he had learned about himself in the last thirty-six hours, from Elspeth, Billie, Anthony and Bern. Had he lost his way slowly and gradually, like a child wandering farther and farther from home? Or was there a turning point, a moment when he had made a bad decision, taken the wrong fork in the road? Was he a weak man, who had drifted into misfortune for lack of a purpose in life? Or did he have some crucial flaw in his character?

He must be a poor judge of people, he thought. He had remained close to Anthony, who had tried to kill him, yet had broken with Bern, who had been a faithful friend. He had quarrelled with Billie and married Elspeth, yet Billie had dropped everything to help him and Elspeth had deceived him.

A large moth bumped into the closed window, and the noise startled Luke out of his reverie. He looked at his watch and was shocked to see that it was past seven.

If he hoped to unravel the mystery of his life, he needed to start with the elusive file. It was not here, so it had to be at Redstone Arsenal. He would turn out the lights and lock up the house, then he would get the black car out of the garage and drive to the base.

Time was pressing. The launch of the rocket was scheduled for ten-thirty. He had only three hours to find out whether there was a plot to sabotage it. Nevertheless, he remained sitting at his desk, staring through the window into the darkened garden, seeing nothing.

7.30 P.M.

*One radio transmitter is powerful but short-lived – it will be
dead in two weeks. The weaker signal from the second will
last two months.*

There were no lights on in Luke's house when Billie
drove by. But what did that mean? There were three
possibilities. One: the house was empty. Two: Anthony
was sitting in the dark, waiting to shoot Luke. Three:
Luke was lying in a pool of blood, dead. The
uncertainty made her crazy with fear.

She had screwed up royally, maybe fatally. A few
hours ago, she had been well placed to warn Luke and
save him – then she had allowed herself to be diverted
by a simple ruse. It had taken her hours to get back to
Huntsville and find Luke's house. She had no idea
whether either of her warning messages had reached
him. She was furious with herself for being so
incompetent, and terrified that Luke might have died
because of her failure.

She turned the next corner and pulled up. She
breathed deeply and made herself think calmly. She
had to find out who was in the house. But what if
Anthony were there? She contemplated sneaking up,

hoping to surprise him; but that was too dangerous. It was never a good idea to startle a man with a gun in his hand. She could go right up to the front door and ring the bell. Would he shoot her down in cold blood, just for being there? He might. And she did not have the right to risk her life carelessly – she had a child who needed her.

On the passenger seat beside her was her attaché case. She opened it and took out the Colt. She disliked the heavy touch of the dark steel on the palm of her hand. The men she had worked with, in the war, had enjoyed handling guns. It gave a man sensual pleasure to close his fist around a pistol grip, spin the cylinder of a revolver, or fit the stock of a rifle into the hollow of his shoulder. She felt none of that. To her, guns were brutal and cruel, made to tear and crush the flesh and bones of living, breathing people. They made her skin crawl.

With the pistol in her lap, she turned the car around and returned to Luke's house.

She screeched to a halt outside, threw the car door open, grabbed her gun and leaped out. Before anyone inside might have time to react, she jumped the low wall and ran across the lawn to the side of the house.

She heard no sound from within.

She ran around to the back, ducked past the door, and looked in at a window. The dim light of a distant street lamp enabled her to see that it was a simple casement with a single latch. The room seemed empty. She reversed her grip on the gun and smashed the glass, all the time waiting for the gunshot that would end her life. Nothing happened. She reached through the broken pane, undid the latch, and pulled open the window. She climbed in, holding the gun in her right hand, and flattened herself against a wall. She could make out vague shapes of furniture, a desk and some bookshelves. This was a little study. Her instinct told her she was alone. But she was terrified of stumbling over Luke's body in the dark.

Moving slowly, she crossed the room and located the doorway. Her dark-accustomed eyes saw an empty hall. She stepped cautiously out, gun at the ready. She moved through the house in the gloom, dreading at every step that she would see Luke on the floor. All the rooms were empty.

At the end of her search she stood in the largest bedroom, staring at the double bed where Luke slept with Elspeth, wondering what to do next. She felt tearfully grateful that Luke was not lying here dead. But where was he? Had he changed his plans, and decided not to come here? Or had the body been spirited away? Had Anthony somehow failed to kill him? Or had one of her warnings got through?

One person who might have some answers was Marigold.

Billie returned to Luke's study and turned on the light. A medical encyclopedia lay on the desk, open at the page about female sterilization. Billie frowned in puzzlement, then put aside her questions. She called information and asked for a number for Marigold Clark. After a moment the voice on the line gave her a Huntsville number.

A man answered. 'She gone to singing practice,' he said. Billie guessed he was Marigold's husband. 'Miz Lucas is down to Florida, so Marigold conducting the choir till she come back.'

Billie recalled that Elspeth had been conductor of the Radcliffe Choral Society, and later of an orchestra for black kids in Washington. It seemed she was doing something of that sort here in Huntsville, and Marigold was her deputy. 'I need to talk to Marigold real bad,' Billie said. 'Do you think it would be all right if I interrupted the choir for a minute?'

'Guess so. They're at the Calvary Gospel Church on Mill Street.'

'Thank you, I sure appreciate it.'

Billie went out to her car. She found Mill Street on the Hertz map and drove there. The church was a fine brick building in a poor neighbourhood. She heard the choir as soon as she opened the car door. When she stepped inside the church, the music washed over her like a tidal wave. The singers stood at the far end. There were only about thirty men and women, but they sounded like a hundred. The hymn went: 'Everybody's gonna have a wonderful time up there – oh! Glory, hallelujah!' They clapped and swayed as they sang. A pianist played a rhythmic barrelhouse accompaniment, and a large woman with her back to Billie conducted vigorously.

The pews were neat rows of wooden folding seats. She sat in the rear, conscious that hers was the only white face in the place. Despite her anxiety, the music tugged at her heartstrings. She had been born in Texas and, to her, these thrilling harmonies represented the soul of the South.

She was impatient to question Marigold, but she felt sure she would get a better response by showing respect and waiting for the end of the song.

They finished on a high chord, and the conductor immediately looked around. 'I wondered what happened to disturb your concentration,' she said to the choir. 'Take a short break.'

Billie walked up the aisle. 'I'm sorry to interrupt,' she said. 'Are you Marigold Clark?'

'Yes,' she said warily. She was a woman of about fifty, wearing fancy spectacles. 'But I don't know you.'

'We spoke on the phone earlier, I'm Billie Josephson.'

'Oh, hi, Dr Josephson.'

They walked a few steps away from the others. Billie said: 'Have you heard from Luke?'

'Not since this morning. I expected him to show up at the base this afternoon, but he didn't. Do you think he's all right?'

'I don't know. I went to his house, but there was no one there. I'm afraid he might have been killed.'

Marigold shook her head in bewilderment. 'I've worked for the army twenty years and I never heard of anything like this.'

'If he is alive, he's in great danger,' Billie said. She looked Marigold in the eye. 'Do you believe me?'

Marigold hesitated for a long moment. 'Yes, ma'am, I do,' she said at last.

'Then you have to help me,' Billie told her.

9.30 P.M.

The radio signal from the more powerful transmitter may be picked up by radio hams all over the world. The weaker signal from the second can be picked up only by specially equipped stations.

Anthony was at Redstone Arsenal, sitting in his army Ford, peering through the darkness, anxiously watching the door of the Computation Laboratory. He was in the parking lot in front of the headquarters building, a couple of hundred yards away.

Luke was in the lab, searching for his file folder. Anthony knew he would not find it there, just as he had known Luke would not find it at his home – because he had already searched there. But Anthony was no longer able to anticipate Luke's movements. He could only wait until Luke decided where to go next, then try to follow him.

However, time was on his side. Every minute that passed made Luke less dangerous. The rocket would be launched in one hour. Could Luke ruin everything in an hour? Anthony knew only that over the last two days his old friend had proved again and again that he should not be underestimated.

As he was thinking this, the door to the lab opened, spilling yellow light into the night, and a figure emerged and approached the black Chrysler parked at the curb. As Anthony had expected, Luke was empty-handed. He got in and drove off.

Anthony's heartbeat quickened. He started his engine, switched on his headlights, and followed.

The road went south in a dead-straight line. After about a mile, Luke slowed in front of a long one-storey building and pulled into its parking lot. Anthony drove past, accelerating into the night. A quarter of a mile down the road, out of sight of Luke, he turned around. When he came back, Luke's car was still there, but Luke had gone.

Anthony pulled into the parking lot and killed his engine.

* * *

Luke had felt sure he would find the folder in the Computation Lab, where his office was. That was why he had spent so long there. He had looked at every file in his own room, then in the main office where the secretaries sat. And he had found nothing.

But there was one more possibility. Marigold had said that he also went to the Engineering Building on Monday. There must have been a reason for that. Anyway, it was his last hope. If the file were not here, he did not know where else to look. And anyway, he would by then have run out of time. In a few minutes, the rocket would either be launched – or be sabotaged.

Engineering had an atmosphere quite different

from that of the Computation Lab. Computation was spotlessly clean, as it had to be for the sake of the massive computers that calculated thrust and speed and trajectories. Engineering was scruffy by comparison, smelling of oil and rubber.

He hurried along a corridor. The walls were painted dark green below waist level and light green above. Most of the doors had nameplates beginning 'Dr', so he presumed they were the offices of scientists but, to his frustration, none said 'Dr Claude Lucas'. Most likely he did not have a second office, but maybe he had a desk here.

At the end of the corridor he came upon a large open room with half a dozen steel tables. On the far side, an open door led into a laboratory with granite bench tops above green metal drawers and, beyond the benches, a big double door that looked as if it led to a loading bay outside.

Along the wall to Luke's immediate left was a row of lockers, each with a name plate. One was his. Maybe he had stashed the file here.

He took out his key ring and found a likely key. It worked, and he opened the door. Inside he saw a hard hat on a high shelf. Below that, hanging from a hook, was a set of blue overalls. On the floor stood a pair of black rubber boots that looked like his size.

There, beside the boots, was a buff-coloured army file folder. This had to be what he was looking for.

The folder contained some papers. When he took them out, he could see immediately that they were blueprints for parts of a rocket.

His heart hammering in his chest, Luke moved quickly to one of the steel tables and spread the papers out under a lamp. After a few moments' rapid study, he knew without doubt that the drawings showed the Jupiter C rocket's self-destruct mechanism.

He was horrified.

Every rocket had a self-destruct mechanism so that, if it should veer off course and threaten human life, it could be blown up in mid-air. In the main stage of the Jupiter rocket, a Primacord igniter rope ran the length of the missile. A firing cap was attached to its top end, and two wires stuck out of the cap. If a voltage was applied across the wires, Luke could see from the drawings, the cap would ignite the Primacord, which would rip the tank, causing the fuel to burn and be dispersed, and destroying the rocket.

The explosion was triggered by a coded radio signal. The blueprints showed twin plugs, one for the transmitter on the ground and the other for the receiver in the satellite. One turned the radio signal into a complex code; the other received the signal and, if the code was correct, applied the voltage across the twin wires. A separate diagram, not a blueprint but a hastily drawn sketch, showed exactly how the plugs were wired, so that anyone having the diagram could duplicate the signal.

It was brilliant, Luke realized. The saboteurs had no need of explosives or timing devices – they could use what was already built in. They did not need access to the rocket. Once they had the code, they did not even have to get inside Cape Canaveral. The radio signal could be broadcast from a transmitter miles away.

The last sheet was a photocopy of an envelope addressed to Theo Packman at the Vanguard Motel. Had Luke prevented the original being mailed? He could not be sure. Standard counter intelligence procedure was to leave a spy network in place and use it for disinformation. But if Luke had confiscated the original, the sender would have mailed another set of blueprints. Either way, Theo Packman was now somewhere in Cocoa Beach with a radio transmitter, ready to blow up the rocket seconds after it took off.

But now Luke could prevent that. He glanced at the electric clock on the wall. It was ten-fifteen. He had time to call Cape Canaveral and have the launch postponed. He snatched up the phone on the desk.

A voice said: 'Put it down, Luke.'

Luke turned slowly, phone in hand. Anthony stood in the doorway in his camel-hair coat, with two black eyes and a swollen lip, holding a gun with a silencer, pointing it at Luke.

Slowly and reluctantly, Luke cradled the phone. 'You were in the car behind me,' he said.

'I figured you were in too much of a rush to check.'

Luke stared at the man whom he had so misjudged. Was there some sign he should have noticed, some feature that should have warned him he was dealing with a traitor? Anthony had a pleasantly ugly face that suggested considerable force of character, but not duplicity. 'How long have you been working for Moscow?' Luke asked him. 'Since the war?'

'Longer. Since Harvard.'

'Why?'

Anthony's lips twisted into a strange smile. 'For a better world.'

Once upon a time, Luke knew, a lot of sensible people had believed in the Soviet system. But he also knew their faith had been undermined by the realities of life under Stalin. 'You still believe that?' he said incredulously.

'Sort of. It's still the best hope, despite all that has happened.'

Maybe it was. Luke had no way of judging. But that was not the real issue. For him, it was Anthony's personal betrayal that was so hard to understand. 'We've been friends for two decades,' he said. 'But you *shot* at me last night.'

'Yes.'

'Would you kill your oldest friend? For this cause that you only half believe in?'

'Yes, and so would you. In the war, we both put lives at risk, our own and other people's, because it was right.'

'I don't think we lied to one another, let alone shot at one another.'

'We would have, if necessary.'

'I don't think so.'

'Listen. If I don't kill you now, you'll try to stop me escaping – won't you?'

Luke was scared, but he angrily told the truth. 'Hell, yes.'

'Even though you know that if I'm caught, I'll finish up in the electric chair.'

'I guess so . . . yes.'

'So you're willing to kill your friend, too.'

Luke was taken aback. Surely he could not be classified with Anthony? 'I might bring you to justice. That's not murder.'

'I'd be just as dead, though.'

Luke nodded slowly. 'I guess you would.'

Anthony raised the gun with a steady hand, aiming at Luke's heart.

Luke dropped behind the steel table.

The silenced gun coughed, and there was a metallic clang as the bullet hit the top of the table. It was cheap furniture, and the steel of which it was made was thin, but it had been enough to deflect the shot.

Luke rolled under the table. He guessed Anthony was now running across the room, trying to get another shot at him. He raised himself so that his back was against the underside of the table. Grabbing the two legs at one end of the table he heaved, standing upright at the same time. The table came up off the floor and teetered forward. As it toppled, Luke blindly ran with it, hoping to collide with Anthony. The table crashed to the floor.

But Anthony was not beneath it.

Luke tripped and tumbled onto the inverted table. He fell on his hands and knees, and banged his head on a steel leg. He rolled sideways and came up into a sitting position, hurt and dazed. He looked up to see

Anthony facing him, framed by the doorway that led into the lab, braced with his feet apart, aiming his gun two-handed. He had dodged Luke's clumsy charge and got behind him. Luke was now, literally, a sitting target, and the end of his life was a second away.

Then a voice rang out: 'Anthony! Stop!'

It was Billie.

Anthony froze, gun pointed at Luke. Luke slowly turned his head and looked behind him. Billie stood by the door, her sweater a flash of red against the army-green wall. Her red lips were set in a determined line. She held an automatic pistol in a steady hand, levelled at Anthony. Behind her was a middle-aged Negro woman, looking shocked and scared.

'Drop the gun!' Billie yelled.

Luke half expected Anthony to shoot him anyway. If he was a truly dedicated communist, he might be willing to sacrifice his life. But that would achieve nothing, for Billie would still have the blueprints, and they told the whole story.

Slowly, Anthony lowered his arms, but he did not drop the gun.

'Drop it, or I'll shoot!'

Anthony gave his twisted smile again. 'No, you won't,' he said. 'Not in cold blood.' Still pointing the gun at the floor, he began to walk backwards, making for the open door that led into the laboratory. Luke remembered noticing a door there that looked as if it led to the outside.

'Stop!' Billie cried.

'You don't believe that a rocket is worth more than

a human life, even if it's a traitor's life,' Anthony said, continuing to walk backward. He was now two steps from the door.

'Don't test me!' she cried.

Luke stared at her, not knowing whether she would shoot or not.

Anthony turned and darted through the doorway.

Billie did not shoot.

Anthony leaped over a lab bench, then threw himself at a double door. It burst open, and he disappeared into the night.

Luke leaped to his feet. Billie came towards him with her arms wide. He looked at the clock on the wall. It said ten twenty-nine. He had a minute left to warn Cape Canaveral.

He turned away from Billie and picked up the phone.

10.29 P.M.

The scientific instruments on board the satellite have been designed to withstand take-off pressure of more than 100 gravities.

When the phone was picked up in the blockhouse, Luke said: 'This is Luke, give me the launch conductor.'

'Right now he's—'

'I know what he's doing! Put him on, quick!'

There was a pause. In the background, Luke could hear the countdown: 'Twenty, nineteen, eighteen—'

A new voice came on the line, tense and impatient. 'This is Willy – what the hell is it?'

'Someone has the self-destruct code.'

'Shit! Who?'

'I'm pretty sure it's a spy. They're going to blow up the rocket. You have to abort the launch.'

The background voice said: 'Eleven, ten—'

'How do you know?' Willy asked.

'I've found diagrams of the wiring of the coded plugs, and an envelope addressed to someone called Theo Packman.'

'That's not proof. I can't cancel the launch on such a flimsy basis.'

Luke sighed, suddenly feeling fatalistic. 'Oh, Christ, what can I say? I've told you what I know. The decision is yours.'

'Five, four—'

'Hell!' Willy raised his voice. 'Stop the countdown!'

Luke slumped in his chair. He had done it. He glanced up at the anxious faces of Billie and Marigold. 'They've aborted the launch,' he said.

Billie lifted the hem of her sweater and stuffed the pistol into the waistband of her ski pants.

'Well,' said Marigold, somewhat lost for words. 'Well, I declare.'

Over the phone, Luke heard a buzz of angry questions in the blockhouse. A new voice came on the line. 'Luke? This is Colonel Hide. What the hell is going on?'

'I've discovered what made me take off for Washington in such a hurry on Monday. Do you know who Theo Packman is?'

'Uh, yeah, I think he's a freelance journalist on the missile beat, writes for a couple of European newspapers.'

'I found an envelope addressed to him containing blueprints of the Explorer's self-destruct system, including a sketch of the wiring of the coded plugs.'

'Jesus! Anyone who had that information could blow up the rocket in mid-air!'

'That's why I persuaded Willy to abort the launch.'

'Thank God you did.'

'Listen, you have to find this Packman character right now. The envelope was addressed to the Vanguard Motel, you may find him there.'

'Got it.'

'Packman was working with someone in the CIA, a double agent called Anthony Carroll. He's the one who intercepted me in Washington before I could get to the Pentagon with the information.'

'I talked to him!' Hide sounded incredulous.

'I'm sure of it.'

'I'll call the CIA and tell them.'

'Good.' Luke hung up. He had done all he could.

Billie said: 'What next?'

'I guess I'll go to Cape Canaveral. The launch will be rescheduled for the same time tomorrow. I'd like to be there.'

'Me, too.'

Luke smiled. 'You deserve it. You saved the rocket.' He stood up and embraced her.

'Your life, you goop. To heck with the rocket, I saved your life.' She kissed him.

Marigold coughed. 'You've missed the last plane from Huntsville airport,' she said in a businesslike tone.

Luke and Billie separated reluctantly.

'Next one is a MATS flight that leaves from the base at 5.30 a.m.,' Marigold went on. 'Or there's a train on the Southern Railway System you could catch. It runs from Cincinnati to Jacksonville and stops in Chattanooga around one a.m. You could get to Chattanooga in a couple of hours in that nice new car of yours.'

Billie said: 'I like the train idea.'

Luke nodded. 'Okay.' He looked at the upturned

table. 'Someone's going to have to talk to army security about these bullet holes.'

Marigold said: 'I'll do it in the morning. You don't want to be waiting around here answering questions.'

They went outside. Luke's car and Billie's rental were in the parking lot. Anthony's car had gone.

Billie embraced Marigold. 'Thank you,' she said. 'You were wonderful.'

Marigold was embarrassed, and turned practical again. 'You want me to return your rental to Hertz?'

'Thank you.'

'Off you go, leave everything to me.'

Billie and Luke got into his Chrysler and drove away.

When they were on the highway, Billie said: 'There's a question we haven't talked about.'

'I know,' Luke said. 'Who sent the blueprints to Theo Packman?'

'It must be someone inside Cape Canaveral, someone on the scientific team.'

'Exactly.'

'Do you have any idea who?'

Luke winced. 'Yes.'

'Why didn't you tell Hide?'

'Because I don't have any evidence, or even much of a reason, for my suspicions. It's just instinct. But, all the same, I'm sure.'

'Who?'

With a heart full of grief, Luke said: 'I think it's Elspeth.'

11 P.M.

The telemetry encoder uses hysteresis loop core materials to establish a series of input parameters from satellite instruments.

Elspeth could not believe it. Just a few seconds before ignition, the launch had been postponed. She had been so close to success. The triumph of her life had been within her grasp – and had slipped through her fingers.

She was not in the blockhouse – that was restricted to key personnel – but on the flat roof of an administration building, with a small crowd of secretaries and clerks, watching the floodlit launch pad through binoculars. The Florida night was warm, the sea-air moist. Their fears had grown as the minutes ticked by and the rocket remained on the ground; and now a collective groan went up as technicians in overalls swarmed out of their bunkers and began the complex procedure of standing down all systems. Final confirmation came when the mobile service tower slowly moved forward on its railway tracks to take the white rocket back into its steel arms.

Elspeth was in an agony of frustration. What the hell had gone wrong?

She left the others without a word and walked back to Hangar R, her long legs covering the ground with purposeful strides. When she reached her office, the phone was ringing. She snatched it up. 'Yes?'

'What's happening?' The voice was Anthony's.

'They've aborted the launch. I don't know why – do you?'

'Luke found the papers. He must have called.'

'Couldn't you stop him?'

'I had him in my sights – literally – but Billie walked in, armed.'

Elspeth had a sick feeling in the pit of her stomach at the thought of Anthony pointing a gun at Luke. It only made things worse that it was Billie who had intervened. 'Is Luke all right?'

'Yes – and so am I. But Theo's name is on those papers, remember?'

'Oh, hell.'

'They'll be on their way to arrest him already. You have to find him first.'

'Let me think . . . he's on the beach . . . I can be there in ten minutes . . . I know his car, it's a Hudson Hornet . . .'

'Then get going!'

'Yep.' She slammed down the phone and rushed out of the building.

She ran across the parking lot and jumped into her car. Her white Bel Air was a convertible, but she kept the top up and the windows tightly shut because of the mosquitoes that plagued the Cape. She drove fast to the gate and was waved through:

security was heavy coming in, but not going out. She headed south.

There was no regular road to the beach. From the highway several narrow, unpaved tracks led between the dunes to the shore. She planned to take the first, then continue south on the beach. That way she could not miss Theo's car. She peered at the rough brush alongside the road, trying to pick out the track in the light of her headlamps. She had to go slowly, even though she was in such a hurry, for fear of missing the turn-off. Then she saw a car emerging.

It was followed by another, and another. Elspeth flashed her left-turn indicator and slowed down. A constant stream of cars was coming from the beach. The spectators had figured out that the launch was cancelled – no doubt they, too, had seen, through their binoculars, the service gantry returning to position – and they were all going home.

She waited to turn left. Infuriatingly, the track was too narrow for two-way traffic. A car behind her honked impatiently. She grunted with exasperation as she saw she was not going to be able to get to the beach this way. She flicked off the indicator and floored the gas pedal.

She soon came to another turn-off, but the picture was the same: an unbroken line of cars emerging from a track too narrow to allow two cars to pass. 'Hell!' she said aloud. She was sweating now, despite the air-conditioning in her car. There was no way for her to get to the beach. She would have to think of something else. Could she wait on the highway in the hope of spotting his car? It was too chancy. What would Theo do after he left the beach? Her best option was to go to his motel and wait there.

She sped on, driving fast through the night. She wondered if Colonel Hide and army security were already at the Vanguard Motel. They might first have called the police or the FBI. They needed a warrant to arrest Theo, she knew – although law enforcement people generally had ways around such inconveniences. Whatever happened, it would take them a few minutes to get themselves together. She had a chance of beating them if she hurried.

The Vanguard was in a short business strip alongside the highway, between a gas station and a bait-and-tackle store. It had a large parking lot out front. There was no sign of police or army security: she was in time. But Theo's car was not there. She parked near the motel office, where she was sure to see anyone going in or out, and switched off her engine.

She did not have to wait long. The yellow-and-brown Hudson Hornet pulled in a couple of minutes later. Theo eased into a slot at the far end of the lot, near the road, and got out, a small man with thinning hair, dressed in chinos and a beach shirt.

Elspeth got out of her own car.

She opened her mouth to call to Theo across the lot. At that moment, two police cruisers arrived.

Elspeth froze.

They were Cocoa County Sheriff's vehicles. They came in fast, but without flashing lights or sirens. Behind them followed two unmarked cars. They parked across the entry, making it impossible for cars to leave.

At first Theo did not see them. He headed across the lot, toward Elspeth and the motel office.

She knew in a flash what she had to do – but it would take a steady nerve. Stay cool, she told herself. She took a deep breath, then started walking towards him.

As he came close he recognized her and said loudly: 'What the hell happened? Did they abort the launch?'

Elspeth said in a low voice: 'Give me your car keys.' She held out her hand.

'What for?'

'Look behind you.'

He glanced over his shoulder and saw the police cars. 'Fuck, what do they want?' he said shakily.

'You. Stay calm. Give me the keys.'

He dropped them into her open hand.

'Keep walking,' she said. 'The trunk of my car is not locked. Get inside.'

'Into the trunk?'

'*Yes!*' Elspeth went on past him.

She recognized Colonel Hide and another vaguely familiar face from Cape Canaveral. With them were four local cops and two tall, well-dressed young men who might have been FBI agents. None of them was looking her way. They gathered around Hide. Distantly, Elspeth heard him say: 'We need two men to check the licence plates of the cars here in the lot while the rest come inside.'

She reached Theo's car and opened the trunk. Inside was the leather suitcase containing the radio transmitter – powerful, and heavy. She was not sure she could carry it. She pulled it to the lip of the trunk and dragged it over the edge. It hit the ground with a thud. She closed the trunk lid quickly.

She looked around. Hide was still giving orders to his men. At the other end of the lot, she saw the trunk lid of her own car slowly closing, as if of its own volition. Theo was inside. That was half the problem solved.

Gritting her teeth, she grasped the handle of the suitcase and lifted it. It felt like a box of lead. She walked a few yards, holding it as long as she could. When her fingers became numb with strain, she dropped the case. Then she picked it up with her left hand. She managed another ten yards before the pain overcame her will and she dropped the case again.

Behind her, Colonel Hide and his men were crossing the lot towards the motel office. She prayed Hide would not look at her face. The darkness made it less likely he would recognize her. Of course, she could make up some story to explain her presence here, but what if he asked to look in the case?

Once more she changed sides and grasped the handle with her right hand. She could not lift the transmitter this time. Giving up, she began to drag it across the concrete, hoping the noise would not attract the attention of the cops.

At last she reached her car. As she opened the trunk, one of the uniformed police approached her with a cheerful smile. 'Help you with that, ma'am?' he said politely.

Theo's face stared at her from inside the trunk, white and scared.

'I got it,' she said to the cop out of the corner of her mouth. With both hands, she heaved up the suitcase and slid it in. There was a quiet grunt of pain from Theo as a corner dug into him. With a quick movement, Elspeth slammed the trunk lid and leaned on it. Her arms felt as if they would fall off.

She looked at the cop. Had he spotted Theo? He gave a puzzled grin. Elspeth said: 'My daddy taught me never to pack a bag I couldn't lift.'

'Strong girl,' the cop said in a mildly resentful tone.

'Thanks, anyway.'

The other men went past, heading purposefully towards the motel office. Elspeth was careful not to catch Hide's eye. The cop lingered a moment. 'Checking out?' he said.

'Yeah.'

'All alone?'

'That's right.'

He bent to the window and looked into the car, front and back seats, then straightened up again. 'Drive safely.' He walked on.

Elspeth got into her car and started the engine.

Two more uniformed cops had stayed behind and were checking licence plates. She pulled up next to one of them. 'Are you going to let me out, or do I have to stay here all night?' she said. She tried a friendly smile.

He checked her licence plate. 'Are you alone?'

'Yes.'

He looked through the window into the back seat. She held her breath. 'Okay,' he said at last. 'You can go.'

He sat in one of the cruisers and moved it out of the way.

She drove through the gap and pulled onto the highway, then floored the gas pedal.

Suddenly she felt limp with relief. Her arms trembled, and she had to slow the car. 'God almighty,' she breathed. 'That was too damn close.'

12 MIDNIGHT

Four whip antennae, protruding from the satellite cylinder, broadcast radio signals to receiving stations around the globe. Explorer will broadcast on a frequency of 108 MHz.

Anthony had to get out of Alabama. The action was in Florida now. Everything he had worked towards for twenty years would be decided at Cape Canaveral in the next twenty-four hours, and he had to be there.

Huntsville Airport was still open, lights blazing on the runway. That meant there was at least one more plane in or out tonight. He parked his army Ford at the roadside in front of the terminal building, behind a limousine and a couple of taxicabs. The place seemed deserted. He did not trouble to lock the car but hurried inside.

The place was quiet but not empty. One girl sat behind an airline counter writing in a book, and two black women in overalls were mopping the floor. Three men stood around waiting, one in chauffeur uniform and the others in the creased clothes and peaked caps of cab drivers. Pete was sitting on a bench.

Anthony had to get rid of Pete, for the man's own sake. The scene in the Engineering Building at

Redstone Arsenal had been witnessed by Billie and
Marigold, and one of them would soon report it. The
army would complain to the CIA. George Cooperman
had already said he could not shield Anthony any
longer. Anthony had to give up the pretence that he
was on a legitimate CIA mission. The game was up,
and Pete had better go home before he got hurt.

Pete might have been bored after twelve hours
waiting at the airport, but instead he seemed excited
and tense as he jumped to his feet. 'At last!' he said.

'What's flying out of here tonight?' Anthony said
abruptly.

'Nothing. One more flight is due in, from
Washington, but nothing is leaving before seven a.m.'

'Damn. I have to get to Florida.'

'There's a MATS flight from Redstone at five-thirty
going to Patrick Air Force Base, near Cape Canaveral.'

'That'll have to do.'

Pete looked embarrassed. Seeming to force the
words out, he said: 'You can't go to Florida.'

So that was why he was so tense. Anthony said coolly:
'How so?'

'I talked to Washington. Carl Hobart spoke to me
himself. We have to go back – and no argument, to
quote him.'

Anthony felt wild with rage, but he pretended to be
merely frustrated. 'Those assholes,' Anthony said. 'You
can't run a field operation from headquarters!'

Pete was not buying this. 'Mr Hobart says we have
to accept there is no operation now. The army is
handling this from here on.'

'We can't let them. Army security is totally incompetent.'

'I know, but I don't think we have a choice, sir.'

Anthony made an effort to breathe calmly. This had to happen sooner or later. The CIA did not yet believe he was a double agent, but they knew he had gone rogue, and they wanted to put him out of action as quietly as possible.

However, Anthony had carefully cultivated the loyalty of his men over the years, and he should still have some credit left. 'Here's what we'll do,' he said to Pete. 'You go back to Washington. Tell them I refused to obey orders. You're out of it – this is my responsibility now.' He half turned away, as if taking Pete's consent for granted.

'Okay,' Pete said. 'I guessed you would say that. And they can't expect me to kidnap you.'

'That's right,' Anthony said casually, concealing his relief that Pete was not going to argue.

'But there's something else,' Pete said.

Anthony rounded on him, letting his irritation show. 'What now?'

Pete blushed, and the birthmark on his face turned purple. 'They told me to take your gun.'

Anthony began to fear he might not be able to get out of this situation easily. There was no way he was giving up his weapon. He forced a smile and said: 'So you'll tell them I refused.'

'I'm sorry, sir, I can't tell you how sorry I am. But Mr Hobart was very specific. If you won't hand it over, I have to call the local police.'

Anthony realized then that he had to kill Pete.

For a moment he was swamped by grief. What depths of treachery he had been led into. It hardly seemed possible that this was the logical conclusion of his commitment, made two decades ago, to dedicate his life to a noble cause. Then a deadly calm descended on him. He had learned about hard choices in the war. This was a different war, but the imperatives were the same. Once you were in, you had to win, whatever it took. 'In that case, I guess it's all over,' he said with a sigh that was genuine. 'I think it's a dumb decision, but I believe I've done all I can.'

Pete made no attempt to conceal his relief. 'Thank you,' he said. 'I'm so glad you're taking it this way.'

'Don't you worry. I won't hold this against you. I know you have to follow a direct order from Hobart.'

Pete's face took on a determined expression. 'So, do you want to give me the firearm now?'

'Sure.' The gun was in Anthony's coat pocket, but he said: 'It's in my trunk.' He wanted Pete to go with him to the car, but he pretended the opposite. 'Wait here, I'll get it.'

As he had expected, Pete feared he was trying to escape. 'I'll come with you,' Pete said hastily.

Anthony pretended to hesitate and then give in. 'Whatever.' He walked through the door, with Pete following. The car was parked at the kerb, thirty yards from the airport entrance. There was no one in sight.

Anthony thumbed the trunk lid and threw it open. 'There you go,' he said.

Pete bent over to look in the trunk.

411

Anthony drew the gun, silencer attached, from inside his coat. For a moment, he was tempted by a mad impulse to put the barrel in his own mouth and pull the trigger, bringing the nightmare to an end.

That moment of delay was a crucial mistake.

Pete said: 'I don't see any gun,' and he turned around.

He reacted fast. Before Anthony could level his gun with its cumbersome silencer, Pete stepped sideways, away from the muzzle, and swung a fist. He caught Anthony with a bone-jarring blow to the side of the head. Anthony staggered. Pete hit him with the other fist, connecting with his jaw, and Anthony stumbled backwards and fell; but as he hit the ground he brought the gun up. Pete saw what was going to happen. His face twisted in fear and he lifted his hands, as if they could protect him from a bullet; then Anthony pulled the trigger three times in rapid succession.

All three bullets found their target on Pete's chest, and blood spurted from three holes in his grey mohair suit. He fell to the road with a thud.

Anthony scrambled to his feet and pocketed the gun. He looked up and down. No one was arriving at the airport, and no one had come out of the building. He bent over Pete's body.

Pete looked at him. He was not dead.

Fighting down nausea, Anthony picked up the bleeding body and tumbled it into the open trunk of the car. Then he drew his gun again. Pete lay in the trunk, twisted in pain, staring at him with terrified eyes. Chest wounds were not always fatal: Pete could live if he were treated in hospital soon. Anthony pointed the gun at Pete's head. Pete tried to speak, and blood came out of his mouth. Anthony pulled the trigger.

Pete slumped, and his eyes closed.

Anthony slammed the trunk lid and collapsed onto it. He had been hit seriously hard for the second time in a day, and his head was swimming; but worse than the physical damage was the knowledge of what he had done.

A voice said: 'Are you okay, buddy?'

Anthony came upright, stuffing the gun inside his coat, and turned around. A taxi had pulled up behind and the driver walked up, looking concerned. He was a black man with greying hair.

How much had the man seen? Anthony did not know if he had the heart to kill him, too.

The cabbie said: 'Whatever you were loading into your trunk, looks like it was heavy.'

'A rug,' Anthony said, breathing hard.

The man looked at him with the candid curiosity of small-town people. 'Someone give you a black eye? Or two?'

'A little accident.'

'Come inside, get a cup of coffee or something.'

'No, thanks. I'm okay.'

'Please yourself.' The driver ambled slowly into the terminal.

Anthony got into his car and drove away.

1.30 A.M.

The first task of the radio transmitters is to provide signals enabling the satellite to be followed by tracking stations on Earth – to prove that it is in orbit.

The train pulled slowly out of Chattanooga. In the cramped roomette, Luke took off his jacket and hung it up, then perched on the edge of the lower bunk and unlaced his shoes. Billie sat cross-legged on the bunk, watching him. The lights of the station flickered then faded as the locomotive gathered speed, heading into the Southern night, bound for Jacksonville, Florida.

Luke undid his tie. Billie said: 'If this is a striptease, it doesn't have much oomph.'

Luke grinned ruefully. He was going slowly because he was undecided. They had been forced to share the roomette: only one was available. He was longing to take Billie in his arms. Everything he had learned about himself and his life told him that Billie was the woman he should be with. Yet, all the same, he hesitated.

'What?' she said. 'What are you thinking?'

'That this is too quick.'

'Seventeen years is nothing?'

'To me it's been a couple of days, that's all I can remember.'

'It feels like forever.'

'I'm still married to Elspeth.'

Billie nodded solemnly. 'But she's been lying to you for years.'

'So I should jump out of her bed into yours?'

She looked offended. 'You should do what you want.'

He tried to explain. 'I don't like the feeling that I'm seizing an excuse.' She said nothing in reply, so he added: 'You don't agree, do you?'

'Hell, no,' she said. 'I want to make love to you tonight. I remember what it was like, and I want it again, right now.' She glanced out of the window as the train flew through a small town: ten seconds of streaking lights and they were in darkness again. 'But I know you,' she went on. 'You've never been one to live for the moment, even when we were kids. You need time to think things through and convince yourself that you're doing the right thing.'

'Is that so bad?'

She smiled. 'No. I'm glad you're like that. It makes you rock-solid reliable. If you weren't this way, I guess I wouldn't have . . .' Her voice tailed off.

'What were you going to say?'

She looked him in the eye. 'I wouldn't have loved you this much, this long.' She was embarrassed, and covered up by saying something flip. 'Anyway, you need a shower.'

It was true. He had been wearing the same clothes since he had stolen them thirty-six hours ago. 'Every time I thought about changing, there was something more urgent to do,' he said. 'I have fresh clothes in my bag.'

'No matter. Why don't you climb up on top, and give me room to take off my shoes.'

Obediently, he climbed the little ladder and lay down on the top bunk. He turned on his side, elbow on the pillow, head resting on his hand. 'Losing your memory is like a new start in life,' he said. 'Like being born again. Every decision you ever made can be revisited.'

She kicked off her shoes and stood up. 'I'd hate that,' she said. With a swift movement, she slipped off her black ski pants and stood there in her sweater and brief white panties. Catching his eye, she grinned and said: 'It's okay, you can watch.' She reached under her sweater at the back and unfastened her brassiere. Then she drew her left arm out of her sleeve, reached inside with her right hand to pull the strap off her shoulder, thrust her left arm back into the sleeve, and drew her bra out of her right sleeve with a conjurer's flourish.

'Bravo,' he said.

She gave him a thoughtful look. 'So, we're going to sleep now?'

'I guess.'

'Okay.' She stood on the edge of the lower bunk and raised herself to his level, tilting her face to be kissed. He leaned forward and touched her lips with his own. She closed her eyes. He felt the tip of her tongue flick over his lips, then she pulled away and her face disappeared.

He lay on his back, thinking about her lying a few

inches below, with her round breasts inside the soft angora sweater, her neat bare legs. In a few moments he was asleep.

He had an intensely erotic dream. He was Bottom in *A Midsummer Night's Dream*, with donkey's ears, and he was being kissed all over his hairy face by Titania's fairies, who were naked girls with slim legs and round breasts. Titania herself, the queen of the fairies, was unbuttoning his pants, while the wheels of the train drummed an insistent beat . . .

He woke up slowly, reluctant to leave fairyland and return to the world of railroads and rockets. His shirt was open and his pants were undone. Billie lay beside him, kissing him. 'Are you awake?' she murmured in his ear – a normal ear, not a donkey's. She giggled. 'I don't want to waste this on a guy who's asleep.'

He touched her, running his hand along her side. She still had on the sweater, but her panties had gone. 'I'm awake,' he said thickly.

She lifted herself on hands and knees so that she was over him, poised in the narrow space below the ceiling of the roomette. Looking into his eyes, she lowered her body onto his. He sighed with intense pleasure as he slid inside her. The train rocked from side to side, and the tracks sang to an erotic rhythm.

He reached inside her sweater to touch her breasts. Her skin was soft and warm. She whispered in his ear: 'They missed you.'

He felt as if he were still half in the dream, as the train rocked and Billie kissed his face and America flew by the window, mile after mile. He wound his arms around her back and held her tightly, to convince himself that she was made of flesh and blood, not fairy gossamer. Just as he was thinking that he wanted this to go on forever, his body took control, and he clung to her as waves of pleasure broke over him.

As soon as it was over she said: 'Keep still. Hold me tight.' He did not move. She buried her face in his neck, her breath hot on his skin. As he lay prone, still inside her, she seemed to twitch with an internal spasm, time and time again, until at last she sighed deeply and relaxed.

They lay still a few minutes longer, but Luke was not sleepy. Billie evidently felt the same, for she said: 'I have an idea. Let's wash.'

He laughed. 'Well, I sure need it.'

She rolled off him and climbed down, and he followed. In the corner of the roomette was a tiny washbasin with a cupboard over it. Billie found a hand towel and a little cake of soap in the cupboard. She filled the basin with hot water. 'I'll wash you, then you can wash me,' she said. She soaked the towel, rubbed soap on it, and began.

It was delightfully intimate and sexy. He closed his eyes. She soaped his belly, then kneeled to wash his legs. 'You missed a bit,' he said.

'Don't worry, I'm leaving the best part till last.'

When she had finished, he did the same for her, which was even more arousing. Then they lay down again, this time on the lower bunk.

'Now,' she said, 'do you remember oral sex?'

'No,' he said. 'But I think I can figure it out.'

PART 6

8.30 A.M.

To help track the satellite accurately, the Jet Propulsion Laboratory has developed a new radio technique called Microlock. The Microlock stations use a phased-lock loop tracking system which is able to lock on to a signal of only one-thousandth of a watt from as far as 20,000 miles away.

Anthony flew to Florida in a small plane that bumped and bucked with every gust of wind all the way across Alabama and Georgia. He was accompanied by a general and two colonels who would have shot him on sight if they had known the purpose of his trip.

He landed at Patrick Air Force Base, a few miles south of Cape Canaveral. The air terminal consisted of a few small rooms at the rear of an aircraft hangar. In his imagination he saw a detachment of FBI agents, with their neat suits and shiny shoes, waiting to arrest him; but there was only Elspeth.

She looked drained. For the first time, he saw signs of approaching middle age in her. The pale skin of her face showed the beginnings of wrinkles, and the posture of her long body was a little stooped. She led him outside to where her white Corvette was parked in the hot sun.

As soon as they were inside the car, he said: 'How's Theo?'

'Pretty shook, but he'll be okay.'

'Do the local police have his description?'

'Yes – Colonel Hide gave it out.'

'Where's he hiding?'

'In my motel room. He'll stay there until dark.' She drove out of the base onto the highway and turned north. 'What about you? Will the CIA give out your description to the police?'

'I don't think so.'

'So you can move around fairly freely. That's good, because you'll need to buy a car.'

'The Agency likes to solve its own problems. Right now, they think I've gone rogue, and their only concern is to take me out of circulation before I embarrass them. Once they start listening to Luke, they'll realize they've been harbouring a double agent for years – but that may make them even more concerned to hush up the whole thing. I can't be sure, but my guess is there will be no high-profile search for me.'

'And no shadow of suspicion has fallen on me. So all three of us are still in play. That gives us a good chance. We can still pull this thing off.'

'Luke doesn't suspect you?'

'He has no reason to.'

'Where is he now?'

'On a train, according to Marigold.' A note of bitterness entered her voice. 'With Billie.'

'When will he get here?'

'I'm not sure. The overnight train takes him to Jacksonville, but from there he has to get a slow train down the coast. Some time this afternoon, I guess.'

They drove in silence for a while. Anthony tried to make himself calm. In twenty-four hours, it would be all over. They would have struck a historic blow for the cause to which they had devoted their lives, and they would go down in history – or they would have failed, and the space race would once again be a two-horse contest.

Elspeth glanced across at him. 'What will you do after tonight?'

'Leave the country.' He tapped the small case in his lap. 'I have everything I need – passports, cash, a few simple items of disguise.'

'And then?'

'Moscow.' He had spent much of the flight thinking about this. 'The Washington desk at the KGB, I imagine.' Anthony was a major in the KGB. Elspeth had been an agent longer – had, in fact, recruited Anthony, back at Harvard – and she was a colonel. 'They'll give me some kind of senior advisory-consultative role,' he went on. 'After all, I'll know more about the CIA than anyone else in the Soviet bloc.'

'How will you like life in the USSR?'

'In the workers' paradise, you mean?' He gave her a wry grin. 'You've read George Orwell. Some animals are more equal than others. I guess a lot will depend on what happens tonight. If we pull this off, we'll be heroes. And if not . . .'

'You're not nervous?'

'Sure I am. I'll be lonely at first – no friends, no family, and I don't speak Russian. But maybe I'll get married and raise a brood of little comrades.' His flip answers disguised the depth of his anxiety. 'I decided, a long time ago, to sacrifice my personal life to something more important.'

'I made the same decision, but I'd still be frightened by the thought of moving to Moscow.'

'It's not going to happen to you.'

'No. They want me to stay in place, at all costs.'

She had obviously talked to her controller, whoever that was. Anthony was not surprised by the decision to leave Elspeth in place. For the last four years, Russian scientists had known everything about the US space programme. They saw every important report, all the test results, each blueprint produced by the Army Ballistic Missile Agency – thanks to Elspeth. It was as good as having the Redstone team working for the Soviet programme. Elspeth was the reason the Soviets had beaten the Americans into space. She was easily the most important spy of the Cold War.

Her work had been done at enormous personal sacrifice, Anthony knew. She had married Luke in order to spy on the space programme. But her love for him was genuine, and it had broken her heart to betray him. However, her triumph was the Soviet victory in the space race, which would be sealed tonight. That would make everything worthwhile.

Anthony's own triumphs were second only to Elspeth's. A Soviet agent, he had penetrated to the highest levels of the CIA. The tunnel he had been responsible for in Berlin, which had tapped into Soviet communications, had in fact been a channel for disinformation. The KGB had used it to mislead the CIA into wasting millions shadowing men who were not spies, penetrating organizations that were never communist fronts, and discrediting Third World politicians who were in fact pro-American. If he was lonely in his Moscow flat, he would think of what he had achieved, and it would warm his heart.

Among the palm trees on the roadside ahead, he saw a huge model of a space rocket above a sign that read 'Starlite Motel'. Elspeth slowed the car and pulled in. The office was in a low building with angular buttresses that gave it a futuristic look. Elspeth parked as far as possible from the road. The rooms were in a two-storey building around a large pool where a few early birds were already sunbathing. Beyond the pool, Anthony could see the beach.

Despite the assurances he had given Elspeth, he wanted to be seen by as few people as possible, so he pulled his hat low and walked quickly as they went from the car to her upstairs room.

The motel was making the most of the space-programme connection. The lamps were shaped like rockets, and there were pictures of stylized planets and stars on the walls. Theo was standing at the window, looking out over the ocean. Elspeth introduced the two men and ordered coffee and doughnuts from room service. Theo said to Anthony: 'How did Luke find me out – did he explain that to you?'

Anthony nodded. 'He was using the Xerox machine in Hangar R. There's a security log book beside the machine. You have to note the date and time and the number of copies you made, and sign the log. Luke noticed that twelve copies had been signed for by "WvB", meaning Wernher von Braun.'

Elspeth said: 'I always used von Braun's name, because no one would dare to question the boss about the Xerox copies he needed.'

Anthony went on: 'But Luke knew something you and everyone else didn't know – that von Braun was in Washington that day. Luke's instinct rang an alarm bell. He went to the mail room and found the copies in an envelope addressed to you. But he had no clue as to who had sent the package. He decided he couldn't trust anyone down here, so he flew to Washington. Fortunately, Elspeth called me and I was able to intercept Luke before he could tell anyone.'

Elspeth said: 'But now we're right back where we were on Monday. Luke has rediscovered what we made him forget.'

Anthony asked her: 'What do you think the army will do now?'

'They could launch the rocket with the self-destruct mechanism disabled. But if it got out that they had done so, there would be hell to pay, and the fuss might spoil the triumph. So my guess is they'll change the code, so that a different signal is required to trigger the explosion.'

'How would they do that?'

'I don't know.'

There was a knock at the door. Anthony tensed, but Elspeth said: 'I ordered coffee.' Theo went into the bathroom. Anthony turned his back to the door. To look natural, he opened the closet and pretended to study the clothes inside. There was a suit of Luke's hanging there, a light grey herringbone, and a stack of blue shirts. Instead of letting the waiter in, Elspeth stood in the doorway to sign the bill, tipped the man, then took the tray from him and closed the door.

Theo came out of the bathroom and Anthony sat down again.

Anthony said: 'What can we do? If they change the code we can't make the rocket self-destruct.'

Elspeth put down the coffee tray. 'I have to find out what their plan is, and figure out a way around it.' She picked up her handbag and slung her jacket over her shoulders. 'Buy a car. Drive to the beach as soon as it's dark. Park as near as you can to the Cape Canaveral fence. I'll meet you there. Enjoy your coffee.' She went out.

After a moment, Theo said: 'You have to give her credit, she's got a cool nerve.'

Anthony nodded. 'It's what she needs.'

4 P.M.

A string of tracking stations stretches from north to south roughly along the line of longitude 65 degrees west of the Greenwich meridian. The network will receive signals from the satellite every time it passes overhead.

The countdown stood at X minus 390 minutes.

Countdown time was moving in step with real time, so far, but Elspeth knew that might not last. If something unexpected happened, causing a delay, the countdown would stop. After the problem had been solved, the countdown would resume where it had left off, even though ten or fifteen minutes had passed. As the moment of ignition approached, the gap often broadened, and countdown time fell farther behind real time.

Today the countdown had started half an hour before noon, at X minus 660 minutes. Elspeth had moved about the base restlessly, updating her timetable, alert for any change in procedure. So far she had gained no clue as to how the scientists planned to guard against sabotage – and she was beginning to feel desperate.

Everyone knew Theo Packman was a spy. The desk

clerk at the Vanguard had told people that Colonel Hide had raided the motel with four cops and two FBI men, and asked at the desk for Theo's room number. The space community quickly linked the news with the last-second cancellation of the launch. The explanation given, that a late weather report had indicated a worsening of the jet stream, was not believed by anyone inside Cape Canaveral's perimeter fence. By this morning everyone had been talking about sabotage. But no one seemed to know what was being done about it; or, if they did, they were not spreading the news. As midday cooled into afternoon, Elspeth's tension mounted. So far she had not asked direct questions, for fear of arousing suspicion, but before too long she would have to abandon caution. If she did not learn the plan soon, it would be too late for her to act to counter it.

Luke had not shown up yet. She was longing to see him, and dreading it at the same time. She missed him when he was not beside her at night. But when he was there, she thought all the time about how she was working to destroy his dream. Her deceit had poisoned their marriage, she knew. All the same, she yearned to see his face, to hear his grave, courteous voice, to touch his hand and make him smile.

The scientists in the blockhouse were taking a break, eating sandwiches and drinking coffee where they sat at their panels. There was normally some joshing when an attractive woman entered the room, but today the atmosphere was quiet and tense. They were waiting for something to go wrong: a warning light, an overload, a broken part or a malfunctioning system. As soon as a glitch appeared, the mood would change: they would all become more cheerful as they got immersed in the problem, trying out explanations, brainstorming solutions, jury-rigging a repair. They were the kind of men who were happiest fixing something.

She sat next to Willy Fredrickson, her boss, who had his headphones around his neck while he ate a grilled-cheese sandwich. 'I guess you know everyone's talking about an attempt to sabotage the rocket,' she said conversationally.

Willy looked disapproving, which she took as a sign that he knew exactly what she was talking about. Before he could reply, a technician at the back of the room said: 'Willy,' and touched his own headphones.

Willy put down his sandwich and replaced his headset, then said: 'Fredrickson here.' He listened for a minute. 'Okay,' he said into his mouthpiece. 'Quick as you can.' Then he looked up and said: 'Stop the countdown.'

Elspeth tensed. Was this the clue she was waiting for? She lifted her notebook and pencil expectantly.

Willy took off his headphones. 'There'll be a ten-minute delay,' he said. His tone of voice betrayed only the normal irritation with any glitch. He took another bite of his sandwich.

Fishing for more information, Elspeth said: 'Shall I say why?'

'We have to replace a feed-through capacitor that seems to be chattering.'

It was possible, Elspeth thought. Capacitors were essential to the tracking system, and 'chattering' – random small electrical discharges – could be a sign that the device was going to fail. But she was not convinced. She made up her mind to check it out, if she could.

She scribbled a note, then got up and left with a cheery wave. Outside the blockhouse, the afternoon shadows were lengthening. The white shaft of the rocket stood like a signpost to the heavens. She imagined it taking off, lifting with agonizing slowness from the launch pad on its tail flame and rising into the night. Then she saw a flash of light brighter than the sun as the rocket exploded, fragments of metal scattering like shards of glass, a ball of red-and-black flame in the night sky, and a roaring sound like the triumphant shout of all the earth's poor and wretched.

She walked briskly across the sandy lawn to the concrete launch pad, circled around the gantry to the back and entered the steel cabin in its base that housed the offices and machinery. The gantry supervisor, Harry Lane, was speaking into a phone, making notes with a thick pencil. When he hung up, she said: 'Ten minutes' delay?'

'Could be more.' He did not look at her, but that did not mean much: he was always rude, not liking to see women on the launch pad.

Writing in her notebook, she said: 'Reason?'

'Replacing a malfunctioning component,' he said.

'Would you care to tell me *which* component?'

'No.'

It was maddening. She still could not tell whether he was covering up for security reasons or being just plain awkward. She turned away. Just then, a technician in oily overalls walked in. 'Here's the old one, Harry,' he said.

In his dirty hand he held a plug.

Elspeth knew exactly what it was: the receiver for the coded self-destruct signal. The pins that stuck out from it were cross-wired in a complex manner, so that only the correct radio signal would cause it to ignite the firing cap.

She walked quickly out the door before Harry could see the triumphant expression on her face. Heart thumping with excitement, she hurried back to her jeep.

She sat in the driving seat, working it out. To prevent sabotage they were replacing the plug. The new one would be wired differently, to work on a different code. A matching broadcast plug must have been fitted to the transmitter. The new plugs had probably been flown here from Huntsville earlier in the day.

It made sense, she thought with satisfaction. At last she knew what the army was doing. But how could she outmanoeuvre them?

The plugs were always made in sets of four, the duplicate pair being a spare in case of malfunction. It was the duplicate pair that Elspeth had examined, last Sunday, when she had sketched the wiring so that Theo could mimic the radio code and trigger the explosion. Now, she thought worriedly, she had to do the same all over again: find the duplicate set, dismantle the transmitter plug, and sketch its wiring.

She started the jeep and drove fast back to the hangars. Instead of going into Hangar R, where her desk was, she entered Hangar D and went to the telemetry room. This was where she had found the duplicate plugs the last time.

Hank Mueller was leaning on a bench with two other scientists, looking solemnly at a complex electrical device. When he saw her he brightened and said: 'Eight thousand.'

His colleagues groaned in mock despair and moved away.

Elspeth suppressed her impatience. She would have to play the numbers game with him before anything else. 'It's the cube of twenty,' she said.

'Not good enough.'

She thought for a moment. 'Okay, it's the sum of four consecutive cubes: $11^3+12^3+13^3+14^3$ equals 8,000.'

'Very good.' He gave her a dime and looked expectant.

She racked her brains for a curious number, then said: 'The cube of 16,830.'

He frowned, and looked affronted. 'I can't work that out, I need a computer!' he said indignantly.

'You haven't heard of it? It's the sum of all the consecutive cubes from 1,134 to 2,133.'

'I didn't know that!'

'When I was in high school, the number of my parents' house was 16,830, that's how I know.'

'This is the first time you've ever kept my dime.' He looked comically despondent.

She could not search the lab: she had to ask him. Fortunately, the other men were out of earshot, just. She blurted out: 'Do you have the duplicate set of new plugs from Huntsville?'

'No,' he replied, looking even more despondent. 'They say security is not good enough here. They put the plugs in a safe.'

She was relieved that he did not question her need to know. 'What safe?'

'They didn't tell me.'

'Never mind.' She pretended to make a note in her book, and went out.

She hurried to Hangar R, running across the sandy earth in her high-heeled shoes. She felt optimistic. But she still had a lot to do. It was getting dark already, she noticed.

There was only one safe that she knew of, in Colonel Hide's office.

Back at her desk, she rolled an army envelope into her typewriter and marked it: 'Dr W. Fredrickson – Eyes Only.' Then she folded two blank sheets of paper, slid them into the envelope, and sealed it.

She went to Hide's office, tapped at the door, and walked in. He was alone, sitting behind his desk, smoking a pipe. He looked up and smiled: like most of the men, he was generally pleased to see a pretty face. 'Elspeth,' he said in his slow drawl. 'What can I do for you?'

'Would you keep this in the safe for Willy?' She handed him the envelope.

'Sure,' he said. 'What is it?'

'He didn't tell me.'

'Naturally.' He spun around in his chair and opened a cupboard behind him. Looking over his shoulder, Elspeth saw a steel door with a dial. She moved closer. The dial was graduated from 0 to 99, but only multiples of 10 were marked with a figure, the other numbers being indicated by a notch. She peered at the dial. She had sharp eyesight, but still it was difficult to see exactly where Hide stopped the dial. She strained forward, leaning over the desk to get closer.

The first number was easy: 10. Then he dialled a number just below 30, either 29 or 28. Finally he moved the dial to between 10 and 15. The combination was something like 10–29–13. It must be his birthday, either the 28th or 29th of October, in 1911, 1912, 1913 or 1914. That gave a total of eight possibilities. If she could get in here alone, she could try them all in a few minutes.

Hide opened the door. Inside were two plugs. 'Eureka,' Elspeth whispered.

'What was that?' Hide said.

'Nothing.'

He grunted, tossed the envelope into the safe, closed the door and spun the dial.

Elspeth was already on her way out. 'Thank you, Colonel.'

'Any time.'

Now she had to wait for him to leave his office. She could not quite see his door from her desk. However, he was farther down the corridor, so he had to pass her office to get out. She propped her door open.

Her phone rang. It was Anthony. 'We're leaving here in a few minutes,' he said. 'Do you have what we need?'

'Not yet, but I will.' She wished she felt as sure as she sounded. 'What kind of car did you buy?'

'A light green Mercury Monterey, fifty-four model, the old-fashioned style, no tail fins.'

'I'll recognize it. How's Theo?'

'Asking me what he should do after tonight.'

'I assumed he'd fly to Europe and continue to work for *Le Monde*.'

'He's afraid they may track him down there.'

'I guess they might. Then he should go with you.'

'He doesn't want to.'

'Promise him anything,' she said impatiently. 'Just make sure he's ready for tonight.'

'Okay.'

Colonel Hide passed her door. 'I gotta go,' she said, and hung up.

She went out, but Hide had not disappeared. He stood in the next doorway, talking to the girls in the typing pool. He was still in sight of his door: Elspeth could not go in. She loitered for a minute, wishing he would move on. But, when he did, he returned to his office.

He stayed there for two hours.

Elspeth almost went crazy. She had the combination, she only needed to get in there and open the safe, and he would not go away. He sent his secretary to get coffee from the mobile refreshment stall they called the Roach Coach. He did not even go to the bathroom. Elspeth began to dream up ways of putting him out of action. She had been taught, in OSS, how to strangle someone with a nylon stocking, but she had never tried it. Anyway, Hide was a big man, he would put up a hell of a struggle.

She did not leave her office. Her timetable was forgotten. Willy Fredrickson would be furious, but what did that matter?

She looked at her wristwatch every few minutes. At eight twenty-five Hide at last walked past. She sprang up and went to her door. She saw him heading down the stairs. Launch was now only a couple of hours away: he was probably heading for the blockhouse.

Another man was walking along the corridor towards her. He said: 'Elspeth?' in an uncertain voice that she recognized. Her heart stopped, and she met his eye.

It was Luke.

8.30 P.M.

Information from the satellite's recording instruments is transmitted via radio by a musical tone. The different instruments use tones of different frequencies, so that the 'voices' can be separated, electronically, when they are received.

Luke had been dreading this moment.

He had dropped Billie off at the Starlite. She planned to check in and freshen up, then get a cab to the base in time to see the launch. Luke had gone straight to the blockhouse and learned that take-off was now scheduled for 10.45 p.m. Willy Fredrickson had explained the precautions the team had taken to prevent the sabotage of the rocket. Luke was not completely reassured. He wished Theo Packman had been arrested, and he would have liked to know where Anthony was. However, neither of them could do anything with the wrong code. And the new plugs were locked in a safe, Willy told him.

He would feel less worried when he had seen Elspeth. He had not told anyone about his suspicions of her – partly because he could not bear to accuse her, partly because he had no evidence. But when he looked into her eyes and asked her to tell him the truth, he would know.

He came up the stairs in Hangar R with a heavy heart. He had to talk to Elspeth about her betrayal, and he had to confess that he had been unfaithful to her. He did not know which was worse.

As he reached the top of the stairs he passed a man in colonel's uniform who spoke without stopping. 'Hey, Luke, good to have you back, see you in the blockhouse.' Then he saw a tall redhead emerge from an office along the corridor, looking anxious. There was a poised tension to her slender body as she stood in the doorway, looking past Luke at the colonel going down the stairs. She was more beautiful than her wedding photograph. Her pale face had a faint glow, like the surface of a lake at dawn. He felt a jolt of emotion like a shot in the arm, a strong feeling of tenderness for her.

He spoke to her, and then she noticed him. 'Luke!' She came quickly towards him. Her smile of welcome showed genuine pleasure, but he saw fear in her eyes. She threw her arms around him and kissed his lips. He realized he should not have been surprised – she was his wife, and he had been away all week. A hug was the most natural thing in the world. She had no idea that he suspected her, so she was continuing to act like a normal wife.

He cut short the kiss and detached himself from her embrace. She frowned and looked hard at him, trying to read his expression. 'What is it?' she said. Then she sniffed, and sudden anger suffused her face.

'You son of a bitch, you smell of sex.' She pushed him away. 'You fucked Billie Josephson, you bastard!' A passing scientist looked startled to hear such language, but she took no notice. 'You fucked her on the goddamn train.'

He did not know what to say. Her betrayal was worse than his, but all the same he was ashamed of what he had done. Anything he said was going to sound like an excuse, and he hated excuses, they made a man pathetic. So he said nothing.

Her mood switched again, just as quickly. 'I don't have time for this,' she said. She looked up and down the corridor, seeming impatient and distracted.

Luke was suspicious. 'What do you have to do that is more important than this conversation?'

'My job!'

'Don't worry about that.'

'What the hell are you talking about? I have to go. We'll talk later.'

'I don't think so,' he said firmly.

She reacted to his tone. 'What do you mean, you don't think so?'

'When I was at the house I opened a letter addressed to you.' He took it out of his jacket pocket and gave it to her. 'It's from a doctor in Atlanta.'

The blood drained from her face. She pulled the letter out of the envelope and began to read it. 'Oh, my God,' she whispered.

'You had your tubes tied six weeks before our wedding,' he said. Even now he could hardly believe it.

Tears came to her eyes. 'I didn't want to do it,' she said. 'I had to.'

He recalled what the doctor had said about Elspeth's state – insomnia, loss of weight, sudden crying, depression – and he felt a surge of compassion. His voice fell to a whisper. 'I'm so sorry you've been unhappy,' he said.

'Don't be nice to me, I couldn't stand it.'

'Let's go into your office.' He took her arm and led her into the room, closing the door. She went automatically to her desk and sat down, fumbling in her purse for a handkerchief. He got the big chair from behind the boss's desk and pulled it over so that he could sit close to her.

She blew her nose. 'I almost didn't have the operation,' she said. 'It broke my heart.'

He looked carefully at her, trying to be cool and detached. 'I guess they forced you to,' he said. He paused. Her eyes widened. 'The KGB,' he went on, and she stared at him. 'They ordered you to marry me so that you could spy on the space programme, and they made you get sterilized so that you would not have children to divide your loyalties.' He saw a terrible grief in her eyes, and he knew he was right. 'Don't lie,' he said quickly. 'I won't believe you.'

'All right,' she said.

She had admitted it. He sat back. It was all over. He felt breathless and bruised, as if he had fallen out of a tree.

'I kept changing my mind,' she said, and tears rolled down her face as she spoke. 'In the morning I'd be determined to do it. Then at lunch time I'd call you on the phone, and you'd say something about a house with a big yard for children to run around in, and I'd make up my mind to defy them. Then, alone in bed at night, I'd think how badly they needed the information I could get if I was married to you, and I'd resolve all over again to do what they wanted.'

'You couldn't do both?'

She shook her head. 'As it was I could hardly stand it, loving you and spying on you at the same time. If we'd had children I never could have done it.'

'What made you decide, in the end?'

She sniffed and wiped her face. 'You're not going to believe me. It was Guatemala.' She gave a queer little laugh. 'Those wretched people only wanted schools for their children and a trade union to protect them and the chance to earn a living. But it would have put a few cents on the price of bananas, and United Fruit didn't want that, so what did the US do? We overthrew their government and put in a fascist puppet. I was working for the CIA at the time, so I knew the truth. It made me so angry – that those greedy men in Washington could screw a poor country, and get away with it, and tell lies about it, and have the press tell Americans that it was a revolt by local anti-communists. You'll say it's a strange thing to get emotional about, but I can't tell you how mad I was.'

'Mad enough to do damage to your body.'

'And betray you, and ruin my marriage.' She lifted her head, and a proud look came over her face. 'But what hope is there for the world, if a nation of penniless peasants can't try to climb up out of the mud without being crushed under the jackboot of Uncle Sam? The only thing I regret is denying you children. That was wicked. The rest, I'm proud of.'

He nodded. 'I guess I understand.'

'That's something.' She sighed. 'What are you going to do? Call the FBI?'

'Should I?'

'If you do, I'll end up in the electric chair, like the Rosenbergs.'

He winced as if someone had stabbed him. 'Christ.'

'There's an alternative.'

'What?'

'Let me go. I'll catch the first plane out. I'll go to Paris, Frankfurt, Madrid, anywhere in Europe. From there I can get a flight to Moscow.'

'Is that what you want to do? Live out your days there?'

'Yes.' She gave a wry grin. 'I'm a KGB colonel, you know. I'd never be a colonel in the US.'

'You'd have to go now, immediately,' he said.

'Okay.'

'I'll escort you to the gate, and you'll have to give me your pass so you can't get back in.'

'Okay.'

He looked at her, trying to imprint her face on his memory. 'I guess this is goodbye.'

She picked up her purse. 'Can I go to the ladies' room first?'

'Of course,' he said.

9.30 P.M.

The main scientific purpose of the satellite is to measure cosmic rays, in an experiment designed by Dr James Van Allen of the State University of Iowa. The most important instrument inside it is a Geiger counter.

Elspeth walked out of her office, turned left, passed the door of the ladies' room, and entered Colonel Hide's office.

It was empty.

She closed the door behind her and stood leaning against it, trembling with relief. The office swam in her sight as her eyes filled with tears. The triumph of her life was within her grasp, but she had just ended her marriage to the best man she had ever known; and she was committed to leave the country of her birth and spend the rest of her days in a land she had never seen.

She closed her eyes and made herself breathe slowly and deeply: one, out, two, out, three, out. After a moment she felt better.

She turned the key in the office door. Then she went to the cupboard behind Hide's desk and kneeled in front of the safe. Her hands were shaking. With an effort of will, she made them steady. For some reason she recalled her Latin lessons at school and the proverb *Festina lente* – hurry slowly.

She repeated the actions Hide had performed when she watched him opening the safe. First she spun the dial four times anticlockwise, stopping at ten. Next she turned it three times in the other direction, stopping at 29. Then she turned it twice anticlockwise, stopping at 14. She tried to turn the handle. It would not move.

She heard footsteps outside, and a woman's voice. The sounds from the corridor seemed unnaturally loud, like noises in a nightmare. But the footsteps receded and the voice faded.

She knew the first number was 10. She dialled it again. The second number could have been 29 or 28. She dialled 28 this time, then 14 again.

The handle still would not turn.

She had tried only two possibilities out of the eight. Her fingers were slippery with sweat, and she wiped them on the hem of her dress. Next she tried 10, 29, 13, then 10, 28, 13.

She was half way through the list.

She heard a distant hooter give a warning blast – two shorts and a long, sounded three times in succession. This meant that all personnel should clear the launch-pad area. The launch was an hour away. She glanced involuntarily at the door, then returned her attention to the dial.

The combination 10, 29, 12 did not work.

But 10, 28, 12 did.

Jubilant, she turned the handle and pulled open the heavy door.

The two plugs were still there. She allowed herself a smile of triumph.

There was no time now to dismantle them and sketch the wiring. She would have to take them to the beach. Theo could either copy the wiring or use the actual plug in his own transmitter.

A danger occurred to her. Was it possible someone might notice the absence of the duplicate plugs during the next hour? Colonel Hide had gone to the blockhouse and was unlikely to return before blast-off. She had to take the risk.

There were footsteps outside the office again, and this time someone tried the door.

Elspeth stopped breathing.

A man's voice called: 'Hey, Bill, you in there?' It sounded like Harry Lane. What the hell did he want? The doorknob rattled. Elspeth kept still and silent. Harry said: 'Bill doesn't normally keep his door locked, does he?'

Another voice replied: 'I don't know, I guess the head of security is entitled to lock his door if he wants to.'

She heard departing footsteps, then the waning voice of Harry, saying: 'Security, hell, he doesn't want anyone stealing his Scotch.'

She grabbed the plugs from the safe and stuffed them into her purse. Then she closed the safe, spun the dial, and shut the cupboard.

She went to the office door, turned the key, and opened it.

Harry Lane was standing outside.

'Oh!' she said in shock.

He frowned accusingly. 'What were you doing in there?'

'Oh, nothing,' she said feebly, and tried to walk around him.

He grabbed her arm in a firm grasp. 'If it was nothing, why did you lock the door?' He squeezed her until it hurt.

That made her mad, and she stopped acting guilty. 'Let go of my arm, you big brainless bear, or I'll scratch your damn eyes out.'

Startled, he let go and stepped back; but he said: 'I still want to know what you were up to in there.'

She was struck by inspiration. 'I had to adjust my garter belt, and the ladies' room was full, so I used Bill's office in his absence. I'm sure he wouldn't mind.'

'Oh.' Harry looked foolish. 'No, I guess he wouldn't.'

Elspeth softened her tone. 'I know we have to be security-conscious, but there was no need to bruise my arm.'

'Yeah, sorry.'

She walked past him, breathing hard.

She re-entered her office. Luke was sitting where she had left him, looking grim. 'I'm ready,' she said.

He stood up. 'After you leave here, you'll go straight to the motel,' he said.

He was sounding brisk and practical, but she could see by his face that he was suppressing powerful emotions. She just said: 'Yes.'

'In the morning, you'll drive to Miami and get on a plane out of the United States.'

'Yes.'

He nodded, satisfied. Together they went down the steps and out into the warm night. Luke walked her to her car. As she opened the door, he said: 'I'll take your security pass now.'

She opened her purse and suffered a moment of sheer panic. The plugs were right there, on top of a yellow silk make-up bag, glaringly visible. But Luke did not see them. He was looking away, too polite to peek into a lady's purse. She took out her Cape Canaveral security pass and gave it to him, then closed her purse with a snap.

He pocketed the pass and said: 'I'll follow you to the gate in the jeep.'

She realized this was goodbye. She found herself unable to speak. She got into her car and slammed the door.

She swallowed her tears and drove off. The lights of Luke's jeep came on and followed her. Passing the launch pad, she saw the gantry inching back on its railroad tracks, ready for take-off. It left the huge white rocket standing alone in the floodlights, looking precarious, as if a careless nudge from a passer-by might topple it. She checked her watch. It was a minute before ten. She had forty-six minutes left.

She drove out of the base without stopping. The

headlights of Luke's jeep diminished in her rear-view mirror and finally disappeared as she rounded a bend. 'Goodbye, my love,' she said aloud, and she began to cry.

This time she could not control herself. As she drove down the coast road, she cried unrestrainedly, tears pouring down her face, her chest heaving with anguished sobs. The lights of other cars swept by in blurred streaks. She almost overshot the beach road. When she saw it, she jammed on her brakes and slewed across the highway in the path of the oncoming traffic. A taxicab braked hard and swerved, honking and skidding, and narrowly missed the tail of her Bel Air. She bumped onto the uneven sand of the beach track and slowed to a halt, heart pounding. She had almost ruined everything.

She wiped her face on her sleeve and drove on, more slowly, to the beach.

* * *

After Elspeth left, Luke stayed at the gate in his jeep, waiting for Billie to arrive. He felt breathless and stunned, as if he had run full-tilt into a wall, and was now lying on the ground trying to recover his senses. Elspeth had admitted everything. He had been sure, for the last twenty-four hours, that she was working for the Soviets, but nonetheless it was shocking to have his beliefs confirmed. Of course there were spies, everyone knew that, and Ethel and Julius Rosenberg had both died in the electric chair for espionage; but reading about such things in the newspapers was nothing. He had been married to a spy for four years. He could hardly take it in.

Billie arrived at ten-fifteen in a taxicab. Luke signed her in with security, then they got in the jeep and headed for the blockhouse. 'Elspeth has gone,' Luke said.

'I think I saw her,' Billie replied. 'Is she in a white Bel Air?'

'Yes, that's her.'

'My cab nearly hit her car. She pulled across the road right in front of us. I saw her face in the headlights. We missed her by about an inch.'

Luke frowned. 'Why did she pull in front of you?'

'She was turning off the road.'

'She told me she'd go straight back to the Starlite.'

Billie shook her head. 'No, she was heading for the beach.'

'The beach?'

'She went down one of those little tracks between the dunes.'

'Shit,' said Luke, and he turned the jeep around.

* * *

Elspeth drove slowly along the beach, staring at the groups of people who had gathered for the launch. Wherever she saw children or women, her eye moved on quickly. But there were many all-male groups of rocket buffs, standing around their cars in shirtsleeves with binoculars and cameras, smoking cigarettes and drinking coffee or beer. She stared hard at their vehicles, looking for a four-year-old Mercury Monterey.

Anthony had told her it was green, but there was not enough light to see colours.

She started at the crowded end of the beach, nearest to the base, but Anthony and Theo were not there, and she guessed they had chosen a more isolated spot. Terrified of missing them, she worked her way gradually south.

At last she saw a tall man in old-fashioned braces leaning against a light-coloured car and looking through binoculars towards the glow of the Cape Canaveral lights. She stopped the car and jumped out. 'Anthony!' she said.

He lowered the binoculars and she saw that it was not him. 'I'm sorry,' she said. She drove on.

She checked her watch. It was ten-thirty. She was almost out of time. She had the plugs, everything was ready: she just had to find two men on a beach.

The cars thinned out until they were a hundred yards or so apart. Elspeth picked up speed. She drove close to a car that looked right, but it seemed to be empty. She accelerated again – then the car honked.

She slowed down and looked back. A man had got out of the car and was waving at her. It was Anthony.'Thank God!' she said. She reversed back to him and leaped out of the car. 'I've got the duplicate plugs,' she said.

Theo got out of the other car and opened its trunk. 'Give them to me,' he said. 'Quickly, for God's sake.'

10.48 P.M.

The countdown reaches zero.

In the blockhouse, the launch conductor says: 'Firing command!' A crewman pulls a metal ring and twists it. This is the action that fires the rocket.

Prevalves open to let the fuel start flowing. The liquid oxygen vent is closed, and the halo of white smoke around the missile suddenly vanishes.

The launch conductor says: 'Fuel tanks pressurized.'

For the next eleven seconds, nothing happens.

The jeep tore along the beach at top speed, dodging in and out of family groups. Luke scanned the cars, ignoring the cries of protest as his tyres showered people with sand. Billie was standing up beside him, holding the top of the windshield. He shouted over the wind noise: 'See a white Bel Air?'

She shook her head. 'It should be easy to spot!'

'Yeah,' Luke said. 'So where the hell are they?'

* * *

The last connection hose drops away from the missile. A second later, the priming fuel ignites, and the first-stage

452

engine thunders into life. A huge orange firelick bursts from the base of the rocket as thrust builds.

* * *

Anthony said: 'For Christ's sake, Theo, hurry!'

'Shut up,' Elspeth told him.

They were bent over the open trunk of the Mercury, watching Theo fiddle with his radio transmitter. He was attaching wires to the pins of one of the plugs Elspeth had given him.

There was a roaring sound like distant thunder, and they all looked up.

* * *

With painful slowness, Explorer I lifts off the launch pad.

In the blockhouse, someone yells: 'Go, baby!'

* * *

Billie saw a white Bel Air parked next to a darker sedan. 'There!' she screamed.

'I see them,' Luke shouted back.

At the rear of the sedan, three people were clustered around the open trunk. Billie recognized Elspeth and Anthony. The other man was presumably Theo Packman. But they were not looking into the trunk. Their heads were raised and they were staring across the sand dunes towards Cape Canaveral.

Billie read the situation instantly. The transmitter was in the trunk. They were in the process of setting it to broadcast the detonation signal. But why were they looking up? She turned towards Cape Canaveral.

There was nothing to see, but she heard a deep, rumbling roar like the sound of a blast furnace in a steel mill.

The rocket was taking off.

'We're out of time!' she yelled.

'Hold tight!' Luke said.

She gripped the windshield as he swung the jeep around in a wide arc.

* * *

The rocket picks up speed suddenly. At one instant it seems to be hovering hesitantly over the launch pad. At the next it moves like a bullet out of a gun, shooting into the night sky on a tail of fire.

* * *

Over the roar of the rocket, Elspeth heard another sound, the scream of a car engine being raced. A second later, the beam of headlights fell on the group around the trunk of the Mercury. She looked up and saw a jeep heading for them at top speed. She realized it was going to ram them. 'Hurry!' she screamed.

Theo connected the last wire.

On his transmitter were two switches, one marked 'Arm' and the other 'Destroy'.

The jeep was on them.

Theo threw the 'Arm' switch.

* * *

On the beach, a thousand faces tip backwards, watching the rocket rise straight and true, and a huge cheer goes up.

* * *

Luke drove straight for the back of the Mercury.

The jeep had slowed as he turned, but he was still travelling at about twenty miles per hour. Billie jumped out, hit the ground running, then fell and rolled.

At the last second Elspeth threw herself out of the way. Then there was a deafening bang and the crash of breaking glass.

The Mercury's rear end crumpled, it jumped forward a yard, and its trunk lid came down with a bang. Luke thought either Theo or Anthony had been crushed between the cars, but he could not be sure. He was thrown forward violently. The bottom of the steering wheel caught his lower chest, and he felt the sharp pain of cracked ribs. A moment later, his forehead hit the top edge of the wheel, and he sensed hot blood flowing down his face.

Luke pulled himself upright and looked at Billie. She seemed to have fared better than he. She was sitting on the ground rubbing her forearms, but she did not appear to be bleeding.

He looked across the hood of the jeep. Theo lay on the ground in a spread-eagle position, not moving. Anthony was on his hands and knees, looking shaken but unhurt. Elspeth had escaped injury and was scrambling to her feet. She dashed to the Mercury and tried to open the trunk.

Luke leaped out of the jeep and ran at her. As the trunk lid lifted, he shoved her aside. She fell to the sand.

Anthony yelled: 'Hold it!'

Luke looked at him. He was standing over Billie with a pistol held to the back of her head.

Luke looked up. The red firetail of the missile was a bright shooting star in the night sky. As long as that was visible, Explorer could still be destroyed. The first stage would burn out when it was sixty miles high. At that point, the rocket would become invisible – for the lesser fire of the second stage would not be bright enough to be seen from the Earth – and this would be the sign that the self-destruct system would no longer work. The first stage, which contained the explosive detonator, would separate and fall away, eventually to splash down in the Atlantic Ocean. After separation, it could no longer damage the satellite.

And separation would take place two minutes and twenty-five seconds after ignition. Luke figured the rocket had been ignited roughly two minutes ago. There had to be about twenty-five seconds left.

It was plenty of time to throw a switch.

Elspeth got to her feet again.

Luke looked at Billie. She was on one knee, like a sprinter at the starting line, frozen in position with the long silencer of Anthony's gun pressing into her curly black hair. Anthony's hand was rock-steady.

Luke asked himself if he was ready to sacrifice Billie's life for the rocket.

The answer was No.

But what would happen, he thought, if he moved? Would Anthony shoot Billie? He might.

Elspeth again bent over the trunk of the car.

Then Billie moved.

She jerked her head to one side, then threw herself backwards, hitting Anthony's legs with her shoulders.

Luke lunged at Elspeth and pushed her away from the car.

The silenced gun coughed as Anthony and Billie fell in a heap.

Luke stared in dread. Anthony had fired, but had he hit Billie? She rolled away from him, apparently unhurt, and Luke breathed again. Then Anthony lifted his gun arm, aiming at Luke.

Luke looked death in the face, and a peculiar calm possessed him. He had done all he could.

There was a long moment of hesitation. Then Anthony coughed, and blood came out of his mouth. Pulling the trigger as he fell, he had shot himself, Luke realized. Now his limp hand dropped the gun and he slumped back on the sand, his eyes staring up at the sky but seeing nothing.

Elspeth sprang to her feet and bent over the transmitter a third time.

Luke looked up. The firetail was a glow-worm in space. As he watched, it winked out.

Elspeth threw the switch and looked up into the sky, but she was too late. The first stage had burned out and separated. The Primacord had probably detonated, but there was no fuel left to burn, and anyway the satellite was no longer connected to the first stage.

Luke sighed. It was all over. He had saved the rocket.

Billie put her hand on Anthony's chest, then checked his pulse. 'Nothing,' she said. 'He's dead.'

At the same moment, Luke and Billie looked at Elspeth. 'You lied again,' Luke said to her.

Elspeth stared at him with a hysterical light in her eyes. 'We weren't wrong!' she yelled. 'We were not wrong!'

Behind her, families of spectators and tourists were beginning to pack their belongings. No one had been close enough to notice the fighting: all eyes had been turned to the sky.

Elspeth looked at Luke and Billie as if she had more to say; but after a long moment she turned away. She got into her car, slamming the door, and started the engine.

Instead of turning towards the road, she headed for the ocean. Luke and Billie watched in horror as she drove straight into the water.

The Bel Air stopped, waves lapping at its fenders, and Elspeth got out. In the car's headlights, Luke and Billie saw her begin to swim out to sea.

Luke moved to go after her, but Billie grabbed his arm and held him back.

'She'll kill herself!' he said in agony.

'You can't catch her now,' Billie said. 'You'll kill yourself!'

Luke still wanted to try. But then Elspeth passed beyond the headlights' beam, swimming strongly, and he realized he would never find her in the dark. He bowed his head in defeat.

Billie put her arms around him. After a moment, he hugged her back.

Suddenly the strain of the last three days fell on him like a tree. He staggered, about to fall, and Billie held him upright.

After a moment he felt better. Standing on the beach, with their arms around one another, they both looked up.

The sky was full of stars.

EPILOGUE

1969

Explorer 1's Geiger counter recorded cosmic radiation a thousand times higher than expected. This information enabled scientists to map the radiation belts above the Earth that became known as the Van Allen belts, named after the State University of Iowa scientist who designed the experiment.

The micrometeorite experiment determined that about two thousand tons of cosmic dust rain down on the Earth annually.

The shape of the Earth turned out to be about one per cent flatter than previously thought.

Most important of all, for the pioneers of space travel, the temperature data from the Explorer showed that it was possible to control the heat inside a missile sufficiently for human beings to survive in space.

Luke was on the NASA team that put Apollo 11 on the moon.

By then he was living in a big, comfortable old house in Houston with Billie, who was Head of Cognitive Psychology at Baylor. They had three children: Catherine, Louis, and Jane. (Luke's stepson, Larry, also lived with them, but that July he was visiting his father, Bern.)

Luke happened to be off duty on the evening of 20 July. Consequently, at a few minutes before nine o'clock, Central time, he was watching TV with his family, as was half the world. He sat on the big couch with Billie beside him and Jane, the youngest, on his lap. The other kids were on the carpet with the dog, a yellow Labrador called Sidney.

When Neil Armstrong stepped on the moon, a tear rolled down Luke's cheek.

Billie took his hand and squeezed it.

Catherine, the nine-year-old, who had Billie's colouring, looked at him with solemn brown eyes. Then she whispered to Billie: 'Mommy, why is Daddy crying?'

'It's a long story, honey,' Billie said. 'I'll tell it to you, one day.'

* * *

Explorer 1 was expected to remain in space for two to three years. In fact, it orbited the Earth for twelve years. On 31 March 1970 it finally re-entered the atmosphere over the Pacific Ocean near Easter Island, and burned up at 5.47 a.m., having circled the Earth 58,376 times and travelled a total of 1.66 billion miles.

THE END.

ACKNOWLEDGEMENTS

Many people generously gave time and effort to help me get the background details right for this story. Most of them were found for me by Dan Starer, of Research for Writers in New York City, who has worked with me on every book since *The Man from St Petersburg* back in 1981. Special thanks to the following:

In Cambridge, Massachusetts: Ruth Helman, Isabelle Yardley, Fran Mesher, Peg Dyer, Sharon Holt and the students of Pforzheimer House, and Kay Stratton.

At the St Regis hotel, formerly the Carlton, in Washington DC: concierge Louis Alexander, bellhop José Muzo, general manager Peter Walterspiel and Mr Walterspiel's assistant, Pat Gibson.

At Georgetown University: archivist Jon Reynolds, retired physics professor Edward J. Finn, and Val Klump of the Astronomy Club.

In Florida: Henry Magill, Ray Clark, Henry Paul, and Ike Rigell, all of whom worked on the early space programme; and Henri Landwirth, the former manager of the Starlite Motel.

In Huntsville, Alabama: Tom Carney, Cathey Carney, and Jackie Gray, of *Old Huntsville* magazine;

Roger Schwerman of Redstone Arsenal; Michael Baker, Command Historian of the US Army Aviation & Missile Command; David Albert, Curator of the US Space & Rocket Center; Dr Ernst Stuhlinger.

Several family members read drafts and offered criticism, including my wife Barbara Follett, my stepdaughters Jann Turner and Kim Turner, and my cousin John Evans. I'm much indebted to editors Phyllis Grann, Neil Nyren, and Suzanne Baboneau; and to agents Amy Berkower, Simon Lipskar and, most of all, Al Zuckerman.

THE MAN FROM
ST PETERSBURG

'One can't love humanity. One can only love people'
Graham Greene

ACKNOWLEDGEMENTS

In writing this book I was helped by many friends. My grateful thanks to Alan Earney, Pat Golbitz, M. E. Hirsh, Elaine Koster, Diana Levine, Caren Meyer and her moles, Sue Rapp, Pamela Robinson and the staff of Bertram Rota Ltd, Hilary Ross, Christopher Sinclair-Stevenson, Daniel Starer, Colin Tennant, and – alphabetically last but in every other way first – Al Zuckerman.

The quotation on pages 71–2 is taken from *The Times* of 4 June 1914.

The quotation on pages 317–18 is taken from *The Times* of 29 June 1914.

'After the Ball' on page 288 was written by Chad K. Harris and published in the UK by Francis Day and Hunter.

'Her Dilemma' on pages 417–18 is taken from *The Complete Poems* by Thomas Hardy, published by Papermac.

CHAPTER ONE

IT WAS A slow Sunday afternoon, the kind Walden loved. He stood at an open window and looked across the park. The broad, level lawn was dotted with mature trees: a Scots pine, a pair of mighty oaks, several chestnuts, and a willow like a head of girlish curls. The sun was high and the trees cast dark, cool shadows. The birds were silent, but a hum of contented bees came from the flowering creeper beside the window. The house was still, too. Most of the servants had the afternoon off. The only weekend guests were Walden's brother George, George's wife Clarissa, and their children. George had gone for a walk, Clarissa was lying down, and the children were out of sight. Walden was comfortable: he had worn a frock coat to church, of course, and in an hour or two he would put on his white tie and tails for dinner, but in the meantime he was at ease in a tweed suit and a soft-collared shirt. Now, he thought, if only Lydia will play the piano tonight, it will have been a perfect day.

He turned to his wife. 'Will you play, after dinner?'

Lydia smiled. 'If you like.'

Walden heard a noise and turned back to the window. At the far end of the drive, a quarter of a mile

1

away, a motor car appeared. Walden felt a twinge of irritation, like the sly stab of pain in his right leg before a rainstorm. Why should a car annoy me? he thought. He was not against motor cars – he owned a Lanchester and used it regularly to travel to and from London – although in the summer they were a terrible nuisance to the village, sending up clouds of dust from the unpaved road as they roared through. He was thinking of putting down a couple of hundred yards of tarmacadam along the street. Ordinarily he would not have hesitated, but roads had not been his responsibility since 1909 when Lloyd George had set up the Roads Boards – and that, he realized, was the source of his irritation. It had been a characteristic piece of Liberal legislation: they took money from Walden in order to do themselves what he would have done anyway, then they failed to do it. I suppose I'll pave the road myself in the end, he thought; it's just annoying to pay for it twice.

The motor car turned into the gravel forecourt and came to a noisy, shuddering halt opposite the south door. Exhaust fumes drifted in at the window, and Walden held his breath. The driver got out, wearing helmet, goggles and a heavy motoring coat, and opened the door for the passenger. A short man in a black coat and a black felt hat stepped down from the car. Walden recognized the man, and his heart sank: the peaceful summer afternoon was over.

'It's Winston Churchill,' he said.

Lydia said: 'How embarrassing.'

The man just refused to be snubbed. On Thursday

he had sent a note which Walden had ignored. On Friday he had called on Walden at his London house, and had been told that the Earl was not at home. Now he had driven all the way to Norfolk on a Sunday. He would be turned away again. Does he think his stubbornness is impressive? Walden wondered.

He hated to be rude to people but Churchill deserved it. The Liberal government in which Churchill was a Minister was engaged in a vicious attack on the very foundations of English society – taxing landed property, undermining the House of Lords, trying to give Ireland away to the Catholics, emasculating the Royal Navy, and yielding to the blackmail of trade unions and damned socialists. Walden and his friends would not shake hands with such people.

The door opened and Pritchard came into the room. He was a tall Cockney with brilliantined black hair and an air of gravity which was transparently fake. He had run away to sea as a boy, and had jumped ship in East Africa. Walden, there on safari, had hired him to supervise the native porters, and they had been together ever since. Now Pritchard was Walden's majordomo, travelling with him from one house to another, and as much of a friend as a servant could be.

'The First Lord of the Admiralty is here, my lord,' Pritchard said.

'I'm not at home,' Walden said.

Pritchard looked uncomfortable. He was not used to throwing out Cabinet Ministers. My father's butler would have done it without turning a hair, Walden thought; but old Thomson is graciously retired, growing roses in the garden of that little cottage in the village, and somehow Pritchard has never acquired that unassailable dignity.

Pritchard began to drop his aitches, a sign that he was either very relaxed or very tense. 'Mr Churchill said you'd say not at 'ome, my lord, and 'e said to give you this letter.' He proffered an envelope on a tray.

Walden did *not* like to be pushed. He said crossly: 'Give it back to him—' Then he stopped, and looked again at the handwriting on the envelope. There was something familiar about the large, clear, sloping letters.

'Oh, dear,' said Walden.

He took the envelope, opened it, and drew out a single sheet of heavy white paper, folded once. At the top was the royal crest, printed in red. Walden read:

Buckingham Palace
May 1st. 1914.

My dear Walden
 You will see young Winston.

George R. I

'It's from the King,' Walden said to Lydia.

He was so embarrassed that he flushed. It was *frightfully* bad form to drag the King into something like this. Walden felt like a schoolboy who is told to stop quarrelling and get on with his prep. For a moment he was tempted to defy the King. But the consequences ... Lydia would no longer be received by the Queen, people would be unable to invite the Waldens to parties at which a member of the Royal Family would be present, and – worst of all – Walden's daughter Charlotte could not be presented at court as a debutante. The family's social life would be wrecked. They might as well go and live in another country. No, there was no question of disobeying the King.

Walden sighed. Churchill had defeated him. In a way it was a relief, for now he could break ranks and no one could blame him. *Letter from the King, old boy*, he would say in explanation; *nothing to be done, you know.*

'Ask Mr Churchill to come in,' he said to Pritchard.

He handed the letter to Lydia. The Liberals really did not understand how the monarchy was supposed to work, he reflected. He murmured: 'The King is just not firm enough with these people.'

Lydia said: 'This is becoming awfully boring.'

She was not bored at all, Walden thought, in fact she probably found it all quite exciting; but she said that because it was the kind of thing an English countess would say, and since she was not English but Russian she liked to say typically English things, the way a man speaking French would say *alors* and *hein?* a lot.

Walden went to the window. Churchill's motor car was still rattling and smoking in the forecourt. The driver stood beside it, with one hand on the door, as if he had to hold it like a horse to stop it wandering away. A few servants were gazing at it from a safe distance.

Pritchard came in and said: 'Mr Winston Churchill.'

Churchill was forty, exactly ten years younger than Walden. He was a short, slender man who dressed in a way Walden thought was a shade too elegant to be quite

5

gentlemanly. His hair was receding rapidly, leaving a peak at the forehead and two curls at the temples which, together with his short nose and the permanent sardonic twinkle in his eye, gave him a mischievous look. It was easy to see why the cartoonists regularly portrayed him as a malign cherub.

Churchill shook hands and said cheerfully: 'Good afternoon, Lord Walden.' He bowed to Lydia. 'Lady Walden, how do you do.' Walden thought: What is it about him that grates so on my nerves?

Lydia offered him tea and Walden told him to sit down. Walden would not make small talk: he was impatient to know what all the fuss was about.

Churchill began: 'First of all my apologies, together with the King's, for imposing myself on you.'

Walden nodded. He was not going to say it was perfectly all right.

Churchill said: 'I might add that I should not have done so, other than for the most compelling reasons.'

'You'd better tell me what they are.'

'Do you know what has been happening in the money market?'

'Yes. The discount rate has gone up.'

'From one-and-three-quarters to just under three per cent. It's an enormous rise, and it has come about in a few weeks.'

'I presume you know why.'

Churchill nodded. 'German companies have been factoring debts on a vast scale, collecting cash and buying gold. A few more weeks of this, and Germany will have got in everything owing to her from other countries, while leaving her debts to them outstanding – and her gold reserves will be higher than they have ever been before.'

'They are preparing for war.'

'In this and other ways. They have raised a levy of one billion marks, over and above normal taxation, to improve an army which is already the strongest in Europe. You will remember that in 1909, when Lloyd George increased British taxation by fifteen million pounds sterling, there was almost a revolution. Well, a billion marks is equivalent to *fifty* million pounds. It's the biggest levy in European history—'

'Yes, indeed,' Walden interrupted. Churchill was threatening to become histrionic: Walden did not want him making speeches. 'We Conservatives have been worried about German militarism for some time. Now, at the eleventh hour, you're telling me that we were right.'

Churchill was unperturbed. 'Germany will attack France, almost certainly. The question is, will we come to the aid of France?'

'No,' Walden said in surprise. 'The Foreign Secretary has assured us that we have no obligations to France—'

'Sir Edward is sincere, of course,' Churchill said. 'But he is mistaken. Our understanding with France is such that we could not possibly stand aside and watch her defeated by Germany.'

Walden was shocked. The Liberals had convinced everyone, him included, that they would not lead England into war; and now one of their leading Ministers was saying the opposite. The duplicity of the politicians was infuriating, but Walden forgot that as he began to contemplate the consequences of war. He thought of the young men he knew who would have to fight: the patient gardeners in his park, the cheeky footmen, the brown-faced farm-boys, the hell-raising undergraduates, the languid idlers in the clubs of St James's ... then that thought was overtaken by another, much more chilling, and he said: 'But can we win?'

Churchill looked grave. 'I think not.'

Walden stared at him. 'Dear God, what have you people done?'

Churchill became defensive. 'Our policy has been to avoid war; and you can't do that and arm yourself to the teeth at the same time.'

'But you have failed to avoid war.'

'We're still trying.'

'But you think you will fail.'

Churchill looked belligerent for a moment, then swallowed his pride. 'Yes.'

'So what will happen?'

'If England and France together cannot defeat Germany, then we must have another ally, a third country on our side: Russia. If Germany is divided, fighting on two fronts, we can win. The Russian army is incompetent and corrupt, of course – like everything else in that country – but it doesn't matter so long as they draw off part of Germany's strength.'

Churchill knew perfectly well that Lydia was Russian, and it was characteristically tactless of him to disparage her country in her presence, but Walden let it pass, for he was highly intrigued by what Churchill was saying. 'Russia already has an alliance with France,' he said.

'It's not enough,' Churchill said. 'Russia is obliged to fight if France is the victim of aggression. It is left to Russia to decide whether France is the victim or the aggressor in a particular case. When war breaks out both sides always claim to be the victim. Therefore the alliance obliges Russia to do no more than fight if she wants to. We need Russia to be freshly and firmly committed to our side.'

'I can't imagine you chaps joining hands with the Czar.'

'Then you misjudge us. To save England, we'll deal with the devil.'

'Your supporters won't like it.'

'They won't know.'

Walden could see where all this was leading, and the prospect was exciting. 'What have you in mind? A secret treaty? Or an unwritten understanding?'

'Both.'

Walden looked at Churchill through narrowed eyes. This young demagogue might have a brain, he thought; and that brain might not be working in my interest. So the Liberals want to do a secret deal with the Czar, despite the hatred which the English people have for the brutal Russian regime – but why tell me? They want to rope me in somehow, that much is clear. For what purpose? So that if it all goes wrong they will have a Conservative on whom to put the blame? It will take a plotter more subtle than Churchill to lead me into such a trap.

Walden said: 'Go on.'

'I have initiated naval talks with the Russians, along the lines of our military talks with the French. They've been going on for a while at a rather low level, and now they are about to get serious. A young Russian admiral is coming to London. His name is Prince Aleksei Andreivitch Orlov.'

Lydia said: 'Aleks!'

Churchill looked at her. 'I believe he is related to you, Lady Walden.'

'Yes,' Lydia said, and for some reason Walden could not even guess at she looked uneasy. 'He is the son of my elder sister, which makes him my . . . cousin?'

'Nephew,' Walden said.

'I didn't know he had become admiral,' Lydia added. 'It must be a recent promotion.' She was her usual, perfectly composed self, and Walden decided he had imagined that moment of unease. He was pleased that Aleks would be coming to London: he was very fond of the lad. Lydia said: 'He is young to have so much authority.'

'He's thirty,' Churchill said to Lydia, and Walden recalled that Churchill, at forty, was very young to be in charge of the entire Royal Navy. Churchill's expression seemed to say: The world belongs to brilliant young men like me and Orlov.

But you need me for something, Walden thought.

'In addition,' Churchill went on, 'Orlov is nephew to the Czar, through his father the late Prince, and – more importantly – he is one of the few people other than Rasputin whom the Czar likes and trusts. If anyone in the Russian naval establishment can swing the Czar on to our side, Orlov can.'

Walden asked the question that was on his mind. 'And my part in all this?'

'I want you to represent England in these talks – and I want you to bring me Russia on a plate.'

The fellow could never resist the temptation to be melodramatic, Walden thought. 'You want Aleks and me to negotiate an Anglo-Russian military alliance?'

'Yes.'

Walden saw immediately how difficult, challenging and rewarding the task would be. He concealed his excitement, and resisted the temptation to get up and pace about.

Churchill was saying: 'You know the Czar personally. You know Russia and speak Russian fluently. You're Orlov's uncle by marriage. Once before you have persuaded the Czar to side with England rather than with Germany – in 1906, when you intervened to prevent the ratification of the Treaty of Bjorko.' Churchill paused. 'Nevertheless, you were not our first choice to represent Britain at these negotiations. The way things are at Westminster . . .'

'Yes, yes.' Walden did not want to start discussing *that*. 'However, something changed your mind.'

'In a nutshell, you were the Czar's choice. It seems you are the only Englishman in whom he has any faith. Anyway, he sent a telegram to his cousin the King, insisting that Orlov deal with you.'

Walden could imagine the consternation among the Radicals when they learned they would have to involve a reactionary old Tory peer in such a clandestine scheme. 'I should think you were horrified,' he said.

'Not at all. In foreign affairs our policies are not so much at odds with yours. And I have always felt that domestic political disagreements were no reason why your talents should be lost to His Majesty's Government.'

Flattery now, Walden thought. They want me badly. Aloud he said: 'How would all this be kept secret?'

'It will seem like a social visit. If you agree, Orlov will stay with you for the London season. You will introduce him to society. Am I right in thinking that your daughter is due to come out this year?' He looked at Lydia.

'That's right,' she said.

'So you'll be going about a good deal anyway. Orlov is a bachelor, as you know, and obviously very eligible, so we can noise it abroad that he's looking for an English wife. He may even find one.'

'Excellent idea.' Suddenly Walden realized that he was enjoying himself. He had once been a kind of semi-official diplomat under the Conservative governments of Salisbury and Balfour, but for the last eight years he had taken no part in international politics. Now he had a chance to go back on stage, and he began to remember how absorbing and fascinating the whole business was: the secrecy; the gambler's art of negotiation; the conflicts of personalities; the cautious use of persuasion, bullying or the threat of war. The Russians were not easy to deal with, he recalled; they tended to be capricious, obstinate and arrogant. But Aleks would be manageable. When Walden married

Lydia, Aleks had been at the wedding, a ten-year-old in
a sailor suit. Later Aleks had spent a couple of years at
Oxford University, and had visited Walden Hall in the
vacations. The boy's father was dead, so Walden gave
him rather more time than he might normally have
spent with an adolescent, and was delightfully rewarded
by a friendship with a lively young mind.

It was a splendid foundation for a negotiation. I
believe I might be able to bring it off, he thought. What
a triumph that would be!

Churchill said: 'May I take it, then, that you'll do it?'

'Of course,' said Walden.

Lydia stood up. 'No, don't get up,' she said as the men
stood with her. 'I'll leave you to talk politics. Will you
stay for dinner, Mr Churchill?'

'I've an engagement in Town, unfortunately.'

'Then I shall say goodbye.' She shook his hand.

She went out of the Octagon, which was where they
always had tea, and walked across the great hall,
through the small hall, and into the flower-room. At
the same time one of the under-gardeners – she did
not know his name – came in through the garden door
with an armful of tulips, pink and yellow, for the dinner
table. One of the things Lydia loved about England in
general and Walden Hall in particular was the wealth
of flowers, and she always had fresh ones cut morning
and evening, even in winter when they had to be grown
in the hothouses.

The gardener touched his cap – he did not have to

take it off unless he was spoken to, for the flower room was notionally part of the garden – and laid the flowers on a marble table, then went out. Lydia sat down and breathed the cool, scented air. This was a good room in which to recover from shocks, and the talk of St Petersburg had unnerved her. She remembered Aleksei Andreivitch as a shy, pretty little boy at her wedding; and she remembered *that* as the most unhappy day of her life.

It was perverse of her, she thought, to make the flower room her sanctuary. This house had rooms for almost every purpose: different rooms for breakfast, lunch, tea and dinner, a room for billiards and another in which to keep guns, special rooms for washing clothes, ironing, making jam, cleaning silver, hanging game, keeping wine, brushing suits ... Her own suite had a bedroom, a dressing-room and a sitting-room. And yet, when she wanted to be at peace, she would come here and sit on a hard chair and look at the crude stone sink and the cast-iron legs of the marble table. Her husband also had an unofficial sanctuary, she had noticed: when Stephen was disturbed about something he would go to the gun-room and read the game book.

So Aleks would be her guest in London for the season. They would talk of home, and the snow and the ballet and the bombs; and seeing Aleks would make her think of another young Russian, the man she had not married.

It was nineteen years since she had seen that man, but still the mere mention of St Petersburg could bring

him to mind, and make her skin crawl beneath the
watered silk of her tea-gown. He had been nineteen,
the same age as she, a hungry student with long black
hair, the face of a wolf and the eyes of a spaniel. He was
as thin as a rail. His skin was white, the hair of his body
soft, dark and adolescent; and he had clever, clever
hands. She blushed now, not at the thought of his body
but at the thought of her own, betraying her, maddening her with pleasure, making her cry out shamefully. I
was wicked, she thought; and I am wicked still, for I
should like to do it again.

She thought guiltily of her husband. She hardly ever
thought of him without feeling guilty. She had not
loved him when they married, but she loved him now.
He was strong-willed and warm-hearted, and he adored
her. His affection was constant and gentle and entirely
lacking in the desperate passion which she had once
known. He was happy, she thought, only because he
had never known that love could be wild and hungry.

I no longer crave that kind of love, she told herself.
I have learned to live without it, and over the years it
has become easier. So it should – I'm almost forty!

Some of her friends were still tempted, and they
yielded, too. They did not speak to her of their affairs,
for they sensed she did not approve; but they gossiped
about others, and Lydia knew that at some country-
house parties there was a lot of . . . well, adultery. Once
Lady Girard had said to Lydia, with the condescending
air of an older woman who gives sound advice to a
young hostess: 'My dear, if you have the Viscountess
and Charlie Stott at the same time you simply *must* put

15

them in adjoining bedrooms.' Lydia had put them at opposite ends of the house, and the Viscountess had never come to Walden Hall again.

People said all this immorality was the fault of the late King, but Lydia did not believe them. It was true that he had befriended Jews and singers, but that did not make him a rake. Anyway, he had stayed at Walden Hall twice – once as Prince of Wales and once as King Edward the Seventh – and he had behaved impeccably both times.

She wondered whether the new King would ever come. It was a great strain, to have a monarch to stay, but such a thrill to make the house look its very best and have the most lavish meals imaginable and buy twelve new dresses just for one weekend. And if this King were to come, he might grant the Waldens the coveted *entrée* – the right to go into Buckingham Palace by the garden entrance on big occasions, instead of queuing up in The Mall along with two hundred other carriages.

She thought about her guests this weekend. George was Stephen's younger brother: he had Stephen's charm but none of Stephen's seriousness. George's daughter Belinda was eighteen, the same age as Charlotte. Both girls would be coming out this season. Belinda's mother had died some years ago and George had married again, rather quickly. His second wife, Clarissa, was much younger than he, and quite vivacious. She had given him twin sons. One of the twins would inherit Walden Hall when Stephen died, unless Lydia gave birth to a boy late in life. I could, she thought; I feel as if I could, but it just doesn't happen.

It was almost time to be getting ready for dinner. She sighed. She felt comfortable and natural in her tea-gown, with her fair hair dressed loosely; but now she would have to be laced into a corset and have her hair piled high on her head by a maid. It was said that some of the young women were giving up corsets altogether. That was all right, Lydia supposed, if you were naturally shaped like the figure 8; but she was small in all the wrong places.

She got up and went outside. That under-gardener was standing by a rose tree, talking to one of the maids. Lydia recognized the maid: she was Annie, a pretty, voluptuous, empty-headed girl with a wide, generous smile. She stood with her hands in the pockets of her apron, turning her round face up to the sun and laughing at something the gardener had said. Now *there* is a girl who doesn't need a corset, Lydia thought. Annie was supposed to be supervising Charlotte and Belinda, for the governess had the afternoon off. Lydia said sharply: 'Annie! Where are the young ladies?'

Annie's smile disappeared and she dropped a curt-sey. 'I can't find them, m'lady.'

The gardener moved off sheepishly.

'You don't appear to be looking for them,' Lydia said. 'Off you go.'

'Very good, m'lady.' Annie ran toward the back of the house. Lydia sighed: the girls would not be there, but she could not be bothered to call Annie back and reprimand her again.

She strolled across the lawn, thinking of familiar and pleasant things, pushing St Petersburg to the back of her mind. Stephen's father, the seventh Earl of Walden, had planted the west side of the park with rhododendrons and azaleas. Lydia had never met the old man, for he had died before she knew Stephen, but by all accounts he had been one of the great larger-than-life Victorians. His bushes were now in full glorious bloom, and made a rather un-Victorian blaze of assorted colours. We must have somebody paint a picture of the house, she thought; the last one was done before the park was mature.

She looked back at Walden Hall. The grey stone of the south front looked beautiful and dignified in the afternoon sunshine. In the centre was the south door. The farther, east wing contained the drawing-room and various dining-rooms, and behind them a straggle of kitchens, pantries and laundries running higgledy-piggledy to the distant stables. Nearer to her, on the west side, were the morning-room, the Octagon, and at the corner the library; then, around the corner along the west front, the billiard-room, the gun-room, her flower-room, a smoking-room and the estate office. On the first floor, the family bedrooms were mostly on the south side, the main guest-rooms on the west side, and the servants' rooms over the kitchens to the north-east, out of sight. Above the first floor was an irrational collection of towers, turrets and attics. The whole facade was a riot of ornamental stonework in the best Victorian rococo manner, with flowers and chevrons and sculpted coils of rope, dragons and lions and cherubim, balconies and battlements, flagpoles and sundials and gargoyles. Lydia loved the place, and she was grateful that Stephen – unlike many of the old aristocracy – could afford to keep it up.

She saw Charlotte and Belinda emerge from the shrubbery across the lawn. Annie had not found them, of course. They both wore wide-brimmed hats and summer frocks with schoolgirls' black stockings and low black shoes. Because Charlotte was coming out this season, she was occasionally permitted to put up her hair and dress for dinner, but most of the time Lydia treated her like the child she was, for it was bad for children to grow up too fast. The two cousins were deep in conversation, and Lydia wondered idly what they were talking about. What was on my mind when I was eighteen? she asked herself; and then she remembered a young man with soft hair and clever hands, and she thought: Please, God, let me keep my secrets.

'Do you think we'll *feel* different after we've come out?' Belinda said.

Charlotte had thought about this before. 'I shan't.'

'But we'll be grown up.'

'I don't see how a lot of parties and balls and picnics can make a person grow up.'

'We'll have to have corsets.'

Charlotte giggled. 'Have you ever worn one?'

'No, have you?'

'I tried mine on last week.'

'What's it like?'

'Awful. You can't walk upright.'

'How did you look?'

Charlotte gestured with her hands to indicate an enormous bust. They both collapsed laughing. Charlotte caught sight of her mother, and put on a contrite face in anticipation of a reprimand; but Mama seemed preoccupied, and merely smiled vaguely as she turned away.

'It will be fun, though,' said Belinda.

'The season? Yes,' Charlotte said doubtfully. 'But what's the point of it all?'

'To meet the right sort of young man, of course.'

'To look for husbands, you mean.'

They reached the great oak in the middle of the lawn, and Belinda threw herself down on the seat beneath the tree, looking faintly sulky. 'You think coming out is all very silly, don't you?' she said.

Charlotte sat beside her and looked across the carpet of turf to the long south front of Walden Hall. The tall Gothic windows glinted in the afternoon sun. From here the house looked as if it might be rationally and regularly planned, but behind that facade it was really an enchanting muddle. She said: 'What's silly is being made to wait so long. I'm not in a hurry to go to balls and leave cards on people in the afternoon and meet young men – I shouldn't mind if I never did those things – but it makes me so angry to be treated like a child still. I hate having supper with Marya, she's quite ignorant, or pretends to be. At least in the dining-room you get some conversation. Papa talks about interesting things. When I get bored Marya suggests we play cards.

I don't want to *play* anything, I've been playing all my life.' She sighed. Talking about it had made her angrier. She looked at Belinda's calm, freckled face with its halo of red curls. Charlotte's own face was oval, with a rather distinctive straight nose and a strong chin, and her hair was thick and dark. Happy-go-lucky Belinda, she thought; these things really don't bother her, *she* never gets intense about anything.

Charlotte touched Belinda's arm. 'Sorry. I didn't mean to carry on so.'

'It's all right.' Belinda smiled indulgently. 'You always get cross about things you can't possibly change. Do you remember that time you decided you wanted to go to Eton?'

'Never!'

'You most certainly did. You made a terrible fuss. Papa had gone to school at Eton, you said, so why shouldn't you?'

Charlotte had no memory of that, but she could not deny that it sounded just like her at ten years old. She said: 'But do you really think these things can't possibly be different? Coming out, and going to London for the season, and getting engaged, and then marriage . . .'

'You could have a scandal and be forced to emigrate to Rhodesia.'

'I'm not quite sure how one goes about having a scandal.'

'Nor am I.'

They were silent for a while. Sometimes Charlotte wished she were passive like Belinda. Life would be simpler – but then again, it would be awfully dull. She

21

said: 'I asked Marya what I'm supposed to *do* after I get married. Do you know what she said?' She imitated her governess's throaty Russian accent. 'Do? Why, my child, you will do *nothing*.'

'Oh, that's silly,' Belinda said.

'Is it? What do my mother and yours do?'

'They're Good Society. They have parties and stay about at country houses and go to the opera and . . .'

'That's what I mean. Nothing.'

'They have babies—'

'Now that's another thing. They make such a *secret* about having babies.'

'That's because it's . . . vulgar.'

'Why? What's vulgar about it?' Charlotte saw herself becoming *enthusiastic* again. Marya was always telling her not to be *enthusiastic*. She took a deep breath and lowered her voice. 'You and I have got to have these babies. Don't you think they might tell us something about how it happens? They're very keen for us to know all about Mozart and Shakespeare and Leonardo da Vinci.'

Belinda looked uncomfortable but very interested. She feels the same way about it as I do, Charlotte thought; I wonder how much she knows?

Charlotte said: 'Do you realize they grow inside you?'

Belinda nodded, then blurted out: 'But how does it start?'

'Oh, it just happens, I think, when you get to about twenty-one. That's really why you have to be a debutante and come out – to make sure you get a husband

22

before you start having babies.' Charlotte hesitated. 'I think,' she added.

Belinda said: 'Then how do they get out?'

'I don't know. How big are they?'

Belinda held her hands about two feet apart. 'The twins were this big when they were a day old. She thought again, and narrowed the distance. 'Well, perhaps this big.'

Charlotte said: 'When a hen lays an egg, it comes out ... behind.' She avoided Belinda's eyes. She had never had such an intimate conversation with anyone, ever. 'The egg seems too big, but it does come out.'

Belinda leaned closer and spoke quietly. 'I saw Daisy drop a calf once. She's the Jersey cow on the Home Farm. The men didn't know I was watching. That's what they call it, "dropping" a calf.'

Charlotte was fascinated. 'What happened?'

'It was horrible. It looked as if her tummy opened up, and there was a lot of blood and things.' She shuddered.

'It makes me scared,' Charlotte said. 'I'm afraid it will happen to me before I find out all about it. Why won't they *tell* us?'

'We shouldn't be talking about such things.'

'We've damn well got a right to talk about them!'

Belinda gasped. 'Swearing makes it worse!'

'I don't care.' It maddened Charlotte that there was no way to find out these things, no one to ask, no book to consult ... She was struck by an idea. 'There's a locked cupboard in the library – I bet there are books about all this sort of thing in there. Let's look!'

'But if it's locked . . .'

'Oh, I know where the key is, I've known for years.'

'We'll be in terrible trouble if we're caught.'

'They're all changing for dinner now. This is our chance.' Charlotte stood up.

Belinda hesitated. 'There'll be a row.'

'I don't care if there is. Anyway, I'm going to look in the cupboard, and you can come if you want.' Charlotte turned and walked toward the house. After a moment Belinda ran up beside her, as Charlotte had known she would.

They went through the pillared portico and into the cool, lofty great hall. Turning left, they passed the morning-room and the Octagon, then entered the library. Charlotte told herself she was a woman and entitled to know, but all the same she felt like a naughty little girl.

The library was her favourite room. Being on a corner of the house it was very bright, lit by three big windows. The leather-upholstered chairs were old and surprisingly comfortable. In winter there was a fire all day, and there were games and jigsaw puzzles as well as two or three thousand books. Some of the books were ancient, having been here since the house was built, but many were new, for Mama read novels and Papa was interested in lots of different things – chemistry, agriculture, travel, astronomy and history. Charlotte liked particularly to come here on Marya's day off, when the governess was not able to snatch away *Far from the Madding Crowd* and replace it with *The Water Babies*. Sometimes Papa would be here with her, sitting at the

Victorian pedestal desk and reading a catalogue of agricultural machinery or the balance sheet of an American railroad, but he never interfered with her choice of books.

The room was empty now. Charlotte went straight to the desk, opened a small, square drawer in one of the pedestals, and took out a key.

There were three cupboards against the wall beside the desk. One contained games in boxes and another had cartons of writing-paper and envelopes embossed with the Walden crest. The third was locked. Charlotte opened it with the key.

Inside were twenty or thirty books and a pile of old magazines. Charlotte glanced at one of the magazines. It was called *The Pearl.* It did not seem promising. Hastily, she picked out two books at random, without looking at the titles. She closed and locked the cupboard and replaced the key in the desk drawer.

'There!' she said triumphantly.

'Where can we go to look at them?' Belinda hissed.

'Remember the hideaway?'

'Oh! Yes!'

'Why are we whispering?'

They both giggled.

Charlotte went to the door. Suddenly she heard a voice in the hall, calling: 'Lady Charlotte ... Lady Charlotte ...'

'It's Annie, she's looking for us,' Charlotte said. 'She's nice, but so dim-witted. We'll go out the other way, quickly.' She crossed the library and went through the far door into the billiard-room, which led in turn to the gun-room; but there was someone in the gun-room. She listened for a moment.

'It's my Papa,' Belinda whispered, looking scared. 'He's been out with the dogs.'

Fortunately there was a pair of French doors from the billiard-room on to the west terrace. Charlotte and Belinda crept out and closed the doors quietly behind them. The sun was low and red, casting long shadows across the lawns.

'Now how do we get back in?' Belinda said.

'Over the roofs. Follow me!'

Charlotte ran around the back of the house and through the kitchen garden to the stables. She stuffed the two books into the bodice of her dress and tightened her belt so that they should not fall out.

From a corner of the stable yard she could climb, by a series of easy steps, to the roof over the servants' quarters. First she stood on the lid of a low iron bunker which was used to store logs. From there she hauled herself on to the corrugated tin roof of a lean-to shed where tools were kept. The shed leaned against the wash-house. She stood upright on the corrugated tin and lifted herself on to the slate roof of the wash-house. She turned to look behind: Belinda was following.

Lying face down on the sloping slates, Charlotte edged along crabwise, holding on with the palms of her hands and the sides of her shoes, until the roof ended up against a wall. Then she crawled up the roof and straddled the ridge.

Belinda caught up with her and said: 'Isn't this dangerous?'

'I've been doing it since I was nine years old.'

Above them was the window of an attic bedroom shared by two parlourmaids. The window was high in the gable, its top corners almost reaching the roof which sloped down on either side. Charlotte stood upright and peeped into the room. No one was there. She pulled herself on to the window-ledge and stood up.

She leaned to the left, got an arm and a leg over the edge of the roof, and hauled herself on to the slates. She turned back and helped Belinda up.

They lay there for a moment, catching their breath. Charlotte remembered being told that Walden Hall had four acres of roof. It was hard to believe until you came up here and realized you could get lost among the ridges and valleys. From here it was possible to reach any part of the roofs by using the footways, ladders and tunnels provided for the maintenance men who came every spring to clean gutters, paint drain-pipes and replace broken tiles.

Charlotte got up. 'Come on, the rest is easy,' she said.

There was a ladder to the next roof, then a board footway, then a short flight of wooden steps leading to a small, square door set in a wall. Charlotte unlatched the door and crawled through, and she was in the hideaway.

It was a low, windowless room with a sloping ceiling and a plank floor which would give you splinters if you were not careful. She imagined it had once been used as a storeroom: anyway, it was now quite forgotten. A door at one end led into a closet off the nursery, which had not been used for many years. Charlotte had discovered the hideaway when she was eight or nine, and had used it occasionally in the game – which she seemed to have been playing all her life – of escaping from supervision. There were cushions on the floor, candles in jars, and a box of matches. On one of the cushions lay a battered and floppy toy dog which had been hidden here eight years ago after Marya, the governess, had threatened to throw him away. A tiny occasional table bore a cracked vase full of coloured pencils, and a red leather writing-case. Walden Hall was inventoried every few years, and Charlotte could recall Mrs Braithwaite, the housekeeper, saying that the oddest things went missing.

Belinda crawled in and Charlotte lit the candles. She took the two books from her bodice and looked at the titles. One was called *Household Medicine* and the other *The Romance of Lust*. The medical book seemed more promising. She sat on a cushion and opened it. Belinda sat beside her, looking guilty. Charlotte felt as if she were about to discover the secret of life.

She leafed through the pages. The book seemed explicit and detailed on rheumatism, broken bones and measles, but when it arrived at childbirth it suddenly became impenetrably vague. There was some mysterious stuff about cramps, waters breaking, and a cord which had to be tied in two places then cut with scissors which had been dipped in boiling water. This chapter was evidently written for people who already knew a lot about the subject. There was a drawing of a naked woman. Charlotte noticed, but was too embarrassed to tell Belinda, that the woman in the drawing had no hair in a certain place where Charlotte had a great deal. Then there was a diagram of a baby inside a woman's tummy, but no indication of a passage by which the baby might emerge.

Belinda said: 'It must be that the doctor cuts you open.'

'Then what did they do in history, before there were doctors?' Charlotte said. 'Anyway, this book's no good.' She opened the other at random and read aloud the first sentence that came to her eye. 'She lowered herself with lascivious slowness until she was completely impaled upon my rigid shaft, whereupon she commenced her delicious rocking movements to and fro.' Charlotte frowned, and looked at Belinda.

'I wonder what it means?' said Belinda.

Feliks Kschessinsky sat in a railway carriage waiting for the train to pull out of Dover Station. The carriage was cold. He was quite still. It was dark outside, and he could see his own reflection in the window: a tall man with a neat moustache, wearing a black coat and a bowler hat. There was a small suitcase on the rack above his head. He might have been the travelling representative of a Swiss watch manufacturer, except that anyone who looked closely would have seen that the coat was cheap, the suitcase was cardboard, and the face was not the face of a man who sold watches.

He was thinking about England. He could remember

when, in his youth, he had upheld England's constitutional monarchy as the ideal form of government. The thought amused him, and the flat white face reflected in the window gave him the ghost of a smile. He had since changed his mind about the ideal form of government.

The train moved off, and a few minutes later Feliks was watching the sun rise over the orchards and hop fields of Kent. He never ceased to be astonished at how *pretty* Europe was. When he first saw it he had suffered a profound shock, for like any Russian peasant he had been incapable of imagining that the world could look this way. He had been on a train then, he recalled. He had crossed hundreds of miles of Russia's thinly populated north-western provinces, with their stunted trees, their miserable villages buried in snow, and their winding mud roads; then, one morning, he had woken up to find himself in Germany. Looking at the neat green fields, the paved roads, the dainty houses in the clean villages, and the flower beds on the sunny station platform, he had thought he was in Paradise. Later, in Switzerland, he had sat on the verandah of a small hotel, warmed by the sun yet within sight of snow-covered mountains, drinking coffee and eating a fresh, crusty roll, and he had thought: People here must be so happy.

Now, watching the English farms come to life in the early morning, he recalled dawn in his home village: a grey, boiling sky and a bitter wind; a frozen swampy field with puddles of ice and tufts of coarse grass rimed with frost; himself in a worn canvas smock, his feet

30

already numb in felt shoes and clogs; his father striding along beside him, wearing the threadbare robes of an impoverished country priest, arguing that God was good. His father had loved the Russian people because God loved them. It had always been perfectly obvious to Feliks that God hated the people, for He treated them so cruelly.

That discussion had been the start of a long journey, a journey which had taken Feliks from Christianity through socialism to anarchist terror, from Tambov province through St Petersburg and Siberia to Geneva. And in Geneva he had made the decision which brought him to England. He recalled the meeting. He had almost missed it . . .

He almost missed the meeting. He had been to Cracow, to negotiate with the Polish Jews who smuggled the magazine, *Mutiny*, across the border into Russia. He arrived in Geneva after dark, and went straight to Ulrich's tiny back-street printing shop. The editorial committee was in session: four men and two girls, gathered around a candle, in the rear of the shop behind the gleaming press, breathing the smells of newsprint and oiled machinery, planning the Russian revolution.

Ulrich brought Feliks up to date on the discussion. He had seen Josef, a spy for the Ochrana, the Russian secret police. Josef secretly sympathized with the revolutionaries, and gave the Ochrana false information for their money. Sometimes the anarchists would give him true but harmless tidbits, and in return Josef warned them of Ochrana activities.

This time Josef's news had been sensational. 'The Czar wants a military alliance with England,' Ulrich told Feliks. 'He is sending Prince Orlov to London to negotiate. The Ochrana know about it because they have to guard the Prince on the journey through Europe.'

Feliks took off his hat and sat down, wondering whether this was true. One of the girls, a sad, shabby Russian, brought him tea in a glass. Feliks took a half-eaten lump of sugar from his pocket, placed it between his teeth, and sipped the tea through the sugar in the peasant manner.

'The point being,' Ulrich went on, 'that England could then have a war with Germany and make the Russians fight it.'

Feliks nodded.

The shabby girl said: 'And it won't be the princes and counts who get killed – it will be the ordinary Russian people.'

She was right, Feliks thought. The war would be fought by the peasants. He had spent most of his life among those people. They were hard, surly and narrow-minded, but their foolish generosity and their occasional spontaneous outbursts of sheer fun gave a hint of how they might be in a decent society. Their concerns were the weather, animals, disease, childbirth and outwitting the landlord. For a few years, in their late teens, they were sturdy and straight, and could smile and run fast and flirt; but soon they became

bowed and grey and slow and sullen. Now Prince Orlov
would take those young men in the springtime of their
lives and march them in front of cannon to be shot to
pieces or maimed for ever, no doubt for the very best
reasons of international diplomacy.

It was things like this that made Feliks an anarchist.

'What is to be done?' said Ulrich.

'We must blaze the news across the front page of
Mutiny!' said the shabby girl.

They began to discuss how the story should be
handled. Feliks listened. Editorial matters interested
him little. He distributed the magazine and wrote
articles about how to make bombs, and he was deeply
discontented. He had become terribly civilized in
Geneva. He drank beer instead of vodka, wore a collar
and a tie, and went to concerts of orchestral music. He
had a job in a bookshop. Meanwhile Russia was in
turmoil. The oil workers were at war with the Cossacks,
the parliament was impotent, and a million workers
were on strike. Czar Nicolas II was the most incompetent and asinine ruler a degenerate aristocracy could
produce. The country was a powder barrel waiting for
a spark, and Feliks wanted to be that spark. But it was
fatal to go back. Joe Stalin had gone back, and no
sooner had he set foot on Russian soil than he had
been sent to Siberia. The secret police knew the exiled
revolutionaries better than they knew those still at
home. Feliks was chafed by his stiff collar, his leather
shoes and his circumstances.

He looked around at the little group of anarchists:
Ulrich, the printer, with white hair and an inky apron,

an intellectual who loaned Feliks books by Proudhon and Kropotkin but also a man of action who had once helped Feliks rob a bank; Olga, the shabby girl, who had seemed to be falling in love with Feliks until, one day, she saw him break a policeman's arm and became frightened of him; Vera, the promiscuous poetess; Yevno, the philosophy student who talked a lot about a cleansing wave of blood and fire; Hans, the watchmaker, who saw into people's souls as if he had them under his magnifying glass; and Piotr, the dispossessed Count, writer of brilliant economic tracts and inspirational revolutionary editorials. They were sincere and hardworking people, and all very clever. Feliks knew their importance, for he had been inside Russia among the desperate people who waited impatiently for smuggled newspapers and pamphlets and passed them from hand to hand until they fell to pieces. Yet it was not enough, for economic tracts were no protection against police bullets, and fiery articles would not burn palaces.

Ulrich was saying: 'This news deserves wider circulation than it will get in *Mutiny*. I want every peasant in Russia to know that Orlov would lead him into a useless and bloody war over something that concerns him not at all.'

Olga said: 'The first problem is whether we will be believed.'

Feliks said: 'The first problem is whether the story is true.'

'We can check,' Ulrich said. 'The London comrades could find out whether Orlov arrives when he is supposed to arrive, and whether he meets the people he needs to meet.'

'It's not enough to spread the news,' Yevno said excitedly. 'We must put a stop to this!'

'How?' said Ulrich, looking at young Yevno over the top of his wire-rimmed spectacles.

'We should call for the assassination of Orlov – he is a traitor, betraying the people, and he should be executed.'

'Would that stop the talks?'

'It probably would,' said Count Piotr. 'Especially if the assassin were an anarchist. Remember, England gives political asylum to anarchists, and this infuriates the Czar. Now, if one of his princes were killed in England by one of our comrades, the Czar might well be angry enough to call off the whole negotiation.'

Yevno said: 'What a story we would have then! We could say that Orlov had been assassinated by one of us for treason against the Russian people.'

'Every newspaper in the world would carry *that* report,' Ulrich mused.

'Think of the effect it would have at home. You know how Russian peasants feel about conscription – it's a death sentence. They hold a funeral when a boy goes into the army. If they learned that the Czar was planning to make them fight a major European war, the rivers would run red with blood . . .'

He was right, Feliks thought. Yevno always talked like that, but this time he was right.

Ulrich said: 'I think you're in dreamland, Yevno.

Orlov is on a secret mission – he won't ride through London in an open carriage waving to the crowds. Besides, I know the London comrades – they've never assassinated anyone. I don't see how it can be done.'

'I do,' Feliks said. They all looked at him. The shadows on their faces shifted in the flickering candle-light. 'I know how it can be done.' His voice sounded strange to him, as if his throat was constricted. 'I'll go to London. I'll kill Orlov.'

The room was suddenly quiet, as all the talk of death and destruction suddenly became real and concrete in their midst. They stared at him in surprise, all except Ulrich, who smiled knowingly, almost as if he had planned, all along, that it would turn out this way.

CHAPTER TWO

LONDON WAS unbelievably rich. Feliks had seen extravagant wealth in Russia, and much prosperity in Europe, but not on this scale. Here *nobody* was in rags. In fact, although the weather was warm, everyone was wearing several layers of heavy clothing. Feliks saw carters, street vendors, sweepers, labourers and delivery boys – all sporting fine factory-made coats without holes or patches. All the children wore boots. Every woman had a hat, and such hats! They were mostly enormous things, as broad across as the wheel of a dog-cart, and decorated with ribbons, feathers, flowers and fruit. The streets were teeming. He saw more motor cars in the first five minutes than he had in all his life. There seemed to be as many cars as there were horse-drawn vehicles. On wheels or on foot, everyone was rushing.

In Piccadilly Circus all the vehicles were at a standstill, and the cause was one familiar in any city: a horse had fallen and its cart had overturned. A crowd of men struggled to get beast and wagon upright, while from the pavement flower-girls and ladies with painted faces shouted encouragement and made jokes.

As he went farther east his initial impression of great

wealth was somewhat modified. He passed a domed cathedral which was called St Paul's, according to the map he had bought at Victoria Station, and thereafter he was in poorer districts. Abruptly, the magnificent facades of banks and office buildings gave place to small row houses in varying states of disrepair. There were fewer cars and more horses, and the horses were thinner. Most of the shops were street stalls. There were no more delivery boys. Now he saw plenty of barefoot children – not that it mattered, for in this climate, it seemed to him, they had no need of boots anyway.

Things got worse as he penetrated deeper into the East End. Here were crumbling tenements, squalid courtyards and stinking alleys, where human wrecks dressed in rags picked over piles of garbage, looking for food. Then Feliks entered Whitechapel High Street, and saw the familiar beards, long hair and traditional robes of assorted Orthodox Jews, and tiny shops selling smoked fish and kosher meat: it was like being in the Russian Pale, except that the Jews did not look frightened.

He made his way to No. 165 Jubilee Street, the address Ulrich had given him. It was a two-storey building that looked like a Lutheran chapel. A notice outside said the Worker's Friend Club and Institute was open to all working men regardless of politics, but another notice betrayed the nature of the place by announcing that it had been opened in 1906 by Peter Kropotkin. Feliks wondered whether he would meet the legendary Kropotkin here in London.

He went in. He saw in the lobby a pile of newspapers,

also called *The Worker's Friend* but in Yiddish: *Der Arbeter Fraint*. Notices on the walls advertised lessons in English, a Sunday school, a trip to Epping Forest, and a lecture on *Hamlet*. Feliks stepped into the hall. The architecture confirmed his earlier instincts: this had definitely been the nave of a nonconformist church once upon a time. However, it had been transformed by the addition of a stage at one end and a bar at the other. On the stage a group of men and women appeared to be rehearsing a play. Perhaps this was what anarchists did in England, Feliks thought; that would explain why they were allowed to have clubs. He went over to the bar. There was no sign of alcoholic drink, but on the counter he saw gefilte fish, pickled herring, and – joy! – a samovar.

The girl behind the counter looked at him and said: 'Nu?'

Feliks smiled.

A week later, on the day that Prince Orlov was due to arrive in London, Feliks had lunch at a French restaurant in Soho. He arrived early and picked a table near the door. He ate onion soup, fillet steak and goat's cheese, and drank half a bottle of red wine. He ordered in French. The waiters were deferential. When he finished, it was the height of the lunch-hour rush. At a moment when three of the waiters were in the kitchen and the other two had their backs to him he calmly got up, went to the door, took his coat and hat, and left without paying.

He smiled as he walked down the street. He enjoyed stealing.

He had quickly learned how to live in this town on almost no money. For breakfast he would buy sweet tea and a slab of bread from a street stall for twopence, but that was the only food he would pay for. At lunchtime he stole fruit or vegetables from street stalls. In the evening he would go to a charity soup kitchen and get a bowl of broth and unlimited bread in return for listening to an incomprehensible sermon and singing a hymn. He had five pounds in cash but it was for emergencies.

He was living at Dunstan Houses in Stepney Green, in a five-storey tenement building where lived half the leading anarchists in London. He had a mattress on the floor in the apartment of Rudolf Rocker, the charismatic blond German who edited *Der Arbeter Fraint*. Rocker's charisma did not work on Feliks, who was immune to charm, but Feliks respected the man's total dedication. Rocker and his wife Milly kept open house for anarchists, and all day – and half the night – there were visitors, messengers, debates, committee meetings, and endless tea and cigarettes. Feliks paid no rent, but each day he brought home something – a pound of sausages, a packet of tea, a pocketful of oranges – for the communal larder. They thought he bought these things, but of course he stole them.

He told the other anarchists he was here to study at the British Museum and finish his book about natural anarchism in primitive communities. They believed him. They were friendly, dedicated and harmless: they sincerely believed the revolution could be brought about by education and trade unionism, by pamphlets and lectures and trips to Epping Forest. Feliks knew that most anarchists outside Russia were like this. He did not hate them, but secretly he despised them, for in the end they were just frightened.

Nevertheless, among such groups there were generally a few violent men. When he needed them he would seek them out.

Meanwhile he worried about whether Orlov would come and about how he would kill him. Such worries were useless, and he tried to distract his mind by working on his English. He had learned a little of the language in cosmopolitan Switzerland. During the long train journey across Europe he had studied a school textbook for Russian children and an English translation of his favourite novel, *The Captain's Daughter*, by Pushkin, which he knew almost by heart in Russian. Now he read *The Times* every morning in the reading-room of the Jubilee Street club, and in the afternoons he walked the streets, striking up conversations with drunks, vagrants and prostitutes – the people he liked best, the people who broke the rules. The printed words in books soon meshed with the sounds all around him, and already he could say anything he needed to. Before long he would be able to talk politics in English.

After leaving the restaurant he walked north, across Oxford Street, and entered the German quarter west of Tottenham Court Road. There were a lot of revolutionists among the Germans, but they tended to be communists rather than anarchists. Feliks admired the

41

discipline of the communists but he was suspicious of their authoritarianism; and besides, he was temperamentally unsuited to party work.

He walked all the way across Regents Park and entered the middle-class suburb to its north. He wandered around the tree-lined streets, looking into the small gardens of the neat brick villas, searching for a bicycle to steal. He had learned to ride a bicycle in Switzerland, and had discovered that it was the perfect vehicle for shadowing someone, for it was manoeuvrable and inconspicuous, and in city traffic it was fast enough to keep up with a motor car or a carriage. Sadly, the bourgeois citizens of this part of London seemed to keep their bicycles locked away. He saw one cycle being ridden along the street, and was tempted to knock the rider off the machine, but at that moment there were three pedestrians and a baker's van in the road, and Feliks did not want to create a scene. A little later he saw a boy delivering groceries, but the boy's cycle was too conspicuous, with a large basket on the front and a metal plate, hanging from the crossbar, bearing the name of the grocer. Feliks was beginning to toy with alternative strategies when at last he saw what he needed.

A man of about thirty came out of one of the gardens wheeling a bicycle. The man wore a straw boater and a striped blazer which bulged over his paunch. He leaned his cycle against the garden wall and bent down to put on his trouser-clips.

Feliks approached him rapidly.

The man saw his shadow, looked up, and muttered: 'Good afternoon.'

Feliks knocked him down.

The man rolled on to his back and looked up at Feliks with a stupid expression of surprise.

Feliks fell on him, dropping one knee into the middle button of the striped blazer. The man's breath left his body in a whoosh, and he was winded, helpless, gasping for air.

Feliks stood up and glanced toward the house. A young woman stood at a window watching, her hand raised to her open mouth, her eyes wide with fright.

He looked again at the man on the ground: it would be a minute or so before he even thought about getting up.

Feliks climbed on the bicycle and rode away rapidly.

A man who has no fear can do anything he wants, Feliks thought. He had learned that lesson eleven years ago, in a railway siding outside Omsk. It had been snowing . . .

It was snowing. Feliks sat in an open railway truck, on a pile of coal, freezing to death.

He had been cold for a year, ever since he escaped from the chain gang in the gold mine. In that year he had crossed Siberia, from the frozen north almost to the Urals. Now he was a mere thousand miles from civilization and warm weather. Most of the way he had walked, although sometimes he rode in railcars or on wagons full of pelts. He preferred to ride with cattle, for they kept him warm and he could share their feed. He was vaguely aware that he was little more than an animal himself. He never washed, his coat was a blanket stolen from a horse, his ragged clothes were full of lice and there were fleas in his hair. His favourite food was raw birds' eggs. Once he had stolen a pony, ridden it to death, then eaten its liver. He had lost his sense of time. He knew it was autumn, by the weather, but he did not know what month he was in. Often he found himself unable to remember what he had done the day before. In his saner moments he realized he was half mad. He never spoke to people. When he came to a town or village he skirted it, pausing merely to rob the garbage tip. He knew only that he had to keep going west, for it would be warmer there.

But the coal train had been shunted into a siding, and Feliks thought he might be dying. There was a guard, a burly policeman in a fur coat, who was there to stop peasants taking coal for their fires ... As that thought occurred to him Feliks realized he was having a lucid moment, and that it might be his last. He wondered what had brought it on, then he smelled the policeman's dinner. But the policeman was big and healthy and had a gun.

I don't care, Feliks thought; I'm dying anyway.

So he stood up, and picked up the biggest lump of coal he could carry, and staggered over to the policeman's hut, and went in, and hit the startled policeman over the head with the lump of coal.

There was a pot on the fire and stew in the pot, too

hot to eat. Feliks carried the pot outside and emptied it out into the snow, then he fell on his knees and ate the food mixed with cooling snow. There were lumps of potato and turnip, and fat carrots, and chunks of meat. He swallowed them whole. The policeman came out of the hut and hit Feliks with his club, a heavy blow across the back. Feliks was wild with rage that the man should try to stop him eating. He got up from the ground and flew at the man, kicking and scratching. The policeman fought back with his club but Feliks could not feel the blows. He got his fingers to the man's throat and squeezed. He would not let go. After a while the man's eyes closed, then his face went blue, then his tongue came out, then Feliks finished the stew.

He ate all the food in the hut, and warmed himself by the fire, and slept in the policeman's bed. When he woke up he was sane. He took the boots and the coat off the corpse and walked to Omsk. On the way he made a remarkable discovery about himself: he had lost the ability to feel fear. Something had happened in his mind, as if a switch had closed. He could think of nothing that could possibly frighten him. If hungry, he would steal; if chased, he would hide; if threatened, he would kill. There was nothing he wanted. Nothing could hurt him any more. Love, pride, desire and compassion were forgotten emotions.

They all came back, eventually, except the fear.

When he reached Omsk he sold the policeman's fur coat and bought trousers and a shirt, a waistcoat and a topcoat. He burned his rags and paid one rouble for a hot bath and a shave in a cheap hotel. He ate in a restaurant, using a knife instead of his fingers. He saw the front page of a newspaper, and remembered how to read; and then he knew he had come back from the grave.

He sat on a bench in Liverpool Street Station, his bicycle leaning against the wall beside him. He wondered what Orlov was like. He knew nothing about the man other than his rank and mission. The Prince might be a dull, plodding, loyal servant of the Czar, or a sadist and a lecher, or a kindly white-haired old man who liked nothing better than to bounce his grandchildren on his knee. It did not matter: Feliks would kill him anyway.

He was confident he would recognize Orlov, for Russians of that type had not the faintest conception of travelling unobtrusively, secret mission or no.

Would Orlov come? If he did come, and arrived on the very train Josef had specified, and if he subsequently met with the Earl of Walden as Josef had said he would, then there could hardly be any further doubt that Josef's information had been accurate.

A few minutes before the train was due a closed coach drawn by four magnificent horses clattered by and drove straight on to the platform. There was a coachman in front and a liveried footman hanging on behind. A railwayman in a military-style coat with shiny buttons strode after the coach. The railwayman spoke to the coachman and directed him to the far end of the platform. Then a stationmaster in a frock coat and top hat arrived, looking important, consulting his fob watch and comparing it critically with the station clocks. He opened the carriage door for the passenger to step down.

The railwayman walked past Feliks' bench, and Feliks grabbed his sleeve. 'Please, sir,' he said, putting on the wide-eyed expression of a naive foreign tourist. 'Is that the King of England?'

The railwayman grinned. 'No, mate, it's only the Earl of Walden.' He walked on.

So Josef had been right.

Feliks studied Walden with an assassin's eye. He was tall, about Feliks' height, and beefy – easier to shoot than a small man. He was about fifty. Except for a slight limp he seemed fit: he could run away, but not very fast. He wore a highly visible light-grey morning coat and a top hat of the same colour. His hair under the hat was short and straight, and he had a spade-shaped beard patterned after that of the late King Edward VII. He stood on the platform, leaning on a cane – potential weapon – and favouring his left leg. The coachman, the footman and the stationmaster bustled about him like bees around the queen. His stance was relaxed. He did not look at his watch. He paid no attention to the flunkies around him. He is used to this, Feliks thought; all his life he has been the important man in the crowd.

The train appeared, smoke billowing from the funnel of the engine. I could kill Orlov now, Feliks thought, and he felt momentarily the thrill of the hunter as he closes with his prey; but he had already decided not to do the deed today. He was here to observe, not to act. Most anarchist assassinations were bungled because of haste or spontaneity, in his view. He believed in planning and organisation, which were anathema to many anarchists; but they did not realize that a man could plan his own actions – it was when he began to organize the lives of others that he became a tyrant.

The train halted with a great sigh of steam. Feliks stood up and moved a little closer to the platform. Toward the far end of the train was what appeared to be a private car, differentiated from the rest by the colours of its bright new paintwork. It came to a stop precisely opposite Walden's coach. The stationmaster stepped forward eagerly and opened a door.

Feliks tensed, peering along the platform, watching the shadowed space in which his quarry would appear.

For a moment everyone waited; then Orlov was there. He paused in the doorway for a second, and in that time Feliks' eye photographed him. He was a small man wearing an expensive-looking heavy Russian coat with a fur collar, and a black top hat. His face was pink and youthful, almost boyish, with a small moustache and no beard. He smiled hesitantly. He looked vulnerable. Feliks thought: So much evil is done by people with innocent faces.

Orlov stepped off the train. He and Walden embraced, Russian fashion, but quickly; then they got into the coach.

That was rather hasty, Feliks thought.

The footman and two porters began to load luggage on to the carriage. It rapidly became clear that they could not get everything on, and Feliks smiled to think of his own cardboard suitcase, half empty.

The coach was turned around. It seemed the footman was being left behind to take care of the rest of the luggage. The porters came to the carriage window, and a grey-sleeved arm emerged and dropped coins into their hands. The coach pulled away. Feliks mounted his bicycle and followed.

In the tumult of the London traffic it was not difficult for him to keep pace. He trailed them through the city, along the Strand, and across St James's Park. On the far side of the park the coach followed the boundary road for a few yards then turned abruptly into a walled forecourt.

Feliks jumped off his bicycle and wheeled it along the grass at the edge of the park until he stood across the road from the gateway. He could see the coach drawn up at the imposing entrance to a large house. Over the roof of the coach he saw two top hats, one black and one grey, disappear into the building. Then the door closed, and he could see no more.

Lydia studied her daughter critically. Charlotte stood in front of a large pier glass, trying on the debutante's gown she would wear to be presented at court. Madame Bourdon, the thin, elegant dressmaker, fussed about her with pins, tucking a flounce here and fastening a ruffle there.

Charlotte looked both beautiful and innocent – just the effect that was called for in a debutante. The dress, of white tulle embroidered with crystals, went down almost to the floor and partly covered the tiny pointed shoes. Its neckline, plunging to waist level, was filled in with a crystal corsage. The train was four yards of cloth-of-silver lined with pale pink chiffon and caught at the end by a huge white-and-silver bow. Charlotte's dark hair was piled high and fastened with a tiara which had belonged to the previous Lady Walden, Stephen's mother. In her hair she wore the regulation two white plumes.

My baby has almost grown up, Lydia thought.

She said: 'It's very lovely, Madame Bourdon.'

'Thank you, my lady.'

Charlotte said: 'It's terribly uncomfortable.'

Lydia sighed. It was just the kind of thing Charlotte *would* say. Lydia said: 'I wish you wouldn't be so frivolous.'

Charlotte knelt down to pick up her train. Lydia said: 'You don't have to kneel. Look, copy me and I'll show you how it's done. Turn to the left.' Charlotte did so, and the train draped down her left side. 'Gather it with your left arm, then make another quarter turn to the left.' Now the train stretched out along the floor in front of Charlotte. 'Walk forward, using your right hand to loop the train over your left arm as you go.'

'It works.' Charlotte smiled. When she smiled, you could feel the glow. She used to be like this all the time, Lydia thought. When she was little, I always knew what was going on in her mind. Growing up is learning to deceive.

Charlotte said: 'Who taught *you* all these things, Mama?'

'Your Uncle George's first wife, Belinda's mother, coached me before I was presented.' She wanted to say: These things are easy to teach, but the hard lessons you must learn on your own.

Charlotte's governess Marya came into the room. She was an efficient, unsentimental woman in an iron-grey dress, the only servant Lydia had brought from St Petersburg. Her appearance had not changed in nineteen years. Lydia had no idea how old she was: fifty? Sixty?

Marya said: 'Prince Orlov has arrived, my lady. Why, Charlotte, you look magnificent!'

It was almost time for Marya to begin calling her 'Lady Charlotte', Lydia thought. She said: 'Come down as soon as you've changed, Charlotte.' Charlotte immediately began to unfasten the shoulder-straps which held her train. Lydia went out.

She found Stephen in the drawing-room, sipping sherry. He touched her bare arm and said: 'I love to see you in summer dresses.'

She smiled. 'Thank you.' He looked rather fine himself, she thought, in his grey coat and silver tie. There was more grey and silver in his beard. *We might have been so happy, you and I* . . . Suddenly she wanted to kiss his cheek. She glanced around the room: there was a footman at the sideboard pouring sherry. She had to restrain the impulse. She sat down and accepted a glass from the footman. 'How is Aleks?'

'Much the same as always,' Stephen replied. 'You'll see, he'll be down in a minute. What about Charlotte's dress?'

'The gown is lovely. It's her attitude that disturbs me. She's unwilling to take anything at face value these days. I should hate her to become *cynical.*'

Stephen refused to worry about that. 'You wait until some handsome Guards officer starts paying attention to her – she'll soon change her mind.'

The remark irritated Lydia, implying as it did that all girls were the slaves of their romantic natures. It was the kind of thing Stephen said when he did not want to think about a subject. It made him sound like a hearty, empty-headed country squire, which he was not. But he was convinced that Charlotte was no different from any other eighteen-year-old girl, and he would not hear otherwise. Lydia knew that Charlotte had in her make-up a streak of something wild and un-English which had to be suppressed.

Irrationally, Lydia felt hostile toward Aleks on account of Charlotte. It was not his fault, but he represented the St Petersburg factor, the danger of the past. She shifted restlessly in her chair, and caught Stephen observing her with a shrewd eye. He said: 'You can't possibly be nervous about meeting little Aleks.'

She shrugged. 'Russians are so unpredictable.'

'He's not very Russian.'

She smiled at her husband, but their moment of intimacy had passed, and now there was just the usual qualified affection in her heart.

The door opened. Be calm, Lydia told herself.

Aleks came in. 'Aunt Lydia!' he said, and bowed over her hand.

'How do you do, Aleksei Andreivitch,' she said formally. Then she softened her tone and added: 'Why, you still look eighteen.'

'I wish I were,' he said, and his eyes twinkled.

She asked him about his trip. As he replied, she found herself wondering why he was still unmarried. He had a title which on its own was enough to knock many girls – not to mention their mothers – off their feet; and on top of that he was strikingly good-looking and enormously rich. I'm sure he's broken a few hearts, she thought.

'Your brother and your sisters send their love,' Aleks was saying, 'and ask for your prayers.' He frowned. 'St Petersburg is very unsettled now – it's not the town you knew.'

Stephen said: 'We've heard about this monk.'

'Rasputin. The Czarina believes that God speaks through him, and she has great influence over the Czar. But Rasputin is only a symptom. All the time there are strikes, and sometimes riots. The people no longer believe that the Czar is holy.'

'What is to be done?' Stephen asked.

Aleks sighed. 'Everything. We need efficient farms, more factories, a proper parliament like England's, land reform, trade unions, freedom of speech . . .'

'I shouldn't be in too much of a hurry to have trade unions, if I were you,' Stephen said.

'Perhaps. Still, somehow Russia must join the twentieth century. Either we, the nobility, must do it, or the people will destroy us and do it themselves.'

Lydia thought he sounded more radical than the Radicals. How things must have changed at home, that a prince could talk like this! Her sister Tatyana, Aleks' mother, referred in her letters to 'the troubles' but gave no hint that the nobility was in real danger. But then, Aleks was more like his father, the old Prince Orlov, a political animal. If he were alive today he would talk like this.

Stephen said: 'There is a third possibility, you know; a way in which the aristocracy and the people might yet be united.'

Aleks smiled, as if he knew what was coming. 'And that is?'

'A war.'

Aleks nodded gravely. They think alike, Lydia reflected; Aleks always looked up to Stephen; Stephen was the nearest thing to a father that the boy had, after the old Prince died.

Charlotte came in, and Lydia stared at her in surprise. She was wearing a frock Lydia had never seen, of cream lace lined with chocolate-brown silk. Lydia would never have chosen it – it was rather *striking* – but there was no denying that Charlotte looked ravishing. Where did she buy it? Lydia wondered. When did she start buying clothes without taking me along? Who told her that those colours flatter her dark hair and brown eyes? Does she have a trace of make-up on? And why isn't she wearing a corset?

Stephen was also staring. Lydia noticed that he had stood up, and she almost laughed. It was a dramatic acknowledgement of his daughter's grown-up status, and what was funny was that it was clearly involuntary. In a moment he would feel foolish, and he would realize that standing up every time his daughter walked into a room was a courtesy he could hardly sustain in his own house.

The effect on Aleks was even greater. He sprang to his feet, spilled his sherry, and blushed crimson. Lydia thought: Why, he's shy! He transferred his dripping glass from his right hand to his left, so that he was unable to shake with either, and he stood there looking helpless. It was an awkward moment, for he needed to compose himself before he could greet Charlotte, but he was clearly waiting to greet her before he would compose himself. Lydia was about to make some inane remark just to fill the silence when Charlotte took over.

She pulled the silk handkerchief from Aleks' breast pocket and wiped his right hand with it, saying: 'How do you do, Aleksei Andreivitch,' in Russian. She shook his now-dry right hand, took the glass from his left hand, wiped the glass, wiped the left hand, gave him back the glass, stuffed the handkerchief back into his pocket, and made him sit down. She sat beside him and said: 'Now that you've finished throwing the sherry around, tell me about Diaghilev. He's supposed to be a strange man. Have you met him?'

Aleks smiled. 'Yes, I've met him.'

As Aleks talked, Lydia marvelled. Charlotte had dealt with the awkward moment without hesitation, and had gone on to ask a question – one which she had presumably prepared in advance – which succeeded in taking Orlov's mind off himself and making him feel at ease. And she had done all that as smoothly as if she had had twenty years' practice. Where had she learned such poise?

Lydia caught her husband's eye. He too had noted Charlotte's graciousness, and he was smiling from ear to ear in a glow of fatherly pride.

Feliks paced up and down in St James's Park, pondering what he had seen. From time to time he glanced across the road at the graceful white facade of Walden's house, rising over the high forecourt wall like a noble head above a starched collar. He thought: They believe they are safe in there.

He sat on a bench, in a position from which he could still see the house. Middle-class London swarmed about him, the girls in their outrageous headgear, the clerks and shopkeepers walking homeward in their dark suits and bowler hats. There were gossiping nannies with babies in perambulators or overdressed toddlers; there were top-hatted gentlemen on their way to and from the clubs of St James's; there were liveried footmen walking tiny ugly dogs. A fat woman with a big bag of shopping plumped herself down on the bench beside him and said: 'Hot enough for you?' He was not sure what would be the appropriate reply, so he smiled and looked away.

It seemed that Orlov had realized his life might be

in danger in England. He had shown himself for only a few seconds at the station, and not at all at the house. Feliks guessed that he had requested, in advance, that he be met by a closed coach, for the weather was fine and most people were driving in open landaus.

Until today this killing had been planned in the abstract, Feliks reflected. It had been a matter of international politics, diplomatic quarrels, alliances and ententes, military possibilities, the hypothetical reactions of far-away Kaisers and Czars. Now, suddenly, it was flesh and blood; it was a real man, of a certain size and shape; it was a youthful face with a small moustache, a face which must be smashed by a bullet; it was a short body in a heavy coat, which must be turned into blood and rags by a bomb; it was a clean-shaven throat above a spotted tie, a throat which must be sliced open to gush blood.

Feliks felt completely capable of doing it. More than that, he was eager. There were questions – they would be answered; there were problems – they would be solved; it would take nerve – he had plenty.

He visualized Orlov and Walden inside that beautiful house, in their fine soft clothes, surrounded by quiet servants. Soon they would have dinner at a long table whose polished surface reflected like a mirror the crisp linen and silver cutlery. They would eat with perfectly clean hands, even the fingernails white, and the women wearing gloves. They would consume a tenth of the food provided and send the rest back to the kitchen. They might talk of racehorses or the new ladies' fashions or a king they all knew. Meanwhile the people who were to fight the war shivered in hovels in the cruel Russian climate – yet could still find an extra bowl of potato soup for an itinerant anarchist.

What a joy it will be to kill Orlov, he thought; what sweet revenge. When I have done that I can die satisfied.

He shivered.

'You're catching a cold,' said the fat woman.

Feliks shrugged.

'I've got him a nice lamb chop for his dinner, and I've made an apple pie,' she said.

'Ah,' said Feliks. What on earth was she talking about? He got up from the bench and walked across the grass toward the house. He sat on the ground with his back to a tree. He would have to observe this house for a day or two and find out what kind of life Orlov would lead in London: when he would go out and to where; how he would travel – coach, landau, motor car or cab; how much time he would spend with Walden. Ideally he wanted to be able to predict Orlov's movements and so lie in wait for him. He might achieve that simply by learning his habits. Otherwise he would have to find a way of discovering the Prince's plans in advance – perhaps by bribing a servant in the house.

Then there was the question of what weapon to use and how to get it. The choice would depend upon the detailed circumstances of the killing. Getting it would depend on the Jubilee Street anarchists. For this purpose the amateur-dramatics group could be ignored, as could the Dunstan Houses intellectuals and indeed all those with visible means of support. But there were four or five angry young men who always had money for drinks and, on the rare occasions when they talked politics, spoke of anarchism in terms of expropriating the expropriators, which was jargon for financing the revolution by theft. They would have weapons or know where to get them.

Two young girls who looked like shop assistants strolled by his tree, and he heard one of them say: '. . . told him, if you think just because you take a girl to the Bioscope and buy her a glass of brown ale you can . . .' Then they were past.

A peculiar feeling came over Feliks. He wondered whether the girls had caused it – but no, they meant nothing to him. Am I apprehensive? he thought. No. Fulfilled? No, that comes later. Excited? Hardly.

He finally figured out that he was happy.

It was very odd indeed.

That night Walden went to Lydia's room. After they had made love she slept, and he lay in the dark with her head on his shoulder, remembering St Petersburg in 1895.

He was always travelling in those days – America, Africa, Arabia – mainly because England was not big enough for him and his father both. He found St Petersburg society gay but prim. He liked the Russian landscape and the vodka. Languages came easily to him but Russian was the most difficult he had ever encountered and he enjoyed the challenge.

As the heir to an earldom, Stephen was obliged to

pay a courtesy call on the British Ambassador; and the Ambassador, in his turn, was expected to invite Stephen to parties and introduce him around. Stephen went to the parties because he liked talking politics with diplomats almost as much as he liked gambling with officers and getting drunk with actresses. It was at a reception in the British Embassy that he first met Lydia.

He had heard of her previously. She was spoken of as a paragon of virtue and a great beauty. She *was* beautiful, in a frail, colourless sort of way, with pale skin, pale blond hair, and a white gown. She was also modest, respectable, and scrupulously polite. There seemed to be nothing to her, and Walden detached himself from her company quite quickly.

But later he found himself seated next to her at dinner, and he was obliged to converse with her. The Russians all spoke French, and if they learned a third language it was German, so Lydia had very little English. Fortunately Stephen's French was good. Finding something to talk about was a bigger problem. He said something about the government of Russia, and she replied with the reactionary platitudes that were two-a-penny at the time. He spoke about his enthusiasm, big-game hunting in Africa, and she was interested for a while, until he mentioned the naked black pygmies, at which point she blushed and turned away to talk with the man on her other side. Stephen told himself he was not very interested in her, for she was the kind of girl one married, and he was not planning to marry. Still she left him with the nagging feeling that there was more to her than met the eye.

Lying in bed with her nineteen years later, Walden thought: She still gives me that nagging feeling; and he smiled ruefully in the dark.

He had seen her once more that evening in St Petersburg. After dinner he had lost his way in the labyrinthine embassy building, and had wandered into the music-room. She was there alone, sitting at the piano, filling the room with wild, passionate music. The tune was unfamiliar and almost discordant; but it was Lydia that fascinated Stephen. The pale, untouchable beauty was gone: her eyes flashed, her head tossed, her body trembled with emotion, and she seemed altogether a different woman.

He never forgot that music. Later he discovered that it had been Tchaikovsky's piano concerto in B flat minor, and since then he went to hear it played at every opportunity, although he never told Lydia why.

When he left the embassy he went back to his hotel to change his clothes, for he had an appointment to play cards at midnight. He was a keen gambler but not a self-destructive one: he knew how much he could afford to lose, and when he had lost it he stopped playing. Had he run up enormous debts he would have been obliged to ask his father to pay them, and that he could not bear to do. Sometimes he won quite large sums. However, that was not the appeal of gambling for him: he liked the masculine companionship, the drinking, and the late hours.

He did not keep that midnight rendezvous. Pritchard, his valet, was tying Stephen's tie when the British Ambassador knocked on the door of the hotel suite.

His Excellency looked as if he had got out of bed and dressed hastily. Stephen's first thought was that some kind of revolution was going on and all the British would have to take refuge in the embassy.

'Bad news, I'm afraid,' said the Ambassador. 'You'd better sit down. Cable from England. It's your father.'

The old tyrant was dead of a heart attack at sixty-five.

'Well, I'm damned,' Stephen said. 'So soon.'

'My deepest sympathy,' the Ambassador said.

'It was very good of you to come personally.'

'Not at all. Anything I can do.'

'You're very kind.'

The Ambassador shook his hand and left.

Stephen stared into space, thinking about the old man. He had been immensely tall, with a will of iron and a sour disposition. His sarcasm could bring tears to your eyes. There were three ways to deal with him: you could become like him, you could go under, or you could go away. Stephen's mother, a sweet, helpless Victorian girl, had gone under, and died young. Stephen had gone away.

He pictured his father lying in a coffin, and thought: You're helpless at last. Now you can't make housemaids cry, or footmen tremble, or children run and hide. You're powerless to arrange marriages, evict tenants, or defeat parliamentary bills. You'll send no more thieves to jail, transport no more agitators to Australia. Ashes to ashes, dust to dust.

In later years he revised his opinion of his father. Now, in 1914, at the age of fifty, Walden could admit to himself that he had inherited some of his father's values: love of knowledge, a belief in rationalism, a commitment to good work as the justification of a man's existence. But back in 1895 there had been only bitterness.

Pritchard had brought a bottle of whisky on a tray and said: 'This is a sad day, my lord.'

That *my lord* startled Stephen. He and his brother had courtesy titles – Stephen's was Lord Highcombe – but they were always called 'sir' by the servants, and 'my lord' was reserved for their father. Now, of course, Stephen was the Earl of Walden. Along with the title, he now possessed several thousands of acres in the south of England, a big chunk of Scotland, six race-horses, Walden Hall, a villa in Monte Carlo, a shooting-box in Scotland and a seat in the House of Lords.

He would have to live at Walden Hall. It was the family seat, and the Earl always lived there. He would put in electric light, he decided. He would sell some of the farms and invest in London property and North American railroads. He would make his maiden speech in the House of Lords – what would he speak on? Foreign policy, probably. There were tenants to be looked after, several households to be managed. He would have to appear in court in the season, and give shooting parties and hunt balls—

He needed a wife.

The role of Earl of Walden could not be played by a bachelor. Someone must be hostess at all those parties, someone must reply to invitations, discuss menus with cooks, allocate bedrooms to guests, and sit at the foot of the long table in the dining-room of Walden Hall. There must be a Countess of Walden.

There must be an heir.

'I need a wife, Pritchard.'

'Yes, my lord. Our bachelor days are over.'

The next day Walden saw Lydia's father and formally asked permission to call on her.

Twenty years later he found it difficult to imagine how he could have been so wickedly irresponsible, even in his youth. He had never asked himself whether she was the right wife for him, only whether she was suited to be a countess. He had never wondered whether he could make her happy. He had assumed that the hidden passion released when she played the piano would be released for him, and he had been wrong.

He called on her every day for two weeks – there was no possibility of getting home in time for his father's funeral – and then he proposed, not to her but to her father. Her father saw the match in the same practical terms as Walden. Walden explained that he wanted to marry immediately, although he was in mourning, because he had to get home and manage the estate. Lydia's father understood perfectly. They were married six weeks later.

What an arrogant young fool I was, he thought. I imagined that England would always rule the world and I would always rule my own heart.

The moon came out from behind a cloud and illuminated the bedroom. He looked down at Lydia's sleeping face. I didn't foresee this, he thought; I didn't know that I would fall helplessly, hopelessly in love with you. I asked only that we should like each other, and in the end that was enough for you but not for me. I never thought that I would *need* your smile, yearn for your kisses, long for you to come to *my* room at night; I never thought that I would be frightened, *terrified* of losing you.

She murmured in her sleep and turned over. He pulled his arm from under her neck, then sat up on the edge of the bed. If he stayed any longer he would nod off, and it would not do to have Lydia's maid find them in bed together when she came in with the morning cup of tea. He put on his dressing-gown and his carpet slippers and walked softly out of the room, through the twin dressing-rooms, and into his own bedroom. I'm such a lucky man, he thought as he lay down to sleep.

Walden surveyed the breakfast table. There were pots of coffee, China tea and Indian tea; jugs of cream, milk and cordial; a big bowl of hot porridge; plates of scones and toast; and little pots of marmalade, honey and jam. On the sideboard was a row of silver dishes, each warmed by its own spirit lamp, containing scrambled eggs, sausages, bacon, kidneys and haddock. On the cold table were pressed beef, ham and tongue. The fruit bowl, on a table of its own, was piled with nectarines, oranges, melons and strawberries.

This ought to put Aleks in a good mood, he thought.

He helped himself to eggs and kidneys and sat down.

The Russians would have their price, he thought; they would want something in return for their promise of military help. He was worried about what the price might be. If they were to ask for something England could not possibly grant, the whole deal would collapse immediately, and then . . .

It was his job to make sure it did not collapse.

He would have to manipulate Aleks. The thought made him uncomfortable. Having known the boy for so long should have been a help, but in fact it might have been easier to negotiate in a tough way with someone about whom one did not care personally.

I must put my feelings aside, he thought; we must have Russia.

He poured coffee and took some scones and honey. A minute later Aleks came in, looking bright-eyed and well-scrubbed. 'Sleep well?' Walden asked him.

'Wonderfully well.' Aleks took a nectarine and began to eat it with a knife and fork.

'Is that all you're having?' Walden said. 'You used to love English breakfast – I remember you eating porridge, cream, eggs, beef and strawberries and then asking cook for more toast.'

'I'm not a growing boy any more, Uncle Stephen.'

I might do well to remember that, Walden thought.

After breakfast they went into the morning-room. 'Our new five-year plan for the army and navy is about to be announced,' Aleks said.

That's what he does, Walden thought; he tells you something before he asks you for something. He remembered Aleks saying: I'm planning to read Clausewitz this summer, Uncle. By the way, may I bring a guest to Scotland for the shooting?'

'The budget for the next five years is seven-and-a-half billion roubles,' Aleks went on.

At ten roubles to the pound sterling, Walden calculated, that made £750 million. 'It's a massive programme,' he said, 'but I wish you had begun it five years ago.'

'So do I,' said Aleks.

'The chances are that the programme will hardly have started before we're at war.'

Aleks shrugged.

Walden thought: He won't commit himself to a forecast of how soon Russia might be at war, of course. 'The first thing you should do is increase the size of the guns on your Dreadnoughts.'

Aleks shook his head. 'Our third Dreadnought is about to be launched. The fourth is being built now. Both will have 12-inch guns.'

'It's not enough, Aleks. Churchill has gone over to 15-inch guns for ours.'

'And he's right. Our commanders know that, but our politicians don't. You know Russia, Uncle: new ideas are viewed with the utmost distrust. Innovation takes for ever.'

We're fencing, Walden thought. 'What *is* your priority?'

'A hundred million roubles will be spent immediately on the Black Sea fleet.'

'I should have thought the North Sea was more important.' For England, anyway.

'We have a more Asian viewpoint than you – our bullying neighbour is Turkey, not Germany.'

'They might be allies.'

'They might indeed.' Aleks hesitated. 'The great weakness of the Russian Navy,' he went on, 'is that we have no warm-water port.'

It sounded like the beginning of a prepared speech. This is it, Walden thought; we're getting to the heart of the matter now. But he continued to fence. 'What about Odessa?'

'On the Black Sea coast. While the Turks hold Constantinople and Gallipoli, they control the passage between the Black Sea and the Mediterranean; so for strategic purposes the Black Sea might as well be an inland lake.'

'Which is why the Russian Empire has been trying to push southward for hundreds of years.'

'Why not? We're Slavs, and many of the Balkan peoples are Slavs. If they want national freedom, of course we sympathize.'

'Indeed. Still, if they get it, they will probably let your navy pass freely into the Mediterranean.'

'Slav control of the Balkans would help us. Russian control would help even more.'

'No doubt – although it's not on the cards, as far as I can see.'

'Would you like to give the matter some thought?'

Walden opened his mouth to speak then closed it abruptly. This is it, he thought; this is what they want, this is the price. We can't give Russia the Balkans, for

God's sake! If the deal depends on that, there will be no deal . . .

Aleks was saying: 'If we are to fight alongside you, we must be strong. The area we are talking about is the area in which we need strengthening, so naturally we look to you for help there.'

That was putting it as plainly as could be: Give us the Balkans and we'll fight with you.

Pulling himself together, Walden frowned as if puzzled and said: 'If Britain had control of the Balkans, we could – at least in theory – give the area to you. But we can't give you what we haven't got, so I'm not sure how we can strengthen you – as you put it – in that area.'

Aleks' reply was so quick that it must have been rehearsed. 'But you might acknowledge the Balkans as a Russian sphere of influence.'

Aah, that's not so bad, Walden thought. That we *might* be able to manage.

He was enormously relieved. He decided to test Aleks' determination before winding up the discussion. He said: 'We could certainly agree to favour you over Austria or Turkey in that part of the world.'

Aleks shook his head. 'We want more than that,' he said firmly.

It had been worth a try. Aleks was young and shy, but he could not be pushed around. Worse luck.

Walden needed time to reflect, now. For Britain to do as Russia wanted would mean a significant shift in international alignments, and such shifts, like movements of the earth's crust, caused earthquakes in unexpected places.

'You may like to talk with Churchill before we go any farther,' Aleks said with a little smile.

You know damn well I will, Walden thought. He realized suddenly how well Aleks had handled the whole thing. First he had scared Walden with a completely outrageous demand; then, when he put forward his real demand, Walden had been so relieved that he welcomed it.

I thought I was going to manipulate Aleks, but in the event he manipulated me.

Walden smiled. 'I'm proud of you, my boy,' he said.

That morning Feliks figured out when, where and how he was going to kill Prince Orlov.

The plan began to take shape in his mind while he read *The Times* in the library of the Jubilee Street club. His imagination was sparked by a paragraph in the 'Court Circular' column:

Prince Aleksei Andreivitch Orlov arrived from St Petersburg yesterday. He is to be the guest of the Earl and Countess of Walden for the London Season. Prince Orlov will be presented to their Majesties the King and Queen at the Court on Thursday, June 4th.

Now he knew for certain that Orlov would be at a certain place, on a certain date, at a certain time.

Information of this kind was essential to a carefully planned assassination. Feliks had anticipated that he would get the information either by speaking to one of Walden's servants or by observing Orlov and identifying some habitual rendezvous. Now he had no need to take the risks involved in interviewing servants or trailing people. He wondered whether Orlov knew that his movements were being advertised by the newspapers, as if for the benefit of assassins. It was typically English, he thought.

The next problem was how to get sufficiently close to Orlov to kill him. Even Feliks would have difficulty getting into a royal palace. But this question also was answered by *The Times*. On the same page as the Court Circular, sandwiched between a report of a dance given by Lady Bailey and the details of the latest wills, he read:

THE KING'S COURT
Arrangements for Carriages

In order to facilitate the arrangements for calling the carriages of the company at their Majesties' Courts at Buckingham Palace, we are requested to state that in the case of the company having the privilege of the entrée at the Pimlico entrance the coachman of each carriage returning to take up is required to leave with the constable stationed on the left of the gateway a card distinctly written with the name of the lady or gentleman to whom the carriage belongs, and in the case of the carriages of the general company returning to take up at the grand entrance a similar card should be handed to the constable stationed on the left of the archway leading to the Quadrangle of the Palace.

To enable the company to receive the advantage of the above arrangements, it is necessary that a footman should accompany each carriage, as no provision can be made for calling the carriages beyond giving the names to the footmen waiting at the door, with whom it rests to bring the carriage. The doors will be open for the reception of the company at 8.30 o'clock.

Feliks read it several times: there was something about the prose style of *The Times* that made it extremely difficult to comprehend. It seemed at least to mean that as people left the palace their footmen were sent running to fetch their carriages, which would be parked somewhere else.

There must be a way, he thought, that I can contrive to be in or on the Walden carriage when it returns to the palace to pick them up.

One major difficulty remained. He had no gun.

He could have got one easily enough in Geneva, but then to have carried it across international frontiers would have been risky: he might have been refused entry into England if his baggage had been searched.

It was surely just as easy to get a gun in London, but he did not know how, and he was most reluctant to make open inquiries. He had observed gun shops in the West End of London and noted that all the customers who went in and out looked thoroughly upper-class: Feliks would not get served in there even if he had the money to buy their beautifully made precision firearms. He had spent time in low-class pubs, where guns were surely bought and sold among criminals, but he had not seen it happen, which was hardly surprising. His only hope was the anarchists. He had got into conversation with those of them whom he thought 'serious', but they never talked of weapons, doubtless because of Feliks' presence. The trouble was that he had not been around long enough to be trusted. There were always police spies in anarchist groups, and while this did not prevent the anarchists welcoming newcomers, it made them wary.

Now the time for surreptitious investigation had run out. He would have to ask directly how guns were to be obtained. It would require careful handling. And immediately afterwards he would have to sever his ties with Jubilee Street and move to another part of London, to avoid the risk of being traced.

He considered the young Jewish tearaways of Jubilee Street. They were angry and violent boys. Unlike their parents, they refused to work like slaves in the sweat-shops of the East End, sewing the suits that the aristocracy ordered from Savile Row tailors. Unlike their parents, they paid no attention to the conservative sermonizing of the rabbis. But as yet they had not decided whether the solutions to their problems lay in politics or in crime.

His best prospect, he decided, was Nathan Sabelinsky. A man of about twenty, he had rather Slavic good looks, and wore very high stiff collars and a yellow waistcoat. Feliks had seen him around the spielers off the Commercial Road: he must have had money to spend on gambling as well as clothes.

He looked around the library. The other occupants were an old man asleep, a woman in a heavy coat reading *Das Kapital* in German and making notes, and a Lithuanian Jew bent over a Russian newspaper, reading with the aid of a magnifying glass. Feliks left the room and went downstairs. There was no sign of Nathan or any of his friends. It was a little early for him: if he worked at all, Feliks thought, he worked at night.

Feliks went back to Dunstan Houses. He packed his razor, his clean underwear and his spare shirt in his cardboard suitcase. He told Milly, Rudolf Rocker's wife: 'I've found a room. I'll come back this evening to say thank you to Rudolf.' He strapped the suitcase to the back seat of the bicycle and rode west, to central London, then north to Camden Town. Here he found a street of high, once-grand houses which had been built for pretentious middle-class families who had now moved to the suburbs at the ends of the new railway lines. In one of them Feliks rented a dingy room from an Irish woman called Bridget. He paid her ten shillings in advance of two weeks' rent.

By midday he was back in Stepney, outside Nathan's home in Sidney Street. It was a small row house of the two-rooms-up-and-two-down type. The front door was wide open. Feliks walked in.

The noise and the smell hit him like a blow. There, in a room about twelve feet square, some fifteen or twenty people were working at tailoring. Men were using machines, women were sewing by hand, and children were pressing finished garments. Steam rose from the ironing-boards to mingle with the smell of sweat. The machines clattered, the irons hissed, and the workers jabbered incessantly in Yiddish. Pieces of cloth cut ready for stitching were piled on every available patch of floor space. Nobody looked up at Feliks: they were all working furiously fast.

He spoke to the nearest person, a girl with a baby at her breast. She was hand-sewing buttons on to the sleeve of a jacket. 'Is Nathan here?' he said.

'Upstairs,' she said without pausing in her work.

Feliks went out of the room and up the narrow staircase. Each of the two small bedrooms had four beds. Most of them were occupied, presumably by people who worked at night. He found Nathan in the back room, sitting on the edge of a bed, buttoning his shirt.

Nathan saw him and said: 'Feliks, *wie gehts?*'

'I need to talk to you,' Feliks said in Yiddish.

'So talk.'

'Come outside.'

Nathan put on his coat and they went out into Sidney Street. They stood in the sunshine, close to the open window of the sweat-shop, their conversation masked by the noise from inside.

'My father's trade,' said Nathan. 'He'll pay a girl fivepence for machining a pair of trousers – an hour's work for her. He'll pay another threepence to the girls who cut, press, and sew on buttons. Then he will take the trousers to a West End tailor and get paid nine-pence. Profit, one penny – enough to buy one slice of bread. If he asks the West End tailor for tenpence he'll be thrown out of the shop, and the work will be given to one of the dozens of Jewish tailors out in the street with their machines under their arms. I won't live like that.'

'Is this why you're an anarchist?'

'Those people make the most beautiful clothes in the world – but did you see how *they* are dressed?'

'And how will things be changed – by violence?'

'I think so.'

'I was sure you would feel this way. Nathan, I need a gun.'

Nathan laughed nervously. 'What for?'

'Why do anarchists usually want guns?'

'You tell me, Feliks.'

'To steal from thieves, to oppress tyrants, and to kill murderers.'

'Which are you going to do?'

'I'll tell you – if you *really* want to know . . .'

Nathan thought for a moment, then said: 'Go to the Frying Pan pub on the corner of Brick Lane and Thrawl Street. See Garfield the Dwarf.'

'Thank you!' said Feliks, unable to keep the note of triumph out of his voice. 'How much will I have to pay?'

'Five shillings for a pinfire.'

'I'd rather have something more reliable.'

'Good guns are expensive.'

'I'll just have to haggle.' Feliks shook Nathan's hand. 'Thank you.'

Nathan watched him climb on his bicycle. 'Maybe you'll tell me about it, afterwards.'

Feliks smiled. 'You'll read about it in the papers.' He waved a hand and rode off.

He cycled along Whitechapel Road and Whitechapel High Street, then turned right into Osborn Street. Immediately, the character of the streets changed. This was the most run-down part of London he had yet seen. The streets were narrow and very dirty, the air smoky and noisome, the people mostly wretched. The gutters were choked with filth. But despite all that the place was as busy as a beehive. Men ran up and down with handcarts, crowds gathered around street stalls, prostitutes worked every corner, and the workshops of carpenters and bootmakers spilled out on to the pavements.

Feliks left his bicycle outside the door of the Frying Pan: if it was taken he would just have to steal another one. To enter the pub he had to step over what looked like a dead cat. Inside was a single room, low and bare, with a bar at the far end. Older men and women sat on benches around the walls, while younger people stood in the middle of the room. Feliks went to the bar and asked for a glass of ale and a cold sausage.

He looked around and spotted Garfield the Dwarf. He had not seen him before because the man was standing on a chair. He was about four feet tall, with a large head and a middle-aged face. A very big black dog sat on the floor beside his chair. He was talking to two large, tough-looking men dressed in leather waist-coats and collarless shirts. Perhaps they were bodyguards. Feliks noted their large bellies and grinned to himself, thinking: I'll eat them up alive. The two men held quart pots of ale, but the dwarf was drinking what looked like gin. The barman handed Feliks his drink and his sausage. 'And a glass of the best gin,' Feliks said.

A young woman at the bar looked at him and said: 'Is that for me?' She smiled coquettishly, showing rotten teeth. Feliks looked away.

When the gin came he paid and walked over to the group, who were standing near a small window which looked on to the street. Feliks stood between them and the door. He addressed the dwarf. 'Mr Garfield?'

'Who wants him?' said Garfield in a squeaky voice.

Feliks offered the glass of gin. 'May I speak to you about business?'

Garfield took the glass, drained it, and said: 'No.'

Feliks sipped his ale. It was sweeter and less fizzy than Swiss beer. He said: 'I wish to buy a gun.'

'I don't know what you've come here for, then.'

'I heard about you at the Jubilee Street club.'

'Anarchist, are you?'

Feliks said nothing.

Garfield looked him up and down. 'What kind of gun would you want, if I had any?'

'A revolver. A good one.'

'Something like a Browning seven-shot?'

'That would be perfect.'

'I haven't got one. If I had I wouldn't sell it. And if I sold it I'd have to ask five pounds.'

'I was told a pound at the most.'

'You was told wrong.'

Feliks reflected. The dwarf had decided that, as a foreigner and an anarchist, Feliks could be rooked. All right, Feliks thought, we'll play it your way. 'I can't afford more than two pounds.'

'I couldn't come down below four.'

'Would that include a box of ammunition?'

'All right, four pounds including a box of ammunition.'

'Agreed,' Feliks said. He noticed one of the bodyguards smothering a grin. After paying for the drinks and the sausage, Feliks had three pounds fifteen shillings and a penny.

Garfield nodded at one of his companions. The man went behind the bar and out through the back door. Feliks ate his sausage. A minute or two later the man came back carrying what looked like a bundle of rags. He glanced at Garfield, who nodded. The man handed the bundle to Feliks.

Feliks unfolded the rags and found a revolver and a small box. He took the gun from its wrappings and examined it.

Garfield said: 'Keep it down, no need to show it to the whole bleeding world.'

The gun was clean and oiled, and the action worked smoothly. Feliks said: 'If I do not look at it, how do I know it is good?'

'Where do you think you are, Harrods?'

Feliks opened the box of cartridges and loaded the chambers with swift, practised movements.

'Put the fucking thing away,' the dwarf hissed. 'Give me the money quick and fuck off out of it. You're fucking mad.'

A bubble of tension rose in Feliks' throat, and he swallowed dryly. He took a step back and pointed the gun at the dwarf.

Garfield said: 'Jesus, Mary and Joseph.'

'Shall I test the gun?' Feliks said.

The two bodyguards stepped sideways in opposite directions so that Feliks could not cover them both with the one gun. Feliks' heart sank: he had not expected them to be that smart. Their next move would be to jump him. The pub was suddenly silent. Feliks realized he could not get to the door before one of the bodyguards reached him. The big dog growled, sensing the tension in the air.

Feliks smiled and shot the dog.

The bang of the gun was deafening in the little room. Nobody moved. The dog slumped to the floor, bleeding. The dwarf's bodyguards were frozen where they stood.

Feliks took another step back, reached behind him, and found the door. He opened it, still pointing the gun at Garfield, and stepped out.

He slammed the door, stuffed the gun in his coat pocket, and jumped on his bicycle.

He heard the pub door open. He pushed himself off and began to pedal. Somebody grabbed his coat sleeve. He pedalled harder and broke free. He heard a shot, and ducked reflexively. Someone screamed. He dodged around an ice-cream vendor and turned a corner. In the distance he heard a police whistle. He looked behind. Nobody was following him.

Half a minute later he was lost in the warrens of Whitechapel.

He thought: Six bullets left.

CHAPTER THREE

C HARLOTTE WAS ready. The gown, agonized over for so long, was perfect. To complete it she wore a single blush rose in her corsage and carried a spray of the same flowers, covered in chiffon. Her diamond tiara was fixed firmly to her upswept hair, and the two white plumes were securely fastened. Everything was fine.

She was terrified.

'As I enter the Throne Room,' she said to Marya, 'my train will drop off, my tiara will fall over my eyes, my hair will come loose, my feathers will lean sideways, and I shall trip over the hem of my gown and go flat on the floor. The assembled company will burst out laughing, and no one will laugh louder than Her Majesty the Queen. I shall run out of the palace and into the park and throw myself into the lake.'

'You ought not to talk like that,' said Marya. Then, more gently, she added: 'You'll be the loveliest of them all.'

Charlotte's mother came into the bedroom. She held Charlotte at arm's length and looked at her. 'My dear, you're beautiful,' she said, and kissed her.

Charlotte put her arms around Mama's neck and

pressed her cheek against her mother's, the way she had used to as a child, when she had been fascinated by the velvet smoothness of Mama's complexion. When she drew away, she was surprised to see a hint of tears in her mother's eyes.

'You're beautiful too, Mama,' she said.

Lydia's gown was of ivory charmeuse, with a train of old ivory brocade lined in purple chiffon. Being a married lady she wore three feathers in her hair as opposed to Charlotte's two. Her bouquet was sweet-peas and petunia roses.

'Are you ready?' she said.

'I've been ready for ages,' Charlotte said.

'Pick up your train.'

Charlotte picked up her train the way she had been taught.

Mama nodded approvingly. 'Shall we go?'

Marya opened the door. Charlotte stood aside to let her mother go first, but Mama said: 'No, dear – it's your night.'

They walked in procession, Marya bringing up the rear, along the corridor and down to the landing. When Charlotte reached the top of the grand staircase she heard a burst of applause.

The whole household was gathered at the foot of the stairs: housekeeper, cook, footmen, maids, skivvies, grooms and boys. A sea of faces looked up at her with pride and delight. Charlotte was touched by their affection: it was a big night for them, too, she realized.

In the centre of the throng was Papa, looking magnificent in a black velvet tail-coat, knee breeches, and silk stockings, with a sword at his hip and a cocked hat in his hand.

Charlotte walked slowly down the stairs.

Papa kissed her and said: 'My little girl.'

The cook, who had known her long enough to take liberties, plucked at her sleeve and whispered: 'You look wonderful, m'lady.'

Charlotte squeezed her hand and said: 'Thank you, Mrs Harding.'

Aleks bowed to her. He was resplendent in the uniform of an admiral in the Russian Navy. What a handsome man he is, Charlotte thought; I wonder whether someone will fall in love with him tonight.

Two footmen opened the front door. Papa took Charlotte's elbow and gently steered her out. Mama followed on Aleks' arm. Charlotte thought: If I can just keep my mind blank all evening, and go automatically wherever people lead me, I shall be all right.

The coach was waiting outside. William the coachman and Charles the footman stood, wearing the Walden livery, at attention on either side of the door. William, stout and greying, was calm; but Charles looked excited. Papa handed Charlotte into the coach, and she sat down gratefully. I haven't fallen over yet, she thought.

The other three got in. Pritchard brought a hamper and put it on the floor of the coach before closing the door.

The coach pulled away.

Charlotte looked at the hamper. 'A picnic?' she said. 'But we're only going half a mile!'

'Wait till you see the queue,' Papa said. 'It will take us almost an hour to get there.'

It occurred to Charlotte that she might be more bored than nervous this evening.

Sure enough, the carriage stopped at the Admiralty end of The Mall, half a mile from Buckingham Palace. Papa opened the hamper and took out a bottle of champagne. The basket also contained chicken sandwiches, hothouse peaches, and a cake.

Charlotte sipped a glass of champagne but she could not eat anything. She looked out of the window. The pavements were thronged with idlers watching the procession of the mighty. She saw a tall man with a thin, handsome face leaning on a bicycle and staring intently at their coach. Something about his look made Charlotte shiver and turn away.

After such a grand exit from the house, she found that the anticlimax of sitting in the queue was calming. By the time the coach passed through the palace gates and approached the grand entrance she was beginning to feel more her normal self – sceptical, irreverent and impatient.

The coach stopped and the door was opened. Charlotte gathered her train in her left arm, picked up her skirts with her right hand, stepped down from the coach and walked into the palace.

The great red-carpeted hall was a blaze of light and colour. Despite her scepticism she felt a thrill of excitement when she saw the crowd of white-gowned women and men in glittering uniforms. The diamonds flashed, the swords clanked and the plumes bobbed.

Red-coated Beefeaters stood at attention on either side.

Charlotte and Mama left their wraps in the cloakroom then, escorted by Papa and Aleks, walked slowly through the hall and up the grand staircase, between the Yeomen of the Guard with their halberds and the massed red and white roses. From there they went through the picture gallery and into the first of three state drawing-rooms with enormous chandeliers and mirror-bright parquet floors. Here the procession ended and people stood around in groups, chatting and admiring one another's clothes. Charlotte saw her cousin Belinda with Uncle George and Aunt Clarissa. The two families greeted each other.

Uncle George was wearing the same clothes as Papa, but because he was so fat and red-faced he looked awful in them. Charlotte wondered how Aunt Clarissa, who was young and pretty, felt about being married to such a lump.

Papa was surveying the room as if looking for someone. 'Have you seen Churchill?' he said to Uncle George.

'Good Lord, what do you want him for?'

Papa took out his watch. 'We must take our places in the Throne Room – we'll leave you to look after Charlotte, if we may, Clarissa.' Papa, Mama and Aleks left.

Belinda said to Charlotte: 'Your dress is gorgeous.'

'It's awfully uncomfortable.'

'I *knew* you were going to say that!'

'You're ever so pretty.'

'Thank you.' Belinda lowered her voice. 'I say, Prince Orlov is rather dashing.'

'He's very sweet.'

'I think he's more than *sweet*.'

'What's that funny look in your eye?'

Belinda lowered her voice even more. 'You and I must have a long talk very soon.'

'About what?'

'Remember what we discussed in the hideaway? When we took those books from the library at Walden Hall?'

Charlotte looked at her uncle and aunt, but they had turned away to talk to a dark-skinned man in a pink satin turban. 'Of course I remember.'

'About that.'

Silence descended suddenly. The crowd fell back toward the sides of the room to make a gangway in the middle. Charlotte looked around and saw the King and Queen enter the drawing-room, followed by their pages, several members of the Royal Family, and the Indian bodyguard.

There was a great sigh of rustling silk as every woman in the room sank to the floor in a curtsey.

In the Throne Room, the orchestra concealed in the Minstrels' Gallery struck up 'God Save the King'. Lydia looked toward the huge doorway guarded by gilt giants. Two attendants walked in backwards, one carrying a gold stick and one a silver. The King and Queen entered at a stately pace, smiling faintly. They mounted the dais and stood in front of the twin thrones. The rest of their entourage took their places near by, remaining standing.

Queen Mary wore a gown of gold brocade and a crown of emeralds. *She's no beauty,* Lydia thought, *but they say he adores her.* She had once been engaged to her husband's elder brother, who had died of pneumonia; and the switch to the new heir to the throne had seemed coldly political at the time. However, everyone now agreed that she was a good queen and a good wife. Lydia would have liked to know her personally.

The presentations began. One by one the wives of ambassadors came forward, curtsied to the King, curtsied to the Queen, then backed away. The ambassadors followed, dressed in a great variety of gaudy comic-opera uniforms, all but the United States Ambassador who wore ordinary black evening clothes, as if to remind everyone that Americans did not really believe in this sort of nonsense.

As the ritual went on, Lydia looked around the room, at the crimson satin on the walls, the heroic frieze below the ceiling, the enormous candelabra, and the thousands of flowers. She loved pomp and ritual, beautiful clothes and elaborate ceremonies; they moved and soothed her at the same time. She caught the eye of the Duchess of Devonshire, the Mistress of the Robes, and they exchanged a discreet smile. She spotted John Burns, the socialist President of the Board of Trade, and was amused to see the extravagant gilt embroidery on his court dress.

When the diplomatic presentations ended, the King and Queen sat down. The Royal Family, the diplomats, and the most senior nobility followed suit. Lydia and Walden, along with the lesser nobility, had to remain standing.

At last the presentation of the debutantes began. Each girl paused just outside the Throne Room while an attendant took her train from her arm and spread it behind her. Then she began the endless walk along the red carpet to the thrones, with all eyes on her. If a girl could look graceful and unselfconscious there, she could do it anywhere.

As the debutante approached the dais she handed her invitation card to the Lord Chamberlain, who read out her name. She curtsied to the King, then to the Queen. Few girls curtsied elegantly, Lydia thought. She had had a great deal of trouble getting Charlotte to practise at all: perhaps other mothers had the same problem. After the curtsies the debutante walked on, careful not to turn her back on the thrones until she was safely hidden in the watching crowd.

The girls followed one another so closely that each was in danger of treading on the train of the one in front. The ceremony seemed to Lydia to be less personal, more perfunctory than it had used to be. She herself had been presented to Queen Victoria in the season of 1896, the year after she married Walden. The old Queen had not sat on a throne, but on a high stool which gave the impression that she was standing. Lydia had been surprised at how little Victoria was. She had had to kiss the Queen's hand. That part of the ceremony had now been dispensed with, presumably to save time. It made the court seem like a factory for turning out the maximum number of debutantes in the shortest possible time. Still, the girls of today did not know the difference and probably would not care if they did.

Suddenly Charlotte was at the entrance, and the attendant was laying down her train, then giving her a gentle push, and she was walking along the red carpet, head held high, looking perfectly serene and confident. Lydia thought: This is the moment I have lived for.

The girl ahead of Charlotte curtsied – and then the unthinkable happened.

Instead of getting up from her curtsey, the debutante looked at the King, stretched out her arms in a gesture of supplication, and cried in a loud voice:

'*Your Majesty, for God's sake stop torturing women!*'

Lydia thought: A suffragette!

Her eyes flashed to her daughter. Charlotte was standing dead still, halfway to the dais, staring at the tableau with an expression of horror on her ashen face.

The shocked silence in the Throne Room lasted only for a split second. Two gentlemen-in-waiting were the fastest to react. They sprang forward, took the girl firmly by either arm, and marched her unceremoniously away.

The Queen was blushing crimson. The King managed to appear as if nothing had happened. Lydia looked again at Charlotte, thinking: Why did my daughter have to be next in line?

Now all eyes were on Charlotte. Lydia wanted to call out to her: Pretend it never happened! Just carry on!

Charlotte stood still. A little colour came back into her cheeks. Lydia could see that she was taking a deep breath.

Then she walked forward. Lydia could not breathe. Charlotte handed her card to the Lord Chamberlain, who said: 'Presentation of Lady Charlotte Walden.' Charlotte stood before the King.

Lydia thought: Careful!

Charlotte curtsied perfectly.

She curtsied again to the Queen.

She half-turned, and walked away.

Lydia let out her breath in a long sigh.

The woman standing next to Lydia – a baroness whom she vaguely recognized but did not really know – whispered: 'She handled that very well.'

'She's my daughter,' Lydia said with a smile.

Walden was secretly amused by the suffragette. Spirited girl! he thought. Of course, if *Charlotte* had done such a thing at the court he would have been horrified, but as it was someone else's daughter he regarded the incident as a welcome break in the interminable ceremony. He had noticed how Charlotte had carried on, unruffled: he would have expected no less of her. She was a highly self-assured young lady, and in his opinion Lydia should congratulate herself on the girl's upbringing instead of worrying all the time.

He had used to enjoy these occasions, years ago. As a young man he had quite liked to put on court dress and cut a dash. In those days he had had the legs for it, too. Now he felt foolish in knee-breeches and silk stockings, not to mention a damn great steel sword. And he had attended so many courts that the colourful ritual no longer fascinated him.

He wondered how King George felt about it. Walden liked the King. Of course, by comparison with his father Edward VII, George was a rather colourless, mild fellow. The crowds would never shout 'Good old Georgie!' the way they had shouted 'Good old Teddy!' But in the end they would like George for his quiet charm and his modest way of life. He knew how to be firm, although as yet he did it too rarely; and Walden liked a man who could shoot straight. Walden thought he would turn out very well indeed.

Finally the last debutante curtsied and passed on, and the King and Queen stood up. The orchestra played the national anthem again, the King bowed, and the Queen curtsied, first to the ambassadors, then to the ambassadors' wives, then the Duchesses, and lastly the Ministers. The King took the Queen by the hand. The pages picked up her train. The attendants went out backwards. The royal couple left, followed by the rest of the company in order of precedence.

They divided to go into three supper-rooms: one for the Royal Family and their close friends, one for the diplomatic corps, and one for the rest. Walden was a friend, but not an intimate friend, of the King: he went with the general assembly. Aleks went with the diplomats.

In the supper-room Walden met up with his family again. Lydia was glowing. Walden said: 'Congratulations, Charlotte.'

Lydia said: 'Who was that awful girl?'

'I heard someone say she's the daughter of an architect,' Walden replied.

'That explains it,' said Lydia.

Charlotte looked mystified. 'Why does that explain it?'

Walden smiled. 'Your Mama means that the girl is not quite out of the top drawer.'

'But why does she think the King tortures women?'

'She was talking about the suffragettes. But let's not go into all that tonight; this is a great occasion for us. Let's have supper. It looks marvellous.'

There was a long buffet table loaded with flowers and hot and cold food. Servants in the scarlet-and-gold royal livery waited to offer the guests lobster, filleted trout, quail, York ham, plovers' eggs, and a host of pastries and desserts. Walden got a loaded plate and sat down to eat. After standing about in the Throne Room for more than two hours he was hungry.

Sooner or later Charlotte would have to learn about the suffragettes, their hunger strikes, and the consequent force-feeding; but the subject was indelicate, to say the least, and the longer she remained in blissful ignorance the better, Walden thought. At her age life should be all parties and picnics, frocks and hats, gossip and flirtation.

But everyone was talking about 'the incident' and 'that girl'. Walden's brother George sat beside him and said without preamble: 'She's a Miss Mary Blomfield, daughter of the late Sir Arthur Blomfield. Her mother was in the drawing-room at the time. When she was told what her daughter had done she fainted right off.' He seemed to relish the scandal.

'Only thing she could do, I suppose,' Walden replied.

'Damn shame for the family,' George said. 'You won't see Blomfields at court again for two or three generations.'

'We shan't miss them.'

'No.'

Walden saw Churchill pushing through the crowd toward where they sat. He had written to Churchill about his talk with Aleks, and he was impatient to discuss the next step – but not *here*. He looked away, hoping Churchill would get the hint. He should have known better than to hope that such a subtle message would get through.

Churchill bent over Walden's chair. 'Can we have a few words together?'

Walden looked at his brother. George wore an expression of horror. Walden threw him a resigned look and got up.

'Let's walk in the picture gallery,' Churchill said.

Walden followed him out.

Churchill said: 'I suppose you, too, will tell me that this suffragette protest is all the fault of the Liberal Party.'

'I expect it is,' Walden said. 'But that isn't what you want to talk about.'

'No indeed.'

The two men walked side by side through the long gallery. Churchill said: 'We can't acknowledge the Balkans as a Russian sphere of influence.'

'I was afraid you'd say that.'

'What do they want the Balkans *for*? I mean, forgetting all this nonsense about sympathy with Slav nationalism.'

'They want passage through to the Mediterranean.'

'That would be to our advantage, if they were our allies.'

'Exactly.'

They reached the end of the gallery and stopped. Churchill said: 'Is there some way we can give them that passage without redrawing the map of the Balkan Peninsula?'

'I've been thinking about that.'

Churchill smiled. 'And you've got a counter-proposal.'

'Yes.'

'Let's hear it.'

Walden said: 'What we're talking about here are three stretches of water: the Bosphorus, the Sea of Marmara, and the Dardanelles. If we can give them those waterways, they won't need the Balkans. Now, suppose that whole passage between the Black Sea and the Mediterranean could be declared an international waterway, with free passage to ships of all nations guaranteed jointly by Russia and England.'

Churchill started walking again, slow and thoughtful. Walden walked beside him, waiting for his answer.

Eventually Churchill said: 'That passage *ought* to be an international waterway, in any event. What you're suggesting is that we offer, as if it were a concession, something which we want anyway.'

'Yes.'

Churchill looked up and grinned suddenly. 'When it comes to Machiavellian manoeuvring, there's no one to beat the English aristocracy. All right. Go ahead and propose it to Orlov.'

'You don't want to put it to the Cabinet?'

'No.'

'Not even to the Foreign Secretary?'

'Not at this stage. The Russians are certain to want to modify the proposal – they'll want details of how the guarantee is to be enforced, at least – so I'll go to the Cabinet when the deal is fully elaborated.'

'Very well.' Walden wondered just how much the Cabinet knew about what Churchill and he were up to. Churchill, too, could be Machiavellian. Were there wheels within wheels?

Churchill said: 'Where is Orlov now?'

'In the diplomatic supper-room.'

'Let's go and put it to him right away.'

Walden shook his head, thinking that people were correct when they accused Churchill of being impulsive. 'This is not the moment.'

'We can't wait for the moment, Walden. Every day counts.'

It will take a bigger man than you to bully me, Walden thought. He said: 'You're going to have to leave that to my judgement, Churchill. I'll put this to Orlov tomorrow morning.'

Churchill seemed disposed to argue, but he restrained himself visibly and said: 'I don't suppose Germany will declare war tonight. Very well.' He looked at his watch. 'I'm going to leave. Keep me fully informed.'

'Of course. Goodbye.'

Churchill went down the staircase and Walden returned to the supper-room. The party was breaking up. Now that the King and Queen had disappeared and everyone had been fed there was nothing to stay for. Walden rounded up his family and took them downstairs. They found Aleks in the great hall.

While the ladies went into the cloakroom Walden asked one of the attendants to summon his carriage.

All in all, he thought as he waited, it had been a rather successful evening.

The Mall reminded Feliks of the streets in the Old Equerries Quarter of Moscow. It was a wide, straight avenue that ran from Trafalgar Square to Buckingham Palace. On one side was a series of grand houses including St James's Palace. On the other side was St James's Park. The carriages and motor cars of the great were lined up on both sides of The Mall for half its length. Chauffeurs and coachmen leaned against their vehicles, yawning and fidgeting, waiting to be summoned to the palace to collect their masters and mistresses.

The Walden carriage waited on the park side of The Mall. Their coachman, in the blue-and-pink Walden livery, stood beside the horses, reading a newspaper by the light of a carriage lamp. A few yards away, in the darkness of the park, Feliks stood watching him.

Feliks was desperate. His plan was in ruins.

He had not understood the difference between the English words 'coachman' and 'footman' and consequently he had misunderstood the notice in *The Times* about summoning carriages. He had thought that the driver of the coach would wait at the palace gate until his master emerged, then would come running to fetch the coach. At that point, Feliks had planned, he would have overpowered the coachman, taken his livery, and driven the coach to the palace himself.

What happened in fact was that the coachman stayed with the vehicle and the footman waited at the palace gate. When the coach was wanted, the footman would come running; then he and the coachman would go with the carriage to pick up the passengers. That meant Feliks had to overpower two people, not one; and the difficulty was that it had to be done surreptitiously, so that none of the hundreds of other servants in The Mall would know anything was wrong.

Since realizing his mistake a couple of hours ago he had worried at the problem, while he watched the coachman chatting with his colleagues, examining a nearby Rolls-Royce car, playing some kind of game with halfpennies, and polishing the carriage windows. It might have been sensible to abandon the plan, and kill Orlov another day.

But Feliks hated that idea. For one thing, there was no certainty that another good opportunity would arise. For another, Feliks wanted to kill him now. He had been anticipating the bang of the gun, the way the Prince would fall; he had composed the coded cable which would go to Ulrich in Geneva; he had pictured the excitement in the little printing shop, and then the headlines in the world's newspapers, and then the final wave of revolution sweeping through Russia. I can't postpone this any longer, he thought; I want it now.

As he watched, a young man in green livery approached the Walden coachman and said: 'What ho, William.'

So the coachman's name is William, Feliks thought.

William said: 'Mustn't grumble, John.'

Feliks did not understand that.

'Anything in the news?' said John.

'Yeah, revolution. The King says that next year all the coachmen can go in the palace for supper and the toffs will wait in The Mall.'

'A likely tale.'

'You're telling me.'

John moved on.

I can get rid of William, Feliks thought, but what about the footman?

In his mind he ran over the probable sequence of events. Walden and Orlov would come to the palace door. The doorman would alert Walden's footman, who would run from the palace to the carriage – a distance of about a quarter of a mile. The footman would see Feliks dressed in the coachman's clothes, and would sound the alarm.

Suppose the footman arrived at the parking-place to find that the carriage was no longer there?

That was a thought!

The footman would wonder whether he had misremembered the spot. He would look up and down. In something of a panic he would search for the coach. Finally he would admit defeat and return to the palace to tell his master that he could not find the coach. By which time Feliks would be driving the coach and its owner through the park.

It could still be done!

It was more risky than before, but it could still be done.

There was no more time for reflection. The first two or three footmen were already running down The Mall. The Rolls-Royce car in front of the Walden coach was summoned. William put on his top hat in readiness.

Feliks emerged from the bushes and walked a little way toward him, calling: 'Hey! Hey, William!'

The coachman looked toward him, frowning.

Feliks beckoned urgently. 'Come here, quick!'

William folded his newspaper, hesitated, then walked slowly toward Feliks.

Feliks allowed his own tension to put a note of panic into his voice. 'Look at this!' he said, pointing to the bushes. 'Do you know anything about this?'

'What?' William said, mystified. He drew level and peered the way Feliks was pointing.

'This.' Feliks showed him the gun. 'If you make a noise I'll shoot you.'

William was terrified. Feliks could see the whites of his eyes in the half-dark. He was a heavily built man, but he was older than Feliks. If he does something foolish and messes this up I'll kill him, Feliks thought savagely.

'Walk on,' Feliks said.

The man hesitated.

I've got to get him out of the *light.* 'Walk, you bastard!'

William walked into the bushes.

Feliks followed him. When they were about fifty yards away from The Mall Feliks said: 'Stop.'

William stopped and turned around.

Feliks thought: If he's going to fight, this is where he will do it. He said: 'Take off your clothes.'

'What?'

'Undress.'

'You're mad,' William whispered.

'You're right – I'm mad! Take off your clothes!'

William hesitated.

If I shoot him, will people come running? Will the bushes muffle the sound? Could I kill him without making a hole in his uniform? Could I take his coat off and run away before anyone arrives?

Feliks cocked the gun.

William began to undress.

Feliks could hear the increasing activity in The Mall: motor cars started, harness jingled, hooves clattered and men shouted to one another and to their horses. Any minute now the footman might come running for the Walden coach. 'Faster!' Feliks said.

William got down to his underwear.

'The rest also,' Feliks said.

William hesitated. Feliks lifted the gun.

William pulled off his undershirt, dropped his underpants, and stood naked, shivering with fear, covering his genitals with his hands.

'Turn around,' said Feliks.

William turned his back.

'Lie on the ground, face down.'

He did so.

Feliks put down the gun. Hurriedly, he took off his coat and hat and put on the livery coat and the top hat which William had dropped on the ground. He contemplated the knee-breeches and white stockings, but decided to leave them: when he was sitting up on the coach no one would notice his trousers and boots, especially in the uncertain light of the street lamps.

He put the gun into the pocket of his own coat and folded the coat over his arm. He picked up William's clothes in a bundle.

William tried to look around.

'Don't move!' Feliks said sharply.

Softly, he walked away.

William would stay there for a while then, naked as he was, he would try to get back to the Walden house unobserved. It was highly unlikely that he would report that he had been robbed of his clothes before he had a chance to get some more, unless he was an extraordinarily immodest man. Of course if he had known Feliks was going to kill Prince Orlov he might have thrown modesty to the winds – but how could he possibly guess that?

Feliks pushed William's clothes under a bush, then walked out into the lights of The Mall.

This was where things might go wrong. Until now he had been merely a suspicious person lurking in the bushes. From this moment on he was plainly an imposter. If one of William's friends – John, for instance – should look closely at his face, the game would be up.

He climbed rapidly on to the coach, put his own coat on the seat beside him, adjusted his top hat, released the brake, and flicked the reins. The coach pulled out into the road.

He sighed with relief. I've got this far, he thought; I'll get Orlov!

As he drove down The Mall he watched the pavements, looking for a running footman in the blue-and-pink livery. The worst possible mischance would be for the Walden footman to see him now, and recognize the colours, and jump on to the back of the coach. Feliks cursed as a motor car pulled out in front of him, forcing him to slow the horses to a halt. He looked around anxiously. There was no sign of the footman. After a moment the road was clear and he went on.

At the palace end of the avenue he spotted an empty space on the right, the side of the road farther from the park. The footman would come along the opposite pavement and would not see the coach. He pulled into the space and set the brake.

He climbed down from the seat and stood behind the horses, watching the opposite pavement. He wondered whether he would get out of this alive.

In his original plan there had been a good chance that Walden would get into the carriage without so much as a glance at the coachman, but now he would surely notice that his footman was missing. The palace doorman would have to open the coach door and pull down the steps. Would Walden stop and speak to the coachman, or would he postpone inquiries until he got home? If he were to speak to Feliks then Feliks would have to reply and his voice would give the game away. What will I do then? Feliks thought.

I'll shoot Orlov at the palace door, and take the consequences.

He saw the footman in blue-and-pink running along the far side of The Mall.

Feliks jumped on to the coach, released the brake, and drove into the courtyard of Buckingham Palace.

There was a queue. Ahead of him, the beautiful women and the well-fed men climbed into their carriages and cars. Behind him, somewhere in The Mall, the Walden footman was running up and down, hunting for his coach. How long before he returned?

The palace servants had a fast and efficient system for loading guests into vehicles. While the passengers were getting into the carriage at the door, a servant was calling the owners of the second in line, and another servant was inquiring the name of the people for the third.

The line moved, and a servant approached Feliks. 'The Earl of Walden,' Feliks said. The servant went inside.

They mustn't come out too soon, Feliks thought.

The line moved forward, and now there was only a motor car in front of him. Pray God it doesn't stall, he thought. The chauffeur held the doors for an elderly couple. The car pulled away.

Feliks moved the coach to the porch, halting it a little too far forward, so that he was beyond the wash of light from inside, and his back was to the palace doors.

He waited, not daring to look around.

He heard the voice of a young girl say, in Russian: 'And how many ladies proposed marriage to you this evening, Cousin Aleks?'

A drop of sweat ran down into Feliks' eye and he wiped it away with the back of his hand.

A man said: 'Where the devil is my footman?'

Feliks reached into the pocket of the coat beside him and got his hand on the butt of the revolver. Six shots left, he thought.

Out of the corner of his eye he saw a palace servant spring forward, and a moment later he heard the door of the coach being opened. The vehicle rocked slightly as someone got in.

'I say, William, where's Charles?'

Feliks tensed. He imagined he could feel Walden's

eyes boring into the back of his head. The girl's voice said: 'Come on, Papa,' from inside the carriage.

'William's getting deaf in his old age . . .' Walden's words were muffled as he got into the coach. The door slammed.

'Right away, coachman!' said the palace servant.

Feliks breathed out, and drove away.

The release of tension made him feel weak for a moment. Then, as he guided the carriage out of the courtyard, he felt a surge of elation. Orlov was in his power, shut in a box behind him, caught like an animal in a trap. Nothing could stop Feliks now.

He drove into the park.

Holding the reins in his right hand, he struggled to get his left arm into his topcoat. That done, he switched the reins to his left hand and got his right arm in. He stood up and shrugged the coat up over his shoulders. He felt in the pocket and touched the gun.

He sat down again and wound a scarf around his neck.

He was ready.

Now he had to choose his moment.

He had only a few minutes. The Walden house was less than a mile from the palace. He had bicycled along this road the night before, to reconnoitre. He had found two suitable places, where a street lamp would illuminate his victim and there was thick shrubbery near by into which he could disappear afterwards.

The first spot loomed up fifty yards ahead. As he approached it he saw a man in evening dress pause beneath the lamp to light his cigar. He drove past the spot.

The second place was a bend in the road. If there was someone there, Feliks would just have to take a chance, and shoot the intruder if necessary.

Six bullets.

He saw the bend. He made the horses trot a little faster. From inside the coach he heard the young girl laugh.

He came to the bend. His nerves were as taut as piano-wire.

Now.

He dropped the reins and heaved on the brake. The horses staggered and the carriage shuddered and jerked to a halt.

From inside the coach he heard a woman cry and a man shout. Something about the woman's voice bothered him, but there was no time to wonder why. He jumped down to the ground, pulled the scarf up over his mouth and nose, took the gun from his pocket and cocked it.

Full of strength and rage, he flung open the coach door.

CHAPTER FOUR

A WOMAN CRIED out, and time stood still.

Feliks knew the voice. The sound hit him like a mighty blow. The shock paralysed him.

He was supposed to locate Orlov, point the gun at him, pull the trigger, make sure he was dead with another bullet, then turn and run into the bushes . . .

Instead he looked for the source of the cry, and saw her face. It was startlingly familiar, as if he had last seen it only yesterday, instead of nineteen years ago. Her eyes were wide with panic, and her small red mouth was open.

Lydia.

He stood at the door of the coach with his mouth open under the scarf, the gun pointing nowhere, and he thought: My Lydia – here in *this carriage* . . .

As he stared at her he was dimly aware that Walden was moving, with uncanny slowness, close by him on his left; but all Feliks could think was: This is how she used to look, wide-eyed and open-mouthed, when she lay naked beneath me, her legs wrapped around my waist, and she stared at me and began to cry out with delight . . .

Then he saw that Walden had drawn a sword –

For God's sake, *a sword*?

– and the blade was glinting in the lamplight as it swept down, and Feliks moved too slowly and too late, and the sword bit into his right hand, and he dropped the gun and it went off with a bang as it hit the road.

The explosion broke the spell.

Walden drew back the sword and thrust at Feliks' heart. Feliks moved sideways. The point of the sword went through his coat and jacket and stuck into his shoulder. He jumped back reflexively and the sword came out. He felt a rush of warm blood inside his shirt.

He stared down at the road, looking for the gun, but he could not see it. He looked up again, and saw that Walden and Orlov had collided as they tried simultaneously to get out through the narrow carriage door. Feliks' right arm hung limply at his side. He realized he was unarmed and helpless. He could not even strangle Orlov, for his right arm was useless. He had failed utterly, and all because of the voice of a woman from the past.

After all that, he thought bitterly; after all that.

Full of despair, he turned and ran away.

Walden roared: 'Damned villain!'

Feliks' wound hurt every step. He heard someone running behind him. The footsteps were too light to be Walden's: Orlov was chasing him. He teetered on the edge of hysteria as he thought: Orlov is chasing *me* – and I am running away!

He darted off the road and into the bushes. He

heard Walden shout: 'Aleks, come back, he's got a gun!' They don't know I dropped it, Feliks thought. If only I still had it I could shoot Orlov now.

He ran a little way farther then stopped, listening. He could hear nothing. Orlov had given up.

He leaned against a tree. He was exhausted by his short sprint. When he had caught his breath he took off his topcoat and the stolen livery coat and gingerly touched his wounds. They hurt like the devil, which he thought was probably a good sign, for if they had been very grave they would have been numb. His shoulder bled slowly, and throbbed. His hand had been sliced in the fleshy part between thumb and forefinger, and it bled fast.

He had to get out of the park before Walden had a chance to raise the hue and cry.

With difficulty he drew on the topcoat. He left the livery coat on the ground where it lay. He squeezed his right hand under his left armpit, to relieve the pain and slow the flow of blood. Wearily, he headed toward The Mall.

Lydia.

It was the second time in his life that she had caused a catastrophe. The first time, in 1895, in St Petersburg—

No. He would not allow himself to think about her, not yet. He needed his wits about him now.

He saw with relief that his bicycle was where he had left it, under the overhanging branches of a big tree. He wheeled it across the grass to the edge of the park. Had Walden alerted the police yet? Were they looking for a tall man in a dark coat? He stared at the scene in

The Mall. The footmen were still running, the car engines roaring, the carriages manoeuvring. How long had it been since Feliks had climbed up on to the Walden coach – twenty minutes? In that time the world had turned over.

He took a deep breath and wheeled the bicycle into the road. Everyone was busy, nobody looked at him. Keeping his right hand in his coat pocket, he mounted the machine. He pushed off and began to pedal, steering with his left hand.

There were bobbies all around the palace. If Walden mobilized them quickly they could cordon off the park and the roads around it. Feliks looked ahead, toward Admiralty Arch. There was no sign of a roadblock.

Once past the arch he would be in the West End and they would have lost him.

He began to get the knack of cycling one-handed, and increased his speed.

As he approached the arch a motor car drew alongside him and, at the same time, a policeman stepped into the road ahead. Feliks stopped the bicycle and prepared to run – but the policeman was merely holding up the traffic to permit another car, belonging presumably to some kind of dignitary, to emerge from a gateway. When the car came out the policeman saluted then waved the traffic on.

Feliks cycled through the arch and into Trafalgar Square.

Too slow, Walden, he thought with satisfaction.

It was midnight, but the West End was bright with street lights and crowded with people and traffic. There were policemen everywhere and no other cyclists: Feliks was conspicuous. He considered abandoning the bicycle and walking back to Camden Town, but he was not sure he could make the journey on foot: he seemed to be tiring.

From Trafalgar Square he rode up St Martin's Lane, then left the main streets for the back alleys of Theatreland. A dark lane was suddenly illuminated as a stage door opened and a bunch of actors came out, talking loudly and laughing. Farther on he heard groans and sighs, and passed a couple making love standing up in a doorway.

He crossed into Bloomsbury. Here it was quieter and darker. He cycled north up Gower Street, past the classical facade of the deserted university. Pushing the pedals became an enormous effort, and he ached all over. Just a mile or two more, he thought.

He dismounted to cross the busy Euston Road. The lights of the traffic dazzled him. He seemed to be having difficulty focusing his eyes.

Outside Euston Station he got on the bicycle again and pedalled off. Suddenly he felt dizzy. A street light blinded him. The front wheel wobbled and hit the kerb. Feliks fell.

He lay on the ground, dazed and weak. He opened his eyes and saw a policeman approaching. He struggled to his knees.

'Have you been drinkin'?' the policeman said.

'Feel faint,' Feliks managed.

The policeman took his right arm and hauled him to his feet. The pain in his wounded shoulder brought

Feliks to his senses. He managed to keep his bleeding right hand in his pocket.

The policeman sniffed audibly and said: 'Hmm.' His attitude became more genial when he discovered that Feliks did not smell of drink. 'Will you be all right?'

'In a minute.'

'Foreigner, are you?'

The policeman had noticed his accent. 'French,' Feliks said. 'I work at the Embassy.'

The policeman became more polite. 'Would you like a cab?'

'No, thank you. I have only a little way to go.'

The policeman picked up the bicycle. 'I should wheel it home if I were you.'

Feliks took the bicycle from him. 'I will do that.'

'Very good, sir. Bong noo-wee.'

'Bonne nuit, officer.' With an effort Feliks produced a smile. Pushing the bicycle with his left hand, he walked away. I'll turn into the next alley and sit down for a rest, he resolved. He looked back over his shoulder: the policeman was still watching him. He made himself keep on walking, although he desperately needed to lie down. The next alley, he thought. But when he came to an alley he passed it, thinking: Not this one, but the next.

And in that way he got home.

It seemed hours later that he stood outside the high terraced house in Camden Town. He peered through a fog at the number on the door to make sure this was the right place.

To get to his room he had to go down a flight of

stone steps to the basement area. He leaned the bicycle against the wrought-iron railings while he opened the little gate. He then made the mistake of trying to wheel the bicycle down the steps. It slid out of his grasp and fell into the area with a loud clatter. A moment later his landlady, Bridget, appeared at the street door in a shawl.

'What the divil is it?' she called.

Feliks sat on the steps and made no reply. He decided he would not move for a while, until he felt stronger.

Bridget came down and helped him to his feet. 'You've had a few too many drinks,' she said. She made him walk down the steps to the basement door.

'Give us your key,' she said.

Feliks had to use his left hand to take the key from his right trouser pocket. He gave it to her and she opened the door. They went in. Feliks stood in the middle of the little room while she lit the lamp.

'Let's have your coat off,' she said.

He let her remove his coat, and she saw the bloodstains. 'Have you been fightin'?'

Feliks went and lay on the mattress.

Bridget said: 'You look as if you lost!'

'I did,' said Feliks, and he passed out.

An agonizing pain brought him around. He opened his eyes to see Bridget bathing his wounds with something that stung like fire. 'This hand should be stitched,' she said.

'Tomorrow,' Feliks breathed.

She made him drink from a cup. It was warm water with gin in it. She said: 'I haven't any brandy.'

He lay back and let her bandage him.

'I could fetch the doctor but I couldn't be payin' him.'

'Tomorrow.'

She stood up. 'I'll look at you first thing in the morning.'

'Thank you.'

She went out, and at last Feliks allowed himself to remember.

It has happened in the long run of ages that everything which permits men to increase their production, or even to continue it, has been appropriated by the few. The land belongs to the few, who may prevent the community from cultivating it. The coal-pits, which represent the labour of generations, belong again to the few. The lace-weaving machine, which represents, in its present state of perfection, the work of three generations of Lancashire weavers, belongs also to the few; and if the grandsons of the very same weaver who invented the first lace-weaving machine claim their right to bring one of these machines into motion, they will be told: 'Hands off! This machine does not belong to you!' The railroads belong to a few shareholders, who may not even know where is situated the railway which brings them a yearly income larger than that of a medieval king. And if the children of those people who died by the thousands in digging the tunnels should gather and go – a ragged and starving crowd – to ask bread or work from the shareholders, they would be met with bayonets and bullets.

Feliks looked up from Kropotkin's pamphlet. The bookshop was empty. The bookseller was an old revolutionist who made his money selling novels to wealthy women, and kept a hoard of subversive literature in the back of the shop. Feliks spent a lot of time in here.

He was nineteen. He was about to be thrown out of the prestigious Spiritual Academy for truancy, indiscipline, long hair and associating with Nihilists. He was hungry and broke, and soon he would be homeless, and life was wonderful. He cared about nothing other than ideas, and he was learning every day new things about poetry, history, psychology, and – most of all – politics.

Laws on property are not made to guarantee either to the individual or to society the enjoyment of the produce of their own labour. On the contrary, they are made to rob the producer of a part of what he has created. When, for example, the law establishes Mr So-and-so's right to a house, it is not establishing his right to a cottage he has built for himself, or to a house he has erected with the help of some of his friends. In that case no one would have disputed his right! On the contrary, the law is establishing his right to a house which is not the product of his labour.

The anarchist slogans had sounded ridiculous when he had first heard them: Property is theft, Government is tyranny, Anarchy is justice. It was astonishing how, when he had really thought about them, they came to seem not only true but crashingly obvious. Kropotkin's point about laws was undeniable. No laws were required to prevent theft in Feliks' home village: if one peasant stole another's horse, or his chair, or the coat his wife had embroidered, then the whole village would see the culprit in possession of the goods and make him give them back. The only stealing that went on was when the landlord demanded rent; and the policeman was there to enforce that theft. It was the same with government. The peasants needed no one to tell them how the plough and the oxen were to be shared between their fields: they decided among themselves. It was only the ploughing of the landlord's fields that had to be enforced.

We are continually told of the benefits conferred by laws and penalties, but have the speakers ever attempted to balance the benefits attributed to laws and penalties against the degrading effects of these penalties upon humanity? Only calculate all the evil passions awakened in mankind by the atrocious punishments inflicted in our streets! Man is the cruellest animal on earth. And who has pampered and developed the cruel instincts if it is not the king, the judge and the priests, armed with law, who caused flesh to be torn off in strips, boiling pitch to be poured into wounds, limbs to be dislocated, bones

117

to be crushed, men to be sawn asunder to maintain their authority? Only estimate the torrent of depravity let loose in human society by the 'informing' which is countenanced by judges, and paid in hard cash by governments, under pretext of assisting in the discovery of 'crime'. Only go into the jails and study what man becomes when he is steeped in the vice and corruption which oozes from the very walls of our prisons. Finally, consider what corruption, what depravity of mind is kept up among men by the idea of obedience, the very essence of law; of chastisement; of authority having the right to punish; of the necessity for executioners, jailers, and informers – in a word, by all the attributes of law and authority. Consider this, and you will assuredly agree that a law inflicting penalties is an abomination which should cease to exist.

Peoples without political organization, and therefore less depraved than ourselves, have perfectly understood that the man who is called 'criminal' is simply unfortunate; and that the remedy is not to flog him, to chain him up, or to kill him, but to help him by the most brotherly care, by treatment based on equality, by the usages of life among honest men.

Feliks was vaguely aware that a customer had come into the shop and was standing close to him, but he was concentrating on Kropotkin.

No more laws! No more judges! Liberty, equality and practical human sympathy are the only effective barriers we can oppose to the anti-social instincts of certain among us.

The customer dropped a book and he lost his train of thought. He glanced away from his pamphlet, saw the book lying on the floor beside the customer's long skirt, and automatically bent down to pick it up for her. As he handed it to her he saw her face.

He gasped. 'Why, you're an angel!' he said with perfect honesty.

She was blonde and petite, and she wore a pale grey fur the colour of her eyes, and everything about her was pale and light and fair. He thought he would never see a more beautiful woman, and he was right.

She stared back at him and blushed, but she did not turn away. It seemed, incredibly, that she found something fascinating in him, too.

After a moment he looked at her book. It was *Anna Karenina*. 'Sentimental rubbish,' he said. He wished he had not spoken, for his words broke the spell. She took the book and turned away. He saw then that there was a maid with her, for she gave the book to the maid and left the shop. The maid paid for the book. Looking through the window, Feliks saw the woman get into a carriage.

He asked the bookseller who she was. Her name was Lydia, he learned, and she was the daughter of Count Shatov.

He found out where the Count lived, and the next day he hung around outside the house in the hope of seeing her. She went in and out twice, in her carriage, before a groom came out and chased Feliks off. He did not mind, for the last time her carriage passed she had looked directly at him.

The next day he went to the bookshop. For hours he read Bakunin's *Federalism, Socialism and Anti-Theologism* without understanding a single word. Every time a carriage passed he looked out of the window. Whenever a customer came into the shop his heart missed a beat.

She came in at the end of the afternoon.

This time she left the maid outside. She murmured a greeting to the bookseller and came to the back of the shop, where Feliks stood. They stared at each other. Feliks thought: She loves me, why else would she come?

He meant to speak to her, but instead he threw his arms around her and kissed her. She kissed him back, hungrily, opening her mouth, hugging him, digging her fingers into his back.

It was always like that with them: when they met they threw themselves at each other like animals about to fight.

They met twice more in the bookshop and once, after dark, in the garden of the Shatov house. That time in the garden she was in her nightclothes. Feliks put his hands under the woollen nightgown and touched her body all over, as boldly as if she were a street girl, feeling and exploring and rubbing; and all she did was moan.

She gave him money so that he could rent a room of his own, and thereafter she came to see him almost every day for six astonishing weeks.

The last time was in the early evening. He was sitting at the table, wrapped in a blanket against the cold, reading Proudhon's *What is Property?* by candlelight. When he heard her footstep on the stairs he took his trousers off.

She rushed in, wearing an old brown cloak with a hood. She kissed him, sucked his lips, bit his chin, and pinched his sides.

She turned and threw off the cloak. Underneath it she was wearing a white evening gown that must have cost hundreds of roubles. 'Unfasten me, quickly,' she said.

Feliks began to undo the hooks at the back of the dress.

'I'm on my way to a reception at the British Embassy, I only have an hour,' she said breathlessly. 'Hurry, please.'

In his haste he ripped one of the hooks out of the material. 'Damn, I've torn it.'

'Never mind!'

She stepped out of the dress, then pulled off her petticoats, her chemise and her drawers, leaving on her corset, hose and shoes. She flung herself into his arms. As she was kissing him she pulled down his underpants.

She said: 'Oh, God, I love the smell of your thing.'

When she talked like that it drove him wild.

She pulled her breasts out of the top of her corset and said: 'Bite them. Bite them hard. I want to feel them all evening.'

A moment later she pulled away from him. She lay

on her back on the bed. Where the corset ended, moisture glistened in the sparse blonde hair between her thighs.

She spread her legs and lifted them into the air, opening herself to him. He gazed at her for a moment, then fell on her.

She grabbed his penis with her hands and pushed it inside her greedily.

The heels of her shoes tore the skin of his back and he did not care.

'Look at me,' she said. 'Look at me!'

He looked at her with adoration in his eyes.

An expression of panic came over her face.

She said: 'Look at me, I'm coming!'

Then, still staring into his eyes, she opened her mouth and screamed.

'Do you think other people are like us?' she said.

'In what way?'

'Filthy.'

He lifted his head from her lap and grinned. 'Only the lucky ones.'

She looked at his body, curled up between her legs. 'You're so compact and strong, you're perfect,' she said. 'Look how your belly is flat, and how neat your bottom is, and how lean and hard your thighs are.' She ran a finger along the line of his nose. 'You have the face of a prince.'

'I'm a peasant.'

'Not when you're naked.' She was in a reflective

mood. 'Before I met you, I *was* interested in men's bodies, and all that; but I used to pretend I wasn't, even to myself. Then you came along and I just couldn't pretend any more.'

He licked the inside of her thigh.

She shuddered. 'Have you ever done this to another girl?'

'No.'

'Did you used to pretend, as well?'

'No.'

'I think I knew that, somehow. There's a look about you, wild and free like an animal, you never obey anyone, you just do what you want.'

'I never before met a girl who would let me.'

'They all wanted to, really. Any girl would.'

'Why?' he said egotistically.

'Because your face is so cruel and your eyes are so kind.'

'Is that why you let me kiss you in the bookshop?'

'I didn't *let* you – I had no choice.'

'You could have yelled for help, afterwards.'

'By then all I wanted was for you to do it again.'

'I must have guessed what you were really like.'

It was her turn to be egotistical. 'What am I really like?'

'Cold as ice on the surface, hot as hell below.'

She giggled. 'I'm such an actor. Everyone in St Petersburg thinks I'm so *good*. I'm held up as an example to younger girls, just like Anna Karenina. Now that I know how bad I really am, I have to pretend to be twice as virginal as before.'

'You can't be twice as virginal as anything.'

'I wonder if they're all pretending,' she resumed. 'Take my father. If he knew I was here, like this, he'd die of rage. But he must have had the same feelings when he was young – don't you think?'

'I think it's an imponderable,' Feliks said. 'But what *would* he do, really, if he found out?'

'Horsewhip you.'

'He'd have to catch me first.' Feliks was struck by a thought. 'How old are you?'

'Almost eighteen.'

'My God, I could go to jail for seducing you.'

'I'd make Father get you out.'

He rolled over on to his front and looked at her. 'What are we going to do, Lydia?'

'When?'

'In the long term.'

'We're going to be lovers until I come of age, and then we'll get married.'

He stared at her. 'Do you mean that?'

'Of *course.*' She seemed genuinely surprised that he had not made the same assumption. 'What else could we do?'

'You want to marry me?'

'Yes! Isn't that what you want?'

'Oh, *yes,*' he breathed. 'That's what I want.'

She sat up, with her legs spread either side of his face, and stroked his hair. 'Then that's what we'll do.'

Feliks said: 'You never tell me how you manage to get away to come here.'

'It's not very interesting,' she said. 'I tell lies, I bribe servants, and I take risks. Tonight, for example. The reception at the embassy starts at half past six. I left home at six o'clock and I'll get there at a quarter past seven. The carriage is in the park – the coachman thinks I'm taking a walk with my maid. The maid is outside this house, dreaming about how she will spend the ten roubles I will give her for keeping her mouth shut.'

'It's ten to seven,' Feliks said.

'Oh, God. Quick, do it to me with your tongue before I have to go.'

That night Feliks was asleep, dreaming about Lydia's father – whom he had never seen – when they burst into his room carrying lamps. He woke instantly and jumped out of bed. At first he thought students from the university were playing a prank on him. Then one of them punched his face and kicked him in the stomach, and he knew they were the secret police.

He assumed they were arresting him on account of Lydia, and he was terrified for her. Would she be publicly disgraced? Was her father crazy enough to make her give evidence in court against her lover?

He watched the police put all his books and a bundle of letters in a sack. The books were all borrowed, but none of the owners was foolish enough to put his name inside. The letters were from his father and his sister Natasha – he had never had any letters from Lydia, and now he was thankful for that.

He was marched out of the building and thrown into a four-wheel cab.

They drove across the Chain Bridge and then followed the canals, as if avoiding the main streets. Feliks asked: 'Am I going to the Litovsky prison?' Nobody replied, but when they went over the Palace Bridge he realized he was being taken to the notorious Fortress of St Peter and St Paul, and his heart sank.

On the other side of the bridge the carriage turned left and entered a dark arched passage. It stopped at a gate. Feliks was taken into a reception hall, where an army officer looked at him and wrote something in a book. He was put in the cab again and driven deeper into the fortress. They stopped at another gate, and waited several minutes until it was opened from the inside by a soldier. From there Feliks had to walk through a series of narrow passages to a third iron gate which led to a large damp room.

The prison governor sat at a table. He said: 'You are charged with being an anarchist. Do you admit it?'

Feliks was elated. So this was nothing to do with Lydia! 'Admit it?' he said. 'I boast of it.'

One of the policemen produced a book which was signed by the governor. Feliks was stripped naked, then given a green flannel dressing-gown, a pair of thick woollen stockings, and two yellow felt slippers much too big.

From there an armed soldier took him through more gloomy corridors to a cell. A heavy oak door closed behind him, and he heard a key turn in the lock.

The cell contained a bed, a table, a stool and a washstand. The window was an embrasure in an enormously thick wall. The floor was covered with painted felt, and the walls were cushioned with some kind of yellow upholstery.

Feliks sat on the bed.

This was where Peter I had tortured and killed his own son. This was where Princess Tarakanova had been kept in a cell which flooded so that the rats climbed all over her to save themselves from drowning. This was where Catherine II buried her enemies alive.

Dostoevsky had been imprisoned here, Feliks thought proudly; so had Bakunin, who had been chained to a wall for two years. Nechayev had died here.

Feliks was at once elated to be in such heroic company and terrified at the thought that he might be here for ever.

The key turned in the lock. A little bald man with spectacles came in, carrying a pen, a bottle of ink, and some paper. He set them down on the table and said: 'Write the names of all the subversives you know.'

Feliks sat down and wrote: Karl Marx, Frederick Engels, Peter Kropotkin, Jesus Christ—

The bald man snatched away the paper. He went to the door of the cell and knocked. Two hefty guards came in. They strapped Feliks to the table and took off his slippers and stockings. They began to lash the soles of his feet with whips.

The torture went on all night.

When they pulled out his fingernails, he began to give them made-up names and addresses, but they told him they knew they were false.

When they burned the skin of his testicles with a candle flame he named all his student friends, but still they said he was lying.

Each time he passed out they revived him. Sometimes they would stop for a while, and allow him to think it was all over at last; then they would begin again and he would beg them to kill him so that the pain would stop. They carried on long after he had told them everything he knew.

It must have been around dawn that he passed out for the last time.

When he came round he was lying on the bed. There were bandages on his feet and hands. He was in agony. He wanted to kill himself but he was too weak to move.

The bald man came into the cell in the evening. When he saw him, Feliks began to sob with terror. The man just smiled and went away.

He never came back.

A doctor came to see Feliks each day. Feliks tried without success to pump him for information: Did anyone outside know that Feliks was here? Had there been any messages? Had anyone tried to visit? The doctor just changed the dressings and went away.

Feliks speculated. Lydia would have gone to his room and found the place in disarray. Someone in the house would have told her that the secret police had taken him away. What would she have done then? Would she make frantic inquiries, careless of her reputation?

Would she have been discreet, and gone quietly to see the Minister of the Interior with some story about the boyfriend of her maid having been jailed in error?

Every day he hoped for word from her, but it never came.

Eight weeks later he could walk almost normally, and they released him without explanation.

He went to his lodging. He expected to find a message from her there, but there was nothing, and his room had been let to someone else. He wondered why Lydia had not continued to pay the rent.

He went to her house and knocked at the front door. A servant answered. Feliks said: 'Feliks Davidovitch Kschessinsky presents his compliments to Lydia Shatova—'

The servant slammed the door.

Finally he went to the bookshop. The old bookseller said: 'Hello! I've got a message for you. It was brought yesterday by *her* maid.'

Feliks tore open the envelope with trembling fingers. It was written, not by Lydia, but by the maid. It read:

> *I have been Let Go and have no job it is all your fault She is wed and gone to England yesterday now you know the wages of Sin.*

He looked up at the bookseller with tears of anguish in his eyes. 'Is that all?' he cried.

He learned no more for nineteen years.

*

Normal regulations had been temporarily suspended in the Walden house, and Charlotte sat in the kitchen with the servants.

The kitchen was spotless, for of course the family had dined out. The fire had gone out in the great range, and the high windows were wide open, letting in the cool night air. The crockery used for servants' meals was racked neatly in the dresser; the cook's knives and spoons hung from a row of hooks; her innumerable bowls and pans were out of sight in the massive oak cupboards.

Charlotte had had no time to be frightened. At first, when the coach stopped so abruptly in the park, she had been merely puzzled; and after that her concern had been to stop Mama screaming. When they got home she had found herself a little shaky, but now, looking back, she found the whole thing rather exciting.

The servants felt the same way. It was very reassuring to sit around the massive bleached wooden table and talk things over with these people who were so much a part of her life: the cook, who had always been motherly; Pritchard, whom Charlotte respected because Papa respected him; the efficient and capable Mrs Mitchell, who as housekeeper always had a solution to any problem.

William the coachman was the hero of the hour. He described several times the wild look in his assailant's eyes as the man menaced him with the gun. Basking in the awestruck gaze of the under-house-parlourmaid, he recovered rapidly from the indignity of having walked into the kitchen stark naked.

'Of course,' Pritchard explained, 'I naturally presumed the thief just wanted William's clothes. I knew Charles was at the palace, so he could drive the coach. I thought, I wouldn't inform the police until after speaking to his lordship.'

Charles the footman said: 'Imagine how I felt when I found the carriage gone! I said to myself, I'm sure it was left here. Oh, well, I thinks, William's moved it. I run up and down The Mall, I look everywhere. In the end I go back to the palace. "Here's trouble," I says to the doorman, "the Earl of Walden's carriage has gone missing." He says to me: "Walden?" he says – not very respectful—'

Mrs Mitchell interrupted: 'Palace servants, they think they're better than the nobility—'

'He says to me: "Walden's gone, mate." I thought Gorblimey, I'm for it! I come running through the park, and halfway home I find the carriage, and my lady having hysterics, and my lord with blood on his sword!'

Mrs Mitchell said: 'And, after all that, nothing stolen.'

'A lewnatic,' said Charles. 'An ingenious lewnatic.'

There was general agreement.

The cook poured the tea and served Charlotte first. 'How is my lady now?' she said.

'Oh, she's all right,' Charlotte said. 'She went to bed and took a dose of laudanum. She must be asleep by now.'

'And the gentlemen?'

'Papa and Prince Orlov are in the drawing-room, having a brandy.'

The cook sighed heavily. 'Robbers in the park and suffragettes at the court – I don't know what we're coming to.'

'There'll be a socialist revolution,' said Charles. 'You mark my words.'

'We'll all be murdered in our beds,' the cook said lugubriously.

Charlotte said: 'What did the suffragette mean about the King torturing women?' As she spoke she looked at Pritchard, who was sometimes willing to explain to her things she was not supposed to know about.

'She was talking about force-feeding,' Pritchard said. 'Apparently it's painful.'

'Force-feeding?'

'When they won't eat, they're fed by force.'

Charlotte was mystified. 'How on earth is that done?'

'Several ways,' said Pritchard with a look which indicated he would not go into detail about all of them. 'A tube through the nostrils is one.'

The under-house-parlourmaid said: 'I wonder what they feed them.'

Charles said: 'Probably 'ot soup.'

'I can't believe this,' Charlotte said. 'Why should they refuse to eat?'

'It's a protest,' said Pritchard. 'Makes difficulties for the prison authorities.'

'Prison?' Charlotte was astonished. 'Why are they in prison?'

'For breaking windows, making bombs, disturbing the peace . . .'

'But what do they want?'

There was a silence as the servants realized that Charlotte had no idea what a suffragette was.

Finally Pritchard said: 'They want votes for women.'

'Oh.' Charlotte thought: Did I know that women couldn't vote? She was not sure. She had never thought about that sort of thing.

'I think this discussion has gone quite far enough,' said Mrs Mitchell firmly. 'You'll be in trouble, Mr Pritchard, for putting wrong ideas into my lady's head.'

Charlotte knew that Pritchard never got into trouble, because he was practically Papa's friend. She said: 'I wonder why they care so much about something like voting?'

There was a ring, and they all looked instinctively at the bellboard.

'Front door!' said Pritchard. 'At this time of night!' He went out, pulling on his coat.

Charlotte drank her tea. She felt tired. The suffragettes were puzzling and rather frightening, she decided; but all the same she wanted to know more.

Pritchard came back. 'Plate of sandwiches, please, Cook,' he said. 'Charles, take a fresh soda-siphon to the drawing-room.' He began to arrange plates and napkins on a tray.

'Well, come on,' Charlotte said. 'Who is it?'

'A gentleman from Scotland Yard,' said Pritchard.

*

Basil Thomson was a bullet-headed man with light-coloured receding hair, a heavy moustache, and a penetrating gaze. Walden had heard of him. His father had been Archbishop of York. Thomson had been educated at Eton and Oxford, and had done service in the Colonies as a Native Commissioner and as Prime Minister of Tonga. He had come home to qualify as a barrister and then had worked in the Prison Service, ending up as Governor of Dartmoor Prison with a reputation as a riot-breaker. From prisons he had gravitated toward police work, and had become an expert on the mixed criminal–anarchist milieu of London's East End. This expertise had got him the top job in the Special Branch, the political police force.

Walden sat him down and began to recount the evening's events. As he spoke he kept an eye on Aleks. The boy was superficially calm, but his face was pale, he sipped steadily at a glass of brandy-and-soda, and his left hand clutched rhythmically at the arm of his chair.

At one point Thomson interrupted Walden, saying: 'Did you notice when the carriage picked you up that the footman was missing?'

'Yes, I did,' Walden said. 'I asked the coachman where he was, but the coachman seemed not to hear. Then, because there was such a crush at the palace door, and my daughter was telling me to hurry up, I decided not to press the matter until we got home.'

'Our villain was relying on that, of course. He must have a cool nerve. Go on.'

'The carriage stopped suddenly in the park, and the door was thrown open by the man.'

'What did he look like?'

'Tall. He had a scarf or something over his face. Dark hair. Staring eyes.'

'All criminals have staring eyes,' Thomson said. 'Earlier on, had the coachman got a better look at him?'

'Not much. At that time the man wore a hat, and of course it was dark.'

'Hm. And then?'

Walden took a deep breath. At the time he had been not so much frightened as angry, but now, when he looked back on it, he was full of fear for what might have happened to Aleks, or Lydia, or Charlotte. He said: 'Lady Walden screamed, and that seemed to disconcert the fellow. Perhaps he had not expected to find any women in the coach. Anyway, he hesitated.' And thank God he did, he thought. 'I poked him with my sword, and he dropped the gun.'

'Did you do him much damage?'

'I doubt it. I couldn't get a swing in that confined space, and of course the sword isn't particularly sharp. I blooded him, though. I wish I had chopped off his damned head.'

The butler came in, and conversation stopped. Walden realized he had been talking rather loudly. He tried to calm himself. Pritchard served sandwiches and brandy-and-soda to the three men. Walden said: 'You'd better stay up, Pritchard, but you can send everyone else to bed.'

'Very good, my lord.'

When he had gone Walden said: 'It is possible that

this was just a robbery. I have let the servants think that, and Lady Walden and Charlotte too. However, a robber would hardly have needed such an elaborate plan, to my mind. I am perfectly certain that it was an attempt on Aleks' life.'

Thomson looked at Aleks. 'I'm afraid I agree. Have you any idea how he knew where to find you?'

Aleks crossed his legs. 'My movements haven't been secret.'

'That must change. Tell me, sir, has your life ever been threatened?'

'I live with threats,' Aleks said tightly. 'There has never been an attempt before.'

'Is there any reason why you in particular should be the target of Nihilists or revolutionists?'

'For them, it is enough that I am a p-prince.'

Walden realized that the problems of the English establishment, with suffragettes and Liberals and trade unions, were trivial by comparison with what the Russians had to cope with, and he felt a surge of sympathy for Aleks.

Aleks went on in a quiet, controlled voice: 'However, I am known to be something of a reformer, by Russian standards. They could pick a more appropriate victim.'

'Even in London,' Thomson agreed. 'There's always a Russian aristocrat or two in London for the season.'

Walden said: 'What are you getting at?'

Thomson said: 'I'm wondering whether the villain knew what Prince Orlov is doing here, and whether his motive for tonight's attack was to sabotage your talks.'

Walden was dubious. 'How would the revolutionists have found that out?'

'I'm just speculating,' Thomson replied. '*Would* this be an effective way to sabotage your talks?'

'Very effective indeed,' Walden said. The thought made him go cold. 'If the Czar were to be told that his nephew had been assassinated in London by a revolutionist – especially if it were an expatriate Russian revolutionist – he would go through the roof. You know, Thomson, how the Russians feel about our having their subversives here – our open-door policy has always caused friction at the diplomatic level. Something like this could destroy Anglo-Russian relations for twenty years. There would be no question of an alliance then.'

Thomson nodded. 'I was afraid of that. Well, there's no more we can do tonight. I'll set my department to work at dawn. We'll search the park for clues, and interview your servants, and I expect we'll round up a few anarchists in the East End.'

Aleks said: 'Do you think you will catch the man?'

Walden longed for Thomson to give a reassuring answer, but it was not forthcoming. 'It won't be easy,' Thomson said. 'He's obviously a planner, so he'll have a bolt-hole somewhere. We've no proper description of him. Unless his wounds take him to hospital, our chances are slim.'

'He may try to kill me again,' Aleks said.

'So we must take evasive action. I propose you should move out of this house tomorrow. We'll take the top floor of one of the hotels for you, in a false name, and give you a bodyguard. Lord Walden will have to meet with you secretly, and you'll have to cut out social engagements, of course.'

'Of course.'

Thomson stood up. 'It's very late. I'll set all this in motion.'

Walden rang for Pritchard. 'You've got a carriage waiting, Thomson?'

'Yes. Let us speak on the telephone tomorrow morning.'

Pritchard saw Thomson out, and Aleks went off to bed. Walden told Pritchard to lock up, then went upstairs.

He was not sleepy. As he undressed he let himself relax, and feel all the conflicting emotions which he had so far held at bay. He felt proud of himself, at first – after all, he thought, I drew a sword and fought off an assailant: not bad for a man of fifty with a gouty leg! Then he became depressed when he recalled how coolly they had all discussed the diplomatic conse-quences of the death of Aleks – bright, cheerful, shy, handsome, clever Aleks, whom Walden had seen grow into a man.

He got into bed and lay awake, reliving the moment when the carriage door flew open and the man stood there with the gun; and now he was frightened, not for himself or Aleks, but for Lydia and Charlotte. The thought that they might have been killed made him tremble in his bed. He remembered holding Charlotte in his arms, eighteen years ago, when she had blonde hair and no teeth; he remembered her learning to walk and forever falling on her bottom; he remembered giving her a pony of her own, and thinking that her joy when she saw it gave him the biggest thrill of his life; he remembered her just a few hours ago, walking into the royal presence with her head held high, a grown woman and a beautiful one. If she died, he thought, I don't know that I could bear it.

And Lydia: if Lydia were dead I would be alone. The thought made him get up and go through to her room. There was a nightlight beside her bed. She was in a deep sleep, lying on her back, her mouth a little open, her hair a blonde skein across the pillow. She looked soft and vulnerable. I have never been able to make you understand how much I love you, he thought. Suddenly he needed to touch her, to feel that she was warm and alive. He got into bed with her and kissed her. Her lips responded but she did not wake up. Lydia, he thought, I could not live without you.

Lydia had lain awake for a long time, thinking about the man with the gun. It had been a brutal shock, and she had screamed in sheer terror – but there was more to it than that. There had been something about the man, something about his stance, or his shape, or his clothes, that had seemed dreadfully sinister in an almost supernatural way, as if he were a ghost. She wished she could have seen his eyes.

After a while she had taken another dose of laudanum, and then she slept. She dreamed that the man with the gun came to her room and got into bed with her. It was her own bed, but in the dream she was eighteen years old again. The man put his gun down on the white pillow beside her head. He still had the scarf around his face. She realized that she loved him. She kissed his lips through the scarf.

He made love to her beautifully. She began to think that she might be dreaming. She wanted to see his face. She said *Who are you?* and a voice said *Stephen*. She knew this was not so, but the gun on the pillow had somehow turned into Stephen's sword, with blood on its point; and she began to have doubts. She clung to the man on top of her, afraid that the dream would end before she was satisfied. Then, dimly, she began to suspect that she was doing in reality what she was doing in the dream; yet the dream persisted. Strong physical pleasure possessed her. She began to lose control. Just as her climax began the man in the dream took the scarf from his face, and in that moment Lydia opened her eyes, and saw Stephen's face above her; and then she was overcome by ecstasy, and for the first time in nineteen years she cried for joy.

CHAPTER FIVE

CHARLOTTE LOOKED forward with mixed feelings to Belinda's coming-out ball. She had never been to a town ball, although she had been to lots of country balls, many of them at Walden Hall. She liked to dance and she knew she did it well, but she hated the cattle-market business of sitting out with the wallflowers and waiting for a boy to pick you out and ask you to dance. She wondered whether this might be handled in a more civilized way among the 'Smart Set'.

They got to Uncle George and Aunt Clarissa's Mayfair house half an hour before midnight, which Mama said was the earliest time one could decently arrive at a London ball. A striped canopy and a red carpet led from the kerb to the garden gate, which had somehow been transformed into a Roman triumphal arch.

But even that did not prepare Charlotte for what she saw when she passed through the arch. The whole side-garden had been turned into a Roman atrium. She gazed about her in wonderment. The lawns and the flower beds had been covered over with a hardwood dance floor stained in black and white squares to look like marble tiles. A colonnade of white pillars, linked with chains of laurel, bordered the floor. Beyond the pillars, in a kind of cloister, there were raised benches for the sitters-out. In the middle of the floor a fountain in the form of a boy with a dolphin splashed in a marble basin, the streams of water lit by coloured spotlights. On the balcony of an upstairs bedroom a band played ragtime. Garlands of smilax and roses decorated the walls, and baskets of begonias hung from the balcony. A huge canvas roof, painted sky-blue, covered the whole area from the eaves of the house to the garden wall.

'It's a miracle!' Charlotte said.

Papa said to his brother: 'Quite a crowd, George.'

'We invited eight hundred. What the devil happened to you in the park?'

'Oh, it wasn't as bad as it sounded,' Papa said with a forced smile. He took George by the arm, and they moved to one side to talk.

Charlotte studied the guests. All the men wore full evening dress – white tie, white waistcoat and tails. It particularly suited the young men, or at least the slim men, Charlotte thought: it made them look quite dashing as they danced. Observing the dresses, she decided that hers and her mother's, though rather tasteful, were a trifle old-fashioned, with their wasp waists and ruffles and sweepers: Aunt Clarissa wore a long, straight, slender gown with a skirt almost too tight to dance in, and Belinda had harem pants.

Charlotte realized she knew nobody. Who will dance with me, she wondered, after Papa and Uncle George? However, Aunt Clarissa's younger brother Jonathan waltzed with her then introduced her to three men who were at Oxford with him, each of whom danced with her. She found their conversation monotonous: they said the floor was good, and the band – Gottlieb's – was good, then they ran out of steam. Charlotte tried: 'Do you believe that women should have the vote?' The replies she got were: 'Certainly not,' 'No opinion,' and 'You're not one of *them*, are you?'

The last of her partners, whose name was Freddie, took her into the house for supper. He was a rather sleek young man, with regular features – handsome, I suppose, Charlotte thought – and fair hair. He was at the end of his first year at Oxford. Oxford was rather jolly, he said, but he confessed he was not much of a one for reading books, and he rather thought he would not go back in October.

The inside of the house was festooned with flowers and bright with electric light. For supper there was hot and cold soup, lobster, quail, strawberries, ice-cream, and hothouse peaches. 'Always the same old food for supper,' Freddie said. 'They all use the same caterer.'

'Do you go to a lot of balls?' Charlotte asked.

''Fraid so. All the time, really, in the season.'

Charlotte drank a glass of champagne-cup in the hope that it would make her feel more gay, then she left Freddie and wandered through a series of reception-rooms. In one of them several games of bridge were under way. Two elderly duchesses held court in another. In a third, older men played billiards while younger men smoked. Charlotte found Belinda there with a cigarette in her hand. Charlotte had never seen the point of tobacco, unless one wanted to look sophisticated. Belinda certainly looked sophisticated.

'I adore your dress,' Belinda said.

'No, you don't. But *you* look sensational. How did you persuade your stepmother to let you dress like that?'

'She'd like to wear one herself!'

'She seems so much younger than my Mama. Which she is, of course.'

'And being a stepmother makes a difference. Whatever happened to you after the court?'

'Oh, it was extraordinary! A madman pointed a gun at us!'

'Your Mama was telling me. Weren't you simply terrified?'

'I was too busy calming Mama. Afterwards I was scared to death. Why did you say, at the palace, that you wanted to have a long talk with me?'

'Ah! Listen.' She took Charlotte aside, away from the young men. 'I've discovered how they come out.'

'What?'

'Babies.'

'Oh!' Charlotte was all ears. 'Do tell.'

Belinda lowered her voice. 'They come out between your legs, where you make water.'

'It's too small!'

'It stretches.'

How awful, Charlotte thought.

'But that's not all,' Belinda said. 'I've found out how they start.'

'How?'

Belinda took Charlotte's elbow and they walked to the far side of the room. They stood in front of a mirror garlanded with roses. Belinda's voice fell almost to a whisper. 'When you get married, you know you have to go to bed with your husband.'

'Do you?'

'Yes.'

'Papa and Mama have separate bedrooms.'

'Don't they adjoin?'

'Yes.'

'That's so that they can get into the same bed.'

'Why?'

'Because, to start a baby, the husband has to put his pego into that place – where the babies come out.'

'What's a pego?'

'Hush! It's a thing men have between their legs – haven't you ever seen a picture of Michelangelo's *David*?'

'No.'

'Well, it's a thing they make water with. Looks like a finger.'

'And you have to do *that* to start babies?'

'Yes.'

'And all married people have to do it?'

'Yes.'

'How dreadful. Who told you all this?'

'Viola Pontadarvy. She swore it was true.'

And somehow Charlotte knew it *was* true. Hearing it was like being reminded of something she had forgotten. It seemed, unaccountably, to make sense. Yet she felt physically shocked. It was the slightly queasy feeling she sometimes got in dreams, when a terrible suspicion turned out to be correct, or when she was afraid of falling and suddenly found she *was* falling.

'I'm jolly glad you found out,' she said. 'If one got married without knowing ... how embarrassing it would be!'

'That happens to some girls, apparently,' Belinda said. 'Your mother is supposed to explain it all to you the night before your wedding, but if your mother is too shy you just ... find out when it happens.'

'Thank Heaven for Viola Pontadarvy.' Charlotte was struck by a thought. 'Has all this got something to do with ... bleeding, you know, every month?'

'I don't know.'

'I expect it has. It's all connected – all the things people don't talk about. Well, now we know why they don't talk about it – it's so disgusting.'

'The thing you have to do in bed is called sexual intercourse, but Viola says the common people call it swiving.'

'She knows a lot.'

'She's got brothers. They told her years ago.'

'How did they find out?'

'From older boys at school. Boys are ever so interested in that sort of thing.'

'Well,' Charlotte said, 'it does have a sort of horrid fascination.'

Suddenly she saw in the mirror the reflection of Aunt Clarissa. 'What are you two doing huddled in a

146

corner?' she said. Charlotte flushed, but apparently Aunt Clarissa did not want an answer, for she went on: 'Do please move around and talk to people, Belinda – it is your party.'

She went away, and the two girls moved on through the reception-rooms. The rooms were arranged on a circular plan so that you could walk through them all and end up where you had started, at the top of the staircase. Charlotte said: 'I don't think I could ever bring myself to do it.'

'Couldn't you?' Belinda said with a funny look.

'What do you mean?'

'I don't know. I've been thinking about it. It might be quite nice.'

Charlotte stared at her.

Belinda looked embarrassed. 'I must go and dance,' she said. 'See you later on!'

She went down the stairs. Charlotte watched her go, and wondered how many more shocking secrets life had to reveal.

She went back into the supper-room and got another glass of champagne-cup. What a peculiar way for the human race to perpetuate itself, she thought. She supposed animals did something similar. What about birds? No, birds had eggs. And such words! *Pego* and *swiving*. All these hundreds of elegant and refined people around her knew those words, but never mentioned them. Because they were never mentioned, they were embarrassing. Because they were embarrassing, they were never mentioned. There was something very *silly* about the whole thing. If the Creator had ordained that people should swive, why pretend that they did not?

She finished her drink and went outside to the dance floor. Papa and Mama were dancing a polka, and doing it rather well. Mama had got over the incident in the park, but it still preyed on Papa's mind. He looked very fine in white tie and tails. When his leg was bad he would not dance, but obviously it was giving him no trouble tonight. He was surprisingly light on his feet for a big man. Mama seemed to be having a wonderful time. She was able to let herself go a bit when she danced. Her usual studied reserve fell away, and she smiled radiantly and let her ankles show.

When the polka was over Papa caught Charlotte's eye and came over. 'May I have this dance, Lady Charlotte?'

'Certainly, my lord.'

It was a waltz. Papa seemed distracted, but he whirled her around the floor expertly. She wondered whether she looked radiant, like Mama. Probably not. Suddenly she thought of Papa and Mama swiving, and found the idea terribly embarrassing.

Papa said: 'Are you enjoying your first big ball?'

'Yes, thank you,' she said dutifully.

'You seem thoughtful.'

'I'm on my best behaviour.' The lights and the bright colours blurred slightly, and suddenly she had to concentrate on staying upright. She was afraid she might fall over and look foolish. Papa sensed her unsteadiness and held her a little more firmly. A moment later the dance ended.

Papa took her off the floor. He said: 'Are you feeling quite well?'

'Yes, but I was dizzy for a moment.'

'Have you been smoking?'

Charlotte laughed. 'Certainly not.'

'That's the usual reason young ladies feel dizzy at balls. Take my advice: when you want to try tobacco, do it in private.'

'I don't think I want to try it.'

She sat out the next dance, and then Freddie turned up again. As she danced with him, it occurred to her that all the young men and girls, including Freddie and herself, were supposed to be looking for husbands or wives during the season, especially at balls like this. For the first time she considered Freddie as a possible husband for herself. It was unthinkable.

Then what kind of husband do I want? she wondered. She really had no idea.

Freddie said: 'Jonathan just said "Freddie, meet Charlotte," but I gather you're called Lady Charlotte Walden.'

'Yes. Who are you?'

'Marquis of Chalfont, actually.'

So, Charlotte thought, we're socially compatible.

A little later she and Freddie got into conversation with Belinda and Freddie's friends. They talked about a new play, called *Pygmalion*, which was said to be absolutely hilarious but quite vulgar. The boys spoke of going to a boxing match, and Belinda said she wanted to go too, but they all said it was out of the question. They discussed jazz music. One of the boys was something of a connoisseur, having lived for a while in the United States; but Freddie disliked it, and talked rather pompously about 'the negrification of society'. They all drank coffee and Belinda smoked another cigarette. Charlotte began to enjoy herself.

It was Charlotte's Mama who came along and broke up the party. 'Your father and I are leaving,' she said. 'Shall we send the coach back for you?'

Charlotte realized she was tired. 'No, I'll come,' she said. 'What time is it?'

'Four o'clock.'

They went to get their wraps. Mama said: 'Did you have a lovely evening?'

'Yes, thank you, Mama.'

'So did I. Who were those young men?'

'They know Jonathan.'

'Were they nice?'

'The conversation got quite interesting, in the end.'

Papa had called the carriage already. As they drove away from the bright lights of the party, Charlotte remembered what had happened last time they rode in a carriage, and she felt scared.

Papa held Mama's hand. They seemed happy. Charlotte felt excluded. She looked out of the window. In the dawn light she could see four men in silk hats walking up Park Lane, going home from some night club perhaps. As the carriage rounded Hyde Park

Corner Charlotte saw something odd. 'What's that?' she said.

Mama looked out. 'What's what, dear?'

'On the pavement. Looks like people.'

'That's right.'

'What are they doing?'

'Sleeping.'

Charlotte was horrified. There were eight or ten of them, up against a wall, bundled in coats, blankets and newspapers. She could not tell whether they were men or women, but some of the bundles were small enough to be children.

She said: 'Why do they sleep there?'

'I don't know, dear,' Mama said.

Papa said: 'Because they've nowhere else to sleep, of course.'

'They have no homes?'

'No.'

'I didn't know there was anyone that poor,' Charlotte said. 'How dreadful.' She thought of all the rooms in Uncle George's house, the food that had been laid out to be picked at by eight hundred people all of whom had had dinner, and the elaborate gowns they wore new each season while people slept under newspapers. She said: 'We should do something for them.'

'We?' Papa said. 'What should *we* do?'

'Build houses for them.'

'All of them?'

'How many are there?'

Papa shrugged. 'Thousands.'

'Thousands! I thought it was just those few.' Charlotte was devastated. 'Couldn't you build small houses?'

'There's no profit in house property, especially at that end of the market.'

'Perhaps you should do it anyway.'

'Why?'

'Because the strong should take care of the weak. I've heard you say that to Mr Samson.' Samson was the bailiff at Walden Hall, and he was always trying to save money on repairs to tenanted cottages.

'We already take care of rather a lot of people,' Papa said. 'All the servants whose wages we pay, all the tenants who farm our land and live in our cottages, all the workers in the companies we invest in, all the government employees who are paid out of our taxes—'

'I don't think that's much of an excuse,' Charlotte interrupted. 'Those poor people are sleeping on the *street*. What will they do in winter?'

Mama said sharply: 'Your Papa doesn't need excuses. He was born an aristocrat and he has managed his estate carefully. He is entitled to his wealth. Those people on the pavement are idlers, criminals, drunkards and ne'er-do-wells.'

'Even the children?'

'Don't be impertinent. Remember you still have a great deal to learn.'

'I'm just beginning to realize how much,' Charlotte said.

As the carriage turned into the courtyard of their

house, Charlotte glimpsed one of the street sleepers beside the gate. She decided she would take a closer look.

The coach stopped beside the front door. Charles handed Mama down, then Charlotte. Charlotte ran across the courtyard. William was closing the gates. 'Just a minute,' Charlotte called.

She heard Papa say: 'What the devil . . . ?'

She ran out into the street.

The sleeper was a woman. She lay slumped on the pavement with her shoulders against the courtyard wall. She wore a man's boots, woollen stockings, a dirty blue coat, and a very large once-fashionable hat with a bunch of grubby artificial flowers in its brim. Her head was slumped sideways and her face was turned toward Charlotte.

There was something familiar about the round face and the wide mouth. The woman was young . . .

Charlotte cried: 'Annie!'

The sleeper opened her eyes.

Charlotte stared at her in horror. Two months ago Annie had been a housemaid at Walden Hall in a crisp clean uniform with a little white hat on her head, a pretty girl with a large bosom and an irrepressible laugh. 'Annie, what happened to you?'

Annie scrambled to her feet and bobbed a pathetic curtsey. 'Oh, Lady Charlotte, I was hoping I would see you, you was always good to me, I've nowhere to turn—'

'But how did you get like this?'

'I was let go, m'lady, without a character, when they found out I was expecting the baby, I know I done wrong—'

'But you're not married!'

'But I was courting Jimmy, the under-gardener . . .'

Charlotte recalled Belinda's revelations, and realized that if all that was true it would indeed be possible for girls to have babies without being married. 'Where is the baby?'

'I lost it.'

'You *lost* it?'

'I mean, it came too early, m'lady, it was born dead.'

'How horrible,' Charlotte whispered. That was something else she had not known to be possible. 'And why isn't Jimmy with you?'

'He run away to sea. He *did* love me, I know, but he was frightened to wed, he was only seventeen . . .' Annie began to cry.

Charlotte heard Papa's voice. 'Charlotte, come in this instant.'

She turned to him. He stood at the gate in his evening clothes, with his silk hat in his hand, and suddenly she saw him as a big, smug, cruel old man. She said: 'This is one of the servants you care for so well.'

Papa looked at the girl. 'Annie! What is the meaning of this?'

Annie said: 'Jimmy run away, m'lord, so I couldn't wed, and I couldn't get another position because you never gave me a character, and I was ashamed to go home, so I come to London . . .'

'You came to London to beg,' Papa said harshly.

'Papa!' Charlotte cried.

'You don't understand, Charlotte—'

'I understand perfectly well—'

Mama appeared and said: 'Charlotte, get away from that creature!'

'She's not a creature, she's Annie.'

'Annie!' Mama shrilled. 'She's a fallen woman!'

'That's enough,' Papa said. 'This family does not hold discussions in the street. Let us go in immediately.'

Charlotte put her arm around Annie. 'She needs a bath, new clothes and a hot breakfast.'

'Don't be ridiculous!' Mama said. The sight of Annie seemed to have made her almost hysterical.

'All right,' Papa said. 'Take her into the kitchen. The parlourmaids will be up by now. Tell them to take care of her. Then come and see me in the drawing-room.'

Mama said: 'Stephen, this is insane—'

'Let us go *in*,' said Papa.

They went in.

Charlotte took Annie downstairs to the kitchen. A skivvy was cleaning the range and a kitchenmaid was slicing bacon for breakfast. It was just past five o'clock: Charlotte had not realized they started work so early. They both looked at her in astonishment when she walked in, in her ball gown, with Annie at her side.

Charlotte said: 'This is Annie. She used to work at

Walden Hall. She's had some bad luck but she's a good girl. She must have a bath. Find new clothes for her and burn her old ones. Then give her breakfast.'

For a moment they were both dumbstruck, then the kitchenmaid said: 'Very good, m'lady.'

'I'll see you later, Annie,' Charlotte said.

Annie seized Charlotte's arm. 'Oh, thank you, m'lady.'

Charlotte went out.

Now there will be trouble, she thought as she went upstairs. She did not care as much as she might have. She almost felt that her parents had betrayed her. What had her years of education been for, when in one night she could find out that the most important things had never been taught her? No doubt they talked of protecting young girls, but Charlotte thought deceit might be the appropriate term. When she thought of how ignorant she had been until tonight, she felt so foolish, and that made her angry.

She marched into the drawing-room.

Papa stood beside the fireplace holding a glass. Mama sat at the piano, playing double-minor chords with a pained expression on her face. They had drawn back the curtains. The room looked odd in the morning, with yesterday's cigar butts in the ashtrays and the cold early light on the edges of things. It was an evening room, and wanted lamps and warmth, drinks and footmen, and a crowd of people in formal clothes.

Everything looked different today.

'Now, then, Charlotte,' Papa began. 'You don't

understand what kind of woman Annie is. We let her go for a reason, you know. She did something very wrong which I cannot explain to you—'

'I know what she did,' Charlotte said, sitting down. 'And I know who she did it with. A gardener called Jimmy.'

Mama gasped.

Papa said: 'I don't believe you have any idea what you're talking about.'

'And if I haven't, whose fault is it?' Charlotte burst out. 'How did I manage to reach the age of eighteen without learning that some people are so poor they sleep in the street, that maids who are expecting babies get dismissed, and that – that – men are not made the same as women? Don't stand there telling me I don't understand these things and I have a lot to learn! I've spent all my life learning and now I discover most of it was lies! How dare you! How dare you!' She burst into tears, and hated herself for losing control.

She heard Mama say: 'Oh, this is too foolish.'

Papa sat beside her and took her hand. 'I'm sorry you feel that way,' he said. 'All young girls are kept in ignorance of certain things. It is done for their own good. We have never lied to you. If we did not tell you just how cruel and coarse the world is, that was only because we wanted you to enjoy your childhood for as long as possible. Perhaps we made a mistake.'

Mama snapped: 'We wanted to keep you out of the trouble that Annie got into!'

'I wouldn't put it quite like that,' Papa said mildly.

Charlotte's rage evaporated. She felt like a child again. She wanted to put her head on Papa's shoulder, but her pride would not let her.

'Shall we all forgive each other, and be pals again?' Papa said.

An idea which had been quietly budding in Charlotte's mind now blossomed, and she spoke without thinking. 'Would you let me take Annie as my personal maid?'

Papa said: 'Well . . .'

'We won't even think of it!' Mama said hysterically. 'It is quite out of the question! That an eighteen-year-old girl who is the daughter of an earl should have a scarlet woman as a maid! No, absolutely and finally, no!'

'Then what will she do?' Charlotte asked calmly.

'She should have thought of that when— She should have thought of that before.'

Papa said: 'Charlotte, we cannot possibly have a woman of bad character to live in this house. Even if I would allow it, the servants would be scandalized. Half of them would give notice. We shall hear mutterings even now, just because the girl has been allowed into the kitchen. You see, it is not just Mama and I who shun such people – it is the whole of society.'

'Then I shall buy her a house,' Charlotte said, 'and give her an allowance and be her friend.'

'You've no money,' Mama said.

'My Russian grandfather left me something.'

Papa said: 'But the money is in my care until you

reach the age of twenty-one, and I will not allow it to be used for that purpose.'

'Then what is to be done with her?' Charlotte said desperately.

'I'll make a bargain with you,' Papa said. 'I will give her money to get decent lodgings, and I'll see that she gets a job in a factory.'

'What would be my part of the bargain?'

'You must promise not to try to make contact with her, ever.'

Charlotte felt very tired. Papa had all the answers. She could no longer argue with him, and she did not have the power to insist. She sighed.

'All right,' she said.

'Good girl. Now, then, I suggest you go and find her and tell her the arrangement, then say goodbye.'

'I'm not sure I can look her in the eye.'

Papa patted her hand. 'She will be very grateful, you'll see. When you've spoken to her, you go to bed. I'll see to all the details.'

Charlotte did not know whether she had won or lost, whether Papa was being cruel or kind, whether Annie should feel saved or spurned. 'Very well,' she said wearily. She wanted to tell Papa that she loved him, but the words would not come. After a moment she got up and left the room.

On the day after the fiasco Feliks was awakened at noon by Bridget. He felt very weak. Bridget stood beside his bed with a large cup in her hand. Feliks sat up and took the cup. The drink was wonderful. It seemed to consist of hot milk, sugar, melted butter and lumps of bread. While he drank it Bridget moved around his room, tidying up, singing a sentimental song about boys who gave their lives for Ireland.

She went away and came back again with another Irishwoman of her own age who was a nurse. The woman stitched his hand and put a dressing on the puncture wound in his shoulder. Feliks gathered from the conversation that she was the local abortionist. Bridget told her that Feliks had been in a fight in a pub. The nurse charged a shilling for the visit and said: 'You won't die. If you'd had yourself seen to straight away you wouldn't have bled so much. As it is you'll feel weak for days.'

When she had gone Bridget talked to him. She was a heavy, good-natured woman in her late fifties. Her husband had got into some kind of trouble in Ireland and they had fled to the anonymity of London, where he died of the booze, she said. She had two sons who were policemen in New York and a daughter who was in service in Belfast. There was a vein of bitterness in her which showed in an occasional sarcastically humorous remark, usually at the expense of the English.

While she was explaining why Ireland should have Home Rule Feliks went to sleep. She woke him again in the evening to give him hot soup.

On the following day his physical wounds began visibly to heal, and he started to feel the pain of his emotional wounds. All the despair and self-reproach which he had felt in the park as he ran away now came back to him. Running away! How could it happen?

Lydia.

She was now Lady Walden.

He felt nauseous.

He made himself think clearly and coolly. He had known that she married and went to England. Obviously the Englishman she married was likely to be both an aristocrat and a man with a strong interest in Russia. Equally obviously, the person who negotiated with Orlov had to be a member of the establishment and an expert on Russian affairs. I couldn't have guessed it would turn out to be the same man, Feliks thought, but I should have realized the possibility.

The coincidence was not as remarkable as it had seemed, but it was no less shattering. Twice in his life Feliks had been utterly, blindly, deliriously happy. The first time was when, at the age of four – before his mother died – he had been given a red ball. The second was when Lydia fell in love with him. But the red ball had never been taken from him.

He could not imagine a greater happiness than that which he had had with Lydia – nor a disappointment more appalling than the one that followed. There had certainly been no such highs and lows in Feliks' emotional life since then. After she left he began to tramp the Russian countryside, dressed as a monk, preaching the anarchist gospel. He told the peasants that the land was theirs because they tilled it; that the wood in the forest belonged to anyone who felled a tree; that nobody had a right to govern them except

161

themselves, and because self-government was no government it was called anarchy. He was a wonderful preacher and he made many friends, but he never fell in love again, and he hoped he never would.

His preaching phase had ended in 1899, during the national student strike, when he was arrested as an agitator and sent to Siberia. The years of wandering had already inured him to cold, hunger and pain; but now, working in a chain gang, using wooden tools to dig out gold in a mine, labouring on when the man chained to his side had fallen dead, seeing boys and women flogged, he came to know darkness, bitterness, despair, and finally hatred. In Siberia he had learned the facts of life: steal or starve, hide or be beaten, fight or die. There he had acquired cunning and ruthlessness. There he had learned the ultimate truth about oppression: that it works by turning its victims against each other instead of against their oppressors.

He escaped, and began the long journey into madness which ended when he killed the policeman outside Omsk, and realized that he had no fear.

He returned to civilization as a full-blooded revolutionist. It seemed incredible to him that he had once scrupled to throw bombs at the noblemen who maintained those Siberian convict mines. He was enraged by the government-inspired pogroms against the Jews in the west and south of Russia. He was sickened by the wrangling between Bolsheviks and Mensheviks at the second congress of the Social Democratic Party. He was inspired by the magazine that came from Geneva, called *Bread and Liberty*, with the quote from Bakunin on its masthead: 'The urge to destroy is also a creative urge.' Finally, hating the government, disenchanted with the socialists, and convinced by the anarchists, he went to a mill town called Bialystock and founded a group called Struggle.

Those had been the glory years. He would never forget young Nisan Farber, who had knifed the mill owner outside the synagogue on the Day of Atonement. Feliks himself had shot the chief of police. Then he took the fight to St Petersburg, where he founded another anarchist group, The Unauthorized, and planned the successful assassination of the Grand Duke Sergei. That year – 1905 – in St Petersburg there were killings, bank robberies, strikes and riots: the revolution seemed only days away. Then came the repression – more fierce, more efficient, and a great deal more bloodthirsty than anything the revolutionists had ever done. The secret police came in the middle of the night to the homes of The Unauthorized, and they were all arrested, except Feliks, who killed one police-man and maimed another and escaped to Switzerland, for by then nobody could stop him, he was so deter-mined and powerful and angry and ruthless.

In all those years, and even in the quiet years in Switzerland which followed, he had never loved anyone. There had been people of whom he had grown mildly fond – a pig-keeper in Georgia, an old Jewish bomb-maker in Bialystock, Ulrich in Geneva – but they tended to pass into and then out of his life. There had been women, too. Many women sensed his violent nature and shied away from him, but those of them who found him attractive found him extremely so. Occasionally he had yielded to the temptation, and he had always been more or less disappointed. His parents were both dead and he had not seen his sister for twenty years. Looking back, he could see his life since Lydia as a slow slide into anaesthesia. He had survived by becoming less and less sensitive, through the experiences of imprisonment, torture, the chain gang, and the long, brutal escape from Siberia. He no longer cared even for himself: this, he had decided, was the meaning of his lack of fear, for one could only be afraid on account of something for which one cared.

He liked it this way.

His love was not for people, it was for *the* people. His compassion was for starving peasants in general, and sick children and frightened soldiers and crippled miners in general. He hated nobody in particular: just all princes, all landlords, all capitalists and all generals.

In giving his personality over to a higher cause he knew he was like a priest, and indeed like one priest in particular: his father. He no longer felt diminished by this comparison. He respected his father's high-mindedness and despised the cause it served. He, Feliks, had chosen the right cause. His life would not be wasted.

This was the Feliks that had formed over the years, as his mature personality emerged from the fluidity of youth. What had been so devastating about Lydia's scream, he thought, was that it had reminded him that there might have been a different Feliks, a warm and loving man, a sexual man, a man capable of jealousy, greed, vanity and fear. Would I rather be that man? he

164

asked himself. That man would long to stare into her wide grey eyes and stroke her fine blonde hair, to see her collapse into helpless giggles as she tried to learn how to whistle, to argue with her about Tolstoy, to eat black bread and smoked herrings with her and to watch her screw up her pretty face at her first taste of vodka. That man would be *playful*.

He would also be *concerned*. He would wonder whether Lydia was happy. He would hesitate to pull the trigger for fear she might be hit by a ricochet. He might be reluctant to kill her nephew in case she were fond of the boy. That man would make a poor revolutionist.

No, he thought as he went to sleep that night; I would not want to be that man. He is not even dangerous.

In the night he dreamed that he shot Lydia, but when he woke up he could not remember whether it had made him sad.

On the third day he went out. Bridget gave him a shirt and a coat which had belonged to her husband. They fitted badly, for he had been shorter and wider than Feliks. Feliks' own trousers and boots were still wearable, and Bridget had washed the blood off.

He mended the bicycle, which had been damaged when he dropped it down the steps. He straightened a buckled wheel, patched a punctured tyre, and taped the split leather of the saddle. He climbed on and rode a short distance, but he realized immediately that he was not yet strong enough to go far on it. He walked instead.

It was a glorious sunny day. At a second-hand clothes

stall in Mornington Crescent he gave a halfpenny and Bridget's husband's coat for a lighter coat that fitted him. He felt peculiarly happy, walking through the streets of London in the summer weather. I've nothing to be happy about, he thought; my clever, well-organized, daring assassination plan fell to pieces because a woman cried out and a middle-aged man drew a sword. What a fiasco!

It was Bridget who had cheered him up, he decided. She had seen that he was in trouble and she had given help without thinking twice. It reminded him of the great-heartedness of the people in whose cause he fired guns and threw bombs and got himself sliced up with a sword. It gave him strength.

He made his way to St James's Park and took up his familiar station opposite the Walden house. He looked at the pristine white stonework and the high, elegant windows. You can knock me down, he thought, but you can't knock me out; if you knew I was back here again, you'd tremble in your patent-leather shoes.

He settled down to watch. The trouble with a fiasco was that it put the intended victim on his guard. It would now be very difficult indeed to kill Orlov because he would be taking precautions. But Feliks would find out what those precautions were, and he would evade them.

At eleven a.m. the carriage went out, and Feliks thought he saw behind the glass a spade-shaped beard and a top hat: Walden. It came back at one. It went out again at three, this time with a feminine hat inside, belonging presumably to Lydia, or perhaps to the daughter of the family; whoever it was returned at five. In the evening several guests came and the family apparently dined at home. There was no sign of Orlov. It rather looked as if he had moved out.

I'll find him, then, he thought.

On his way back to Camden Town he bought a newspaper. When he arrived home Bridget offered him tea, so he read the paper in her parlour. There was nothing about Orlov either in the Court Circular or the Social Notes.

Bridget saw what he was reading. 'Interesting material, for a fellow such as yourself,' she said sarcastically. 'You'll be making up your mind which of the balls to attend tonight, no doubt.'

Feliks smiled and said nothing.

Bridget said: 'I know what you are, you know. You're an anarchist.'

Feliks was very still.

'Who are you going to kill?' she said. 'I hope it's the bloody King.' She drank tea noisily. 'Well, don't stare at me like that. You look as if you're about to slit me throat. You needn't worry, I won't tell on you. My husband did for a few of the English in his time.'

Feliks was nonplussed. She had guessed – and she approved! He did not know what to say. He stood up and folded his newspaper. 'You're a good woman,' he said.

'If I was twenty years younger I'd kiss you. Get away before I forget myself.'

'Thank you for the tea,' Feliks said. He went out.

He spent the rest of the evening sitting in the drab

basement room, staring at the wall, thinking. Of course Orlov was lying low, but where? If he was not at the Walden house, he might be at the Russian Embassy, or at the home of one of the embassy staff, or at an hotel, or at the home of one of Walden's friends. He might even be out of London, at a house in the country. There was no way to check all the possibilities.

It was not going to be so easy. He began to worry.

He considered following Walden around. It might be the best he could do, but it was unsatisfactory. Although it was possible for a bicycle to keep pace with a carriage in London, it could be exhausting for the cyclist, and Feliks knew that he could not contemplate it for several days. Suppose then that, over a period of three days, Walden visited several private houses, two or three offices, an hotel or two and an embassy – how would Feliks find out which of those buildings Orlov was in? It was possible, but it would take time.

Meanwhile the negotiations would be progressing and war was drawing nearer.

And suppose that, after all that, Orlov was still living in Walden's house and had decided simply not to go out?

Feliks went to sleep gnawing at the problem and woke up in the morning with the solution.

He would ask Lydia.

He polished his boots, washed his hair, and shaved. He borrowed from Bridget a white cotton scarf which, worn around his throat, concealed the fact that he had neither collar nor tie. At the second-hand clothes stall in Mornington Crescent he found a bowler hat which fitted him. He looked at himself in the stallholder's cracked, frosted mirror. He looked dangerously respectable. He walked on.

He had no idea how Lydia would react to him. He was quite sure that she had not recognized him on the night of the fiasco: his face had been covered and her scream had been a reaction to the sight of an anonymous man with a gun. Assuming he could get in to see her, what would she do? Would she throw him out? Would she immediately begin to tear off her clothes, the way she had used to? Would she be merely indifferent, thinking of him as someone she knew in her youth and no longer cared for?

He wanted her to be shocked and dazed and still in love with him, so that he would be able to make her tell him a secret.

Suddenly he could not remember what she looked like. It was very odd. He knew she was a certain height, neither fat nor thin, with pale hair and grey eyes; but he could not bring to mind a picture of her. If he concentrated on her nose he could see that, or he could visualize her vaguely, without definite form, in the bleak light of a St Petersburg evening; but when he tried to focus on her she faded away.

He arrived at the park and hesitated outside the house. It was ten o'clock. Would they have got up yet? In any event, he thought he should probably wait until Walden left the house. It occurred to him that he might even see Orlov in the hall – at a time when he had no weapon.

If I do I'll strangle him with my hands, he thought savagely.

He wondered what Lydia was doing right now. She might be dressing. Ah, yes, he thought, I can picture her in a corset, brushing her hair before a mirror. Or she might be eating breakfast. There would be eggs and meat and fish, but she would eat a small piece of a soft roll and a slice of apple.

The carriage appeared at the entrance. A minute or two later someone got in and it drove to the gate. Feliks stood on the opposite side of the road as it emerged. Suddenly he was looking straight at Walden, behind the window of the coach, and Walden was looking; at him. Feliks had an urge to shout: 'Hey, Walden, I fucked her first!' Instead he grinned and doffed his hat. Walden inclined his head in acknowledgement, and the carriage passed on.

Feliks wondered why he felt so elated.

He walked through the gateway and across the courtyard. He saw that there were flowers in every window of the house, and he thought: Ah, yes, she always loved flowers. He climbed the steps to the porch and pulled the bell at the front door.

Perhaps she will call the police, he thought.

A moment later a servant opened the door. Feliks stepped inside. 'Good morning,' he said.

'Good morning, sir,' the servant said.

So I *do* look respectable. 'I should like to see the Countess of Walden. It is a matter of great urgency. My name is Constantine Dmitrich Levin. I am sure she will remember me from St Petersburg.'

'Yes, sir. Constantine . . . ?'

'Constantine Dmitrich Levin. Let me give you my

card.' Feliks fumbled inside his coat. 'Ach! I brought none.'

'That's all right, sir. Constantine Dmitrich Levin.'

'Yes.'

'If you will be so good as to wait here, I'll see if the Countess is in.'

Feliks nodded, and the servant went away.

CHAPTER SIX

THE QUEEN ANNE bureau-bookcase was one of Lydia's favourite pieces of furniture in the London house. Two hundred years old, it was of black lacquer decorated in gold with vaguely Chinese scenes of pagodas, willow trees, islands and flowers. The flap front folded down to form a writing-table and to reveal red-velvet-lined pigeonholes for letters and tiny drawers for paper and pens. There were large drawers in the bombé base, and the top, above her eye-level as she sat at the table, was a bookcase with a mirrored door. The ancient mirror showed a cloudy, distorted reflection of the morning-room behind her.

On the writing-table was an unfinished letter to her sister, Aleks' mother, in St Petersburg. Lydia's handwriting was small and untidy. She had written, in Russian: *I don't know what to think about Charlotte* and then she had stopped. She sat, looking into the cloudy mirror, musing.

It was turning out to be a very eventful season in the worst possible way. After the suffragette protest at the court and the madman in the park she had thought there could be no more catastrophes. And for a few days life had been calm. Charlotte was successfully launched. Aleks was no longer around to disturb Lydia's equanimity, for he had fled to the Savoy Hotel and did not appear at society functions. Belinda's ball had been a huge success. That night Lydia had forgotten her troubles and had a wonderful time. She had danced the waltz, the polka, the two-step, the tango and even the Turkey Trot. She had partnered half the House of Lords, several dashing young men, and – most of all – her husband. It was not really chic to dance with one's own husband quite as much as she had. But Stephen looked so fine in his white tie and tails, and he danced so well, that she had given herself up to pleasure. Her marriage was definitely in one of its happier phases. Looking back over the years, she had the feeling that it was often like this in the season. And then Annie had turned up to spoil it all.

Lydia had only the vaguest recollection of Annie as a housemaid at Walden Hall. One could not possibly know all the servants at an establishment as large as that: there were some fifty indoor staff, and then the gardeners and grooms. Nor was one known to all the servants: on one famous occasion, Lydia had stopped a passing maid in the hall and asked her whether Lord Walden was in his room, and had received the reply: 'I'll go and see, madam – what name shall I say?'

However, Lydia remembered the day Mrs Braithwaite, the housekeeper at Walden Hall, had come to her with the news that Annie would have to go because she was pregnant. Mrs Braithwaite did not say 'pregnant', she said 'overtaken in moral transgression'. Both Lydia and Mrs Braithwaite were embarrassed, but neither was shocked: it had happened to housemaids before and it would happen again. They had to be let go – it was the only way to run a respectable house – and naturally they could not be given references in those circumstances. Without a 'character' a maid could not get another job in service, of course; but normally she did not need a job, for she either married the father of the child or went home to mother. Indeed, years later, when she had brought up her children, such a girl might even find her way back into the house, as a laundrymaid or kitchenmaid, or in some other capacity which would not bring her into contact with her employers.

Lydia had assumed that Annie's life would follow that course. She remembered that a young under-gardener had left without giving notice and run away to sea – that piece of news had come to her attention because of the difficulty of finding boys to work as gardeners for a sensible wage these days – but of course no one ever told her the connection between Annie and the boy.

We're not harsh, Lydia thought; as employers we're relatively generous. Yet Charlotte reacted as if Annie's plight were my fault. I don't know where she gets her ideas. What was it she said? 'I know what Annie did and I know who she did it with.' In Heaven's name, where did the child learn to speak like that? I dedicated my whole life to bringing her up to be pure and clean and decent, not like me *don't even think that*—

She dipped her pen in the inkwell. She would have liked to share her worries with her sister, but it was so hard in a letter. It was hard enough in person, she thought. Charlotte was the one with whom she really wanted to share her thoughts. Why is it that when I try I become shrill and tyrannical?

Pritchard came in. 'A Mr Constantine Dmitrich Levin to see you, my lady.'

Lydia frowned. 'I don't think I know him.'

'The gentleman said it was a matter of urgency, m'lady, and seemed to think you would remember him from St Petersburg.' Pritchard looked dubious.

Lydia hesitated. The name was distinctly familiar. From time to time Russians whom she hardly knew would call on her in London. They usually began by offering to take back messages, and ended by asking to borrow the passage money. Lydia did not mind helping them. 'All right,' she said. 'Show him in.'

Pritchard went out. Lydia inked her pen again, and wrote: *What can one do when the child is eighteen years old and has a will of her own? Stephen says I worry too much. I wish—*

I can't even talk to Stephen properly, she thought. He just makes soothing noises.

The door opened, and Pritchard said: 'Mr Constantine Dmitrich Levin.'

Lydia spoke over her shoulder in English. 'I'll be with you in a moment, Mr Levin.' She heard the butler close the door as she wrote: *– that I could believe him.* She put down her pen and turned around.

He spoke to her in Russian. 'How are you, Lydia?'

Lydia whispered: 'Oh, my *God*.'

It was as if something cold and heavy had descended

over her heart, and she could not breathe. Feliks stood in front of her: tall, and thin as ever, in a shabby coat with a scarf, holding a foolish English hat in his left hand. He was as familiar as if she had seen him yesterday. His hair was still long and black, without a hint of grey. There was that white skin, the nose like a curved blade, the wide, mobile mouth, and the sad soft eyes.

He said: 'I'm sorry to shock you.'

Lydia could not speak. She struggled with a storm of mixed emotions: shock, fear, delight, horror, affection and dread. She stared at him. He was *older*. His face was lined: there were two sharp creases in his cheeks, and downturning wrinkles at the corners of his lovely mouth. They seemed like lines of pain and hardship. In his expression there was a hint of something which had not been there before – perhaps ruthlessness, or cruelty, or just inflexibility. He looked tired.

He was studying her, too. 'You look like a girl,' he said wonderingly.

She tore her eyes away from him. Her heart pounded like a drum. Dread became her dominant feeling. If Stephen should come back early, she thought, and walk in here now, and give me that look that says Who is this man? and I were to blush, and mumble, and—

'I wish you'd say something,' Feliks said.

Her eyes returned to him. With an effort, she said: 'Go away.'

'No.'

Suddenly she knew she did not have the strength of will to make him leave. She looked over to the bell which would summon Pritchard. Feliks smiled as if he knew what was in her mind.

'It's been nineteen years,' he said.

'You've aged,' she said abruptly.

'You've changed.'

'What did you expect?'

'I expected this,' he said. 'That you would be afraid to admit to yourself that you are happy to see me.'

He had always been able to see into her soul with those soft eyes. What was the use of pretending? He knew all about pretending, she recalled. He had understood her from the moment he first set eyes on her.

'Well?' he said. 'Aren't you happy?'

'I'm frightened, too,' she said, and then she realized she had admitted to being happy. 'And you?' she added hastily. 'How do you feel?'

'I don't feel much at all, any more,' he said. His face twisted into an odd, pained smile. It was a look she had never seen on him in the old days. She felt intuitively that he was telling the truth at that moment.

He drew up a chair and sat close to her. She jerked back convulsively. He said: 'I won't hurt you—'

'Hurt me?' Lydia gave a laugh that sounded unexpectedly brittle. 'You'll ruin my life!'

'You ruined mine,' he replied; then he frowned as if he had surprised himself.

'Oh, Feliks, I didn't mean to.'

He was suddenly tense. There was a heavy silence. He gave that hurt smile again, and said: 'What happened?'

She hesitated. She realized that all these years she

177

had been longing to explain it to him. She began: 'That night you tore my gown . . .'

'What are you going to do about this tear in your gown?' Feliks asked.

'The maid will put a stitch in it before I arrive at the embassy,' Lydia replied.

'Your maid carries needles and thread around with her?'

'Why else would one take one's maid when one goes out to dinner?'

'Why indeed?' He was lying on the bed watching her dress. She knew that he loved to see her put her clothes on. He had once done an imitation of her pulling up her drawers which had made her laugh until it hurt.

She took the gown from him and put it on. 'Everybody takes an hour to dress for the evening,' she said. 'Until I met you I had no idea it could be done in five minutes. Button me up.'

She looked in the mirror and tidied her hair while he fastened the hooks at the back of her gown. When he had finished he kissed her shoulder. She arched her neck. 'Don't start again,' she said. She picked up the old brown cloak and handed it to him.

He helped her on with it. He said: 'The lights go out when you leave.'

She was touched. He was not often sentimental. She said: 'I know how you feel.'

'Will you come tomorrow?'

'Yes.'

At the door she kissed him and said: 'Thank you.'

'I love you dearly,' he said.

She left him. As she went down the stairs she heard a noise behind her and looked back. Feliks' neighbour was watching her from the door of the next apartment. He looked embarrassed when he caught her eye. She nodded politely to him, and he withdrew. It occurred to her that he could probably hear them making love through the wall. She did not care. She knew that what she was doing was wicked and shameful but she refused to think about it.

She went out into the street. Her maid was waiting on the corner. Together they walked to the park where the carriage was waiting. It was a cold evening, but Lydia felt as if she were glowing with her own warmth. She often wondered whether people could tell, just by looking at her, that she had been making love.

The coachman put down the step of the carriage for her and avoided her eyes. He knows, she thought with surprise; then she decided that that was fanciful.

In the coach the maid hastily repaired the back of Lydia's gown. Lydia changed the brown cloak for a fur wrap. The maid fussed with Lydia's hair. Lydia gave her ten roubles for her silence. Then they were at the British Embassy.

Lydia composed herself and went in.

It was not difficult, she found, to assume her other personality and become the modest, virginal Lydia whom polite society knew. As soon as she entered the real world she was terrified by the brute power of her passion for Feliks and she became quite genuinely a trembling lily. It was no act. Indeed, for most of the hours in the day she felt that this well-behaved maiden was her real self, and she thought she must be somehow possessed while she was with Feliks. But when he was there, and also when she was alone in bed in the middle of the night, she knew that it was her official persona that was evil, for it would have denied her the greatest joy she had ever known.

So she entered the hall, dressed in becoming white, looking young and a little nervous.

She met her cousin Kiril, who was nominally her escort. He was a widower of thirty-something years, an irritable man who worked for the Foreign Minister. He and Lydia did not much like each other, but because his wife was dead, and because Lydia's parents did not enjoy going out, Kiril and Lydia had let it be known that they should be invited together. Lydia always told him not to trouble to call for her. This was how she managed to meet Feliks clandestinely.

'You're late,' Kiril said.

'I'm sorry,' she replied insincerely.

Kiril took her into the salon. They were greeted by the Ambassador and his wife, and then introduced to Lord Highcombe, elder son of the Earl of Walden. He was a tall, handsome man of about thirty, in well-cut but rather sober clothes. He looked very English, with his short, light-brown hair and blue eyes. He had a smiling, open face which Lydia found mildly attractive. He spoke good French. They made polite conversation for a few moments, then he was introduced to someone else.

'He seems rather pleasant,' Lydia said to Kiril.

'Don't be fooled,' Kiril told her. 'Rumour has it that he's a tearaway.'

'You surprise me.'

'He plays cards with some officers I know, and they were telling me that he drinks them under the table some nights.'

'You know so much about people, and it's always bad.'

Kiril's thin lips twisted in a smile. 'Is that my fault or theirs?'

Lydia said: 'Why is he here?'

'In St Petersburg? Well, the story is that he has a very rich and domineering father, with whom he doesn't see eye to eye; so he's drinking and gambling his way around the world while he waits for the old man to die.'

Lydia did not expect to speak to Lord Highcombe again, but the Ambassador's wife, seeing them both as eligible, seated them side by side at dinner. During the second course he tried to make conversation. 'I wonder whether you know the Minister of Finance?' he said.

'I'm afraid not,' Lydia said coldly. She knew all about the man, of course, and he was a great favourite of the Czar; but he had married a woman who was not only divorced but also Jewish, which made it rather awkward for people to invite him. She suddenly thought how scathing Feliks would be about such prejudices; then the Englishman was speaking again.

'I should be most interested to meet him. I understand

he's terribly energetic and forward-looking. His Trans-Siberian Railway project is marvellous. But people say he's not very refined.'

'I'm sure Sergei Yulevitch Witte is a loyal servant of our adored sovereign,' Lydia said politely.

'No doubt,' Highcombe said, and turned back to the lady on his other side.

He thinks I'm boring, Lydia thought.

A little later she asked him: 'Do you travel a great deal?'

'Most of the time,' he replied. 'I go to Africa almost every year, for the big game.'

'How fascinating! What do you shoot?'

'Lion, elephant . . . a rhinoceros, once.'

'In the jungle?'

'The hunting is in the grasslands to the east, but I did once go as far south as the rain forest, just to see it.'

'And is it how it is pictured in books?'

'Yes, even to the naked black pygmies.'

Lydia felt herself flush, and she turned away. Now why did he have to say that? she thought. She did not speak to him again. They had conversed enough to satisfy the dictates of etiquette, and clearly neither of them was keen to go farther.

After dinner she played at the Ambassador's wonderful grand piano for a while, then Kiril took her home. She went straight to bed to dream of Feliks.

The next morning after breakfast a servant summoned her to her father's study.

The Count was a small, thin, exasperated man of

fifty-five. Lydia was the youngest of his four children – the others were a sister and two brothers, all married. Their mother was alive but in continual bad health. The Count saw little of his family. He seemed to spend most of his time reading. He had one old friend who came to play chess. Lydia had vague memories of a time when things were different, and they were a jolly family around a big dinner-table; but it was a long time ago. Nowadays a summons to the study meant only one thing: trouble.

When Lydia went in he was standing in front of the writing-table, his hands behind his back, his face twisted with fury. Lydia's maid stood near the door with tears on her cheeks. Lydia knew then what the trouble was, and she felt herself tremble.

There was no preamble. Her father began by shouting: 'You have been seeing a boy secretly!'

Lydia folded her arms to stop herself shaking. 'How did you find out?' she said with an accusing look at the maid.

Her father made a disgusted noise. 'Don't look at *her*,' he said. 'The coachman told me of your extraordinarily long walks in the park. Yesterday I had you followed.' His voice rose again. 'How could you act like that – like a peasant girl?'

How much did he know? Not everything, surely! 'I'm in love,' Lydia said.

'In love?' he roared. 'You mean you're in heat!'

Lydia thought he was about to strike her. She took several paces backward and prepared to run. He knew everything. It was total catastrophe. What would he do?

He said: 'The worst of it is, you can't possibly marry him.'

Lydia was aghast. She was prepared to be thrown out of the house, cut off without a penny, and humiliated; but he had in mind worse punishment than that. 'Why can't I marry him?' she cried.

'Because he's practically a serf and an anarchist to boot. Don't you understand – you're ruined!'

'Then let me marry him and live in ruin!'

'No!' he yelled.

There was a heavy silence. The maid, still in tears, sniffed monotonously. Lydia heard a ringing in her ears.

'This will kill your mother,' the Count said.

Lydia whispered: 'What are you going to do?'

'You'll be confined to your room for now. As soon as I can arrange it, you'll enter a convent.'

Lydia stared at him in horror. It was a sentence of death.

She ran from the room.

Never to see Feliks again – the thought was utterly unbearable. Tears rolled down her face. She ran to her bedroom. She could not possibly suffer this punishment. I shall die, she thought; I shall die.

Rather than leave Feliks for ever she would leave her family for ever. As soon as this idea occurred to her she knew it was the only thing to do – and the time to do it was now, before her father sent someone to lock her into the room.

She looked in her purse: she had only a few roubles.

She opened her jewellery case. She took out a diamond bracelet, a gold chain, and some rings, and stuffed them into her purse. She put on her coat and ran down the back stairs. She left the house by the servants' door.

She hurried through the streets. People stared at her, running in her fine clothes, with tears on her face. She did not care. She had left society for good. She was going to elope with Feliks.

She quickly became exhausted and slowed to a walk. Suddenly the whole affair did not seem so disastrous. She and Feliks could go to Moscow, or to a country town, or even abroad, perhaps Germany. Feliks would have to find work. He was educated, so he could at least be a clerk, possibly better. She might take in sewing. They would rent a small house and furnish it cheaply. They would have children, strong boys and pretty girls. The things she would lose seemed worthless: silk dresses, society gossip, ubiquitous servants, huge houses and delicate foods.

What would it be like, living with him? They would get into bed and actually go to sleep together – how romantic! They would take walks, holding hands, not caring who saw that they were in love. They would sit by the fireside in the evenings, playing cards or reading or just talking. Any time she wanted, she could touch him, or kiss him, or take off her clothes for him.

She reached his house and climbed the stairs. What would his reaction be? He would be shocked, then elated; then he would become practical. They would have to leave immediately, he would say, for her father could send people after them to bring her back. He would be decisive. 'We'll go to X,' he would say, and he would talk about tickets and a suitcase and disguises.

She took out her key, but the door to his apartment hung open and askew on its hinges. She went in, calling: 'Feliks, it's me – oh!'

She stopped in the doorway. The whole place was in a mess, as if it had been robbed, or there had been a fight. Feliks was not there.

Suddenly she was terribly afraid.

She walked around the small apartment, feeling dazed, stupidly looking behind the curtains and under the bed. All his books were gone. The mattress had been slashed. The mirror was broken, the one in which they watched themselves making love one afternoon when it had been snowing outside.

Lydia wandered aimlessly into the hallway. The occupant of the next apartment stood in his doorway. Lydia looked at him. 'What happened?' she said.

'He was arrested last night,' the man replied.

And the sky fell in.

She felt faint. She leaned against the wall for support. Arrested! Why? Where was he? Who had arrested him? How could she elope with him if he was in jail?

'It seems he was an anarchist.' The neighbour grinned suggestively and added: 'Whatever else he might have been.'

It was too much to bear, that this should have happened on the very day that Father had—

'Father,' Lydia whispered. 'Father did this.'

'You look ill,' the neighbour said. 'Would you like to come in and sit down for a moment?'

Lydia did not like the look on his face. She could not cope with this leering man on top of everything else. She pulled herself together and, without answering him, made her way slowly down the stairs and went out into the street.

She walked slowly, going nowhere, wondering what to do. Somehow she had to get Feliks out of jail. She had no idea how to go about it. Should she appeal to the Minister of the Interior? To the Czar? She did not know how to reach them except by going to the right receptions. She could write – but she needed Feliks *today*. Could she visit him in jail? At least then she would know how he was, and he would know she was fighting for him. Maybe, if she arrived in a coach, dressed in fine clothes, she could overawe the jailer . . . But she did not know where the jail was – there might be more than one – and she did not have her carriage; and if she went home her father would lock her up and she would never see Feliks—

She fought back the tears. She was so ignorant of the world of police and jails and criminals. Whom could she ask? Feliks' anarchist friends would know all about that sort of thing, but she had never met them and did not know where to find them.

She thought of her brothers. Maks was managing the family estate in the country, and he would see Feliks from Father's point of view and would completely approve of what Father had done. Dmitri – empty-headed, effeminate Dmitri – would sympathize with Lydia but be helpless.

There was only one thing to do. She must go and plead with her father for Feliks' release.

Wearily, she turned around and headed for home.

Her anger toward her father grew with every step she took. He was supposed to love her, care for her, and ensure her happiness – and what did he do? Tried to ruin her life. She knew what she wanted, she knew what would make her happy. Whose life was it? Who had the right to decide?

She arrived home in a rage.

She went straight to the study and walked in without knocking. 'You've had him arrested,' she accused.

'Yes,' her father said. His mood had altered. His mask of fury had gone, to be replaced by a thoughtful, calculating look.

Lydia said: 'You must have him released immediately.'

'They are torturing him, at the moment.'

'No,' Lydia whispered. 'Oh, no.'

'They are flogging the soles of his feet – '

Lydia screamed.

Father raised his voice. ' – with thin, flexible, canes – '

There was a paper-knife on the writing-table.

' – which quickly cut the soft skin – '

I will kill him—

' – until there is so much blood—'

Lydia went berserk.

She picked up the paper-knife and rushed at her father. She lifted the knife high in the air and brought it down with all her might, aiming at his skinny neck, screaming all the while: 'I hate you, I hate you, I hate you—'

He moved aside, caught her wrist, forced her to drop the knife, and pushed her into a chair.

She burst into hysterical tears.

After a few minutes her father began to speak again, calmly, as if nothing had happened. 'I could have it stopped immediately,' he said. 'I can have the boy released whenever I choose.'

'Oh, please,' Lydia sobbed. 'I'll do anything you say.'

'Will you?' he said.

She looked up at him through her tears. An access of hope calmed her. Did he mean it? Would he release Feliks? 'Anything,' she said, 'anything.'

'I had a visitor while you were out,' he said conversationally. 'The Earl of Walden. He asked permission to call on you.'

'Who?'

'The Earl of Walden. He was Lord Highcombe when you met him last evening, but his father died in the night so now he's the Earl. "Earl" is the English for "Count".'

Lydia stared at her father uncomprehendingly. She remembered meeting the Englishman, but she could not understand why her father was suddenly rambling on about him. She said: 'Don't torture me. Tell me what I must do to make you release Feliks.'

'Marry the Earl of Walden,' her father said abruptly.

Lydia stopped crying. She stared at him, struck dumb. Was he really saying this? It sounded insane.

He continued: 'Walden will want to marry quickly. You would leave Russia and go to England with him. This appalling affair could be forgotten and nobody need know. It's the ideal solution.'

'And Feliks?' Lydia breathed.

'The torture would stop today. The boy would be released the moment you leave for England. You would never see him again as long as you live.'

'No,' Lydia whispered. 'In God's name, no.'

They were married eight weeks later.

'You really tried to stab your father?' Feliks said with a mixture of awe and amusement.

Lydia nodded. She thought: Thank God, he had not guessed the rest of it.

Feliks said: 'I'm proud of you.'

'It was a terrible thing to do.'

'He was a terrible man.'

'I don't think so any more.'

There was a pause. Feliks said softly: 'So, you never betrayed me, after all.'

The urge to take him into her arms was almost irresistible. She made herself sit frozen still. The moment passed.

'Your father kept his word,' he mused. 'The torture stopped that day. They let me out the day after you left for England.'

190

'How did you know where I had gone?'

'I got a message from the maid. She left it at the bookshop. Of course she didn't know of the bargain you had made.'

The things they had to say were so many and so weighty that they sat in silence. Lydia was still afraid to move. She noticed that he kept his right hand in his coat pocket all the time. She did not remember his having that habit before.

'Can you whistle yet?' he said suddenly.

She could not help laughing. 'I never got the knack.'

They lapsed into quiet again. Lydia wanted him to leave, and with equal desperation she wanted him to stay. Eventually she said: 'What have you been doing since then?'

Feliks shrugged. 'A good deal of travelling. You?'

'Bringing up my daughter.'

The years in between seemed to be an uncomfortable topic for both of them.

Lydia said: 'What made you come here?'

'Oh . . .' Feliks seemed momentarily confused by the question. 'I need to see Orlov.'

'Aleks? Why?'

'There's an anarchist sailor in jail – I have to persuade Orlov to release him . . . You know how things are in Russia, there's no justice, only influence.'

'Aleks isn't here any more. Someone tried to rob us in our carriage, and he got frightened.'

'Where can I find him?' Feliks said. He seemed suddenly tense.

'The Savoy Hotel – but I doubt if he'll see you.'

'I can try.'

'This is important to you, isn't it?'

'Yes.'

'You're still . . . political?'

'It's my life.'

'Most young men lose interest as they grow older.'

He smiled ruefully. 'Most young men get married and have a family.'

Lydia was full of pity. 'Feliks, I'm so sorry.'

He reached out and took her hand.

She snatched it back and stood up. 'Don't touch me,' she said.

He looked at her in surprise.

'I've learned my lesson, even if you haven't,' she said. 'I was brought up to believe that lust is evil, and destroys. For a while, when we were . . . together . . . I stopped believing that, or at least I pretended to stop. And look what happened – I ruined myself and I ruined you. My father was right – lust does destroy. I've never forgotten that, and I never will.'

He looked at her sadly. 'Is that what you tell yourself?'

'It's true.'

'The morality of Tolstoy. Doing good may not make you happy, but doing wrong will certainly make you unhappy.'

She took a deep breath. 'I want you to go away now, and never come back.'

He looked at her in silence for a long moment, then he stood up. 'Very well,' he said.

Lydia thought her heart would break.

He took a step toward her. She stood still, knowing she should move away from him, unable to do so. He put his hands on her shoulders and looked into her eyes, and then it was too late. She remembered how it used to be when they looked into each other's eyes, and she was lost. He drew her to him and kissed her, folding her into his arms. It was just as always, his restless mouth on her soft lips, busy, loving, gentle; she was melting. She pushed her body against his. There was a fire in her loins. She shuddered with pleasure. She searched for his hands and held them in her own, just to have something to hold, a part of his body to grip, to squeeze with all her might—

He gave a shout of pain.

They broke apart. She stared at him, nonplussed.

He held his right hand to his mouth. She saw that he had a nasty wound, and in squeezing his hand she had made it bleed. She moved to take his hand, to say sorry, but he stepped back. A change had come over him, the spell was broken. He turned and strode to the door. Horrified, she watched him go out. The door slammed. Lydia gave a cry of loss.

She stood for a moment gazing at the place where he had been. She felt as if she had been ravaged. She fell into a chair. She began to shake uncontrollably.

Her emotions whirled and boiled for minutes, and she could not think straight. Eventually they settled, leaving one predominant feeling: relief that she had not yielded to the temptation to tell him the last chapter of the story. That was a secret lodged deep within her, like a piece of shrapnel in a healed-over wound; and there it would stay until the day she died, when it would be buried with her.

Feliks stopped in the hall to put on his hat. He looked at himself in the mirror, and his face twisted into a grin of savage triumph. He composed his features and went out into the midday sunshine.

She was so gullible. She had believed his half-baked story about an anarchist sailor, and she had told him, without a second's hesitation, where to find Orlov. He was exultant that she was still so much in his power. *She married Walden for my sake*, he thought, *and now I have made her betray her husband.*

Nevertheless, the interview had had its dangerous moments for him. As she was telling her story he had watched her face, and a dreadful grief had welled up within him, a peculiar sadness that made him want to cry; but it had been so long since he shed tears that his body seemed to have forgotten how, and those dangerous moments had passed. *I'm not really vulnerable to sentiment*, he told himself: *I lied to her, betrayed her trust in me, kissed her and ran away; I used her.*

Fate is on my side today. It's a good day for a dangerous task.

He had dropped his gun in the park, so he needed a new weapon. For an assassination in an hotel room a bomb would be best. It did not have to be aimed accurately, for wherever it landed it would kill everyone in the room. If Walden should happen to be there with Orlov at the time, so much the better, Feliks thought.

It occurred to him that then Lydia would have helped him kill her husband.

So?

He put her out of his mind and began to think about chemistry.

He went to a chemist's shop in Camden Town and bought four pints of a common acid in concentrated form. The acid came in two two-pint bottles, and cost four shillings and fivepence including the price of the bottles, which was returnable.

He took the bottles home and put them on the floor of the basement room.

He went out again, and bought another four pints of the same acid in a different shop. The chemist asked him what he was going to use it for. 'Cleaning,' he said, and the man seemed satisfied.

In a third chemist's he bought four pints of a different acid. Finally he bought a pint of pure glycerine and a glass rod a foot long.

He had spent sixteen shillings and eightpence, but he would get four shillings and threepence back for the bottles when they were empty. That would leave him with just under three pounds.

Because he had bought the ingredients in different shops, none of the chemists had any reason to suspect that he was going to make explosives.

He went up to Bridget's kitchen and borrowed her largest mixing bowl.

'Would you be baking a cake?' she asked him.

He said: 'Yes.'

'Don't blow us all up, then.'

'I won't.'

Nevertheless, she took the precaution of spending the afternoon with a neighbour.

Feliks went back downstairs, took off his jacket, rolled up his sleeves, and washed his hands.

He put the mixing bowl in the washbasin.

He looked at the thirteen large brown bottles, with their ground-glass stoppers, lined up on the floor.

The first part of the job was not very dangerous.

He mixed the two kinds of acid together in Bridget's kitchen bowl, waited for the bowl to cool, then re-bottled the two-to-one mixture.

He washed the bowl, dried it, put it back into the sink, and poured the glycerine into it.

The sink was fitted with a rubber plug on a chain. He wedged the plug into the drain-hole sideways, so that it was partly blocked. He turned on the tap. When the water level reached almost to the rim of the kitchen bowl he turned the tap partly but not completely off, so that the water was flowing out as fast as it was flowing in and the level in the sink stayed constant without overflowing into the kitchen bowl.

The next part had killed more anarchists than the Ochrana.

Gingerly, he began to add the mixed acids to the glycerine, stirring gently but constantly with the glass rod.

The basement room was very warm.

Occasionally a wisp of reddish-brown smoke came off the bowl, a sign that the chemical reaction was beginning to get out of control; then Feliks would stop adding acid, but carry on stirring, until the flow of water through the washbasin cooled the bowl and moderated the reaction. When the fumes were gone he waited a minute or two then carried on mixing.

This is how Ilya died, he recalled; standing over a sink in a basement room, mixing acids and glycerine: perhaps he was impatient. When they finally cleared the rubble, there was nothing left of Ilya to bury.

Afternoon turned into evening. The air became cooler but Feliks perspired all the same. His hand was as steady as a rock. He could hear children in the street outside, playing a game and chanting a rhyme: 'Salt, mustard, vinegar *pepper*, salt, mustard, vinegar *pepper*.' He wished he had ice. He wished he had electric light. The room filled with acid fumes. His throat was raw. The mixture in the bowl stayed clear.

He found himself daydreaming about Lydia. In the daydream she came into the basement room, stark naked, smiling, and he told her to go because he was busy.

'Salt, mustard, vinegar *pepper*.'

He poured the last bottle of acid as slowly and gently as the first.

Still stirring, he increased the stream of water from the tap so that it overflowed into the bowl, then he meticulously washed away the surplus acids.

When he had finished he had a bowl of nitroglycerine.

It was an explosive liquid twenty times as powerful as gunpowder. It could be detonated by a blasting cap, but such a detonator was not essential, for it could also be set off by a lighted match or even the warmth from a nearby fire. Feliks had known a foolish man who carried a bottle of nitroglycerine in the breast pocket of his coat until the heat of his body detonated it and killed him and three other people and a horse in a St Petersburg street. A bottle of nitroglycerine would explode if smashed, or just dropped on the floor, or shaken or even jerked hard.

With the utmost care, Feliks dipped a clean bottle into the bowl and let it fill slowly with the explosive. When it was full he closed the bottle, making sure that there was no nitroglycerine caught between the neck of the bottle and the ground-glass stopper.

There was some liquid left in the bowl. Of course it could not be poured down the sink.

Feliks went over to his bed and picked up the pillow. The stuffing seemed to be cotton waste. He tore a small hole in the pillow and pulled out some of the stuff. It was chopped rag mixed with a few feathers. He poured some of it into the nitroglycerine remaining in the bowl. The stuffing absorbed the liquid quite well. Feliks added more stuffing until all the liquid was soaked up then he rolled it into a ball and wrapped it in newspaper. It was now much more stable, like dynamite – in fact dynamite was what it was. It would detonate much less readily than the pure liquid. Lighting the newspaper might do it, and it might not: what was really required was a paper drinking-straw packed with gunpowder. But Feliks did not plan to use the dynamite, for he needed something reliable and immediate.

He washed and dried the mixing bowl again. He

plugged the sink, filled it with water, then gently placed the bottle of nitroglycerine in the water, to keep cool.

He went upstairs and returned Bridget's kitchen bowl.

He came back down and looked at the bomb in the sink. He thought: I wasn't afraid. All afternoon, I was never frightened of dying. I still have no fear.

That made him glad.

He went off to reconnoitre the Savoy Hotel.

CHAPTER SEVEN

WALDEN OBSERVED that both Lydia and Charlotte were subdued at tea. He, too, was thoughtful. The conversation was desultory.

After he had changed for dinner, Walden sat in the drawing-room sipping sherry, waiting for his wife and his daughter to come down. They were to dine out, at the Pontadarvies'. It was another warm evening. So far it had been a fine summer for weather, if for nothing else.

Shutting Aleks up in the Savoy Hotel had not done anything to hasten the slow pace of negotiating with the Russians. Aleks inspired affection like a kitten, and had the kitten's surprisingly sharp teeth. Walden had put to him the counter-proposal, an international waterway from the Black Sea to the Mediterranean. Aleks had said flatly that this was not good enough, for in wartime – when the strait would become vital – neither Britain nor Russia, with the best will in the world, could prevent the Turks closing the channel. Russia wanted not only the right of passage but also the power to enforce that right.

While Walden and Aleks argued about how Russia might be given that power, the Germans had completed the widening of the Kiel Canal, a strategically crucial project which would enable their Dreadnoughts to pass from the North Sea battleground to the safety of the Baltic. In addition, Germany's gold reserves were at a record high, as a result of the financial manoeuvres which had prompted Churchill's visit to Walden Hall in May. Germany would never be better prepared for war: every day which passed made an Anglo-Russian alliance more indispensable. But Aleks had true nerve – he would make no concessions in haste.

And, as Walden learned more about Germany – its industry, its government, its army, its natural resources – he realized that it had every chance of replacing Britain as the most powerful nation in the world. Personally he did not much mind whether Britain was first, second or ninth, so long as she was free. He loved England. He was proud of his country. Her industry provided work for millions, and her democracy was a model for the rest of the world. Her population was becoming more educated, and following that process more of her people had the vote. Even the women would get it sooner or later, especially if they stopped breaking windows. He loved the fields and the hills, the opera and the music-hall, the frenetic glitter of the metropolis and the slow, reassuring rhythms of country life. He was proud of her inventors, her playwrights, her businessmen and her craftsmen. England was a damn good place, and it was not going to be spoiled by squareheaded Prussian invaders, not if Walden could help it.

He was worried because he was not sure he *could*

help it. He wondered just how far he really understood modern England, with its anarchists and suffragettes, ruled by young firebrands like Churchill and Lloyd George, swayed by even more disruptive forces such as the burgeoning Labour Party and the ever-more-powerful trade unions. Walden's kind of people still ruled – the wives were Good Society and the husbands were the Establishment – but the country was not as governable as it had used to be. Sometimes he had a terribly depressing feeling that it was all slipping out of control.

Charlotte came in, reminding him that politics was not the only area of life in which he seemed to be losing his grip. She was still wearing her tea-gown. Walden said: 'We must go soon.'

'I'll stay at home, if I may,' she said. 'I've a slight headache.'

'There'll be no hot dinner, unless you warn Cook quickly.'

'I shan't want it. I'll have a tray in my room.'

'You look a little pale. Have a small glass of sherry, it'll give you an appetite.'

'All right.'

She sat down and he poured the drink for her. As he gave it to her he said: 'Annie has a job and a home, now.'

'I'm glad,' she replied coldly.

He took a deep breath. 'It must be said that I was at fault in that affair.'

'Oh!' Charlotte said, astonished.

Is it so rare for me to admit that I'm in the wrong?

he wondered. He went on: 'Of course, I didn't know that her ... young man ... had run off and she was ashamed to go to her mother. But I should have inquired. As you quite rightly said, the girl was my responsibility.'

Charlotte said nothing, but sat beside him on the sofa and took his hand. He was touched.

He said: 'You have a kind heart, and I hope you'll always stay that way. Might I also be permitted to hope that you will learn to express your generous feelings with a little more ... equanimity?'

She looked up at him. 'I'll do my best, Papa.'

'I often wonder whether we've protected you too much. Of course, it was your Mama who decided how you should be brought up, but I must say I agreed with her nearly all the time. There are people who say that children ought not to be protected from, well, what might be called the facts of life; but those people are very few, and they tend to be an awfully coarse type.'

They were quiet for a while. As usual, Lydia was taking for ever to dress for dinner. There was more that Walden wanted to say to Charlotte, but he was not sure he had the courage. In his mind he rehearsed various openings, none of which was less than acutely embarrassing. She sat with him in contented silence, and he wondered whether she had some idea of what was going on in his mind.

Lydia would be ready in a moment. It was now or never. He cleared his throat. 'You'll marry a good man, and together with him you'll learn about all sorts of things that are mysterious and perhaps a little worrying to you now.' That might be enough, he thought; this was the moment to back down, to duck the issue. Courage! 'But there is one thing you need to know in advance. Your mother should tell you, really, but somehow I think she may not, so I shall.'

He lit a cigar, just to have something to do with his hands. He was past the point of no return. He rather hoped Lydia would come in now to put a stop to the conversation; but she did not.

'You said you know what Annie and the gardener did. Well, they aren't married, so it was wrong. But when you are married, it's a very fine thing to do indeed.' He felt his face redden and hoped she would not look up just now. 'It's very good just physically, you know,' he plunged on. 'Impossible to describe, perhaps a bit like feeling the heat from a coal fire . . . However, the main thing is, the thing I'm sure you don't realize, is how wonderful the whole thing is spiritually. Somehow it seems to express all the affection and tenderness and respect and . . . well, just the love there is between a man and his wife. You don't necessarily understand that when you're young. Girls especially tend to see only the, well, coarse aspect; and some unfortunate people never discover the good side of it at all. But if you're expecting it, and you choose a good, kind, sensible man for your husband, it's sure to happen. So that's why I've told you. Have I embarrassed you terribly?'

To his surprise she turned her head and kissed his cheek. 'Yes, but not as much as you've embarrassed yourself,' she said.

That made him laugh.

Pritchard came in. 'The carriage is ready, my lord, and her ladyship is waiting in the hall.'

Walden stood up. 'Not a word to Mama, now,' he murmured to Charlotte.

'I'm beginning to see why everybody says you're such a good man,' Charlotte said. 'Enjoy your evening.'

'Goodbye,' he said. As he went out to join his wife he thought: Sometimes I get it right, anyway.

After that, Charlotte almost changed her mind about going to the suffragette meeting.

She had been in a rebellious mood, following the Annie incident, when she saw the poster stuck to the window of a jeweller's shop in Bond Street. The headline VOTES FOR WOMEN had caught her eye, then she had noticed that the hall in which the meeting was to be held was not far from her house. The notice did not name the speakers, but Charlotte had read in the newspapers that the notorious Mrs Pankhurst often appeared at such meetings without prior warning. Charlotte had stopped to read the poster, pretending (for the benefit of Marya, who was chaperoning her) to be looking at a tray of bracelets. As she was reading a boy came out of the shop and began to scrape the poster off the window. There and then Charlotte decided to go to the meeting.

Now Papa had shaken her resolution. It was a shock to see that he could be fallible, vulnerable, even humble; and even more of a revelation to hear him talk of sexual intercourse as if it were something beautiful.

She realized that she was no longer raging inwardly at him for allowing her to grow up in ignorance. Suddenly she saw his point of view.

But none of that altered the fact that she was still horribly ignorant, and she could not trust Mama and Papa to tell her the whole truth about things, especially about things like suffragism. I *will* go, she decided.

She rang the bell for Pritchard, and asked for a salad to be brought up to her room, then she went upstairs. One of the advantages of being a woman was that no one ever cross-questioned you if you said you had a headache: women were *supposed* to have headaches every now and then.

When the tray came she picked at the food for a while, until the time came when the servants would be having their supper, then she put on a hat and coat and went out.

It was a warm evening. She walked quickly toward Knightsbridge. She felt a peculiar sense of freedom, and realized that she had never before walked the streets of a city unaccompanied. I could do anything, she thought. I have no appointments and no chaperone. Nobody knows where I am. I could have dinner in a restaurant. I could catch a train to Scotland. I could take a room in an hotel. I could ride on an omnibus. I could eat an apple in the street, and drop the core in the gutter.

She felt conspicuous but nobody looked at her. She had always had the vague impression that if she went out alone strange men would embarrass her in unspecified ways. In reality they did not seem to see her.

The men were not lurking, they were all going somewhere, wearing their evening clothes or their worsted suits or their frock coats. How could there be any danger? she thought. Then she remembered the madman in the park, and she began to hurry.

As she approached the hall she noticed more and more women heading the same way. Some were in pairs or in groups, but many were alone like Charlotte. She felt safer.

Outside the hall was a crowd of hundreds of women. Many wore the suffragette colours of purple, green and white. Some were handing out leaflets or selling a newspaper called *Votes For Women*. There were several policemen about, wearing rather strained expressions of amused contempt. Charlotte joined the queue to get in.

When she reached the door a woman wearing a steward's armband asked her for sixpence. Charlotte turned, automatically, then realized she did not have Marya, or a footman, or a maid, to pay for things. She was alone, and she had no money. She had not anticipated that she would have to pay to get into the hall. She was not quite sure where she would have got sixpence even if she had foreseen the need.

'I'm sorry,' she said. 'I haven't any money . . . I didn't know . . .' She turned to leave.

The steward reached out to stop her. 'It's all right,' the woman said. 'If you've no money you get in free.' She had a middle-class accent, and although she spoke kindly Charlotte imagined that she was thinking: Such fine clothes, and no money!

Charlotte said: 'Thank you ... I'll send you a cheque ...' Then she went in, blushing furiously. Thank Heaven I didn't try to have dinner in a restaurant or catch a train, she thought. She had never needed to worry about carrying money around with her. Her chaperone always had petty cash, Papa kept accounts with all the shops in Bond Street, and if she wanted to have lunch at Claridge's or morning coffee in the Café Royal she would simply leave her card on the table and the bill would be sent to Papa. But this was one bill he would not pay.

She took her seat in the hall quite close to the front: she did not want to miss anything, after all this trouble. If I'm going to do this kind of thing often, she thought, I'll have to think of a way to get my hands on proper money, grubby pennies and gold sovereigns and crumpled banknotes.

She looked around her. The place was almost full of women, with just a scattering of men. The women were mostly middle-class, wearing serge and cotton rather than cashmere and silk. There were a few who looked distinctly more well-bred than the average – they talked more quietly and wore less jewellery – and those women seemed – like Charlotte – to be wearing last year's coats and rather undistinguished hats, as if to disguise themselves. As far as Charlotte could see there were no working-class women in the audience.

Up on the platform was a table draped with a purple, green and white 'Votes for Women' banner. A small lectern stood on the table. Behind it was a row of six chairs.

Charlotte thought: All these women – rebelling against men! She did not know whether to be thrilled or ashamed.

The audience applauded as five women walked on to the stage. They were all impeccably dressed in rather less-than-fashionable clothes – not a hobble skirt or a cloche hat among them. Were these really the people who broke windows, slashed paintings and threw bombs? They looked too respectable.

The speeches began. They meant little to Charlotte. They were about organization, finance, petitions, amendments, divisions and by-elections. She was disappointed: she was learning nothing. Ought she to read books about this before going to a meeting, in order to understand the proceedings? After almost an hour she was ready to leave. Then the current speaker was interrupted.

Two women appeared at the side of the stage. One was an athletic-looking girl in a motoring coat. Walking with her, and leaning on her for support, was a small, slight woman in a pale green spring coat and a large hat. The audience began to applaud. The women on the platform stood up. The applause grew louder, with shouts and cheers. Someone near Charlotte stood up, and in seconds a thousand women were on their feet.

Mrs Pankhurst walked slowly to the lectern.

Charlotte could see her quite clearly. She was what people called a handsome woman. She had dark, deep-set eyes, a wide, straight mouth, and a strong chin. She would have been beautiful but for a rather fat, flat nose. The effects of her repeated imprisonments and hunger strikes showed in the fleshlessness of her face and hands and the yellow colour of her skin. She seemed weak, thin and feeble.

She raised her hands, and the cheering and applause died down almost instantly.

She began to speak. Her voice was strong and clear, although she did not seem to shout. Charlotte was surprised to notice that she had a Lancashire accent.

She said: 'In 1894 I was elected to the Manchester Board of Guardians, in charge of the workhouse. The first time I went into that place I was horrified to see little girls seven and eight years old on their knees scrubbing the cold stones of the long corridors. These little girls were clad, summer and winter, in thin cotton frocks, low in the neck and short-sleeved. At night they wore nothing at all, nightdresses being considered too good for paupers. The fact that bronchitis was epidemic among them most of the time had not suggested to the Guardians any change in the fashion of the clothes. I need hardly add that, until I arrived, all the Guardians were men.

'I found that there were pregnant women in that workhouse, scrubbing floors, doing the hardest kind of work, almost until their babies came into the world. Many of them were unmarried women; very, very young, mere girls. These poor mothers were allowed to stay in the hospital after confinement for a short two weeks. Then they had to make a choice of staying in the workhouse and earning their living by scrubbing and other work, in which case they were separated from their babies; or of taking their discharges. They could stay and be paupers, or they could leave – leave with a two-week-old baby in their arms, without hope, without home, without money, without anywhere to go. What became of those girls, and what became of their hapless infants?'

Charlotte was stunned by the public discussion of such delicate matters. Unmarried mothers ... mere girls ... without home, without money ... And why should they be separated from their babies in the workhouse? Could this be true?

There was worse to come.

Mrs Pankhurst's voice rose a fraction. 'Under the law, if a man who ruins a girl pays down a lump sum of twenty pounds, the boarding home is immune from inspection. As long as a baby-farmer takes only one child at a time, the twenty pounds being paid, the inspectors cannot inspect the house.'

Baby-farmers ... a man who ruins a girl ... the terms were unfamiliar to Charlotte, but they were dreadfully self-explanatory.

'Of course the babies die with hideous promptness, and then the baby-farmers are free to solicit another victim. For years women have tried to get the Poor Law changed, to protect all illegitimate children, and to make it impossible for any rich scoundrel to escape liability for his child. Over and over again it has been tried, but it has always failed – ' Here her voice became a passionate cry. ' – because the ones who really care about the thing are mere women!'

The audience burst into applause, and a woman next to Charlotte cried: 'Hear, hear!'

Charlotte turned to the woman and grabbed her arm. 'Is this true?' she said. 'Is this *true*?'

But Mrs Pankhurst was speaking again.

'I wish I had time, and strength, to tell you of all the tragedies I witnessed while I was on that board. In our out-relief department I was brought into contact with widows who were struggling desperately to keep their homes and families together. The law allowed these women relief of a certain very inadequate kind, but for herself and one child it offered no relief except the workhouse. Even if the woman had a baby at her breast she was regarded, under the law, as an able-bodied man. Women, we are told, should stay at home and take care of their children. I used to astound my men colleagues by saying to them: "When women have the vote they will see that mothers *can* stay at home and care for their children!"

'In 1899 I was appointed to the office of Registrar of Births and Deaths in Manchester. Even after my experience on the Board of Guardians I was shocked to be reminded over and over again of what little respect there was in the world for women and children. I have had little girls of thirteen come to my office to register the births of their babies, illegitimate, of course. There was nothing that could be done in most cases. The age of consent is sixteen years, but a man can usually claim that he thought the girl was over sixteen. During my term of office a very young mother of an illegitimate child exposed her baby, and it died. The girl was tried for murder and sentenced to death. The man who was, from the point of view of justice, the real murderer of the baby, received no punishment at all.

'Many times in those days I asked myself what was to be done. I had joined the Labour Party, thinking that through its councils something vital might come, some demand for the women's enfranchisement that the politicians could not possibly ignore. Nothing came.

'All these years my daughters had been growing up. One day Christabel startled me with the remark: "How long you women have been trying for the vote. For my part, I mean to get it." Since that day I have had two mottoes. One has been: "Votes for women." The other: "For my part, I mean to get it!"'

Someone shouted: 'So do I!' and there was another outburst of cheering and clapping. Charlotte was feeling dazed. It was as if she, like Alice in the story, had walked through the looking-glass and found herself in a world where nothing was what it seemed. When she had read in the newspapers about suffragettes, no mention had been made of the Poor Law, of thirteen-year-old mothers (was it *possible*?) or of little girls catching bronchitis in the workhouse. Charlotte would have believed none of it had she not seen with her own eyes Annie, a decent ordinary maid from Norfolk, sleeping on a London pavement after being 'ruined' by a man. What did a few broken windows matter while this sort of thing was going on?

'It was many years before we lighted the torch of militancy. We had tried every other measure, and our years of work and suffering and sacrifice had taught us that the Government would not yield to right and justice, but it would yield to expediency. We had to make England and every department of English life insecure and unsafe. We had to make English law a failure and the courts theatres of farce; we had to discredit the Government and Parliament in the eyes of the world; we had to spoil English sports, hurt business, destroy valuable property, demoralize the world of Society, shame the churches, upset the whole orderly conduct of life! We had to do as much of this guerrilla warfare as the people of England would tolerate. When they came to the point of saying to the Government: "Stop this, in the only way it can be stopped, by giving the women of England representation," then we should extinguish our torch.

'The great American statesman Patrick Henry summed up the causes that led to the American revolution like this: "We have petitioned, we have remonstrated, we have supplicated, we have prostrated ourselves at the foot of the throne, and it has all been in vain. We must fight – I repeat it, sir, we must fight." Patrick Henry was advocating killing people as the proper means of securing the political freedom of *men*. The suffragettes have not done that and never will. In fact, the moving spirit of militancy is a deep and abiding reverence for human life.

'It was in this spirit that our women went forth to war. On January 31st a number of putting greens were burned with acids. On February 7th and 8th telegraph and telephone wires were cut in several places and for some hours all communication between London and

Glasgow was suspended. A few days later windows in various of London's smartest clubs were broken, and the orchid houses at Kew were wrecked and many valuable blooms destroyed by cold. The jewel room at the Tower of London was invaded and a showcase broken. On February 18th a country house which was being built at Walton-on-the-Hill for Mr Lloyd George was partially destroyed, a bomb having been exploded in the early morning before the arrival of the workmen.

'Over one thousand women have gone to prison in the course of this agitation, have suffered their imprisonment, have come out of prison injured in health, weakened in body, but not in spirit. Not one of those women would, if women were free, be law-breakers. They are women who seriously believe that the welfare of humanity demands this sacrifice; they believe that the horrible evils which are ravaging our civilization will never be removed until women get the vote. There is only one way to put a stop to this agitation; there is only one way to break down this agitation. It is not by deporting us!'

'No!' someone shouted.

'It is not by locking us up in jail!'

The whole crowd shouted: 'No!'

'It is by doing us justice!'

'Yes!'

Charlotte found herself shouting with the rest. The little woman on the platform seemed to radiate righteous indignation. Her eyes blazed, she clenched her fists, she tilted up her chin, and her voice rose and fell with emotion.

'The fire of suffering whose flame is upon our sisters in prison is burning us also. For we suffer with them, we partake of their affliction, and we shall share their victory by-and-by. This fire will breathe into the ear of many a sleeper the one word "Awake", and she will arise to slumber no more. It will descend with the gift of tongues upon many who have hitherto been dumb, and they will go forth to preach the news of deliverance. Its light will be seen afar off by many who suffer and are sorrowful and oppressed, and will irradiate their lives with a new hope. For the spirit which is in women today cannot be quenched; it is stronger than all tyranny, cruelty and oppression; it is stronger – even – than – death – itself!'

During the day a dreadful suspicion had dawned on Lydia.

After lunch she had gone to her room to lie down. She had been unable to think about anything but Feliks. She was still vulnerable to his magnetism: it was foolish to pretend otherwise. But she was no longer a helpless girl. She had resources of her own. And she was determined that she would not lose control, would not let Feliks wreck the placid life she had so carefully made for herself.

She thought of all the questions she had not asked him. What was he doing in London? How did he earn his living? How had he known where to find her?

He had given Pritchard a false name. Clearly he had been afraid that she would not let him in. She realized why 'Constantine Dmitrich Levin' had seemed familiar: it was the name of a character in *Anna Karenina*, the book she had been buying when she first met Feliks. It was an alias with a double meaning, a sly mnemonic which lit up a host of dim memories, like a taste recalled from childhood. They had argued about the novel. It was brilliantly real, Lydia had said, for she knew what it was like when passion was released in the soul of a respectable woman; Anna *was* Lydia. But the book was not about Anna, said Feliks; it was about Levin and his search for the answer to the question: 'How should I live?' Tolstoy's answer was: 'In your heart you know what is right.' Feliks argued that it was this kind of empty-headed morality – deliberately ignorant of history, economics and psychology – which had led to the utter incompetence and degeneracy of the Russian ruling class. That was the night they ate pickled mushrooms and she tasted vodka for the first time. She had been wearing a turquoise dress which turned her grey eyes blue. Feliks had kissed her toes, and then—

Yes, he was sly, to remind her of all that.

Had been in London a long time, she wondered, or had he come just to see Aleks? There was presumably a reason for approaching an admiral in London about the release of a sailor imprisoned in Russia. For the first time it occurred to Lydia that Feliks might not have told her the truth about that. After all, he was still an anarchist. In 1895 he had been determinedly non-violent, but he might have changed.

If Stephen knew that I had told an anarchist where to find Aleks . . .

She had worried about it through tea. She had worried about it while the maid was putting up her hair, with the result that the job was not properly done and she looked a fright. She had worried about it through dinner, with the result that she had been less than vivacious with the Marchioness of Quort, Mr Chamberlain, and a young man called Freddie who kept hoping aloud that there was nothing seriously wrong with Charlotte.

She recalled Feliks' cut hand, which had caused him to give such a shout when she squeezed it. She had only glimpsed the wound but it looked as if it had been bad enough to need stitches.

Nevertheless, it was not until the end of the evening, when she sat in her bedroom at home brushing her hair, that it occurred to her to connect Feliks with the madman in the park.

The thought was so frightening that she dropped a gold-backed hair-brush on to the dressing-table and broke a glass vial of perfume.

What if Feliks had come to London to kill Aleks?

Suppose it were Feliks who had attacked the coach in the park, not to rob them but to get at Aleks? Had the man with the gun been Feliks' height and build? Yes, roughly. And Stephen had wounded him with his sword . . .

Then Aleks had left the house because he was frightened (or perhaps, she now realized, because he *knew* the 'robbery' had been an assassination attempt) and Feliks had not known where to find him, so he had asked Lydia . . .

She stared at herself in the mirror. The woman she saw there had grey eyes, fair eyebrows, blonde hair, a pretty face, and the brain of a sparrow.

Could it be true? Could Feliks have deceived her so? Yes – because he had spent nineteen years imagining that she had betrayed him.

She picked up the pieces of broken glass from the vial and put them in a handkerchief, then she mopped up the spilled perfume. She did not know what to do now. She had to warn Stephen, but how? 'By the way, an anarchist called this morning and asked me where Aleks had gone; and because he used to be my lover I told him . . .' She would have to make up a story. She thought for a while. Once upon a time she had been an expert barefaced liar, but she was out of practice. Eventually she decided she could get away with a combination of the lies Feliks had told to her and to Pritchard.

She put on a cashmere robe over the silk nightgown and went through to Stephen's bedroom.

He was sitting at the window, in pyjamas and a dressing-gown, with a small glass of brandy in one hand and a cigar in the other, looking out over the moonlit park. He was surprised to see her come in, for it was always he who went to her room in the night. He stood up with a welcoming smile and embraced her. She realized that he misunderstood her visit: he thought she had come to make love.

She said: 'I want to talk to you.'

He released her. He looked disappointed. 'At this time of night?'

'I think I may have done something awfully silly.'

'You'd better tell me about it.'

They sat down on opposite sides of the cold fire-place. Suddenly Lydia wished she *had* come to make love. She said: 'A man called this morning. He said he had known me in St Petersburg. Well, the name was familiar and I thought I vaguely recalled him ... You know how it is, sometimes—'

'What was his name?'

'Levin.'

'Go on.'

'He said he wanted to see Prince Orlov.'

Stephen was suddenly very attentive. 'Why?'

'Something to do with a sailor who had been unjustly imprisoned. This ... Levin ... wanted to make a personal plea for the man's release.'

'What did you say?'

'I told him the Savoy Hotel.'

'Damn,' Stephen cursed, then apologized: 'Forgive me.'

'Afterwards it occurred to me that Levin might have been up to no good. He had a cut hand – and I remembered that you had cut the madman in the park ... so, you see, it dawned on me gradually ... I've done something dreadful, haven't I?'

'It's not your fault. In fact it's mine. I should have told you the truth about the man in the park, but I thought it better not to frighten you. I was wrong.'

'Poor Aleks,' Lydia said. 'To think that someone would want to kill him. He's so sweet.'

'What was Levin like?'

The question unsettled Lydia. For a moment she had been thinking of 'Levin' as an unknown assassin; now she was forced to describe Feliks. 'Oh . . . tall, thin, with dark hair, about my age, obviously Russian; a nice face, rather lined . . .' She tailed off. *And I yearn for him.*

Stephen stood up. 'I'll go and rouse Pritchard. He can drive me to the hotel.'

Lydia wanted to say: No, don't, take me to bed instead, I need your warmth and tenderness. She said: 'I'm so sorry.'

'It may be for the best,' Stephen said.

She looked at him in surprise. 'Why?'

'Because, when he comes to the Savoy Hotel to assassinate Aleks, I shall catch him.'

And then Lydia knew that before this was over one of the two men she loved would surely kill the other.

Feliks gently lifted the bottle of nitroglycerine out of the sink. He crossed the room as if he were walking on eggshells. His pillow was on the mattress. He had enlarged the rip until it was about six inches long, and now he put the bottle through the hole and into the pillow. He arranged the stuffing all around the bottle so that the bomb lay cocooned in shock-absorbing material. He picked up the pillow and, cradling it like a baby, placed it in his open suitcase. He closed the case and breathed more easily.

He put on his coat, his scarf, and his respectable hat. Carefully, he turned the cardboard suitcase on to its edge, then picked it up.

He went out.

The journey into the West End was a nightmare.

Of course he could not use the bicycle, but even walking was nerve-racking. Every second he visualized that green glass bottle in its pillow; every time his foot hit the pavement he imagined the little shock wave which must travel up his body and down his arm to the case; in his mind he saw the molecules of nitroglycerine vibrating faster and faster under his hand.

He passed a woman washing the pavement in front of her house. He went by on the road, in case he should slip on the wet flagstones, and she jeered: 'A-scared of getting yer feet wet, toff?'

Outside a factory in Euston a crowd of apprentices poured through the gates chasing a football. Feliks stood stock still as they rushed all around him, jostling and fighting for the ball. Then someone kicked it clear and they were gone as quickly as they had arrived.

Crossing the Euston Road was a dance with death. He stood at the kerb for five minutes, waiting for a good-sized gap in the stream of traffic; and then he had to walk across so fast he was almost running.

In Tottenham Court Road he went into a high-class stationer's. It was calm and hushed in the shop. He set the suitcase down gently on the counter. An assistant in a morning-coat said: 'Can I help you, sir?'

'I need an envelope, please.'

The assistant raised his eyebrows. 'Just the one, sir?'

'Yes.'

'Any particular kind, sir?'

'Just plain, but good quality.'

'We have blue, ivory, eau-de-nil, cream, beige—'

'White.'

'Very good, sir.'

'And a sheet of paper.'

'One sheet of paper, sir.'

They charged him threepence. On principle he would have preferred to run off without paying, but he could not run with the bomb in his case.

Charing Cross Road teemed with people on their way to work in shops and offices. It was impossible to walk at all without getting buffeted. Feliks stood in a doorway for a while, wondering what to do. Finally he decided to carry the case in his arms to protect it from the scurrying hordes.

In Leicester Square he took refuge in a bank. He sat at one of the writing-tables where the customers made out their cheques. There were a tray of pens and an inkwell. He put the case on the floor between his feet. He relaxed for a moment. Frock-coated bank clerks padded softly by with papers in their hands. Feliks took a pen and wrote on the front of his envelope:

Prince A. A. Orlov
The Savoy Hotel
Strand, London W.

He folded the blank sheet of paper and slipped it inside the envelope, just for the sake of its weight: he did not want the envelope to seem empty. He licked the gummed flap and sealed it shut. Then he reluctantly picked up the suitcase and left the bank.

In Trafalgar Square he dipped his handkerchief in the fountain and cooled his face with it.

He passed Charing Cross Station and walked east along the embankment. Near Waterloo Bridge a small group of urchins lounged against the parapet, throwing stones at the seagulls on the river. Feliks spoke to the most intelligent-looking boy.

'Do you want a penny?'

'Yes, guv!'

'Are your hands clean?'

'Yes, guv!' The boy showed a pair of filthy hands.

They would have to do, Feliks thought. 'Do you know where the Savoy Hotel is?'

'Too right!'

Feliks assumed this meant the same as 'Yes, guv.' He handed the boy the envelope and a penny. 'Count to a hundred slowly, then take this letter to the hotel. Do you understand?'

'Yes, guv!'

Feliks mounted the steps to the bridge. It was thronged with men in bowler hats coming across the river from the Waterloo side. Feliks joined the procession.

He went into a newsagent's and bought *The Times*. As he was leaving a young man rushed in through the door. Feliks stuck out his arm and stopped the man, shouting: 'Look where you're going!'

The man stared at him in surprise. As Feliks went out he heard the man say to the shopkeeper: 'Nervous type, is he?'

'Foreigner,' said the shopkeeper, and then Feliks was outside.

He turned off the Strand and went into the hotel. In the lobby he sat down and placed the suitcase on the floor between his feet. Not much farther now, he thought.

From his seat he could see both doors and the hall porter's desk. He put his hand inside his coat and consulted an imaginary fob watch, then opened his newspaper and settled down to wait, as if he were early for an appointment.

He pulled the suitcase closer to his seat and stretched out his legs either side of it, to protect it against an accidental kick from a careless passer-by. The lobby was crowded: it was just before ten o'clock. This is when the ruling class has breakfast, Feliks thought. He had not eaten: he had no appetite today.

He examined the other people in the lobby over the top of *The Times*. There were two men who might be detectives. Feliks wondered whether they might impede his escape. But even if they hear the explosion, he thought, how will they know which of the dozens of people walking through this lobby was responsible for it? Nobody knows what I look like. Only if I were being chased would they know. I'll have to make sure I'm not chased.

He wondered whether the urchin would come. After all, the boy had his penny already. Perhaps by now he had thrown the envelope into the river and gone off to the sweet shop. If so, Feliks would simply have to go through the whole rigmarole again until he found an honest urchin.

Looking up every few seconds, he read an article in the newspaper. The Government wanted to make those who gave money to the Women's Social and Political Union liable to pay for damage done by suffragettes. They planned to bring in special legislation to make this possible. How foolish governments are when they become intransigent, Feliks thought; everyone will just give money anonymously.

Where was that urchin?

He wondered what Orlov was doing right now. In all probability he was in one of the rooms of the hotel, a matter of yards above Feliks' head, eating breakfast, or shaving, or writing a letter, or having a discussion with Walden. I'd like to kill Walden too, Feliks thought.

It was not impossible that the two of them should walk through the lobby at any minute. That was too much to hope for. What would I do if it happened? thought Feliks.

I would throw the bomb, and die happy.

Through the glass door he saw the urchin.

The boy came along the narrow road which led to the hotel entrance. Feliks could see the envelope in his hand: he held it by one corner, almost distastefully, as if it were dirty and he were clean instead of the reverse. He approached the door but was stopped by a commissionaire in a top hat. There was some discussion, inaudible from inside, then the boy went away. The commissionaire came into the lobby with the envelope in his hand.

Feliks tensed. Would it work?

The commissionaire handed in the envelope at the hall porter's desk.

The hall porter looked at it, picked up a pencil, scribbled something in the top right-hand corner – a room number? – and summoned a pageboy.

It was working!

Feliks stood up, gently lifted his case, and headed for the stairs.

The pageboy passed him on the first floor and went on up.

Feliks followed.

It was almost too easy.

He allowed the pageboy to get one flight of stairs ahead, then he quickened his step to keep him in view.

On the fifth floor the boy walked along the corridor.

Feliks stopped and watched.

The boy knocked on a door. It was opened. A hand came out and took the envelope.

Got you, Orlov.

The pageboy made a pantomime of going away and was called back. Feliks could not hear the words. The boy received a tip. He said: 'Thank you very much indeed, sir, very kind of you.' The door closed.

Feliks started to walk along the corridor.

The boy saw his case and reached for it, saying: 'Can I help you with that, sir?'

'No!' Feliks said sharply.

'Very good, sir,' said the boy, and he passed on.

Feliks walked to the door of Orlov's room. Were there no more security precautions? Walden might imagine that a killer could not get into a London hotel room, but Orlov would know better. For a moment Feliks was tempted to go away and do some more thinking, or perhaps more reconnaissance; but he was too close to Orlov now.

He put the suitcase down on the carpet outside the door.

He opened the case, reached inside the pillow, and carefully withdrew the green bottle.

He straightened up slowly.

He knocked on the door.

CHAPTER EIGHT

WALDEN LOOKED at the envelope. It was addressed in a neat, characterless hand. It had been written by a foreigner, for an Englishman would have put *Prince Orlov* or *Prince Aleksei* but not *Prince A. A. Orlov*. Walden would have liked to know what was inside, but Aleks had moved out of the hotel in the middle of the night, and Walden could not open it in his absence – it was, after all, another gentleman's mail.

He handed it back to Basil Thomson, who had no such scruples.

Thomson ripped it open and took out a single sheet of paper. 'Blank!' he said.

There was a knock at the door.

They all moved quickly. Walden went over to the windows, away from the door and out of the line of fire, and stood behind a sofa, ready to duck. The two detectives moved to either side of the room and drew their guns. Thomson stood in the middle of the room behind a large overstuffed easy chair.

The knock came again.

Thomson called: 'Come in – it's open.'

The door opened, and there he stood.

Walden clutched at the back of the sofa. He *looked* frightening.

He was a tall man in a bowler hat and a black coat buttoned to the neck. He had a long, gaunt, white face. In his left hand he held a large green bottle. His eyes swept the room, and he understood in a flash that this was a trap.

He lifted the bottle and said: 'Nitro!'

'Don't shoot!' Thomson barked at the detectives.

Walden was sick with fear. He knew what nitroglycerine was: if the bottle fell they would all die. He wanted to live; he did not want to die in an instant of burning agony.

There was a long moment of silence. Nobody moved. Walden stared at the face of the killer. It was a shrewd, hard, determined face. Every detail was imprinted on Walden's mind in that short, terrible pause: the curved nose, the wide mouth, the sad eyes, the thick black hair showing beneath the brim of the hat. Is he mad? Walden wondered. Bitter? Heartless? Sadistic? The face showed only that he was fearless.

Thomson broke the silence. 'Give yourself up,' he said. 'Put the bottle on the floor. Stop being a fool.'

Walden was thinking: If the detectives shoot, and the man falls, could I get to him in time to catch the bottle before it crashes on to the floor—

No.

The killer stood motionless, bottle raised high. He's looking at me, not Thomson, Walden realized; he's studying me, as if he finds me fascinating; taking in the details, wondering what makes me tick. It's a personal look. He's as interested in me as I am in him.

He has realized Aleks isn't here – what will he do now?

The killer spoke to Walden in Russian: 'You're not as stupid as you look.'

Walden thought: Is he suicidal? Will he kill us all and himself too? Better keep him talking—

Then the man was gone.

Walden heard his footsteps running down the corridor.

Walden made for the door. The other three were ahead of him.

Out in the corridor, the detectives knelt on the floor, aiming their guns. Walden saw the killer running away with a queer fluid step, his left arm hanging straight down by his side, holding the bottle as steady as possible while he ran.

If it goes off now, Walden thought, will it kill us at this distance? Probably not.

Thomson was thinking the same. He said: 'Shoot!'

Two guns crashed.

The killer stopped and turned.

Was he hit?

He swung back his arm and hurled the bottle at them.

Thomson and the two detectives threw themselves flat. Walden realized in a flash that if the nitroglycerine exploded anywhere near them it would be no use to be lying flat.

The bottle turned over and over in the air as it flew at them. It was going to hit the floor five feet away from Walden. If it landed it would surely explode.

Walden ran *toward* the flying bottle.

It descended in a flat arc. He reached for it with both hands. He caught it. His fingers seemed to slip on the glass. He fumbled it, panicking; he almost lost it; then he grasped it again –

Don't slip Christ Jesus don't slip—

– and like a goalkeeper catching a football he drew it to his body, cushioning it against his chest, and spun around in the direction the bottle was travelling; then he lost his balance, and fell to his knees, and steadied himself, still holding the bottle, and thinking: I'm going to die.

Nothing happened.

The others stared at him, on his knees, cradling the bottle in his arms like a new-born baby.

One of the detectives fainted.

Feliks stared in amazement at Walden for a split second longer, then he turned and raced down the stairs.

Walden was amazing. What a nerve, to catch that bottle!

He heard a distant shout: 'Go after him!'

It's happening again, he thought; I'm running away again. What is the matter with me?

The stairs were endless. He heard running footsteps behind him. A shot rang out.

On the next landing he crashed into a waiter with a tray. The waiter fell, and crockery and food flew everywhere.

The pursuer was one or two flights behind him. He reached the foot of the staircase. He composed himself and walked into the lobby.

It was still crowded.

He felt as if he were walking a tightrope.

Out of the corner of his eye he spotted the two men he had identified as possibly detectives. They were deep in conversation, looking worried: they must have heard distant gunfire.

He walked slowly across the lobby, fiercely resisting the urge to break into a run. He had the illusion that everyone was staring at him. He looked ahead fixedly.

He reached the door and went out.

'Cab, sir?' said the doorman.

Feliks jumped into a waiting cab and it pulled away.

As it turned into the Strand he looked back at the hotel. One of the detectives from upstairs burst out of the door, followed by the two from the lobby. They spoke to the doorman. He pointed at Feliks' cab. The detectives drew their guns and ran after the cab.

The traffic was heavy. The cab stopped in the Strand.

Feliks jumped out.

The cabbie shouted: 'Oi! What's on, John?'

Feliks dodged through the traffic to the far side of the road and ran north.

He looked back over his shoulder. They were still after him.

He had to stay ahead until he could lose himself somewhere, in a maze of back alleys, or a railway station.

A uniformed policeman saw him running and watched suspiciously from the other side of the street. A minute later the detectives saw the policeman and yelled at him. He joined the chase.

Feliks ran faster. His heart pounded and his breath came in ragged gasps.

He turned a corner and found himself in the fruit and vegetable market of Covent Garden.

The cobbled streets were jammed with motor lorries and horsedrawn wagons. Everywhere there were market porters carrying wooden trays on their heads or pushing handcarts. Barrels of apples were being man-handled off wagons by heavily muscled men in undershirts. Boxes of lettuce and tomatoes and straw-berries were bought and sold by men in bowler hats, and fetched and carried by men in caps. The noise was terrific.

Feliks plunged into the heart of the market.

He hid behind a stack of empty crates and peered through the slats. After a moment he saw his pur-suers. They stood still, looking around. There was some conversation, then the four of them split up to search.

So Lydia betrayed me, Feliks thought as he caught his breath. Did she know in advance that I was after Orlov to kill him? No, she can't have. She wasn't acting a part that morning; she wasn't dissembling when she kissed me. But if she believed the story about getting a sailor out of jail, surely she would never have said anything to Walden. Well, perhaps later she realized that I had lied to her, so then she warned her husband, because she didn't want to have any part in the killing of Orlov. She didn't exactly betray me.

She won't kiss me next time.

There won't be a next time.

The uniformed policeman was coming his way.

He moved around the stack of crates and found himself alone in a little backwater, concealed by the boxes all around him.

Anyway, he thought, I escaped their trap. Thank God for nitroglycerine.

But *they* are supposed to be afraid of *me*.

I am the hunter; I am the one who sets traps.

It's Walden, he's the danger. Twice now he has got in the way. Who would have thought an aristocrat with grey hair would have had so much spunk?

He wondered where the policeman was. He peeped out.

He came face to face with the man.

The policeman's face was forming into an expression of astonishment when Feliks grabbed him by the coat and jerked him into the little enclosure.

The policeman stumbled.

Feliks tripped him. He fell on the floor. Feliks dropped on top of him and got him by the throat. He began to squeeze.

Feliks hated policemen.

He remembered Bialystock, when the strike-breakers – thugs with iron bars – had beaten up the workers outside the mill, while the police looked on unmoving. He remembered the pogrom, when the hooligans ran wild in the Jewish quarter, setting fire to houses and kicking old men and raping the young girls, while the police watched, laughing. He recalled Bloody Sunday, when the troops fired round after round into the peaceful crowd in front of the Winter Palace, and the police watched, cheering. He saw in his mind the police who had taken him to the Fortress of St Peter and St Paul to be tortured, and those who escorted him to Siberia and stole his coat, and those who had burst into the strike meeting in St Petersburg with their truncheons waving, hitting the women's heads, they always hit the women.

A policeman was a worker who had sold his soul.

Feliks tightened his grip.

The man's eyes closed, and he stopped struggling.

Feliks squeezed harder.

He heard a sound.

His head whipped around.

A small child of two or three years stood there, eating an apple, watching him strangle the policeman.

Feliks thought: What am I waiting for?

He let the policeman go.

The child walked over and looked down at the unconscious man.

Feliks looked out. He could not see any of the detectives.

The child said: 'Is he sleepy?'

Feliks walked away.

He got out of the market without seeing any of his pursuers.

He made his way to the Strand.

He began to feel safe.

In Trafalgar Square he caught an omnibus.

I almost died, Walden kept thinking; I almost died.

He sat in the hotel suite while Thomson gathered his team of detectives. Somebody gave him a glass of brandy-and-soda, and that was when he noticed that his hands were shaking. He could not put from his mind the image of that bottle of nitroglycerine in his hands.

He tried to concentrate on Thomson. The policeman changed visibly as he spoke to his men: he took his hands out of his pockets, he sat on the edge of his chair, and his voice altered from a drawl to a crisp snap.

Walden began to calm down as Thomson was talking. 'This man has slipped through our fingers,' Thomson said. 'It is not going to happen a second time. We know something about him now, and we're going to find out a great deal more. We know he was in St Petersburg during or before 1895, because Lady Walden remembers him. We know he's been to Switzerland, because the suitcase in which he carried the bomb was Swiss. And we know what he looks like.'

That face, Walden thought; and he clenched his fists.

Thomson went on: 'Watts, I want you and your lads

to spend a little money in the East End. The man is almost certainly Russian, so he's probably an anarchist and Jewish, but don't count on it. Let's see if we can put a name to him. If we can, cable Zurich and St Petersburg and ask for information.

'Richards, you start with the envelope. It was probably bought singly, so a shop assistant might remember the sale.

'Woods, you work on the bottle. It's a Winchester bottle with a ground-glass stopper. The name of the manufacturer is stamped on the bottom. Find out who in London they supply it to. Send your team around all the shops and see whether any chemists remember a customer answering to the description of our man. He will have bought the ingredients for nitroglycerine in several different shops, of course; and if we can find those shops we will know where in London to look for him.'

Walden was impressed. He had not realized that the killer had left behind so many clues. He began to feel better.

Thomson addressed a young man in a felt hat and a soft collar. 'Taylor, yours is the most important job. Lord Walden and I have seen the killer briefly, but Lady Walden has had a good long look at him. You'll come with us to see her ladyship, and with her help and ours you'll draw a picture of this fellow. I want the picture printed tonight and distributed to every police station in London by midday tomorrow.'

Surely, Walden thought, the man cannot escape us now. Then he remembered that he had thought the same when they set the trap here in the hotel room; and he began to tremble again.

Feliks looked in the mirror. He had had his hair cut very short, like a Prussian, and he had plucked his eyebrows until they were thin lines. He would stop shaving immediately, so that in a day he would look scruffy and in a week his beard and moustache would cover his distinctive mouth and chin. Unfortunately there was nothing he could do about his nose. He had bought a pair of second-hand spectacles with wire rims. The lenses were small so he could look over the top of them. He had changed his bowler hat and black coat for a blue sailor's pea-jacket and a tweed cap with a peak.

A close look would still reveal him as the same man, but to a casual glance he was completely different.

He knew he had to leave Bridget's house. He had bought all his chemicals within a mile or two of here, and when the police learned that they would begin a house-to-house search. Sooner or later they would end up in this street, and one of the neighbours would say: 'I know him, he stops in Bridget's basement.'

He was on the run. It was humiliating and depressing. He had been on the run at other times, but always after killing someone, never before.

He gathered up his razor, his spare underwear, his home-made dynamite, and his book of Pushkin stories, and tied them all up in his clean shirt. Then he went to Bridget's parlour.

'Jesus, Mary and Joseph, what have you done to your eyebrows?' she said. 'You used to be a handsome man.'

'I must leave,' he said.

She looked at his bundle. 'I can see your luggage.'

'If the police come, you don't have to lie to them.'

'I'll say I threw you out because I suspected you were an anarchist.'

'Goodbye, Bridget.'

'Take off those daft glasses and kiss me.'

Feliks kissed her cheek and went out.

'Good luck, boy,' she called after him.

He took the bicycle and, for the third time since he had arrived in London he went looking for lodgings.

He rode slowly. He was no longer weak from the sword wounds, but his spirit was sapped by his sense of failure. He went through North London and the City, then crossed the river at London Bridge. On the far side he headed south-east, passing a pub called The Elephant and Castle.

In the region of the Old Kent Road he found the kind of slum where he could get cheap accommodation and no questions asked. He took a room on the fourth floor of a tenement building owned, the caretaker told him lugubriously, by the Church of England. He would not be able to make nitroglycerine here: there was no water in the room, nor indeed in the building – just a stand-pipe and a privy in the courtyard.

The room was grim. There was a tell-tale mousetrap in the corner, and the one window was covered with a sheet of newspaper. The paint was peeling and the mattress stank. The caretaker, a stooped, fat man shuffling in carpet-slippers and coughing, said: 'If you want to mend the window, I can get glass cheap.'

Feliks said: 'Where can I keep my bicycle?'

'I should bring it up here if I were you, it'll get nicked anywhere else.'

With the bicycle in the room there would be just enough space to get from the door to the bed.

'I'll take the room,' Feliks said.

'That'll be twelve shillings, then.'

'You said three shillings a week.'

'Four weeks in advance.'

Feliks paid him. After buying the spectacles and trading in the clothes, he now had one pound and nineteen shillings.

The caretaker said: 'If you want to decorate, I can get you half-price paint.'

'I'll let you know,' said Feliks. The room was filthy but that was the least of his problems.

Tomorrow he had to start looking for Orlov again.

'Stephen! Thank Heaven you're all right!' said Lydia.

He put his arm around her.

'Of course I'm all right.'

'What happened?'

'I'm afraid we didn't catch our man.'

Lydia almost fainted with relief. Ever since Stephen had said, 'I shall catch the man,' she had been terrified twice over: terrified that Feliks would kill Stephen, and terrified that if not, she would be responsible for putting Feliks in jail for the second time in her life. She knew what he had gone through the first time, and the thought sickened her.

'You know Mr Basil Thomson, I think,' Stephen said, 'and this is Mr Taylor, the police artist. We're all going to help him draw the face of the killer.'

Lydia's heart sank. She would have to spend hours visualizing her lover in the presence of her husband. When will this end? she thought.

Stephen said: 'By the way, where is Charlotte?'

'Shopping,' Lydia told him.

'Good. I don't want her to know anything about this. In particular I don't want her to know where Aleks has gone.'

'Don't tell me, either,' Lydia said. 'I'd rather not know. That way I shan't be able to make the same mistake again.'

They sat down, and the artist got out his sketchbook.

Over and over again he drew that face. Lydia could have drawn it herself in five minutes. At first she tried to make the artist get it wrong, by saying 'Not quite' when something was exactly right and 'That's it' when something was crucially awry; but Stephen and Thomson had both seen Feliks clearly, if briefly, and they corrected her. In the end, fearful of being found out, she co-operated properly, knowing all the time that she might still be helping them to put Feliks in prison again. They ended up with a very good likeness of the face Lydia loved.

After that her nerves were so bad that she took a dose of laudanum and went to sleep. She dreamed that she was going to St Petersburg to meet Feliks. With the devastating logic of dreams, it seemed that she drove to catch the ship in a carriage with two duchesses who, in real life, would have expelled her from polite society had they known of her past. However, they made a mistake and went to Bournemouth instead of Southampton. There they stopped for a rest, although it was five o'clock and the ship sailed at seven. The duchesses told Lydia that they slept together at night and caressed each other in a perverted way. Somehow this came as no surprise at all, although they were both extremely old. Lydia kept saying, 'We must go, now,' but they took no notice. A man came with a message for Lydia. It was signed 'Your anarchist lover'. Lydia said to the messenger: 'Tell my anarchist lover that I'm *trying* to get the seven o'clock boat.' There: the cat was out of the bag. The duchesses exchanged knowing winks. At twenty minutes to seven, still in Bournemouth, Lydia realized that she had not yet packed her luggage. She raced around throwing things into cases but she could never find anything and the seconds ticked by and she was already too late and somehow her case *would not* fill up, and she panicked and went without her luggage and climbed on the carriage and drove herself, and lost her way on the sea front at Bournemouth and could not get out of town and woke up without getting anywhere near Southampton.

Then she lay in bed with her heart beating fast, her eyes wide open and staring at the ceiling, and she thought: It was only a dream. Thank God. Thank God!

*

Feliks went to bed miserable and woke up angry.

He was angry with himself. The killing of Orlov was not a superhuman task. The man might be guarded, but he could not be locked away in an underground vault like money in a bank; besides, even bank vaults could be robbed. Feliks was intelligent and determined. With patience and persistence he would find a way around all the obstacles they would put in his path.

He was being hunted. Well, he would not be caught. He would travel by the back streets, avoid his neighbours, and keep a constant look-out for blue police uniforms. Since he began his career of violence he had been hunted many times, but he had never been caught.

So he got up, washed at the stand-pipe in the courtyard, remembered not to shave, put on his tweed cap, his pea-jacket and his spectacles, had breakfast at a tea-stall, and cycled, avoiding the main roads, to St James's Park.

The first thing he saw was a uniformed policeman pacing up and down outside the Walden house.

That meant he could not take up his usual position for observing the house. He had to retreat much farther into the park and watch from a distance. He could not stay in the same place for too long, either, in case the policeman was alert and keen-eyed enough to notice.

At about midday a motor car emerged from the house. Feliks ran for his bicycle.

He had not seen the car go in, so presumably it was Walden's. Previously the family had always travelled in a coach, but there was no reason why they should not have both horse-drawn and motor vehicles. Feliks was too far away to be able to guess who was inside the car. He hoped it was Walden.

The car headed for Trafalgar Square. Feliks cut across the grass to intercept it.

The car was a few yards ahead of him when he reached the road. He kept up with it easily around Trafalgar Square, then it drew ahead of him as it headed north on Charing Cross Road.

He pedalled fast, but not desperately so. For one thing he did not want to draw attention to himself, and for another he wanted to conserve his strength. But he was too cautious, for when he reached Oxford Street the car was out of sight. He cursed himself for a fool. Which direction had it taken? There were four possibilities: left, straight on, right or sharp right.

He guessed, and went straight on.

In the traffic jam at the north end of Tottenham Court Road he saw the car again, and breathed a sigh of relief. He caught up with it as it turned east. He risked going close enough to see inside. In the front was a man in a chauffeur's cap. In the back was someone with grey hair and a beard: Walden!

I'll kill him too, Feliks thought; by Christ, I'll kill him.

In the traffic jam outside Euston Station he passed the car and got ahead, taking the chance that Walden might look at him when the car caught up again. He stayed ahead all down Euston Road, looking back over his shoulder continually to check that the car was still following him. He waited at the junction by King's

Cross, breathing hard, until the car passed him. It turned north. He averted his face as it went by, then followed.

The traffic was fairly heavy, and he was able to keep pace, although he was tiring. He began to hope that Walden was going to see Orlov. A house in North London, discreet and suburban, might be a good hiding-place. His excitement mounted. He might be able to kill them both.

After half a mile or so the traffic began to thin out. The car was large and powerful. Feliks had to pedal faster and faster. He was sweating heavily. He thought: How much farther?

Heavy traffic at Holloway Road gave him a brief rest, then the car picked up speed along Seven Sisters Road. He went as fast as he could. Any minute now the car might turn off the main road; it might be only minutes from its destination. All I want is some luck! he thought. He summoned up his last reserves of strength. His legs hurt now, and his breath came in ragged gasps. The car pulled remorselessly away from him. When it was a hundred yards ahead and still accelerating, he gave up.

He coasted to a halt and sat on the bicycle at the side of the road, bent over the handlebars, waiting to recover. He felt faint.

It was always the way, he thought bitterly: the ruling class fought in comfort. There was Walden, sitting comfortably in a big smooth car, smoking a cigar, not even having to drive.

Walden was plainly going out of town. Orlov could be anywhere north of London within half a day's journey by fast motor car. Feliks was utterly defeated – again.

For want of a better idea, he turned around and headed back toward St James's Park.

Charlotte was still tingling from Mrs Pankhurst's speech.

Of course there would be misery and suffering while all power was in the hands of one half of the world, and that half had no understanding of the problems of the other half. Men accepted a brutish and unjust world because it was brutish and unjust not to them but to women. If women had power, there would be nobody left to oppress.

The day after the suffragette meeting her mind teemed with speculations of this kind. She saw all the women around her – servants, shop assistants, nurses in the park, even Mama – in a new light. She felt she was beginning to understand how the world worked. She no longer resented Mama and Papa for lying to her. They had not really lied to her, except by omission; besides, insofar as deceit was involved, they deceived themselves almost as much as they had deceived her. And Papa had spoken frankly to her, against his evident inclinations. Still she wanted to find out things for herself, so that she could be sure of the truth.

In the morning she got hold of some money by the simple expedient of going shopping with a footman and saying to him: 'Give me a shilling.' Later, while he waited with the carriage at the main entrance to

Liberty's in Regent Street, she slipped out of a side entrance and walked to Oxford Street where she found a woman selling the suffragette newspaper *Votes For Women.* The paper cost a penny. Charlotte went back to Liberty's and, in the ladies' cloakroom, hid the newspaper under her dress. Then she returned to the carriage.

She read the paper in her room after lunch. She learned that the incident at the palace during her debut had not been the first time that the plight of women had been brought to the attention of the King and Queen. Last December three suffragettes in beautiful evening gowns had barricaded themselves inside a box at Covent Garden. The occasion was a gala performance of *Jeanne d'Arc* by Raymond Roze, attended by the King and Queen with a large entourage. At the end of the first act one of the suffragettes stood up and began to harangue the King through a megaphone. It took them half an hour to break down the door and get the women out of the box. Then forty more suffragettes in the front rows of the gallery stood up, threw showers of pamphlets down into the stalls, and walked out en masse.

Before and after this incident the King had refused to give an audience to Mrs Pankhurst. Arguing that all subjects had an ancient right to petition the King about their grievances, the suffragettes announced that a deputation would march to the palace, accompanied by thousands of women.

Charlotte realized that the march was to take place today – this afternoon – now.

She wanted to be there.

It was no good understanding what was wrong, she told herself, if one did nothing about it. And Mrs Pankhurst's speech was still ringing in her ears: 'The spirit which is in women today cannot be quenched . . .'

Papa had gone off with Pritchard in the motor car. Mama was lying down after lunch, as usual. There was nobody to stop her.

She put on a dowdy dress and her most unprepossessing hat and coat, then she went quietly down the stairs and out of the house.

Feliks walked about the park, keeping the house always in view, racking his brains.

Somehow he had to find out where Walden was going in the motor car. How might that be achieved? Could he try Lydia again? He might, at some risk, get past the policeman and into the house, but would he get out again? Would Lydia not raise the alarm? Even if she let him go, she would hardly tell him the secret of Orlov's hiding-place, now that she knew why he wanted to know. Perhaps he could seduce her – but where and when?

He could not follow Walden's car on a bicycle. Could he follow in another car? He could steal one, but he did not know how to drive them. Could he learn? Even then, would Walden's chauffeur not notice that he was being followed?

If he could hide in Walden's motor car . . . That meant getting inside the garage, opening the boot, spending several hours inside – all in the hope that nothing would be put inside the boot before the journey. The odds against success were too high for him to risk everything on that gamble.

The chauffeur must know, of course. Could he be bribed? Made drunk? Kidnapped? Feliks' mind was elaborating these possibilities when he saw the girl come out of the house.

He wondered who she was. She might be a servant, for the family always came and went in coaches; but she had left by the main entrance, and Feliks had never seen servants do that. She might be Lydia's daughter. She might know where Orlov was.

Feliks decided to follow her.

She walked toward Trafalgar Square. Leaving his bicycle in the bushes, Feliks went after her and got a closer look. Her clothes did not look like those of a servant. He recalled that there had been a girl in the coach on the night he had first tried to kill Orlov. He had not taken a good look at her, because all his attention had been – disastrously – riveted to Lydia. During his many days observing the house he had glimpsed a girl in the carriage from time to time. This was probably the girl, Feliks decided. She was sneaking out on a clandestine errand while her father was away and her mother was busy.

There was something vaguely familiar about her, he thought, as he tailed her across Trafalgar Square. He was quite sure he had never looked closely at her, yet he had a strong sense of *déjà vu* as he watched her trim figure walk, straight-backed and with a determined quick pace, through the streets. Occasionally he saw her face in profile when she turned to cross a road, and the tilt of her chin, or perhaps something about her eyes, seemed to strike a chord deep in his memory. Did she remind him of the young Lydia? Not at all, he realized: Lydia had always looked small and frail, and her features were all delicate. This girl had a strong-looking, angular face. It reminded Feliks of a painting by an Italian artist which he had seen in a gallery in Geneva. After a moment the name of the painter came back to him: Modigliani.

He got closer still to her, and a minute or two later he saw her full-face. His heart skipped a beat, and he thought: she's just beautiful.

Where was she going? To meet a boyfriend, perhaps? To buy something forbidden? To do something of which her parents would disapprove, such as go to a moving-picture show or a music-hall?

The boyfriend theory was the likeliest. It was also the most promising possibility from Feliks' point of view. He could find out who the boyfriend was, and threaten to give away the girl's secret unless she would tell him where Orlov was. She would not do it readily, of course, especially if she had been told that an assassin was after Orlov; but, given the choice between the love of a young man and the safety of a Russian cousin, Feliks reckoned that a young girl would choose romance.

He heard a distant noise. He followed the girl around a corner. Suddenly he was in a street full of marching women. Many of them wore the suffragette colours of green, white and purple. Many carried banners. There were *thousands* of them. Somewhere a band played marching tunes.

The girl joined the demonstration and began to march.

Feliks thought: Wonderful!

The route was lined with policemen, but they mostly faced inward, toward the women, so Feliks could dodge along the pavement behind their backs. He went with the march, keeping the girl in sight. He had been in need of a piece of luck, and he had been given one. She was a secret suffragette! She was vulnerable to blackmail, but there might be more subtle ways of manipulating her.

One way or another, Feliks thought, I'll get what I want from her.

Charlotte was thrilled. The march was orderly, with female stewards keeping the women in line. Most of the marchers were well-dressed, respectable-looking types. The band played a jaunty two-step. There were even a few men, carrying a banner which read: 'Fight the Government that Refuses to give Women the Parliamentary Vote'. Charlotte no longer felt like a misfit with heretical views. Why, she thought, all these thousands of women think and feel as I do! At times in the last twenty-four hours she had wondered whether men were right in saying that women were weak, stupid and ignorant, for she sometimes *felt* weak and stupid and she really was ignorant. Now she thought: If we educate ourselves we won't be ignorant; if we think for ourselves we won't be stupid; and if we struggle together we won't be weak.

The band began to play the hymn *Jerusalem*, and the women sang the words. Charlotte joined in lustily:

> *I will not cease from mental fight*
> *Nor shall my sword sleep in my hand*

I don't care if anybody sees me, she thought defiantly – not even the duchesses!

> *Till we have built Jerusalem*
> *In England's green and pleasant land.*

The march crossed Trafalgar Square and entered The Mall. Suddenly there were many more policemen, watching the women intently. There were also many spectators, mostly male, along either side of the road. They shouted and whistled derisively. Charlotte heard one of them say: 'All you need is a good swiving!' and she blushed crimson.

She noticed that many women carried a staff with a silver arrow fixed to its top. She asked the woman nearest her what that symbolized.

'The arrows on prison clothing,' the woman replied. 'All the women who carry that have been to jail.'

'To jail!' Charlotte was taken aback. She had known that a few suffragettes had been imprisoned, but as she looked around she saw hundreds of silver arrows. For the first time it occurred to her that she might end the day in prison. The thought made her feel weak. I won't go on, she thought. My house is just there, across the park; I can be there in five minutes. Prison! I would die! She looked back. Then she thought: I've done nothing wrong! Why am I afraid that I shall go to prison? Why should I not petition the King? Unless we do this women will always be weak, ignorant and stupid. Then the band began again, and she squared her shoulders and marched in time.

The facade of Buckingham Palace loomed up at the end of The Mall. A line of policemen, many on horseback, stretched across the front of the building. Charlotte was near the head of the procession: she wondered what the leaders intended to happen when they reached the gates.

She remembered once coming out of Derry & Toms and seeing an afternoon drunk lurching at her across the pavement. A gentleman in a top hat had pushed the drunk aside with his walking-cane, and the footman had quickly helped Charlotte up into the carriage which was waiting at the kerb.

Nobody would rush to protect her from a jostling today.

They were at the palace gates.

Last time I was here, Charlotte thought, I had an invitation.

The head of the procession came up against the line of policemen. For a moment there was deadlock. The people behind pressed forward. Suddenly Charlotte saw Mrs Pankhurst. She wore a jacket and skirt of purple velvet, a high-necked white blouse, and a green waistcoat. Her hat was purple with a huge white ostrich feather and a veil. She had detached herself from the body of the march and somehow had managed, unnoticed, to reach the far gate of the palace courtyard. She was such a brave little figure, marching with her head held high to the King's gate!

She was stopped by a police inspector in a flat hat. He was a huge, burly man, and looked at least a foot taller than she. There was a brief exchange of words. Mrs Pankhurst stepped forward. The inspector barred her way. She tried to push past him. Then, to Charlotte's horror, the policeman grabbed Mrs Pankhurst in a bear-hug, lifted her off her feet, and carried her away.

Charlotte was enraged – and so was every other woman in sight. The marchers pressed fiercely against the police line. Charlotte saw one or two break through and run toward the palace, chased by constables. The horses shifted, their iron hooves clattering threateningly on the pavement. The line began to break up. Several women struggled with policemen and were thrown to the ground. Charlotte was terrified of being manhandled. Some of the male bystanders rushed to the aid of the police, and then jostling turned into fighting. A middle-aged woman close to Charlotte was grabbed by the thighs. 'Unhand me, sir!' she said indignantly. The policeman said: 'My old dear, I can grip you where I like today!' A group of men in straw boaters waded into the crowd, pushing and punching the women, and Charlotte screamed. Suddenly a team of suffragettes wielding Indian clubs counter-attacked, and straw boaters flew everywhere. There were no longer any spectators: everyone was in the mêlée. Charlotte wanted to run away but every way she turned she saw violence. A fellow in a bowler picked up a young woman by getting one arm across her breasts and one hand in the fork of her thighs, and Charlotte heard him say: 'You've been wanting this for a long time, haven't you?' The bestiality of it all horrified Charlotte: it was like one of those medieval paintings of Purgatory in which everyone is suffering unspeakable tortures; but it was real and she was in the middle of it. She was pushed from behind and fell down, grazing her hands and bruising her knees. Someone trod on her hand. She tried to get up and was knocked down again. She realized she might be trampled by a horse and die. Desperately, she grabbed the skirts of a woman's coat and hauled herself to her feet.

Some of the women were throwing pepper into the eyes of the men, but it was impossible to throw accurately and they succeeded in incapacitating as many women as men. The fighting became vicious. Charlotte saw a woman lying on the ground with blood streaming from her nose. She wanted to help the woman but she could not move – it was as much as she could do to stay upright. She began to feel angry as well as scared. The men, police and civilians alike, punched and kicked women with relish. Charlotte thought hysterically: Why do they *grin* so? To her horror she felt a large hand grasp her breast. The hand squeezed and twisted. She turned, clumsily shoving the arm away from her. She was confronted by a man in his middle twenties, well-dressed in a tweed suit. He put out his hands and grabbed both her breasts, digging his fingers in hard. Nobody had *ever* touched her there. She struggled with the man, seeing on his face a wild look of mingled hatred and desire. He yelled: 'This is what you need, ain't it?' then he punched her in the stomach with his fist. The blow seemed to sink into her belly. The shock was bad and the pain was worse, but what made her panic was that she could not breathe. She stood, bending forward, with her mouth open. She wanted to gasp, she wanted to scream, but she could do neither. She felt sure she was going to die. She was vaguely aware of a very tall man pushing past her, dividing the crowd as if it were a field of corn. The tall man grabbed the lapel of the man in the tweed suit and hit him on the chin. The blow seemed to knock the young man off his feet and lift him into the air. The look of surprise on his face was almost comical. At last Charlotte was able to breathe, and she sucked in air with a great heave. The tall man put his arm firmly around her shoulders and said in her ear: 'This way.' She realized she was being rescued, and the sense of being in the hands of someone strong and protective was such a relief that she almost fainted.

The tall man propelled her toward the edge of the crowd. A police sergeant struck at her with a truncheon. Charlotte's protector raised his arm to ward off the blow, then gave a shout of pain as the wooden club landed on his forearm. He let go of Charlotte. There was a brief flurry of blows, then the sergeant was lying on the ground, bleeding, and the tall man was once again leading Charlotte through the crush.

Suddenly they were out of it. When Charlotte realized she was safe she began to cry, sobbing softly as tears ran down her cheeks. The man made her keep walking. 'Let's get right away,' he said. He spoke with a foreign accent. Charlotte had no will of her own: she went where he led her.

After a while she began to recover her composure. She realized they were in the Victoria area. The man stopped outside a Lyons Corner House and said: 'Would you like a cup of tea'

She nodded, and they went in.

He led her to a chair, then sat opposite her. She looked at him for the first time. For an instant she was frightened again. He had a long face with a curved nose. His hair was very short but his cheeks were unshaven. He looked somehow rapacious. But then she saw that there was nothing but compassion in his eyes.

She took a deep breath and said: 'How can I ever thank you?'

He ignored the question. 'Would you like something to eat?'

'Just tea.' She recognized his accent, and she began to speak Russian. 'Where are you from?'

He looked pleased that she could speak his language. 'I was born in Tambov province. You speak Russian very well.'

'My mother is Russian, and my governess.'

A waitress came, and he said: 'Two teas, please, love.'

Charlotte thought: He is learning English from Cockneys. She said in Russian: 'I don't even know your name. I'm Charlotte Walden.'

258

'Feliks Kschessinsky. You were brave, to join that march.'

She shook her head. 'Bravery had nothing to do with it. I simply didn't know it would be like that.' She was thinking: Who and what is this man? Where did he come from? He *looks* fascinating. But he's guarded. I'd like to know more about him.

He said: 'What did you expect?'

'On the march? I don't know . . . Why do those men *enjoy* attacking women?'

'This is an interesting question.' He was suddenly animated, and Charlotte saw that he had an attractive, expressive face. 'You see, we put women on a pedestal and pretend they are pure in mind and helpless in body. So, in polite society at least, men must tell themselves that they feel no hostility toward women, ever; nor do they feel lust for women's bodies. Now, here come some women – the suffragettes – who plainly are not helpless and need not be worshipped. What is more, they break the law. They deny the myths that men have made themselves believe, and they can be assaulted with impunity. The men feel cheated, and they give expression to all the lust and anger which they have been pretending not to feel. This is a great release to tension, and they enjoy it.'

Charlotte looked at him in amazement. It was fantastic – a complete explanation, just like that, off the top of his head! I like this man, she thought. She said: 'What do you do for a living?'

He became guarded again. 'Unemployed philosopher.'

The tea came. It was strong and very sweet, and it

259

restored Charlotte somewhat. She was intrigued by the weird Russian, and she wanted to draw him out. She said: 'You seem to think that all this – the position of women in society and so on – is just as bad for men as it is for women.'

'I'm sure of it.'

'Why?'

He hesitated. 'Men and women are happy when they love.' A shadow passed briefly across his face and was gone. 'The relation of love is not the same as the relation of worship. One worships a god. Only human beings can be loved. When we worship a woman we cannot love her. Then, when we discover she is not a god, we hate her. This is sad.'

'I never thought of that,' Charlotte said wonderingly.

'Also, every religion has good gods and bad gods. The Lord and the Devil. So, we have good women and bad women; and you can do anything you like to the bad women, for example suffragettes and prostitutes.'

'What are prostitutes?'

He looked surprised. 'Women who sell themselves for—' He used a Russian word that Charlotte did not know.

'Can you translate that?'

'Swiving,' he said in English.

Charlotte flushed and looked away.

He said: 'Is this an impolite word? I'm sorry, I know no other.'

Charlotte screwed up her courage and said in a low voice: 'Sexual intercourse.'

He reverted to Russian. 'I think *you* have been put on a pedestal.'

'You can't imagine how awful it is,' she said fiercely. 'To be so ignorant! Do women really sell themselves that way?'

'Oh, yes. Respectable married women must pretend not to like sexual intercourse. This sometimes spoils it for the men, so they go to the prostitutes. The prostitutes pretend to like it very much, although since they do it so often with so many different people they don't really enjoy it. Everyone ends up pretending.'

These things are *just* what I need to know! thought Charlotte. She wanted to take him home and chain him up in her room, so that he could explain things to her day and night. She said: 'How did we get like this – all this pretending?'

'The answer is a lifetime study. At least. However, I'm sure it has to do with power. Men have power over women, and rich men have power over poor men. A great many fantasies are required to legitimize this system – fantasies about monarchy, capitalism, breeding, and sex. These fantasies make us unhappy, but without them someone would lose his power. And men will not give up power, even if it makes them miserable.'

'But what is to be done?'

'A famous question. Men who will not give up power must have it taken from them. A transfer of power from one faction to another faction *within the same class* is called a coup and this changes nothing. A transfer of power from one *class* to another is called a revolution, and this does change things.' He hesitated. 'Although

the changes are not necessarily the ones the revolutionaries sought.' He went on: 'Revolutions occur only
when the people rise up en masse against their oppressors – as the suffragettes seem to be doing. Revolutions
are always violent, for people will always kill to retain
power. Nevertheless, they happen, for people will
always give their lives in the cause of freedom.'

'Are you a revolutionary?'

He said in English: 'I'll give you three guesses.'

Charlotte laughed.

It was the laugh that did it.

While he spoke, a part of Feliks' mind had been
watching her face, gauging her reactions. He warmed
to her, and the affection he felt was somehow familiar.
He thought: I am supposed to bewitch her, but she is
bewitching me.

And then she laughed.

She smiled widely; crinkles appeared in the corners
of her brown eyes; she tipped back her head so that
her chin pointed forward; she held up her hands, palms
forward, in a gesture that was almost defensive; and she
chuckled richly, deep in her throat.

Feliks was transported back in time twenty-five years.
He saw a three-roomed hut leaning against the side of
a wooden church. Inside the hut a boy and a girl sat
opposite one another at a crude table made of planks.
On the fire was a cast-iron pot containing a cabbage, a
small piece of bacon fat and a great deal of water. It
was almost dark outside and soon the father would be

home for his supper. Fifteen-year-old Feliks had just told his eighteen-year-old sister Natasha the joke about the traveller and the farmer's daughter. She threw back her head and laughed.

Feliks stared at Charlotte. She looked exactly like Natasha. He said: 'How old are you?'

'Eighteen.'

There occurred to Feliks a thought so astonishing, so incredible and so devastating that his heart stood still.

He swallowed, and said: 'When is your birthday?'

'The second of January.'

He gasped. She had been born exactly seven months after the wedding of Lydia and Walden; nine months after the last occasion on which Feliks had made love to Lydia.

And Charlotte looked exactly like Feliks' sister Natasha.

And now Feliks knew the truth.

Charlotte was his daughter.

CHAPTER NINE

'WHAT IS IT?' Charlotte said.

'What?'

'You look as if you'd seen a ghost.'

'You reminded me of someone. Tell me all about yourself.'

She frowned at him. He seemed to have a lump in his throat, she thought. She said: 'You've got a cold coming.'

'I never catch colds. What's your earliest memory?'

She thought for a moment. 'I was brought up in a country house called Walden Hall, in Norfolk. It's a beautiful grey stone building with a very lovely garden. In summer we had tea outdoors, under the chestnut tree. I must have been about four years old when I was first allowed to have tea with Mama and Papa. It was very dull. There was nothing to investigate on the lawn. I always wanted to go around to the back of the house, to the stables. One day they saddled a donkey and let me ride it. I had seen people ride, of course, and I thought I knew how to do it. They told me to sit still or I would fall off, but I didn't believe them. First somebody took the bridle and walked me up and down. Then I was allowed to take the reins myself. It all seemed so easy that I gave him a kick, as I had seen people do to horses, and made him trot. Next thing I knew, I was on the ground in tears. I just couldn't *believe* I had really fallen!' She laughed at the memory.

'It sounds like a happy childhood,' Feliks said.

'You wouldn't say that if you knew my governess. Her name is Marya and she's a Russian dragon. "Little ladies *always* have clean hands." She's still around – she's my chaperone now.'

'Still – you had good food, and clothes, and you were never cold, and there was a doctor when you were sick.'

'Is that supposed to make you happy?'

'I would have settled for it. What's your *best* memory?'

'When Papa gave me my own pony,' she said immediately. 'I had wanted one so badly, it was like a dream come true. I shall never forget that day.'

'What's he like?'

'Who?'

Feliks hesitated. 'Lord Walden.'

'Papa? Well . . .' It was a good question, Charlotte thought. For a complete stranger, Feliks was remarkably interested in her. But she was even more interested in him. There seemed to be some deep melancholy beneath his questions: it had not been there a few minutes ago. Perhaps that was because he had had an unhappy childhood and hers seemed so much better. 'I think Papa is probably a terribly *good* man . . .'

'But?'

'He will treat me as a child. I know I'm probably frightfully naive, but I'll never be anything else unless I learn. He won't explain things to me the way – well, the way you do. He gets very embarrassed if he talks about . . . men and women, you know . . . and when he speaks of politics his views seem a bit, I don't know, smug.'

'That's completely natural. All his life he's got everything he wanted, and got it easily. Of course he thinks the world is wonderful just as it is, except for a few small problems which will get ironed out in time. Do you love him?'

'Yes, except for the moments when I hate him.' The intensity of Feliks' gaze was beginning to make her uncomfortable. He seemed to be drinking in her words and memorizing her facial expressions. 'Papa is a very lovable man. Why are you so interested?'

He gave a peculiar, twisted smile. 'I've been fighting the ruling class all my life but I rarely get the chance to talk to one of them.'

Charlotte could tell that this was not the real reason, and she wondered vaguely why he should lie to her. Perhaps he was embarrassed about something – that was usually the reason why people were less than honest with her. She said: 'I'm not a member of the ruling class, any more than one of my father's dogs is.'

He smiled. 'Tell me about your mother.'

'She has bad nerves. Sometimes she has to take laudanum.'

'What's laudanum?'

'Medicine with opium in it.'

He raised his eyebrows. 'That sounds ominous.'

'Why?'

'I thought the taking of opium was considered degenerate.'

'Not if it's for medical reasons.'

'Ah.'

'You're sceptical.'

'Always.'

'Come, now, tell me what you mean.'

'If your mother needs opium, I suspect it is because she is unhappy, rather than because she is ill.'

'Why should she be unhappy?'

'You tell me, she's your mother.'

Charlotte considered. Was Mama unhappy? She certainly was not *content* in the way Papa seemed to be. She worried too much, and she would fly off the handle without much provocation. 'She's not relaxed,' she said. 'But I can't think of any reason why she should be unhappy. I wonder if it has to do with leaving your native country?'

'That's possible,' Feliks said, but he did not sound convinced. 'Have you any brothers and sisters?'

'No. My best friend is my cousin Belinda, she's the same age as me.'

'What other friends have you got?'

'No other friends, just acquaintances.'

'Other cousins?'

'Twin boys, six years old. Of course I've loads of cousins in Russia but I've never seen any of them, except Aleks, who's much older than me.'

'And what are you going to do with your life?'

'What a question!'

267

'Don't you know?'

'I haven't made up my mind.'

'What are the alternatives?'

'That's the big question, really. I mean, I'm expected to marry a young man of my own class and raise children. I suppose I shall have to marry.'

'Why?'

'Well, Walden Hall won't come to me when Papa dies, you know.'

'Why not?'

'It goes with the title – and I can't be the Earl of Walden. So the house will be left to Peter, the elder of the twins.'

'I see.'

'And I couldn't make my own living.'

'Of course you could.'

'I've been trained for nothing.'

'Train yourself.'

'What would I do?'

Feliks shrugged. 'Raise horses. Be a shopkeeper. Join the civil service. Become a professor of mathematics. Write a play.'

'You talk as if I might do anything I put my mind to.'

'I believe you could. But I have one quite serious idea. Your Russian is perfect – you could translate novels into English.'

'Do you really think I could?'

'I've no doubt whatsoever.'

Charlotte bit her lip. 'Why is it that you have such faith in me and my parents don't?'

He thought for a minute, then smiled. 'If I had

brought you up, you would complain that you were forced to do serious work all the time and never allowed to go dancing.'

'You've no children?'

He looked away. 'I never married.'

Charlotte was fascinated. 'Did you want to?'

'Yes.'

She knew she ought not to go on, but she could not resist it: she wanted to know what this strange man had been like when he was in love. 'What happened?'

'The girl married someone else.'

'What was her name?'

'Lydia.'

'That's my mother's name.'

'Is it?'

'Lydia Shatova, she was. You must have heard of Count Shatov, if you ever spent any time in St Petersburg.'

'Yes, I did. Do you carry a watch?'

'What? No.'

'Nor do I.' He looked around and saw a clock on the wall.

Charlotte followed his glance. 'Heavens, it's five o'clock! I intended to get home before Mother came down for tea.' She stood up.

'Will you be in trouble?' he said, getting up.

'I expect so.' She turned to leave the café.

He said: 'Oh, Charlotte . . .'

'What is it?'

'I don't suppose you could pay for the tea? I'm a very poor man.'

'Oh! I wonder whether I've any money. Yes! Look, elevenpence. Is that enough?'

'Of course.' He took sixpence from the palm of her hand and went to the counter to pay. It's funny, Charlotte thought, the things you have to remember when you're not in Society. What would Marya think of me, buying a cup of tea for a strange man? She would have apoplexy.

He gave her the change and held the door for her. 'I'll walk part of the way with you.'

'Thank you.'

Feliks took her arm as they walked along the street. The sun was still strong. A policeman came toward them, and Feliks made her stop and look in a shop window while he passed. She said: 'Why don't you want him to see us?'

'They may be looking for people who were seen on the march.'

Charlotte frowned. That seemed a bit unlikely, but he would know better than she.

They walked on. Charlotte said: 'I love June.'

'The weather in England is wonderful.'

'Do you think so? You've never been to the South of France, then.'

'You have, obviously.'

'We go every winter. We've a villa in Monte Carlo.' She was struck by a thought. 'I hope you don't think I'm boasting.'

'Certainly not.' He smiled. 'You must have realized by now that I think great wealth is something to be ashamed of, not proud of.'

'I suppose I should have realized, but I hadn't. Do you despise me, then?'

'No, but the wealth isn't yours.'

'You're the most interesting person I've ever met,' Charlotte said. 'May I see you again?'

'Yes,' he said. 'Have you got a handkerchief?'

She took one from her coat pocket and gave it to him. He blew his nose. 'You *are* catching a cold,' she said. 'Your eyes are streaming.'

'You must be right.' He wiped his eyes. 'Shall we meet at that café?'

'It's not a frightfully attractive place, is it?' she said. 'Let's think of somewhere else. I know! We'll go to the National Gallery. Then, if I see somebody I know, we can pretend we aren't together.'

'All right.'

'Do you like paintings?'

'I'd like you to educate me.'

'Then it's settled. How about the day after tomorrow, at three o'clock?'

'Fine.'

It occurred to her that she might not be able to get away. 'If something goes wrong, and I have to cancel, can I send you a note?'

'Well ... er ... I move about a lot ...' He was struck by a thought. 'But you can always leave a message with Mrs Bridget Callahan at number nineteen, Cork Street, in Camden Town.'

She repeated the address. 'I'll write that down as soon as I get home. My house is just a few hundred yards away.' She hesitated. 'You must leave me here. I hope you won't be offended, but it really would be best if no one saw me with you.'

'Offended?' he said with his funny, twisted smile. 'No, not at all.'

She held out her hand. 'Goodbye.'

'Goodbye.' He shook her hand firmly.

She turned around and walked away. There will be trouble when I get home, she thought. They will have found out that I'm not in my room, and there will be an inquisition. I'll say I went for a walk in the park. They won't like it.

Somehow she did not care what they thought. She had found a true friend. She was very happy.

When she reached the gate she turned and looked back. He stood where she had left him, watching her. She gave a discreet wave. He waved back. For some reason he looked vulnerable and sad, standing there alone. That was silly, she realized as she remembered how he had rescued her from the riot: he was very tough indeed.

She went into the courtyard and up the steps to the front door.

Walden arrived at Walden Hall suffering from nervous indigestion. He had rushed away from London before lunch, as soon as the police artist had finished drawing the face of the assassin, and he had eaten a picnic and drunk a bottle of Chablis on the way down, without stopping the car. As well as that he was nervous.

Today he was due for another session with Aleks. He guessed that Aleks had a counter-proposal and expected the Czar's approval of it by cable today. He hoped the Russian Embassy had had the sense to forward cables to Aleks at Walden Hall. He hoped the counter-proposal was something reasonable, something he could present to Churchill as a triumph.

He was fiercely impatient to get down to business with Aleks, but he knew that in reality a few minutes made no difference, and it was always a mistake to appear eager during a negotiation; so he paused in the hall and composed himself before walking into the Octagon.

Aleks sat at the window, brooding, with a great tray of tea and cakes untouched beside him. He looked up eagerly and said: 'What happened?'

'The man came, but I'm afraid we failed to catch him,' Walden said.

Aleks looked away. 'He came to kill me . . .'

Walden felt a surge of pity for him. He was young, he had a huge responsibility, he was in a foreign country and a killer was stalking him. But there was no point in letting him brood. Walden put on a breezy tone of voice. 'We have the man's description now – in fact the police artist has made a drawing of him. Thomson will catch him in a day or so. And you're safe here – he can't possibly find out where you are.'

'We thought I was safe at the hotel – but he found out I was there.'

'That can't happen again.' This was a bad start to a

negotiating session, Walden reflected. He had to find a way to turn Aleks' mind to more cheerful subjects. 'Have you had tea?'

'I'm not hungry.'

'Let's go for a walk – it will give you an appetite for dinner.'

'All right.' Aleks stood up.

Walden got a gun – for rabbits, he told Aleks – and they walked down to the Home Farm. One of the two bodyguards provided by Basil Thomson followed ten yards behind them.

Walden showed Aleks his champion sow, the Princess of Walden. 'She's won first prize in the East Anglian Agricultural Show for the last two years.' Aleks admired the sturdy brick cottages of the tenants, the tall white-painted barns, and the magnificent shire horses.

'I don't make any money out of it, of course,' Walden said. 'All the profit is spent on new stock, or drainage, or buildings, or fencing . . . but it sets a standard for the tenanted farms; and the Home Farm will be worth a lot more when I die than it was when I inherited it.'

'We can't farm like this in Russia,' Aleks said. Good, thought Walden; he's thinking of something else. Aleks went on: 'Our peasants won't use new methods, won't touch machinery, won't take care of new buildings or good tools. They are still serfs, psychologically if not legally. When there is a bad harvest and they are starving, do you know what they do? They burn the empty barns.'

The men were mowing hay in the South Acre.

Twelve labourers made a ragged line across the field, stooped over their scythes, and there was a steady swish, swish as the tall stalks fell like dominoes.

Samuel Jones, the oldest of the labourers, finished his row first. He came over, scythe in hand, and touched his cap to Walden. Walden shook his calloused hand. It was like grasping a rock.

'Did your lordship find time to go to that there exhibition in Lunnun?' Samuel said.

'Yes, I did,' Walden replied.

'Did you see that mowing machine you are talking about?'

Walden put on a dubious face. 'It's a beautiful piece of engineering, Sam – but I don't know . . .'

Sam nodded. 'Machinery never does the job as well as a labourer.'

'On the other hand, we could cut the hay in three days instead of a fortnight – and by getting it in that much faster we run less risk of rain. Then we could rent the machine to the tenanted farms.'

'You'd need fewer labourers, too,' Sam said.

Walden pretended to be disappointed. 'No,' he said, 'I couldn't let anyone go. It would just mean we need not take on gypsies to help around harvest-time.'

'It wouldn't make that much difference, then.'

'Not really. And I'm a bit concerned about how the men would take to it – you know young Peter Dawkins will find any excuse to make trouble.'

Sam made a non-committal sound.

'Anyway,' Walden continued, 'Mr Samson is going to take a look at the machine next week.' Samson was the bailiff. 'I say!' Walden said as if he had been struck by an idea. 'I don't suppose you'd want to go with him, Sam?'

Sam pretended not to care much for the idea. 'To Lunnun?' he said. 'I went there in 1888. Didn't like it.'

'You could go up on the train with Mr Samson – perhaps take young Dawkins with you – see the machine, have your dinner in London, and come back in the afternoon.'

'I dunno what my missus would say.'

'I'd be glad to have your opinion of the machine, though.'

'Well, I should be interested.'

'That's settled, then. I'll tell Samson to make the arrangements.' Walden smiled conspiratorially. 'You can give Mrs Jones to understand I practically forced you to go.'

Sam grinned. 'I'll do that, m'lord.'

The mowing was almost done. The men stopped work. Any rabbits would be hidden within the last few yards of hay. Walden called Dawkins over and gave him the gun. 'You're a good shot, Peter. See if you can get one for yourself and one for the Hall.'

They all stood on the edge of the field, out of the line of fire, then cut the last of the hay from the side, to drive the rabbits into the open field. Four came out, and Dawkins got two with his first round and one with his second. The gunfire made Aleks wince.

Walden took the gun and one of the rabbits, then he and Aleks walked back toward the Hall. Aleks shook his head in admiration. 'You have a wonderful way with the men,' he said. 'I never seem to be able to strike the right balance between discipline and generosity.'

'It takes practice,' Walden said. He held up the rabbit. 'We don't really need this at the Hall – but I took it to remind them that the rabbits are mine, and that any they have are a gift from me, not theirs by right.' If I had a son, Walden thought, this is how I would explain things to him.

'One proceeds by discussion and consent,' Aleks said.

'It's the best method – even if you have to give something away.'

Aleks smiled. 'Which brings us back to the Balkans.'

Thank Heaven – at last, Walden thought.

'Shall I sum up?' Aleks went on. 'We are willing to fight on your side against Germany, and you are willing to recognize our right to pass through the Bosphorus and the Dardanelles. However, we want not just the right but the power. Our suggestion, that you should recognize the whole of the Balkan Peninsula from Rumania to Crete as a Russian sphere of influence did not meet with your approval: no doubt you felt it was giving us too much. My task, then, was to formulate a lesser demand: one which would secure our sea passage without committing Britain to an unreservedly pro-Russian Balkan policy.'

'Yes.' Walden thought: He has a mind like a surgeon's knife. A few minutes ago I was giving him fatherly advice, and now, suddenly, he seems my equal – at the least. I suppose this is how it is when your son becomes a man.

'I'm sorry it has taken so long,' Aleks said. 'I have to send coded cables via the Russian Embassy to St Petersburg, and discussion at this distance just can't be as quick as I should like.'

'I understand,' said Walden, thinking: Come on – out with it!

'There is an area of about ten thousand square miles, from Constantinople to Adrianople – it amounts to half of Thrace – which is at present part of Turkey. Its coastline begins in the Black Sea, borders the Bosphorus, the Sea of Marmara, and the Dardanelles, and finishes in the Aegean Sea. In other words it guards the whole of the passage between the Black Sea and the Mediterranean.' He paused. 'Give us that, and we're on your side.'

Walden concealed his excitement. Here was a real basis for bargaining. He said: 'The problem remains, that it isn't ours to give away.'

'Consider the possibilities if war breaks out,' Aleks said. 'One: If Turkey is on our side we will have the right of passage anyway. However, this is unlikely. Two: If Turkey is neutral, we would expect Britain to insist on our right of passage as a sign that Turkey's neutrality was genuine; and, failing that, to support our invasion of Thrace. Three: If Turkey is on the German side – which is the likeliest of the three possibilities – then Britain would concede that Thrace is ours as soon as we can conquer it.'

Walden said dubiously: 'I wonder how the Thracians would feel about all this.'

'They would rather belong to Russia than to Turkey.'

'I expect they'd like to be independent.'

Aleks gave a boyish smile. 'Neither you nor I – nor, indeed, either of our governments – is in the least concerned about what the inhabitants of Thrace might prefer.'

'Quite,' Walden said. He was forced to agree. It was Aleks' combination of boyish charm and thoroughly grown-up brains which kept putting Walden off balance. He always thought he had the discussion firmly under control, until Aleks came out with a punch line which showed that *he* had been controlling it all along.

They walked up the hill that led to the back of Walden Hall. Walden noticed the bodyguard scanning the woods on either side. Dust puffed around his heavy brown brogues. The ground was dry: it had hardly rained for three months. Walden was excited about Aleks' counter-proposal. What would Churchill say? Surely the Russians could be given part of Thrace – who cared about Thrace?

They crossed the kitchen garden. An under-gardener was watering lettuces. He touched his cap to them. Walden searched for the man's name, but Aleks beat him to it. 'A fine evening, Stanley,' said Aleks.

'We could do with a shower, your highness.'

'But not too much, eh?'

'Quite so, your highness.'

Aleks is learning, Walden thought.

They went into the house. Walden rang for a footman. 'I'll send a telegram to Churchill making an appointment for tomorrow morning. I'll motor to London first thing.'

'Good,' Aleks said. 'Time is running short.'

Charlotte got a big reaction from the footman who opened the door to her.

'Oh! Thank goodness you're home, Lady Charlotte!' he said.

Charlotte gave him her coat. 'I don't know why you should thank goodness, William.'

'Lady Walden has been worried about you,' he said. 'She asked that you should be sent to her as soon as you arrived.'

'I'll just go and tidy myself up,' Charlotte said.

'Lady Walden did say "immediately"—'

'And I said I'll go and tidy myself.' Charlotte went up to her room.

She washed her face and unpinned her hair. There was a dull, muscular ache in her stomach, from the punch she had received, and her hands were grazed, but not badly. Her knees were sure to be bruised, but no one ever saw them. She went behind the screen and took off her dress. It seemed undamaged. I don't *look* as if I've been in a riot, she thought. She heard her bedroom door open.

'Charlotte!' It was Mama's voice.

Charlotte slipped into a robe, thinking: Oh, dear, she's going to be hysterical. She came from behind the screen.

'We've been frantic with worry!' Mama said.

Marya came into the room behind her, looking self-righteous and steely-eyed.

Charlotte said: 'Well, here I am, safe and sound, so you can stop worrying now.'

Mama reddened. 'You impudent child!' she shrilled. She stepped forward and slapped Charlotte's face.

Charlotte fell back and sat down heavily on the bed. She was stunned, not by the blow but by the idea of it. Mama had never struck her before. Somehow it seemed to hurt more than all the blows she had received during the riot. She caught Marya's eye and saw a peculiar look of satisfaction on her face.

Charlotte recovered her composure and said: 'I shall never forgive you for that.'

'That you should speak of forgiving me!' In her rage Mama was speaking Russian. 'And how soon should I forgive you for joining a mob outside Buckingham Palace?'

Charlotte gasped. 'How did you know?'

'Marya saw you marching along The Mall with those . . . those suffragettes. I feel so *ashamed*. God knows who else saw you. If the King ever finds out we shall be banished from the court.'

'I see.' Charlotte was still smarting from the slap. She said nastily: 'So you weren't worried about my safety, just the family reputation.'

Mama looked hurt. Marya butted in: 'We were worried about both.'

'Keep quiet, Marya,' said Charlotte. 'You've done enough damage with your tongue.'

'Marya did the right thing!' Mama said. 'How could she *not* tell me?'

Charlotte said: 'Don't you think women should have the vote?'

'Certainly not – and you shouldn't think so, either.'

'But I do,' Charlotte said. 'There it is.'

'You know nothing – you're still a child.'

'We always come back to that, don't we? I'm a child, and I know nothing. Who is responsible for my ignorance? Marya has been in charge of my education for fifteen years. As for being a child, you know perfectly well that I'm nothing of the kind. You would be quite happy to see me married by Christmas. And some girls are mothers by the age of thirteen, married or not.'

Mama was shocked. 'Who tells you such things?'

'Certainly not Marya. She never told me anything important. Nor did you.'

Mama's voice became almost pleading. 'You have no need of such knowledge – you're a lady.'

'You see what I mean? You want me to be ignorant. Well, I don't intend to be.'

Mama said plaintively: 'I only want you to be happy!'

'No, you don't,' Charlotte said stubbornly. 'You want me to be like you.'

'No, no, no!' Mama cried. 'I don't want you to be like me! I don't!' She burst into tears, and ran from the room.

Charlotte stared after her, mystified and ashamed.

Marya said: 'You see what you've done.'

Charlotte looked her up and down: grey dress, grey hair, ugly face, smug expression. 'Go away, Marya.'

'You've no conception of the trouble and heartache you've caused this afternoon.'

Charlotte was tempted to say: If you had kept your mouth shut there would have been no heartache. Instead she said: 'Get out.'

'You listen to me, little Charlotte—'

'I'm *Lady* Charlotte to you.'

'You're little Charlotte, and—'

Charlotte picked up a hand mirror and hurled it at Marya. Marya squealed. The missile was badly aimed, and smashed against the wall. Marya scuttled out of the room.

Now I know how to deal with *her*, Charlotte thought.

It occurred to her that she had won something of a victory. She had reduced Mama to tears and chased Marya out of her room. That's something, she thought; I may be stronger than they after all. They deserved rough treatment: Marya went to Mama behind my back, and Mama slapped me. But I didn't grovel and apologize and promise to be good in future. I gave as good as I got. I should be proud.

So why do I feel so ashamed?

I hate myself, Lydia thought.

I know how Charlotte feels, but I can't *tell* her that I understand. I always lose control. I never used to be like this. I was always calm and dignified. When she was a little girl I could laugh at her peccadilloes. Now she's a woman. Dear God, what have I done? She's tainted with the blood of her father, of Feliks, I'm sure of it.

What am I going to do? I thought if I pretended she were Stephen's daughter she might actually become like a daughter of Stephen – innocent, ladylike, English. It was no good. All those years the bad blood was in her, dormant, and now it's coming out; now the amoral Russian peasant in her ancestry is taking her over. When I see those signs I panic, I can't help it. I'm cursed, we're all cursed, the sins of the fathers are visited upon the children, even unto the third and fourth generation, when will I be forgiven? Feliks is an anarchist and Charlotte is a suffragette, Feliks is a fornicator and Charlotte talks about thirteen-year-old mothers; she has no idea how awful it is to be possessed by passion; my life was ruined, hers will be too, that's what I'm afraid of, that's what makes me shout and cry and get hysterical and smack her, but, sweet Jesus, don't let her ruin herself, she's all I've lived for. I shall lock her away. If only she would marry a nice boy, soon, before she has time to go right off the rails, before everybody realizes there is something wrong with her breeding. I wonder if Freddie will propose to her before the end of the season – that would be the answer – I must make sure he does, I *must* have her married, quickly! Then it will be too late for her to ruin herself; besides, with a baby or two she won't have time. I must make sure she meets Freddie more often. She's quite pretty, she'll be a good enough wife to a strong man who can keep her under control, a decent man who will love her without unleashing her dark desires, a man who will sleep in an adjoining room and share her bed once a week with the light out, Freddie is just right for her, then she'll never have to go through what I've been through, she'll never have to learn the hard way that lust is wicked and destroys, the sin won't be passed down yet another generation, she won't be wicked like me. She thinks I want her to be like me. If only she knew. If only she knew!

Feliks could not stop crying.

People stared at him as he walked through the park to retrieve his bicycle. He shook with uncontrollable sobs and the tears poured down his face. This had never happened to him before and he could not understand it. He was helpless with grief.

He found the bicycle where he had left it, beneath a bush, and the familiar sight calmed him a little. What is happening to me? he thought. Lots of people have children. Now I know that I have too. So what? And he burst into tears again.

He sat down on the dry grass beside the bicycle. She's so beautiful, he thought. But he was not weeping for what he had found, he was weeping for what he had lost. For eighteen years he had been a father without knowing it. While he was wandering from one grim village to another, while he was in jail, and in the gold mine, and walking across Siberia, and making bombs in Bialystock, she had been growing up. She had learned to walk, and to talk, and to feed herself and tie her bootlaces. She had played on a green lawn under a chestnut tree in summer, and had fallen off a donkey and cried. Her 'father' had given her a pony while

Feliks had been working on the chain gang. She had worn white frocks in summer and woollen stockings in winter. She had always been bilingual in Russian and English. Someone else had read story-books to her; someone else had said 'I'll catch you!' and chased her, screaming with delight, up the stairs; someone else had taught her to shake hands and say 'How do you do?'; someone else had bathed her and brushed her hair and made her finish up her cabbage. Many times Feliks had watched Russian peasants with their children and had wondered how, in their lives of misery and grinding poverty, they managed to summon up affection and tenderness for the infants who took the bread from their mouths. Now he knew: the love just came, whether you wanted it or not. From his recollections of other people's children he could visualize Charlotte at different stages of development: as a toddler with a protruding belly and no hips to hold up her skirt; as a boisterous seven-year-old, tearing her frock and grazing her knees; as a lanky, awkward girl of ten with ink on her fingers and clothes always a little too small; as a shy adolescent, giggling at boys, secretly trying her mother's perfume, passionate about horses, and then—

And then this beautiful, brave, alert, inquisitive, admirable young woman.

And I'm her father, he thought.

Her *father*.

What was it she had said? *You're the most interesting person I've ever met – may I see you again?* He had been preparing to say goodbye to her for ever. When he

286

knew that he would not have to, his self-control had begun to disintegrate. She thought he had a cold. Ah, she was young still, to make such bright, cheerful remarks to a man whose heart was breaking.

I'm becoming maudlin, he thought; I must pull myself together.

He stood up and picked up the bicycle. He mopped his face with the handkerchief she had given him. It had a bluebell embroidered in one corner, and he wondered whether she had done that herself. He mounted the bicycle and headed for the Old Kent Road.

It was supper time but he knew he would not be able to eat. That was just as well, for his money was running low and tonight he did not have the spirit to steal. He looked forward now to the darkness of his tenement room, where he could spend the night alone with his thoughts. He would go over every minute of this encounter, from the moment she emerged from the house to that last goodbye wave.

He would have liked a bottle of vodka for company, but he could not afford it.

He wondered whether anyone had ever given Charlotte a red ball.

The evening was mild but the city air was stale. The pubs of the Old Kent Road were already filling up with brightly dressed working-class women and their husbands, boyfriends or fathers. On impulse, Feliks stopped outside one. The sound of an elderly piano wafted through the open door. Feliks thought: I'd like someone to smile at me, even if it's only a barmaid. I could afford half a pint of ale. He tied his bicycle to a railing and went in.

The place was stifling, full of smoke and the unique beery smell of an English pub. It was early, but already there was a good deal of loud laughter and feminine squeals. Everyone seemed enormously cheerful. Feliks thought: Nobody knows how to spend money better than the poor. He joined the crush at the bar. The piano began a new tune, and everyone sang.

> *Once a young maiden climbed an old man's knee*
> *Begged for a story, 'Do, uncle, please,*
> *Why are you single, why live alone?*
> *Have you no babies, have you no home?'*
> *'I had a sweetheart, years, years ago;*
> *Where is she now, pet, you will soon know*
> *List to my story, I'll tell it all*
> *I believed her faithless, after the ball.'*

The stupid, sentimental, empty-headed damn song brought tears to Feliks' eyes and he left the pub without ordering his beer.

He cycled away, leaving the laughter and music behind. That kind of jollity was not for him, it never had been and never would be. He made his way back to the tenement and carried the bicycle up the stairs to his room on the top floor. He took off his hat and coat and lay on the bed. He would see her again in two days. They would look at paintings together. He would go to the municipal bath house before meeting her, he decided. He rubbed his chin: there was nothing he could do to make the beard grow decently in two days. He cast his mind back to the moment when she came out of the house. He had seen her from a distance, never dreaming . . .

What was I thinking of at that moment? he wondered.

And then he remembered.

I was asking myself whether she might know where Orlov is.

I haven't thought about Orlov all afternoon.

In all probability she *does* know where he is; if not she could find out.

I might use her to help me kill him.

Am I capable of that?

No, I am not. I will not do it. No, no, no!

What is happening to me?

Walden saw Churchill at the Admiralty at twelve noon. The First Lord was impressed. 'Thrace,' he said. 'Surely we can give them half of Thrace. Who the devil cares if they have the whole of it!'

'That's what I thought,' Walden said. He was pleased with Churchill's reaction. 'Now, will your colleagues agree?'

'I believe they will,' Churchill said thoughtfully. 'I'll see Grey after lunch and Asquith this evening.'

'And the Cabinet?' Walden did not want to do a deal with Aleks only to have it vetoed by the Cabinet.

'Tomorrow morning.'

Walden stood up. 'So I can plan to go back to Norfolk late tomorrow.'

'Splendid. Have they caught that damned anarchist yet?'

'I'm having lunch with Basil Thomson of the Special Branch – I'll find out then.'

'Keep me informed.'

'Naturally.'

'And thank you. For this proposal, I mean.' Churchill looked out of the window dreamily. 'Thrace!' he murmured to himself. 'Who has ever even heard of it?'

Walden left him to his reverie.

He was in a buoyant mood as he walked from the Admiralty to his club in Pall Mall. He usually ate lunch at home, but he did not want to trouble Lydia with policemen, especially as she was in a rather strange mood at the moment. No doubt she was worried about Aleks, as Walden was. The boy was the nearest thing to a son that they had: if anything should happen to him—

He went up the steps of his club and, just inside the door, handed his hat and gloves to a flunkey. 'What a lovely summer we're having, my lord,' the man said.

The weather had been remarkably fine for months, Walden reflected as he went up to the dining-room. When it broke there would probably be storms. We shall have thunder in August, he thought.

Thomson was waiting. He looked rather pleased with himself. What a relief it will be if he's caught the assassin, Walden thought. They shook hands, and Walden sat down. A waiter brought the menu.

'Well?' said Walden. 'Have you caught him?'

'All but,' Thomson said.

That meant No, Walden thought. His heart sank. 'Oh, *damn*,' he said.

The wine waiter came. Walden asked Thomson: 'Do you want a cocktail?'

'No, thank you.'

Walden approved. Cocktails were a nasty American habit. 'Perhaps a glass of sherry?'

'Yes, please.'

'Two,' Walden said to the waiter.

They ordered Brown Windsor soup and poached salmon, and Walden chose a bottle of hock to wash it down.

Walden said: 'I wonder if you realize quite how important this is? My negotiations with Prince Orlov are almost complete. If he were to be assassinated now the whole thing would fall through – with serious consequences for the security of this country.'

'I do realize, my lord,' Thomson said. 'Let me tell you what progress we've made. Our man is Feliks Kschessinsky. That's so hard to say that I propose we call him Feliks. He is forty, the son of a country priest, and he comes from Tambov province. My opposite number in St Petersburg has a very thick file on him. He has been arrested three times and is wanted in connection with half a dozen murders.'

'Dear God,' Walden muttered.

'My friend in St Petersburg adds that he is an expert bomb-maker and an extremely vicious fighter.' Thomson paused. 'You were terribly brave, to catch that bottle.'

291

Walden gave a thin smile: he preferred not to be reminded.

The soup came and the two men ate in silence for a while. Thomson sipped his hock frugally. Walden liked this club. The food was not as good as he got at home, but there was a relaxed atmosphere. The chairs in the smoking-room were old and comfortable, the waiters were old and slow, the wallpaper was faded and the paintwork was dull. They still had gas lighting. Men such as Walden came here because their homes were spick and span and feminine.

'I thought you said you had all but caught him,' Walden said as the poached salmon arrived.

'I haven't told you the half of it yet.'

'Ah.'

'At the end of May he arrived at the Jubilee Street anarchist club in Stepney. They didn't know who he was, and he told them lies. He's a cautious man – quite rightly so, from his point of view, for one or two of those anarchists are working for me. My spies reported his presence, but the information didn't come to my notice at that stage because he appeared to be harmless. Said he was writing a book. Then he stole a gun and moved on.'

'Without telling anyone where he was going, of course.'

'That's right.'

'Slippery fellow.'

A waiter collected their plates and said: 'Will you have a slice off the joint, gentlemen? It's mutton today.'

They both had mutton with redcurrant jelly, roast potatoes and asparagus.

Thomson said: 'He bought the ingredients for his nitroglycerine in four different shops in Camden Town. We made house-to-house inquiries there.' Thomson took a mouthful of mutton.

'And?' Walden asked impatiently.

'He's been living at nineteen Cork Street, Camden, in a house owned by a widow called Bridget Callahan.'

'But he's moved on.'

'Yes.'

'Damn it, Thomson, can't you see the fellow's cleverer than you?'

Thomson looked at him coolly and made no comment.

Walden said: 'I beg your pardon, that was discourteous of me, the fellow's got me rattled.'

Thomson went on: 'Mrs Callahan says she threw Feliks out because she thought he was a suspicious character.'

'Why didn't she report him to the police?'

Thomson finished his mutton and put down his knife and fork. 'She says she had no real reason to. I found that suspicious, so I checked up on her. Her husband was an Irish rebel. If she knew what our friend Feliks was up to, she might well have been sympathetic.'

Walden wished Thomson would not call Feliks 'our friend'. He said: 'Do you think she knows where the man went?'

'If she does, she won't say. But I can't think why he should tell her. The point is, he may come back.'

'Are you having the place watched?'

'Surreptitiously. One of my men has already moved into the basement room as a tenant. Incidentally, he found a glass rod of the kind used in chemistry laboratories. Evidently Feliks made up his nitroglycerine right there in the sink.'

It was chilling to Walden to think that in the heart of London anyone could buy a few chemicals, mix them together in a washhand-basin, and make a bottle of dreadfully explosive liquid – then walk with it into a suite in a West End hotel.

The mutton was followed by a savoury of foie gras. Walden said: 'What's your next move?'

'The picture of Feliks is hanging up in every police station in the County of London. Unless he locks himself indoors all day, he's bound to be spotted by an observant bobby sooner or later. But just in case that should be later rather than sooner, my men are visiting cheap hotels and lodging-houses, showing the picture.'

'Suppose he changes his appearance?'

'It's a bit difficult in his case.'

Thomson was interrupted by the waiter. Both men refused the Black Forest gateau and chose ices instead. Walden ordered half a bottle of champagne.

Thomson went on: 'He can't hide his height, nor his Russian accent. And he has distinctive features. He hasn't had time to grow a beard. He may wear different clothes, shave himself bald, or wear a wig. If I were he I should go about in a uniform of some kind – as a sailor, or a footman, or a priest. But policemen are alert to that sort of thing.'

After their ices they had Stilton cheese and sweet biscuits with some of the club's vintage port.

It was all too vague, Walden felt. Feliks was *loose*, and Walden would not feel safe until the fellow was locked up and chained to the wall.

Thomson said: 'Feliks is clearly one of the top killers of the international revolutionist conspiracy. He is very well informed: for example, he knew that Prince Orlov was going to be here in England. He is also clever, and formidably determined. However, we have hidden Orlov away.'

Walden wondered what Thomson was getting at.

'By contrast,' Thomson went on, 'you are still walking about the streets of London as large as life.'

'Why should I not?'

'If I were Feliks, I would now concentrate on you. I would follow you in the hope that you might lead me to Orlov; or I would kidnap you and torture you until you told me where he was.'

Walden lowered his eyes to hide his fear.

'How could he do that alone?'

'He may have help. I want you to have a bodyguard.'

Walden shook his head. 'I've got my man Pritchard. He would risk his life for me – he has done, in the past.'

'Is he armed?'

'No.'

'Can he shoot?'

'Very well. He used to come with me to Africa in my

295

big-game hunting days. That's when he risked his life for me.'

'Then let him carry a pistol.'

'All right,' Walden assented. 'I'll be going to the country tomorrow. I've got a revolver there which he can have.'

To finish the meal Walden had a peach and Thomson took a melba pear. Afterwards they went into the smoking-room for coffee and biscuits. Walden lit a cigar. 'I think I shall walk home, for my digestion's sake.' He tried to say it calmly, but his voice sounded oddly high-pitched.

'I'd rather you didn't,' Thomson said. 'Haven't you brought your carriage?'

'No—'

'I should be happier about your safety if you were to go everywhere in your own vehicles from now on.'

'Very well,' Walden sighed. 'I shall have to eat less.'

'For today, take a cab. Perhaps I'll accompany you.'

'Do you really think that's necessary?'

'He might be waiting for you outside this club.'

'How would he find out which club I belong to?'

'By looking you up in *Who's Who.*'

'Yes, of course.' Walden shook his head. 'One just doesn't think of these things.'

Thomson looked at his watch. 'I should get back to the Yard . . . if you're ready.'

'Certainly.'

They left the club. Feliks was not lying in wait outside. They took a cab to Walden's house, then Thomson took the cab on to Scotland Yard. Walden went into the house. It felt empty. He decided to go to his room. He sat at the window and finished his cigar.

He felt the need to talk to someone. He looked at his watch: Lydia would have had her siesta, and would now be putting on a gown ready to have tea and receive callers. He went through to her room.

She was sitting at her mirror in a robe. She looks strained, he thought; it's all this trouble. He put his hands on her shoulders, looking at her reflection in the mirror, then bent to kiss the top of her head. 'Feliks Kschessinsky.'

'*What?*' She seemed frightened.

'That's the name of our assassin. Does it mean something to you?'

'No.'

'I thought you seemed to recognize it.'

'It . . . it rings a bell.'

'Basil Thomson has found out all about the fellow. He's a killer, a thoroughly evil type. It's not impossible that you might have come across him in St Petersburg – that would explain why he seemed vaguely familiar when he called here, and why his name rings a bell.'

'Yes – that must be it.'

Walden went to the window and looked out over the park. It was the time of day when nannies took their charges for a walk. The paths were crowded with perambulators, and every bench was occupied by gossiping women in unfashionable clothes. It occurred to Walden that Lydia might have had some connection with Feliks, back in St Petersburg – some connection which she did not want to admit. The thought was

shaming, and he pushed it out of his mind. He said:
'Thomson believes that, when Feliks realizes Aleks is
hidden away, he will try to kidnap me.'

Lydia got up from her chair and came to him. She
put her arms around his waist and laid her head on his
chest. She did not speak.

Walden stroked her hair. 'I must go everywhere in
my own coach, and Pritchard must carry a pistol.'

She looked up at him, and to his surprise he saw that
her grey eyes were full of tears. She said: 'Why is this
happening to us? First Charlotte gets involved in a
riot, then you're threatened – it seems we're all in
jeopardy.'

'Nonsense. You're in no danger, and Charlotte is
only being a silly girl. And I'll be well protected.' He
stroked her sides. He could feel the warmth of her body
through the thin robe – she was not wearing her corset.
He wanted to make love to her, right now. They had
never done it in daylight.

He kissed her mouth. She pressed her body against
his, and he realized that she, too, wanted to make love.
He could not remember her being like this ever before.
He glanced toward the door, thinking to lock it. He
looked at her, and she gave a barely perceptible nod. A
tear rolled down her nose. Walden went to the door.

Someone knocked.

'Damn!' Walden said quietly.

Lydia turned her face away from the door and
dabbed at her eyes with a handkerchief.

Pritchard came in. 'Excuse me, my lord. An urgent
telephone communication from Mr Basil Thomson.

They have tracked the man Feliks to his lodging. If you want to be in at the kill, Mr Thomson will pick you up here in three minutes.'

'Get my hat and coat,' Walden told him.

CHAPTER TEN

WHEN FELIKS went out to get the morning
paper he seemed to see children every way
he turned. In the courtyard a group of girls played a
game involving dancing and chanting. The boys were
playing cricket with a wicket chalked on the wall and a
piece of rotten planking for a bat. In the street, older
boys were pushing handcarts. He bought his newspaper
from an adolescent girl. Coming back to his room, his
way was blocked by a naked baby crawling up the stairs.
As he looked at the child – it was a girl – she stood up
unsteadily and slowly toppled backwards. Feliks caught
her and put her down on the landing. Her mother
came out of an open door. She was a pale young
woman with greasy hair, already very pregnant with
another child. She scooped the baby girl up off the
floor and disappeared back into her room with a
suspicious look at Feliks.

Every time he considered exactly how he would
trick Charlotte into telling him the whereabouts of
Orlov, he seemed to run up against a brick wall in his
mind. He visualized getting the information out of her
sneakily, without her knowing she was telling him; or
by giving her a cock-and-bull story like the one he had

given Lydia; or by telling her straight out that he wanted to kill Orlov; and his imagination recoiled at each scene.

When he thought about what was at stake he found his feelings ridiculous. He had a chance to save millions of lives and possibly spark the Russian Revolution – and he was worried about lying to an upper-class girl! It was not as if he intended to do her any harm – just use her, deceive her, and betray her trust, his own daughter, whom he had only just met . . .

To occupy his hands he began to fashion his home-made dynamite into a primitive bomb. He packed the nitroglycerine-soaked cotton waste into a cracked china vase. He considered the problem of detonation. Burning paper alone might not be sufficient. He stuffed half a dozen matches into the cotton so that only their bright red heads showed. It was difficult to get the matches to stand upright because his hands were unsteady.

My hands *never* shake.

What is happening to me?

He twisted a piece of newspaper into a taper and stuck one end into the middle of the match heads, then tied the heads together with a length of cotton. He found it very difficult to tie the knot.

He read all the international news in *The Times*, ploughing doggedly through the turgid English sentences. He was more or less sure that there would be a war, but more or less sure no longer seemed enough. He would have been happy to kill a useless idler like Orlov then find out that it had been to no purpose. But to destroy his relationship with Charlotte to no purpose . . .

Relationship? What relationship?

You know what relationship.

Reading *The Times* made his head ache. The print was too small and his room was dark. It was a wretchedly conservative newspaper. It ought to be blown up.

He longed to see Charlotte again.

He heard shuffling footsteps on the landing outside, then there was a knock at the door.

'Come in,' he called carelessly.

The caretaker came in, coughing. 'Morning.'

'Good morning, Mr Price.' What did the old fool want now?

'What's that?' said Price, nodding at the bomb on the table.

'Home-made candle,' Feliks said. 'Lasts months. What do you want?'

'I wondered if you needed a spare pair of sheets. I can get them at a very low price—'

'No, thank you,' Feliks said. 'Goodbye.'

'Goodbye, then.' Price went out.

I should have hidden that bomb, Feliks thought.

What is happening to me?

'Yes, he's in there,' Price said to Basil Thomson.

Tension knotted in Walden's stomach.

They sat in the back of a police car parked around the corner from Canada Buildings, where Feliks was. With them was an inspector from the Special Branch and a uniformed superintendent from Southwark police station.

If they could catch Feliks now, then Aleks would be safe: what a relief that will be, Walden thought.

Thomson said: 'Mr Price went to the police station to report that he had rented a room to a suspicious character with a foreign accent who had very little money and was growing a beard as if to change his appearance. He identified Feliks from our artist's drawing. Well done, Price.'

'Thank you, sir.'

The uniformed superintendent unfolded a large-scale map. He was maddeningly slow and deliberate. 'Canada Buildings consists of three five-storey tenements around a courtyard. Each building has three stairwells. As you stand at the entrance to the courtyard, Toronto House is on your right. Feliks is on the middle staircase and the top floor. Behind Toronto House is the yard of a builder's merchant.'

Walden contained his impatience.

'On your left is Vancouver House, and behind Vancouver House is another street. The third building, straight ahead of you as you stand at the courtyard entrance, is Montreal House, which backs on to the railway line.'

Thomson pointed to the map. 'What's that, in the middle of the courtyard?'

'The privy,' replied the superintendent. 'And a real stinker, too, with all those people using it.'

Walden thought: Get on with it!

Thomson said: 'It seems to me that Feliks has three

ways out of the courtyard. First, the entrance: obviously we'll block that. Second, at the opposite end of the courtyard on the left, the alley between Vancouver House and Montreal House. It leads to the next street. Put three men in the alley, superintendent.'

'Very good, sir.'

'Third, the alley between Montreal House and Toronto House. This alley leads to the builder's yard. Another three men in there.'

The superintendent nodded.

'Now, do these tenements have back windows?'

'Yes, sir.'

'So Feliks has a fourth escape route from Toronto House: out of the back window and across the builder's yard. Better put six men in the builder's yard. Finally, let's have a nice show of strength right here in the middle of the courtyard, to encourage him to come along quietly. Does all that meet with your approval, Superintendent?'

'More than adequate, I'd say, sir.'

He doesn't know what kind of man we're dealing with, Walden thought.

Thomson said: 'You and Inspector Sutton here can make the arrest. Got your gun, Sutton?'

Sutton pulled aside his coat to show a small revolver strapped under his arm. Walden was surprised: he had thought that no British policeman ever carried a fire-arm. Obviously the Special Branch was different. He was glad.

Thomson said to Sutton: 'Take my advice – have it in your hand when you knock on his door.' He turned to the uniformed superintendent. 'You'd better take my gun.'

The superintendent was mildly offended. 'I've been twenty-five years in the force and never felt the lack of a firearm, sir, so if it's all the same to you I shan't begin now.'

'Policemen have died trying to arrest this man.'

'I'm afraid I've never been taught to shoot, sir.'

Good God, Walden thought despairingly, how can people like us deal with people like Feliks?

Thomson said: 'Lord Walden and I will be at the courtyard entrance.'

'You'll stay in the car, sir?'

'We'll stay in the car.'

Let's *go*, thought Walden.

'Let's go,' said Thomson.

Feliks realized he was hungry. He had not eaten for more than twenty-four hours. He wondered what to do. Now that he had stubble on his chin and working-class clothes he would be watched by shopkeepers so it would be more difficult for him to steal.

He pulled himself up at that thought. It's *never* difficult to steal, he told himself. Let's see: I could go to a suburban house – the kind where they are likely to have only one or two servants – and walk in at the tradesman's entrance. There would be a maid in the kitchen, or perhaps a cook. 'I am a madman,' I would say with a smile, 'but if you make me a sandwich I won't rape you.' I would move toward the door to block her escape. She might scream, in which case I should go away and try another house. But, most likely, she would give me the food. 'Thank you,' I would say. 'You are kind.' Then I would walk away. It is never difficult to steal.

Money was a problem. Feliks thought: As if I could afford a pair of sheets! The caretaker was an optimist. Surely he knew that Feliks had no money . . .

Surely he knows I've no money.

On reflection, Price's reason for coming to Feliks' room was suspicious. Was he just optimistic? Or was he *checking*? I seem to be slowing down, Feliks thought. He stood up and went to the window.

Jesus *Christ*.

The courtyard was alive with blue-uniformed policemen.

Feliks stared down at them in horror.

The sight made him think of a nest of worms, wriggling and crawling over one another in a hole in the ground.

His instincts screamed: Run! Run! Run!

Where?

They had blocked all exits from the courtyard.

Feliks remembered the back windows.

He ran from his room and along the landing to the back of the tenement. There a window looked out on to the builder's yard behind. He peered down into the yard and saw five or six policemen taking up positions among the piles of bricks and stacks of planking. There was no escape that way.

That left only the roof.

He ran back to his room and looked out. The policemen were still, all but two men – one in uniform and one in plain clothes – who were walking purposefully across the courtyard toward Feliks' stair.

He picked up his bomb and the box of matches and ran down to the landing below. A small door with a latch gave access to a cupboard beneath the stairs. Feliks opened the door and placed the bomb inside. He lit the paper fuse and closed the cupboard door. He turned around. He had time to run up the stairs before the fuse burned down—

The baby girl was crawling up the stairs.

Shit.

He picked her up and dashed through the door into her room. Her mother sat on the dirty bed, staring vacantly at the wall. Feliks thrust the baby into her arms and yelled: 'Stay here! Don't move!' The woman looked scared.

He ran out. The two men were one floor down. Feliks raced up the stairs –

Don't blow now don't blow now don't—

– to his landing. They heard him, and one shouted: 'Hey, you!' They broke into a run.

Feliks dashed into his room, picked up the cheap straight-backed chair, carried it out to the landing and positioned it directly under the trapdoor leading to the loft.

The bomb had not exploded.

Perhaps it would not work.

Feliks stood on the chair.

The two men hit the stairs.

Feliks pushed open the trapdoor.

The uniformed policeman shouted: 'You're under arrest!'

The plain-clothes man raised a gun and pointed it at Feliks.

The bomb went off.

There was a big dull thud like something very heavy falling and the staircase broke up into matchwood which flew everywhere and the two men were flung backward and the debris burst into flames and Feliks hauled himself up into the loft.

'Damn, he's exploded a damn bomb!' Thomson shouted.

Walden thought: It's going wrong – again.

There was a crash as shards of glass from a third-floor window hit the ground.

Walden and Thomson jumped out of the car and ran across the courtyard.

Thomson picked two uniformed policemen at random. 'You and you – come inside with me.' He turned to Walden. 'You stay here.' They ran inside.

Walden backed across the courtyard, looking up at the windows of Toronto House.

Where is Feliks?

He heard a policeman say: 'He've gorn out the back, you mark my words.'

Four or five slates fell off the roof and shattered in the courtyard – loosened, Walden assumed, by the explosion.

Walden kept feeling the urge to look back over his shoulder, as if Feliks might suddenly appear behind him, from nowhere.

The residents of the tenements were coming to their doors and windows to see what was going on, and the courtyard began to fill with people. Some of the policemen made half-hearted attempts to send them back inside. A woman ran out of Toronto House screaming: 'Fire!'

Where is Feliks?

Thomson and a policeman came out carrying Sutton. He was unconscious, or dead. Walden looked more closely. No, he was not dead: his pistol was gripped in his hand.

More slates fell off the roof.

The policeman with Thomson said: 'It's a bloody mess in there.'

Walden said: 'Did you see where Feliks is?'

'Couldn't see anything.'

Thomson and the policeman went back inside.

More slates fell—

Walden was struck by a thought. He looked up.

There was a hole in the roof, and Feliks was climbing up through it.

'There he is!' Walden yelled.

They all watched, helpless, as Feliks crawled out of the loft and scrambled up the roof to the ridge.

If I had a gun—

Walden knelt over the unconscious body of Sutton and prised the pistol from his fingers.

He looked up. Feliks was kneeling on the peak of

the roof. I wish it was a rifle, Walden thought as he lifted the gun. He sighted along the barrel. Feliks looked at him. Their eyes met.

Feliks moved.

A shot rang out.

He felt nothing.

He began to run.

It was like running along a tightrope. He had to hold out his arms for balance, he had to place his feet squarely on the narrow ridge, and he had to avoid thinking about the fifty-foot drop to the courtyard.

There was another shot.

Feliks panicked.

He ran at top speed. The end of the roof loomed up. He could see the down-sloping roof of Montreal House ahead. He had no idea how wide was the gap between the two buildings. He slowed down, hesitating; then Walden fired again.

Feliks ran full-tilt at the end of the ridge.

He jumped.

He flew through the air. He heard his own voice, as if distantly, screaming.

He caught a momentary glimpse of three policemen, in the alley fifty feet below him, staring up at him open-mouthed.

Then he hit the roof of Montreal House, landing hard on his hands and knees.

The impact winded him. He slid backwards down

the roof. His feet hit the gutter. It seemed to give under the strain, and he thought he was going to slide right off the edge of the roof and fall, fall, endlessly – but the gutter held and he stopped sliding.

He was frightened.

A distant corner of his mind protested: But I'm never frightened!

He scrambled up the roof to the peak and then down the other side.

Montreal House backed on to the railway. There were no policemen on the lines or the embankment. They didn't anticipate this, Feliks thought exultantly; they thought I was trapped in the courtyard, it never occurred to them I might escape over the rooftops.

Now all I have to do is get down.

He peered over the gutter at the wall of the building beneath him. There were no drainpipes – the gutters emptied through spouts which jutted out from the edge of the roof, like gargoyles. But the top-floor windows were close to the eaves and had wide ledges.

With his right hand Feliks grasped the gutter and pulled it, testing its strength.

Since when have I cared whether I live or die?

(You know since when.)

He positioned himself over a window, gripped the gutter with both hands, and slowly eased himself over the edge.

For a moment he hung free.

His feet found the window-ledge. He took his right hand from the gutter and felt the brickwork around the window for a handhold. He got his fingers into a shallow groove, then let go of the gutter with his other hand.

He looked through the window. Inside, a man saw him and shouted in fright.

Feliks kicked the window in and dropped into the room. He pushed the frightened occupant aside and rushed out through the doorway.

He ran down the stairs four at a time. If he could reach the ground floor he could get out through the back windows and on to the railway line.

He reached the last landing and stopped at the top of the last flight of stairs, breathing hard. A blue uniform appeared at the front entrance. Feliks spun around and raced to the back of the landing. He lifted the window. It stuck. He gave a mighty heave and threw it open. He heard boots running up the stairs. He clambered over the windowsill, eased himself out, hung by his hands for a moment, pushed himself away from the wall and dropped.

He landed in the long grass of the railway embankment. To his right, two men were jumping over the fence of the builders' yard. A shot came from his far left. A policeman came to the window from which Feliks had jumped.

He ran up the embankment to the railway.

There were four or five pairs of lines. In the distance a train was approaching fast. It seemed to be on the farthermost track. He suffered a moment of cowardice, frightened to cross in front of the train; then he broke into a run.

The two policemen from the builders' yard and the one from Montreal House chased him across the tracks. From the far left a voice shouted: 'Clear the field of fire!' The three pursuers were making it difficult for Walden to get a shot.

Feliks glanced over his shoulder. They had fallen back. A shot rang out. He began to duck and zig-zag. The train sounded very loud. He heard its whistle. There was another shot. He turned aside suddenly, then stumbled and fell on to the last pair of railway lines. There was a terrific thunder in his ears. He saw the locomotive bearing down on him. He jerked convulsively, catapulting himself off the track on to the gravel on the far side. The train roared past his head. He caught a split-second glimpse of the engineman's face, white and scared.

He stood up and ran down the embankment.

Walden stood at the fence watching the train. Basil Thomson came up beside him.

Those policemen who had got on to the railway line ran across to the last track then stood there, helpless, waiting for the train to pass. It seemed to take for ever.

When it had gone, there was no sign of Feliks.

'The bugger's got away,' a policeman said.

Basil Thomson said: 'God damn it all to hell.'

Walden turned away and walked back to the car.

*

Feliks dropped down on the far side of a wall and found himself in a poor street of small row houses. He was also in the goalmouth of an improvised soccer pitch. A group of small boys in large caps stopped playing and stared at him in surprise. He ran on.

It would take them a few minutes to redeploy the police on the far side of the railway line. They would come looking for him, but they would be too late: by the time they got a search under way he would be half a mile from the railway and still moving.

He kept running until he reached a busy shopping street. There, on impulse, he jumped on an omnibus.

He had escaped, but he was terribly worried. This kind of thing had happened to him before, but previously he had never been scared, he had never panicked. He remembered the thought that had gone through his mind as he slid down the roof: I don't want to die.

In Siberia he had lost the ability to feel fear. Now it had come back. For the first time in years, he wanted to stay alive. I have become human again, he thought.

He looked out of the window at the mean streets of south-east London, wondering whether the dirty children and the white-faced women could look at him and see a reborn man.

It was a disaster. It would slow him down, cramp his style, interfere with his work.

I'm afraid, he thought.

I want to live.

I want to see Charlotte again.

CHAPTER ELEVEN

THE FIRST tram of the day woke Feliks with its noise. He opened his eyes and watched it go by, striking bright blue sparks from the overhead cable. Dull-eyed men in working clothes sat at its windows, smoking and yawning, on their way to jobs as street cleaners and market porters and road menders.

The sun was low and bright, but Feliks was in the shade of Waterloo Bridge. He lay on the pavement with his head to the wall, wrapped in a blanket of newspapers. On one side of him was a stinking old woman with the red face of a drunkard. She looked fat, but now Feliks could see, between the hem of her dress and the tops of her man's boots, a few inches of dirty white legs like sticks; and he concluded that her apparent obesity must be due to several layers of clothing. Feliks liked her: last night she had amused all the vagrants by teaching him the vulgar English words for various parts of the body. Feliks had repeated them after her and everyone had laughed.

On his other side was a red-haired boy from Scotland. For him, sleeping in the open was an adventure. He was tough and wiry and cheerful. Looking now at his sleeping face, Feliks saw that he had no morning

315

beard: he was terribly young. What would happen to him when winter came?

There were about thirty of them in a line along the pavement, all lying with their heads to the wall and their feet toward the road, covered with coats or sacks or newspapers. Feliks was the first to stir. He wondered whether any of them had died in the night.

He got up. He ached after a night on the cold street. He walked out from under the bridge into the sunshine. Today he was to meet Charlotte. No doubt he looked and smelled like a tramp. He contemplated washing himself in the Thames, but the river appeared to be dirtier than he was. He went looking for a municipal bath-house.

He found one on the south side of the river. A notice on the door announced that it would open at nine o'clock. Feliks thought that characteristic of social-democratic government: they would build a bath-house so that working men could keep clean, then open it only when everyone was at work. No doubt they complained that the masses failed to take advantage of the facilities so generously provided.

He found a tea-stall near Waterloo Station and had breakfast. He was severely tempted by the fried-egg sandwiches but he could not afford one. He had his usual bread and tea and saved the money for a newspaper.

He felt contaminated by his night with the dead-beats. That was ironic, he thought, for in Siberia he had been glad to sleep with pigs for warmth. It was not difficult to understand why he felt differently now: he was to meet his daughter, and she would be fresh and clean, smelling of perfume and dressed in silk, with gloves and a hat and perhaps a parasol to shade her from the sun.

He went into the railway station and bought *The Times*, then sat on a stone bench outside the bath-house and read the paper while he waited for the place to open.

The news shocked him to the core.

AUSTRIAN HEIR AND HIS WIFE MURDERED
SHOT IN BOSNIAN TOWN
A STUDENT'S POLITICAL CRIME
BOMB THROWN EARLIER IN THE DAY
THE EMPEROR'S GRIEF

The Austro-Hungarian Heir-Presumptive, the Archduke Francis Ferdinand, and his wife, the Duchess of Hohenberg, were assassinated yesterday morning at Sarajevo, the capital of Bosnia. The actual assassin is described as a high school student, who fired bullets at his victims with fatal effect from an automatic pistol as they were returning from a reception at the Town Hall.

The outrage was evidently the fruit of a carefully laid plot. On their way to the Town Hall the Archduke and his Consort had narrowly escaped death. An individual, described as a compositor from Trebinje, a garrison town in the extreme south of Herzegovina, had thrown a bomb at their motor car. Few details of this first outrage have been received. It is stated that the Archduke warded off the bomb with his arm, and that it exploded behind the car, injuring the occupants of the second carriage.

The author of the second outrage is stated to be a native of Grahovo, in Bosnia. No information as to his race or creed is yet forthcoming. It is presumed that he belongs to the Serb or Orthodox section of the Bosnian population.

Both criminals were immediately arrested, and were with difficulty saved from being lynched.

While this tragedy was being enacted in the Bosnian capital, the aged Emperor Francis Joseph was on his way from Vienna to his summer residence at Ischl. He had an enthusiastic send-off from his subjects in Vienna and an even more enthusiastic reception on reaching Ischl.

Feliks was stunned. He was delighted that another useless aristocratic parasite had been destroyed, another blow struck against tyranny; and he felt ashamed that a schoolboy had been able to kill the heir to the Austrian throne while he, Feliks, had failed repeatedly to kill a Russian prince. But what occupied his mind most was the change in the world political picture that must surely follow. The Austrians, with the Germans backing them, would take their revenge on Serbia. The Russians would protest. Would the Russians mobilize their army? If they were confident of British support, they probably would. Russian mobilization would mean German mobilization; and once the Germans had mobilized no one could stop their generals going to war.

Feliks painstakingly deciphered the tortured English of the other reports, on the same page, to do with the assassination. There were stories headlined OFFICIAL REPORT OF THE CRIME, AUSTRIAN EMPEROR AND THE NEWS, TRAGEDY OF A ROYAL HOUSE, and SCENE OF THE MURDER (From Our Special Correspondent). There was a good deal of nonsense about how shocked and horrified and grieved everyone was; plus repeated assertions that there was no cause for undue alarm, and that tragic though it was the murder would make no real difference to Europe – sentiments which Feliks had already come to recognize as being characteristic of *The Times,* which would have described the Four Horsemen of the Apocalypse as strong rulers who could do nothing but good for the stability of the international situation.

So far there was no talk of Austrian reprisals, but it would come, Feliks was sure. And then—

Then there would be war.

There was no real reason for Russia to go to war, Feliks thought angrily. The same applied to England. It was France and Germany that were belligerent: the French had been wanting since 1871 to win back their lost territories of Alsace and Lorraine, and the German generals felt that Germany would be a second-class power until she began to throw her weight about.

What might stop Russia going to war? A quarrel with her allies. What would cause a quarrel between Russia and England? The killing of Orlov.

319

If the assassination in Sarajevo could start a war, another assassination in London could stop a war.

And Charlotte could find Orlov.

Wearily, Feliks contemplated afresh the dilemma that had haunted him for the last forty-eight hours. Was anything changed by the murder of the Archduke? Did that give him the right to take advantage of a young girl?

It was almost time for the bath-house to open. A small crowd of women carrying bundles of washing gathered around the door. Feliks folded his newspaper and stood up.

He knew that he *would* use her. He had not resolved the dilemma – he had simply decided what to do. His whole life seemed to lead up to the murder of Orlov. There was a momentum in his progress toward that goal, and he could not be deflected, even by the knowledge that his life had been founded on a mistake.

Poor Charlotte.

The doors opened, and Feliks went into the bath-house to wash.

Charlotte had it all planned. Lunch was at one o'clock when the Waldens had no guests. By two-thirty Mama would be in her room, lying down. Charlotte would be able to sneak out of the house in time to meet Feliks at three. She would spend an hour with him. By four-thirty she would be at home in the morning-room, washed and changed and demurely ready to pour tea and receive callers with Mama.

It was not to be. At midday Mama ruined the whole plan by saying: 'Oh, I forgot to tell you – we're lunching with the Duchess of Middlesex at her house in Grosvenor Square.'

'Oh, dear,' Charlotte said. 'I really don't feel like a luncheon party.'

'Don't be silly, you'll have a lovely time.'

I said the wrong thing, Charlotte thought immediately. I should have said I've got a splitting headache and I can't possibly go. I was too half-hearted. I could have lied if I'd known in advance but I can't do it on the spur of the moment. She tried again. 'I'm sorry, Mama, I don't want to go.'

'You're coming, and no nonsense,' Mama said. 'I want the Duchess to get to know you – she really is most useful. And the Marquess of Chalfont will be there.'

Lunch parties generally started at one-thirty and went on past three. I might be home by three-thirty, so I could get to the National Gallery by four, Charlotte thought; but by then he will have given up and gone away, and besides, even if he is still waiting, I would have to leave him almost immediately in order to be home for tea. She wanted to talk to him about the assassination: she was eager to hear his views. She did not want to have lunch with the old Duchess and—

'Who is the Marquess of Chalfont?'

'You know, Freddie. He's charming, don't you think?'

'Oh, him. Charming? I haven't noticed.' I could write a note, address it to that place in Camden Town, and leave it on the hall table on my way out for the footman to post; but Feliks doesn't actually live at that address, and anyway he wouldn't get the note before three o'clock.

Mama said: 'Well, notice him today. I fancy you may have bewitched him.'

'Who?'

'*Freddie.* Charlotte, you really must pay a little attention to a young man when he pays attention to you.'

So that was why she was so keen on this lunch party. 'Oh, Mama, don't be silly—'

'What's silly about it?' Mama said in an exasperated voice.

'I've hardly spoken three sentences to him.'

'Then it's not your conversation that has bewitched him.'

'Please!'

'All right, I won't tease. Go and change. Put on that cream dress with the brown lace – it suits your colouring.'

Charlotte gave in, and went up to her room. I suppose I should be flattered about Freddie, she thought, as she took off her dress. Why can't I get interested in any of these young men? Maybe I'm just not ready for all that yet. At the moment there's too much else to occupy my mind. At breakfast Papa said there would be a war, because of the shooting of the Archduke. But girls aren't supposed to be too interested in that sort of thing. The summit of my ambition should be to get engaged before the end of my first season – that's what Belinda is thinking about.

But not all girls are like Belinda – remember the suffragettes.

She got dressed and went downstairs. She sat and made idle conversation while Mama drank a glass of sherry, then they went to Grosvenor Square.

The Duchess was an overweight woman in her sixties: she made Charlotte think of an old wooden ship rotting beneath a new coat of paint. The lunch was a real hen-party. If this were a play, Charlotte thought, there would be a wild-eyed poet, a discreet Cabinet Minister, a cultured Jewish banker, a Crown Prince, and at least one remarkably beautiful woman. In fact the only men present, apart from Freddie, were a nephew of the Duchess and a Conservative M.P. Each of the women was introduced as the wife of so-and-so. If I ever get married, Charlotte thought, I shall insist on being introduced as myself, not as somebody's wife.

Of course it was difficult for the Duchess to have interesting parties because so many people were banned from her table: all Liberals, all Jews, anybody in trade, anybody who was on the stage, all divorcees, and all of the many people who had at one time or another offended against the Duchess's idea of what was the done thing. It made for a dull circle of friends.

The Duchess's favourite topic of conversation was the question of what was ruining the country. The main candidates were subversion (by Lloyd George and Churchill), vulgarity (Diaghilev and the post-impressionists), and supertax (one shilling and threepence in the pound).

Today, however, the ruin of England took second place to the death of the Archduke. The Conservative M.P. explained at somewhat tedious length why there would be no war. The wife of a South American ambassador said in a little-girlish tone which infuriated Charlotte: 'What I don't understand is why these nihilists want to throw bombs and shoot people.'

The Duchess had the answer to that. Her doctor had explained to her that all suffragettes had a nervous ailment known to medical science as hysteria; and in her view the revolutionists suffered from the male equivalent of this disease.

Charlotte, who had read *The Times* from cover to cover that morning, said: 'On the other hand, perhaps the Serbs simply don't want to be ruled by Austria.' Mama gave her a black look and everyone else glanced at her for a moment as if she were quite mad and then ignored what she had said.

Freddie was sitting next to her. His round face always seemed to gleam slightly. He spoke to her in a low voice. 'I say, you do say the most outrageous things.'

'What was outrageous about it?' Charlotte demanded.

'Well, I mean to say, anyone would think you approved of people shooting archdukes.'

'I think if the Austrians tried to take over England, you would shoot archdukes, wouldn't you?'

'You're priceless,' Freddie said.

Charlotte turned away from him. She was beginning to feel as if she had lost her voice: nobody seemed to hear anything she said. It made her very cross.

Meanwhile the Duchess was getting into her stride. The lower classes were idle, she said; and Charlotte thought: You who have never done a day's work in your life! Why, the Duchess said, she understood that nowadays each workman had a lad to carry his tools around: surely a man could carry his own tools, she said as a footman held out for her a silver salver of boiled potatoes. Beginning her third glass of sweet wine, she said that they drank so much beer in the middle of the day that they were incapable of working in the afternoon. People today wanted to be mollycoddled, she said as three footmen and two maids cleared away the third course and served the fourth; it was no business of the Government's to provide Poor Relief and medical insurance and pensions. Poverty would encourage the lower orders to be thrifty, and that was a virtue, she said, at the end of a meal which would have fed a working-class family of ten for a fortnight. People must be self-reliant, she said, as the butler helped her rise from the table and walk into the drawing-room.

By this time Charlotte was boiling with suppressed rage. Who could blame revolutionists for shooting people like the Duchess?

Freddie handed her a cup of coffee and said: 'She's a marvellous old warhorse, isn't she?'

Charlotte said: 'I think she's the nastiest old woman I've ever met.'

Freddie's round face became furtive and he said: 'Hush!'

At least, Charlotte thought, no one could say I'm encouraging him.

A carriage clock on the mantel struck three with a tinkling chime. Charlotte felt as if she were in jail. Feliks was now waiting for her on the steps of the National Gallery. She had to get out of the Duchess's house. She thought: What am I doing here when I could be with someone who talks sense?

The Conservative M.P. said: 'I must get back to the House.' His wife stood up to go with him. Charlotte saw her way out.

She approached the wife and spoke quietly. 'I have a slight headache,' she said. 'May I come with you? You must pass my house on the way to Westminster.'

'Certainly, Lady Charlotte,' said the wife.

Mama was talking to the Duchess. Charlotte interrupted them and repeated the headache story. 'I know Mama would like to stay a little longer, so I'm going with Mrs Shakespeare. Thank you for a lovely lunch, your grace.'

The Duchess nodded regally.

I managed that rather well, Charlotte thought, as she walked out into the hall and down the stairs.

She gave her address to the Shakespeares' coachman and added: 'There's no need to drive into the courtyard – just stop outside.'

On the way, Mrs Shakespeare advised her to take a spoonful of laudanum for the headache.

The coachman did as he had been told, and at three-twenty Charlotte was standing on the pavement outside her home, watching the coach drive off. Instead of going into the house she headed for Trafalgar Square.

She arrived just after three-thirty and ran up the

steps of the National Gallery. She could not see Feliks. He's gone, she thought; after all that. Then he emerged from behind one of the massive pillars, as if he had been lying in wait, and she was so pleased to see him she could have kissed him.

'I'm sorry to have made you wait about,' she said as she shook his hand. 'I got involved in a dreadful luncheon party.'

'It doesn't matter, now that you're here.' He was smiling, but uneasily, like – Charlotte thought – someone saying hello to a dentist before having a tooth pulled.

They went inside. Charlotte loved the cool, hushed museum, with its glass domes and marble pillars, grey floors and beige walls, and the paintings shouting out colour and beauty and passion. 'At least my parents taught me to look at pictures,' she said.

He turned his sad dark eyes on her. 'There's going to be a war.'

Of all people who had spoken of that possibility today, only Feliks and Papa had seemed to be *moved* by it. 'Papa said the same thing. But I don't understand why.'

'France and Germany both think they stand to gain a lot by war. Austria, Russia and England may get sucked in.'

They walked on. Feliks did not seem to be interested in the paintings. Charlotte said: 'Why are you so concerned? Shall you have to fight?'

'I'm too old. But I think of all the millions of innocent Russian boys, straight off the farm, who will be crippled or blinded or killed in a cause they don't understand and wouldn't care about if they did.'

Charlotte had always thought of war as a matter of men killing one another, but Feliks saw it as men being killed by war. As usual, he showed her things in a new light. She said: 'I never looked at it that way.'

'The Earl of Walden never looked at it that way either. That's why he will let it happen.'

'I'm sure Papa wouldn't let it happen if he could help—'

'You're wrong,' Feliks interrupted. 'He is making it happen.'

Charlotte frowned, puzzled. 'What do you mean?'

'That's why Prince Orlov is here.'

Her puzzlement deepened. 'How do you know about Aleks?'

'I know more about it than you do. The police have spies among the anarchists, but the anarchists have spies among the police spies. We find things out. Walden and Orlov are negotiating a treaty, the effect of which will be to drag Russia into the war on the British side.'

Charlotte was about to protest that Papa would not do such a thing, then she realized that Feliks was right. It explained some of the remarks passed between Papa and Aleks while Aleks was staying at the house, and it explained why Papa was shocking his friends by consorting with Liberals like Churchill.

She said: 'Why would he do that?'

'I'm afraid he doesn't care how many Russian peasants die so long as England dominates Europe.'

Yes, of course, Papa would see it in those terms, she thought. 'It's awful,' she said. 'Why don't you *tell* people? Expose the whole thing – shout it from the rooftops!'

'Who would listen?'

'Wouldn't they listen in Russia?'

'They will if we can find a dramatic way of bringing the thing to their notice.'

'Such as?'

Feliks looked at her. 'Such as kidnapping Prince Orlov.'

It was so outrageous that she laughed, then stopped abruptly. It crossed her mind that he might be playing a game, pretending in order to make a point; then she looked at his face and knew that he was deadly serious. For the first time she wondered whether he was perfectly sane. 'You don't mean that,' she said incredulously.

He smiled awkwardly. 'Do you think I'm crazy?'

She knew he was not. She shook her head. 'You're the sanest man I ever met.'

'Then sit down, and I'll explain it to you.'

She allowed herself to be led to a seat.

'The Czar already distrusts the English, because they let political refugees like me come to England. If one of us were to kidnap his favourite nephew there would be a real quarrel – then they could not be sure of each other's help in a war. And, when the Russian people learn what Orlov was trying to do to them, they will be so angry that the Czar will not be able to make them go to war anyway. Do you see?'

Charlotte watched his face as he talked. He was quiet, reasonable, and only a little tense. There was no mad light of fanaticism in his eye. Everything he said made sense, but it was like the logic of a fairy tale – one thing followed from another, but it seemed to be a story about a different world, not the world she lived in.

'I do see,' she said, 'but you can't kidnap Aleks, he's such a nice man.'

'That *nice man* will lead a million other nice men to their deaths if he's allowed to. This is *real*, Charlotte; not like the battles in these paintings of gods and horses. Walden and Orlov are discussing *war* – men cutting each other open with swords, boys getting their legs blown off by cannonballs, people bleeding and dying in muddy fields, screaming in pain with no one to help them. This is what Walden and Orlov are trying to arrange. Half the misery in the world is caused by nice young men like Orlov who think they have the right to organize wars between nations.'

She was struck by a frightening thought. 'You've already tried once to kidnap him.'

He nodded. 'In the park. You were in the carriage. It went wrong.'

'Oh, my word.' She felt sickened and depressed.

He took her hand. 'You know I'm right, don't you?'

It seemed to her that he *was* right. His world was the real world: she was the one who lived in a fairy tale. In fairyland the debutantes in white were presented to the King and Queen, and the Prince went to war, and the

Earl was kind to his servants who all loved him, and the
Duchess was a dignified old lady, and there was no such
thing as sexual intercourse. In the real world Annie's
baby was born dead because Mama let Annie go without
a reference, and a thirteen-year-old mother was condemned to death because she had let her baby die, and
people slept on the streets because they had no homes,
and there were baby farms, and the Duchess was a
vicious old harridan, and a grinning man in a tweed
suit punched Charlotte in the stomach outside Buckingham Palace.

'I know you're right,' she said to Feliks.

'That's very important,' he said. 'You hold the key to
the whole thing.'

'Me? Oh, no!'

'I need your help.'

'No, please don't say that!'

'You see, I can't find Orlov.'

It's not fair, she thought; it has all happened too
quickly. She felt miserable and trapped. She wanted to
help Feliks, and she could see how important it was,
but Aleks was her cousin, and he had been a guest in
her house – how could she betray him?

'Will you help me?' Feliks said.

'I don't know where Aleks is,' she said evasively.

'But you could find out.'

'Yes.'

'Will you?'

She sighed. 'I don't know.'

'Charlotte, you must.'

'There's no *must* about it!' she flared. 'Everyone tells me what I *must* do – I thought you had more respect for me!'

He looked crestfallen. 'I wish I didn't have to ask you.'

She squeezed his hand. 'I'll think about it.'

He opened his mouth to protest, and she put a finger to his lips to silence him. 'You'll have to be satisfied with that,' she said.

At seven-thirty Walden went out in the Lanchester, wearing evening dress and a silk hat. He was using the motor car all the time, now: in an emergency it would be faster and more manoeuvrable than a carriage. Pritchard sat in the driving seat with a revolver holstered beneath his jacket. Civilized life seemed to have come to an end. They drove to the back entrance of Number Ten, Downing Street. The Cabinet had met that afternoon to discuss the deal Walden had worked out with Aleks. Now Walden was to hear whether or not they had approved it.

He was shown into the small dining-room. Churchill was already there with Asquith, the Prime Minister. They were leaning on the sideboard drinking sherry. Walden shook hands with Asquith.

'How do you do, Prime Minister.'

'Good of you to come, Lord Walden.'

Asquith had silver hair and a clean-shaven face. There were traces of humour in the wrinkles around his eyes, but his mouth was small, thin-lipped and stubborn-looking, and he had a broad, square chin. Walden thought there was in his voice a trace of a Yorkshire accent which had survived the City of London School and Balliol College, Oxford. He had an unusually large head which was said to contain a brain of machine-like precision; but then, Walden thought, people always credit Prime Ministers with more brains than they've got.

Asquith said: 'I'm afraid the Cabinet would not approve your proposal.'

Walden's heart sank. To conceal his disappointment he adopted a brisk manner. 'Why not?'

'The opposition came mainly from Lloyd George.'

Walden looked at Churchill and raised his eyebrows.

Churchill nodded. 'You probably thought, like everyone else, that L.G. and I vote alike on every issue. Now you know otherwise.'

'What's his objection?'

'Matter of principle,' Churchill answered. 'He says we're passing the Balkans around like a box of chocolates: help yourself, choose your favourite flavour, Thrace, Bosnia, Bulgaria, Serbia. Small countries have their rights, he says. That's what comes of having a Welshman in the Cabinet. A Welshman and a solicitor too, I don't know which is worse.'

His levity irritated Walden. This is his project as much as mine, he thought: why isn't the man as dismayed as I am?

They sat down to dinner. The meal was served by

the butler. Asquith ate sparingly. Churchill drank too much, Walden thought. Walden was gloomy, mentally damning Lloyd George with every mouthful.

At the end of the first course Asquith said: 'We must have this treaty, you know. 'There will be a war between France and Germany sooner or later; and, if the Russians stay out of it, Germany will conquer Europe. We can't have that.'

Walden asked: 'What must be done to change Lloyd George's mind?'

Asquith smiled thinly. 'If I had a pound note for every time that question has been asked I'd be a rich man.'

The butler served quail and poured claret. Churchill said: 'We must come up with a modified proposal which will meet L.G.'s objection.'

Churchill's casual tone infuriated Walden. 'You know perfectly well it's not that simple,' he snapped.

'No indeed,' Asquith said mildly. 'Still, we must try. Thrace to be an independent country under Russian protection, something like that.'

'I've spent the past month beating them down,' Walden said wearily.

'Still, the murder of poor old Francis Ferdinand changes the complexion of things,' Asquith said. 'Now that Austria is getting aggressive in the Balkans again, the Russians need more than ever that toehold in the area which, in principle, we're trying to give them.'

Walden set aside his disappointment and began to think constructively. After a moment he said: 'What about Constantinople?'

'What do you mean?'

'Suppose we offered Constantinople to the Russians – would Lloyd George object to that?'

'He might say it was like giving Cardiff to the Irish Republicans,' Churchill said.

Walden ignored him and looked at Asquith.

Asquith put down his knife and fork. 'Well. Now that he has made his principled stand, he may be keen to show how reasonable he can be when offered a compromise. I think he may agree to it. Will it be enough for the Russians?'

Walden was not sure, but he was buoyed up by his new idea. Impulsively he said: 'If you can sell it to Lloyd George, I can sell it to Orlov.'

'Splendid!' said Asquith. 'Now, then, what about this anarchist?'

Walden's optimism was punctured. 'They're doing everything possible to protect Aleks, but still it's damned worrying.'

'I thought Basil Thomson was a good man.'

'Excellent,' Walden said. 'But I'm afraid Feliks might be even better.'

Churchill said: 'I don't think we should let the fellow *frighten* us—'

'I am frightened, gentlemen,' Walden interrupted. 'Three times Feliks has slipped through our grasp: the last time we had thirty policemen to arrest him. I don't see how he can get at Aleks now, but the fact that I can't see a way doesn't mean that he can't see a way. And we know what will happen if Aleks is killed: our alliance with Russia will fall through. Feliks is the most dangerous man in England.'

Asquith nodded, his expression sombre. 'If you're less than perfectly satisfied with the protection Orlov is getting, please contact me directly.'

'Thank you.'

The butler offered Walden a cigar, but he sensed that he was finished here. 'Life must go on,' he said, 'and I must go to a crush at Mrs Glenville's. I'll smoke my cigar there.'

'Don't tell them where you had dinner,' Churchill said with a smile.

'I wouldn't dare – they'd never speak to me again.' Walden finished his port and stood up.

'When will you put the new proposal to Orlov?' Asquith asked.

'I'll motor to Norfolk first thing in the morning.'

'Splendid.'

The butler brought Walden's hat and gloves and he took his leave.

Pritchard was standing at the garden gate, chatting to the policeman on duty. 'Back to the house,' Walden told him.

He had been rather rash, he reflected as they drove. He had promised to secure Aleks' consent to the Constantinople plan, but he was not sure now. It was worrying. He began to rehearse the words he would use tomorrow.

He was home before he had made any progress. 'We'll need the car again in a few minutes, Pritchard.'

'Very good, my lord.'

Walden entered the house and went upstairs to wash

his hands. On the landing he met Charlotte. 'Is Mama getting ready?' he said.

'Yes, she'll be a few minutes. How goes your politicking?'

'Slowly.'

'Why have you suddenly got involved in all that sort of thing again?'

He smiled. 'In a nutshell: to stop Germany conquering Europe. But don't you worry your pretty little head—'

'I shan't worry. But where on earth have you hidden cousin Aleks?'

He hesitated. There was no harm in her knowing; yet, once she knew, she would be capable of accidentally letting the secret out. Better for her to be left in the dark. He said: 'If anyone asks you, say you don't know.' He smiled and went on up to his room.

There were times when the charm of English life wore thin for Lydia.

Usually she liked crushes. Several hundred people would gather at someone's home to do nothing whatsoever. There was no dancing, no formal meal, no cards. You shook hands with the hostess, took a glass of champagne, and wandered around some great house chatting to your friends and admiring people's clothes. Today she was struck by the pointlessness of the whole thing. Her discontent took the form of nostalgia for Russia. There, she felt, the beauties would surely be more ravishing, the intellectuals less polite, the conversations deeper, the evening air not so balmy and soporific. In truth she was too worried – about Stephen, about Feliks and about Charlotte – to enjoy socializing.

She ascended the broad staircase with Stephen on one side of her and Charlotte on the other. Her diamond necklace was admired by Mrs Glenville. They moved on. Stephen peeled off to talk to one of his cronies in the Lords: Lydia heard the words 'Amendment Bill' and listened no more. They moved through the crowd, smiling and saying hello. Lydia kept thinking: What am I doing here?

Charlotte said: 'By the way, Mama, where has Aleks gone?'

'I don't know, dear,' Lydia said absently. 'Ask your father. Good evening, Freddie.'

Freddie was interested in Charlotte, not Lydia. 'I've been thinking about what you said at lunch,' he said. 'I've decided that the difference is, we're English.'

Lydia left them to it. In my day, she thought, political discussions were decidedly *not* the way to win a man; but perhaps things have changed. It begins to look as if Freddie will be interested in whatever Charlotte wants to talk about. I wonder if he will propose to her. Oh Lord, what a relief that would be.

In the first of the reception-rooms, where a string quartet played inaudibly, she met her sister-in-law Clarissa. They talked about their daughters, and Lydia was secretly comforted to learn that Clarissa was terribly worried about Belinda.

'I don't mind her buying those ultra-fashionable

clothes and showing her ankles, and I shouldn't mind her smoking cigarettes if only she were a little more discreet about it,' Clarissa said. 'But she goes to the most dreadful places to listen to nigger bands playing jazz music, and last week she went to a boxing match!'

'What about her chaperone?'

Clarissa sighed. 'I've said she can go out without a chaperone if she's with girls we know. Now I realize that was a mistake. I suppose Charlotte is always chaperoned.'

'In theory, yes,' Lydia said. 'But she's frightfully disobedient. Once she sneaked out and went to a suffragette meeting.' Lydia was not prepared to tell Clarissa the whole disgraceful truth: 'a suffragette meeting' did not sound quite as bad as 'a demonstration'. She added: 'Charlotte is interested in the most unladylike things, such as politics. I don't know where she gets her ideas.'

'Oh, I feel the same,' Clarissa said. 'Belinda was always brought up with the very best of music, and good society, and wholesome books and a strict governess . . . so naturally one wonders where on earth she got her taste for vulgarity. The worst of it is, I can't make her realize that I am worried for her happiness, not my own.'

'Oh, I'm so glad to hear you say that!' Lydia said. 'It's *just* how I feel. Charlotte seems to think there's something false or silly about our protecting her.' She sighed. 'We must marry them off quickly, before they come to any harm.'

'Absolutely! Is anyone interested in Charlotte?'

'Freddie Chalfont.'

'Ah, yes, I'd heard that.'

'He even seems to be prepared to talk politics to her. But I'm afraid she's not awfully interested in him. What about Belinda?'

'The opposite problem. She likes them all.'

'Oh, dear!' Lydia laughed, and moved on, feeling better. In some ways Clarissa, as a stepmother, had a more difficult task than Lydia. I suppose I have much to be thankful for, she thought.

The Duchess of Middlesex was in the next room. Most people stayed on their feet at a crush, but the Duchess, characteristically, sat down and let people come to her. Lydia approached her just as Lady Gay-Stephens was moving away.

'I gather Charlotte is quite recovered from her headache,' the Duchess said.

'Yes, indeed; it's kind of you to inquire.'

'Oh, I wasn't inquiring,' the Duchess said. 'My nephew saw her in the National Gallery at four o'clock.'

The National Gallery! What in Heaven's name was she doing there? She had sneaked out again! But Lydia was not going to let the Duchess know that Charlotte had been misbehaving. 'She has always been fond of art,' she improvised.

'She was with a man,' the Duchess said. 'Freddie Chalfont must have a rival.'

The little minx! Lydia concealed her fury. 'Indeed,' she said, forcing a smile.

'Who is he?'

'Just one of their set,' Lydia said desperately.

'Oh, no,' said the Duchess with a malicious smile. 'He was about forty, and wearing a tweed cap.'

'A tweed cap!' Lydia was being humiliated, and she knew it, but she hardly cared. Who could the man be? What was Charlotte thinking of? Her reputation—

'They were holding hands,' the Duchess added, and she smiled broadly, showing rotten teeth.

Lydia could no longer pretend that everything was all right. 'Oh, my God,' she said. 'What has the child got into now?'

The Duchess said: 'In my day the chaperone system was found effective in preventing this sort of thing.'

Lydia was suddenly very angry at the pleasure the Duchess was taking in this catastrophe. 'That was a hundred years ago,' she snapped. She walked away. A tweed cap! Holding hands! Forty years old! It was too appalling to be contemplated. The cap meant he was working class, the age meant he was a lecher, and the hand-holding implied that matters had already gone far, perhaps too far. What can I do, she thought helplessly, if the child goes out of the house without my knowledge? Oh, Charlotte, Charlotte, you don't know what you're doing to yourself!

'What was the boxing match like?' Charlotte asked Belinda.

'In a horrid sort of way it was terribly exciting,' Belinda said. 'These two enormous men wearing nothing but their shorts, standing there trying to beat each other to death.'

341

Charlotte did not see how that could be exciting. 'It sounds dreadful.'

'I got so worked up – ' Belinda lowered her voice – 'that I almost let Peter Go Too Far.'

'What do you mean?'

'You know. Afterwards, in the cab on the way home. I let him . . . kiss me, and so on.'

'What's *and so on?*'

Belinda whispered: 'He kissed my bosom.'

'Oh!' Charlotte frowned. 'Was it nice?'

'Heavenly!'

'Well, well.' Charlotte tried to picture Freddie kissing her bosom, and somehow she knew it would not be heavenly.

Mama walked past and said: 'We're leaving, Charlotte.'

Belinda said: 'She looks cross.'

Charlotte shrugged. 'Nothing unusual in that.'

'We're going to a coon show afterwards – why don't you come with us?'

'What's a coon show?'

'Jazz. It's wonderful music.'

'Mama wouldn't let me.'

'Your Mama is so old-fashioned.'

'You're telling me! I'd better go.'

'Bye.'

Charlotte went down the stairs and got her wrap from the cloakroom. She felt as if two people were inhabiting her skin, like Dr Jekyll and Mr Hyde. One of them smiled and made polite conversation and talked to Belinda about girlish matters; the other thought about kidnapping and treachery, and asked sly questions in an innocent tone of voice.

Without waiting for her parents she went outside and said to the footman: 'The Earl of Walden's car.'

A couple of minutes later the Lanchester pulled up at the kerb. It was a warm evening, and Pritchard had the hood down. He got out of the car and held the door for Charlotte.

She said: 'Pritchard, where is Prince Orlov?'

'It's supposed to be a secret, m'lady.'

'You can tell me.'

'I'd rather you asked your Papa, m'lady.'

It was no good. She could not bully these servants who had known her as a baby. She gave up, and said: 'You'd better go into the hall and tell them I'm waiting in the car.'

'Very good, m'lady.'

Charlotte sat back on the leather seat. She had asked the three people who might have known where Aleks was, and none of them would tell her. They did not trust her to keep the secret, and the maddening thing was that they were of course quite right. She still had not decided whether to help Feliks, however. Now, if she could not get the information he wanted, perhaps she would not have to make the agonizing decision. What a relief that would be.

She had arranged to meet Feliks the day after tomorrow, same place, same time. What would he say when she turned up empty-handed? Would he despise her for failing? No, he was not like that. He would be terribly disappointed. Perhaps he would be able to think of another way to find out where Aleks was. She could not wait to see him again. He was so interesting, and she learned so much from him, that the rest of her life seemed unbearably dull without him. Even the anxiety of this great dilemma into which he had thrown her was better than the boredom of choosing dresses for yet another day of empty social routine.

Papa and Mama got into the car and Pritchard drove off. Papa said: 'What's the matter, Lydia? You look rather upset.'

Mama looked at Charlotte. 'What were you doing in the National Gallery this afternoon?'

Charlotte's heart missed a beat. She had been found out. Someone had spied on her. Now there would be trouble. Her hands started to shake and she held them together in her lap. 'I was looking at pictures.'

'You were with a man.'

Papa said: 'Oh, *no. Charlotte*, what *is* all this?'

'He's just somebody I met,' Charlotte said. 'You wouldn't approve of him.'

'Of course we wouldn't approve!' Mama said. 'He was wearing a tweed cap!'

Papa said: 'A tweed cap! Who the devil is he?'

'He's a terribly *interesting* man, and he understands things—'

'And he holds your hand!' Mama interrupted.

Papa said sadly: 'Charlotte, how vulgar! In the National Gallery!'

'There's no romance,' Charlotte said. 'You've nothing to fear.'

'Nothing to fear?' Mama said with a brittle laugh.

'That evil old Duchess knows all about it, and she'll tell everyone.'

Papa said: 'How could you do this to your Mama?'

Charlotte could not speak. She was close to tears. She thought: I did nothing wrong, just held a conversation with someone who talks sense! How can they be so – so brutish? I hate them!

Papa said: 'You'd better tell me who he is. I expect he can be paid off.'

Charlotte shouted: 'I should think he's one of the few people in the world who can't!'

'I suppose he's some Radical,' Mama said. 'No doubt it is he who has been filling your head with foolishness about suffragism. He probably wears sandals and eats potatoes with the skins on.' She lost her temper. 'He probably believes in Free Love! If you have—'

'No, I haven't,' Charlotte said. 'I told you, there's no romance.' A tear rolled down her nose. 'I'm not the romantic type.'

'I don't believe you for a minute,' Papa said disgustedly. 'Nor will anyone else. Whether you realize it or not, this episode is a social catastrophe for all of us.'

'We'd better put her in a convent!' Mama said hysterically, and she began to cry.

'I'm sure that won't be necessary,' Papa said.

Mama shook her head. 'I didn't mean it. I'm sorry to be so shrill, but I just get so *worried* . . .'

'However, she can't stay in London, after this.'

'Certainly not.'

The car pulled into the courtyard of their house. Mama dried her eyes so that the servants would not see her upset. Charlotte thought: And so they will stop me from seeing Feliks, and send me away, and lock me up. I wish now I had promised to help him, instead of hesitating and saying I would think about it. At least then he would know I'm on his side. Well, they won't win. I shan't live the life they have mapped out for me. I shan't marry Freddie and become Lady Chalfont and raise fat, complacent children. They can't keep me locked away for ever. As soon as I'm twenty-one I'll go and work for Mrs Pankhurst, and read books about anarchism, and start a rest home for unmarried mothers, and if I ever have children I will never, never tell them lies.

They went into the house. Papa said: 'Come into the drawing-room.'

Pritchard followed them in. 'Would you like some sandwiches, my lord?'

'Not just now. Leave us alone for a while, would you, Pritchard?'

Pritchard went out.

Papa made a brandy-and-soda and sipped it. 'Think again, Charlotte,' he said. 'Will you tell us who this man is?'

She wanted to say: He's an anarchist who is trying to prevent you starting a war! But she merely shook her head.

'Then you must see,' he said almost gently, 'that we can't possibly trust you.'

You could have, once, she thought bitterly; but not any more.

Papa spoke to Mama. 'She'll just have to go to the

country for a month, it's the only way to keep her out of trouble. Then, after the Cowes Regatta, she can come to Scotland for the shooting.' He sighed. 'Perhaps she'll be more manageable by next season.'

Mama said: 'We'll send her to Walden Hall, then.'

Charlotte thought: They're talking about me as if I weren't here.

Papa said: 'I'm driving down to Norfolk in the morning, to see Aleks again. I'll take her with me.'

Charlotte was stunned.

Aleks was at Walden Hall.

I never even thought of that!

Now I know!

'She'd better go up and pack,' Mama said.

Charlotte stood up and went out, keeping her face down so that they should not see the light of triumph in her eyes.

CHAPTER TWELVE

A T A QUARTER to three Feliks was in the lobby
of the National Gallery. Charlotte would probably be late, like last time, but anyway he had nothing
better to do.

He was nervy and restless, sick of waiting and sick of
hiding. He had slept rough again the last two nights,
once in Hyde Park and once under the arches of
Charing Cross. During the day he had hidden in alleys
and railway sidings and patches of waste ground,
coming out only to get food. It reminded him of being
on the run in Siberia, and the memory was unpleasant.
Even now he kept moving, going from the lobby into
the domed rooms, glancing at the pictures, and returning to the lobby to look for her. He watched the clock
on the wall. At half past three she still had not come.
She had got involved in another dreadful luncheon
party.

She would surely be able to find out where Orlov
was. She was an ingenious girl, he was certain. Even if
her father would not tell her straightforwardly, she
would think of a way to discover the secret. Whether
she would pass the information on was another matter.
She was strong-willed, too.

348

He wished . . .

He wished a lot of things. He wished he had not deceived her. He wished he could find Orlov without her help. He wished human beings did not make themselves into Princes and Earls and Kaisers and Czars. He wished he had married Lydia and known Charlotte as a baby. He wished she would come: it was four o'clock.

Most of the paintings meant nothing to him: the sentimental religious scenes, the portraits of smug Dutch merchants in their lifeless homes. He liked Bronzino's *Allegory*, but only because it was so sensual. Art was an area of human experience which he had passed by. Perhaps one day Charlotte would lead him into the forest and show him the flowers. But it was unlikely. First, he would have to live through the next few days, and escape after killing Orlov. Even that much was not certain. Then he would have to retain Charlotte's affection despite having used her, lied to her, and killed her cousin. That was close to impossible, but even if it happened he would have to find ways of seeing her while avoiding the police . . . No, there was not much chance he would know her after the assassination. He thought: Make the most of her now.

It was four-thirty.

She's not just late, he thought with a sinking heart: she is unable to come. I hope she's not in trouble with Walden. I hope she didn't take risks and get found out. I wish she would come running up the steps, out of breath and a little flushed, with her hat slightly awry and an anxious look on her pretty face, and say: 'I'm

terribly sorry to have made you wait about, I got
involved in . . .'

The building seemed to be emptying out. Feliks
wondered what to do next. He went outside and down
the steps to the pavement. There was no sign of her.
He went back up the steps and was stopped at the door
by an attendant. 'Too late, mate,' the man said. 'We're
closing.' Feliks turned away.

He could not wait about on the steps, in the hope
that she would come later, for he would be too conspicuous right here in Trafalgar Square. Anyway, she was
now two hours late: she was not going to come.

She was not going to come.

Face it, he thought: she has decided to have nothing
more to do with me, and quite sensibly. But would she
not have come, if only to tell me that? She might have
sent a note—

She might have sent a note.

She had Bridget's address. She *would* have sent a note.

Feliks headed north.

He walked through the alleys of Theatreland and
the quiet squares of Bloomsbury. The weather was
changing. All the time he had been in England it had
been sunny and warm, and he had yet to see rain. But
for the last day or so the atmosphere had seemed
oppressive, as if a storm were slowly gathering.

He thought: I wonder what it is like to live in
Bloomsbury, in this prosperous middle-class atmosphere, where there is always enough to eat and money
left over for books. But after the revolution we will take
down the railings around the parks.

He had a headache. He had not suffered headaches since childhood. He wondered whether it was caused by the stormy air. More likely it was worry. After the revolution, he thought, headaches will be prohibited.

Would there be a note from her waiting at Bridget's house? He imagined it. 'Dear Mr Kschessinsky, I regret I am unable to keep our appointment today. Yours truly, Lady Charlotte Walden.' No, it would surely not be like that. 'Dear Feliks, Prince Orlov is staying at the home of the Russian Naval Attaché, 25A Wilton Place, second floor, left front bedroom. Your affectionate friend, Charlotte.' That was more like it. 'Dear Father, Yes – I have learned the truth. But my "Papa" has locked me in my room. Please come and rescue me. Your loving daughter, Charlotte Kschessinsky.' Don't be a damned fool.

He reached Cork Street and looked along the road. There were no policemen guarding the house, no hefty characters in plain clothes reading newspapers outside the pub. It looked safe. His heart lifted. There's something marvellous about a warm welcome from a woman, he thought, whether she's a slip of a girl like Charlotte or a fat old witch like Bridget. I've spent too much of my life with men – or alone.

He knocked on Bridget's door. As he waited, he looked down at the window of his old basement room, and saw that there were new curtains. The door opened.

Bridget looked at him and smiled widely. 'It's my favourite international terrorist, begod,' she said. 'Come in, you darling man.'

He went into her parlour.

'Do you want some tea? It's hot.'

'Yes, please.' He sat down. 'Did the police trouble you?'

'I was interrogated by a superintendent. You must be a big cheese.'

'What did you tell him?'

She looked contemptuous. 'He'd left his truncheon at home – he got nothing out of me.'

Feliks smiled. 'Have you got a letter—'

But she was still talking. 'Did you want your room back? I've let it to another fellow, but I'll chuck him out – he's got side-whiskers, and I never could abide side-whiskers.'

'No, I don't want my room—'

'You've been sleeping rough, I can tell by the look on you.'

'That's right.'

'Whatever it was you came to London to do, you haven't done it yet.'

'No.'

'Something's happened – you've changed.'

'Yes.'

'What, then?'

He was suddenly grateful for someone to whom he could talk about it. 'Years ago I had a love affair. I didn't know it, but the woman had a baby. A few days ago . . . I met my daughter.'

'Ah.' She looked at him with pity in her eyes. 'You poor bugger. As if you didn't have enough on your mind already. Is she the one that wrote the letter?'

Feliks gave a grunt of satisfaction. 'There's a letter.'

'I supposed that's what you came for.' She went to the mantelpiece and reached behind the clock. 'And is the poor girl mixed up with oppressors and tyrants?'

'Yes.'

'I thought so from the crest. You don't get much luck, do you?' She handed him the letter.

Feliks saw the crest on the back of the envelope. He ripped it open. Inside were two pages covered with neat, stylish handwriting.

> *Walden Hall*
> *July 1st, 1914*

Dear Feliks,

> *By the time you get this you will have waited in vain for me at our rendezvous. I am most awfully sorry to let you down. Unfortunately I was seen with you on Monday and it is assumed I have a clandestine lover!!!*

If she's in trouble she seems cheerful enough about it, Feliks thought.

> *I have been banished to the country for the rest of the season. However, it is a blessing in disguise. Nobody would tell me where Aleks was, but now I know because he is here!!!*

Feliks was filled with savage triumph. 'So that's where the rats have their nest.'

Bridget said: 'Is this child helping you?'

'She was my only hope.'

'Then you deserve to look troubled.'
'I know.'

Take a train from Liverpool Street Station to Walden-hall Halt. This is our village. The house is three miles out of the village on the north road. However, don't come to the house of course!!! On the left-hand side of the road you will see a wood. I always ride through the wood, along the bridle path, before breakfast between 7 and 8 o'clock. I will look out for you each day until you come.

Once she decided whose side she was on, Feliks thought, there were no half measures.

I'm not sure when this will get sent. I will put it on the hall table as soon as I see some other letters for posting there: that way, nobody will see my handwriting on an envelope, and the footman will just pick it up along with all the rest when he goes to the post office.

'She's a brave girl,' Feliks said aloud.

I am doing this because you are the only person I ever met who talks sense to me.
Yours most affectionately,
Charlotte.

Feliks sat back in his seat and closed his eyes. He was so proud of her, and so ashamed of himself, that he felt close to tears.

Bridget took the letter from his unresisting fingers and began to read.

'So she doesn't know you're her father,' she said.

'No.'

'Why is she helping you, then?'

'She believes in what I'm doing.'

Bridget made a disgusted noise. 'Men like yourself always find women to help them. I should know, bechrist.' She read on. 'She writes like a schoolgirl.'

'Yes.'

'How old is she?'

'Eighteen.'

'Old enough to know her own mind. Aleks is the one you're after?'

Feliks nodded.

'What is he?'

'A Russian prince.'

'Then he deserves to die.'

'He's dragging Russia into war.'

Bridget nodded. 'And you're dragging Charlotte into it.'

'Do you think I'm doing wrong?'

She handed the letter back to him. She seemed angry. 'We'll never be sure, will we?'

'Politics is like that.'

'Life is like that.'

Feliks tore the envelope in half and dropped it in the waste-paper basket. He intended to rip up the letter but he could not bring himself to do it. When it's all over, he thought, this may be all I have to remember her by. He folded the two sheets of paper and put them in his coat pocket.

He stood up. 'I've got a train to catch.'

'Do you want me to make you a sandwich to take with you?'

He shook his head. 'Thank you, I'm not hungry.'

'Have you money for your fare?'

'I never pay train fares.'

She put her hand into the pocket of her apron and took out a sovereign. 'Here. You can buy a cup of tea as well.'

'It's a lot of money.'

'I can afford it this week. Away with you before I change my mind.'

Feliks took the coin and kissed her goodbye. 'You have been kind to me.'

'It's not for you, it's for my Sean, God rest his merry soul.'

'Goodbye.'

'Good luck to you, boy.'

Feliks went out.

Walden was in an optimistic mood as he entered the Admiralty building. He had done what he had promised: he had sold Constantinople to Aleks. The previous afternoon Aleks had sent a message to the Czar recommending acceptance of the British offer. Walden was confident that the Czar would follow the advice of his favourite nephew, especially after the assassination in Sarajevo. He was not so sure that Lloyd George would bend to the will of Asquith.

He was shown into the office of the First Lord of the Admiralty. Churchill bounced up out of his chair and came around his desk to shake hands. 'We sold it to Lloyd George,' he said triumphantly.

'That's marvellous!' Walden said. 'And I sold it to Orlov!'

'I knew you would. Sit down.'

I might have known better than to expect a thank you, Walden thought. But even Churchill could not damp his spirits today. He sat on a leather chair and glanced around the room, at the charts on the walls and the naval memorabilia on the desk. 'We should hear from St Petersburg at any time,' he said. 'The Russian Embassy will send a note directly to you.'

'The sooner the better,' Churchill said. 'Count Hoyos has been to Berlin. According to our intelligence, he took with him a letter asking the Kaiser whether Germany would support Austria in a war against Serbia. Our intelligence also says the answer was yes.'

'The Germans don't want to fight Serbia—'

'No,' Churchill interrupted, 'they want an excuse to fight France. Once Germany mobilizes, France will mobilize, and that will be Germany's pretext for invading France. There's no stopping it now.'

'Do the Russians know all this?'

'We've told 'em. I hope they believe us.'

'Can nothing be done to make peace?'

'Everything is being done,' Churchill said. 'Edward Grey is working night and day, as are our ambassadors in Berlin, Paris, Vienna and St Petersburg. Even the King is firing off telegrams to his cousins, Kaiser "Willy" and Czar "Nicky". It'll do no good.'

There was a knock at the door, and a young male secretary came in with a piece of paper. 'A message from the Russian Ambassador, sir,' he said.

Walden tensed.

Churchill glanced at the paper and looked up with triumph in his eyes. 'They've accepted.'

Walden beamed. 'Bloody good show!'

The secretary went out. Churchill stood up. 'This calls for a whisky-and-soda. Will you join me?'

'Certainly.'

Churchill opened a cupboard. 'I'll have the treaty drafted overnight and bring it down to Walden Hall tomorrow afternoon. We can have a little signing ceremony tomorrow night. It will have to be ratified by the Czar and Asquith, of course, but that's a formality – so long as Orlov and I sign as soon as possible.'

The secretary knocked and came in again. 'Mr Basil Thomson is here, sir.'

'Show him in.'

Thomson came in and spoke without preamble. 'We've picked up the trail of our anarchist again.'

'Good!' said Walden.

Thomson sat down. 'You'll remember that I put a man in his old basement room in Cork Street, just in case he should go back there.'

'I remember,' Walden said.

'He did go back there. When he left, my man followed him.'

'Where did he go?'

'To Liverpool Street Station.' Thomson paused. 'And he bought a ticket to Waldenhall Halt.'

CHAPTER THIRTEEN

WALDEN WENT cold.

His first thought was for Charlotte. She was vulnerable there: the bodyguards were concentrating on Aleks, and she had nobody to protect her but her servants. How could I have been so stupid? he thought.

He was nearly as worried for Aleks. The boy was almost like a son to Walden. He thought he was safe in Walden's home – and now Feliks was on his way there, with a gun or a bomb, to kill him, and perhaps Charlotte too, and sabotage the treaty—

Walden burst out: 'Why the devil haven't you stopped him?'

Thomson said mildly: 'I don't think it's a good idea for one man alone to go up against our friend Feliks, do you? We've seen what he can do against several men. He seems not to care about his own life. My chappie has instructions to follow him and report.'

'It's not enough—'

'I *know*, my lord,' Thomson interrupted.

Churchill said: 'Let us be calm, gentlemen. At least we know where the fellow is. With all the resources of His Majesty's Government at our disposal we shall catch him. What do you propose, Thomson?'

'As a matter of fact I've already done it, sir. I spoke by telephone with the chief constable of the county. He will have a large detachment of men waiting at Waldenhall Halt to arrest Feliks as he gets off the train. Meanwhile, in case anything should go wrong, my chappie will stick to him like glue.'

'That won't do,' Walden said. 'Stop the train and arrest him before he gets anywhere near my home.'

'I did consider that,' Thomson said. 'The dangers outweigh the advantages. Much better to let him go on thinking he's safe, then catch him unawares.'

Churchill said, 'I agree.'

'It's not your home!' Walden said.

'You're going to have to leave this to the professionals,' Churchill said.

Walden realized he could not overrule them. He stood up. 'I shall motor to Walden Hall immediately. Will you come, Thomson?'

'Not tonight. I'm going to arrest the Callahan woman. Once we've caught Feliks, we have to mount a prosecution, and she may be our chief witness. I'll come down tomorrow to interrogate Feliks.'

'I don't know how you can be so confident,' Walden said angrily.

'We'll catch him this time,' Thomson said.

'I hope to God you're right.'

The train steamed into the falling evening. Feliks watched the sun setting over the English cornfields. He was not young enough to take mechanical transport for granted: he still found travelling by train almost magical. The boy who had walked in clogs across the muddy Russian meadows could not have dreamed this.

He was alone in the carriage but for a young man who seemed intent on reading every line of that evening's *Pall Mall Gazette*. Feliks' mood was almost gay. Tomorrow morning he would see Charlotte. How fine she would look on a horse, with the wind streaming her hair. They would be working together. She would tell him where Orlov's room was, where he was to be found at different times of day. She would help him get hold of a weapon.

It was her letter that had made him so cheerful, he realized. She was on *his* side now, come what may. Except—

Except that he had told her he was going to kidnap Orlov. Each time he recalled this he wanted to squirm in his seat. He tried to put it out of his mind, but the thought was like an itch that could not be ignored and had to be scratched. Well, he thought, what is to be done? I must begin to prepare her for the news, at least. Perhaps I should tell her that I am her father. What a shock it will be!

For a moment he was tempted by the idea of going away, vanishing, and never seeing her again; leaving her in peace. No, he thought; that is not her destiny, nor is it mine.

I wonder what *is* my destiny, after the killing of Orlov? Shall I die? He shook his head, as if he could get rid of the thought like shaking off a fly. This was not time for gloom. He had plans to make.

How will I kill Orlov? There will be guns to steal in an earl's country house: Charlotte can tell me where they are, or bring me one. Failing that there will be knives in the kitchen. And I have my bare hands.

He flexed his fingers.

Will I have to go into the house, or will Orlov come out? Shall I do it by day or by night? Shall I kill Walden too? Politically the death of Walden would make no difference, but I should like to kill him anyway. So it's personal – so what?

He thought again of Walden catching the bottle. Don't underestimate that man, he told himself.

I must be careful that Charlotte has an alibi – no one must ever know she helped me.

The train slowed down and entered a little country station. Feliks tried to recall the map he had looked at in Liverpool Street Station. He seemed to remember that Waldenhall Halt was the fourth station after this one.

His travelling companion at last finished the *Pall Mall Gazette* and put it down on the seat beside him. Feliks decided that he could not plan the assassination until he had seen the lie of the land, so he said: 'May I read your newspaper?'

The man seemed startled. Englishmen did not speak to strangers on trains, Feliks recalled. 'By all means,' the man said.

Feliks had learned that this phrase meant yes. He picked up the paper. 'Thank you.'

He glanced at the headlines. His companion stared out of the window, as if embarrassed. He had the kind of facial hair that had been fashionable when Feliks was a boy. Feliks tried to remember the English word . . . 'side-whiskers', that was it.

Side-whiskers.

Did you want your room back? I've let it to another fellow, but I'll chuck him out – he's got side-whiskers, and I never could abide side-whiskers.

And now Feliks recalled that this man had been behind him in the queue at the ticket office.

He felt a stab of fear.

He held the newspaper in front of his face in case his thoughts should show in his expression. He made himself think calmly and clearly. Something Bridget had said had made the police suspicious enough to place a watch on her house. They had done that by the simple means of having a detective live in the room Feliks had vacated. The detective had seen Feliks call, had recognized him, and had followed him to the station. Standing behind Feliks in the queue, he had heard him ask for Waldenhall Halt and bought himself a ticket to the same destination. Then he had boarded the train along with Feliks.

No, not quite. Feliks had sat in the train for ten minutes or so before it pulled out. The man with the side-whiskers had jumped aboard at the last minute. What had he been doing in those few missing minutes?

He had probably made a telephone call.

Feliks imagined the conversation as the detective sat in the stationmaster's office speaking into a telephone:

'The anarchist returned to the house in Cork Street, sir. I'm following him now.'

'Where are you?'

'At Liverpool Street Station. He bought a ticket to Waldenhall Halt. He's on the train now.'

'Has it left?'

'Not for another . . . seven minutes.'

'Are there any police in the station?'

'Just a couple of bobbies.'

'It's not enough . . . this man is dangerous.'

'I can have the train delayed while you get a team down here.'

'Our anarchist might get suspicious and bolt for it. No. You stay with him . . .'

And what, Feliks wondered, would they do then? They could either take him off the train somewhere along the route, or wait to catch him at Waldenhall Halt.

Either way he had to get off the train, fast.

What to do about the detective? He must be left behind, on the train, unable to give the alarm, so that Feliks would have time to get clear.

I could tie him up, if I had anything to tie him with, Feliks thought. I could knock him out if I had something heavy and hard to hit him with. I could strangle him, but that would take time, and someone might see. I could throw him off the train, but I want to leave him on the train . . .

The train began to slow down. They might be waiting for me at the next station, he thought. I wish I had a weapon. Does the detective have a gun? I doubt it. I could break the window and use a shard of glass to cut his throat – but that would surely draw a crowd.

I must get off the train.

A few houses could be seen alongside the railway track. They were coming into a village or a small town. The brakes of the train squealed, and a station slid into view. Feliks watched intently for signs of a police trap. The platform appeared empty. The locomotive shuddered to a halt with a hiss of steam.

People began to get off. A handful of passengers walked past Feliks' window, heading for the exit: a family with two small children, a woman with a hat-box, a tall man in tweeds.

I could hit the detective, he thought, but it's so hard to knock somebody unconscious just with your fists.

The police trap could be at the next station. I must get off now.

A whistle blew.

Feliks stood up.

The detective looked startled.

Feliks said: 'Is there a lavatory on the train?'

The detective was thrown by this. 'Er . . . sure to be,' he said.

'Thank you.' He doesn't know whether to believe me, Feliks thought.

He stepped out of the compartment and into the corridor.

He ran to the end of the carriage. The train chuffed and jerked forward. Feliks looked back. The detective poked his head out of the compartment. Feliks went into the lavatory, and came back out again. The detective was still watching. The train moved a little faster. Feliks went to the carriage door. The detective came running.

Feliks turned back and punched him full in the face. The blow stopped the detective in his tracks. Feliks hit him again, in the stomach. A woman screamed. Feliks got him by the coat and dragged him into the lavatory. The detective struggled and threw a wild punch which caught Feliks in the ribs and made him gasp. He got the detective's head in his hands and banged it against the edge of the washbasin. The train picked up speed. Feliks banged the detective's head again, and then again. The man went limp. Feliks dropped him and stepped out of the lavatory. He went to the door and opened it. The train was moving at running speed. A woman at the other end of the corridor watched him, white-faced. Feliks jumped. The door banged shut behind him. He landed running. He stumbled and regained his balance. The train moved on, faster and faster.

Feliks walked to the exit.

'You left it a bit late,' said the ticket man.

Feliks nodded and handed over his ticket.

'This ticket takes you three more stations,' the ticket man said.

'I changed my mind at the last minute.'

There was a squeal of brakes. They both looked along the track. The train was stopping: someone had pulled the emergency brake. The ticket man said: 'Here, what's going on?'

Feliks forced himself to shrug unconcernedly. 'Search me,' he said. He wanted to run, but that would be the worst thing he could do.

The ticket man hovered, torn between his suspicion of Feliks and his concern for the train. Finally he said: 'You wait here,' and ran along the platform. The train stopped a couple of hundred yards out of the station. Feliks watched the ticket man run to the end of the platform and down on to the embankment.

He looked around. He was alone. He walked briskly out of the station and into the town.

A few minutes later a car with three policemen in it went past him at top speed, heading for the station.

On the outskirts of the town Feliks climbed over a gate and went into a cornfield, where he lay down to wait for nightfall.

The big Lanchester roared up the drive to Walden Hall. All the lights were on in the house. A uniformed policeman stood at the door, and another was patrolling, sentry-fashion, along the terrace. Pritchard brought the car to a halt. The policeman at the entrance stood to attention and saluted. Pritchard opened the car door and Walden got out.

Mrs Braithwaite, the housekeeper, came out of the house to greet him. 'Good evening, my lord.'

'Hello, Mrs Braithwaite. Who's here?'

'Sir Arthur is in the drawing-room with Prince Orlov.'

Walden nodded and they entered the house

together. Sir Arthur Langley was the Chief Constable and an old school friend of Walden's.

'Have you dined, my lord?' said Mrs Braithwaite.

'No.'

'Perhaps a piece of game pie, and a bottle of burgundy?'

'I leave it to you.'

'Very good, my lord.'

Mrs Braithwaite went away and Walden entered the drawing-room. Aleks and Sir Arthur were leaning on the mantelpiece with brandy glasses in their hands. Both wore evening dress.

Sir Arthur said: 'Hello, Stephen. How are you?'

Walden shook his hand. 'Did you catch the anarchist?'

'I'm afraid he slipped through our fingers—'

'Damnation!' Walden exclaimed. 'I was afraid of that! No one would listen to me.' He remembered his manners, and shook hands with Aleks. 'I don't know what to say to you, dear boy – you must think we're a lot of fools.' He turned back to Sir Arthur. 'What the devil happened, anyway?'

'Feliks hopped off the train at Tingley.'

'Where was Thomson's precious detective?'

'In the lavatory with a broken head.'

'Marvellous,' Walden said bitterly. He slumped into a chair.

'By the time the town constabulary had been roused, Feliks had melted away.'

'He's on his way here, do you realize that?'

'Yes, of course,' said Sir Arthur in a soothing tone.

'Your men should be instructed that next time he is sighted he's to be shot.'

'Ideally, yes – but of course they don't have guns.'

'They damn well should have!'

'I think you're right, but public opinion—'

'Before we discuss that, tell me what is being done.'

'Very well. I've got five patrols covering the roads between here and Tingley.'

'They won't see him in the dark.'

'Perhaps not, but at least their presence will slow him down, if not stop him altogether.'

'I doubt it. What else?'

'I've brought a constable and a sergeant to guard the house.'

'I saw them outside.'

'They'll be relieved every eight hours, day and night. The Prince already has two bodyguards from the Special Branch, and Thomson is sending four more down here by car tonight. They'll take twelve-hour shifts, so he'll always have three men with him. My men aren't armed but Thomson's are – they have revolvers. My recommendation is that until Feliks is caught, Prince Orlov should remain in his room and be served his food and so on by the bodyguards.'

Aleks said: 'I will do that.'

Walden looked at him. He was pale but calm. He's very brave, Walden thought. If I were he, I should be raging about the incompetence of the British police. Walden said: 'I don't think a few bodyguards is enough. We need an army.'

'We'll have one by tomorrow morning,' Sir Arthur

replied. 'We're mounting a search, beginning at nine o'clock.'

'Why not at dawn?'

'Because the army has to be mustered. A hundred and fifty men will be coming here from all over the county. Most of them are now in bed – they have to be visited and given their instructions, and they have to make their ways here.'

Mrs Braithwaite came in with a tray. There was cold game pie, half a chicken, a bowl of potato salad, bread rolls, cold sausages, sliced tomatoes, a wedge of Cheddar cheese, several kinds of chutney and some fruit. A footman followed with a bottle of wine, a jug of milk, a pot of coffee, a dish of ice-cream, an apple tart and half of a large chocolate cake. The footman said: 'I'm afraid the burgundy hasn't had time to breathe, my lord – shall I decant it?'

'Yes, please.'

The footman fussed with a small table and a place setting. Walden was hungry but he felt too tense to eat. I don't suppose I shall be able to sleep, either, he thought.

Aleks helped himself to more brandy. He is drinking steadily, Walden realized. His movements were deliberate and machine-like, as if he had himself rigidly under control.

'Where is Charlotte?' Walden said suddenly.

Aleks answered: 'She went to bed.'

'She mustn't leave the house while all this is going on.'

Mrs Braithwaite said: 'Shall I tell her, my lord?'

370

'No don't wake her. I'll see her at breakfast.' Walden took a sip of wine, hoping it would relax him a little. 'We could move you again, Aleks, if it would make you feel better.'

Aleks gave a tight little smile. 'I don't think there's much point, do you? Feliks always manages to find me. The best plan is for me to hide in my room, sign the treaty as soon as possible, and then go home.'

Walden nodded. The servants went out. Sir Arthur said: 'Um, there is something else, Stephen.' He seemed embarrassed. 'I mean, the question of just what made Feliks suddenly catch a train to Waldenhall Halt.'

In all the panic Walden had not even considered that. 'Yes – how in Heaven's name did he find out?'

'As I understand it, only two groups of people knew where Prince Orlov had gone. One is the embassy staff, who of course have been passing telegrams and so on to and fro. The other group is your people here.'

'A traitor among my servants?' Walden said. The thought was chilling.

'Yes,' said Sir Arthur hesitantly. 'Or, of course, among the family.'

Lydia's dinner party was a disaster. With Stephen away, his brother George had to sit in as host, which made the numbers uneven. More seriously, Lydia was so distracted that her conversation was barely polite, let alone sparkling. All but the most kind-hearted guests asked after Charlotte, knowing full well that she was in disgrace. Lydia just said that she had gone to the country for a few days' rest. She spoke mechanically, hardly knowing what she was saying. Her mind was full of nightmares: Feliks being arrested, Stephen being shot, Feliks being beaten, Stephen bleeding, Feliks running, Stephen dying. She longed to tell someone how she felt, but with her guests she could talk only of last night's ball, the prospects for the Cowes Regatta, the Balkan situation and Lloyd George's budget.

Fortunately they did not linger after dinner: they were all going to a ball, or a crush, or a concert. As soon as the last one had left Lydia went into the hall and picked up the telephone. She could not speak to Stephen, for Walden Hall was not yet on the telephone, so she called Winston Churchill's home in Eccleston Square. He was out. She tried the Admiralty, Number Ten, and the National Liberal Club without success. She *had* to know what had happened. Finally she thought of Basil Thomson, and she telephoned Scotland Yard. Thomson was still at his desk, working late.

'Lady Walden, how are you?' he said.

Lydia thought: People *will* be polite! She said: 'What is the news?'

'Bad, I'm afraid. Our friend Feliks has slipped through our fingers again.'

Relief washed over Lydia in a tidal wave. 'Thank . . . thank you,' she said.

'I don't think you need to worry too much,' Thomson went on. 'Prince Orlov is well guarded, now.'

Lydia blushed with shame: she had been so pleased that Feliks was all right that she had momentarily forgotten to worry about Aleks and Stephen. 'I . . . I'll try not to worry,' she said. 'Good night.'

'Good night, Lady Walden.'

She put down the telephone.

She went upstairs and rang for her maid to come and unlace her. She felt distraught. Nothing was resolved, everyone she loved was still in danger. How long could it go on? Feliks would not give up, she was sure, unless he got caught.

The maid came and unbuttoned her gown and unlaced her corset. Some ladies confided in their maids, Lydia knew. She did not. She had once, in St Petersburg . . .

She decided to write to her sister, for it was too early to go to bed. She told the maid to bring writing paper from the morning-room. She put on a wrap and sat by the open window, staring into the darkness of the park. The evening was close. It had not rained for three months, but during the last few days the weather had become thundery, and soon there would surely be storms.

The maid brought paper, pens, ink and envelopes. Lydia took a sheet of paper and wrote: *Dear Tatyana*—

She did not know where to begin. How can I explain about Charlotte, she thought, when I don't understand her myself? And I daren't say anything about Feliks, for

Tatyana might tell the Czar, and if the Czar knew how close Aleks had come to being killed . . .

Feliks is so *clever*. How on earth did he find out where Aleks is hiding? We wouldn't even tell Charlotte!

Charlotte.

Lydia went cold.

Charlotte?

She stood upright and cried: 'Oh, no!'

He was about forty, and wearing a tweed cap.

A sense of inevitable horror possessed her. It was like one of those crucifying dreams in which you think of the worst thing that could possibly happen and that thing immediately begins to happen: the ladder falls, the child is run over, the loved one dies.

She buried her face in her hands. She felt dizzy.

I must think, I must try to *think*.

Please, God, help me think.

Charlotte met a man in the National Gallery. That evening, she asked me where Aleks was. I didn't tell her. Perhaps she asked Stephen, too: he wouldn't have told her. Then she was sent home, to Walden Hall, and of course she discovered that Aleks was there. Two days later Feliks went to Waldenhall Halt.

Make this be a dream, she prayed; make me wake up, now, please, and find myself in my own bed, make it be morning.

It was not a dream. Feliks was the man in the tweed cap. Charlotte had met her father. They had been holding hands.

It was horrible, horrible.

Had Feliks told Charlotte the truth, had he said: 'I

am your real father,' had he revealed the secret of nineteen years? Did he even know? Surely he must have. Why else would she be ... collaborating with him?

My daughter, conspiring with an anarchist to commit murder.

She must be helping him still.

What can I do? I must warn Stephen – but how can I do that without telling him he's not Charlotte's father? I wish I could *think*.

She rang for her maid again. I must find a way to put an end to this, she thought. I don't know what I'm going to do but I must do something. When the maid came she said: 'Start packing. I shall leave first thing in the morning. I have to go to Walden Hall.'

After dark Feliks headed across the fields. It was a warm, humid night, and very dark: heavy cloud hid the stars and the moon. He had to walk slowly for he was almost blind. He found his way to the railway line and turned north.

Walking along the tracks he could go a little faster, for there was a faint shine on the steel lines, and he knew there would be no obstacles. He passed through dark stations, creeping along the deserted platforms. He heard rats in the empty waiting-rooms. He had no fear of rats: once upon a time he had killed them with his hands and eaten them. The names of the stations were stamped on sheet-metal signs, and he could read them by touch.

When he reached Waldenhall Halt he recalled Charlotte's directions: *The house is three miles out of the village on the north road.* The railway line was running roughly north-north-east. He followed it another mile or so, measuring the distance by counting his paces. He had reached one thousand six hundred when he bumped into someone.

The man gave a shout of surprise and then Feliks had him by the throat.

An overpowering smell of beer came from the man. Feliks realized he was just a drunk going home, and relaxed his grip.

'Don't be frightened,' the man said in a slurred voice.

'All right,' Feliks said. He let go.

'It's the only way I can get home see, without getting lost.'

'On your way, then.'

The man moved on. A moment later he said: 'Don't go to sleep on the line – the milk train comes at four o'clock.'

Feliks made no reply and the drunk shuffled off.

Feliks shook his head, disgusted with himself for being so jumpy: he might have killed the man. He was weak with relief. This would not do.

He decided to find the road. He moved off the railway line, stumbled across a short stretch of rough ground, then came up against a flimsy three-wire fence. He waited for a moment. What was in front of him? A field? Someone's back garden? The village

green? There was no darkness like a dark night in the
country, with the nearest street light a hundred miles
away. He heard a sudden movement close to him, and
out of the corner of his eye he saw something white.
He bent down and fumbled on the ground until he
found a small stone, then threw it in the direction of
the white thing. There was a whinny, and a horse
cantered away.

Feliks listened. If there were dogs near by the whinny
ought to make them bark. He heard nothing.

He stooped and clambered through the fence. He
walked slowly across the paddock. Once he stumbled
into a bush. He heard another horse but did not see it.

He came up against another wire fence, climbed
through it, and bumped into a wooden building.
Immediately there was a tremendous noise of chickens
clucking. A dog started to bark. A light came on in the
window of a house. Feliks threw himself flat and lay
still. The light showed him that he was in a small
farmyard. He had bumped into the hen-house. Beyond
the farmhouse he could see the road he was looking
for. The chickens quieted, the dog gave a last disappointed howl, and the light went out. Feliks walked to
the road.

It was a dirt road bordered by a dry ditch. Beyond
the ditch there seemed to be woodland. Feliks remembered: *On the left hand side of the road you will see a wood.*
He was almost there.

He walked north along the uneven road, his hearing
strained for the sound of someone approaching. After

more than a mile he sensed that there was a wall on his left. A little farther on, the wall was broken by a gate, and he saw a light.

He leaned on the iron bars of the gate and peered through. There seemed to be a long drive. At its far end he could see, dimly illuminated by a pair of flickering lamps, the pillared portico of a vast house. As he watched, a tall figure walked across the front of the house: a sentry.

In that house, he thought, is Prince Orlov. I wonder which is his bedroom window?

Suddenly he heard the sound of a car approaching very fast. He ran back ten paces and threw himself into the ditch. A moment later the car's headlights swept along the wall and it pulled up in front of the gate. Someone got out.

Feliks heard knocking. There must be a gatehouse, he realized: he had not seen it in the darkness. A window was opened and a voice shouted: 'Who's there?'

Another voice replied: 'Police, from the Special Branch of Scotland Yard.'

'Just a minute.'

Feliks lay perfectly still. He heard footsteps as the man who had got out of the car moved around restlessly. A door was opened. A dog barked, and a voice said: 'Quiet, Rex!'

Feliks stopped breathing. Was the dog on a lead? Would it smell Feliks? Would it come snuffling along the ditch and find him and start to bark?

The iron gates creaked open. The dog barked again. The voice said: 'Shut *up*, Rex!'

A car door slammed and the car moved off up the drive. The ditch was dark again. Now, Feliks thought, if the dog finds me I can kill it and the gatekeeper and run away . . .

He tensed, ready to jump up as soon as he heard a snuffling sound near to his ear.

The gates creaked shut.

A moment later the gatehouse door slammed.

Feliks breathed again.

CHAPTER FOURTEEN

CHARLOTTE WOKE at six o'clock. She had
drawn back the curtains of her bedroom windows so that the first rays of the sun would shine on her
face and rouse her from sleep: it was a trick she had
used years ago, when Belinda was staying, and the two
of them had liked to roam around the house while the
grown-ups were still in bed and there was no one to tell
them to behave like little ladies.

Her first thought was for Feliks. They had failed to
catch him – he was so clever! Today he would surely be
waiting for her in the wood. She jumped out of bed
and looked outside. The weather had not yet broken:
he would have been dry in the night, anyway.

She washed in cold water and dressed quickly in a
long skirt, riding boots and a jacket. She never wore a
hat for these morning rides.

She went downstairs. She saw nobody. There would
be a maid or two in the kitchen, lighting fires and
heating water, but otherwise the servants were still in
bed. She went out of the south front door and almost
bumped into a large uniformed policeman.

'Heavens!' she exclaimed. 'Who are you?'

'Constable Stevenson, Miss.'

He called her *Miss* because he did not know who she was. 'I'm Charlotte Walden,' she said.

'Pardon me, m'lady.'

'That's all right. What are you doing here?'

'Guarding the house, m'lady.'

'Oh, I see: guarding the Prince, you mean. How reassuring. How many of you are there?'

'Two outside and four inside. The inside men are armed. But there'll be a lot more later.'

'How so?'

'Big search party, m'lady. I hear there'll be a hundred and fifty men here by nine. We'll get this anarchist chappie – never you fear.'

'How splendid.'

'Was you thinking of going riding, m'lady? I shouldn't, if I was you. Not today.'

'No, I shan't,' Charlotte lied.

She walked away, around the east wing of the house to the back. The stables were deserted. She went inside and found her mare, Spats, so called because of the white patches on her forelegs. She talked to her for a minute, stroking her nose, and gave her an apple. Then she saddled her, led her out of the stable, and mounted her.

She rode away from the back of the house and around the park in a wide circle, staying out of sight and out of earshot of the policeman. She galloped across the west paddock and jumped the low fence into the wood. She walked Spats through the trees until she came to the bridle path, then let her trot.

It was cool in the wood. The oak and beech trees

were heavy with leaf, shading the path. In the patches where the sun came through, dew rose from the ground like wisps of steam. Charlotte felt the heat of those stray sunbeams as she rode through them. The birds were very loud.

She thought: What can he do against a hundred and fifty men? His plan was impossible, now: Aleks was too well guarded and the hunt for Feliks was too well organized. At least Charlotte could warn him off.

She reached the far end of the wood without seeing him. She was disappointed: she had been sure he would be here today. She began to worry, for if she did not see him she could not warn him, and then he would surely be caught. But it was not yet seven o'clock: perhaps he had not begun to watch out for her. She dismounted and walked back, leading Spats. Perhaps Feliks had seen her and was waiting to check whether she had been followed. She stopped in a glade to watch a squirrel. They did not mind people, although they would run away from dogs. Suddenly she felt she was being watched. She turned around, and there he was, looking at her with a peculiarly sad expression.

He said: 'Hello, Charlotte.'

She went to him and held both his hands. His beard was quite full, now. His clothes were covered with bits of greenery. 'You look dreadfully tired,' she said in Russian.

'I'm hungry. Did you bring food?'

'Oh, dear, no!' She had brought an apple for her horse and nothing for Feliks. 'I didn't think of it.'

'Never mind. I've been hungrier.'

'Listen,' she said. 'You must go away, immediately. If you leave now you can escape.'

'Why should I escape? I want to kidnap Orlov.'

She shook her head. 'It's impossible, now. He has armed bodyguards, the house is patrolled by policemen, and by nine o'clock there will be a hundred and fifty men searching for you.'

He smiled. 'And if I escape, what will I do with the rest of my life?'

'But I won't help you commit suicide!'

'Let's sit on the grass,' he said. 'I have something to explain to you.'

She sat with her back against a broad oak tree. Feliks sat in front of her and crossed his legs, like a Cossack. Dappled sunlight played across his weary face. He spoke rather formally, in complete sentences which sounded as if they might have been rehearsed. 'I told you I was in love, once, with a woman called Lydia; and you said: "That's my mother's name." Do you remember?'

'I remember everything you've ever said to me.' She wondered what this was all about.

'It *was* your mother.'

She stared at him. 'You were in love with Mama?'

'More than that. We were lovers. She used to come to my rooms, alone – do you understand what I mean?'

Charlotte blushed with confusion and embarrassment. 'Yes, I do.'

'Her father, your grandfather, found out. The old Count had me arrested, then he forced your mother to marry Walden.'

'Oh, how terrible,' Charlotte said softly. For some reason she was frightened of what he might say next.

'You were born seven months after the wedding.'

He seemed to think that was very significant. Charlotte frowned.

Feliks said: 'Do you know how long it takes for a baby to grow and be born?'

'No.'

'It takes nine months, normally, although it can take less.'

Charlotte's heart was pounding. 'What are you getting at?'

'You might have been conceived before the wedding.'

'Does that mean you might be my father?' she said incredulously.

'There's more. You look *exactly* like my sister Natasha.'

Charlotte's heart seemed to rise into her throat and she could hardly speak. 'You think you *are* my father?'

'I'm sure of it.'

'Oh, God.' Charlotte put her face in her hands and stared into space, seeing nothing. She felt as if she were waking from a dream and could not yet make out which aspects of the dream had been real. She thought of Papa, but he was not her Papa; she thought of Mama, having a lover; she thought of Feliks, her friend and suddenly her father . . .

She said: 'Did they lie to me even about this?'

She was so disoriented that she felt she would not be able to stand upright. It was as if someone had told her that all the maps she had ever seen were forgeries and she really lived in Brazil; or that the real owner of Walden Hall was Pritchard; or that horses could talk but merely kept silent by choice; but it was much worse than all those things. She said: 'If you were to tell me that I am a boy, but my mother always dressed me in girl's clothing . . . it would be like this.'

She thought: Mama . . . and Feliks? That made her blush again.

Feliks took her hand and stroked it. He said: 'I suppose all the love and concern that a man normally gives to his wife and children went, in my case, into politics. I have to try to get Orlov, even if it's impossible; the way a man would have to try to save his child from drowning, even if the man could not swim.'

Charlotte suddenly realized how confused Feliks must feel about *her*, the daughter he never really had. She understood, now, the odd, painful way he had looked at her sometimes.

'You poor man,' she said.

He bit his lip. 'You have such a generous heart.'

She did not know why he should say that. 'What are we going to do?'

He took a deep breath. 'Could you get me inside the house and hide me?'

She thought for a moment. 'Yes,' she said.

He mounted the horse behind her. The beast shook its head and snorted, as if offended that it should be expected to carry a double weight. Charlotte urged it

385

into a trot. She followed the bridle path for a while, then turned off it at an angle and headed through the wood. They went through a gate, across a paddock, and into a little lane. Feliks did not yet see the house: he realized she was circling around it to approach from the north side.

She was an astonishing child. She had such strength of character. Had she inherited it from him? He wanted to think so. He was very happy to have told her the truth about her birth. He had the feeling she had not quite accepted it, but she would. She had listened to him turn her world upside down, and she had reacted with emotion but without hysteria – she did not get *that* kind of equanimity from her mother.

From the lane they turned into an orchard. Now, looking between the tops of the trees, Feliks could see the roofs of Walden Hall. The orchard ended in a wall. Charlotte stopped the horse and said: 'You'd better walk beside me from here. That way, if anyone should glance out of a window, they won't be able to see you very easily.'

Feliks jumped off. They walked alongside the wall and followed it around a corner. 'What's behind the wall?' Feliks asked.

'Kitchen garden. Better not talk, now.'

'You're marvellous,' Feliks whispered, but she did not hear.

They stopped at the next corner. Feliks could see some low buildings and a yard. 'The stables,' Charlotte murmured. 'Stay here for a moment. When I give you the signal, follow me as fast as you can.'

'Where are we going?'

'Over the roofs.'

She rode into the yard, dismounted, and looped the reins over a rail. Feliks watched her cross to the far side of the little yard, look both ways, then come back and look inside the stables.

He heard her say: 'Oh, hello, Peter.'

A boy of about twelve years came out, taking off his cap. 'Good morning, m'lady.'

Feliks thought: How will she get rid of him?

Charlotte said: 'Where's Daniel?'

'Having his breakfast, m'lady.'

'Go and fetch him, will you, and tell him to come and unsaddle Spats.'

'I can do it, m'lady.'

'No, I want Daniel,' Charlotte said imperiously. 'Off you go.'

Marvellous, Feliks thought.

The boy ran off. Charlotte turned toward Feliks and beckoned. He ran to her.

She jumped on to a low iron bunker, then climbed on to the corrugated tin roof of a lean-to shed, and from there got on to the slate roof of a one-storey stone building.

Felix followed.

They edged along the slate roof, moving sideways on all fours, until it ended up against a brick wall, then they crawled up the slope to the ridge of the roof.

Feliks felt dreadfully conspicuous and vulnerable.

Charlotte stood upright and peeped through a window in the brick wall.

Feliks whispered: 'What's in there?'

'Parlourmaids' bedroom. But they're downstairs by now, laying the breakfast table.'

She clambered on to the window-ledge and stood upright. The bedroom was an attic room and the window was in the gable end, so that the roof peaked just above the window and sloped down either side. Charlotte moved along the sill, then cocked her leg over the edge of the roof.

It looked dangerous. Feliks frowned, frightened that she would fall. But she hauled herself on to the roof with ease.

Feliks did the same.

'Now we're out of sight,' Charlotte said.

Feliks looked around. She was right: they could not be seen from the ground. He relaxed a fraction.

'There are four acres of roof,' Charlotte told him.

'Four acres! Most Russian peasants haven't got that much land.'

It was quite a sight. On all sides were roofs of every material, size and pitch. Ladders and strips of decking were provided so that people could move around without treading on the slates and tiles. The guttering was as complex as the piping in the oil refinery Feliks had seen at Batum. 'I've never seen such a big house,' he said.

Charlotte stood up. 'Come on, follow me.'

She led him up a ladder to the next roof, along a board footway, then up a short flight of wooden steps leading to a small, square door set in a wall. She said: 'At one time this must have been the way they got out on to the roofs for maintenance – but now everybody has forgotten about it.' She opened the door and crawled through.

Gratefully, Feliks followed her into the welcoming darkness.

Lydia borrowed a motor car and driver from her brother-in-law George and, having lain awake all night, left London very early. The car entered the drive at Walden Hall at nine o'clock, and she was astonished to see, in front of the house and spreading over the park, hundreds of policemen, dozens of vehicles, and scores of dogs. George's driver threaded the car through the crowd to the south front of the house. There was an enormous tea-urn on the lawn, and the policemen were queuing up with cups in their hands. Pritchard walked by carrying a mountain of sandwiches on a huge tray and looking harassed. He did not even notice that his mistress had arrived. A trestle table had been set up on the terrace, and behind it sat Stephen with Sir Arthur Langley, giving instructions to half a dozen police officers who stood in front of them in a semicircle. Lydia went over to them. Sir Arthur had a map in front of him. She heard him say: 'Each team will have a local man, to keep you on the correct route, and a motor-cyclist to dash back here and report progress every hour.' Stephen looked up, saw Lydia, and left the group to speak to her.

'Good morning, my dear, this is a pleasant surprise, how did you get here?'

'I borrowed George's car. What is going on?'

'Search parties.'

'Oh.' With all these men looking for him, how could Feliks possibly escape?

Stephen said: 'Still, I wish you had stayed in Town. I should have been happier for your safety.'

'And I should have spent every minute wondering whether bad news was on its way.' And what would count as good news? she wondered. Perhaps if Feliks were simply to give up and go away. But he would not do that, she was sure. She studied her husband's face. Beneath his customary poise there were signs of tiredness and tension. Poor Stephen: first his wife, and now his daughter, deceiving him. A guilty impulse made her reach up and touch his cheek. 'Don't wear yourself out,' she said.

A whistle blew. The policemen hastily drained their teacups, stuffed the remains of sandwiches into their mouths, put on their helmets, and formed themselves into six groups, each around a leader. Lydia stood with Stephen, watching. There were a lot of shouted orders and a good deal more whistling. Finally they began to move out. The first group went south, fanning out across the park, and entered the wood. Two more headed west, into the paddock. The other three groups went down the drive toward the road.

Lydia regarded her lawn. It looked like the site of a Sunday-school outing when all the children have gone home. Mrs Braithwaite began to organize the clearing-up with a pained expression on her face. Lydia went into the house.

She met Charlotte in the hall. Charlotte was surprised to see her. 'Hello, Mama,' she said. 'I didn't know you were coming down.'

'One gets so bored in Town,' Lydia said automatically, then she thought: What rubbish we talk.

'How did you get here?'

'I borrowed Uncle George's car.' Lydia saw that Charlotte was making small talk, and thinking of something else.

'You must have started very early,' Charlotte said.

'Yes.' Lydia wanted to say: Stop it! Let's not pretend! Why don't we speak the truth? But she could not bring herself to do it.

'Have all those policemen gone yet?' Charlotte asked. She was looking at Lydia in a strange way, as if seeing her for the first time. It made Lydia uncomfortable. I wish I could read my daughter's mind, she thought.

She replied: 'Yes, they've all gone.'

'Splendid.'

That was one of Stephen's words – splendid. There was, after all, something of Stephen in Charlotte: the curiosity, the determination, the poise – since she had not inherited those things, she must have acquired them simply by imitating him . . .

Lydia said: 'I hope they catch this anarchist,' and watched Charlotte's reaction.

'I'm sure they will,' Charlotte said gaily.

She's very bright-eyed, Lydia thought. Why should she look that way, when hundreds of policemen are combing the county for Feliks? Why is she not

391

depressed and anxious, as I am? It must be that she does *not* expect them to catch him. For some reason she thinks he is safe.

Charlotte said: 'Tell me something, Mama. How long does it take for a baby to grow and be born?'

Lydia's mouth fell open and the blood drained from her face. She stared at Charlotte, thinking: She knows! She knows!

Charlotte smiled and nodded, looking faintly sad. 'Never mind,' she said. 'You've answered my question.' She went on down the stairs.

Lydia held on to the banister, feeling faint. Feliks had told Charlotte. It was just too cruel, after all these years. She felt angry at Feliks: why had he ruined Charlotte's life this way? The hall spun around her head, and she heard a maid's voice say: 'Are you all right, my lady?'

Her head cleared. 'A little tired, after the journey,' she said. 'Take my arm.'

The maid took her arm and together they walked upstairs to Lydia's room. Another maid was already unpacking Lydia's cases. There was hot water ready for her in the dressing-room. Lydia sat down. 'Leave me now, you two,' she said. 'Unpack later.'

The maids went out. Lydia unbuttoned her coat but did not have the energy to take it off. She thought about Charlotte's mood. It had been almost vivacious, even though there was obviously a lot on her mind. Lydia understood that; she recognized it; she had sometimes felt that way. It was the mood you were in when you had spent time with Feliks. You felt that life was endlessly fascinating and surprising, that there were important things to be done, that the world was full of colour and passion and change. Charlotte had seen Feliks, and she believed him to be safe.

Lydia thought: What am I going to do?

Wearily, she took off her clothes. She spent time washing and dressing again, taking the opportunity to calm herself. She wondered how Charlotte felt about Feliks being her father. She obviously liked him very much. People do, Lydia thought; people love him. Where had Charlotte got the strength to hear such news without collapsing?

Lydia decided she had better take care of the house-keeping. She looked in the mirror and composed her face, then she went out. On the way downstairs she met a maid with a tray laden with sliced ham, scrambled eggs, fresh bread, milk, coffee and grapes. 'Who is that for?' she asked.

'For Lady Charlotte, m'lady,' said the maid.

Lydia passed on. Had Charlotte not even lost her appetite? She went into the morning-room and sent for Cook. Mrs Rowse was a thin, nervous woman who never ate the kind of rich food she prepared for her employers. She said: 'I understand Mr Thomson will be arriving for lunch, m'lady, and Mr Churchill also for dinner.' Lydia discussed the menus with her, then sent her away. Why on earth was Charlotte having such a massive breakfast in her room? she wondered. And so late! In the country Charlotte was normally up early, and had finished breakfast before Lydia surfaced.

She sent for Pritchard and made the table plan with

him. Pritchard told her that Aleks was having all his meals in his room until further notice. It made little difference to the table plan: they still had too many men, and in the present situation Lydia could hardly invite people to make up the right numbers. She did the best she could, then sent Pritchard away.

Where had Charlotte seen Feliks? And why was she confident that he would not be caught? Had she found him a hiding-place? Was he in some impenetrable disguise?

She moved around the room, looking at the pictures, the little bronzes, the glass ornaments, the writing-desk. She had a headache. She began to rearrange the flowers in a big vase by the window, and knocked over the vase. She rang for someone to clear up the mess, then left the room.

Her nerves were very bad. She contemplated taking some laudanum. These days it did not help her as much as it had used to.

What will Charlotte do now? Will she keep the secret? Why don't children talk to one?

She went along to the library with the vague idea of getting a book to take her mind off everything. When she walked in she gave a guilty start on seeing that Stephen was there, at his desk. He looked up at her as she entered, smiled in a welcoming way, and went on writing.

Lydia wandered along the bookshelves. She wondered whether to read the Bible. There had been a great deal of Bible-reading in her childhood, and family prayers and much church-going. She had had stern nurses who were keen on the horrors of hell and the penalties of uncleanliness, and a Lutheran German governess who talked a great deal about sin. But, since Lydia had committed fornication and brought retribution upon herself and her daughter, she had never been able to take any consolation from religion. *I should have gone into that convent*, she thought, *and put myself right with God; my father's instinct was correct.*

She took a book at random and sat down with it open on her lap. Stephen said: 'That's an unusual choice for you.' He could not read the title from where he was sitting, but he knew where all the authors were placed on the shelves. He read so many books, Lydia did not know how he found the time. She looked at the spine of the book she was holding. It was Thomas Hardy's *Wessex Poems*. She did not like Hardy: did not like those determined, passionate women nor the strong men whom they made helpless.

They had often sat like this, she and Stephen, especially when they first came to Walden Hall. She recalled nostalgically how she would sit and read while he worked. He had been less tranquil in those days, she remembered: he used to say that nobody could make money out of agriculture any more, and that if this family were to continue to be rich and powerful it would have to get ready for the twentieth century. He had sold off some farms at that time, many thousands of acres at very low prices, then he had put the money into railroads and banks and London property. The plan must have worked, for he soon stopped looking worried.

It was after the birth of Charlotte that everything seemed to settle down. The servants adored the baby and loved Lydia for producing her. Lydia got used to English ways and was well liked by London society. There had been eighteen years of tranquillity.

Lydia sighed. Those years were coming to an end. For a while she had buried the secrets so successfully that they tormented nobody but her, and even she had been able to forget them at times; but now they were coming out. She had thought that London was at a safe distance from St Petersburg, but perhaps California would have been a better choice; or it might be that nowhere was far enough. The time of peace was over. It was all falling apart. What would happen now?

She looked down at the open page, and read:

> *She would have given a world to breathe 'yes' truly,*
> *So much his life seemed hanging on her mind,*
> *And hence she lied, her heart persuaded thoroughly*
> *'Twas worth her soul to be a moment kind.*

Is that me? she wondered. Did I give my soul when I married Stephen in order to save Feliks from incarceration in the Fortress of St Peter and St Paul? Ever since then I've been playing a part, pretending I'm not a wanton, sinful, brazen whore. But I am! And I'm not the only one. Other women feel the same. Why else would the Viscountess and Charlie Stott want adjoining bedrooms? And why would Lady Girard tell me about them with a wink, if she did not understand how they felt? If I had been just a little wanton, perhaps Stephen would have come to my bed more often, and we might have had a son. She sighed again.

'Penny for 'em,' Stephen said.

'What?'

'A penny for your thoughts.'

Lydia smiled. 'Will I never stop learning English expressions? I've never heard that one.'

'Nobody ever stops learning. It means tell me what you're thinking.'

'I was thinking about Walden Hall going to George's son when you die.'

'Unless we have a son.'

She looked at his face: the bright blue eyes, the neat grey beard. He was wearing a blue tie with white spots.

He said: 'Is it too late?'

'I don't know,' she said, thinking: That depends on what Charlotte does next.

'Do let's keep trying,' he said.

This was an unusually frank conversation: Stephen had sensed that she was in a mood to be candid. She got up from her chair and went over to stand beside him. He had a bald spot on the back of his head, she noticed. How long had that been there? 'Yes,' she said, 'let's keep trying.' She bent down and kissed his forehead: then, on impulse, she kissed his lips. He closed his eyes.

After a moment she broke away. He looked a little embarrassed: they rarely did this sort of thing during the day, for there were always so many servants about. She thought: Why do we live the way we do, if it doesn't make us happy? She said: 'I *do* love you.'

He smiled. 'I know you do.'

Suddenly she could stand it no longer. She said: 'I must go and change for lunch before Basil Thomson arrives.'

He nodded.

She felt his eyes following her as she left the room. She went upstairs, wondering whether there might still be a chance that she and Stephen could be happy.

She went into her bedroom. She was still carrying the book of poems. She put it down. Charlotte held the key to all this. Lydia had to talk to her. One *could* say difficult things, after all, if one had the courage; and what now was left to lose? Without having a clear idea of what she would say, she headed for Charlotte's room on the next floor.

Her footsteps made no noise on the carpet. She reached the top of the staircase and looked along the corridor. She saw Charlotte disappearing into the old nursery. She was about to call out, then stopped herself. What had Charlotte been carrying? It had looked very like a plate of sandwiches and a glass of milk.

Puzzled, Lydia went along to Charlotte's bedroom. There on the table was the tray Lydia had seen the maid carrying. All the ham and all the bread had gone. Why would Charlotte order a tray of food, then make sandwiches of it and eat it in the nursery? There was nothing in the nursery, as far as Lydia knew, except furniture covered with dust-sheets. Was Charlotte so anxious that she needed to retreat into the cosy world of childhood?

Lydia decided to find out. She felt uneasy about interrupting Charlotte's private ritual, whatever it was; but then she thought: It's my house, she's my daughter, and perhaps I ought to know. And it might create a moment of intimacy, and help me say what I need to say. So she left Charlotte's bedroom and went along the corridor and into the nursery.

Charlotte was not there.

Lydia looked around. There was the old rocking-horse, his ears making twin peaks in the dust-sheet. Through an open door she could see the schoolroom, with maps and childish drawings on the wall. Another door led to the bedroom: that, too, was empty but for shrouds. Will all this ever be used again? Lydia wondered. Will we have nurses, and nappies, and tiny, tiny clothes; and a nanny, and toy soldiers, and exercise books filled with clumsy handwriting and ink blots?

But where was Charlotte?

The closet door was open. Suddenly Lydia remembered: of course! Charlotte's hideaway! The little room she thought no one else knew of, where she used to go when she had been naughty. She had furnished it herself, with bits and pieces from around the house, and everyone had pretended not to know how certain things had disappeared. One of the few indulgent decisions Lydia had made was to allow Charlotte her hideaway, and to forbid Marya to 'discover' it; for Lydia herself hid away sometimes, in the flower-room, and she knew how important it was to have a place of your own.

So Charlotte still used that little room! Lydia moved closer, more reluctant now to disturb Charlotte's privacy, but tempted all the same. No, she thought; I'll leave her be.

Then she heard voices.

Was Charlotte talking to herself?

Lydia listened carefully.

Talking to herself in Russian?

Then there was another voice, a man's voice, replying in Russian, in low tones; a voice like a caress, a voice which sent a sexual shudder through Lydia's body.

Feliks was in there.

Lydia thought she would faint. Feliks! Within touching distance! Hidden, in Walden Hall, while the police searched the county for him! Hidden by Charlotte.

I mustn't scream!

She put her fist to her mouth and bit herself. She was shaking.

I must get away. I can't think straight. I don't know what to do.

Her head ached horribly. I need a dose of laudanum, she thought. That prospect gave her strength. She controlled her trembling. After a moment she tip-toed out of the nursery.

She almost ran along the corridor and down the stairs to her room. The laudanum was in the dresser. She opened the bottle. She could not hold the spoon steady, so she took a gulp directly from the bottle. After a few moments she began to feel calmer. She put the bottle and the spoon away and closed the drawer. A feeling of mild contentment began to come over her as her nerves settled down. Her head ached less. Nothing would really matter now for a while. She went to her wardrobe and opened the door. She stood staring at the rows of dresses, totally unable to make up her mind what to wear for lunch.

Feliks paced the tiny room like a caged tiger, three steps each way, bending his head to avoid the ceiling, listening to Charlotte.

'Aleks' door is always locked,' she said. 'There are two armed guards inside and one outside. The inside ones won't unlock the door unless their colleague outside tells them to.'

'One outside, and two inside.' Feliks scratched his head and cursed in Russian. Difficulties, there are always difficulties, he thought. Here I am, right in the house, with an accomplice in the household, and still it isn't easy. Why shouldn't I have the luck of those boys in Sarajevo? Why did it have to turn out that I'm a part of this family? He looked at Charlotte and thought: Not that I regret it.

She caught his look, and said: 'What?'

'Nothing. Whatever happens, I'm glad I found you.'

'Me too. But what are you going to do about Aleks?'

'Could you draw a plan of the house?'

Charlotte made a face. 'I can try.'

'You must know it, you've lived here all your life.'

'Well, I know this part, of course – but there are bits of the house I've never been in. The butler's bedroom, the housekeeper's rooms, the cellars, the place over the kitchens where they store flour and things . . .'

'Do your best. One plan for each floor.'

She found a piece of paper and a pencil among her childish treasures and knelt at the little table.

Feliks ate another sandwich and drank the rest of the milk. She had taken a long time to bring him the food because the maids had been working in her corridor. As he ate he watched her draw, frowning and biting the end of her pencil. At one point she said: 'One doesn't realize how difficult this is until one tries it.' She found an eraser among her old crayons and used it frequently. Feliks noticed that she was able to draw perfectly straight lines without using a rule. He found the sight of her like this very touching. So she must have sat, he thought, for years in the schoolroom, drawing houses, then Mama and 'Papa', and later the map of Europe, the leaves of the English trees, the park in winter . . . Walden must have seen her like this many times.

'Why have you changed your clothes?' Feliks asked.

'Oh, everybody has to change all the time here. Every hour of the day has its appropriate clothes, you see. You must show your shoulders at dinner-time but not at lunch. You must wear a corset for dinner but not for tea. You can't wear an indoors gown outside. You can wear woollen stockings in the library but not in the morning-room. You can't imagine the rules I have to remember.'

He nodded. He was no longer capable of being surprised by the degeneracy of the ruling class.

She handed him her sketches, and he became businesslike again. He studied them. 'Where are the guns kept?' he said.

She touched his arm. 'Don't be so abrupt,' she said. 'I'm on your side – remember?'

Suddenly she was grown-up again. Feliks smiled ruefully. 'I had forgotten,' he said.

'The guns are kept in the gun-room.' She pointed it out on the plan. 'You really did have an affair with Mama.'

'Yes.'

'I find it so hard to believe that she would do such a thing.'

'She was very wild, then. She still is, but she pretends otherwise.'

'You really think she's still like that?'

'I know it.'

'Everything, *everything* turns out to be different from how I thought it was.'

'That's called growing up.'

She was pensive. 'What should I call you, I wonder?'

'What do you mean?'

'I should feel very strange, calling you Father.'

'Feliks will do for now. You need time to get used to the idea of me as your father.'

'Shall I have time?'

Her young face was so grave that he held her hand. 'Why not?'

'What will you do when you have Aleks?'

He looked away so that she should not see the guilt in his eyes. 'That depends just how and when I kidnap him, but most likely I'll keep him tied up right here. You'll have to bring us food, and you'll have to send a telegram to my friends in Geneva, in code, telling them what has happened. Then, when the news has achieved what we want it to achieve, we'll let Orlov go.'

'And then?'

'They will look for me in London, so I'll go north. There seem to be some big towns – Birmingham, Manchester, Hull – where I could lose myself. After a few weeks I'll make my way back to Switzerland, then eventually to St Petersburg – that's the place to be, that's where the revolution will start.'

'So I'll never see you again.'

You won't want to, he thought. He said: 'Why not? I may come back to London. You may go to St Petersburg. We might meet in Paris. Who can tell? If there is such a thing as Fate, it seems determined to bring us together.' I wish I could believe this, I wish I could.

'That's true,' she said with a brittle smile, and he saw that she did not believe it either. She got to her feet. 'Now I must get you some water to wash in.'

'Don't bother. I've been a good deal dirtier than this. I don't mind.'

'But I do. You smell awful. I'll be back in a minute.'

With that she went out.

It was the dreariest luncheon Walden could remember in years. Lydia was in some kind of daze. Charlotte was

404

silent but uncharacteristically nervy, dropping her cutlery and knocking over a glass. Thomson was taciturn. Sir Arthur Langley attempted to be convivial but nobody responded. Walden himself was withdrawn, obsessed by the puzzle of how Feliks had found out that Aleks was at Walden Hall. He was tortured by the ugly suspicion that it had something to do with Lydia. After all, Lydia had told Feliks that Aleks was at the Savoy Hotel; and she had admitted that Feliks was 'vaguely familiar' from St Petersburg days. Could it be that Feliks had some kind of hold on her? She had been behaving oddly, as if distracted, all summer. And now, as he thought about Lydia in a detached way for the first time in nineteen years, he admitted to himself that she was sexually lukewarm. Of course, well-bred women were supposed to be like that; but he knew perfectly well that this was a polite fiction, and that women generally suffered the same longings as men. Was it that Lydia longed for someone else, someone from her past? That would explain all sorts of things which until now had not seemed to need explanation. It was perfectly horrible, he found, to look at his lifetime companion and see a stranger.

After lunch Sir Arthur went back to the Octagon, where he had set up his headquarters. Walden and Thomson put on their hats and took their cigars out on to the terrace. The park looked lovely in the sunshine, as always. From the distant drawing-room came the crashing opening chords of the Tchaikovsky piano concerto: Lydia was playing. Walden felt sad. Then the music was drowned by the roar of a motor-cycle as another messenger came to report the progress of the search to Sir Arthur. So far there had been no news.

A footman served coffee then left them alone. Thomson said: 'I didn't want to say this in front of Lady Walden, but I think we may have a clue to the identity of the traitor.'

Walden went cold.

Thomson said: 'Last night I interviewed Bridget Callahan, the Cork Street landlady. I'm afraid I got nothing out of her. However, I left my men to search her house. This morning they showed me what they had found.' He took from his pocket an envelope which had been torn in half, and handed the two pieces to Walden.

Walden saw with a shock that the envelope bore the Walden Hall crest.

Thomson said: 'Do you recognize the handwriting?'

Walden turned the pieces over. The envelope was addressed:

> *Mr F. Kschessinksy*
> *c/o 19 Cork Street*
> *London, N.*

Walden said: 'Oh, dear God, not Charlotte.' He wanted to cry.

Thomson was silent.

'She led him here,' Walden said. 'My own daughter.' He stared at the envelope, willing it to disappear. The handwriting was quite unmistakable, like a juvenile version of his own script.

'Look at the postmark,' Thomson said. 'She wrote it as soon as she arrived here. It was mailed from the village.'

'How could this happen?' Walden said.

Thomson made no reply.

'Feliks was the man in the tweed cap,' Walden said. 'It all fits.' He felt hopelessly sad, almost bereaved, as if someone dear to him had died. He looked out over his park, at trees planted fifty years ago by his father, at a lawn that had been cared for by his family for a hundred years, and it all seemed worthless, worthless. He said quietly: 'You fight for your country, and you are betrayed from within by socialists and revolutionists; you fight for your class, and you're betrayed by Liberals; you fight for your family, and even they betray you. Charlotte! Why, Charlotte, why?' He felt a choking sensation. 'What a damnable life this is, Thomson. What a damnable life.'

'I'll have to interview her,' Thomson said.

'So will I.' Walden stood up. He looked at his cigar. It had gone out. He threw it away. 'Let's go in.'

They went in.

In the hall Walden stopped a maid. 'Do you know where Lady Charlotte is?'

'I believe she's in her room, my lord. Shall I go and see?'

'Yes. Tell her I wish to speak to her in her room immediately.'

'Very good, m'lord.'

Thomson and Walden waited in the hall. Walden looked around. The marble floor, the carved staircase,

the stucco ceiling, the perfect proportions – worthless.
A footman drifted by silently, eyes lowered. A motorcycle messenger came in and headed for the Octagon.
Pritchard crossed the hall and picked up the letters for
posting from the hall table, just as he must have the day
Charlotte's treacherous letter to Feliks was written. The
maid came down the stairs.

'Lady Charlotte is ready to see you, my lord.'

Walden and Thomson went up.

Charlotte's room was on the second floor at the
front of the house, looking over the park. It was sunny
and light, with pretty fabrics and modern furniture. It's
a long time since I've been in here, Walden thought
vaguely.

'You look rather fierce, Papa,' Charlotte said.

'I've reason to be,' Walden replied. 'Mr Thomson
has just given me the most dreadful piece of news of
my whole life.'

Charlotte frowned.

Thomson said: 'Lady Charlotte, where is Feliks?'

Charlotte turned white. 'I've no idea, of course.'

Walden said: 'Don't be so damned cool!'

'How dare you swear at me!'

'I beg your pardon.'

Thomson said: 'Perhaps if you'd leave it to me, my
lord . . .'

'Very well.' Walden sat down in the window-seat,
thinking: How did I find myself apologizing?

Thomson addressed Charlotte. 'Lady Charlotte, I'm
a policeman, and I can prove that you have committed

conspiracy to murder. Now my concern, and your father's, is to let this go no farther; and, in particular, to ensure that you will not have to go to jail for a period of many years.'

Walden stared at Thomson. Jail! Surely he's merely frightening her. But no, he realized with a sense of overwhelming dread; he's right, she's a criminal . . .

Thomson went on: 'As long as we can prevent the murder, we feel we can cover up your participation. But, if the assassin succeeds, I will have no option but to bring you to trial – and then the charge will not be conspiracy to murder, but accessory to murder. In theory you could be hanged.'

'No!' Walden shouted involuntarily.

'Yes,' Thomson said quietly.

Walden buried his face in his hands.

Thomson said: 'You must save yourself that agony – and not only yourself, but your Mama and Papa. You must do everything in your power to help us find Feliks and save Prince Orlov.'

It could not be, Walden thought desperately. He felt as if he was going insane. My daughter could not be hanged. But if Aleks is killed Charlotte will have been one of the murderers. But it would never come to trial. Who was Home Secretary? McKenna. Walden did not know him. But Asquith would intervene to prevent a prosecution . . . wouldn't he?

Thomson said: 'Tell me when you last saw Feliks.'

Walden watched Charlotte, waiting for her response. She stood behind a chair, gripping its back with both hands. Her knuckles showed white, but her face appeared calm. Finally she spoke. 'I have nothing to tell you.'

Walden groaned aloud. How could she continue to be like this now that she was found out? What was going on in her mind? She seemed a stranger. He thought: When did I lose her?

'Do you know where Feliks is now?' Thomson asked her.

She said nothing.

'Have you warned him of our security precautions here?'

She looked blank.

'How is he armed?'

Nothing.

'Each time you refuse to answer a question, you become a little more guilty, do you realize that?'

Walden noticed a change of tone in Thomson's voice, and looked at him. He seemed genuinely angry now.

'Let me explain something to you,' Thomson said. 'You may think that your Papa can save you from justice. He is perhaps thinking the same thing. But, if Orlov dies, I swear to you that I will bring you to trial for murder. Now think about that!'

Thomson left the room.

Charlotte was dismayed to see him go. With a stranger in the room she had just about managed to keep her composure. Alone with Papa she was afraid she would break down.

'I'll save you if I can,' Papa said sadly.

Charlotte swallowed thickly and looked away. I wish he'd be angry, she thought; I could cope with that.

He looked out of the window. 'I'm responsible, you see,' he said painfully. 'I chose your mother, I fathered you, and I brought you up. You're nothing but what I've made you. I can't understand how this has happened, I really can't.' He looked back at her. 'Can you explain it to me, please?'

'Yes, I can,' she said. She was eager to make him understand, and she was sure he would, if she could tell it right. 'I don't want you to succeed in making Russia go to war, because if you do, millions of innocent Russians will be killed or wounded to no purpose.'

He looked surprised. 'Is that it?' he said. 'Is *that* why you've done these awful things? Is that what Feliks is trying to achieve?'

Perhaps he *will* understand, she thought joyfully. 'Yes,' she said. She went on enthusiastically: 'Feliks also wants a revolution in Russia – even you might think that could be a good thing – and he believes it will begin when the people there find out that Aleks has been trying to drag them into war.'

'Do you think I want a war?' he said incredulously. 'Do you think I would like it? Do you think it would do me any good?'

'Of course not – but you'd let it happen, under certain circumstances.'

'Everyone would – even Feliks, who wants a revolution, you tell me. And if there's to be a war, we must win it. Is that an evil thing to say?' His tone was almost pleading.

She was desperate for him to understand. 'I don't know whether it's evil, but I do know it's wrong. The Russian peasants know nothing of European politics, and they care less. But they will be shot to pieces, and have their legs blown off, and all awful things like that because you made an agreement with Aleks!' She fought back tears. 'Papa, can't you see that's wrong?'

'But think of it from the British point of view – from your own personal point of view. Imagine that Freddie Chalfont and Peter and Jonathan go to war as officers, and their men are Daniel the groom, and Peter the stable-lad, and Jimmy the boot-boy, and Charles the footman, and Peter Dawkins from the Home Farm – wouldn't you want them to get some help? Wouldn't you be *glad* that the whole of the Russian nation was on their side?'

'Of course – especially if the Russian nation had chosen to help them. But they won't choose, will they, Papa? You and Aleks will choose. You should be working to prevent war, not to win it.'

'If Germany attacks France, we have to help our friends. And it would be a disaster for Britain if Germany conquered Europe.'

'How could there be a bigger disaster than a war?'

'Should we never fight, then?'

'Only if we're invaded.'

'If we don't fight the Germans in France, we'll have to fight them here.'

'Are you sure?'

'It's likely.'

'When it happens, then we should fight.'

'Listen. This country hasn't been invaded for eight hundred and fifty years. Why? Because we've fought other people on their territory, not ours. That is why you, Lady Charlotte Walden, grew up in a peaceful and prosperous country.'

'How many wars were fought to prevent war? If we had not fought on other people's territory, would they have fought at all?'

'Who knows?' he said wearily. 'I wish you had studied more history. I wish you and I had talked more about this sort of thing. With a son, I would have – but, Lord! I never dreamed my daughter would be interested in foreign policy! And now I'm paying the price of that mistake. What a price. Charlotte, I promise you that the arithmetic of human suffering is not as straightforward as this Feliks has led you to believe. Could you not believe me when I tell you that? Could you not trust me?'

'No,' she said stubbornly.

'Feliks wants to *kill* your cousin. Does that make no difference?'

'He is going to kidnap Aleks, not kill him.'

Papa shook his head. 'Charlotte, he's tried twice to kill Aleks and once to kill me. He has killed many people in Russia. He's not a kidnapper, Charlotte, he's a murderer.'

413

'I don't believe you.'

'But why?' he said plaintively.

'Did you tell me the truth about suffragism? Did you tell me the truth about Annie? Did you tell me that in democratic Britain most people still can't vote? Did you tell me the truth about sexual intercourse?'

'No, I didn't.' To her horror, Charlotte saw that his cheeks were wet with tears. 'It may be that everything I ever did, as a father, was mistaken. I didn't know the world would change the way it has. I had no idea of what a woman's role would be in the world of 1914. It begins to look as if I have been a terrible failure. But I did what I thought best for you, because I loved you, and I still do. It's not your politics that are making me cry. It's the betrayal, you see. I mean, I shall fight tooth and nail to keep you out of the courts, even if you do succeed in killing poor Aleks, because you're my daughter, the most important person in the world to me. For you I will let justice and reputation and England go to hell. I would do wrong for you, without a moment's hesitation. For me, you come above all principles, all politics, everything. That's how it is in families. What hurts me so much is that you will not do the same for me. Will you?'

She wanted desperately to say yes.

'Will you be loyal to me, for all that I may be in the wrong, just because I am your father?'

But you're not, she thought. She bowed her head: she could not look at him.

They sat in silence for a minute. Then Papa blew his nose. He got up and went to the door. He took the key out of the lock, and went outside. He closed the door behind him. Charlotte heard him turn the key, locking her in.

She burst into tears.

It was the second appalling dinner party Lydia had given in two days. She was the only woman at the table. Sir Arthur was glum because his vast search operation had utterly failed to turn up Feliks. Charlotte and Aleks were locked in their rooms. Basil Thomson and Stephen were being icily polite to each other, for Thomson had found out about Charlotte and Feliks, and had threatened to send Charlotte to jail. Winston Churchill was there. He had brought the treaty with him and he and Aleks had signed it, but there was no rejoicing on that account, for everyone knew that if Aleks were to be assassinated then the Czar would refuse to ratify the deal. Churchill said that the sooner Aleks was off English soil the better. Thomson said he would devise a secure route and arrange a formidable bodyguard, and Aleks could leave tomorrow. Everyone went to bed early, for there was nothing else to do.

Lydia knew she would not sleep. Everything was unresolved. She had spent the afternoon in an indecisive haze, drugged with laudanum, trying to forget that Feliks was there in her house. Aleks would leave tomorrow: if only he could be kept safe for a few more hours ... She wondered whether there might be some way she could make Feliks lie low for another day. Could she go to him and tell him a lie, say that he would have his opportunity of killing Aleks tomorrow night? He would never believe her. The scheme was hopeless. But once she had conceived the idea of going to see Feliks she could not get it out of her mind. She thought: Out of this door, along the passage, up the stairs, along another passage, through the nursery, through the closet, and there . . .

She closed her eyes tightly and pulled the sheet up over her head. Everything was dangerous. It was best to do nothing at all, to be motionless, paralysed. Leave Charlotte alone, leave Feliks alone, forget Aleks, forget Churchill.

But she did not know what was going to *happen*. Charlotte might go to Stephen and say: 'You're not my father.' Stephen might kill Feliks. Feliks might kill Aleks. Charlotte might be accused of murder. Feliks might come here, to my room, and kiss me.

Her nerves were bad again and she felt another headache coming on. It was a very warm night. The laudanum had worn off, but she had drunk a lot of wine at dinner and she still felt woozy. For some reason her skin was tender tonight, and every time she moved, the silk of her nightdress seemed to scrape her breasts. She was irritable, both mentally and physically. She half-wished Stephen would come to her, then she thought: No, I couldn't bear it.

Feliks' presence in the nursery was like a bright light shining in her eyes, keeping her awake. She threw off the sheet, got up, and went to the window. She opened it wider. The breeze was hardly cooler than the air in the room. Leaning out and looking down, she could see the twin lamps burning at the portico, and the policeman walking along the front of the house, his boots crunching distantly on the gravel drive.

What was Feliks doing up there? Was he making a bomb? Loading a gun? Sharpening a knife? Or was he sleeping, content to wait for the right moment? Or wandering around the house, trying to find a way to get past Aleks' bodyguards?

There's nothing I can do, she thought; nothing.

She picked up her book. It was Hardy's *Wessex Poems*. Why did I choose this? she thought. It opened at the page she had looked at that morning. She turned up the night-light, sat down, and read the whole poem. It was called 'Her Dilemma'.

The two were silent in a sunless church,
Whose mildewed walls, uneven paving-stones,
And wasted carvings passed antique research;
And nothing broke the clock's dull monotones.

Leaning against a wormy poppy-head,
So wan and worn that he could scarcely stand,
– For he was soon to die, – he softly said,
'Tell me you love me!' – holding hard her hand.

She would have given a world to breathe 'yes' truly,
So much his life seemed hanging on her mind,
And hence she lied, her heart persuaded thoroughly
'Twas worth her soul to be a moment kind.

But the sad need thereof, his nearing death,
So mocked humanity that she shamed to prize
A world conditioned thus, or care for breath
Where Nature such dilemmas could devise.

That's right, she thought; when life is like this, who can do right?

Her headache was so bad she thought her skull would split. She went to the drawer and took a gulp from the bottle of laudanum. Then she took another gulp.

Then she went to the nursery.

CHAPTER FIFTEEN

SOMETHING HAD gone wrong. Feliks had not seen Charlotte since midday, when she had brought him a basin, a jug of water, a towel and a cake of soap. There must have been some kind of trouble to keep her away – perhaps she had been forced to leave the house, or perhaps she felt she might be under observation. But she had not given him away, evidently, for here he was.

Anyway, he did not need her any more.

He knew where Orlov was and he knew where the guns were. He was not able to get into Orlov's room, for the security seemed too good; so he would have to make Orlov come out. He knew how to do that.

He had not used the soap and water, because the little hideaway was too cramped to allow him to stand up straight and wash himself, and anyway he did not care much about cleanliness; but now he was very hot and sticky, and he wanted to feel fresh before going about his work, so he took the water out into the nursery.

It felt very strange, to be standing in the place where Charlotte had spent so many hours of her childhood. He put the thought out of his mind: this was no time for sentiment. He took off all his clothes and washed himself by the light of a single candle. A familiar, pleasant feeling of anticipation and excitement filled him, and he felt as if his skin were glowing. I shall win tonight, he thought savagely, no matter how many I have to kill. He rubbed himself all over roughly with the towel. His movements were jerky, and there was a tight sensation in the back of his throat which made him want to shout. This must be why warriors yell war-cries, he thought. He looked down at his body and saw that he had the beginnings of an erection.

Then he heard Lydia say: 'Why, you've grown a beard.'

He spun around and stared into the darkness, stupefied.

She came forward into the circle of candlelight. Her blonde hair was unpinned and hung around her shoulders. She wore a long, pale nightdress with a fitted bodice and a high waist. Her arms were bare and white. She was smiling.

They stood still, looking at one another. Several times she opened her mouth to speak, but no words came out. Feliks felt the blood rush to his loins. How long, he thought wildly, how long since I stood naked before a woman?

She moved, but it did not break the spell. She stepped forward and knelt at his feet. She closed her eyes and nuzzled his body. As Feliks looked down on her unseeing face, candlelight glinted off the tears on her cheeks.

*

Lydia was nineteen again, and her body was young and strong and tireless. The simple wedding was over, and she and her new husband were in the little cottage they had taken in the country. Outside, snow fell quietly in the garden. They made love by candlelight. She kissed him all over, and he said: 'I have always loved you, all these years,' although it was only weeks since they had met. His beard brushed her breasts, although she could not remember his growing a beard. She watched his hands, busy all over her body, in all the secret places, and she said: 'It's you, you're doing this to me, it's you, Feliks, Feliks,' as if there had ever been anyone else who did these things to her, who gave her this rolling, swelling pleasure. With her long fingernail she scratched his shoulder. She watched as the blood welled up, then leaned forward and licked it greedily. 'You're an animal,' he said. They touched each other busily, all the time; they were like children let loose in a sweet shop, moving restlessly from one thing to another, touching and looking and tasting, unable to believe in their astonishing good fortune. She said: 'I'm so glad we ran away together,' and for some reason that made him look sad, so she said: 'Stick your finger up me,' and the sad look went and desire masked his face, but she realized that she was crying, and she could not understand why. Suddenly she realized that this was a dream, and she was terrified of waking up, so she said: 'Let's do it now, quickly,' and they came together, and she smiled through her tears and said: 'We fit.' They seemed to move like dancers, or courting butterflies, and she said: 'This is so nice, dear Jesus this is so nice,' and then she said: 'I thought this would never happen to me again,' and her breath came in sobs. He buried his face in her neck, but she took his head in her hands and pushed it away so that she could see him. Now she knew that this was not a dream. She was awake. There was a taut string stretched between the back of her throat and the base of her spine, and every time it vibrated, her whole body sang a single note of pleasure which got louder and louder. 'Look at me!' she said as she lost control, and he said gently: 'I'm looking,' and the note got louder. 'I'm wicked!' she cried as the climax hit her, 'Look at me, I'm wicked!' and her body convulsed, and the string got tighter and tighter and the pleasure more piercing until she felt she was losing her mind, and then the last high note of joy broke the string and she slumped and fainted.

Feliks laid her gently on the floor. Her face in the candlelight was peaceful, all the tension gone; she looked like one who had died happy. She was pale, but breathing normally. She had been half asleep, probably drugged, Feliks knew, but he did not care. He felt drained and weak and helpless and grateful, and very much in love. We could start again, he thought: she's a free woman, she could leave her husband, we could live in Switzerland, Charlotte could join us—

This is not an opium dream, he told himself. He and Lydia had made such plans before, in St Petersburg nineteen years ago; and they had been utterly impotent against the wishes of respectable people. It doesn' happen, not in real life, he thought; they would frustrate us all over again.

They will never let me have her.

But I shall have my revenge.

He got to his feet and quickly put on his clothes. He picked up the candle. He looked at her once more. Her eyes were still closed. He wanted to touch her once more, to kiss her soft mouth. He hardened his heart. Never again, he thought. He turned and went through the door.

He walked softly along the carpeted corridor and down the stairs. His candle made weird moving shadows in the doorways. I may die tonight, but not before I have killed Orlov and Walden, he thought. I have seen my daughter, I have lain with my wife; now I will kill my enemies, and then I can die.

On the first-floor landing he stepped on a hard floor and his boot made a loud noise. He froze and listened. He saw that there was no carpet here, but a marble floor. He waited. There was no noise from the rest of the house. He took off his boots and went on in his bare feet – he had no socks.

The lights were out all over the house. Would anyone be roaming around? Might someone come down to raid the larder, feeling hungry in the middle of the night? Might a butler dream he heard noises and make a tour of the house to check? Might Orlov's bodyguards need to go to the lavatory? Feliks strained his hearing, ready to snuff out the candle and hide at the slightest noise.

He stopped in the hall and took from his coat pocket

the plans of the house Charlotte had drawn for him. He consulted the ground-floor plan briefly, holding the candle close to the paper, then turned to his right and padded along the corridor.

He went through the library into the gun-room.

He closed the door softly behind him and looked around. A great hideous head seemed to leap at him from the wall, and he jumped, and grunted with fear. The candle went out. In the darkness he realized he had seen a tiger's head, stuffed and mounted on the wall. He lit the candle again. There were trophies all around the walls: a lion, a deer, and even a rhinoceros. Walden had done some big-game hunting in his time. There was also a big fish in a glass case.

Feliks put the candle down on the table. The guns were racked along one wall. There were three pairs of double-barrelled shotguns, a Winchester rifle and something that Feliks thought must be an elephant gun. He had never seen an elephant gun. He had never seen an elephant. The guns were secured by a chain through their trigger-guards. Feliks looked along the chain. It was fastened by a large padlock to a bracket screwed into the wooden end of the rack.

Feliks considered what to do. He had to have a gun. He thought he might be able to snap the padlock, given a tough piece of iron such as a screwdriver to use as a lever; but it seemed to him that it might be easier to unscrew the bracket from the wood of the rack and then pass chain, padlock and bracket through the trigger-guards to free the guns.

He looked again at Charlotte's plan. Next to the

gun-room was the flower-room. He picked up his candle and went through the communicating door. He found himself in a small, cold room with a marble table and a stone sink. He heard a footstep. He doused his candle and crouched down. The sound had come from outside, from the gravel path: it had to be one of the sentries. The light of a torch flickered outside. Feliks flattened himself against the door, beside the window. The light grew stronger and the footsteps became louder. They stopped right outside and the torch shone in through the window. By its light Feliks could see a rack over the sink and a few tools hanging by hooks: shears, secateurs, a small hoe and a knife. The sentry tried the door against which Feliks stood. It was locked. The footsteps moved away and the light went. Feliks waited a moment. What would the sentry do? Presumably he had seen the glimmer of Feliks' candle. But he might think it had been the reflection of his own torch. Or someone in the house might have had a perfectly legitimate reason to go into the flower-room. Or the sentry might be the ultra-cautious type, and come and check.

Leaving the doors open, Feliks went from the flower-room, through the gun-room, and into the library, feeling his way in the dark, holding his unlit candle in his hand. He sat on the floor in the library behind a big leather sofa and counted slowly to one thousand. Nobody came. The sentry was not the cautious type.

He went back into the gun-room and lit the candle. The windows were heavily curtained here – there had been no curtains in the flower-room. He went cautiously into the flower-room, took the knife he had seen over the sink, came back into the gun-room, and bent over the gun rack. He used the blade of the knife to undo the screws which held the bracket to the wood of the rack. The wood was old and hard, but eventually the screws came loose and he was able to unchain the guns.

There were three cupboards in the room. One held bottles of brandy and whisky together with glasses. Another held bound copies of a magazine called *Horse and Hound* and a huge leather-bound ledger marked 'Game Book'. The third was locked: that must be where the ammunition was kept.

Feliks broke the lock with the garden knife.

Of the three types of gun available – Winchester, shotgun or elephant gun – he preferred the Winchester. However, as he searched through the boxes of ammunition he realized there were no cartridges here either for the Winchester or for the elephant gun: those weapons must have been kept as souvenirs. He had to be content with a shotgun. All three pairs were twelve-bore, and all the ammunition consisted of cartridges of number six shot. To be sure of killing his man he would have to fire at close range – no more than twenty yards, to be absolutely certain. And he would have only two shots before reloading.

Still, he thought, I only want to kill two people.

The image of Lydia lying on the nursery floor kept coming back to him. When he thought of how they had made love, he felt exultant. He no longer felt the fatalism which had gripped him immediately after wards. Why should I die? he thought. And when I have killed Walden, who knows what might happen then?

He loaded the gun.

And now, Lydia thought, I shall have to kill myself.

She saw no other possibility. She had descended to the depths of depravity for the second time in her life. All her years of self-discipline had come to nothing, just because Feliks had returned. She could not live with the knowledge of what she was. She wanted to die, now.

She considered how it might be done. What could she take that was poisonous? There must be rat poison somewhere on the premises, but of course she did not know where. An overdose of laudanum? She was not sure she had enough. You could kill yourself with gas, she recalled, but Stephen had converted the house to electric light. She wondered whether the top storeys were high enough for her to die by jumping from a window. She was afraid she might merely break her back and be paralysed for years. She did not think she had the courage to slash her wrists; and besides, it would take so long to bleed to death. The quickest way would be to shoot herself. She thought she could probably load a gun and fire it: she had seen it done innumerable times. But, she remembered, the guns were locked up.

Then she thought of the lake. Yes, that was the answer. She would go to her room and put on a robe, then she would leave the house by a side door, so that the policemen should not see her; and she would walk

across the west side of the park, beside the rhododendrons, and through the woods until she came to the
water's edge; then she would just keep walking, until
the cool water closed over her head; then she would
open her mouth, and a minute or so later it would be
all over.

She left the nursery and walked along the corridor
in the dark. She saw a light under Charlotte's door, and
hesitated. She wanted to see her little girl one last time.
The key was in the lock on the outside. She unlocked
the door and went in.

Charlotte sat in a chair by the window, fully dressed
but asleep. Her face was pale but for the redness around
her eyes. She had unpinned her hair. Lydia closed the
door and went over to her. Charlotte opened her eyes.

'What's happened?' she said.

'Nothing,' Lydia said. She sat down.

Charlotte said: 'Do you remember when Nannie
went away?'

'Yes. You were old enough for a governess, and I
didn't have another baby.'

'I had forgotten all about it for years. I've just
remembered. You never knew, did you, that I thought
Nannie was my mother?'

'I don't know . . . did you think so? You always called
me Mama, and her Nannie . . .'

'Yes.' Charlotte spoke slowly, almost desultorily, as if
she were lost in the fog of distant memory. 'You were
Mama, and Nannie was Nannie, but everybody had a
mother, you see, and when Nannie said you were my
mother, I said don't be silly, Nannie, *you* are my mother.

And Nannie just laughed. Then you sent her away. I was broken-hearted.'

'I never realized . . .'

'Marya never told you, of course – what governess would?'

Charlotte was just repeating the memory, not accusing her mother, just explaining something. She went on: 'So you see, I have the wrong mother, and now I have the wrong father, too. The new thing made me remember the old, I suppose.'

Lydia said: 'You must hate me. I understand. I hate myself.'

'I don't hate you, Mama. I've been dreadfully angry toward you, but I've never hated you.'

'But you think I'm a hypocrite.'

'Not even that.'

A feeling of peace came over Lydia.

Charlotte said: 'I'm beginning to understand why you're so fiercely respectable, why you were so determined that I should never know anything of sex . . . you just wanted to save me from what happened to you. And I've found out that there are hard decisions, and that sometimes one can't tell what's good and right to do; and I think I've judged you harshly, when I had no right to judge you at all . . . and I'm not very proud of myself.'

'Do you know that I love you?'

'Yes . . . and I love you, Mama, and that's why I feel so wretched.'

Lydia was dazed. This was the last thing she had expected. After all that had happened – the lies, the treachery, the anger, the bitterness – Charlotte still loved her. She was suffused with a kind of tranquil joy. Kill myself? she thought. Why should I kill myself?

'We should have talked like this before,' Lydia said.

'Oh, you've no idea how much I wanted to,' Charlotte said. 'You were always so good at telling me how to curtsey, and carry my train, and sit down gracefully, and put up my hair ... and I longed for you to explain important things to me in the same way – about falling in love and having babies – but you never did.'

'I never could,' Lydia said. 'I don't know why.'

Charlotte yawned. 'I think I'll sleep now.' She stood up. Lydia kissed her cheek, then embraced her.

Charlotte said: 'I love Feliks, too, you know; that hasn't changed.'

'I understand,' said Lydia. 'I do, too.'

'Goodnight, Mama.'

'Goodnight.'

Lydia went out quickly and closed the door behind her. She hesitated outside. What would Charlotte do if the door were left unlocked? Lydia decided to save her the anxiety of the decision. She turned the key in the lock.

She went down the stairs, heading for her own room. She was so glad she had talked to Charlotte. Perhaps, she thought, this family could be mended, after all; I've no idea how, but surely it might be done. She went into her room.

'Where have you been?' said Stephen.

*

Now that Feliks had a weapon, all he had to do was get Orlov out of his room. He knew how to do that. He was going to burn the house down.

Carrying the gun in one hand and the candle in the other, he walked – still barefoot – through the west wing and across the hall into the drawing-room. Just a few more minutes, he thought; give me just a few more minutes and I will be done. He passed through two dining-rooms and a serving-room and entered the kitchens. Here Charlotte's plans became vague, and he had to search for the way out. He found a large rough-hewn door closed with a bar. He lifted the bar and quietly opened the door.

He put out his candle and waited in the doorway. After a minute or so he found he could just about make out the outlines of the buildings. That was a relief: he was afraid to use the candle outside because of the sentries.

In front of him was a small cobbled courtyard. On its far side, if the plan was right, there was a garage, a workshop, and – a petrol tank.

He crossed the yard. The building in front of him had once been a barn, he guessed. Part of it was enclosed – the workshop, perhaps – and the rest was open. He could vaguely make out the great round headlamps of two large cars. Where was the fuel tank? He looked up. The building was quite high. He stepped forward, and something hit his forehead. It was a length of flexible pipe with a nozzle at the end. It hung down from the upper part of the building.

It made sense: they put the cars in the barn and the

431

petrol tank in the hayloft. They simply drove the cars into the courtyard and filled them with fuel from the pipe.

Good! he thought.

Now he needed a container. A two-gallon can would be ideal. He entered the garage and walked around the cars, feeling with his feet, careful not to stumble over anything noisy.

There were no cans.

He recalled the plans again. He was close to the kitchen garden. There might be a watering-can in that region. He was about to go and look when he heard a sniff.

He froze.

The policeman went by.

Feliks could hear the beat of his own heart.

The light from the policeman's oil-lamp meandered around the courtyard. Did I shut the kitchen door? Feliks thought in a panic. The lamp shone on the door: it looked shut.

The policeman went on.

Feliks realized he had been holding his breath, and he let it out in a long sigh.

He gave the policeman a minute to get some distance away, then he went in the same direction, looking for the kitchen garden.

He found no cans there, but he stumbled over a coil of hose. He estimated its length at about a hundred feet. It gave him a wicked idea.

First he needed to know how frequently the policeman patrolled. He began to count. Still counting, he carried the garden hose back to the courtyard and concealed it and himself behind the motor cars.

He had reached nine hundred and two when the policeman came around again.

He had about fifteen minutes.

He attached one end of the hose to the nozzle of the petrol pipe, then walked across the courtyard, paying out the hose as he went. He paused in the kitchen to find a sharp meat skewer and to relight his candle. Then he retraced his steps through the house, laying the hose through the kitchen, the serving-room, the dining-rooms, the drawing-room, the hall and the passage, and into the library. The hose was heavy, and it was difficult to do the job silently. He listened all the while for footsteps, but all he heard was the noise of an old house settling down for the night. Everyone was in bed, he was sure: but would someone come down to get a book from the library, or a glass of brandy from the drawing-room, or a sandwich from the kitchen?

If that were to happen now, he thought, the game would be up.

Just a few more minutes – just a few more minutes!

He had been worried about whether the hose would be long enough, but it just reached through the library door. He walked back, following the hose, making holes in it every few yards with the sharp point of the meat skewer.

He went out through the kitchen door and stood in the garage. He held his shotgun two-handed, like a club.

He seemed to wait an age.

At last he heard footsteps. The policeman passed him and stopped, shining his torch on the hose, and gave a grunt of surprise.

Feliks hit him with the gun.

The policeman staggered.

Feliks hissed: 'Fall down, damn you!' and hit him again with all his might.

The policeman fell down, and Feliks hit him again with savage satisfaction.

The man was still.

Feliks turned to the petrol pipe and found the place where the hose was connected. There was a tap to stop and start the flow of petrol.

Feliks turned on the tap.

'Before we were married,' Lydia said impulsively, 'I had a lover.'

'Good lord!' said Stephen.

Why did I say that? she thought. Because lying about it has made everyone unhappy, and I'm finished with all that.

She said: 'My father found out about it. He had my lover jailed and tortured. He said that if I would agree to marry you, the torture would stop immediately; and that as soon as you and I had left for England, my lover would be released from jail.'

She watched his face. He was not hurt as she had expected, but he was horrified. He said: 'Your father was wicked.'

'I was wicked, to marry without love.'

'Oh . . .' Now Stephen looked pained. 'For that matter, I wasn't in love with you. I proposed to you because my father had died and I needed a wife to be Countess of Walden. It was later that I fell so desperately in love with you. I'd say I forgive you, but there's nothing to forgive.'

Could it be this easy? she thought. Might he forgive me everything and go on loving me? It seemed that, because death was in the air, anything was possible. She found herself plunging on. 'There's more to be told,' she said, 'and it's worse.'

His expression was painfully anxious. 'You'd better tell me.'

'I was . . . I was already with child when I married you.'

Stephen paled. 'Charlotte!'

Lydia nodded silently.

'She . . . she's not mine?'

'No.'

'Oh, God.'

Now I have hurt you, she thought; this you never dreamed. She said: 'Oh, Stephen, I am so dreadfully sorry.'

He stared at her. 'Not mine,' he said stupidly. 'Not mine.'

She thought of how much it meant to him: more than anyone else the English nobility talked about breeding and bloodlines. She remembered him looking at Charlotte and murmuring: 'Bone of my bones, and flesh of my flesh;' it was the only verse of the Bible she had ever heard him quote. She thought of her own feelings, of the mystery of the child starting life as part of oneself and then becoming a separate individual, but never completely separate: it must be the same for men, she thought; sometimes one thinks it isn't, but it must be.

His face was grey and drawn. He looked suddenly older. He said: 'Why are you telling me this now?'

I can't, she thought; I can't reveal any more, I've hurt him so much already. But it was as if she was on a downhill slope and could not stop. She blurted: 'Because Charlotte has met her real father, and she knows everything.'

'Oh, the poor child.' Stephen buried his face in his hands.

Lydia realized that his next question would be: Who is the father? She was overcome by panic. She could not tell him that. It would kill him. But she *needed* to tell him; she wanted the weight of these guilty secrets to be lifted for ever. Don't ask, she thought; not yet, it's too much.

He looked up at her. His face was frighteningly expressionless. He looked like a judge, she thought, impassively pronouncing sentence; and she was the guilty prisoner in the dock.

Don't ask.

He said: 'And the father is Feliks, of course.'

She gasped.

He nodded, as if her reaction was all the confirmation he needed.

What will he do? she thought fearfully. She watched

436

his face, but she could not read his expression: he was like a stranger to her.

He said: 'Oh, dear God in Heaven, what have we done.'

Lydia was suddenly garrulous. 'He came along just when she was beginning to see her parents as frail human beings, of course: and there he was, full of life and ideas and iconoclasm ... just the kind of thing to enchant an independent-minded young girl ... I know, something like that happened to me ... and so she got to know him, and became fond of him, and helped him ... but she loves you. Stephen, she's yours in that way. People can't help loving you ... can't help it ...'

His face was wooden. She wished he would curse, or cry, or abuse her, or even beat her, but he sat there looking at her with that judge's face, and said: 'And you? Did you help him?'

'Not intentionally, no ... but I haven't helped you, either. I am such a hateful, evil woman.'

He stood up and held her shoulders. His hands were cold as the grave. He said: 'But are you mine?'

'I wanted to be, Stephen – I really did.'

He touched her cheek, but no love showed in his face. She shuddered. She said: 'I told you it was too much to forgive.'

He said: 'Do you know where Feliks is?'

She made no reply. If I tell, she thought, it will be like killing Feliks. If I don't tell, it will be like killing Stephen.

'You do know,' he said.

She nodded dumbly.

'Will you tell me?'

She looked into his eyes. If I tell him, she thought, will he forgive me?

Stephen said: 'Choose.'

She felt as if she were falling headlong into a pit.

Stephen raised his eyebrows expectantly.

Lydia said: 'He's in the house.'

'Good God! Where?'

Lydia's shoulders slumped. It was done. She had betrayed Feliks for the last time. 'He's been hiding in the nursery,' she said dejectedly.

His expression was no longer wooden. His cheeks coloured and his eyes blazed with fury.

Lydia said: 'Say you forgive me . . . please?'

He turned around and ran from the room.

Feliks ran through the kitchen and through the serving-room, carrying his candle, the shotgun and his matches. He could smell the sweet, slightly nauseating vapour of petrol. In the dining-room a thin, steady jet was spouting through a hole in the hosepipe. Feliks shifted the hose across the room, so that the fire would not destroy it too quickly, then struck a match and threw it on to a petrol-soaked patch of rug. The rug burst into flames.

Feliks grinned and ran on.

In the drawing-room he picked up a velvet cushion and held it to another hole in the hosepipe for a minute. He put the cushion down on a sofa, set fire to

t, and threw some more cushions on to it. They blazed
merrily.

He ran across the hall and along the passage to the
library. Here the petrol was gushing out of the end of
the pipe and running over the floor. Feliks pulled
handfuls of books off the shelves and threw them on
the floor into the spreading puddle. Then he crossed
the room and opened the communicating door to the
gun-room. He stood in the doorway for a moment, then
threw his candle into the puddle.

There was a noise like a huge gust of wind and the
library caught fire. Books and petrol burned fiercely.
In a moment the curtains were ablaze, then the seats
and the panelling caught. The petrol continued to
pour out of the hosepipe, feeding the fire. Feliks
laughed aloud.

He turned into the gun-room. He stuffed a handful
of extra cartridges into the pocket of his coat. He went
from the gun-room into the flower-room. He unbolted
the door to the garden, opened it quietly, and stepped
out.

He walked directly west, away from the house, for
two hundred paces, containing his impatience. Then
he turned south for the same distance, and finally he
walked east until he was directly opposite the main
entrance to the house, looking at it across the darkened
lawn.

He could see the second police sentry standing in
front of the portico, illuminated by the twin lamps,
smoking a pipe. His colleague lay unconscious, perhaps

dead, in the kitchen courtyard. Feliks could see the flames in the windows of the library, but the policeman was some distance away from there and he had not noticed them yet. He would see them at any moment.

Between Feliks and the house, about fifty yards from the portico, was a big old chestnut tree. Feliks walked toward it across the lawn. The policeman seemed to be looking more or less in Feliks' direction, but he did not see him. Feliks did not care: if he sees me, he thought, I'll shoot him dead. It doesn't matter now. No one could stop the fire. Everyone will have to leave the house. Any minute now, any minute now, I'll kill them both.

He came up behind the tree and leaned against it, with the shotgun in his hands.

Now he could see flames at the opposite end of the house, in the dining-room windows.

He thought: What are they doing in there?

Walden ran along the corridor to the bachelor wing and knocked on the door of the Blue Room, where Thomson was sleeping. He went in.

'What is it?' Thomson's voice said from the bed.

Walden turned on the light. 'Feliks is in the house.'

'Good God!' Thomson got out of bed. 'How?'

'Charlotte let him in,' Walden said bitterly.

Thomson was hastily putting on trousers and a jacket. 'Do we know where?'

'In the nursery. Have you got your revolver?'

'No, but I've got three men with Orlov, remember? I'll peel two of them off and then take Feliks.'

'I'm coming with you.'

'I'd rather—'

'Don't argue!' Walden shouted. 'I want to see him die.'

Thomson gave a queer, sympathetic look, then ran out of the room. Walden followed.

They went along the corridor to Aleks' room. The bodyguard outside the door stood up and saluted Thomson. Thomson said: 'It's Barrett, isn't it?'

'Yes, sir.'

'Who's inside?'

'Bishop and Anderson, sir.'

'Get them to open up.'

Barrett tapped on the door.

Immediately a voice said: 'Password?'

'Mississippi,' said Barrett.

The door opened. 'What's on, Charlie? Oh, it's you, sir.'

Thomson said: 'How is Orlov?'

'Sleeping like a baby, sir.'

Walden thought: Let's get on with it!

Thomson said: 'Feliks is in the house. Barrett and Anderson, come with me and his lordship. Bishop, stay inside the room. Check that your pistols are loaded, please, all of you.'

Walden led the way along the bachelor wing and up the back stairs to the nursery suite. His heart was pounding, and he felt the curious mixture of fear and eagerness which had always come over him when he got a big lion in the sights of his rifle.

He pointed at the nursery door.

Thomson whispered: 'Is there electric light in that room?'

'Yes,' Walden replied.

'Where's the switch?'

'Left-hand side of the door, at shoulder height.'

Barrett and Anderson drew their pistols.

Walden and Thomson stood either side of the door, out of the line of fire.

Barrett threw open the door, Anderson dashed in and stepped to one side, and Barrett threw the light switch.

Nothing happened.

Walden looked into the room.

Anderson and Barrett were checking the schoolroom and the bedroom. A moment later Barrett said: 'No one here, sir.'

The nursery was bare and bright with light. There was a bowl of dirty water on the floor, and next to it a crumpled towel.

Walden pointed to the closet door. 'Through there is a little attic.'

Barrett opened the closet door. They all tensed. Barrett went through with his gun in his hand.

He came back a moment later. 'He *was* there.'

Thomson scratched his head.

Walden said: 'We must search the house.'

Thomson said: 'I wish we had more men.'

'We'll start with the west wing,' Walden said. 'Come *on*.'

They followed him out of the nursery and along the

corridor to the staircase. As they went down the stairs Walden smelled smoke. 'What's that?' he said.

Thomson sniffed.

Walden looked at Barrett and Anderson: neither of them was smoking.

The smell became more powerful, and now Walden could hear noise like wind in the trees.

Suddenly he was filled with fear. 'My house is on fire!' he shouted. He raced down the stairs.

The hall was full of smoke.

Walden ran across the hall and pushed open the door of the drawing-room. Heat hit him like a blow and he staggered back. The room was an inferno. He despaired: it could never be put out. He looked along to the west wing, and saw that the library was afire too. He turned. Thomson was right behind him. Walden shouted: 'My house is burning down!'

Thomson took his arm and pulled him back to the staircase. Anderson and Barrett stood there. Walden found he could breathe and hear more easily in the centre of the hall. Thomson was very cool and collected. He began to give orders.

'Anderson, go and wake up those two bobbies outside. Send one to find a garden hose and a tap. Send the other running to the village to telephone for a fire engine. Then run up the back stairs and through the servants' quarters, waking everyone. Tell them to get out the quickest way they can then gather on the front lawn to be counted. Barrett, go and wake up Mr Churchill and make sure he gets out. I'll fetch Orlov. Walden, you get your wife and daughter. Move!'

Walden ran up the stairs and into Lydia's room. She was sitting on the chaise-longue in her nightdress, and her eyes were red with weeping. 'The house is on fire,' Walden said breathlessly. 'Go out quickly on to the front lawn. I'll get Charlotte.' Then he thought of something: the dinner bell. 'No,' he said. 'You get Charlotte. I'll ring the bell.'

He raced down the stairs again, thinking: Why didn't I think of this before? In the hall was a long silk rope which would ring bells all over the house to warn guests and servants that a meal was about to be served. Walden pulled on the rope, and heard faintly the response of the bells from various parts of the house. He noticed a garden hose trailing through the hall. Was somebody fighting the fire already? He could not think who. He kept on pulling the rope.

Feliks watched anxiously. The blaze was spreading too quickly. Already large areas of the first floor were burning – he could see the glow in the windows. He thought: Come out, you fools. What were they doing? He did not want to burn everyone in the house – he wanted them to come out. The policeman in the portico seemed to be asleep. I'll give the alarm myself, Feliks thought desperately; I don't want the wrong people to die—

Suddenly the policeman looked around. His pipe fell out of his mouth. He dashed into the porch and began to hammer on the door. At last! thought Feliks. Now raise the alarm, you fool! The policeman ran around to a window and broke it.

Just then the door opened and someone rushed out in a cloud of smoke. It's happening, Feliks thought. He raised the shotgun and peered through the darkness. He could not see the face of the newcomer. The man shouted something, and the policeman ran off. I've got to be able to see their faces, Feliks thought; but if I go too close I'll be seen too soon. The newcomer rushed back into the house before Feliks could recognize him. I'll have to get nearer, Feliks thought, and take the chance. He moved across the lawn. Within the house, bells began to ring.

Now they will come, thought Feliks.

Lydia ran along the smoke-filled corridor. How could this happen so *quickly*? In her room she had smelled nothing, but now there were flames flickering underneath the doors of the bedrooms she passed. The whole house must be blazing. The air was too hot to breathe. She reached Charlotte's room and turned the handle of the door. Of course, it was locked. She turned the key. She tried again to open the door. It would not move. She turned the handle and threw her weight against the door. Something was wrong, the door was jammed, Lydia began to scream and scream—

'Mama!' Charlotte's voice came from within the room.

Lydia bit her lip hard and stopped screaming. 'Charlotte!'

'Open the door!'

'I can't I can't I can't—'

445

'It's locked!'

'I've unlocked it and it won't open and the house is on fire oh dear Jesus help me help—'

The door shook and the handle rattled as Charlotte tried to open it from the inside.

'Mama!'

'Yes!'

'Mama, stop screaming and listen carefully to me – the floor has shifted and the door is wedged in its frame – it will have to be broken down – go and fetch help!'

'I can't leave you—'

'MAMA! GO AND GET HELP OR I'LL BURN TO DEATH!'

'Oh, God – all right!' Lydia turned and ran, choking, toward the staircase.

Walden was still ringing the bell. Through the smoke he saw Aleks, flanked by Thomson and the third detective, Bishop, coming down the stairs. Lydia and Churchill and Charlotte should be here too, he thought, then he realized that they might come down any one of several staircases: the only place to check was out on the front lawn where everyone had been told to gather.

'Bishop!' shouted Walden. 'Come here!'

The detective ran across.

'Ring this. Keep going as long as you can.'

Bishop took the rope and Walden followed Aleks out of the house.

*

It was a very sweet moment for Feliks.

He lifted the gun and walked toward the house.

Orlov and another man walked toward him. They had not yet seen him. As they came closer Walden appeared behind them.

Like rats in a trap, Feliks thought triumphantly.

The man Feliks did not know looked back over his shoulder and spoke to Walden.

Orlov was twenty yards away.

This is it, Feliks thought.

He put the stock of the gun to his shoulder, aimed carefully at Orlov's chest, and – just as Orlov opened his mouth to speak – pulled the trigger.

A large black hole appeared in Orlov's nightshirt as an ounce of number six shot, about four hundred pellets, tore into his body. The other two men heard the bang and stared at Feliks in astonishment. Blood gushed from Orlov's chest, and he fell backward.

I did it, Feliks thought exultantly; I killed him.

Now for the other tyrant.

He pointed the gun at Walden. 'Don't move!' he yelled.

Walden and the other man stood motionless.

They all heard a scream.

Feliks looked in the direction from which the sound came.

Lydia was running out of the house with her hair on fire.

Feliks hesitated for a split second, then he dashed toward her.

Walden did the same.

As he ran, Feliks dropped the gun and tore off his coat. He reached Lydia a moment before Walden. He wrapped the coat around her head, smothering the flames.

She pulled the coat off her head and yelled at them: 'Charlotte is trapped in her room!'

Walden turned and ran toward the house.

Feliks ran with him.

Lydia, sobbing with fright, saw Thomson dart forward and pick up the shotgun Feliks had dropped.

She watched in horror as Thomson raised it and took aim at Feliks' back.

'No!' she screamed. She threw herself at Thomson, knocking him off balance.

The gun discharged into the ground.

Thomson stared at her in bewilderment.

'Don't you know?' she shouted hysterically. 'He's suffered enough!'

Charlotte's carpet was smouldering.

She put her fist to her mouth and bit her knuckles to stop herself screaming.

She ran to her washstand, picked up the jug of water, and threw it into the middle of the room. It made more smoke, not less.

She went to the window, opened it, and looked out. Smoke and flames poured out of the windows below her. The wall of the house was faced with smooth stone:

there was no way to climb down. If I have to I'll jump; it will be better than burning, she thought. The idea terrified her and she bit her knuckles again.

She ran to the door and shook the handle impotently.

'Somebody, help, quickly!' she screamed.

Flames rose from the carpet, and a hole appeared in the centre of the floor.

She ran around the edge of the room to be near the window, ready to jump.

She heard someone sobbing and realized it was her.

The hall was full of smoke. Feliks could hardly see. He stayed close behind Walden, thinking: Not Charlotte, I won't let Charlotte die, not Charlotte.

They ran up the staircase. The whole first floor was ablaze. The heat was terrific. Walden dashed through a wall of flame and Feliks followed him.

Walden stopped outside a door and was seized by a fit of coughing. Helpless, he pointed at the door. Feliks rattled the handle and pushed the door with his shoulder. It would not move. He shook Walden and shouted: 'Run at the door!' He and Walden – still coughing – stood on the other side of the corridor, facing the door.

Feliks said: 'Now!'

They threw themselves at the door together.

The wood split but the door stayed shut.

Walden stopped coughing. His face showed sheer terror. 'Again!' he shouted at Feliks.

They stood against the opposite wall.

'Now!'

They threw themselves at the door.

It cracked a little more.

From the other side of the door, they heard Charlotte scream.

Walden gave a roar of anger. He looked about him desperately. He picked up a heavy oak chair. Feliks thought it was too heavy for Walden to lift but Walden raised it above his head and smashed it against the door. The wood began to splinter.

In a frenzy of impatience Feliks put his hands into the crack and began to tear at the splintered wood. His fingers became slippery with blood.

He stood back and Walden swung with the chair again. Again Feliks pulled out the shards. His hands were full of splinters. He heard Walden muttering something and realized it was a prayer. Walden swung the chair a third time. The chair broke, its seat and legs coming away from its back; but there was a hole in the door big enough for Feliks – but not for Walden – to crawl through.

Feliks dragged himself through the hole and fell into the bedroom.

The floor was on fire, and he could not see Charlotte.

'Charlotte!' he shouted at the top of his voice.

'Here!' Her voice came from the far side of the room.

Feliks ran around the outside of the room where the fire was less. She was sitting on the sill of the open window, breathing in ragged gulps. He picked her up by the waist and threw her over his shoulder. He ran back around the edge of the room to the door.

Walden reached through the door to take her.

Walden put his head and one shoulder through the hole to take Charlotte from Feliks. He could see that Feliks' face and hands were burned black and his trousers were on fire. Charlotte's eyes were open and wide with terror. Behind Feliks, the floor began to collapse. Walden got one arm beneath Charlotte's body. Feliks seemed to stagger. Walden withdrew his head, put his other arm through the hole, and got his hand under Charlotte's armpit. Flames licked around her nightdress and she screamed. Walden said: 'All right, Papa's got you.' Suddenly he was taking her entire weight. He drew her through the hole. She fainted and went limp. As he pulled her out the bedroom floor fell in, and Walden saw Feliks' face as Feliks dropped into the inferno.

Walden whispered: 'May God have mercy on your soul.'

Then he ran downstairs.

Lydia was held in an iron grip by Thomson, who would not let her go into the blazing house. She stood, staring at the door, willing the two men to appear with Charlotte.

A figure appeared. Who was it?

It came closer. It was Stephen. He was carrying Charlotte.

Thomson let Lydia go. She ran to them. Stephen laid Charlotte gently on the grass. Lydia stared at him in a panic. She said: 'What – what—'

'She's not dead,' Stephen said. 'Just fainted.'

Lydia got down on the grass, cradled Charlotte's head in her lap, and felt her chest beneath her left breast. There was a strong heartbeat.

'Oh, my baby,' Lydia said.

Stephen sat beside her. She looked at him. His trousers had burned and his skin was black and blistered. But he was alive.

She looked toward the door.

Stephen saw her glance.

Lydia became aware that Churchill and Thomson were standing near, listening.

Stephen took Lydia's hand. 'He saved her,' he said. 'Then he passed her to me. Then the floor fell in. He's dead.'

Lydia's eyes filled with tears. Stephen saw, and squeezed her hand. He said: 'I saw his face as he fell. I don't think I'll ever forget it, as long as I live. You see, his eyes were open, and he was conscious, but – he wasn't frightened. In fact he looked . . . satisfied.'

The tears streamed down Lydia's face.

Churchill spoke to Thomson. 'Get rid of the body of Orlov.'

Poor Aleks, Lydia thought, and she cried for him too.

Thomson said incredulously: 'What?'

Churchill said: 'Hide it, bury it, throw it into the fire,

I don't care how you do it, I just want you to get rid of that body.'

Lydia stared at him aghast, and through a film of tears she saw him take a sheaf of papers from the pocket of his dressing-gown.

'The agreement is signed,' Churchill said. 'The Czar will be told that Orlov died by accident, in the fire that burned down Walden Hall. Orlov was not murdered, do you understand? There was no assassin.' He looked around at each of them with his aggressive, pudgy face set in a fierce scowl. 'There was never anybody called Feliks.'

Stephen stood up and went over to where Aleks' body lay. Someone had covered his face. Lydia heard Stephen say: 'Aleks, my boy ... what am I going to say to your mother?' He bent down and folded the hands over the hole in the chest.

Lydia looked at the fire, burning down all those years of history, consuming the past.

Stephen came over and stood beside her. He whispered: 'There was never anybody called Feliks.'

She looked up at him. Behind him, the sky in the east was pearly grey. Soon the sun would rise, and it would be a new day.

EPILOGUE

O N 2 AUGUST 1914 Germany invaded Belgium. Within days the German army was sweeping through France. Toward the end of August, when it seemed that Paris might fall, vital German troops were withdrawn from France to defend Germany against a Russian invasion from the east; and Paris did not fall.

In 1915 the Russians were officially given control of Constantinople and the Bosphorus.

Many of the young men Charlotte had danced with at Belinda's ball were killed in France. Freddie Chalfont died at Ypres. Peter came home shell-shocked. Charlotte trained as a nurse and went to the front.

In 1916 Lydia gave birth to a boy. The delivery was expected to be difficult because of her age, but in the event there were no problems. They called the boy Aleks.

Charlotte caught pneumonia in 1917 and was sent home. During her convalescence she translated *The Captain's Daughter* by Pushkin into English.

After the war, women got the vote. Lloyd George became Prime Minister. Basil Thomson got a knighthood.

Charlotte married a young officer she had nursed in France. The war had made him a pacifist and a socialist, and he was one of the first Labour Members of Parliament. Charlotte became the leading English translator of nineteenth-century Russian fiction. In 1931 the two of them went to Moscow and came home declaring that the U.S.S.R. was a workers' paradise. They changed their minds at the time of the Nazi–Soviet pact. Charlotte's husband was a Junior Minister in the Labour government of 1945.

Charlotte is still alive. She lives in a cottage on what used to be the Home Farm. The cottage was built by her father for his bailiff, and it is a spacious, sturdy house full of comfortable furniture and bright fabrics. The Home Farm is now a housing estate but Charlotte likes to be surrounded by people. Walden Hall was rebuilt by Lutyens and is now owned by the son of Aleks Walden.

Charlotte is sometimes a little confused about the recent past but she remembers the summer of 1914 as if it were yesterday. A rather distant look comes into those sad brown eyes, and she's off on one of her hair-raising stories.

She's not all memories, though. She denounces the Communist Party of the Soviet Union for giving socialism a bad name and Margaret Thatcher for giving feminism a bad name. If you tell her that Mrs Thatcher is no feminist she will say that Brezhnev is no socialist.

She doesn't translate any more, of course, but she is reading *The Gulag Archipelago* in the original Russian. She says Solzhenitsyn is self-righteous but she's determined to finish the book. As she can read only for half an hour in the morning and half an hour in the afternoon, she calculates that she will be ninety-nine by the time she gets to the end.

Somehow I think she'll make it.